Cage Without Bars

A Forrest Spencer Novel

Book 3

Gerald Neufeld

Novel Voices Press
Radnor, Pennsylvania
Ottawa, Ontario

Novel Voices Press

Neufeld, Gerald
Cage Without Bars / Gerald Neufeld.—1st ed.

ISBN 978-0-9854464-8-2

www.novelvoicespress.com

Printed in the United States of America

Since I began writing fiction, like most, I have come to appreciate the necessity for uncompromising editors for form and content. More surprising to me is how much I've come to rely upon editors who, apart from their valuable contributions to my work, are there for me to hear my insecurities and doubts as well as flights of fancy that they sensitively manage to dissuade. And who among us does not like to hear that at least someone out there thinks what we've managed to produce so far is good.

I've had the good fortune to have found an editor who plays all these roles most admirably who's been with me since the inception of this trilogy. It is to her to whom I dedicate this last book of the series. May Sadie Scapillato always remain a close friend and may she never drift far from her keyboard, her forthcoming progeny notwithstanding.

PART ONE

"Sometimes you put walls up not to keep people out, but to see who cares enough to break them down."

— Socrates, circa 469-399 BCE

Chapter 1

It was near seven in the evening in mid-July as I wended my way up a steep hill in Ojai, about an hour's drive from Santa Lucia where I lived. So different this place was from other small California towns, quiet and secluded with tall oak trees everywhere. There'd been a film made in the Ojai Valley years ago, hadn't there, called *Shangri-La*?

I was so caught up by the majesty of the tall stately trees that I missed my turn. I'd left quaint shops and artists' outdoor displays behind and had been swallowed up by a tunnel of vegetation so dense that little light showed through. It was eerie, stifling almost, the pungent odors of all that greenery, overwhelming.

I had no idea where I was, my little Mustang was too big to turn around and I was late. The trees thickened as I moved ahead, the light having all but disappeared. The effect was not unlike the gloom of deep water dives I'd made. I felt claustrophobic, accustomed as I was to the openness of California cities and terrain.

At last, what might pass for an access road. I did the only thing I could. I turned left and burrowed in, bushes clawing at the top and both sides of my new muscle car. Much further and I wouldn't be going anywhere.

I turned my flashlight on and looked down at the crumpled piece of paper she'd sent me. Meaningless lines and a few hastily scribbled words. Libbie's Park in the center of the village. Yes, that park I'd seen, but where were the dirt roads I was to take? No trace of them.

No way I could miss the turnoff to her little place, halfway between the village and Lake Casitas, she'd casually assured me on the telephone. I'd receive a map to her house in a day or so. A map, she called it. Only lifetime residents of this area could possibly decipher these hieroglyphics and cryptic language.

I had two options—either back up and retrace my steps and go back home or forge ahead down a path not wide enough for a horse and, very possibly, spend the night out here. The prospect of returning to a lonely house versus what I might find with a little luck if I persevered decided me. This path, recently used I was relieved to see, had to go somewhere.

I inched ahead. The trail—it was little more than that—had no holes or bumps but was narrower than my little car. So much for the polishing and wax job I'd done. The further I went, the more certain I was this could be no access road. It was a path hikers used that went God knew where.

I began to curse myself for the idiot I'd been when the path abruptly widened and there was much more light. The topography entirely changed. Trees everywhere of a kind I'd never seen in California. Though not as visible as they'd be during the day, I saw beautiful hardwoods nestled between conifers that looked for all the world like Norfolk pines.

Inconceivable. Sculptured-looking bushes that had to have been transplanted here long ago crowded small trees that were reaching out for light. The term that came to mind as I gazed out my open car window was *enchanted.* I felt a bit like Carroll's awestruck Alice in Wonderland. Whoever could have created a forest like this that was not overrun by tourists?

I wanted to stop and explore the place despite the hour, but I moved on, now very curious about what lay beyond.

There was just sufficient brightness to make out a lodging of some kind with a porch light on about a hundred feet ahead. Hopefully, I could get some idea where I was and how I might reach my destination, a fool's errand though it might turn out to be.

With only my parking lights on—my headlights were of little use—I advanced to the edge of a small clearing and turned my engine off. How extraordinary to live in a hidden place like this in California. Not a soul in sight. No harm, then, to get out of my cramped car and look around. I'd likely be sleeping in my vehicle here anyway, not something I looked forward to.

With the aid of my parking lights and the faux lantern above the porch, I saw the outline of what looked like a Swiss chalet. From where I was, the ground floor appeared almost obscured by flowers and climbing vines. Was that a gabled roof and row of upper windows to let in light? My imagination working overtime.

For minutes I stood there, breathing in fragrant air and feeling better. I'd missed what promised to be an exciting night, okay, but I'd discovered a secret place that delighted me. After a long night curled up in my little car, I'd be less euphoric, but it was the price I had to pay.

I was wrong about being unobserved. As I reached for my remote control to lock my Mustang, I was startled—more accurately, I nearly peed my pants—when a voice, out of nowhere, came at my back.

"Put that thing away, Mr. Spencer. No need for such things out here. There's nobody within a quarter of a mile of us, just you and me."

I was glad cardiac arrest didn't run in my family, little consolation for the prairie of new gray hairs I'd have. I turned around to see her illuminated by the light above her door. By pure accident, I'd found her.

"I've been watching you gazing at my trees. Did you come to see my forest or visit me? It wasn't so hard for you to get out here, now was it. Hmmm?"

My heart rate nearly back to normal, dragging out my words, I said, "Vicky, you have no idea."

Inexplicably, her right hand came out, palm up. Like a moron, half mesmerized as I was, I stared at it.

"Forrest, your face, what I can see of it. You look addled. It's your car keys I'm looking for. You're not going anywhere tonight, not with the amount of alcohol I'll be giving you. Now hand them over."

There was the hint of a smile on her full mouth as I reached into my blazer pocket to extract them. We both knew it wasn't the alcohol she was thinking of. Happy to comply, I crossed the forty feet of clearing to where she stood.

Unusual for Santa Lucia's District Attorney and my long-time friend and colleague, there was nothing flamboyant or provocative in Vicky's dress. Skinny jeans and an embroidered white blouse failed to hide contours that I'd seen often in my dreams. She'd managed somehow to retain the hourglass figure that some Mexican girls have who are half her age.

Even more appealing than her Latina curves was her exceptionally lovely face and abundant lustrous dark hair that fell just past her shoulders. Closer up, I could see real warmth in those liquid brown oval-shaped eyes of hers.

Handing her my keys, I said, "You know, I haven't a clue how I got here. That map of yours wasn't of much use."

"Well, the important thing is, you're here. I hope my invitation didn't come too soon."

How long ago had that dreadful day been when my divorce with Claire was finalized, eight months? Though she'd tried several times previously to lure me to her hideaway, to Vicky's credit, she'd been an especially good friend to me this past year, never venturing beyond platonic warmth and sympathy. She knew how catastrophic my unanticipated loss of Claire had been to me. My reflections must have been evident on my face.

Empathy in her voice, Vicky said, "Come, come in,

Forrest. It's wonderful to finally have you here."

Her arm on mine as we entered her secluded home, I wondered if her invitation had been an act of kindness or whether she'd decided that she'd waited long enough. It was the latter, I was fairly sure. To be honest, it didn't matter all that much, not at that moment, anyway. Trina and Andy were with their mother for July and I was alone. I was glad for Vicky's company and to be with an exquisite woman who was unafraid to show that she wanted me.

Inside, the front door closed, she continued, "It's small, but it's very cozy. I'll show you around the place in a little while. Make yourself comfortable over there," she told me, pointing to a loveseat in the corner of the living room. "It's scotch on the rocks, isn't it?"

"That would do very nicely about now, thanks, but how do you know what I drink?"

Halfway to what I assumed was her kitchen, Vicky stopped and turned back toward me. Hands on hips, a slightly mocking expression on her face, she said, "Well now, let's see. I've heard when a man drinks too much, he tends to forget things he does. That true?"

As I'd learned over the years, Vicky loved her little games. Her look and posture had all the makings of something I wasn't sure I'd like. We'd met frequently for lunch and met at a party or two, but I couldn't remember drinking scotch at those occasions.

Taunting me, she said, "Need a clue?"

What I wanted was that drink she promised and not playing the role of mouse, but I humored her.

"Santa Barbara a couple of years ago, remember?" Seeing my blank expression, she continued, a grin beginning to form on her full mouth, "You were in a bar with Ben and doing your best to keep up with him, as I recall. Oh yes. Jack Chambers was there too, I think. From what I heard, you three were a little down on the Prosecutor who was trouncing you. That ring a bell?"

That bell she was metaphorically referring to hadn't stopped clanging in my head for at least a day. The hangover lasted longer. "The Martinez trial."

Vicky smiled.

"What were you doing there anyway?"

"Hey," she responded, her smile a mile wide, "a girl deserves a night out once in a while, doesn't she, especially when she's been dueling in court with the renowned defense attorney. I was with Allan Resnik at the other end of the bar. You were too busy downing scotches to notice us. Satisfied? Now may I get that drink?"

"I'd be much obliged, Madame Prosecutor," I said in my most pompous voice, "if you'd refrain from reminding me of that night."

She either hadn't heard or was paying no attention. In a minute, she was back, handing me my glass.

Grinning, she said, "Sorry that's no double as you seem to like, but I want your full attention when we eat. Give me a few moments and I'll be back."

I'd been right about the row of upper windows I'd seen outside. The chalet, entirely of wood, was elegant in its simplicity and quite small. The construction was of notched round logs with a beamed ceiling over the open-space living room that was fifteen feet up, at least.

Above the kitchen and what I assumed the bathroom was a half floor with a balcony-like railing, presumably where Vicky's bedroom was. An attractive if rather steep set of wooden steps led up to it. Standing behind that railing on the second floor, one could look across the living room to four ornate little windows whose function doubtless was to provide more light.

No paint or stain anywhere apart from sealants to protect and preserve the natural colors of the wood. The floor, pitted with time but highly polished, might have been made from old barn boards. The effect was intimate and warm.

There were a few prints, some family pictures and a few shelves of DVDs and books. In a blown-up photograph was a striking lady of Mexican descent who was clearly Vicky's mother. Next to her stood a distinguished-looking light-skinned man who could have been from Spain. Hadn't Vicky told me that her father was European?

The furniture, though stylish, was sparse, a loveseat and two end tables, a small coffee table and two lamps. The prints that I thought to be Mexican by Clemente and Tamayo, I hadn't seen. Neither spoke to me. I was perusing what appeared to be a book of poetry in Spanish by Alberto Blanco when Vicky reappeared.

"You like poetry? I didn't know. I write poems sometimes, especially when I'm out here. You didn't expect that of me, did you. Now tell the truth."

Saying anything at that moment that made the slightest sense would be difficult. She'd moved up close beside me.

"Poetry, yes," I mumbled distractedly, "I like it when I can understand it. I can't read a word of this."

"Hmmm," she murmured under her breath. "The one you're looking at's not all that interesting. I can find another one though that is, or, maybe I should do that after dinner."

The vixen was aware of the effect she had on me, hell, on any man who was within a foot of her. Despite the sumptuous odors emanating from the kitchen, her fragrance, the one I'd always liked, wafted all about me. There was that fragrance, yes, but there was more. Vicky had an animal-like quality about her that I'd detected at inauspicious times before. I couldn't concentrate.

Laughing, nudging me, she said, "Sometimes I think it's best not to try to understand poetry when you read. Don't you agree? Just lie back and let it flow over you."

Vicky was prouder than she should be about her double entendres.

Watching her move back toward her kitchen door, I saw a third print that was partially hidden by the lamp. The abstract was anachronistic in this rustic setting, with blobs of metallic gray and blue that intersected with wavy lines that went nowhere.

"Oh, that," Vicky exclaimed dismissively as she emerged with a glass of something clear. Waving it at the print, spilling not a drop, she added, "I wanted to take that down before you got here. I must have been really high when I bought the thing. What people think about when they do this stuff, I can't imagine."

"It's, it's—"

"Yeah, yeah, I know. It'll be gone before you leave." With her elbow nudging my arm, she steered me toward the loveseat. Close beside me, clinking glasses, she said, "To the next time you're here."

"Hey, Vic, is it already time to leave? Here I thought you were going to feed me."

She smiled and made a throaty noise. My companion wasn't being coy. Both of us knew exactly what that noise meant. Vicky's nearness and her not-so-subtle innuendoes were making it hard to think and to camouflage the changing dimensions of my lap. I needed rather hurriedly to talk about something else.

"Hey, before we get on to other topics, I've got a question, if Ms. Rodriguez doesn't mind."

"No shop talk here, counselor, remember?"

"It's not about law stuff."

"If it's about where this girl sleeps, I'm not about to tell you. I did offer you a tour of the place later, though, didn't I."

"Nothing about your boudoir, Madame, not at all. It's more prosaic, I'm afraid."

"Hmmm. What might that be?"

"Where did all those magnificent trees and bushes near your house come from? I've never seen anything like them anywhere, particularly in California."

Mercurial, a chameleon, a good actress—Vicky was all of these. If I hadn't known her the ten years I had, she might have fooled me.

Her face fell and the mouth I couldn't stop looking at began to droop. Her heretofore animated voice was gone. Sliding an inch or two away, she said, "I was watching you out there, you know? I saw how fascinated you were by my little place. Now here we are, after all these years, in what most people would call a romantic atmosphere, and what do you think is on his mind. Trees, if you can believe it, trees! Tell me, Forrest, what does a girl have to do to get to you?"

She'd carried it off pretty well, but by the end, she couldn't keep the twinkle from her eyes. "And to think of all the trouble I went to."

I lightly tapped her a safe distance below those luscious breasts of hers and said, "Now about that forest. Where did it come from?"

Grinning and moving back close to me, Vicky replied, her little act forgotten, "The property's been in my family for generations. My grandfather planted most of the trees when he was young. The Norfolks, they never grew all that much but the hardwoods have done okay. You really like them?"

"My God, what's not to like? They're extraordinary. How far back on the property do the trees go? When I was standing out there and everything was quiet, the forest felt enchanted."

Vicky glowed with pride and she looked happy. "I wonder why others don't see it like you do. The trees don't go back that far, worst luck. They were planted to look like that, but the property isn't all that wide. It's pretty deep, though, about three hundred feet. The trees go back for about forty feet on either side of my access road."

Thinking about what I'd seen, I had to say, "Everything's so beautifully maintained out there, from what I could tell at that hour, anyway, somebody who loves the place a lot has gotta be taking very good care of it."

"Yes. It's my uncle who owns half the property. He's retired now and that's all he does." The grin back and looking more relaxed than I'd ever seen her, Vicky said, "You ought to see him. He's so possessive about the place that he won't let anyone near unless I say so."

This time, it was her turn to tap me, only she didn't

have to worry about what she touched. "Just so you know, it wasn't me who drew that map, if that's what you want to call it. Why do you think our road is so hard to find? You won't see it unless you're really looking for it, and even then."

"That's God's truth," I said. "It's a miracle I'm here."

"No it's not," she retorted. "My uncle was watching out for you. If you hadn't showed up in another quarter of an hour, he'd have gone and found you. Me finally getting you to come out here? No way you were going to get away. Before we go in to eat," she went on without segue, "tell me. How are things at home without the twins? You must be missing them a lot, I guess."

She knew I did. The answer to her question must have registered on my face. Vicky was female, every molecule of her, but, as she'd told me several times, motherhood had no appeal. What she was saying to me, in so many words, was how could a man be missing kids at a time like this if he had her?

"Put it this way. I'm at the office early these days and am still there after everybody's gone."

"Hmmm. Sounds like getting you out here was a good thing to do."

I looked at my near-empty glass then back at her. "You couldn't have picked a better time."

"Now that's what I like to hear. And, just think, Forrest. We've only started."

I looked surreptitiously at my drink. My glance hadn't gone unnoticed. Much more alcohol and the evening could end disastrously. I'd surely have the will when the moment came to perform, but embarrassing moments when I'd been imbibing had demonstrated that I might lack the way.

Wise to the vagaries of male plumbing as the lady doubtless was, Vicky just perceptibly shook her head as she relieved me of my glass. "Much more of this and you won't taste my wine. It's not Two Buck Chuck I'm serving you. Let's go eat."

I'd noticed but hadn't paid much attention to Vicky's

unique walk-through curtain that separated her kitchen from the living room. Six-foot-long round bamboo rods hung nearly to the floor, obscuring everything beyond.

Vicky was in front of me—there came a light rustle of the rods as she passed through and she was gone. I was thinking about where I might install an attractive door like that in my house when she called me. Stepping closer, I saw that what I'd taken to be rods were actually articulating strips. Fascinated by the design, I stepped through to the other side.

I did a double-take, perhaps a triple if such a thing can be done. Lulled by the warm and welcoming sensation all-wood structures impart to me, I was flabbergasted by what I saw. Now I understood the reason for the wood strip screen. One instant, I was in a sylvan hideaway, ideal for these woods, the next, I was in an ultra-modern kitchen that surpassed my own. I blinked as though the tableau was a mirage. In the seconds I was still in the other room, Vicky had donned an apron and stood regarding me.

"Surprised you, didn't I. You thought I ate out of packages and cans, didn't you."

My senses back, I said, "No one with that figure and that complexion could eat like that."

"Mmhmm," she said, a pleased look on her face. "We'll see."

Granite countertops, Florentine-style tile floor and stainless steel everywhere. The room was half again as big as the one we left. Her cupboards—there were lots of them—were of an exquisite hardwood I didn't recognize with a beautiful round table made of oak. The room was stunning. The walls were attractively stained pine. Two chairs, again of oak with the bark left on, turned out to be more comfortable than they looked.

Vicky smiled as I toured the room and stopped at her little pantry. It was stocked, floor to ceiling and side to side, with common and exotic spices and gourmet things. I knew, as only a devotee of culinary arts could, that a cook worked here.

"That's right," there a lilt in Vicky's voice, "you're at home in the kitchen, aren't you."

"I am," I answered, coveting her space-age gas range. "Propane?"

"That's right. I keep the tanks in a hidden shed outside. Now sit."

Cutlery and small plates were stacked in the middle of the table. I set two places.

"That's what I like to see," Vicky quipped, "a man who knows his place."

"Hey," I said, "unless I'm much mistaken, I'm getting the better end of this."

Her back to me, she replied, "Now that, we're about to see."

I couldn't escape her pull, even in the kitchen, surrounded by high-end equipment I lusted after and by all that food. If raising my voltage level had been on her mind in the living room, she'd been successful. I was famished, but I wanted her.

Her efficient but languid movements as she worked told me she was aware. She was an artist in more ways than one. She was too expert to be rushed. She'd be abstemious with the wine and heighten my anticipation with verbal foreplay.

I suppressed a laugh as two wine glasses came out, a pair of four-ounce goblets some potter friend had made.

Feigning reproach, Vicky queried, "What, you don't approve of these?"

"No, no, they're great. They're very nice. You didn't make them, did you?"

"You kidding me? I tried the wheel once and all I could make looked like blinis." Reaching for the wine and holding the bottle up, she said, a tad condescendingly, "You do like rosé, don't you?"

"That kind, I do, a Château d'Esclans, no less."

Vicky looked indignant, but she forgot to hide her eyes. "I didn't know my hero was such a snob."

"Hey," I protested. "I'm a guest here. Be nice to me."

Vicky's expression became predatory. "I think that can be arranged. It's about what time now, nine o'clock? If you're not satisfied with your treatment by midnight, say, you're free to leave. That sound fair to you?"

"Entirely," I answered, settling back contentedly in my chair.

With no hint of mockery in her tone this time, Vicky asked, "Does our sommelier know what gazpacho is?"

What to say to this? Could I beat her at her own game? I doubted it, but...

"Gazpacho," I whispered to myself before putting on what I hoped was a puzzled look.

A characteristic of hers I'd seen several times in court, Vicky was overeager. "Aha," she almost crowed. "He happens to recognize one wine, but he doesn't know what gazpacho is." Tossing all that hair that she hadn't bothered to put up before she served, she said, "And here I thought you knew international cuisine. I'll have to explain to you what this special soup is and the rest of what I cooked, I guess."

Was that triumph or disappointment on her face? It may well have been the latter. I could appreciate. How often had I prepared good cuisine for people who couldn't distinguish it from the meat and potato-based diets they typically had. I had to rescue her. Vicky definitely wasn't happy. Wordlessly, she served the soup.

"Don't worry, Forrest. I didn't forget to heat it. It's served cold. It's a specialty from Madrid, Spain."

I mouthed 'Andalusia,' but I didn't say it.

Vexed though she was, Vicky had been watching. Her spoon stopped halfway to her mouth.

I wanted so very much to laugh, but my puzzled look, or at least a part of it, stayed on.

"What's that you said? You were mumbling." Putting her full spoon back in her bowl, displeasure on her lovely face, she asked, "What's the matter. You don't like cold soup? Forrest, honestly!"

This time, I whispered the name of the Spanish

region a little louder. Her eyes narrowed and her nostrils flared. I couldn't help it. I burst out laughing. While Vicky spluttered, I hastily took a bite and then another.

"Smart-ass. You're such a snob, know that? So how do you make that soup?"

"Not as good as this," I responded, meaning it. "Vicky, I've never lied to you, not once. This gazpacho's even better than Barb Austin's, no mean achievement. She's a superb cook. Don't tell her I like your soup more than hers. She'll never speak to me again."

Vicky's smile was back and she was laughing. "You know what started to bother me the most?"

"I can guess," I said.

"I went to a lot of trouble to make these things 'cuz I know you like good food."

"I understand, Vicky love, believe me, I do. Have no fear. I'll taste everything you've done."

"And am going to do," she added, her eyes intent on me.

"You don't like giving clues to a guy, do you."

She laughed. "Forrest, something I've learned over the years with you. You need every one. The first course, as you gentlemanly pointed out, was from Andalusia, Spain. The second is from France." Winking at me, she declared, "I won't tell you what the last course is."

I didn't ask. Reaching for the rosé, I saw that the bottle was two-thirds gone. Protecting her interests was one thing, but this was a little much. On the other hand, humiliation later on tonight with this spectacular female I didn't need. I'd sip my wine and treat it like eau de vie.

Vicky cleared away the bowls. With panache, off came two metal covers from serving platters to reveal the pièce de resistance. A third cover was removed. Very prettily, she lifted the first plate and held it out. There were two rows of what appeared to be small filets, each pair smothered in a different sauce.

"I hope you like red meat, monsieur," she said.

"Beef, pork and lamb."

Incredulous, I got up to get a closer look. Emily Post forgotten, I bent unceremoniously to sniff. It was true. In color, in smell and assuredly in taste, each of the three sauces that blanketed the medallions was distinct.

"How ever did you manage to keep those mouthwatering sauces intact like that?"

Pleased that I was aware of the difficulty of the task, she tilted her head slightly and said, "Come back another time and I'll show you. Does take some careful handling. They're not ladled on from bottles, I can tell you." Putting down the platter, she pointed to the second, the contents of which I recognized right away.

'Gratin dauphinois,' I mouthed, my favorite potato dish from France. "Vicky, you astound me. I had no idea."

Standing at her range, lifting out the upper level of a stainless steel double boiler, she remarked, "How could you? You've been playing so hard to get for all these years. I'll serve the broccoli now and we can eat. I'm starved."

After one of the most delectable meals I'd had in years, finished with a perfect Grand Marnier soufflé, Vicky excused herself, dipped into her pantry and promptly vanished.

Mystified, I got up to look. She wasn't there. I was sitting back down, wondering what the lady was up to when she reappeared, a wine bottle in her left hand. I saw the label.

"My, my. The very best for our secretive DA out here."

Setting the bottle on the counter, she said, "So you approve?"

"Well now, let me think. When did I last taste a glass of Delaforce vintage port. I know I've had the pleasure, but I can't remember when."

"You're mistaken, sir, if you think I serve this to just anyone. You know as well as I do that most wouldn't know the difference."

"I have to ask. Where did you dredge that up? It certainly wasn't in the pantry."

"One of your more attractive features, Forrest. You notice things. No, I could hardly store wines in the chalet. The heat, especially in the summer, would destroy them. I keep my bottles underground beneath the shed out back. My pantry has a back door you didn't see. Now, if curiosity is satisfied, I'll pour us some of this Portuguese elixir and we can return to the living room."

This time, Vicky left no space between us. Her head, with its masses of dark soft wavy hair, rested on my right shoulder as I breathed her in. The ends of her wide sensual mouth went up as she regarded me.

Sounding drowsy yet looking quite awake, she said, "Something I've never been able to figure out. Now don't take this wrong. You really shouldn't, not with me snuggled up with you like this. You're really not my type, you know? You're attractive in a kind of homey way and you're refined, and you've got a lot more upstairs compared to most of the guys I know."

As if to soften what she just said, she snuggled closer. Another move like that and she'd be on my lap. "I'm not especially proud of it, but I tend to go for men who look at me as just another babe." Hesitating briefly, she speculated out loud, "Hmmm. Do I still qualify as a babe or am I a cougar? Hmmm. Anyway, most of those guys are macho types who think women are their play things. I can't help it. They're usually the ones I go for. Stupid, isn't it. Nothing like that in you."

Putting a warm hand over mine that I had placed there to hide the bulge, she continued, with a little squeeze, "I've gotta say, I've been so furious with you sometimes in court that I wanted to hang you up by this. Other times, like now, when I think about you, I'm wet. Explain that, will you?" Turning to nibble on my earlobe, not something an unhurried girl should do to me, she murmured, "Why can't I wait to feel you inside of me?"

I like foreplay as much as anyone, especially when a

good part of it is verbal. My problem at the moment was that I was on overload. The entire evening had been contrived by this beguiling female to stir me up. I put my empty port glass down and took Vicky a bit more roughly than is my habit in my arms and pulled her close.

"Mmhmm..." was all she said.

Though I was aroused, I wanted to remain on the loveseat long enough to see if that luscious mouth I had tasted only twice before was a figment of embellished memory or if it was real.

The ineffable softness I remembered was still there as was the nectar, every drop of which I craved. No tentative probing with her soft tongue this time. Vicky's incendiary strategy had ricocheted.

Minutes later, we were unbuttoning clothes when the sound came. I felt Vicky freeze. It was the cell phone in my blazer pocket. I tried to pull away, but Vicky, not so gently, grasped both my ears. She didn't appear upset, but the dreamy look was gone.

"Shame on you, Forrest Spencer." She hadn't let go of my ears. "I don't allow cell phones here. I thought you'd know. You're not going to answer it."

"Vic," I said, pulling her hands away, "my regular cell's still in my car. I keep this one for emergencies. Only Ben and Claire know the number. If it rings again after going to voice mail, I'll have to answer. It'll be something about the twins."

We waited, my heartbeat quickening not with passion but alarm.

The phone buzzed again. I drew away from Vicky who was in disarray and swiftly crossed the room. Ben, my partner and a long-time friend, wouldn't be calling me on the weekend. It must be bad news from Claire. I felt my chest loosen when I retrieved the tiny cell phone and looked at the display. It was Ben. Hopefully, nothing about the twins.

"Sorry to bother you, boyo, but we've gotta problem, a big one, I'm afraid."

"What's up, Ben," I asked as I heard Vicky sigh.

"Lucy Jackson, that's what. She shot Pete six times at point-blank range according to what she told the cops. Couldn't get you on the phone so she called me."

Hardly able to process what I heard, I parroted, "Shot Pete six times? Lucy Jackson? Is that what I heard you say? That's impossible, Ben. There's got to be some mistake."

Except, there wasn't. There couldn't be. Ben would have checked things out thoroughly before he called.

"I'm only tellin' you what I heard from the boys downtown. She waived rights to counsel and signed on the dotted line, but she wants to see you anyway. No clue why. Where the hell are you anyway? Cell coverage isn't worth a damn."

"She confessed and they've booked her?"

"So I've heard."

"Christ. Thanks, Ben. I've gotta go." I hit the end call button and, in a daze, I pocketed my cell.

Understandably, Vicky looked downcast. She'd refastened her blouse and was running her fingers through her hair. The consummate professional she was, she'd surely understand my need to get away. She knew the Jacksons and, as Santa Lucia's Public Prosecutor, she'd be in charge of the People's case. Still, as evident from her expression, she wasn't happy. Nor was I, but for very different reasons.

I went to console her, but she shook her head. In a resigned tone, she said, "Forrest, you're aware, aren't you, that you won't really have access to her until tomorrow morning when she's moved to the county jail. You know that, right?"

Remaining where I was, I nodded.

"Chief Nash refuses to loosen up on this."

"That's right," I acknowledged. "He likes to ignore the principle that no one is supposed to come between attorneys and their clients."

"True, but Lucy's not officially your client yet, is she." Vicky's comments were not intended to hold me there. She knew that would be a waste of time. Shaking her head, as though speaking to herself, she said, "Your head wouldn't be with me anyway. What is it, I'd like to know, that keeps you and me from being lovers? Do you believe in fate?"

"Not really," I responded.

Smiling a little with a hint of irony, she quipped, "Well then, there may be hope for us, sometime in the future, anyway."

Temporizing, not knowing what else to do, I said, "Lucy, she was—"

"Yes, yes, I know," she cut in as she came to me and draped her arms around my neck. "She's a dear friend and you want to see her right away. You've known her for a long time, haven't you." She contemplated me for a few seconds, then smiled. "If she comes out of this okay, I'll have to ask her what her secret was." Leaning into me, her face against my chest, Vicky murmured, "I'll call someone and see what I can do. I'm sticking out my neck here, you know." She was. "Friends with benefits can be useful sometimes, can't they." Wistfully, she added, "Trouble is, the benefits never seem to come our way."

"We'll have to correct that, won't we."

"Not for the next little while, counselor, we won't, but when the weather clears, you'd better make your way back here now that you know how or you'll be in for it, understand? I'll send my uncle after you and you don't want that."

After hugs and a quick kiss goodbye, I turned to go.

"You can find your way back alright? It gets very dark out here at night with all these trees." She handed me my keys.

"I'll be okay," I said as I took my blazer from the closet. "It's gotta be easier to go back than come."

Laughing, she said, "Not true always."

Vicky's parting double entendre still resonating in my head, I turned my little car around and headed back.

She was right. I could scarcely see a thing, even

with my parking lights, it was so dark. My inability to concentrate didn't help. Reliable though Ben was, the idea that Lucy could kill anyone, especially Pete, was so absurd that I couldn't credit it, not as it had been reported to me, anyway. Without question, there had to be an alternate explanation.

And, I felt badly for my sweet friend, who had finally managed to contrive our tryst, only to see me leave her at the eleventh hour and drive away. Had that call come a little later...

God, had I turned right or left? There was no way I could tell, immersed in all these trees. I'd been so preoccupied with what Ben had said that, like an idiot, I hadn't paid attention. I'd either end up at Lake Casitas, miles and miles from home, unable to get back until the next day, or I'd soon see the village that I came through. How could a day that had begun so spectacularly end this way?

I knew I was okay when I saw headlights crisscrossing in front of me. Then came lit-up signs from stores and a café. Now I could breathe easily again and think.

I met Lucy over twenty years ago when we were sophomores in college. We were lovers for about six months and had remained close friends. I remembered how happy she looked when she married Pete just after graduation. I could still see her in her snow-white wedding gown, radiantly happy and proud of her protruding belly, six months pregnant with Pete's child. A marriage made in Heaven, that one.

Years after, I came to know their son well as his soccer coach. Alex was a great kid. Lucy gave birth to their daughter, Mia, at about that time. Where were the Jackson children now? Alex, nineteen, might be alright, but what about the little girl? Both would doubtless be with Lucy's brother whom I'd met several times. I'd have to check.

Claire and I used to exchange visits with the Jackson family at least once a year. One of those inevitable hiatuses in relationships, I mused, that accounted for my lack of contact with Lucy during the last two years.

As I exited the Ojai Valley and headed for the 101, I continued to think about Lucy and her husband, Pete. Both were well known to Santa Lucians, she for her leadership in charitable events, in the past, at least, and he as the affable owner of Jackson Motors where vehicles valued at less than a hundred thousand dollars were hard to find. Two or three years ago, Pete offered me a low price on a used Porsche in tip-top shape. Claire urged me to grab it, but I couldn't see spending ninety thousand plus for a sports car. Ruefully, I thought about the costly vehicle I was in.

What could have driven Lucy to such a thing if it really happened? I felt close enough to her that I should know. How close were friends, I chided myself, who, because of events in their own lives, neglected people they loved who might have needed them? But if she'd needed me, I would have heard, or so I hoped. It made no sense. True, I knew little how she and her husband were behind closed doors, but they appeared to get along.

The strongest assurance I had that events were not as they'd been reported was Lucy's alleged willingness to confess to murder without counsel. Though no scholar, she was bright and reasonably well-educated. She'd read more these last few years than I would in a lifetime. She had to be aware of how indispensable an attorney was in her situation. She also had to know what the penalties were in California for capital crimes.

It was after midnight when I reached the station. As Santa Lucia's DA, Vicky carried weight, but she was in no position to issue orders to the police on behalf of the defense. To the contrary, she'd be in trouble if she tried. The only chance I had to get at Lucy at this late hour was if Vicky had a discreet friend within the Force who had some clout. Whether or not she managed it, I appreciated her offer, especially after all she'd done.

I sat in my car in the half filled parking lot, listening to the ticks of my engine as it cooled down. What next to do? I could hardly confront the desk sergeant and demand to see a client I didn't have who'd just been booked. During the years I'd been practicing as a criminal attorney, I'd never been in circumstances quite like these. Since Vicky hadn't called, I must assume she'd been unsuccessful in reaching anyone. Disconsolately, I reached in my blazer pocket for my keys.

Chapter 2

I saw the shadow before I heard the light tap at my car window. Low-slung as my Mustang was, I couldn't make out the face.

"Mr. Spencer, come this way, please."

Though his back was to me as we walked, I recognized the gravelly voice of Sergeant Micky Barns, whom I'd known for years. He'd always been outspoken about his disdain for lawyers, but we two got along. I attributed this to my children, whom he'd met at a picnic once and really liked.

"We'll go around to the side door. Lieutenant Schulz is waitin' for you inside."

In a hurry to get away, I'm not sure he heard me thank him.

I had to smile. It was to be good cop and bad for me tonight. Of all people, why send Schulz? Foxy Kate, Ben's sobriquet for her, was certainly no friend of ours. By all accounts, she'd never forgiven us for the outcome of the Martinez trial two years ago. Detective Johnny Parker, who'd died during that affair, had apparently been a friend. Knowing that Schulz had become involved, I hoped Vicky had insulated herself well.

Kate Schulz hadn't changed a bit. A wolverine in disguise. Another line or two on her not-unfriendly face, she made quite a picture with her outmoded blue-gray hair and that poster board grandmother look of hers. Behind that facade was a hardened police combatant with a mind like a steel trap.

With a smile that didn't reach her eyes, she said, "Someone thinks Mr. Spencer's pretty special. I'd be curious to know who that someone is." Gesturing to a corridor to my left, she added, "Last door on the right. You've got fifteen minutes in there, that's it. You'll be doing everyone a favor if you're out of there by then."

Not waiting for my reply, the pear-shaped lady turned away, took several steps, then stopped. Over her shoulder, with an edge, she said, "You know, counselor, we ought to have lunch sometime, my treat. I'd give somethin' to know what made Cap Lonigan break his rule." I could feel her eyes boring into me.

'Vicky friend,' I said to myself as I made my way down the hall, 'I hope you didn't compromise yourself on account of me. It could have waited until tomorrow.'

Lucy was seated at the far side of the table in an interrogation room. Her blond hair was in disarray and she looked pale and gaunt. More troubling was the absence of expression in her eyes when she looked at me. They might have been made of glass.

For a moment, I forgot why I was there, so shocked I was by her appearance and by her lack of response to me. No semblance of the connection that had been there since our late teens.

Devoid of feeling though her soft blue eyes were, Lucy was alert. Had she not been, I would have thought her drugged. I sat down and was about to reach out to her when she promptly drew back her arms.

In a clear flat voice, she said, "Thanks for coming. I wasn't sure you would. We need to talk. They said I'd have fifteen minutes with you, that's all."

"Lucy, for the love of God, what's happened? What's going on? Why did you wait so long to call me?"

"There was no need. They asked me if I wanted an attorney during the interrogation, but I told them no. I told them what I did, and that was that. I didn't need a lawyer."

"You actually signed a confession that you killed Pete. Is that what you did?" This was easier to believe now that I'd seen her.

Impatience now in her tone, Lucy replied, "Of course I did. What was there to deny? I shot Pete in the chest and in the head, six times. What else was there to do?"

In the more than twelve years that I'd been practicing criminal law, I'd never heard a sane client with no criminal background speak in such a sang froid manner about having killed someone.

As though I were some lawyer off the street to whom she was issuing orders, she said, "The arraignment is to take place on Monday, they told me. I need you to get me out on bail."

I regarded her, beginning to wonder just how sane she was. Contrary to what I knew of her, she appeared to have no knowledge of California law concerning homicide. What could I explain to her in the minutes we had left that would make sense to her?

"Look, Lucy, you don't understand. That's not how the system works. I'll explain this tomorrow when I come to see you. I need to know something before I go. We have no time now so just answer yes or no. Did you say anything in your confession about why you shot Pete? It's important."

Lucy frowned and shook her head. "All I said was that I shot him when he came back home."

"They didn't ask you why?"

"Yes, of course they did, but I didn't see why they had to know. I told them that I shot him, that's all. That's all I said and all I wrote. Now what about getting me out of here long enough to arrange things for the kids before I go to prison? You can do that, can't you?"

"Lucy, we don't have time to talk about this now. We've got two minutes according to my watch, and they're serious out there, believe me. The important thing now is to say absolutely nothing to anyone about what happened, not to anyone at all. Do you understand?"

Still in a flat voice, Lucy replied, "Don't be so dramatic. Of course I understand. I just need to get out for a little while, that's all."

Standing up, I told her I'd be back before noon to talk more with her. I left before the Lieutenant could have the pleasure of having me escorted out.

Schulz and a sergeant I didn't recognize stood at the door where I'd come in. There was nothing grandmotherly about the lady now.

"Nothing's free, Mr. Spencer. Remember that. Now get out of here."

The child voice in me wanted to let her know how eager I was to get her in the witness box to work her over, but the older brother voice prevailed. Schulz was a seasoned warrior in the courtroom. Her ability to humiliate overconfident defense attorneys was renowned.

Was it my depressed mood and loneliness that generated the smell or were there still molecules of Claire's perfume in our front closet that refused to go away?

I didn't tear up often but, at that moment, my eyes were wet. Though she'd been gone for many months, I missed her still. More pressing, I missed our children. They'd been with their mother for two of four weeks that seemed like months. This was the first time I'd been away from them for more than days.

Our house was like a mausoleum, particularly at night. I'd become so accustomed to the tic-toc of the grandfather clock in the living room that I failed to notice it until it stopped days before Trina and Andy left. No wonder people attribute lifelike qualities to old clocks like those.

A nightcap before I went to bed?

"God, no," I said out loud. "This day's been too long as it is."

The sadness on Vicky's face when I left her and Lucy's refusal to receive me as her friend had about done me in. What I needed was an Ambien or two and sleep.

"Well, well, if it isn't our hotshot criminal defense guy. Haven't seen you in a while. Who you here to see?"

Sam Jones, who looked out at me from his perch behind the counter in the lawyer's waiting room at Cabrillo Jail, looked much the same—heavy jowls and a khaki shirt that hadn't seen soap in weeks.

Grinning, I said, "You must have been home sick or sleeping it off somewhere. I was here three times last month. I'm here to see Lucy Jackson."

Emitting a noise of pretended fright through thick rounded lips, in a loud whisper, Sam advised, "If I was you, I'd be careful with that one. You never know what she's got up that orange suit a hers. You know what she did, don't you?"

"Get her for me, Sam, okay?"

"Your funeral. One husband-shooter comin' up."

I had ten straight-back wooden chairs to choose from. The place was empty, unusual for Sunday morning. How long had it been since city planners had agreed to modernize this place, at least ten years. In the interim, companies that made up what was euphemistically called an industrial park near the county jail relocated, leaving CO—our abbreviated name for the facility—to muddle along on its own. The only thing I knew of that had changed since Claire and I settled in Santa Lucia was the increase in inmates the jail housed. Renovations here at CO had long since been deprioritized or just forgotten.

Nearly thirty minutes later, Sam called out, "Room six for Mr. Spencer." Jonesy would have doubtless said more were it not for five other lawyers who had drifted in.

The objection I was about to voice to Lucy's standoffish attitude faltered the moment I saw her. In orange jail garb, she sat at the table in the lawyer's consultation room, only a shell of what she'd once been.

Though she'd done something with her hair, she couldn't hide the circles beneath her eyes and her exhausted look. She obviously hadn't slept. Her eyes that sought mine each time we met to reconnect didn't flicker in the smallest bit, as had been the case last night.

Distressed though I was by the trouble she was in, what disturbed me most was my sense that something inside my friend had died. Her demeanor did little to hearten me. Perhaps it was my emotional vulnerability at that moment, but I wanted my connection with Lucy that we'd always had. Hopeless or not, I had to try.

"Luce," I said, sitting down across from her, "before we talk about your situation,"—her frown deepened as I spoke—"I need to know something. Do we have to continue behaving like we're strangers? I'm here as a friend and I want to help. You know that."

Vehemently, she shook her head. "I'm going to say this only once, and I mean only once. If I have to talk about this again, you'll have to go and I'll have to find someone else. You're here, not as my friend but as the only man and attorney I can trust. What I want is your help to get me out of jail long enough to arrange for the future of my children. That's all. Do you understand? That's all. I know this must be difficult for you to understand, but if we're going to work together, you'll have to believe me when I tell you that I have no choice. Ludicrous as this may sound to you, the last thing in this world that I need at this point is the sympathy and, very frankly, the nosiness of well-intending friends. If you're not willing to work with me on this, then the last thing I'll ask you to do for me is to recommend a criminal lawyer I can count on. Are we clear on this?"

The last thing I'd do would be to turn my friend over to an attorney who, in light of Lucy's intransigence, might advise her to bargain with the DA for her life. If Lucy had no viable choice other than to act in the way she was, there was little I could do but follow. Somehow, some way, I'd have to get past her guard if I was to help her in any real way.

"Alright then, Lucy. We'll work according to your rules. Can we get started?"

Lucy nodded.

"There are some things about the bail system you need to understand. I think it very likely that tomorrow at the arraignment the DA's office will bring a charge of premeditated murder."

Lucy wanted to interrupt, but I cut her off.

"No, listen. It's legal help you're looking for, so let me talk. You can ask questions when I'm done."

A woman I no longer knew looked back at me, clearly impatient to get on.

"You'll have to respond to this charge as guilty or not guilty."

Her tone dismissive, she said, "Since I'm going to plead guilty, we need to move onto other things, so let's do that, please."

"Lucy, I'll say this once again, not as your friend but as your attorney. There are some things you need to know before we can go on. Please don't interrupt me anymore until I'm through. If you plead guilty, it is improbable in the extreme that you'll be released on your own recognizance or on bail. If you admit guilt, there's no need for a trial and no reason to let you loose. If you refuse to plead, by default, the judge will interpret your silence as a not guilty plea. Your refusal to respond will not help you in our request for bail. The only avenue that may be open to you to be set free for a time is to plead not guilty. Even then, there is no guarantee in capital cases like this. The judge may or may not set bail."

Lucy looked alarmed.

"Do you understand what I've told you?"

"This doesn't make any sense to me. How can I plead not guilty when I've confessed to killing Pete? That seems illogical to me."

"Look. The first thing the judge will do at the arraignment is decide whether or not the People have a case. In this instance, he or she will definitely decide they do. The next thing the judge will want to know is how you plead. It's a little more complicated than this, but, basically, it comes down to your statement about whether or not you believe yourself to be guilty. If you say guilty, you'll be returned to jail to await sentencing at a later date, very probably by another judge. If you say not guilty, the judge will bind you over for trial. It is at this point when we request the judge to hear our motion that bail be set in order to set you free until the trial. What you told the police and what you signed have nothing to do with how you plead. At present, we're concerned with what happens at the arraignment and not with what comes after. Understand?"

"What do you mean by request the judge and motion to set bail? You're scaring me. Do you mean that I might not get bail at all?"

"If the judge agrees to hear our motion as they almost always do, I'll move that you be released on bail, pending the trial. The prosecution will contest my motion. They'll insist that you're a risk to flee so bail should not be granted. I'll counter this with arguments that there is no risk and that you have children to see to and care for. The judge will then rule on our motion. In my opinion, given the circumstances, I'm confident bail will be granted. If the amount the judge sets is too high, I'll argue to get it lowered. Are you with me?"

Wrinkles I didn't know Lucy had appeared as she frowned again. "So," she said, "if I understand you, to get out, I have to lie. That means there'll be a trial for nothing. I don't want my children to have to go through such a thing, especially Mia."

"Lucy, you haven't told me and I'm not asking now why you killed Pete. I don't believe you'll be lying when you plead not guilty. I know you too well for that. There has to be a reason for what you did and a damn good one. There's something else you need to understand. As your attorney, it's not my job to determine whether or not you're guilty of a crime or whether your reasons for doing what you did are good or bad. I'm here to get the best deal for you I can, whether it's acquittal or shorter time in jail. Something provoked you to do what you did. Eventually, I'll have to know more about what that something was so I can build a strategy for your defense. Let's get through the arraignment first before worrying about the rest."

Lucy's expression darkened. She looked obstinate.

"Consider this," I said. I needed to be sure that she wasn't agreeing with me today, only to reverse herself at the arraignment. "If you remain adamant about not wanting your case to be heard in court, you can always change your plea later before the trial. At least that way, you may have the time you need to make your arrangements for the children."

Her head came up. "I can do that? Are you sure?"

"Yes. Many people do, in fact. That's what plea bargaining's all about, but let's not talk about this now. Let's get through tomorrow and try to get you released."

Lucy had visibly relaxed. She slowly nodded. "Alright," she said. "I thought everyone was entitled to bail if they had the funds. Why do you keep saying that it's not a sure thing for me?"

"In cases involving murder, especially if it's premeditated, bail is occasionally refused or set so high that the defendant can't possibly get the funds."

"How much do you think my bail might be?"

"Between five hundred thousand and a million dollars would be my guess. You'll need to put up ten percent of that for the bail bondsman that is nonrefundable."

"Could it be higher than a million dollars?"

"Improbable, I think. Amounts higher than that are very rare."

"Forrest, listen." Some progress, maybe? She actually used my name. "We have well over ten percent of that amount at the Wells Fargo bank on La Marina. How can I get money to whatever you said that guy is?"

"Is the money under Pete's name, yours or both?"

"Funny you ask that. He was going to change that a

long time ago, but he never did. Forgot about it, I suppose. Except for the business accounts he has, the accounts I'm talking about are in both our names."

"Glad to hear it. There are several ways we can go about this, but probably the best is to give me what's called durable power of attorney that will allow me to instruct your bank to prepare a certified check for a bail bondsman. This power of attorney will remain in effect until you cancel it. Your signature must be witnessed by a notary, so if that's what you choose to do, I'll come in again tomorrow morning with our legal secretary and her stamp."

Some color had come back into Lucy's face. "That's fine. We can do that. Now how do we get the bail bondsman? Can you recommend anyone?"

"I think they're pretty much cut from the same cloth. Some may be a little more vigorous than others, shall we say, in going after clients who skip town."

Lucy looked mystified.

"Say your bail is a million dollars. You'll pay a hundred thousand and the bondsman pays the rest. Provided you don't run away, his nine hundred thousand is returned to him and he keeps the hundred thousand that you paid. Run, and he's very likely to send a bounty hunter after you. Either that or you put up the entire amount of the bail yourself."

"Oh, right. I see. So can you find someone so I can be released as soon as possible?"

"Yes, assuming bail is granted as I said."

"Would you please stop reminding me about that. I absolutely have to get out of here for a while. I told you."

Vexed by her obstinacy and her rude behavior toward me, I retorted, "Lucy, I'm not here just to tell you what you want to hear. You want to find someone to lead you down a garden path, then get another lawyer. I'm not the one sitting behind the bench. Like it or not, there is a possibility, slim, I think, that the judge won't grant you bail. Frankly, you've got more serious things to worry about."

For a moment, I thought I'd gone too far. She looked angry.

After taking a few breaths, she said, "Alright. I'll plead not guilty. There's something I need to know. Obviously, I'm not well-informed about these things." She was having some difficulty finding words. "I don't want to talk about what attorneys do in court. What I want to know is, who decides what happens in my case, I mean, do you make all the decisions or do I have anything to say?"

Her question was much more complicated than she realized, but I thought I knew what she was after. "Most clients, Lucy, are smart enough to follow their lawyer's advice. But that's all it is, advice. It is the client who makes final decisions, not the counselor."

She nodded, then, more emphatically, nodded again. "I thought that was how it was supposed to be. Now I need to tell you something before you go. Two things, actually. First off, I'm not looking for any favors. You charge me what any other high-profile criminal attorney in Santa Lucia would charge, nothing less. Don't screw around with me on this, okay? I'll know. Second thing—this is important—you're here to buy me time at home to arrange things for my kids. Alex is pretty much on his own. It's Mia I have to worry about. I'm not interested in the slightest in a trial. There won't be one. Once I'm back in jail, there'll be nothing else for you to do except take care of the trust funds for my children if you'll do that."

Lucy looked irritated as though she thought I hadn't understood. "I'm going to be blunt with you. I'm sorry about this, but there's no other way. Don't try to change my mind once I've made it up. And I mean this—don't try to coax details about anything out of me. That'll be the end of us, I promise, if you do that. All I ask of you is you get me out of here for a few weeks, at least. I'll need that to get things done." Lucy's face turned hard. "Are we clear on this?"

"Crystal clear, Lucy, crystal clear." Getting up and

replacing my little notebook—in which I hadn't written down a thing—in my shirt pocket, I said, "I'll be here tomorrow at about eleven to get your signature, then I'll see you again at the arraignment in the afternoon."

She acted as though she hadn't heard. She was up and out of the consultation room before my guard arrived.

For reasons I was unable to even speculate about, my friend had decided upon a self-destructive course, not because of remorse, that much was clear. Her intransigence and her promise that I believed she'd keep were not going to make it easy for me to intervene. Hopefully, in the weeks to come, assuming she'd be set free, something would occur to make it easier to intercede.

While I was having lunch at home Sunday afternoon, I thought of Pete, more effusive than I preferred, but a solid guy. He and his son, Alex, were very close. They had been as far back as I could remember. I knew little of his relationship with his young daughter, who was shy and inclined to remain in the background when we were at their home. When I thought about how Pete and Lucy were as a couple, compared to our other long-time friends, I was perplexed by how little information I could conjure up. True, we hadn't seen the Jackson family for some time. Still...

The only rational explanation for Lucy's behavior was that she was covering up for her son, whom she adored. But, given how bonded he and his father were, why would Alex kill Pete? If he had, why would he allow his mother to take the rap? It wasn't like him, not the stable and respectful boy I knew. I was inclined to discount his one misadventure with the police the previous year that had been satisfactorily resolved. Nonetheless?

Some of the pieces did fit together, but too much was missing. Lucy would defend him with her life if it came to that. But that wasn't where the answer lay. I was sure of it. Apart from the strong relationship between father and son, a young man I knew well and liked, even were he capable of murder, he would never let his mother claim responsibility for what he'd done, not as I saw things, anyway. Nor could little Mia, twelve years old, scarcely big enough to hold a gun, have done the deed. The key lay somewhere else.

Lucy was as aloof Monday morning as she'd been the day before. She was barely civil, not even bothering to sit down in the consultation room. Glancing briefly at the durable power of attorney form that Cheryl Bloomfield, who had come with me, was to notarize, she signed and turned to go.

"You're going to arrange for bail now, aren't you?" Lucy said.

"Everything's set up as we discussed," I answered. "I'll see you in Court this afternoon. Remember, Lucy, no surprises."

In reply, she turned away and tapped on the door for the guard to take her back.

Frowning, Cheryl inquired, "That woman always behave like that? She was downright rude."

"Yes she was," I responded, "and, no she isn't, normally like that, I mean. I'd appreciate it if you'd not talk about this in the office."

Cheryl was indignant. "Mr. Spencer, please."

We didn't exchange one word on our return. Cheryl was efficient, but she was a gossip, as Garrett, Ben and I had come to know. She'd respect my admonition, but she wouldn't like it.

Grant MacElroy, whose face I knew, sat behind his bench looking bored. I could hardly blame him. Superior court judges who had more weighty matters to attend to also found themselves presiding at arraignments during which there was often little more exciting than debates concerning bail.

Vicky, in her exalted position as DA, rarely

appeared in court, though she would have had it otherwise. Across from me at the prosecution table was Deputy DA Allan Resnik, impressive as he was debonair. Soft-spoken but very bright, he reminded me of a quiet bird of prey with his hawkish eyes and narrow chiseled face. For the first time in the four or five years I'd known him, I saw him smile and raise his hand in greeting. Magnanimous this time he could afford to be.

I glanced at MacElroy, who was pointedly looking at the clock. It was five minutes past the hour and no sign of Lucy yet. Not an auspicious way to start. This judge was known to be unfriendly to anyone who arrived in his courtroom late.

'Grant.' Didn't that mean large? A poor moniker for the judge, who couldn't have reached five feet six in platform shoes. Moon-faced and overweight with closely spaced pig's eyes, the man hadn't improved with time. He was once a highly respected jurist who'd, sadly, gone to seed.

A door at the side opened and Lucy, garbed in an oversized orange jumpsuit and flanked by two female guards, came toward me. Her escort sat down behind us.

His eyes pinned on them, caustically, MacElroy said, "Kindly inform your superiors that, in this court, we start on time."

Wordlessly and stone-faced, both guards looked straight ahead.

The judge's clerk called out the case.

"The People are ready to proceed?"

The People were. Allan Resnik, in no hurry, rose. Almost sleepily, he declared, "Your Honor, this is a prima facie case of premeditated murder. Prior to interrogation, Ms. Lucy Jackson was duly informed of her rights to have an attorney present, which she waived. Without coercion or duress, Ms. Jackson signed a confession, copies of which I have here, in which she freely admits to having executed her plan to kill her husband with his sidearm. Ms. Jackson has been charged with first degree murder."

Refreshingly, no arrogance or braggadocio in his presentation. It was short and to the point as was his style. During his four years in the District Attorney's office, Resnik had acquitted himself very well at the bar. I'd not faced him, but I'd been peripherally involved in several cases where I'd watched him contrive traps for witnesses who'd misjudged his nonchalance. It was doubtless he who would lead the charge if this case came to trial, an adversary I would have been happy to do without.

"Thank you, Mr. Resnik," the judge said. "You may sit down." Turning to Lucy to my left, MacElroy went on, "Ms. Jackson. Are you fully aware of these charges and the possible penalties for them?"

"I am, Your Honor," Lucy answered in a robotic voice.

"At this time, Ms. Jackson, you are to enter a plea of guilty or not guilty to this charge. How do you plead?"

As though she were denying that she'd left her garbage can too long in the street, she responded with the same tone, "Not guilty, your Honor."

"Very well. You are hereby bound over for trial in the superior court."

The judge's clerk handed him a document, which he promptly signed. At that point, I stood.

"Your Honor, will you hear our motion at this time for bail?"

"Yes, yes, Mr. Spencer, carry on."

"We request that Ms. Jackson be released on her own recognizance, pending trial. The accused is a well-established person in Santa Lucia, a respected member of the community and the mother of two children. It is unlikely in the extreme that she would flee."

This pro forma request, as everyone knew, would be denied.

Observing the scowl on MacElroy's face, I continued, "Short of this, we request that Ms. Jackson be freed on bail. She has two children to care for and arrangements for them to make, pending the outcome of the trial."

MacElroy swiveled his chair to take in Resnik who, predictably, shook his head. He didn't rise. The Deputy DA as well as I was familiar with this judge's dislike of formality.

Laying a hand on a file folder in front of him and looking right at Lucy, Resnik said, "The People oppose bail in this case, Your Honor. The accused is financially able to collect her children, one of whom is nineteen, by the way, and flee to a country where extradition will be difficult if not impossible. The accused may be well-established, but premeditatedly shooting her husband six times is not the act of a reliable or sane person. For this reason and because of the seriousness of the crime, I would urge the Court to deny bail in this case."

Again, succinctly put as was evident in the expression on the judge's face.

Lucy had turned white. If I'd divined correctly what she intended, her lack of freedom during the next few weeks would seriously hamper her.

Pensive, MacElroy tapped his right index finger on the bench for too long a time. With reason, my client had begun to tremble. If my motion were denied, the judge would not recant. There'd be little I could do.

Nodding slightly, the frown still on his pudgy face, MacElroy said, "Premeditated murder, if that is what it was, is indeed a serious offense. Bail is set at one million dollars."

Wobbling a little as she stood, Lucy stated more than asked, "I can go now, right?"

Before the guards behind her could react, I replied, "Not yet, no you can't. You'll be free within an hour or so, but they have to process you out first."

Frowning, Lucy hesitated while her escorts took firm hold of her and ushered her out the door.

A half hour later, my business with the bail bondsman done, I headed for the office.

"So," Garrett asked as I sat down, "Lucy Jackson free on bail?"

I nodded. "She is. It was a close thing, though. MacElroy almost turned us down. Part of the problem was Allan Resnik."

"Ah yes, Vicky's protégé. He used to work for me, you know. He handling this?"

"It's a high-profile case, Garrett, so I suspect so."

"I don't know a thing about this case, but I can tell you this. Resnik's focused and he's sharp. He's one of the best young litigators I've seen. You find out any more about what's going on?"

Frustrated and out of sorts, I said, "Not a goddamn thing. She's behaving like she's covering for someone, but I can't imagine who. Pete and Alex were that close. If Alex killed his father, he'd be in custody by now. He'd never let his mother take the blame. Anyway, he didn't shoot him. I'm sure of it. They loved each other like no father and son I ever knew. Plus he'd need a powerful motive for doing such a thing. I know that family, and it just doesn't wash."

My partner's hound-dog face lengthened as it often did when he was thinking. "No," he said, "not to you, it doesn't. But maybe you're too close. So how do you want to handle things? Want me to take it?"

"If Lucy has her way, Garrett, it'll never go to trial. The only reason she pleaded not guilty was to get out on bail. I can't tell you why. Frankly, I don't have a clue. The only thing she wants now is to make arrangements for her two kids before she goes to prison. None of it makes a lick of sense. She swore to me, and she meant it, that if I tried to get information out of her, she'd fire me on the spot. Whatever went down at the Jackson house, she doesn't want anyone to know."

"There's only one explanation for this, Forrest, like it or not. She's covering up for her son. If that's the case and she stands pat, there's not a lot any of us can do."

With what must have been a rueful smile on my face, I said, "Thing I like about you, Garrett, is you always brighten up my day."

"Hey, hey, go easy on me, chum. I'm not telling you

to throw in the towel. It'd be a waste of time. All I'm saying is, keep an open mind in every way you can. Won't hurt to talk to Bree. She has a lotta common sense."

I agreed.

As evident from the overloaded to-do tray on my desk, we had more than we could handle at the Spencer-Austin firm. We needed help. She came to us about six months ago, a USC-trained lawyer with a PhD in psychology from Berkeley.

Brianna Dixon, thirty-eight, liked by everyone in the office except for Cheryl, was unflappable and level-headed with a keen mind, an altogether felicitous addition to our little group. We hired her for her background in psychology and, more important, for her experience in family law. Ben liked to goad her from time to time, but it was more badinage than anything.

Bree, who mightn't have been that pleased with the simile, was rather like the Advil or Tylenol we take for a nagging headache. Garrett or I, even sometimes Ben, would seek her out when we needed someone to listen to us vent. Infallibly, we felt better when we left. My stack of untouched files too large to contemplate, I got up and headed for her office.

I grinned as I frequently did when I went in, less at the lady than at the inviting full-length couch that was perpendicular to her desk. It dominated a pleasantly decorated room with a few pictures and a half a dozen plants, all collected from Bree's garden. Her office was spacious enough to accommodate a chair in front of her desk but to the side that looked unused.

Pointing at the sofa, I said, "Now that's precisely what this man needs."

"Well then," came her contralto voice, "be my guest." Grinning back at me, she added, "Either sit or lie down, depending on what you came here for."

"Now, now, Bree," I replied, half sitting, half lying

back, "you mustn't make offers I can't refuse. You think I don't know that you use that line on everyone who comes in here? Please!"

Raising her hands in mock protest, she countered, "Mr. Spencer, you've got me wrong. Who's been telling stories around here? When I lie down over there, I go to sleep. Alone, okay? You've been looking a little peaked these last few days so I thought you might like a nap. I take one every day or so in the middle of the afternoon. You knew that, didn't you?"

"Brianna Dixon, you're an unmitigated flirt. You put this couch in here so you'd always have the upper hand."

"A flirt? Me? That's Sara Pringle's domain as you of all people ought to know. That couch, since you bring it up, is a lot more comfortable than that excuse for a client chair you have. Come on, admit it. That couch, if you must know, is there mostly for me. I meant it about my naps. Now since you didn't come to seduce me, tell me why you're here."

There were no subtexts or ambiguities in that exchange. Bree could be playful when we were together because I was safe. It wasn't that I found her unappealing, not at all. It was just too soon for me to be in hunting mode as I'm sure she sensed, perceptive as she was. Now she'd go from friendly small talk to attentive colleague.

For the next half hour, I summarized Lucy's situation. I was candid about the relationship we'd had. Perhaps it was her training or just her nature. Bree was one of the best listeners I knew. She didn't take notes anymore when I came in since I told her I felt like a patient when she wrote as I talked to her from her couch. She didn't need notes anyway as it turned out. She was able to recall nearly everything I said.

There'd be silences from time to time as she processed things. I could see by the expression in her eyes that she'd temporarily gone away to think. I could contemplate her with impunity at such times.

No real beauty there, nothing I'd write poetry about.

She had green eyes that seemed unusually alive, probably because of little golden flecks I thought I saw that were like fish in an aquarium that were constantly on the move. If I couldn't see them, she was distressed or deep in thought.

Her face was heart-shaped with even features and a full, rather sensual mouth. She had curly brown hair that fell just past her ears. Short, no more than a hundred pounds, her body, while pleasing to the eye, would not turn heads.

Apart from those rather special eyes, her most outstanding feature was her voice. It was low but unmistakably female. It was less the timbre that one paid attention to than the warmth, so it was for me, at least, and others I'd talked to. The best way I can describe it is that, at our first meeting, I felt that I'd be glad to have her as a friend. It was perhaps this attribute, more than other factors, that accounted for the number of visitors she had.

The only person in our office Bree rarely saw was Sara Pringle. She was to have left us months ago to attend law school. She'd decided to stay another year. This fact, when occasionally pointed out, made Bree smile.

"Lucy has two children, you said?"

"Yes, a boy, nineteen, and a daughter who's twelve now, I think."

"No current pictures of them, I assume?"

Curious about why she asked this, I told her no. I could get them, I supposed, if it was important.

"Later on, perhaps," Bree said. "I concur with Garrett about the way it looks. To save a son she loved, a mother might do a thing like that. No matter how you feel, I do think we have to look into it as unobtrusively as we can. When did you see the younger child last?"

Shamefaced, I admitted that it had to have been two, possibly three years ago.

Bree leaned forward slightly and regarded me. "Forrest, a couple of things. Whatever Lucy's motives were for killing Pete, it doesn't seem very likely to me that a few visits by you now and then would have changed things very much, if at all. Related to this, a fair amount of time's gone by since you saw any of the Jackson family. Two years or so, you said."

I nodded.

"Do you know Lucy's friends? Will any of them be willing to talk to you?"

Feeling miserable and guilty, despite what Bree implied, I said, "The truth is, because of my own problems, I neglected Lucy, very badly, I'm afraid. The last couple of times I saw her, she looked pretty woebegone, pretty down. There was no sparkle anymore. Bree, you should have seen the way she used to be, so outgoing, so full of life, a free spirit if I ever saw one. I should have been there for her. I should have seen."

"Forrest, what about her friends?"

"I have no idea who her friends are, if she has any. She's got a brother and sister-in-law in town. They might be of help. How much, though, I don't know. The two families didn't see much of each other as I understand."

Perhaps it was the warmth and sympathy on Bree's face that made me choke up. I just managed to hold back the tears. On the one hand, talking to her was good. On the other, my own words had made me understand what I'd failed to see.

I knew why Lucy reacted to me in the way she did, or at least I thought I knew. She trusted me as a lawyer, yes, but I had abandoned her as a friend. And—I knew I was not at fault for this—how could she maintain the resolve to carry out her plan, devastating though it was, if she had to fend off people close to her who would attempt to save her? Who, in God's name, was Lucy trying to protect? It had to be someone or none of this would have happened. I said as much to Bree.

In that quiet low-pitched voice of hers, she replied, "Find that out, Forrest, and we'll have the key to this. At this point, there's no way to know if your confidence in

Alex is justified." Several seconds after, she continued, her voice even more subdued than before, "If it's not Alex she's protecting, then..."

It took a moment for me to process what she'd just said. I blinked. "Good lord, not Mia, not the child!"

Bree got up and came to sit by me. "It may have nothing to do with either of the children. It's too soon to tell. Until we have further information, we're shooting in the dark. It's troubling that Lucy's doing her utmost to keep things secret. I have a feeling there's a lot involved in this that won't come out unless you force it. I'd like to work with you on this if you'll allow me. The case interests me."

I very nearly hugged her. She must have read this on my face, for she moved away a bit.

"Allow you?" I expostulated. "Are you kidding? I can't think of anyone I'd sooner have. I know you understand that, no matter how this turns out, there's no way I can abandon her any more than I already have. I'm so glad you're willing to help me on this. The way Lucy's behaving, I'm going to need all the assistance I can get."

"Forrest, there's no conflict of interest problem in this, is there, you being a close friend?"

I shook my head. "There's nothing I know of in the Rules of Professional Conduct that prevents me from representing her. Except for our friendship, I'm not involved in her situation in any way. Besides, even if there was some risk, there's no way I'd abandon her, no way at all."

Bree reached for my hand and squeezed.

PART TWO

"When you give another person the power to define you, then you also give them the power to control you."

— Leslie Vernick, *The Emotionally Destructive Relationship: Seeing It, Stopping It, Surviving It*, 2007

Chapter 3

It was done and I was now alone at home, released on bail, Alex and Mia having fled to my brother's home. I was still reeling from the aftermath of a brutal storm that seemed to have come upon our family overnight.

But, reflecting there at my kitchen table with my cup of tea, I knew that the clouds had been gathering for years. In recent weeks, the atmosphere in our home had become intense. A word or look and Pete and Alex were at each other's throats. Dinner served a few minutes late and Pete would berate me as a bad homemaker and lousy wife. A comment by me at the wrong moment about the appropriateness of Mia's clothes would cause my daughter to fly at me or run to her father for support.

And, there were smoldering issues between me and my husband that had grown larger over time, due at any moment to erupt.

Had I done the right thing or should I have stepped back and allowed matters to take their course? Not an issue, really. If I had it to do again, I'd intervene just as I had on the weekend. More important to me at the moment was how we'd ever reached this point.

The ideal couple with a handsome child, people twenty years ago would have said, no way they'd fail. Pete claimed that the blame was mine because of my refusal to be a devoted mother and a proper spouse. For me, it was my husband's determination to rob me of my independence and wear me down until I became his 1950s-style wife.

With everything going for us as we had, I knew there had to be more things involved than my doubtless oversimplified view of things. I no longer knew who I was, but I did remember who I'd been.

What mystified me was how the young woman I recalled had not foreseen the obvious, that the man she'd fallen for wanted a hausfrau for a mate rather than the social, independent female I was. How could I have allowed someone to steal my identity that way and turn me into the codependent weakling I'd become?

As I poured my second cup of tea, I wondered if there might not be a way to get more clarity on some things. For reasons that have always remained a bit of a mystery to me, I began a diary in my late teens. Except for a dry period of two years, I kept it up until a week ago.

I should be able to resurrect a lot of things, important things that took place during the last two years that might help me understand how we could have ended up where we are. And, I'd have the benefit of confirming if I'd been the young woman I remembered myself to be.

I'd have six volumes to go through, mostly trivia and junk, but there had to be some things worthwhile in there. Anyway, what else did I have to keep me occupied for the next few days. One thing for certain—I wouldn't be seeing much of those six volumes where I was going. If nothing else came of it, at least I could revisit the happier years of my life.

Gazing at the dark corner of our basement where my old worn-out trunk was, I wondered if anyone would ever have discovered the six handwritten books I had in there before they were thrown out as trash. I opened the trunk lid whose hinges didn't make a sound. I'd been careful with the 3-IN-ONE to oil them.

No one to worry about seeing me down here now. Where to start? If I wanted insight about who I'd been and how I'd gotten to where I was, best go to the first volume in the set. It wasn't as though I didn't have the time. I'd skip things that didn't really tell me anything—that'd be most of the pages in the books—and focus on the things that did. When I finished, if I thought there was anything worth keeping, I'd leave the books here with a note. They might help the children in some beneficial way, at least, I hoped.

Dragging over a small rolled up rug that I meant to discard months ago, I spread it out near the trunk and sat down on the floor to read.

I was astounded by how much of the past my words brought back, hastily written and telegraphic though many were. Entire scenes, smells, songs, voices, whole conversations returned to me. Within minutes, I was in another world and back with that girl that I'd begun to think was just a fantasy, a girl who was outgoing and had so much zest for life.

Chapter 4

1991

April

"Step by Step" by New Kids on the Block's playing loud in my ears as I get home from high school this afternoon. Mom's calling out to me and waving her hand at me.

"Lucy, would you take off those stupid headphones for a minute, please?"

I hit the button on my Walkman and put my backpack down.

"There's a letter for you on the kitchen table from some university. Don't know which one."

I throw my backpack on the floor, kick off my shoes and run to see. Another turndown, no doubt, just like the other four. Unless I do something outrageous by the end of the school year like packing up and moving to Timbuktu, I'm going to be stuck here in Modesto, which nobody in their right mind would look forward to. My grades just haven't been good enough. Too much partying and fooling around, I know.

My heart sinks as I pick up the envelope. No way the University of California at Santa Barbara, the first school on everybody's lists, is going to let me in.

The print turns into squiggles and my heart stops when I see the first few words: *We are pleased to inform you that...* When the letters on the page come back into focus and I begin to breathe again, I see that the acceptance is conditional. So what! I have to take a remedial English class and maintain at least a C average during the first year.

Mom runs back in, looking scared, as I'm jumping up and down and making a lot of noise. I wave the letter in her face.

"Child, for heaven sake, calm down. What's going on? You frightened me half to death with all that racket."

I'm still waving the letter and I practically shout, "I've only been accepted to absolutely the most fantastic university in California where every girl I know wants to go, that's all. The campus is on the beach!"

"Lucy, stop waving that at me and make some sense. What school are you talking about, anyway?"

"UCSB at Santa Barbara, of course, where else? Can you believe it?"

"Why, that's wonderful, dear," Mom says, but I know she doesn't really mean it. She's always hoped Jimmy and I would go on to school here and live close by. No way, Jose, am I going to be pinned down here, not when I could be in Santa Barbara. I didn't hear Jimmy come in.

"Sis, what are you jumpin' all around about? You look like Sonia Sheedy with those blue pants and big sweater." Sonia's the biggest slut in our high school. I don't listen to what my dorky little brother says. He always says stuff like that.

I turn around to face him with the letter that's changed my life still in my hand and I tell him, "I've been accepted at UC in Santa Barbara. How's that!"

Pretending he doesn't know what UC Santa Barbara is, he says, "You gonna be a waitress there or what?"

Screw him! I can't get the smile off my face. It's like it's painted on. Jimmy goes off to his room upstairs while Mom's watching me reread my letter.

God, just five months and I'll be there, two and a half to finish school and graduate, then two and a half more in this grubby place before I'm free.

"Well," Mom says, looking at the sheet of paper in my hands, "your father will be pleased. He always did want you to go to a good school. Now why don't you try to settle down a bit and get your homework done so you can help me with the veggies. George'll be home a little late. A lot of root canals he had to do today, he said."

"Screw homework," I say. "I've gotta call Lynne and Jenny first. They'll be so jealous! I'll have time for homework after we finish dinner."

August

I feel like a prisoner who's about to be let out. God, I hate this town. First, that earthquake in Southern California in late June that everybody was going on about that I barely felt, then July, the hottest and longest month I can remember, then these last three weeks that seemed like they'd never end.

I've been working my butt off since graduation and putting every cent aside to buy new clothes. No more sweaty shifts in the restaurant, putting up with all kinds of crap. My tips were good, but God, what I had to go through to get them. I finished up yesterday. This morning I'm gonna hit the clothing stores, cosmetic counters and shoe shops, something I've been dreaming about since the letter came.

Mom's against me buying nice stuff. She doesn't understand why I spend so much time looking at fashion magazines. Lucky for me, Dad understands. He must read my mind. How can I have money for myself at school if I use most of it to shop?

Mom's in the bedroom doing I don't know what and I'm finishing the dishes when Dad comes into the kitchen and sits down, holding his paper. He's a news junkie, I swear.

"You realize the Soviet Union's soon to be no more?" he says.

I know I shouldn't feel like this, but I don't really give a damn. I have more exciting things to think about.

Dad's disappointed, I can tell, that here I am going off to university and I could care less about world events.

He folds his paper and puts it on the table. "So, Cee-Cee," he says, "feeling homesick already, baby girl?" My dad has a lotta nicknames for me. I love 'em all. He's quiet but he likes to tease.

Grinning, I say, "Oh, Daddy, how'd you know? It's gonna kill me to leave all of this behind."

"Put your dish towel down for a minute and come sit."

I take the chair at the table across from him.

"You've been workin' real hard this summer at the restaurant to save up for your new clothes, haven't you. That's not gonna leave you much for school, is it?"

I shake my head.

"How much did you save?"

"Just over a thousand bucks," I tell him.

"Good stuff, Chicken, but that's not going to take you very far. You're good with money, lot better than Jimmy is, so this is what we're gonna do. I've gotten a Visa card with your name on it. The account's mine so it's me who pays the bills. You can spend up to fifteen hundred with the card for your new things this week for school and go on using it for stuff you really need at the university. If you're careful with the card and don't overspend, I'll take care of the bills and we'll be fine. We'll just keep this between ourselves, okay? Your mother doesn't have to know."

He takes an envelope from his shirt pocket and hands it to me. "Be careful with this thing. You'll have to sign it and activate it, by the way. The instructions are inside. You ever lose it, you call me right away, okay?"

I want to jump up and go around to hug him, but that's not something we do in this family so I don't. I just smile at him. He nods and understands.

September

The campus is like a different world. It's better than

I ever dreamed. There are attractive wide walkways and lots of grass and pretty plants everywhere. The whole place smells like lilacs. The kids are nice, the whole place is beautiful and the food in the dining commons, wow! I'm going to have to watch it or I'll gain weight.

My dorm room is a little cramped and gloomy, looks like it was built in the last century, but better than what I've got at home. It's boxy with a window that looks out on to a grove of trees. Two sets of wide single beds with attached closets at the foot and desks with bookshelves, small but good enough for two girls.

"Hey Lucy," my roommate says. Her name is Jan. "You gonna try out for a sorority? It's the best way to meet guys. That's what I've heard, anyway." Tapping her cheek then her smallish boobs then her waist, she says, "No way they'll take me. You won't have any problem getting in, not with what you've got."

I'm not sure why she says this. She's cute.

There are some real babes here, let me tell you. No way I compare to them. I'm about five feet seven, one hundred and twenty-five pounds—sometimes I go a little over. I've got nice blue eyes and pretty hair, I'll say that—it's naturally blond and usually shoulder length—and good size boobs and an okay face, but there's not a lot to talk about after that. Just the same, guys hit on me all the time in high school, a lot more than with prettier girls than me.

It's something I don't understand. They say I'm sexy, some girls say so too, but I haven't a clue why. Can't be just because I like sex. I do, a lot, but so do most of the girls I know. I can't see how my pheromones or whatever it is I've got's gonna help me get the sorority I want. The only way to get together with hot guys, everybody says, is to get into one of the better ones.

I apply to four and two invite me. I'm super excited since one of these is the Delta Gamma sorority. Two days later, I'm a DG pledge and about as happy as an action girl—that's kinda how I see myself—can be.

The DGs are involved in a lot of things, I learn. They're very active as volunteers in public service, but that's not all. My DG sisters aren't shy when it comes to hooking up with guys. Doesn't take long for partying to start.

I'm glad to see that whatever I have that attracts Modesto boys works here too, so much so that I have little time for books.

Some of the pledges I talk to seem okay with it, but I'm a bit pissed off by expectations of many of the frat boys. Hey, I like sex in just about every way, but wanting the whole tamale on the first date seems a little much.

I can't believe how fast word gets around that I'm not going to fuck every guy I go out with on the first date and I don't like to swallow. Some of the guys I do like stop calling me. If I'm really into someone or if I'm in the mood, I'll go all the way first time, but fucking just to fuck isn't my thing.

I stop talking about sex with my DG friends. I'm starting to wonder if being in a sorority is right for me. There's a lot of things pledges have to do. I don't really need it to meet guys. And, I find that most of the girls in my dorm who aren't in sororities feel a lot like me.

C's and D's and one F in my midterms and I decide that one trimester is enough. I'll drop out of the sorority when the term ends.

How lucky can a girl get? I don't like living in a messy place, but I don't always pick up after myself. I come back to our room and, magic—it's all done. Jannie insists she just did her own stuff, but I know it's her.

Another thing that I like. For some reason, she makes me feel good. Don't ask me why. Maybe it's just good energy and vibes. I'm a big believer in that stuff.

Jannie and I get along really well. She's not at all like the friends I usually have. She studies nearly all the time. I don't. She's gentle and refined. Next to her, I feel like, what do they call it, a diamond in the rough. She cares about people in a way I'm not used to.

I come into our room one afternoon and she's standing in the middle of the floor. She's so mad her red-orange hair actually looks puffed up.

"Jannie, what's going on?" I ask.

She bunches up her fists like she's going to hit something. "My jerk of a professor in my physics class refuses to let a student in because he's blind. The guy's a math genius from high school, some people say, but the prof still won't let him in. Says he won't be able to do the work and he doesn't want to be responsible. Can you believe that?"

Not something to get all riled up about, seems to me. Maybe the teacher's right. If the kid's blind, how can he do the work?

I'm about to say this when Jannie says, "No way. Not going to put up with this!" She whirls around and leaves.

Overreaction, I think as I put my books and stuff on my desk. My mind's on a guy I'm going out with this coming Friday.

I don't see my roommate again until dinner in the dining commons.

"So where have you been?" I ask.

"In the Dean's office, that's where."

"What, over the physics thing?"

"Yes. He wasn't about to do anything until I told him that I was going to get up a petition against the instructor. He hemmed and hawed a little bit after that but he told me not to bother. He'd make sure the student was let in. I told him that a bunch of us in the class were going to make sure the student's tests were fair. He said not to worry. He'd see about that too."

"Jannie to the rescue," I say. "Way to go. I wish I had your spirit."

December

Christmas at home is pretty nice this year. Our

three-bedroom tract house isn't all that much, but Mom's done a lot of decorating and has a nice tree up.

I feel kinda bad when Dad asks me about my grades. We're sitting together in the living room the day after Christmas. As usual, he's got the newspaper on his lap.

"So, Cee-Cee, how's school? You have all you need?" My dad's rather quiet and indirect in the way he talks sometimes. He doesn't like making me uncomfortable. What he really wants to know is how my grades are, but he won't say so. He just hopes that I'll tell him. Mom doesn't ask me anything at all about my classes.

I turn my face away a little when I answer, "I'm doin' okay. Our grades for the trimester aren't in yet. Courses are a little harder than I expected, there's so much reading."

He nods as he correctly translates my BS as, 'My grades are low.'

"One good thing we can be thankful about," Dad says, glancing down at his lap.

It'll be something in the news so I don't ask.

"We won't have to worry about nuclear warheads anymore, not for the present, anyway. The USSR shuts down today. Incredible, isn't it."

"Yes it is," I respond, with only the vaguest idea why.

Even Jimmy's decent toward me. Mom says he misses me. Like a bad toothache, he does.

Jenny and Lynne just don't seem the same. Neither of them went on to school. Both have jobs in department stores. I go to a few parties with them, but things just aren't the same. The guys are pretty much like before, undressing me with their eyes. The girls are nice enough, but I'm not on the inside anymore. This makes me kinda sad. Lynne called me on the twenty-seventh and invited me to a girls' night out. Wasn't so long ago she would have called me first to see if I was available before arranging things.

"That'd be great," I tell her, "only my parents have

people coming over that evening and they want me to be there."

The girls know it's a lie, but they don't seem to care. It's like they think I'm stuck up or something. It's going to be like this from now on, worse the longer I'm away from here. Maybe things will get better when summer comes.

1992

January

My grades turn out a little better than I thought, but they're not good, mostly C's and a D+. I'll have to improve this trimester or I'm out. I can't let that happen, especially for my dad. He'd be super disappointed.

I don't know how I'd survive without my roommate. She manages to get A's and B's and still have time for me.

"Jannie," I say, upset with a D on a paper I worked hard on, "what's wrong with this? I did everything the prof told us we had to do."

She looks at the comments for a while, then pats the space beside her on her bed. "Luce, there are three things I see that you need to work on." She smiles to soften her comments, then says, "You write about a lot of stuff, but it's not organized very well. I'll help you out with that next time. You don't have much of an introduction to tell us what you're gonna do, and you forgot your bibliography." Smiling at me again, she adds, "Don't sweat it. I can help you with all of this."

She's super, my roommate is.

I'm out on the weekends pretty much all the time, but, from the beginning of the term, I work harder to keep up.

The dorm's okay and my social life is fine, but I need more action, something more exciting. Not the kind my friend down the hall, Ruby Stein, had this afternoon. Poor thing had a miscarriage. The fire department and every other service on the campus came—a real mess. She seems to be okay now.

For kicks, I join a sky diving club. I won't tell my parents or they'd really flip. We have to learn a lot of stuff before we go out, but I can't wait. I'm more scared than I've ever been when the plane door opens and it's my turn to jump.

"Come on, Lucy Goosey," Tony, our jump instructor says. "You're up next. There'll be a line between you and Dan all the way so you'll be okay."

It turns out to be the funnest thing I've ever done except maybe for having sex.

Tony Valdez has thirty jumps. He's really cute. The three other girls in our group want him, but they'll have to stand in line. Tony and I hit it off right away. The chemistry between us is something else! He loves my cowgirl get-up with boots, jeans and matching denim jacket that does nice things for my top.

The night after our first jump, he asks me out. We go to see *The Silence of the Lambs*—creepy—then back to his apartment in Santa Barbara.

February

Yay! First B on a midterm, a C+ and the others C's. I owe the B to Jannie.

She looks funny with those big headphones she has on. For once, I'm not wearing mine that are quite small.

"Earth to Jannie," I say as I come in. She doesn't hear. I tap her on the shoulder. "What are you listening to, anyway?"

"Sorry, Luce. I work better when I have music on. It's 'Black or White,' the Michael Jackson song. What's that in your hands?"

I wave the midterm at her. "The one you stayed up almost all night on to help me with," I say. "My first B."

"Go, girl!" she says. "We were up 'til about three o'clock, weren't we?"

"At least," I say. "Thanks a bunch. I needed that."

Jannie blushes a little and turns away. She blushes

quite a lot, actually.

We complement each other in good ways. She's cute but kinda shy. I help her find guys to go out with. She makes me study more and continues to help me with my exams and essays. I'd flunk out for sure if it wasn't for her help. She was on the Dean's List last trimester.

Except for a sprained ankle that I got on my fourth jump, I'm good. I drop out of the sky diving club, but Tony and I are still going strong. He's a little on the wild side, but hey, so am I. Life's good.

May

Students are in an uproar over the Rodney King killing by police in Los Angeles. When the riots die down, many of them who are still on campus board buses to L.A. to go to demonstrate. Mary Bickerton, who's another friend of mine in my dorm, asks me to go with her so I do.

Jannie also wants to come. She doesn't say much, but I can tell that she's really upset about what happened. The whole place feels like a powder keg ready to explode.

Some of my friends seem to get off on the whole thing but I don't like any of it at all. I feel bad about what happened to King and I expect the police who beat him up will all get off, but I wish I hadn't come. The tension and the violence are just too much. Jannie seems to be crying half the time.

June

Not too bad for an action girl who likes to play: two B's, three C's. Probation period over.

The weather in Modesto drives me nuts. I have to take showers twice a day, it's so damn hot. It's good to be with Mom and Dad again—and Jimmy, too, I guess. My little brother's growing up.

The people in the restaurant where I worked before want me back so, even though I think I could do better if

I looked around, I take the job. It's a steak house where the majority of clients are men. There's no salary as such but the tips are good if you're willing to smile at stupid jokes and pretend to be impressed by jerks who hit on you all the time.

The owner almost fires me when I slap the smirk off of some asshole who doesn't stop groping me. "Lucy," my boss says, "you know what kinda trouble that guy could cause? He could get us for assault or something like that. I know it's tough for you girls sometimes, but we've gotta put up with it, so take it easy."

It's not him who has to put up with anything but his bank account. It's me! I do the same thing again a couple of weeks later and he has to let me go.

August

My God, when will summer end! Jimmy and I are back to fighting all the time and Mom's driving me nuts with her questions about my social life. What she really wants to know but doesn't say is, have I met anyone who might make a decent son-in-law. She just shakes her head and clicks her tongue at me when I tell her that girls don't worry about things like that these days until they're thirty.

I miss having Jannie around to talk to. She always puts me in a better mood when I'm feeling down. I owe her two letters that she wrote from her parents' place in Fresno. She's working as a server too and hates it. I should write back, but I'm no good with letters. Never have been. I'll call her and see what she's up to.

Dad's busy at work, but he's had some time to do a little work on the house with Jimmy's help. God knows, it needed it. It looks shabby compared to other places in our neighborhood.

Dad's also found time to get back to teaching me how to drive. I'll finish up my driver's ed course in about a week, then take my test. I don't need a car at school, but it'll be good to have my license.

I miss Jannie quite a bit, actually. I've never met

anyone quite like her. She always seems cheerful when I'm down, a really good thing for me. I wish I had some way to pay her back for all the things she does. I'm hoping we can room again together this coming year.

September

Can't say how good it is to be back at UCSB. I'm in the same dorm and yay! They honored my request! I've got Jannie back. It must have been a done deal, I guess, since she asked for the same thing. I really get along with her.

October

Like usual, I'm walking around the campus with my earphones on and listening to my Walkman. I can't get "Baby, Baby" by Amy Grant out of my mind. I'm beginning to hate that song. No matter what I listen to, it keeps coming back.

I'm fiddling with my Walkman when I almost bump into my psych instructor I had last year. He can't be much older than I am, thirty-two, maybe, max. I had to move from the front row to the back 'cause he kept giving me the eye all the time. It looks like he hasn't given up.

"Lucy," he says, acting surprised. "Fancy meeting you here. I wondered if you'd dropped out of school." The guy's a jerk. Thinks he's hot stuff. I'm not watching where I'm going, okay, but it was him who bumped into me on purpose. "It's almost lunch time. You want to join me?"

"Thanks, but I'm eating with my boyfriend," I lie. "Thanks for asking."

"There's always a next time," he says.

'In your dreams,' I want to say out loud.

I like English lit well enough because of what we read, but I can't stand writing papers. I'm coming out of a class and heading out the door of the English building, staring at the D that I just got and not looking where

I'm going, when I run smack into a guy who's coming up the steps.

My books fly out of my half open backpack and I'm headed for the ground and he grabs me. Lucky thing. I could have hurt something. He catches me in my armpits where his hands end up against my boobs. Where most guys would hold on a little longer, he doesn't, smiling at me as I stand up.

Nothing particular about him I'd shout about, but he does look warm and nice. His name is Forrest, of all things, Forrest Spencer, weird name. The least I can do to thank the guy is to offer him a cup of coffee.

After looking at his watch, he says, "Sounds good. I'd love to have a cup. In fact, I need to eat something. Haven't had a bite all day." He's still got my books, which I take back and off to the Student Union we go.

I look at him sitting across from me—dark brown hair, a friendly face with widely spaced brown eyes that I really like. There's something solid about him, a little on the serious side, maybe.

"Do I get to know your name?" he says.

I grin and hold out my hand. "I'm Lucy, Lucy Evans. I'm really glad you were where you were when I was going down those steps. They're kinda steep and slippery."

He nods and looks at me, not in the way most guys do who are obsessing about my chest. He is looking at my eyes. The experience is kinda nice.

For something to say, I ask, "What are you studying here?" He looks like a graduate student to me.

"I'm a sophomore in poli sci," he tells me. "And you?"

"I'm in English lit, but I ought to be in something else, something that doesn't require a lot of writing. I'm thinking about minoring in education in case I ever want to teach. You live around here, when you're not in school, I mean?"

"No such luck. My family lives in Sacramento, not all that bad a place, but nothing to compare with Santa Barbara. How about you?"

"I come from beautiful downtown Modesto. You'll know what I mean if you've ever been there."

Forrest grins as he says, "Oh yeah, I know the place. Drove through there last summer with a friend. Pretty hot it was if I remember."

"If it wasn't for my family, I'd be happy if I never saw the place again." Still looking at him while he eats, I say, "Poli sci. That must be tough. You have a lot to write?"

"Not a lot, not as much as I do in English. That's my minor. If I can find a decent school that'll accept me, I'm going into law when I graduate."

Laughing, I say, "Now I know why you look like the serious type. I can see you as a lawyer."

Forrest puts down the rest of his sandwich and regards me. Then he says, "Serious? In a way, I guess. I do have to hit the books pretty hard to get the grades I need. Now as to being serious, let's see." Looking very sober, he says, "You're all fired up about the coming elections, of course, aren't you. Now your prediction, please. Mr. Clinton or Mr. Bush."

At the blank look that must have been on my face, Forrest relents. With a hint of a smile, he goes right on. "I like to play as well, when and if I get the time."

Reviving, aware that he'd been teasing me, I look for that expression in men's eyes that I know so well when they say 'play,' but I don't see it. I can't make up my mind if I'm miffed or pleased. So I say, "What exactly do you mean by play?"

Again that smile. "Well, when I find a girl whose company I enjoy, like now, I think about how nice it'd be to get to know her."

Teasing him back, I say, "That's what you mean by play?"

Now the smile moves up to his eyes. "I could have used a better word, I guess," he says, "but play, one aspect of it, at least, is the getting-to-know process. Don't you agree?"

I'm not sure I've ever been with a guy like this—

young, yet more man than boy, a little on the deep thinker side, maybe, but with possibilities. What I like most of all is that he's respectful. Play, in the minds of most of the guys I know, is just another word for sex. There's that feeling deep in my belly I recognize. What will it take to break through that shell of his?

I ask, "And just how does this process of yours work?"

"By finding out if that person I'd like to get to know is available this coming Friday to go out to dinner and maybe see a movie."

Now it's my turn to smile at this silly but kind of cute fencing game. "Is this the way you talk to every girl you meet?"

"No, not at all," he assures me. "Only to the ones that interest me."

"I can see why you're going into law. Now if you really get to know me, you may find me too direct. When I want something, I go for it. When I don't, I walk away. Does the fact that I'm still sitting with you here tell you anything?"

Without a pause, Forrest says, "Six-thirty be okay?"

I grin and nod. He can be taught. Hmmm. I get a pad and pencil from my purse and write down the name of my dorm and my phone number. He looks at his watch and I quickly look at mine.

"See you Friday, Lucy. I look forward to it."

'So do I,' I'm saying to myself as he walks away.

What am I so excited about, I think, as the week drags by. The guy's almost a nerd, not my type. It's not that I'm all gooey inside about him, I'm really not. What I want, I guess, is for him to put his respect for my gender aside for a little while and make him come after me as a girl. So, it's a game, not one I'm used to but sorta fun.

No candlelight and music in the background as we eat. It's fluorescent lights and so much noise we can hardly talk. Forrest wants to take me to a nice place in Santa Barbara, but he's only got just enough money left for the month, he tells me. Frankie's Place in Goleta where a lot of students go is fine with me.

Now what, I wonder, does Mr. Spencer have in mind when we don't find any movie we like in town? He invites me to his apartment for a drink, predictable, a cheap one-room bachelor, he says. We get into his beat-up Chevrolet and off we go.

Books everywhere, but at least it's neat and clean. We sit on a folded futon that's Forrest's bed and drink cold beer. I keep expecting him to fidget, then drop the act and make his move. Instead, easy as you please, he talks to me and listens. What's this guy made of anyway, I think. Not gay, I'm sure. He doesn't have the look.

I'm just not used to this. You go to a guy's apartment at night alone and you sleep with him. I didn't really come for that, I realize. In fact, I'll be sort of disappointed if he asks. Still...

"Lucy, it's crazy how people meet, isn't it. There we were, people everywhere, and—"

"It was your arms I tumbled into. Beats meeting in a bar."

"Yeah, well, if Miss Evans has no objections, I'd like to get to know her better. How would she react to such a thing?"

This guy's unbelievable. Here I am, sitting on his futon that in a minute could be a double bed, and he's asking me if I'll let him get to know me better. Is this some corny way to ask me to sleep with him?

I have the answer when he says, "I'd love to keep on talking, but I've got only the intro done for a twenty-page essay due for Monday. I'll drive you to your dorm then come back here and hit the sack. Sorry we couldn't find a movie that you liked."

Stammering—now I'm disappointed—I say, "That's, that's okay, Forrest, that's fine. I've got work to do tomorrow anyway."

*

'Oh no you don't,' I'm saying to myself as Forrest reaches for the car door handle on my side to let me out.

"Remember what I told you about what I do when I want something?"

I have to keep from laughing at the confused expression on his face. I reach out and put both my hands behind his head and pull him to me. A kiss that starts as a surprise doesn't finish up that way. I hold him there for at least half a minute while I explore every area of his mouth before I let him go. He looks dazed and thoroughly aroused. Precisely what I'm looking for. Mr. Spencer and I are going to get along. I'm thinking I haven't seen the last of that futon yet.

November

Everybody on campus is jubilant about the outcome of the election. I'm pretty happy about it myself although I'd have a hard time saying why. To quote my father, 'It's just that twelve years of Republicans in the Oval Office is a bit too much.'

With two dreaded papers and three midterms done, I can breathe again. Little social life these last two weeks. Jannie's been quizzing me and helping me with papers.

I realize something's wrong the minute I come in. Jannie's where she nearly always is, at her desk, and staring at a closed notebook. I always get a smile when I get back. This time I only get a nod. Something's up.

I walk over to her chair, pick up a limp right hand and pull her over to her bed where we sit down. She looks upset.

"Hey, what happened?"

She makes a poor effort at a smile and shakes her head. "Nothing, Luce, nothing to worry about. I'll be fine." One tear then two.

Words aren't going to be enough. Jannie's willing to take on everybody else's problems but she doesn't like the thought of burdening others with her own. She's told me so. I slide closer and put an arm around her shoulders.

"Hey. Our friendship goes two ways. I want to know what's wrong."

A few more tears then she tells me. "I was on my way back here when I saw a lady whose little boy was running along in front of her. I happened to be near him when he fell down. He wasn't hurt, but he was scared, I think. I ran over to him and picked him up and cuddled him. He's about twelve months old, I think. I gave him a little kiss on his fat baby cheek and was turning around to take him to his mother when, there she was, screaming at me. She threatened to call the police. I should never pick other people's children up like that, she said, and I certainly shouldn't touch them with my mouth. I gave her the child and apologized and went away as fast as I could. Why did she yell at me, Luce? What did I do?"

Poor Jannie, poor sweet Jannie just wanting to help someone. Lucky I wasn't there or that bitch would have gotten a piece of my mind.

My arm still around her shoulder, I say, "Jannie, you did what any decent person would have done. You ran into some stupid germaphobe who went off the rails. It's her fault, not yours." I bend over and peck Jannie on the cheek. "You're the sweetest most generous person I know."

Another of Jannie's blushes. "Thanks for making me talk about it," she says. "That helps so much."

"What do you think you do for me all the time? I don't know what I'd do if I didn't have you."

This time I get a smile.

I've got cabin fever and need to go out somewhere. I've seen Forrest twice, but only to have drinks. He's been busy too. Finally, after a fantastic dinner at Giovanna's in Santa Barbara, the second invitation to his apartment comes.

No talk this time. We're not in his room for more than minutes when we're pulling off each other's clothes. Forrest wants me, wants me a lot. I can see it in his eyes, but he's too slow.

"Forrest, love," I say when we're in the sack, "I'm a hungry girl and I'm not fragile. I know what your mouth tastes like. Now I'm going to find out about the rest. When I'm finished, you're going to do the same. Then I'm going to find out what it's like to have this big boy inside of me. You up to this? I told you I wasn't bashful."

Reserved Forrest might be in public, but not on that three-inch-thick futon of his. Four hours later, I'm as loved out as I can remember being and so ready for a good night's sleep.

December

If it hadn't been for Forrest and for Jannie, I'd have given up and gone back home. After two more papers and five finals, I'm a wreck. I need recreation. When I'm at Forrest's, I keep looking longingly at his bed, but he won't let me pull him over there until we've got a couple of hours of studying in.

I'm getting restless and a bit antsy in my dorm. I keep wanting to get up and walk around, but I don't want to disturb Jannie at her desk who's got her curly red head bent over three open books.

Lounging on my bed, pretending to read, I watch her. She's so absorbed in what she's doing that she doesn't see. Like other redheads I know, she's got tons of freckles with light brown eyes and a little nose—most unusual. She's petite, size zero max, her face, her hands, her feet, everything. Nice body, no more than a hundred pounds. She has a kinda pouty mouth that's sort of cute.

It's late and I'm in my favorite babydoll nightie and ready to go to bed, but not Jannie. She's fully dressed and up for an hour yet. Maybe if I interrupt her just this once, I can get her to call it quits and we can get some sleep.

I get up and wander over to her chair and put my

hands lightly on her shoulders. They feel quite tight. I'm no masseuse so I don't offer, but I think she needs one. For once, she doesn't have those humungous headphones on.

"Hey there," I say. "Earth to Jannie. You look like you're working pretty hard."

She heard me, she has to have, but she doesn't answer. Also, she doesn't move.

I begin to worry that something may be wrong when I hear her whisper, "Luce, I can't concentrate on anything when you're near me like this."

For a moment, I don't process what she says. I'm still concerned about why she hasn't moved. She seems almost frightened. Then the impact of what I hear hits me. Those frequent blushes, the countless times I've caught her looking at me when I wasn't watching.

My God! Jannie, Jannie has a crush on me or something. I stand there like an idiot, not knowing what to do. If this was just some girl hitting on me—it's happened lots of times before at parties—I'd try to be nice about it but I'd brush her off. But this isn't just some other girl and something tells me in Jannie's voice and the way she's acting that hitting on isn't what's happening here.

I want to suggest that we sit down and talk, so I bend down and start to speak. I stop when I feel her flinch and hear her sharp intake of breath. She stands up quickly and faces me. What's going on here, anyway? Tears are running down Jannie's face and she's trembling.

In a choked voice, she says, "Lucy, no! This has to stop."

Stop? What has to stop? Is Jannie having a breakdown of some kind?

"This isn't right. Luce, oh Lucy," she goes on, covering her little face with her hands, "you don't understand. You mustn't pity me, please don't."

Pity her? What is she going on about?

Trembling and still crying, she looks at me for a

long time. She's obviously upset. I don't know what to think or say so I just stand there.

Finally, she continues, trying to control herself, "There are things about you and me that aren't the same. They can never be." Now she's sobbing and looking at the floor.

I'm confused. Could this be what I think?

"I wish things were different, but I know they can never be, so let's try to go back to the way we were and forget about what I said."

Now I understand. My best friend is attached to me in a way I'd never guessed. What to do? My need at that moment is to comfort her and calm her down. I step forward and reach out for her. She resists, standing stiff as a board, then, as if the energy has all gone out of her, she collapses in my arms and buries her face in my chest.

"I didn't want this to happen," I hear through her sobs. "I didn't want you to ever know. I didn't want to destroy the relationship we have and I didn't want you to ever feel sorry for me. Now see what a mess I've made of things."

Jannie can't stop shaking, even pressed up against me as she is. I walk backwards until my legs touch her bed, then I urge her to sit down, she at one end while I sit at the other to give her space.

Looking at me with tear-stained cheeks, Jannie says, "Now you know part of it, since things will have to change, I may as well tell you the rest. Lucy, I had no way of knowing it would happen to me, I swear, but I fell in love with you the first week we were together in the dorm last year. I tried not to, Luce. I did everything I could. I went out with boys like I did in high school. You even helped me, remember? I joined clubs and I got immersed in my school work, but it didn't help."

Closing her eyes tight, she goes on, "I thought about you all the time, all the time. I wanted to be close to you, but... Luce, I know this is hard for you to hear, but please listen a little longer and I'll be done."

She blinks and I see her swallow several times. "I've never thought about myself as very sexual. I like guys well enough—I've never been with a girl—so I had no way to know what was going to happen. I say I wanted to be close to you, but, I don't even know if any of that's physical or if it's mainly emotional and my need to be near you. Does that make sense?"

Woah! I'm in water way over my head. I haven't a clue what to say so I just let her talk.

"Now that you know, things will have to change for us. We'll have to see if they'll let us change roommates in the middle of the year. That way, you won't have to worry about me anymore."

Jannie wants to go? I wouldn't have predicted it, but the idea shakes me up. Jannie, my roommate, my best friend, the most wonderful girl I know? Jannie who's always there for me, no matter what?

"No, Jannie, no," I say to her. "I couldn't stand it if you go. We've been together too long! There's no need for such a crazy thing. I won't let you go."

Jannie's looking intently at me as I speak. "Luce, how can I say this? I can hardly talk about leaving you, let alone do it. But we have no choice. Loving someone at a distance is bad enough. If I could have held out, it might have worked, for a while, at least. But now that you know, imagine how hard it will be for you and for me to be close to you all the time, you knowing how much I need you. It will destroy me." Again Jannie's hands cover her face and she begins to cry.

I'm not proud of myself as I realize how self-focused about this I am. She can't bear to stay with me anymore, she says, and I can't bear the thought of her not here. I would be so lonely. I must find some way to calm her down and get us back to normal if I can. It won't be like it was before, I understand that, but we can work it out.

"Jannie, listen," I say. "It's late and it's not a good time to solve things like this. Get ready for bed, then come cuddle with me for a while. You'll soon be asleep and tomorrow things will be better, you'll see. I'm not confident they will, but, for the moment, it's the best thing I can think of."

Jannie's tears have dried. I'm surprised to see sorrow in her eyes. After a long pause, she says, "Luce, I've dreamt about doing that since we met, but I'm afraid. I truly am. I dream about going to sleep in your arms, but how will I survive once I've experienced it? Once a child tastes candy, they want more, something I can never have. I want to be with you more than anything else in this world, but I think maybe it's best that we leave things as they are and we make arrangements to change rooms."

She bows her head and begins to cry again. "I'm so sorry, Luce, that I broke down like this. If I hadn't, we'd be okay. Imagine."

What this girl needs right now, it seems to me, is reassurance from someone who cherishes her and a good cuddle, something all of us need sometimes.

"Come on now," I say. "Come be with me for a little while, then we can get some sleep."

"You don't make it easy for a girl to refuse," Jannie says, smiling slightly and looking down. "I'm not sure it's a good idea, but I'd never be able to forgive myself if I refused to be with you." Sounding bashful, she says, "So what should I wear, then?"

"Whatever. Pajamas or something, I don't care. We'll just cuddle for a while, then we can go to sleep."

When I invite Jannie to my bed, I'm interested in two things—to calm her down and try to make her change her mind about switching rooms, and to get some sleep in. I've got a quiz in my first class in the morning. I love Jannie, yes, but not in a sexual way.

I've kissed and played around with a girl or two on the dance floor when I was drunk, but I did it just for fun. I tend to like more aggressive sex, the feel of men's working hands, muscled bellies and real dicks, not things girls are going to give me. What others prefer is up to them. As a sexual person, I know what wanting is. If guys prefer guys or girls prefer girls or whatever, then they should be free to get on with it. That's how I see it, anyway. Sex is natural and to be enjoyed. Since I was a young teenager, I've been fantasizing about and fucking guys. I'm straight, not that the label really means anything.

So it's truly a physical shock when I feel how satiny smooth Jannie's skin is next to mine. She has a nightshirt on or something that doesn't cover much. No wonder guys become so entranced when they touch us. It's mind-blowing in a way, not a sensation I expect.

For the first half hour, Jannie's face is pressed up against me and she's clinging to me so tight I can hardly breathe, from sadness or gladness I can't tell. She keeps murmuring my name while she's like this. I stroke her hair and shoulders just like I would a child. Slowly, she relaxes and lets go of me. It seems as though she's about to go to sleep. I turn my face to give her a quick good night kiss and send her off to bed.

I suppose I should have been expecting it. After all, my body talks to me and I know the signs. There's just no way, the sexual creature that I am, that I'm not gonna get eventually aroused by the feel of a warm body of a beautiful person lying next to me. Still, I'm not actively thinking about it and I'm not really feeling all that much until I experience the second physical whammy of the night, the unexpected softness and taste of Jannie's mouth. If I hadn't kissed her, our cuddling would have probably ended there. But that's not the way things turn out, need I say.

If I had the power, I'd write down more because there's much more to tell. What I can say is that Jannie's gifts to me that night will always count as some of the most beautiful things in my life. She helped me understand how nurturing gentleness and unconditional love can be.

As hours pass, I discover how much more prolonged and joyful sensual pleasure is when with someone who loves deeply like she does and who needs to give. Jannie teaches me without a word that sex is not to be confused with making love. With my experience, maybe I should already know these things. But until that night and early morning, I did not.

For the next few days, I think a lot about what we did. Am I bisexual or lesbian because I've slept with another girl? I decide that the question makes no sense. What difference do labels make, anyway? They're social tags that do more harm than good. I'll be who I am, that's all. I don't tend to get hot and bothered about such things.

I wonder how many girls who consider themselves straight, at some point in their lives, do what Jannie and I did. A lot, I bet. We just don't talk about it all that much. Speaking of Jannie, she's given up her plans to move.

I don't detect any real change in me as sexual desire goes. Loving Jannie doesn't make me more attentive to other girls, not at all. Except for often reliving in my head what my roommate and I do, my fantasies and get-togethers involve guys.

The question is, I guess, does a heterosexual female who enjoys sex with one other girl make her abnormal? From a social perspective, maybe, from a natural or biological perspective, in my opinion, no.

There is no real change in me, but there is in Jannie. One moment she glows with happiness when she looks at me, the next she's trying to hide her sadness when she knows I'm about to go out to be with Forrest or another guy.

She's not all that happy either to see me with a girl. Maria Rosselli, who also lives in our dorm, comes over to see us quite a lot. I'm not sure why. We don't have a thing in common. Maria's into horses, jumping and all of that. She's a bit too rough and masculine for me. She comes over tonight about nine and stays until eleven, well past our bedtime. Maria looks at my roommate a lot which makes me want to laugh. Jannie doesn't like her and wishes she wouldn't come.

When Maria finally leaves, Jannie says, "She likes

you, Luce, you know that? I think she wants you."

I can't help it. I burst out laughing. "Jannie, baby, you gotta be kidding me. It's you that girl wants, not me. Haven't you seen the way she looks at you?"

"I was worried a little," Jannie says, "why Maria keeps coming over here. I thought you and she might have something going, maybe."

Again I laugh and reach out for her. "Hey," I say, "there's one girl in the world I want to be with, that's absolutely all, and I'm holding her. You understand?"

She hugs me and buries her face against my chest and makes a happy sound.

I worry about my relationship with her sometimes. Will continuing to love her physically worsen things for her? Wouldn't it be better if she found someone who could give her what she needs? She goes into orbit when I say this.

"There's nobody else I want to be with," she insists, "and what's the matter with the way things are? I used to be afraid that you'd get tired of me and not want to be with me anymore, but that hasn't happened, so, what's wrong with keeping things the way they are?"

Objectively, she's right. If being with her doesn't hurt her, then I'm glad. One couldn't ask for a sweeter and more giving lover.

I'm just not up to this academic stuff. They say my junior and senior years won't be this hard. God knows, I hope they're right.

I'll miss Forrest's company when I go home, and, of course, I'll miss his loving. Unlike most guys, he knows exactly what I want when he goes down on me which drives me wild. Who would guess he'd be that way by the look of him, serious and all that? You just never know.

1993

February

Easier courses this trimester, I'm glad to say. We

get lots of invitations to parties and sometimes Forrest comes. I know he doesn't like it much when I go alone. I turn guys down who want me to go home with them, but I still flirt and have a lot of fun. I can't help it. That's the way I am. Our loving's as good as it's always been, but I can see something in Forrest's eyes. He's not jealous. That's not what I mean. He's worried about something. Can't quite say what.

Forrest comes down with a bad cold that's later diagnosed as viral pneumonia. I'm at his apartment four days running for several hours, cooking and taking care of him. His fever rises and he loses his appetite. He keeps telling me it's nothing, that I'm an alarmist, but I'm sure he's getting worse.

March

Nearly the end of my sophomore year. I can't believe it. I've been going out a lot, alone sometimes but usually with girlfriends. When I want sex, which seems to be just about all the time, I spend the night at Forrest's or just snuggle up with Jannie, who'd be in my bed every night if I'd let her. I used to think she was confused about her sexuality. She's not.

A lot of times during the week Forrest and I meet for lunch. He's a great guy to be with. I can tell him anything I'm feeling and I know he understands. He's my lover and he's also my best friend, next to Jannie, that is. It's real nice.

Everybody's getting ready to go home. I'm glad school is over, but I wish I could get an apartment and work here. Trouble is, no jobs here and my friends'll all be gone and Forrest too. If I stay in Goleta for the summer, Jannie will too, she says. Otherwise, she'll go back to Fresno with her family.

So it'll be Modesto again that I get to look forward to.

*

It's Friday noon and I'm with Forrest for lunch. I'll be going over to his place tonight for the last time in a while. The idea of being without him for five months doesn't make me happy. I think it's bothering him as well 'cause he's very quiet.

"Luce," he says, "I need to talk about something."

I feel my chest get tight. I think I know what he's going to ask me to do, but, oh boy, how wrong I am.

He says, "You know how much you mean to me, don't you."

I nod. What's this leading up to?

"We're different in some important ways, you and I. You're vital and full of life and, of course, you're beautiful."

I'm starting to get a bad feeling about all this. Why is he saying these things to me?

"As you've pointed out before, I'm more the serious type, not nearly as social as you are. You need people around you more than I do, and you need attention. Attention of the male kind, I mean."

I start to object, but he stops me. "I think you'd be faithful to me if I asked you to while you're at home, but there's no way I'm going to hold you down like that."

Again, I try to interrupt, but he won't let me. "And even if you said you would, I'd worry, and I don't want to. I really like you a lot, maybe more than like, but I don't want to be in a relationship like that, and nor do you. It's not the right thing for either of us to do. Don't you agree?"

I want to say no, that he's wrong, that we are fine the way we are, that nothing has to change. I want to tell him that I don't need to make love with anybody else and I'll wait for him.

I start to say these things, then stop. I know down deep, based on what I've seen these last few months, that Forrest hasn't been totally okay with the way we are.

He needs somebody more like him. Still, the idea that we won't be close anymore makes me want to cry.

It's not the sex, even though that's super good. He makes me feel grounded like no guy ever has. No matter what, I know he's there for me.

I blurt out, and I don't care who hears me, "There's no way you're going to get rid of me tonight, and don't look sad like that or I'm going to lose it, right here."

After a long pause, in a quiet voice, Forrest says, "Lucy, listen, I don't want to get rid of you, not now, not ever. Of course tonight we'll be together. Does any of what I've been saying make sense to you?"

I sit there, not knowing what to say or what to do. He's not exactly telling me goodbye. I wouldn't let him do it anyway. It's the kind of relationship we have, a more open kind, I mean, that he's afraid of. He's worried about how long I'll be happy in one man's bed and how much partying there'll be in his life. The trouble is, I know he's right.

It's stupid, but what I say is, "So we can never be together again like tonight?" I realize, as my words come out, that it's not our lovemaking that I'm afraid to lose. It's the special kind of closeness that we have.

"That's not at all what I mean, Lucy," he says. "You know something? I think you want pretty much the same thing I do. I've found someone very special, you, who I don't want to lose. If we make love again after tonight, then that's fine. Better than fine. I couldn't find a better lover anyway. What I'm saying is we don't need that to keep the special closeness that we have."

I'm trying not very successfully to hold back my tears as I reach my hand out to him. I don't give a damn who's watching.

Trying to be positive even though I feel bad, I smile and tell him, "I hope you haven't got anything important going on tomorrow 'cause you're not gonna get much sleep tonight, got that?"

Squeezing my hand and smiling back, Forrest says, "We'll see who'll be the one to give out first. It was you last time if I remember."

*

July

I'm so sick of hearing Mom go on about Michael Jackson, I could scream. Jimmy's turned into a first-class prick. He doesn't even say hello when he gets home from work. I pity the poor girl who hooks up with him.

As usual, Dad's the only member of our family I get along with. He likes to talk to me about the news 'cause I'm the only person in the house who'll listen to him. I don't really most of the time, but I pretend.

I should have found a waitress job again instead of lifeguarding at one of our Modesto public pools. It's boring and the pay's no good. The only good part is the suntan and the excuse to wear cute bathing suits. I have Sundays and Thursdays off, not good for a girl who likes to party.

I miss Forrest and Jannie and campus life. I try to make up for it by going out a lot, but it's not the same. All the guys around here want to do is drink and fuck. Jannie writes to me every week, but I don't write back. I think she understands. I just don't like writing letters. Never have. I do call her in Goleta once in a while which makes her happy.

As usual, I can't wait 'til school starts again.

September

With money from Mom and Dad, first thing I do back at UCSB is buy a car. It's old and doesn't look like much but it's okay for me.

No more dorm life for this girl. I find a two-bedroom apartment in Goleta that I share with Jannie. It's cramped and has leaky faucets but it's pretty cheap. Jannie and I will have to do some painting and get some pictures up.

We both freak out when a neighbor tells us there are roaches in the apartment across from us. It's only a matter of time, the lady says, until we get them. We didn't have to sign a lease—don't ask me why—so the first beasty we see, we're out of here.

Lots of fast food since neither of us cook. Expensive but it works.

I see Forrest quite a lot, but we're just good friends. I'm glad that being lovers didn't ruin things.

Tony's back in my life. He stays over at our apartment sometimes when he's had too much to drink to drive, but I try to keep that down. Jannie's not happy when he's here. Tony doesn't know we're lovers. He'd flip out if he did. How stupid people are sometimes.

Jannie and I wake up together maybe twice a week, sometimes more.

Everybody told me my third year would be easy. It's not. The courses in education are a snap, but I have papers in every English lit class I take. Jannie is an angel. She'd write my papers if I asked her to. Instead, she insists on writing the outlines. I should have gotten into another field.

October

Jannie's got the TV news on about the wildfires in Laguna Canyon when I go out. It looks really bad. I'm sure I can smell smoke outside and the sky's all clouded over.

I stop in at the pharmacy. I'm late and I'm a little worried. When I get back and run the tests, Jannie leaves the room. I can see she's crying. I must have missed a day or two of my pills. I'm pregnant with Tony's kid. I don't know what to do. I'm not exactly the hausfrau type, but Tony wants the baby and wants to live with me.

I'm tempted, I have to say, especially since university work's just not my thing. Trouble is, Tony rubs me the wrong way sometimes and he's the jealous type. He gets really pissed off if I look at another guy. Like I'm ever gonna change! He'd go ballistic if he knew about Jannie and me. He pushes me too hard about that and I'll dump him. I guess that tells me how committed to him I am.

I doubt very much I'll keep the kid. It's kinda nice, the feeling that there's life inside me, but there's just no way.

December

Turns out, there's no decision I have to make. The first Saturday in December, close to exam time, I get bad cramps and I start to bleed. I'm in my third month and I miscarry.

Tony's in the L.A. area somewhere with his jump team. Just as well, maybe, since he's not exactly the nurturing type.

Fortunately, Jannie is. The miscarriage upsets me quite a lot. Physically, I'm okay after a day or two, but emotionally, I'm a wreck and I don't know why. It's not like I was looking forward to motherhood, and I know for sure that I couldn't stand Tony around all the time. So why am I tearing up so much?

Jannie does everything possible for me, but I still feel down. She calls Forrest who comes over a lot the next few days. When Tony arrives and sees him there, he turns around and leaves.

I don't know how, but Forrest, just being there, settles me. Between him and Jannie, in a few days I'm okay. I wish Forrest and I could be the way we were last year, but I know he doesn't. He's super careful about not letting us get into things. Aggravatingly so sometimes.

She hasn't said so, but I know Jannie's secretly glad that the baby's gone.

With a medical excuse, I get two of my hardest exams postponed. I'll have to turn in my papers and take the tests in late January. Better then than now.

With the pressure off, I convince Forrest and Jannie to go out to eat and to see a movie that just came out. It's *Wayne's World 2*.

*

1994

January

No way I can get these late papers in with all of the other things I have to do. I'm not proud of it, but I turn in two essays written last year by a couple of friends of mine. The same professors are involved so it's kinda risky, but I do it anyway. I'm desperate.

I'm ashamed and I don't tell Jannie. She finds out anyway as I should have known. It was a stupid thing to do and unethical. My judgment's not all that good sometimes. Jannie doesn't say anything, but I know it makes her sad that I didn't come to her.

Funny thing is, I get a B on one that got a C+ from the same prof last year. I get a C- on the other one.

Forrest also knows. I don't know how since Jannie would never tell, but I know he knows. He always asks me how my classes are. He doesn't mention them this time.

Another year plus and I'll be out of here. Then what—Lucy Evans with a useless BA with nowhere to go. Not back to Modesto, that's for sure!

Chapter 5

1994

May

My old boss at the restaurant's happy to have me back. I'm good for business, he says. I have to promise I won't smack guys who try to touch me. As long as they don't go too far, I say. They try to grope me and I'm gonna whack 'em. He thinks about this for a while, then says okay, but try to take it easy.

I haven't gained weight, but I've filled out a little more and that whatever-I've-got that appeals to guys hasn't gone away.

Dad doesn't get on my case, but he's worried about me. I can see it in his eyes. It's because I'm out late or don't come home at all some nights.

Mom's on me all the time. "Lucy," she says, "what are we sending you to college for if you come home like this? You get wilder every year! Makes no sense. Next thing we know, you're gonna end up pregnant, then God knows what. Girl, what's gotten into you?"

She goes on every week like this while I'm at home. I don't pay attention anymore. She's right in a lot of ways, I have to say. I'm drinking too much this summer and I'm doing a few drugs, nothing heavy, mind you, but still...

And, I'm sleeping around too much. There's got to be a reason for me doing these things, but I guess I'm not smart enough to figure out what it is. I feel like there's nothing or no one to hang onto. If Forrest or someone like him was around, I'd be better, or so I tell myself.

July

Everybody's talking about O. J. Simpson these days. They charge him for killing his ex-wife and her friend, but you just watch. No way they're gonna put an American hero with the social clout he has in the pen. Not a chance. The asshole will get off.

Jannie worries me. I get letters from her at least three times a week. She's in Fresno, working at a museum of some kind which she likes, but she's unhappy.

She doesn't say it right out, but I know she's lonely when she's away from me. She's friendly and attractive and could easily find friends and have some fun as I keep telling her, but she doesn't listen. All she does is focus on her work.

Her family's invited me to visit if I have the chance. I'm tempted—I have so little going on these days—but I don't think it's wise. I'm sure Jannie's parents don't know anything about the kind of relationship we have. Twenty minutes after getting there, they'd guess by the way Jannie looks at me, so I continue making excuses why I can't go.

I feel bad for my friend who's the most loving person I know and has so much to offer. I'll be jealous in a way—I know that—but I wish she would look for someone she could be with. I want her to be happy.

Chlamydia, holy shit, is what I've got, so the nurse tells me. No surprise given who I've been with. I'm lucky I haven't caught a dose before.

I quit my job and stay home a couple weeks. I'm seriously depressed—no girls around here I'm really close to, no real boyfriend, nothing to look forward to. Used to be that I couldn't wait for school. Now I could care less about going back. I've got just enough smarts to know that something's going on with me. Dad suggests that I see a therapist, but I say no. What can a shrink do for me, anyway?

August

I go to San Francisco to visit my friend Ruby from UCSB who's got a job up there, but it's no good. She's in a bad relationship with an abusive guy. Somebody like that hits me and I'll deck him, then cut off his balls. I can't believe she puts up with it. I stay only for a couple days, then leave. Just before I go, I call Forrest. He invites me to come and stay with him in Sacramento for a while.

Sanity, at last. He's got a little apartment in some family's house, but it's independent with an outside door. No one sees who comes and goes. Forrest has a job with an accounting firm that he doesn't like, but his mom doesn't have enough to pay everything at school so he has no choice.

It's comfortable with him like it was before. I'm with him one day and I start to feel calmed down. I stay with him a couple weeks—nothing else to do—and we make love a lot, but it's not the same. He wants to, I think, but he won't let himself get attached to me. He needs somebody stable in his life. He's not looking, though. He's got his mind on school.

We lighten up on the sex stuff and just talk a lot. Well, not just talk. We've just come back from dinner, if that's what one can call it, from a crummy joint just down the street. We've got about an hour or so before we go to bed. Neither of us like TV much and his doesn't work very well anyway, so what to do? It comes to me.

"Luce, I know that look. What's on that devious mind of yours?"

"Actually, something fun," I say. "Hang on just a minute. I'll be right back." I'd forgotten I had about a hundred grams of grass. Pretty dried out by now, probably, but still I get it from my travel bag and return to the living room. Forrest takes one look and shakes his head.

"I should have known," he says. "Lucy, I must have tried that stuff fifty times and it never did a thing. Besides, I can't stand the burning in my throat. I'm not used to inhaling 'cause I never smoked."

I consider. "It probably had no effect 'cause you never got enough THC in you if you didn't take it in."

"Probably," Forrest says, "but that's how it is with me. What do you expect me to do?" When I start to smile, he says, "Luce, no way you're gonna get me to eat that wicked-looking stuff. You can forget it." My smile stays on. "Lucy, put that stuff away. It's almost time to go to bed anyway."

"Forrest Spencer, you're pretty smart, but you don't know everything. I can show you a very pleasant way to take this stuff where, I promise, you won't cough once and your throat won't burn and, here's the best, you'll feel the effect just fine, I guarantee. How's that?"

Forrest looks at me, very suspicious-like, but says, "You tell me in words what you're going to do and then we'll see."

"Fine with me," I say. "Here's how all this works. I roll a joint and I take as much as I can into my lungs, then I let it all out to you, mouth-to-mouth. In other words, I give you a big long kiss. Now does that sound so bad to you?"

Forrest smiles and I know I've got him. In two minutes, I've rolled as much of the dry weed into the paper as I can and I start taking long breaths in and out, then, holding a deep breath inside, I go over to him. I don't have to tell him what to do. With our mouths clamped tight together, I breathe out and he breathes in, and then it's done. I take another hit—that's all that's left—and we do it all again.

I'm up and flying. Forrest looks like a judge. And then it happens. He looks kinda pale and he falls into his chair.

"Holy shit, Lucy, you shoulda warned me. This feels

very weird. How long is this gonna last?"

"Oh, just a little while," I say. "I'll make it nicer." I plop down on his lap and try to kiss him on the mouth, but he won't let me, so I kiss him everywhere I can. My hopes that the pot might turn him on as it does with some guys go down the drain when, a minute after putting up with me nibbling on him, he pushes me off and, mumbling, stumbles off to bed.

We have fun our last two days, both of us a little sad that the time's about to end. I could learn to love this man a lot if he'd just let me.

I'm so much better when I leave, teary and sad, but up. I feel like I have my rudder back.

School's starting to look okay again.

September

Another apartment in Goleta that I'll share again with Jannie. She's been in Fresno with her family but will be back late tonight, now that she knows I'm here. I can't wait. I miss her.

I have a heavy load because of a paper I didn't finish for a course last trimester that's due by the end of this month. I feel cooped up in my apartment with all my work and I'm desperate to get out.

The only time I see Forrest these days is on weekends. He's worried about getting in at Berkeley. I see him on campus with different girls—that makes me kind of jealous, but I don't think he goes out very much with them.

I'm putting down my backpack after a Wednesday class when I look over at our kitchen table. In the center is a beautifully decorated cake with tiny candles that surround a heart. September 14, my birthday. I look around for Jannie who's peeking at me with a big smile from behind her bedroom door. I run to swoop her up.

"Who else but you, sweet girl, would remember."

With her face pressed up against me, I barely hear, "Happy birthday, love."

"Well," I reply, touched but a bit unsettled by the scene, "it's a lot happier now than it was when I got my big paper back today. That damn teaching assistant gave me a C+. I think she's got something against me, that girl."

Jannie gently pulls away and reaches for a small package hidden behind the cake. With a shy smile, she hands it to me. "Go sit down and open it," she says.

A picture frame? It turns out to be a small framed watercolor painting with the initials *J. S.* on the bottom right. It's an abstract which, when I first look at it, makes zero sense to me.

"You did this?" I ask.

"Yes. I do watercolors when I'm at home in Fresno, remember? I've been doing it since I was a little girl." Jannie's smiling. "Turn it over and open the little stand."

I do as she tells me and see the inscription in Jannie's hand: *To L with all the love I have to give.* I glance at the cake, then back to the abstract, then back to the girl who's looking tenderly at me. I try to show only the love I have for Jannie and not the trepidation and sadness I feel for her, but she reads me like a book. The expression in her soft brown eyes changes to concern.

"Did I do something wrong? The cake? The painting?"

With the watercolor in my left hand, I reach out and pull Jannie to me with my right. "No, love, no, of course not," I say. "The painting's lovely. It's just that I can't figure out what it means, that's all."

Jannie's face clears. "You're looking at it too close. Try holding it further away."

I release her and take the painting in both my hands and hold it out at arm's length. I hate abstracts. You never know... Swirls of colors that come together with no pattern anywhere. The picture could be a light blue sky with grayish clouds—nimbus I think they're called. A lighter cloud crosses over a darker one and...

Jannie smiles when she sees I've found it. You have to be looking for it, maybe, but the lighter cloud looks sort of like a bent *L* with lots of other little cloud-like things around it, and crossing diagonally over the *L*, if that's what it is, is a straight line of little darker clouds with a bend-off the end, sort of looking like a *J*. Abstract enough, I realize, that only she and I would see. My eyes fill with tears and Jannie hugs me.

What a pain all this crap is about O. J. Simpson. It looks like they're going to televise the trial. Why do people want to stay inside, watching the tube, when they can be outdoors having fun? Different strokes, I guess.

I'm bored out of my mind in my apartment early Saturday afternoon, sick of studying and no date that night, when Forrest calls. There's some beach party starting around five and would I like to come.

"Sounds dull," I say. "Better off sitting here watching TV. How soon can you be here? Who's going to the party, do you know?"

"Haven't got a clue. We're supposed to bring steaks and anything we want to drink. We can get all that when I pick you up. I'll be at your apartment about five o'clock, okay?"

"Jannie's out at a play this afternoon," I say. "If you can pop over a little earlier, I could find ways to keep you entertained."

"Sounds tempting, Luce, but no can do. I'm up to my ears in work. I wasn't going to go this afternoon, then I thought of you cooped up there alone and—"

"I could learn to love you, Forrest. Know that?"

Laughing, he says, "Yeah? Do that and think about what would happen. We'd have four babies in three years, then what would we six do? Hmmm? That prospect tempt you?"

"Well, now that you put it that way, might not be

the best idea."

"Yeah, and just think. With all those kids, how many parties would you miss?"

'Oh, Forrest, love,' I reflect as he's talking, 'you kid about the children, but it's the girl who loves to party that you fear. I might be able to give all that up if I had someone like you.'

What I say is, "Not good. Best we just stay good friends for a while except when we're playing house later on tonight, okay?"

He laughs and says, "See you at five, temptress."

The beach party's big with lots of people I don't know. Some of them are not students at UCSB, to look at them. Bonfires, some big barbecues and tons of food.

I've had at least five beers by eight but I haven't eaten very much and I'm feeling good. Typical, Forrest's had only two, I think. Better for me, I guess, when I get him into bed—if I can coax him to stay with me, that is.

But then I see him, and I forget all about my plan. He's just plain gorgeous, what can I say. He stands almost a head above everybody else, six four or five, at least. He's got broad shoulders and a narrow waist, but that's not mainly what attracts me. It's that strong square masculine face of his that's looking right at me. Forrest's laughing and nudging me.

"I see he's finally caught your eye. He's only been staring at you for the last ten minutes."

"Forrest, where's he been all my life? Would you look at him, standing there? I've gotta have me some of that."

"Go for it," Forrest says. "By the way he's been eating you up with his eyes, you shouldn't have a problem."

I've been with a lot of guys since high school, more than is good for me, I know. I don't remember ever being hit like this! He's coming over. God, he's gonna think I'm here with Forrest. Shit! How am I going to show him we're not together?

"Luce," he says like he reads my mind, "I'm gonna move around a bit. I think I see a couple of friends at the next fire over there. I'll be back a little later to see how things are."

I must seem like an idiot, gawking at the guy the way I am. When he's closer, I see he's huge, two hundred and fifty pounds, easy, and he's fit. I feel my insides go all funny when he talks to me.

"I'm Pete Jackson from Santa Barbara, not from the school here." His voice is nice enough, but nowhere near as low as I'd expect for someone his size.

"I didn't think you were from here. I'd have recognized you, I think." A totally dumb thing to say, but Pete is smiling.

'God, ditz,' I'm thinking as I gaze up at him, 'the guy's gonna take you for an empty-headed blonde which, right now, you are.' I can't believe the effect this guy's having on me.

"Not much to sit on around here, is there," Pete says. "I think I missed your name."

"A few too many beers," I say. "I'm Lucy Evans. There almost never are at beach parties like these—places to sit, I mean. People just stand around or they bring blankets."

Is that a twinkle in Pete's eyes? The thought of him and me on a blanket when it's dark makes me damp and giddy.

"Sounds a lot cozier than most of the parties I go to," he says. "Have to come out here more often. There's some driftwood or something over there that might do the trick," he adds, holding out his arm.

There's just enough room for the two of us when we sit down. I'm so blitzed that I barely process what Pete says.

"I've gotta keep an eye out for my baby sister, Marcia. She's staying with me for a few days at my apartment. She's not even sixteen and she's already checking out colleges in the state. Typical Marcia. She'll be around here some place." He's definitely got a glint in his eye when he tells me this.

Is he thinking of that blanket too? It's probably my overactive imagination and those five or six beers I drank. I'm sure he knows exactly what's on my mind, though, on mine and hundreds of other girls' around here. 'Just ask and I'll bed down with you in a New York minute right here on the sand.'

"So what is it that you study here?" Pete asks.

I'm embarrassed to tell him. I don't know why. "English lit with a minor in education," I say. "Studying's not my forte though."

Pete grins. "Well, that makes two of us. Barely made it through high school, but I'm doin' okay."

"So, what is it that you do? You live in Santa Barbara, you said, don't you?"

"Yes, and, what do I do? I sell new cars."

Is he serious or is he making fun of me? I look up at him to see. He's laughing. "You don't believe me, do you. I'll have you know, Lucy Evans, that I'm probably the most successful car salesman in town with a healthy bank account to prove it." I feel his arm go around my waist and pull me close.

Like the empty-headed female I am, my mind goes blank and I just sit there.

In a lowered voice, he says, "I bet I know what one of those fortes of yours is."

I try not to, but I grin.

"Mmhmm. Well I can tell you, you look good enough to eat."

God, what kind of a slut am I, anyway! I'm behaving like a teenager who can't wait for her first lay.

I hear a girl somewhere calling out Pete's name.

"Over here, Marcia," he says. "Come meet Lucy."

And there she is, a blonde like me but small, a pretty girl with nice brown eyes, the same shade as Pete's. "I've been looking everywhere for you," she says, frowning. "The guys around here don't waste time. They've been coming onto me since you left me."

"Sorry, Marsh," Pete says. "Didn't mean to abandon

you to the wolves. Now you know what to look forward to in college."

Marcia, hands on hips, glares back at him. "It's funny, isn't it Pete, that we girls are so much more serious than you guys." She suddenly seems to become aware of me, pressed up against her brother's side. After a pause, her eyes on me, she says, "Well, some of us are, anyway. So when are we going back?"

Sounding a bit annoyed, Pete says, "Hey, sis, we just got here. Go find yourself something to eat, then we'll head back."

"There's nothing for me here," she says. "I'm a vegetarian. You know that."

Looking at his watch and sighing, Pete tells her, "We'll go back at nine, Marcia. That's twenty minutes you have to wait, that's all." The girl flounces off.

I hope I don't show my disappointment. The man any girl would die for arrives, and then he goes. I don't like his younger sister very much.

"Doesn't seem very happy, does she," I say.

"Marcia's a good kid, but she's always got something to complain about. I forgot all about the vegetarian kick she's on." He squeezes me again. "To change the subject before Marcia's back, I'd like to see you again if that's okay with you."

"I'd like that too," is all I manage to get out. This guy has got me in a state!

Pulling me even closer, he says, "Marcia's going back to Fresno on Monday morning, so as of then I'm free. I work during the day, but there's Monday night. Is that too soon for you?"

I shake my head, then, feeling like a moron, I say, "Monday night will be fine." I dig out my notebook and a pen and write down my number and address. "I have an apartment just off Hollister in Goleta."

"Mind if I borrow your notebook for a minute," Pete says, "and I'll give you my phone number and address."

I sit there, snuggled up to him, wishing the day would never end. He hands me my notebook back and I tuck it in my purse.

"Six-thirty, Monday, then?"

I nod just in time. The little blonde is back, frowning like before.

"Listen, Pete," she says. "I'm not putting up with any more of this. There's lots of girls around here, so why do they have to pick on me?"

Exasperated, clearly aware that this will annoy her, he says, "Because you're juicy like a ripe fruit and the poor guys want a bite."

Marcia looks furious and stomps her foot.

Giving me a final squeeze, he says, "See you this coming Monday. I've gotta get this drop-dead gorgeous female home before they eat her up." Marcia takes a swing at him and Pete ducks and laughs.

They're not very far from the driftwood stack where I'm still sitting when I hear Marcia say, "Are the girls at UCSB all like her?"

In the distance, I think I hear Pete reply, "Be a damn nice place to be if they were."

For an instant, I feel happy, then, sitting there alone on the driftwood, I feel like a total twit. Am I the airhead blonde that I must have sounded like? I'm no crybaby, but the tears are close. Pete must think I'm some horny chick that he'll take to bed then dump. The guy can have his pick.

Maybe I've had too many beers and not enough to eat. I feel like shit. I look around for Forrest, but I don't see him anywhere. Next thing I know, some dude's sitting next to me with his arm around my waist. Before he goes any further, I get up and walk away.

What's come over me anyway? The guy's a real hunk, okay, and he's really sexy, but so? He's definitely knocked me for a loop. Everything around me seems dull compared to him. I'll see Pete in two days and go to bed with him, who knows how many times, then I'll be one more notch for him. I'm nothing but a new plaything. His sister's got so much more class.

Meeting Pete, beers and too little food and I'm not

feeling well. Several friends say hello to me as I'm wandering along the beach, looking for Forrest, but I don't stop to talk. Finally, I find him chatting with a girl I've never seen.

"Hey, Luce," he says, "you don't look so good. Are you alright?" Before I can answer, he says goodbye to his friend and takes me by the arm. "Come on. I'll drive you home. Something happen with that guy?"

"No, no," I tell him, "nothing like that. I should have eaten something before I drank, that's all."

"Hey. I personally gave you two hotdogs. You sure it's not something else?"

I tell him no. In fifteen minutes, I'm home. Jannie hasn't come back yet. I go straight to bed.

It's Monday and I go to two classes, but I don't process a thing. It's like I'm coming down with something and I can't concentrate.

I'm looking forward to tonight with Pete, but, for some reason, I'm kinda scared. If I'm just lusting after him, that's fine. That'd be okay. I'll just fuck and forget like the guys say. I can do that.

Trouble is—and this is new for me—I've got this feeling that it's more than that. I don't believe in this love at first sight stuff, never have. Sad fact of my life is, I've done a lot of loving in the sexual sense, but never really loved, except for Forrest, maybe, and maybe Jannie. If that's what it is with Pete—sounds so stupid, I know—and it's not the same for him—how could it be—I'm dead and no good for anything for a while.

Back outside and heading for my car around 4 p.m., I mentally shake myself and try to get into a better mood. I've gotta stop acting like some inexperienced teenage girl on her first date. That drivel you read about in books about falling for someone just like that's a bunch of crap. Of all people, I should know. I've been around enough, in and out of love so many times I can't count. He's just another hot guy I hang out with.

*

Fifteen minutes to go and I'm so nervous that I feel nauseous. What if he doesn't come? He's gotta come! I take out my little notebook and look for his number. I won't call him, but just in case...

When I find it, I feel my eyes blink like what I'm seeing isn't real. But it is! I can't believe it. Right under his address are two sketched faces, portraits I guess you'd call them. One's Pete—anyone could see that—and the other face is me. It's wild how he did that and I didn't even notice. There's a little tiny heart underneath each face with a line joining them. Cloud nine, here I come.

My buzzer rings at six-thirty on the dot. Pete's right on time. No makeup—I don't need it—and my hair's blow-dried and down. Nothing special about the short royal blue sleeveless dress I've got on. It's a little tight on top, maybe, but so is just about everything I buy. I have a hard time getting things to fit. I'm trying not to overdress.

Pete's kinda quiet on our way in and I don't say much, wondering what might be on his mind. He looks more serious today. I start to worry. Maybe he's regretting that he asked me out.

Then he says, without turning to look at me, "Not a very good conversationalist today, am I."

What do I say to that? I said too many dumb things on Saturday so I just sit there while he drives. This was a bad idea, going out this quick. I should have put him off a few more days.

"I've got a reason if you want to know," he says.

I'm starting to get uncomfortable. I don't know what to say to him. 'Yeah, I'm dying to know' or 'I won't bother asking since you're about to tell me.' I don't say these things, of course. I just turn to look at him, hoping I seem a little smarter than before.

"It's this way." His expression is kinda odd as he says this. "If I don't explain it very well, you've gotta understand. This sort of thing is new to me." He hasn't looked once at me so far. "You see, it's this way." At last he smiles. "I met someone on the weekend who's been a real pest." What's this? "She's gotten inside my head and, in other places too, maybe, and she won't let me be."

I swear my heart skips a beat or two. Can he possibly be talking about me?

"There's something very special about this girl. Maybe you can help me. She looks an awful lot like you and her last name's Evans if I remember right."

Elation. Unadulterated joy, I think I heard someone call it once. Why in the world do I want to cry? I'm trying to smile as I attempt to choke it back.

At last, I feel just the smile and I say to him, "Then it won't come as any surprise to you that it's been just the same for me. You haven't been off my mind one minute since I saw you."

He reaches for my hand. "That's a relief, I've got to tell you. I wasn't sure what kind of a chance I'd have with a girl like you with all the guys where you go to school."

I laugh. "Funny thing about all those guys you're talking about, I don't see any of them when I think of you. After all the confessions I've made tonight, don't make me feel like a fool, please."

He looks at me briefly before turning back to the road. "Somehow, I don't think that's gonna happen. It's good that we both feel the same."

"Hey," I say, "I saw those tiny portraits of us you did in your note. How did you do that? They're so good and you did them so fast!"

"Nah," he says, "that's just somethin' I like to do. I'm no good at it, really. It's my kind of doodlin' so-to-speak."

I feel like a romantic schoolgirl. Forrest smiles at my happiness when I tell him.

"Luce, from what I've seen, I think the guy's as stuck on you as you are on him. It's like one of those relationships you see in the movies or read about. I'm very glad for you. Pete seems like a real solid guy. Good thing you're not the jealous type. From what I saw on the beach the other day, there are a lot of females who'd trade places with you right now."

The very thought makes me burn inside. "Who told you I'm not the jealous kind. Don't be fooled by the color of my eyes."

Forrest's hands come up like I'm about to hit him. "Hey girl, back off," he says, grinning. "I'm not after him, not me. It's all those hungry unattached girls out there you've gotta worry about."

"Stop teasing me," I say. "Any girl who gets too close to him and I'll scratch her eyes out."

For the first time in my life, I am in love, so deeply that it makes me scared. Fortunately, Pete seems to feel the same. Each time we're together—that's very often—it's stronger for the both of us. Within a month, we're talking about serious things like moving in together, like what it'd be like to have a baby and stuff like that. Marriage hasn't been brought up so far, but, hey. We've only known each other for a month.

Jannie's known about us from the start, of course. She's doing her best not to let her feelings show, but I hear sorrow in her voice and see it in her eyes. We haven't slept together since I met Pete. I've been so caught up with him that I haven't really wanted to and—I'm absolutely certain about this—I know he'd leave me if he knew. From comments he's made on different things and because of his conservative outlook, he'd never understand. For him, it would be like sleeping with a guy. I love Jannie and can't stand to see her sad, but there's nothing in this world that would make me risk losing Pete.

One afternoon after classes, I come into our apartment to see boxes everywhere and two suitcases. I stand there, stricken by what I see. Jannie's leaving me.

When she comes out of the bathroom, I can see that she's been crying. I run to her and take her in my arms. She resists at first, then collapses against me and begins to sob. I lead her over to our sofa and pull her down on my lap. She feels like a child, she's so light and small.

Holding her, waiting until her tears stop, I say, "Baby, I'm so sorry. I know how hard this is for you." I don't, of course, since I've never lost anyone. The shame that I've often felt when with Jannie comes back. I should have helped her go as soon as I realized how emotionally involved she was. Instead, selfishly, I let her convince me to stay together. Now poor Jannie is suffering and I have no way to help her.

"I knew this day would come, Luce. It had to. I'm sorry to be a burden to you like this."

"Hush, you silly girl," I say to her. "I love you. I always will. Not the same way you love me, I know, but I love you all the same. You could never be a burden to me, sweet love, never. What are all these boxes for? What do you think you're doing?"

She raises her head and looks at me. "It won't be long before you move in with Pete," she says. "Three weeks? Four? I won't be able to stand it in this apartment when you're gone. I'll see you and smell your fragrance everywhere, everywhere. I've got to find someplace else to live before you go, Luce. Do you understand? Please say you do. I need your strength to help me leave."

I hold her for a long time until she's quiet. I make her promise to call me every day. Otherwise, I'll worry. She nods. I kiss away the tears on both her cheeks and whisper in her ear. I feel troubled by the joy and gratitude I see on her face when she hears me. At the same time, I feel warmth at the prospect of Jannie's loving. How contrary I am. Tonight may be the last time I'll be with her.

November

I can't believe how lonely the apartment is since

Jannie left. We manage to get in a phone call pretty much every day, but it's not the same. It's got to be that much harder for her.

Studying's easier now that I have Pete. I think about him all the time. My social life's not really an issue anymore. I get my incomplete finished up and am doing better in my courses. No A's and not very many B's, but at least I'm not flunking anything so I'm okay.

The three of us, Forrest, Pete and I, hang out together quite a lot, especially on weekend afternoons. It makes me happy that my new love and my friend get along so well. Pete was a little concerned at first, but not anymore. He seems to appreciate the kind of relationship Forrest and I have.

December

My parents expect me home like they always do, but I can't bear the thought of being without Pete. He invites me to move in with him and spend Christmas in Santa Barbara, so I agree. Mom and Dad are so upset that I'm not coming home that I decide to go to Modesto for a couple of days to see them. I want Pete to come, but he says no. It's too soon, and they want to be with me, not him, he says. So I buy a bus ticket and I go to spend Christmas Eve and Christmas day with them.

1995

January

The results of the second test agree with the first. I'm pregnant again. I should be devastated, but I'm not, probably 'cause I'm pretty sure Pete will be happy. He seems eager to have a child. At his age, twenty-five, I can't imagine why, but hey. I pat my tummy and think, one more way to bring us even closer. I'm happier than I've ever been and Pete seems so too. We love each other's company. The sex, I have to say, isn't quite what I hoped for, but I don't really care that much. Pete's absolutely wonderful in every other way. Sex doesn't have to be the best, does it, when you've got the rest.

February

I've missed a lot of classes this trimester because of morning sickness. I'm lucky to have friends who share their notes. My midterms don't turn out so bad so I should be okay.

I haven't seen Jannie now for over three months although we talk on the phone frequently. I'm happy with Pete and delighted about the baby, but I miss the very special friendship she and I had. I'm not talking about the sex. That was something new and wonderful for me in many ways. I don't feel the need for that anymore. It's the sweet and thoughtful girl herself I miss. Just having her nearby comforts me.

No, that's not it exactly. There's something more. I'm not very introspective and I tend not to analyze things all that much, but I'm aware that there's something unique and very beautiful between us that never would have existed if we hadn't shared each other in the way we did. I can't speak for Jannie since her feelings aren't the same, but for me, for someone who considers Jannie as a close friend, our intimacy brought that friendship to another level that will never change, even if we never touch each other again.

I think Jannie's doing okay when, one morning, she's at my door. I should be in class, but I don't go 'cause I'm not feeling all that well. Pete, as usual at that hour, is at work.

Jannie looks awful. Her red hair that I love so much is dull, her skin's all broken out and she's thin, and I mean thin. There's something about her eyes that alarms me. They look all washed out. I reach out and pull her to me and hold her. I can feel her bones sticking out all over.

"Jannie, baby, what's wrong with you? What's happened? You look sick." Before she can answer, I pull her to our couch and make her sit down next to me.

There's no resistance, no reaction from her at all when I do this. I pull her against me as I used to do and just hold her. We don't talk. We just sit like that for a good quarter of an hour. I'm afraid to ask, but I need answers. I gently push her away so I can look at her.

As I'm opening my mouth to talk, she says, "Luce, you're such an alarmist. You're always worried about things that aren't going to happen. I've had a bad case of the flu, that's all. I haven't been eating very much lately and haven't been taking very good care of myself."

I want to believe her, the worst way. I'd feel so much easier if it was true. I reach out for both her hands.

"Sweetheart," I say, feeling a huge lump in my throat, "you're the worst liar there ever was, 'specially with me." Before I know it's going to happen, I burst into tears, an occasion you won't see often with this Evans girl. "I can't stand to think of you like this. What have I done to you, Jannie, baby, what have I done?"

She surprises me by pulling her hands away and firmly grabbing both my arms. In a stern tone I've never heard her use, she says, squeezing hard, "What have you done? You've given me the most precious thing a person could ask for, that's what. You've given me love and allowed me to give you mine in ways most people only dream of. That's what you've done, so no self-recriminations, please."

I'm not sure about the meaning of all Jannie's words, but I get her drift.

"Alright," she continues, "I guess I knew you'd see through me as you always do. I haven't been coping all that well, it's true. Part of it, I think, is that I haven't found a roommate yet to talk to. I'll have to try a little harder to do that, I guess. Truth is, Luce, I just had to see you, that's all. I fought against it, but it was no good. I had to come. I'm very glad I did. I now know two things that are going to help me. Our relationship is as strong as it ever was—I can see it in your face—and I know, just seeing and holding you, that I can go home now and be better than I've been. What I was so afraid of didn't happen." She doesn't go on talking because she's crying.

"Afraid of what, my love?" I ask, reflecting as I speak that it is still so easy to use that term with her.

"Afraid our connection would be weakened or maybe even gone because of Pete and the baby that's going to come."

I think about this for a few seconds, wanting to be careful, then, taking both her hands, I say, "Jannie, our connection is too special and too strong to ever die. You mean more to me than my family members do. I've thought about our situation quite a lot. I love you as the closest friend I could ever have, but the love involves more than that. I know that, even if I don't have the words to tell you why. Does that make sense to you?"

For answer, she reaches for me and puts her face against my chest. I pull her tight against me and we sit there for a while, neither of us saying anything. Finally, she pulls back and smiles.

Whispering, with a quaver in her voice, she says, "Thank you, my darling Luce. I know we can't be together again like we used to, but that's okay. The important things to me are what you just said. I can't tell you how much I needed to hear them and how much the things you said will help me."

Because I live in Santa Barbara rather than Goleta now, I don't see much of my old friends except for Forrest. He comes over at least once a week to visit me, sometimes during the day and other times in the evening when Pete's here. I always feel better when he comes.

April

Yay! Exams over and I passed everything. Even better, I'm feeling great. I haven't felt the baby yet, but I'm showing. Not all that much yet, but I know it's there.

I'm jubilant, at least I think that's the right word to use. Pete wants a wedding after I graduate in June. He's over the moon about the baby. To celebrate me getting my BA, he wants to drive down to Baja to a place he knows. He says I'll love it, so we go.

It's a kind of fancy villa near Tecate, the town where they make good beer. Since I'm pregnant, I have to sit and watch while everybody else gets smashed on booze of just about every kind. Pete said he wouldn't drink for my sake, but I tell him to go ahead and enjoy himself. That's why we came.

The people at the villa are kinda strange. There are thirteen of us in all, eight women, mostly Mexican, and five men, all of them from L.A. except Pete. There's another girl who's pregnant, about nineteen, who's at least seven months along. I don't much like the way some of the guys look at her. What I find odd about this group is that the women aren't here with anybody. They came together in two cars, but they're alone.

To tell the truth, it's a little creepy, this place. I'm not at all relaxed, and the people don't look like they're having all that much fun. Pete's friends with most of the guys so it's not too bad for him. I don't know anyone. I wish we'd gone somewhere else to celebrate.

I'm not the kind who gets bent out of shape because of sex. I've done threesomes with guys and even a couple groups. There's something funny going on with this bunch, though, not the sort of stuff I'm used to. After we're served dinner—the quality's really great—people toke up and things get a little wild. The girls start dancing on their own while taking off their clothes, then end up on different laps, male or female, makes no difference.

The more we drink and smoke—there's a lotta hash here, I think—the more sexually active out in the open people get, doing just about everything. I'm pretty high and feeling good, even though I know I shouldn't be doing a lot of this with a baby inside me. Pete and I have stayed out of much of it so far, though he hasn't been his usual jealous self when guys and girls come up to kiss and play with me.

It all seems weird. I haven't been to many orgies, but the ones I've seen, people were high and having a good time. There's hardly anybody talking here and the sex seems staged. It's probably just me. One thing about it's good. Pete's a lot more laidback and less hung up than he usually is.

A different kind of Mexican drink's served up to everyone, in paper cups this time. Stuff's good. I and a lot of other people ask for more. It's hot in here and I'm about to go out and get some air but I feel dizzy when I stand up so I sit back down. Too much to smoke and drink tonight, so I'll just sit here and wait for Pete when he's ready and we can go to bed. A pretty wild night. Place is alright after all, I guess.

It's the next morning and I decide to stay in bed because of a headache while Pete goes off for breakfast. He promises to bring me something back. But the headache which I don't have isn't why I stay. I want to try to write things down in my diary before I forget everything that happened after those new drinks. It's like trying to hold on to bits of dreams when you wake up. Everything's disappearing, most things, that is.

The last thing I clearly remember is sitting on my stool, waiting for Pete 'cause I was too drunk or high or whatever to go anywhere. After that, things start getting real fuzzy. I have sensations that are familiar to me, but nothing else.

I remember lying on the floor 'cause it was cold. I remember distinctly wondering why I have somebody's cock pushing down my throat and somebody else's fucking me. I remember something hurting me quite a lot down there, but I have no idea what. I remember people's voices, shouting and laughing and saying things, but I can't remember what. The last thing I recall, at least I think I do, is a girl sitting on my face. I wouldn't remember that, probably, except the feeling was new and strange to me.

I'm sure the drinks were drugged and we were told to do stuff we'd never normally do. It's not the sexual things that bother me so much although I prefer to know what I'm doing with who and when. What worries me a little is how much Pete knew about all this before we came. I can't imagine how he couldn't know since he knew nearly everybody. But if he knew, why wouldn't he tell me and why would he be so open to people having sex with me. I'm going to ask him straight off and see what he tells me.

When Pete gets back to the room—he brings me a full plate like he promises—I tell him, "We're supposed to stay here two more days, but I don't want to, so can we go back home today? I really don't like it here."

"Absolutely, baby, if that's what you want to do. We can leave whenever you want to."

I'm reassured. "After I finish breakfast? Will that be okay?"

"Sure thing," he says. "We can say goodbye to people here, then go."

I'm hesitant to bring it up, but I say, "What all did we do after those new drinks in paper cups came? Do you remember?" I watch his face carefully. His eyebrows come together as though he's thinking.

"Funny you should ask that, Luce. This'll sound stupid to you, I know, but I can't really say. To tell you the honest truth, I think somebody drugged those drinks. I don't remember much. I can remember girls all over me, I can tell you that—glad you're not the jealous type—but not much else. I don't even know how we got back to our room. I don't remember how we got back here. Do you?"

Smiling and much relieved, I shake my head and tell him no. I decide I don't really give a damn about what happened the night before. It's Pete I was concerned about. He passes my little test with flying colors.

*

Pete's such a love. While I'm buckling my seatbelt on, he sticks something on my chest. It's a note. I pull it off and smile. It says, *I'm sorry baby*. Instead of signing it, he drew a real good picture of my face, the best one so far. I think he signs a lotta his notes like that. Sometimes he draws them on menus while we're in restaurants. Sometimes, I even see them on receipts. I give him a big hug to thank him and tell him I love him.

May

Everything's back to normal, I'm glad to say. Pete's happy and brings home champagne when I tell him I think I feel the baby move. A couple of glasses of bubbly aren't gonna hurt me, he says. How stupid I was to drink and smoke things in Mexico.

He's even more thoughtful and loving than he used to be. It's nice. Problem is, I'm bored, bored out of my mind. Santa Barbara's gorgeous, but how many walks can a girl do? I've been everywhere dozens of times. I start to watch TV a lot. I'm learning to cook and some of the shows are good.

Like a bad dream that keeps coming back, that weird trip to Baja we took still bothers me. I want to talk about it with someone, but who? I think of Forrest, but that's no good. It would worry him.

June

My parents know about the baby and about our plans to marry. They've been pestering me constantly to meet Pete. He agrees to go this time. We'll drive this coming Saturday to Modesto. Pete will stay over Saturday night and leave me for a few days to finish up plans for our wedding in late June.

As I knew would happen, Pete's a huge hit at home. After a long conversation with him, Dad says to me, "Now there, my chicken, you've got a man who'll take good care of you. He knows what he wants and he's got a good business head, important things these days."

Mom's enchanted. "Lucy," she says, "I'm real proud of you. Your Pete's a real good catch. There's a lot of things to do so we can't waste time. Now, about your dress. We should start by..."

Actually, there's little I have to do. My mom's planned it all, including the invitation list.

"Mom," I try to tell her, "I don't know even half of these. Most of 'em are your friends, not mine."

She doesn't pay attention. Fortunately, Pete says he's okay with whatever my parents want to do. I think sometimes that the only reason we're getting married from his point of view is the baby.

For some reason—it's a man thing, Jimmy says—Pete and my brother don't really hit it off. He makes excuses to be away most of the time Pete's here.

Graduation's early this year. The ceremony's a real bore, more for the parents than anything. Jimmy doesn't come because he's got the flu, he says. He's lying again, I know.

"I get the impression your brother's not entirely in favor of me," Pete says. I deny this and give excuses, but he's not convinced.

A hundred and fifty people are at the wedding in Modesto, most of them I don't recognize. Over a hundred at the reception. Some of my high school friends are there but not a lot. I've lost contact with nearly all of them which makes me a little sad. Of course, Forrest comes.

When I call, Jannie hesitates for a few seconds while she looks for an excuse not to come. I want her close to me and to be my Maid of Honor, but I know how painful this would be for her. I feel bad that the most important person in the world for me except for Pete and maybe Forrest can't be with me, but I understand. Both of us are crying when we hang up.

I'm relieved in a way that most of the people there

are my parents' friends since I know the wedding and the reception cost so much. It would have been fine with me and Pete if just my family and Pete's and my friends were at our wedding in Santa Barbara, but hey. That's what parent-planned weddings are for, I guess.

What I'm looking forward to is our honeymoon that's coming up. We'll fly to Barcelona in Spain and board a ship for a one-week cruise across the Mediterranean. We'll disembark—that's the word the guide books use—in Italy where we'll spend eight days, four in Tuscany and four in Rome. I can barely wait. I've never been out of the United States.

Then we'll come back and move to Santa Lucia where our real life will begin. That's where Pete wants to work. How wonderful it all is. A girl couldn't ask for a better husband.

Chapter 6

1995

July

Just before we leave for Europe, Pete receives a phone call from a lady who is willing to take over his apartment that has four months remaining on the lease. He's pleased because we're now free to move to Santa Lucia where he's wanted to live for a long time. I visited the little city years ago but don't remember much.

I love the place right away. It's a lot like Santa Barbara, a little smaller, maybe. We stay in an apartment that we rent month by month until we find a little house that's not outrageously expensive. Not an easy thing to do in this wealthy town.

I'm so proud of Pete and his ability to manage money. He's saved almost everything he's earned during the last four years, which turns out to be quite a lot. How different we are that way. I don't have much financial sense when it comes to the long term. I'm amazed when Pete tells me he's put away almost five hundred thousand dollars. I had no idea a car salesman could earn that much.

He's been negotiating with a man here in Santa Lucia who owns the Toyota dealership. He's managed to bring the price way down for half interest in the company, from six to four hundred thousand, he says. Pete wants some big changes which are part of the agreement the two men make. The rest is for our little house, if we ever find one, and for our furniture.

I've gotten huge with the baby—the ultrasound says it's a boy—so I don't go out much. It's hot this summer and I'm uncomfortable.

Jannie seems okay according to her letters I get about once a week. She's back in Fresno with her parents and working again for her old boss at the museum. I try hard not to read between the lines.

The house we find needs a lot of work, but it's a place to live. I was beginning to be afraid we wouldn't find one before the baby came. Even though it's old and small, it cost six hundred and fifty thousand dollars to buy the place. We put fifty thousand dollars down and shop for furniture.

I say 'we,' but it's really Pete. I don't have a cent. This bothers me because it makes me feel like everything belongs to him. Legally, it doesn't, so my friends tell me, but still...

It's fun to go from store to store with Pete. He has good taste from what I can tell, and even though it's his money that we use, he asks for my opinion on everything. If I don't like something, we look elsewhere. For some things, we have to go outside of Santa Lucia because of prices. Everything is so expensive here.

We move in on September 1 with all our furniture. I'm exhausted but I'm happy.

September

My ankles swell up and I can hardly walk. The baby's due anytime, the doctor says. I wish to God he'd come. They offer to induce me, but I say no. I want everything to be as natural as possible.

I'm sitting in the kitchen on a Thursday morning about an hour after Pete leaves when the phone rings. I'm expecting our new sound system to arrive, so I think it's the store calling to arrange delivery.

"Mrs. Jackson?"

I say it is, the second time I've heard my new name on the telephone.

"This is Janine Stuart, Jan Stuart's mother."

"Mrs. Stuart," I say, "hello. It's nice to hear from you. Call me Lucy, by the way. Everybody does."

A second or so pause, then Mrs. Stuart says, "No. I'd prefer not, thank you."

Her words and a quaver or something in her voice make me shiver. I go all cold and feel the muscles in my belly tighten up.

"I didn't... want... I didn't want to call you or hear your voice, but my husband said I had no choice."

"Please, Mrs. Stuart, you're beginning to frighten me. Jannie's okay, isn't she?"

Silence at the other end of the line.

"Please"—I hear the desperation in my voice—"tell me she is."

"So you don't know," Mrs. Stuart says with a bitter tone. "You don't know our baby's dead."

With no warning, my stomach convulses and I throw my breakfast up. I want to scream and scream to make what I heard go away, but I can't talk. Cereal, milk and berries keep coming up while I clamp the phone against my head. Not Jannie. No. Please no—

"Are you still there?"

I make a croaking sound to tell her that I am.

Stammering, the voice continues, "Mrs. Jackson, you'll—you'll forgive me if I sound unkind, but I don't exactly feel charitable toward you right now. Robert said I had to call and he was right. Jan wouldn't forgive us if we didn't." Mrs. Stuart begins to cry. "This isn't easy for me. I have several things to tell you so listen, please. I'll say these things one time, then I'll hang up. I don't ever want to talk to you again."

I feel the blood drain from my face and I'm going to faint. I hold the phone against my left ear while I try to bend over to get my head down, but my beach ball stomach doesn't let me. I can just make out the garbled words in the receiver.

"Jan went to see her aunt outside of town two days ago so she took my car. She hit a tree." Sobbing. "Mercifully, she was killed instantly. The police say she was driving at high speed, a hundred miles an hour, at least, they say. I leave it to you, Mrs. Jackson, to explain why our Jan would do such a reckless thing." More crying at the other end.

I fall from my chair and am lying on my side on the kitchen floor.

"We were going through Jan's things this morning in her bedroom where we found a watercolor she finished last week that she wanted us to package up and send to you. Part of the cardboard backing... the backing came off and a letter to you tucked inside came out."

For what seemed to me a long time, Mrs. Stuart didn't say anything.

"We knew who you were, of course. Jan talked about you all the time, but we had no idea how attached to you she was and... and for how long it had been going on. We packaged the painting and the rest like she wanted us to do and sent it off this morning by FedEx. You'll have it tomorrow before noon. Goodbye now, Mrs. Jackson. I hope you can live with what you've done."

There was a click and then the dial tone.

I want to die, I feel so bad. Jannie, my sweet, sweet Jannie, what have I done? My darling Jannie, what have I done to you? Why couldn't I have done more to help you? Jannie, baby, why didn't you call me? You hate driving and you're afraid to death of going fast. Jannie, love, why didn't you call me?

I feel my baby moving around inside me while I lie there on the floor, but what I feel most is the part of me that has been torn away. I feel Jannie's soft hands caress my face and her head against my chest and I sob as I never have in my life.

I'm still crying and on the floor when Pete finds me. Far above, I hear his alarmed voice.

"My God, Lucy, what's the matter? What happened

here? We need to go to the hospital right away!"

"No, love," I say. "It's not the baby."

"Then what's wrong? Is there something wrong with you? You've been sick all over here. What's going on?" He picks me up off the floor and gently puts me on my chair.

"Jannie's dead," I manage to get out before I start to cry again.

"Jannie, dead? When? How? When did you find out? You were on the floor when I came in. Do you think you hurt the baby when you fell?"

I shake my head as Pete's cleaning up my face. I tell him that I slipped off the chair, that's all, when I heard the news.

"I'm so glad you're here," I say. "How did you know to come?"

Pete can't stand messes of any kind. While I talk, he's cleaning up the kitchen table and the floor.

"I tried calling you but got voicemail all the time. Finally, I got worried and came home. Jesus, Luce. How did Jannie die?"

"An auto accident near Fresno," I say. I don't have the heart to tell him more. "Her mother called this morning to let me know."

"Gee, I'm sorry, babe," Pete says. "I know how close you two were." He's looking straight at me and has an odd expression on his face when he says this. Does Pete know how close we really were? No way he can. "Do you think we should check to see if everything's okay with the baby? That must have been quite a shock."

I think about this for a moment, then shake my head. "If I don't feel any movement in the next little while or if anything seems abnormal, then yes, I think we should."

Next morning, as I expect, physically I'm fine and so is baby. If anything, he's more active than before. Emotionally, I'm a wreck. Pete's not sure he should go to work, but, an hour later than he usually goes, he does.

*

About eleven-thirty, the doorbell rings. I'd forgotten all about the package Mrs. Stuart said she sent. I'm afraid to open it, to see the painting and the letter. Finally, I do.

A much larger picture and no abstract this time. Jannie's signature is at the bottom right. There's a beautiful tree—I can't identify the kind—that's growing in the center of a lovely pond with lily pads, a small frog sunning himself and lots of pretty rocks. I love it. It's very peaceful. Other than the mood the picture sets, there's no message in it that I can see.

I'm about to turn the painting over to check the back to get at the letter Mrs. Stuart talked about when I see, almost hidden among the leaves, a little green parrot with a gray head peeking out at me. Where have I seen that kind of bird before? I know I have.

Suddenly, I turn cold and it feels like my heart stops when I remember. My grandparents had two birds like those, almost identical. No ordinary parrots. They were lovebirds, the kind you see only in pairs that mate only one time in their lives. My grandmother was so sad when one died and the other died two days after. I burst into tears.

It takes me a quarter of an hour to recover enough to rewrap the painting and put it in the far back of my closet. It's the saddest picture I've ever seen. I know Jannie didn't paint it for me to make me feel bad. She's telling me she wishes it was otherwise, but she has no choice. There'll be only one real love in her life.

The letter will have to wait. I don't have the courage now to read it.

No matter what Pete does to cheer me up, I feel depressed. I know how impractical it would have been, but if I'd known something bad like this was going to happen, I would have kept Jannie closer to me and hoped that our nearness to one another would have been enough.

But as I think this, I realize that Jannie, with the kind of love she had, needed more than knowing I was nearby. She needed more than what I, as a happily married woman about to have a baby, could possibly have given her.

Jannie's mother's words haunt me and I feel guilty all the time. I wish I had some way to know how much I was to blame. I need someone to talk to who might understand. Pete is loving and attentive but not the one. Instinctively, I know not to confide in him on this. I could talk to Forrest, I know, but he's in Berkeley, at least I think he is, and I'm here. He'd come to me if I called, but it wouldn't work. Pete would get suspicious and want to know why he's here. I'm going to have to deal with this alone.

I'm so fortunate to have Pete and our baby who's soon to come. Without them, I don't know how I'd cope. Every moment that I'm not with someone, I hear Jannie's soft voice or feel her gentle touch. I constantly play over and over in my head so many conversations that we had.

While I don't know quite how I could have done it without being cruel to her, I keep thinking that there must have been a better way to help. I can't escape knowing that at least part of our relationship was selfishness on my part, my inability to let go of someone I'd come to love.

Love, from a physical standpoint, yes, but much more for who Jannie herself was—generous, sensitive and sweet beyond description. If I could only talk to someone I could trust about it all.

It's the twenty-third and I'm about to throw in the towel and phone my obstetrician to tell her I want to be induced. I feel heavy and bloated and can barely move, I'm so enormous. Baby Alex—we refer to him like that now every day—kicks and moves around so much that I'd swear I'm having twins. Right now, he's giving me a little break.

That break goes on for a couple of days and I get worried. The baby's died in me. That's why I don't feel him. I panic and call Pete.

"Hey there," he says, sounding calm. "What I know about babies you can put in a thimble, but isn't the baby supposed to quieten down before he comes? Isn't that right? If you're worried, call your obstra-whatever-they-call-it and talk to them. Call me back if there's a problem."

Already I feel better and a little silly. I call anyway and get the nurse. She tells me everything's absolutely normal and not to worry. It's one of those doom and gloom things I get into sometimes.

Jannie's still on my mind a lot, but the shock of losing her decreases a little bit each day. I'm sitting in the kitchen just after Pete leaves for work and writing in my diary when I feel a gush of warm liquid under me that starts dripping on the floor. It's my waters, thank God. I feel myself smiling for the first time since that awful phone call. 'So, Alex,' I think, 'you're about to join us in the big bad world. Get on with it then.'

I keep waiting for the pains to start, but nothing happens. I can't feel the baby move anymore and I get worried.

"Isn't that the way it's supposed to be?" Pete asks while we're eating Thai take-out that he's brought home.

I call Linda who lives just next door and has three young kids and she agrees. "Your baby's getting ready for the big escape," she says. "Your husband's there with you, right?" I assure her that he is.

I'm still anxious at about eleven when we've just gone to bed when the first pain comes. Did I put everything I'm supposed to in my duffle bag? When I go to check, Pete makes me sit down and tells me to relax. He's happy—I can see he is—and he's so calm and strong. Whatever did I do to deserve him?

By midnight, I'm installed in a birthing room at

Socorro hospital. The people here are really nice. The pains are coming quicker and they're getting pretty bad. Pete's with me every minute and helps me breathe. We didn't take a prenatal class, but he's been reading up.

It's about five-thirty in the morning and the pains are pretty constant and they're strong. They're not as bad as I thought they'd be though.

When I'm fully dilated—four inches I think they say—they wheel me into a delivery room where there's only one dim light on I can see and it's very quiet. It's hurting pretty bad when Dr. Patrikova comes in. She's foreign. I'm not sure from where.

I don't want anesthetic so they don't give me any, except I wish they had when they have to cut me to let the baby out. The worst part of giving birth for me is when they sew me up after Alex comes.

Later, Pete brings a big bouquet of roses to me with a real cute note. It says, *To the mother of our beautiful baby boy*. He drew his own face on the left at the bottom with a baby in the middle and me on the right side. Underneath, it says, *The Jackson family*.

My milk comes down and everything is fine while I stay in the hospital for three days. I don't remember very much about that time. Pete is with me most of the time.

Mom comes for two weeks to help me when I go home. I'm super glad she's there. She knows exactly what to do and she takes care of our darling little boy so I can rest.

Pete's over the moon with our baby son. He buys cigars and hands them out at work, even though nobody smokes them, he says. He's taking pictures all the time. Alex is beautiful and strong from the first day. He weighed nine pounds, four ounces when he was born. No wonder I was big and they had to cut me.

October

Two nights before Mom leaves, I start to have

problems getting back to sleep after feeding Alex. It's not the baby. He wakes up every two hours, nurses on both sides and drops right off. Pete's so used to this after one week that he doesn't wake up, not usually, anyway. I'm having to take little catnaps during the day just to keep up, especially now that Mom's gone back home.

I'm more or less okay when I'm taking care of Alex, feeding him, changing him, bathing him and stuff, but, otherwise, I feel down. I want to cry most of the time.

I don't know how poor Pete puts up with me. For no reason sometimes, I snap at him. He gives me hugs and tells me things will be okay.

We luck out with our pediatrician at Socorro. Dr. Paxton—she insists I call her Donna—is the motherly type, about forty or so with three kids of her own. She tells us that Alex is in perfect shape. He's going to be a big one like his daddy, she says.

The second time I see her, it's just me and the baby. I talk to her about my ups and downs at home.

"Normal as apple pie," she says. "Baby blues, we call it. Not all, but a lot of mothers with newborns get them. Just hang in there and they'll go away."

When she asks me if my husband is supportive, I tell her he's terrific, and he is.

When I ask her how long these mood changes of mine will last, she says, "It varies. Some women are in and out of them in a week, others sometimes take months. Just remember that it's normal, nothing to worry about."

More days go by and I feel worse. I try to hide as much of it as I can from Pete. He mustn't know that it's Jannie that I'm grieving for. I miss her company and I miss her special kind of love that is always there and always, always gentle. I don't think very much about the physical things we did. They will be beautiful to me always, but they're in the past.

It's Jannie herself, her voice, her laughter, her sensitivity to me that I miss. She's why I cry and why I feel so low. At night when I'm half asleep, I feel her little hand in mine and I see her smiling face with all those freckles and her little nose. Sometimes, I actually reach for her, but, of course, she isn't there. If I hadn't been so focused on my own needs, sweet Jannie would still be alive. It is I who killed her. I know I did.

I must see Donna Paxton again soon. I feel much worse. Pete tries not to show it, but I know he's worried. I don't call for an appointment because I know as well as I know my name that Donna can't take away the reason for my pain. No one can. Absolutely no one can.

I've just put Alex down and am washing my face in the bathroom when the doorbell rings. I'm in my bathrobe and I look a mess. I'll ignore it and maybe they'll go away. But they don't. The doorbell rings for the fourth time. Like a zombie, I go to the front door and open it. Whatever they're selling, they can take it and go away.

A man and woman who I've seen somewhere but don't recognize stand there. The woman looks about to cry and the man seems very sad. I'm trying to figure out where I've seen them, then I remember. The picture of Jannie's parents on her desk. I must look as frightened as I feel. Tears are running down Mrs. Stuart's cheeks. She's holding out both of her hands to me.

"Lucy, oh Lucy, please, do please forgive us. We didn't know."

Her husband says the same thing. "We didn't know. When Janine called you, we didn't know. We had no idea. May we please come in and talk to you for a while? It's important, Lucy, please."

None of this is making any sense. What didn't they know before the call, and why are they being nice to me? Not knowing what else to do, I step back and let them in. Pray God, Pete doesn't come home for lunch. I take them to the living room and the three of us sit down, the Stuarts together on the loveseat and me in my favorite chair across from them.

"I know how rude I was on the phone," Mrs. Stuart says. "May I call you Lucy? My name is Janine and this is my husband, Robert."

"Yes, yes of course you can."

"Lucy," Janine says, "two days after Jan's death, we found a letter in her desk that she wrote to the both of us last July. It was a long letter that was very hard for Robert and me to read. There were things in it that are very difficult for us to understand, at least, for a while, they were. We and our daughter have always been very close. We never lied to one another and we never hid things from each other either. We're sure this is why she wanted to tell us things about her life that she knew we didn't know, things that were very important to her. There's no hint in her letter about things that happened in September. You understand what I'm saying here."

I nod. Jannie's parents are doing their best to play down the significance of Jannie's high-speed wreck. I can hardly blame them.

"Now about the letter. Forgive me if I don't express these things very well. They're concepts I'm not accustomed to, that's all. It's taken us a long time to process what Jan was trying to tell us."

"I understand," I say, though I really don't.

"Thank you. Jan spent a lot of time talking to us about you. You'd be proud to know what those things were."

Tears jump to my eyes and I look down, shaking my head over and over. "No, please don't tell me. I cry for Jannie all the time as it is."

"Jan came to love you very much as you know, in some very special ways as we've finally realized. She told us how she tried her best to hide her love from you, but, as these things happen, it finally came out. Jan said that you treated her very gently and that you were always very sensitive to her. She told us how you tried to give her all the love you could and how hard you tried to help her break away, so to speak. She knew you loved her in your own way."

I'm still crying, so all I can do is nod.

Robert continues, "We could talk to you about the letter for a long time since there's so much in it but I'm not sure how useful that would be. The most important things are that our daughter loved you very strongly and that you gave her the most joyful moments of her life. She said that you allowed her to express her love, something she needed desperately to do. She said she was sad that she couldn't have you for her own, but that you gave her more, in her opinion, than most married people ever have." Now Robert stops, seeing how choked up I am.

Janine goes on. "She needed us to understand how important to her you were and what kind of a person you are."

Now both of them are crying, making no attempt to stop. At last, there is quiet in the room.

"Jan begged us," Janine says, "she begged us to get to know you and to protect you and to love you for her if we could." Sobbing, she says, "'we're so sorry for what we've done, how we've been to you. You must have been suffering as much as us, you with a new baby, I understand."

Again, all I can do is nod.

Robert says, "We pray a lot, Lucy. It helps us get through this. Both Janine and I feel sometimes that our Jan is looking down and trying to talk to us. Maybe it's the letter that we're hearing, I don't know. We believe Jan knows you're mourning for her and she wants us to help you. We don't know yet how we can do that other than thank you with all our hearts for being there for her and not rejecting our daughter's love. You mustn't blame yourself for what happened. Please think of the good things you brought to Jan and nothing else."

"I said a terrible thing to you on the phone," Janine says. "I'm so sorry. I don't mean it in any way. You're not at all to blame. Jan was one of these people who loves in a strong way—that's the only way I can describe it—and it's not clear how happy she would have been had she lived. Jan was always a rather quiet girl but very deep."

I'm crying as I get up and walk toward them, holding out my hands. I feel like Jannie's smiling and in the room with us.

"Thank you so much," I say. "There's no way I can tell you how much your visit means to me."

"You don't have to," Robert says. "We feel the same."

"We feel that Jan is finally with the three of us, all together," Janine says. "Will you keep in touch with us, phone us, write us, come to see us when you can? Please?"

I hug them both and promise that I will.

Drying his eyes with his handkerchief, Robert says, "Did you receive the painting that I sent? Did you hang it up?"

I shake my head. "I received it, yes. Thank you. It's in my closet. I can't bear to look at it 'cause each time I do, I cry, and it takes me a long time to stop."

Both Jannie's parents nod.

"Now, Lucy," Janine says, "try to grieve less and take care of that husband and son of yours. That baby needs all your love—well, much of it anyway. Send us pictures of him and please keep in touch."

I hug them again and, in my head, send a little message. 'Jannie, love, thank you for being here with us, and thanks for sending Robert and Janine to me.'

Within two days after the Stuarts leave, I'm feeling better. I miss Jannie still, but the sadness and hurt are less. I don't feel as guilty as I did before.

I hope I'll have the chance to visit the Stuarts someday soon though I don't know how I'll manage. Unlike Jannie's parents, Pete just won't understand. I know there's no way that he can.

Why, I wonder, was I so drawn to Jannie? Why did she become so vital to me? And, while I think of it, why has Forrest always been so important in my life, as a lover and a friend? He's not the type I usually go for, nothing at all like Pete. So why was I so attached to him, still am in a way? As a lover, he was vigorous as I prefer it, but he was careful to do things he knew I liked. He always seemed to be watching after me, sort of. Tender and sensitive toward me? Yes, I guess he was, is. Jannie, my sweet love, if you were only still alive!

I'm not so bored as I was before Alex came. I take little catnaps while he sleeps during the day since he wakes us up at least two times during the night to nurse. We don't use cloth diapers, of course, but there's still a lot of laundry and things for me to do. Nobody comes to see me 'cause I haven't had time to make new friends here, but that's okay.

I do wonder sometimes how mothers stand to stay at home all day with just chores to do. I haven't said anything to Pete yet, but I know I will. After five months of being stuck at home, I'm going to need fresh air. I need people around me.

November

I still think about Jannie much of the time and I still miss her, but the pain of her loss is beginning to go away. I called the Stuarts once and it helped a lot. I think it also helps them to talk to me.

We plan our first dinner party to celebrate Pete's birthday, November 9. I don't know the people who are going to come, his partner Dexter and his wife and another couple. I'm nervous, but I can't wait. I've never prepared a fancy dinner like Pete wants and I'm no cook. Pete is, fortunately for me, and he says he'll help. He's pretty good in about everything he does.

I feel great about the party. The food turns out and the people all are nice, especially Pete's partner who is very complimentary. I feel good about it—that is, until everybody leaves.

I can have drinks once in a while now, and we're sitting on our sofa in the living room when Pete turns to me.

He's looking kind of serious when he says, "Babe"—he uses that nickname for me quite a lot now which I don't like much—"what do you think of Dexter?"

"I like him," I say. "He was very nice about the food and how we've decorated our house and everything."

Pete waits a few seconds while he's looking at me in a funny way, then he says, "He had his eyes on you most of the time, didn't he."

I'm confused. I don't understand the expression on Pete's face. Not knowing what he's expecting, I say, "I didn't notice anything special. He looked okay to me."

"Dexter's wife sure noticed. He's getting an earful right now, I can tell you."

What is Pete going on about? Is he jealous? Whatever it is, he isn't happy.

"Did I do anything to upset you, love?" I ask.

Pete shakes his head. "It's not so much you, Lucy. Thing is, men look at you all the time. You know that."

A bit surprised, pointing at my waist and belly where I still have a few pounds to lose, I say, "That's crazy, Pete. Who'd look at me twice the way I am. I'm fat, just look at me." I'm really just a few pounds over.

Finally, Pete cracks a little smile and I'm relieved. "Honey, it's that hair and face and that gorgeous top of yours that they're lookin' at, not something you can help all that much, I suppose. I just wish Dexter'd behaved a little better, that's all."

December

My first Christmas tree in my first home. Pete and I have a lot of fun decorating it while we listen to Christmas carols on our stereo. We eat gingerbread cookies I made earlier and pieces of fruitcake that my Mom sent us.

I'm usually not in the best of moods at Christmas time, but this year I am. We just had our first full night's sleep since Alex's birth and our son is about as close to perfection as a baby can be. Pete adores him.

Trying to be as casual as I can while I hang tinsel, I say, "Pete, love, in the spring, I'd like to look for work. We'll have to find a sitter or nanny or whatever who can watch Alex while I'm out."

Contrary to what I expect, Pete doesn't seem to be bothered by what I say. He goes right on putting doodads on the tree. "What kind of work do you want to do?" he asks.

"I don't really know," I say. "Editing or something like that, maybe. I did major in English lit."

"You think there's work like that here in Santa Lucia?"

"I don't know," I answer, "but I can try. Thing is, I love being with little Alex—you know that—but I'm just not the stay-at-home type of mom. I'm too used to being out with people to do that."

"Well," Pete says, still putting up decorations, "we can think about it and see what happens."

"Good," I say, glad that he didn't try to discourage me. Somehow, I thought he would. He's a traditional kind of guy as I've come to know. "I'll start looking for someone."

1996

February

Alex is already trying to stand up in his crib. He's also trying to crawl. It's amazing how bonded to our little boy Pete is. The moment our front door opens and he comes in from work, Alex starts sliding on his tummy toward him, smiling and making cooing sounds. Pete has a big grin on his face as he bends down to pick him up. They play together on the floor until I put dinner on.

Alex is in his high chair with little bolsters around him to hold him up. I don't think they're necessary, but Pete does.

When we're eating, I say, "I've got good news."

Pete turns his face toward me. It's usually Alex who

he's looking at.

"I finally found a nanny who I like. She's a Filipino lady with grown kids. She seems real nice. She can come five days a week and isn't too high."

"What's not too high?" Pete asks. I tell him. "Sounds okay. You haven't found work yet though, have you?"

"No, but I'm working on it. There's a small publisher here I'm in contact with. They have an opening for a copy editor. If I get the job, it'll start in March. I'd like to get this lady to come in while I'm still home so we can see how things go with her."

"Not a bad idea," Pete says. "What's the lady's name?"

"Lily Santos," I say. "She'll be coming in next Monday."

I'm nervous as I go to my second interview at Swallowtail Publishing. I'm supposed to meet with the owner of the small company this time.

I'm surprised when the guy comes in and sits down next to the art director who was the one who saw me the first time. He can't be more than twenty-four or -five. He's about my height and can't outweigh me very much. His curly dark hair, heart-shaped face and warm brown eyes are almost pretty. I feel comfortable with him right away.

"Hi Lucy," he says as he holds out his hand. "Officially, I'm Robert Burke, but everybody calls me Bobby. You've already met Nancy, haven't you?" I say I have. "We publish mainly non-fiction stuff, just to stay alive, but our real loves are poetry and contemporary fiction. We're pretty small-time and we don't pay very much, I'm afraid. If you decide to join us, your starting salary will be two thousand per month with benefits. Can you manage that?" He could have offered me half that much and I would have agreed.

"That'll be fine," I say. "It's not so much the money that interests me. It's the experience." Bobby smiles.

He starts off by asking me what I like to read. I

squirm a little inside. I don't dare tell him the honest truth, that I almost don't read anything at all. I can think of lots of stuff we had to read in my twentieth century lit classes, but I can hardly mention those.

"Contemporary fiction?" Bobby asks.

I haven't a clue what to say to him. I feel embarrassed and wish I hadn't come. I'm blushing and Nancy rescues me.

"That's exactly what happened to me when I applied for my first job. It wasn't with Bobby, by the way. My mind went completely blank."

Bobby smiles and says, "I think we can extrapolate from Lucy's résumé, Nancy, don't you think?"

"I think we can," she says. If they only knew.

God, what am I doing, applying to be an editor when I don't even read books these days. That's going to have to change if I'm going to work here.

We spend another half hour or so chatting about this and that, then Bobby says, "Nancy tells me you've got a baby boy at home. Can you manage nine to four-thirty, Monday through Friday?"

I tell him we have a full-time sitter so that'll be okay.

"This coming Monday morning, then," he says. "Linda, who does our bookkeeping and everything else the rest of us can't do, will help you with the paperwork when you come in. See you next week, Lucy. Welcome to our little group."

I feel like a first-class fraud as I thank both of them and leave. Whatever possessed me to think that I could work as a professional in a place like this? They'll find out how really weak I am very soon.

At supper, Pete says, "So, how'd it go? Did you get the job?"

I want to tell him about my fears that I'm no way up to what they need, but I don't want to give him ammunition to keep me home.

"Yup," I say. "I did. Start work on Monday."

"How much are they paying you?" He wouldn't be happy at twice the amount, but I have to tell him.

He has that 'I knew it would be that way' expression on his face when he says, "Well, at least that'll cover the cost for Lily and maybe a few groceries, but, hey. If that's what you want to do... It's the publisher place, right? What will you be doing there?"

What do I tell him. He won't know what a copy editor does. I'm not so sure I know, myself.

"I'll be checking manuscripts people send in for mistakes and stuff."

Alex is banging a plastic toy on his high chair tray. It gets me off the hook.

March

I realize pretty soon that Bobby wasn't fooled at my interview. Instead of manuscripts to read, he's told Linda to show me examples of corrected work by editors who worked for him in the past. I feel a bit ashamed, but I'm grateful. I have serious doubts whether I'll be able to do what Bobby needs. I wouldn't have made a single one of the corrections others did.

By the end of my first week, my head is swimming. The rules I learned in high school and college English don't apply. Things I change, I discover, should have been left as is and things that needed correcting I don't recognize. I'm scared shitless when, on Friday morning of my first week at work, Bobby comes into my tiny office, a carton under his arm.

"Ta-da," he says. "Your first edit job. Shouldn't be all that hard. The manuscript comes from one of our experienced writers who has a good voice but never learned how to punctuate. The digital copy's on the office server if you need it. Let Linda know if you need any help with this, okay? It'd be nice if you could have this back to us by the end of next week. Believe me, I'd prefer to be where you are right now. I'm off to my dentist for two root canals."

God, I think, what was all that about? 'A good voice.'

What did Bobby mean by that, and what's an office server anyway? I'm totally out of my depth here. If I wasn't so desperate to be out of the house and to make new friends, I could be more honest with these people and just tell them that I'm in no way qualified for this job. By all rights, I shouldn't accept a penny from them.

I look down at the carton on my desk like it's a bomb. Open it and I'll have to do something.

Punctuation. Why, I ask myself over and over, do teachers make us learn rules that writers don't seem to use? Commas are going out of style, it appears, and what about sentence fragments that none of the editors in the package Linda gave me were concerned about? I'm having to unlearn everything I was taught. I've gotta go by Barnes & Noble this weekend and buy some books.

Pete's almost bubbly, he's so happy. The changes he's made at the dealership are increasing sales and have improved their repair record. Pete's been featured on TV and radio in Santa Lucia several times.

He comes home most days full of enthusiasm about the future. He makes me all warm inside when he tells me that he loves his work and he loves his life at home. He's worried a little, I know, about how many hours Alex spends with Lily rather than with me, but he doesn't make too big a thing of it.

Pete's wonderful with our son. He changes him almost as much as I do and bathes him. I'm so lucky, I think, compared to other women who complain about their husbands.

We're out at dinner parties more and more. I think it's because Pete's getting to be well-known. It certainly isn't because of me. Nobody in this hoity-toity town knows who Lucy Jackson is. Lucky for us, Lily seems to be available nearly all the time so we don't have to worry about getting sitters.

Every home we go to, I hear glowing things about my spouse—he's the most reliable and honest auto dealer in Santa Lucia, he stands behind the people who work for him, he's fun at parties.

Funny thing. He doesn't mind the attention of women we meet who follow him with their eyes, but he gets on my case right away if he thinks I'm flirting. Men do look at me, but I have to pretend I'm not aware of them. Makes no difference to me, actually. They still want me and that's all I really need to know.

April

I'm on my third manuscript, but things aren't going very well. I'm nervous when I turn in the first one, but I don't get a single comment. What bothers me is that Bobby and Nancy look at me in a sort of funny way, kind of worried-like. I want to ask them how I'm doing but I don't dare.

Then it happens. Bobby comes into my office on Friday morning and sits down. He's not smiling. I feel my stomach clench.

"Lucy," he says, "we know how hard you've been working on the manuscripts, but, frankly, I don't think you're ready for this kind of stuff. Thing is, we really like you and we'd like to have you back. I can't guarantee anything, the publishing industry and bookstore sales so down these days, but if in, six months, say, you can get some reading done that I'll give you, come back and we'll give you another manuscript to do. If everything works out as I'm sure it will, you'll be back with us. That sound okay to you?"

Bobby's such a sweetheart, trying to make it as gentle as he can. Being willing, no less, to take me back if I can cut it. I want to hug him to express my thanks. I don't want to seem too needy so I don't. He wouldn't mind it though, I think. He's absolutely right and I tell him so.

Smiling, I say, "Thanks for being so nice to me and offering me another chance. I'll know those books you give me inside and out before I come back."

"That's the spirit," he says. "Linda will give you a bunch before you leave."

"Could I ask you for something, Bobby, please?" He nods. "I'd appreciate it very much if you don't pay me for the last two weeks. I haven't—"

"No, no, Lucy, none of that. I have a suggestion, if you don't mind. I'm going to give you some material on copy editing that I think you need. Something else, though. You need to read, not pulp fiction, but decent stuff if you're going to develop a sense of style. You don't need to be a writer to edit well. Not at all. In the package we'll give you, there's a list I've made up for you. I think there's about a hundred titles there. Promise me you'll read every one of them while you're boning up on copy editing work."

I thank him for having confidence in me and for giving me the books and list. "I'll be back for sure if there's space for me," I say.

I'd feel like a failure if he'd just sacked me. Instead, I feel good, not bad. I'll be embarrassed to tell Pete what's happened but, hey. Super people are going out of their way to help me. What more can I ask?

Pete seems sympathetic when I talk to him, but I'm not fooled. I'm getting to know how to read between the lines. He wants me home, full time, to be here for the baby.

I think he's going to object when I tell him that I want to spend most of my daytime hours in the public library to study what Bobby gave me. He looks thoughtful, but doesn't say anything. In a way, that's supportive and I'm grateful. I go to hug him. This arouses him more than usual and after a long kiss, he bodily picks me up—he's very strong—and carries me off to our bedroom.

In fifteen minutes, lovemaking is done. Pete's up when he hears Alex cry. As usually happens with Pete and me, I don't finish. I just pretend.

Pete is masculine in every sense. His cock's not super long but thick, just what a girl like me looks for. So where are those orgasms, multiple sometimes, I used to have? Pete's not rough and he doesn't force himself on me, so what's the problem? Lack of foreplay? Not really since I never needed much. A deep kiss and touch me just about anywhere and I'm ready. So what's going on?

I ponder this as Pete goes off to our son. I'm as sexual as I've ever been, even more, maybe. The difference is that my orgasms don't come from others but from me. I know the answer to my questions, at least I think I do, but I don't want to face them. Why not? Either because I'm ashamed or because I don't want to admit that there's a problem in Pete's and my sexual relationship.

Why would I be ashamed? Because I want the sensitivity and tenderness I got to know and want? With who and when? Forrest? Jannie? Pete is a hunk as some women call it, a man's man in every way. I love him a lot, even though I knew from the start of our physical relationship that there's a barrier of some kind we probably won't cross. It's just... he makes love *to* me, not *with* me.

Moments after Pete leaves the room, my mind's back on Swallowtail and what I want to do.

October

Out of the blue, I get a call from Jimmy. He doesn't like it when I use that name. I'm supposed to call him Jim. He tells me he's going to marry Evelyn Shewster, who I met once or twice in high school. She was two years behind me.

"Listen, sis," Jimmy says. "Here's the thing. We're fucked if we stay here in Modesto. First off, Evie's mom and dad don't like me much. They won't go for their daughter marryin' me. The other thing, Mom and Dad—you know how Mom is—they'll want a wedding like they had for you. Evie and I, we don't want that. It's a fucking waste of money, all that crap. It's an excuse for

Mom to get together with her friends and Dad foots the bill. We're not gonna tell anybody what we're doin'. We're gonna get married here by a Justice of the Peace or whatever you call them, then we're gonna split. Evie wants to live in Santa Lucia. That's why I'm callin' you."

A little pissed, I say, "Oh that's nice, Jimmy, real nice. You're not calling me to let your sister know you're getting married. You just want her help, right? That right, Jimmy-o?"

Now he's ticked off. I can hear his breathing at the other end. "Just as mouthy as you always were, huh. All I'm askin' is a little help in findin' a place to live, nothin' special, just cheap. I've got my degree in accounting so it shouldn't be too hard to find a job."

He actually finished his degree. I'm surprised. He's smart enough, but he talks and dresses like a hick. I wonder what Evelyn sees in him.

"Santa Lucia's not exactly like Modesto," I tell him. "You won't find anything inexpensive here. Don't try. Find a job before you move here. It'll be real hard otherwise."

"So you won't help us at all, right?"

I tell him that's not it. "It'll be kinda nice to have you here, if you must know," I say. "I'll do whatever I can, but unless I know how much you can pay for an apartment here, there's not much I can do. Something else. Santa Lucians won't just rent to anybody who comes along. Pete says you need credit and definitely a decent-paying job for them to look at you."

Jimmy's still breathing hard. I agree to send him anything I can find on accounting jobs and listings for apartments here.

"So, when are you getting married?" I ask him.

"Already done," he says. In a snarky voice, he adds, "Evie says she's pregnant, so, you of all people ought to understand."

"Jimmy boy hasn't lost his charm. You've gotta heck of a way of asking someone for help."

"Screw you," he says and hangs up.

What a jerk my brother is.

Wouldn't you know, by Christmas they're in town. Jimmy's got a good job in an accountant firm, he says, and they found a place to live out near Cabrillo Jail. Not the best place to set up house, but they've gotta start somewhere.

1997

January

I keep in touch with Bobby. He invites me to come by, which I agree to do just to say hello. I've made a lot of progress in my studying, or at least I think so, but I don't feel ready to be tested yet. I go in to see everyone just after New Year's.

Pete and Dexter aren't getting along very well. Pete wants more changes that his partner won't support. It's going to take every cent we have, but Pete's going to make an offer to buy Dexter out. It's not a very good offer, Pete says, but all we can afford. To our surprise, Dexter accepts.

Pete's happy again when he comes home. Fighting with Dexter all the time really gets him down.

Pete comes home one day and says, "Luce, we're doing okay at work, but it's nip and tuck. The changes and expansion I made are taking pretty much all we have." I know what's coming next. "We're going to have to cut back at home for a little while. We can't afford Lily staying on right now. You understand why, right?"

I do. Pete's not one to sit back and leave things as they are. He's successful because he looks ahead and plans. I nod.

"Yes, Pete," I say. "I understand. I'm about to go back to Swallowtail to try again. They're going to give me one manuscript to do. If my work is good enough, Bobby says, I'm on. If I'm successful, can we keep her?"

Pete's not expecting this—I can see it in his eyes—

so he thinks a bit before he answers. I can see the struggle on his face. He wants to tell me no. It's that stay-at-home wife and mom thing again.

Finally, he says, "Okay, Luce, how's this. You take your test and if they put you on, then we can keep Lily for the present. It's hard for me to understand why you're so willing to work for nothing, but, if that's what you want to do..."

"Good," I say. "I'll contact Bobby tomorrow and make an appointment to go in."

Bobby isn't in the office when I arrive. A family emergency of some kind in L.A., Nancy says. She hands me a familiar-looking carton that I am to copy edit and return to them within a week.

"Please say hi to Bobby and thank him for me," I say.

"It'll be very nice to have you back," Nancy replies. "See you next week."

Back at the library—it's too distracting to work at home with Alex there—I'm hesitant at first to make corrections. This time, though, mistakes seem to jump out at me, not at all like it was before.

I'm not naive enough to think that I'm on top of things, but I feel much more confident as I move through the work. I'll have to hustle to get through the manuscript, a long one, in under seven days.

On Saturday afternoon, the phone rings and I run to pick it up. No reason to think that it's Swallowtail on the weekend, but I can hope.

It's Pete, wanting to know if he can bring his new sales manager and his wife for dinner. I think about whether or not I have food on hand and decide I do.

"Good stuff," he says, a favorite expression of his these days. "We should be there by six. I'll nip in at the liquor store before we come."

*

I'm getting ready to leave the house on Monday morning when the phone rings. It's Bobby. "Good job, Lucy," he says. "I read your corrections over the weekend and, apart from a few things you missed, it looks fine. I think we're good to go this time. Can you start tomorrow?"

I feel great. Elated is a better word. "I'll be in at nine with bells on."

"Well, you can leave the bells at home. It's Lucy we're looking for. Gotta go. Signing a new printing contract today."

August

I signed up for a creative writing class today at Santa Lucia City College. I have no ambitions to be a writer, but the course may help with my work at Swallowtail.

Little Alex is growing like a weed and talking all the time. For a child his age, his speech is very clear. We're very proud of him. He and Pete seem to get closer day by day. Alex prefers his father's company to mine, something that makes me sad sometimes. It would be different, maybe, if I stayed at home like Pete wants me to, but I'd go stir-crazy within a month. To give Pete his due, he plays with Alex more than me. More than me, or is it more than I? It's I, I think.

Pete's talking more and more about another baby. It's the only real problem the two of us have. He wants more children—I know this—and I wouldn't mind that too except that another child will make it difficult for me to work outside the home. Understandably, Pete's impatient with me when I don't commit myself.

"Luce, I don't understand you," he says. "You knew before you married me that I wanted kids. Not just one but several. That's what you wanted too, you told me. Every time I raise the subject, you back off. What's going on?"

I worry about this. Pete's right, or partially so anyway, about what I said. I wanted children, yes, but I never agreed to stay home full time to care for them. I'm afraid to point this out to him. It could cause him to draw away from me and look for someone else who would be only too pleased to give him what he wants.

Pete's like steel in many ways, bending when it suits him and remaining inflexible otherwise. It's taken me two years to learn this. I tend to take things as they come without worrying too much about tomorrow, but not him. He's strategic—another good word I've learned—and he's always making plans.

Sometimes, I think he's willing to wait on things to eventually wear me down. The milk and cookies wife he wants me to be is an example. I know what being locked down at home will do to me. I couldn't take a social life involving women who want to talk only about their babies. I have to be careful about what I say. Pete seems like a modern man, but he's really traditional in many ways.

"You're right," I say. "I did tell you I wanted children, and I still do. The thing is, Pete, I don't want to end up like my mother. Now that her two children aren't at home anymore, her life is empty. Dad has his work as a dentist to keep him busy, but all Mom has is homemaking skills because that's all she's ever done. I'm just not like women who can stay at home all the time."

"You don't think children should have the benefit of a full-time parent who can care for them?"

It's a little risky and I know what he's going to say, but I answer, "Suppose our roles were reversed and it was me who worked outside and you stayed home to watch the children. How long could you put up with that? Tell me."

Now he's angry. He'll say for the tenth time that men and women aren't the same, that the world doesn't work that way.

"So, what do you think we ought to do, just be

content with Alex and let Lily be his mother?"

Now I'm upset too, but I try to control myself. I don't want this to become a bigger issue between us than it already is.

"Pete, I'm twenty-three, that's all. I've hardly had time to live. I love you and I love our son and I love our life. I'd like to carry on working for a while to develop my skills so that one day, when our children have left home, I have something to go back to. Does that make sense to you?"

The discussion's over as I can tell by the closed-down expression on Pete's face. "Fine," he says. "We'll take this up another time."

If I want to preserve our relationship and our marriage, I'm going to have to give in at some point and give him another baby. How long I'll have my independence after that, God knows.

The news for days is all about Princess Diana and how and why she died. Sometimes I think the U.S. would be happier with a king and queen, the way people carry on.

Diana's death brings Jannie back. I think of her and miss her a lot sometimes, but not as much as before. Pete and Alex and my work keep me preoccupied, I guess. I go back and reread for the tenth time Jannie's letter to me that she put behind the painting.

My darling Lucy,

It is joy and happiness I would send to you if I could instead of the sorrow I know my letter to you will bring. Before I begin, I need you to understand how fortunate I feel I am in having known a kind of love that I didn't believe could exist. You know that I love you with every fiber of my being. The only thing possibly more beautiful that one could ask for in one's life is to have such love returned. This said, I'm much comforted and warmed to know that your love for me is closer in kind to mine than it might have been. What I would have given in my life to have been able to turn you a little more toward me.

But, my precious Lucy, to tell you of my love and my wishes for what might have been is not why I'm writing this. You already know these things. You have always sought to shield me from the fallout of a relationship that couldn't be. I have not been as strong as you in this regard. Nonetheless, my need to protect you is very strong. I would have said something to you before if I knew more precisely what the threat to you that I intuit is.

Lucy, I'm no alarmist as you know. It's not my nature to see monsters behind every tree. At the risk of sounding like the jealous lover, I'll tell you the little I can see. If my intuitions are off base as I hope they are, then no harm done. You'll not reproach me for wanting to watch over you. If, on the other hand, something untoward lies ahead, then, what is it they say—forewarned, forearmed.

Lucy, love, to me you have always been two in one, that is, a person with two conflicting sets of needs. The first set is the one everybody sees—the lively, free-spirited girl who likes to socialize and have a lot of fun. For people who don't know you as I do, you might be thought of by some as that sexy blonde with a top that just won't stop. But there's another set, the one I love the best. It involves a girl who's sensitive and kind and very loyal, a girl who Jannie thinks will be happiest in a loving relationship with a man who is respectful and sensitive as she.

Here, Lucy, is my problem. Please don't think bad things of me for saying this. I know how enamored with Pete you are, and you know that I would never do anything in the world to cause problems between the two of you. I wouldn't, that is, unless I saw something that alarmed me. I don't know Pete well so, very possibly, I'm wrong. But, from the first day—and my impressions never changed, they just grew stronger—I saw a self-made man who would always be number one who would control my angel if he could. You're smart, Lucy, much smarter than you think. If, as years go by, you see no signs of the kind of things I'm talking about, then just smile and think of your Jannie being jealous. Please, please, my love, don't ever let anyone take away that zest for life you have.

Now comes the hardest thing I've ever had to do, that's say goodbye. Adieu, alas, is the better word. I have talked about how beautiful your gift of love to me has been, true in every sense. But, my darling, for reasons I don't understand, I appear to be one of those unfortunate people who loves in such a way that their adoration comes to dominate them in every way. Every woman's voice, every woman's face is yours. With this domination, if that's a word to use, comes a pain of a kind I know, but never at this strength. I have tried, I swear to you, my love, to distract myself, but to no effect. My heart and soul yearn constantly for you and you're not there. I want to be strong enough to resist thoughts I have more and more each day. My darling Lucy, if something should happen to me that causes this pain to go away, please love me as you always have and please forgive me.

Entirely yours as long as my spirit lives,
Your Jannie

I can't write about it in my diary now any more than I could when I first read it. It makes me cry. How wonderful it would be if she was here in Santa Lucia and we were friends. That would cause real problems between Pete and me since he wouldn't allow it.

December

I love my writing course at the college. I know most of my stuff's no good, but the instructor always finds encouraging things to say, not like my classes at UCSB. I don't know how good the guy is as a writing teacher—he's never published anything—but he makes me want to try and the class is fun.

*

Pete brings home a huge eight-foot Christmas tree that bends over at the ceiling until it's trimmed. Like last year, the house smells of cookies and baked things, all made by Lily this time. I try to stop him, but goaded on by Pete, like a cat, Alex circles the tree, trying to decide which ornament he'll pull down next. I'm glad Lily's here to clean up after him.

Pete's done wonders at the dealership this year. Nearly everyone I meet seems to know him and has nothing but praise for him. He donated a new SUV to the Needy Children fund. The car's right in the middle of our biggest mall where the auction will be on Christmas Eve. It was a brilliant move. He says they've sold more cars in the last six months than in the previous year. He's in his element, that's for sure. It's incredible, the change in him when he's at work.

He's considerate and affectionate with Alex at home but on the quiet side. I've watched him in his showroom with people who come in to look. He's warm and outgoing but never pushy. It's obvious that he inspires confidence the way his customers look at him.

We're struggling at Swallowtail this year. Distributors accept fewer and fewer of our books and sales are down. It's that way for all publishers of decent stuff, Bobby says. I'm not fast, but the quality of my work's okay, so everyone at the office says, anyway. I feel a real member of the family there.

1998

June

Mom's been diagnosed with breast cancer. She's had a mastectomy on the right side and she's on chemo and radiation. Dad tells me she's pretty down. Can I come to spend a little time with her, he wants to know.

Pete frowns when I ask him—he'll miss Alex more than me, I think—but he agrees to drive us this coming Sunday. We'll stay in Modesto for a week, then he'll return to get us.

I'm afraid for Mom. They caught the tumor quite late, Dad says. He's very worried about it, I can tell.

October

Mom's feeling better now that she's finished up with her treatments. Dad says she was nauseous during most of them. She's joined a breast cancer support group, which she likes.

Things are up at Swallowtail because of two of our books that are selling very well. I didn't edit either of them. Bobby's smiling again, which makes everybody happy. I love working here.

Chapter 7

1999

February

"Blow jobs in the Oval Office, my God. Couldn't Clinton choose a better place, stupid son of a bitch? How 'bout Kennedy screwing women in the White House swimming pool. What the Democrats don't get away with, I'm telling you." Pete looks up from his paper and turns to me with one of those odd looks. He's not in the best of moods. "Hey, Luce. Say you're workin' in the White House and the President calls you in."

Disgusted, knowing what he's going to say, I head back to the kitchen.

"Now, remember, this is the President talking to you and not some dick who works for him. Would you blow him like Lewinsky did? Fast ticket to a good job, wouldn't you say?"

A nasty side of Pete I see more and more. I don't pay attention to him when he's like this.

April

Pete's going on about what he'd have done to Harris and Klebold if he'd gotten his hands on them before they committed suicide. We're watching the TV evening news and listening to comments about the shooting at Columbine in Colorado.

I'm getting nauseous and feel the tears come as I look at the faces of dead and wounded kids. It's selfish, I know, but I keep thinking how awful it would be if our own son was hurt or killed like that. Not even schools are safe anymore in the U.S. I can't stand watching anymore and get up to go peek at our little boy. It's not rational, but I need to know he's safe.

Pete's sounding off at advocates of gun control. If he's like this at twenty-eight, how far right will he be by the time he's forty? I don't keep up on world affairs as much as I should, but I know more than I did because of all my reading, enough to realize that my husband and I have different opinions on some important things.

Alex, almost four, is by far the biggest boy at nursery school where he goes half days. He'll be a large man like his father who he looks like more and more as he grows. Pete adores our son and Alex adores him, following his father like a puppy dog when Pete gets home.

He loves me too—I know that—but it's clear who he prefers.

We have three couples over tonight for a dinner party, each one of them with kids. Three stay-at-home mothers who are very proud of it. That's what gets Pete going after they leave, I know. One of the women has four kids, all boys, the youngest eleven months and the oldest six. The idea overwhelms me. I'd never have a moment's peace.

After our guests leave, he stands in front of me with this stern look on his face and says, "Luce, I'm tired of waiting. Alex is almost four and we still don't have another child, nothing even on the way. I swear, I'm going to throw out those birth control pills of yours. I'm tired of waiting."

Maybe it's because I've had too much wine or because he's standing there and scowling down at me, but his attitude upsets me. A little voice inside me tells me to button up, that this isn't the time to talk, but I don't listen. "Throw away my pills. What a stupid thing to say. You're tired of waiting, so what are you going to do, force me to have a baby?"

He glares at me. "Don't push me, Lucy. It's not something you want to do. Maybe I shouldn't a brought it up this way, but we're going to talk about it tomorrow, guaranteed. You've stalled long enough."

I'm glad he leaves before I say something I'd regret.

Next morning, Pete has that hard look when we sit down for breakfast. He's been patient, he really has, and I know this. Alex should have a sibling and not grow up an only child. I agree. It's just that I love my work and I need to be out with people as I always have.

What's been hanging over us for a couple of years now will become a real battle when the second child comes. Pete will put pressure on me to remain at home and keep it up 'til I give in. The idea turns my stomach. There's got to be another way. It's called compromise, husband, compromise.

Before he can start, I say, "About the baby thing."

Pete blinks, surprised that I'd bring it up.

"I'd like another child too, and you're right. Alex needs a brother or a sister. You've gotta agree, though. This house is just too small. The children will be far enough apart in age that it won't be good to put them in the same room. Before we think seriously about another baby, we should start looking for a bigger house." How I come up with this on the spot, I don't know.

Pete's expression turns thoughtful. My God! He's going to go for it. "We could do with a bigger house, that's true."

I sit quietly, letting the idea do its work.

"One of my clients owns a real estate office. I'll get in touch with her."

We finish our meal, each of us in our own world, Pete doubtless thinking about what he'd like, and as for me, I'm grateful that I may have up to a year of independence left.

*

July

Houses are so expensive here. None that interest us are less than a million plus. In Modesto, we could get the same thing for a third of that, maybe less. We have the money, Pete says, but it irks him to have a half million dollar mortgage.

Finally, we find a place we really like at 1415 Sycamore: four bedrooms, three baths and a big double garage. It also has a huge backyard. The house will double in value in four years, the agent says. Our closing date is September 1. Alex and I will celebrate our birthdays there.

In the meantime, Jimmy and Evelyn's first child is born. They name him James Jr. of all things. Jimmy swears it was his wife's idea, but I'm not so sure.

How different newborns are. When I go to visit Evie at Socorro, their baby she thinks is beautiful looks like a shriveled up old man to me. Alex was gorgeous from the first day.

Poor Evie's out of it when I see her. Because of the wrong position of the baby, she had to have a C-section and she's in a lot of pain.

Jimmy's with her the second time I go. He says hello to me, but he doesn't smile. My brother and Pete don't get along. Jimmy thinks he's superficial and arrogant. He's one to talk.

September

We're still unpacking boxes when our birthdays come. We love the house, but it's almost too big, too flashy, it seems to me—ornate carved wooden front door, fancy bathroom fixtures, humongous chandeliers, you get the picture. It was Pete who really chose it, more for prestige than anything else, I think.

Pete goes all out on the twenty-fifth. Instead of a birthday party for Alex with his little friends, he takes off time and arranges flights for the three of us to go to San Diego and the zoo.

We have a great time, both Pete and I very proud of our little boy. He loves the animals and gets excited when he's close to them but, compared to other children we see there, he's so grown-up and well-behaved.

As to my birthday on the fourteenth, they make more of it at the office than we do at home.

2000

January

Pete surprises me one late afternoon when he gets home. He usually arrives between seven and eight rather than at six. He's got a determined look when he walks in, but at least he's smiling. He comes up behind me and puts his arms around me while I'm working in the kitchen.

"So, wife," he says. Suddenly, my stomach's in a knot. "Alex is going on five and I bought the house you asked me for. Now where's that baby you promised me?"

The quick hard squeeze he gives me doesn't feel very nice. Quite the opposite in fact. He holds me tight so I can't turn around. I feel trapped. He has a right to be pushing me like this, I think. I can't really put him off anymore.

If we're going to talk about this, it'll be face to face. I pull his arms off of me and turn around. He's looking down at me in a way I've never seen before. This frightens me. There's nothing at all tender or loving in his face. I walk to the sofa and sit down. A moment after, Alex is in the room. He's heard his father.

"Honey," I say, "go back in your room for a few minutes, please. Daddy and I need to talk."

I'm surprised when Pete contradicts me. "No way," he says as he scoops our child up. "Our boy's staying right here with us."

"Yay," Alex says as he climbs up on his father's shoulders. "See Mommy? Daddy wants me here."

I can't put it into words, but I realize that something has just happened that's not good for us.

"Mommy's going to talk to us about the brother or

sister you're going to have. How's that?"

Another yay.

"Pete, please. We can talk about it, yes, but not like this. Alex shouldn't be a part of this discussion."

"To the contrary. He's old enough to know what's going on, aren't you, chum. You understand what a baby brother or sister means, don't you."

Alex keeps jumping up and down on Pete's wide shoulders, but when he looks at me, his little face grows serious and he doesn't answer. Pray God, don't let this be the start of something new. Pete looks like a stone statue that won't budge.

I sigh and say, "Okay, Pete. I agree with you. It's time."

Pete nods. "Hear that, big man?" he says. "By the time you're six, who knows, maybe before, you're going to have that little brother you've been waiting for. It could be a little girl which'll be just fine with me. Now I'd like you to go to your bedroom for a few minutes until suppertime. Can you do that for me?"

Alex doesn't want to go, but anything his adored father asks him to do, he does. Pete puts him down and off he goes. Without a word, Pete walks over to me, bends down and grasps my hand. I'm not fooled into thinking this is over. His face looks like granite.

He pulls me up and says, "Now for those birth control pills of yours. Let's have them and throw them out. There's only one way to handle this."

I stop and push his hand away. "Pete, why are you being like this with me? You've never treated me like this before."

In a hard voice, he answers, "Lucy, you've been putting me off for years and I've put up with it. No more. Either you give me the baby you promised me before we got married, or I'll be looking for a divorce. Do you understand?"

Stunned, all I do is nod. Feeling numb, I go into our bedroom and to my chest of drawers where my dispenser is.

With it in his hands, he says, "I see any more of these and it's quits for us. You can take that to the bank." He turns on his heel and leaves.

July

Good news! Forrest and his new wife, Claire, are moving from Sacramento to Santa Lucia. They'll live in a big house on Maple Street that Claire inherited from her mother. Forrest, he says, will set up his own office in criminal law and his wife will begin her residency in pediatrics at Socorro.

How wonderful it will be to have Forrest here. It'll be a little strange, maybe, to see him with his new wife, but that had to happen. Pete seems pleased about the news. He and Forrest always got on well. Why, I have no idea, since they're about as different as two men can be. Anyway, I'm glad since it means we'll be able to see more of them.

There's no lovemaking between Pete and me anymore, just procreative sex. He drives into me and pounds away until he's finished, then rolls off of me and goes to sleep. Each time he empties himself into me, I wonder if this day marks the beginning of the end of the life I've known. How much longer will I experience the freedom I feel each time I leave the house for work?

The tenderness Pete used to display toward me is gone. He no longer calls to tell me he'll be late. He's perturbed if dinner isn't ready for him right away when he gets home. Eight o'clock used to be the latest he'd come in. Now it's nine or ten.

I'm not suspicious about there being someone else. I know the demands on him at work. The dealership has doubled in size since he took over. Also, I know he wouldn't give up his evening time with Alex unless he had no choice.

Still, I start to worry. How could Pete be home late so often unless, unless... One of these premonition things again. If he's with someone after work, there'll be perfume or something that I'll notice. My God, what'll I do if he has another girl?

As usual, I get worked up for nothing. There's not a single woman's hair I find on Pete's clothes and there's no perfume. I call his office on two nights when he's late, wanting him to stop and get milk one time. I forget what my excuse was the other time. He's talking with a guy while he listens to me the first time I call and he's typing at his computer the second time. I think he suspects why I call, but he doesn't say anything.

October

I dread it as each day I miss goes by. Two weeks it's been so, on my way home, I stop at a CVS and pick up two kits. According to both of them, I see when I get home, I'm pregnant.

Unbelievable change in Pete. The moment I tell him, his face lights up and he's around the table to hug me. "My God, that's fantastic, Luce," he says. "Aren't you glad?"

I nod and put on a smile for him, but in truth, I'm down. I wish this wasn't the case. I'm ashamed of it. I'm willing to deprive my husband and my son of the baby they want to preserve my freedom. If I'm lucky, I have eight more months.

November

It's worse than what it was with Alex, much worse. Back then, I was only nauseous in the morning. It's so bad some days that I can't go into work. Thank God, Lily's there to care for things.

At first, Pete's solicitous as he used to be. But as the weeks go by and things don't improve by my fourth month, he spends less and less time with me and more with Alex.

It's a girl according to the ultrasound, which doesn't help. Pete said many times that a girl was fine. I learn from Alex that what Pete was hoping for was another boy.

*

I want to continue work, desperately, in fact, but there's just no way. Unless I'm resting or lying down, I feel faint or nauseous. Bobby and the crew are wonderful. They can manage, they all say. Come in when I can. Then, once the baby's come and I've had some time at home with her, I can come back and it'll be like before.

But something deep inside me tells me that it won't. Pete has never come right out and said it, but when the second baby's born, he'll find ways to make it impossible for me to be outside the home.

2001

July

Little Mia—her middle name is Josephine after Pete's mother—comes into the world at four-fifteen in the morning of July 13. Pete's first comment when he sees her makes me sad.

"Pale little thing. Looks like she'd prefer to be back inside." He's comparing her with the way Alex was, I know.

I come through it fine, but my Mia's not very happy with the world. She nurses irregularly and cries nearly all the time she's awake. Almost every time Pete puts her on his shoulder and pats her back after I feed her, she throws up on him, or more precisely, on the pad he has draped over him. After a week of this and little sleep, he gives it up. I don't blame him, he gets so little rest. Until things improve, he'll move into the guest room. Actually, I'm relieved. Now I don't have to worry about him each time she wakes.

September

It's eight-thirty on Tuesday morning, just after breakfast. I'm putting a diaper on Mia at the changing table when the phone rings. Pete answers as he's going out.

"Fuck! ... Fuck!" I hear him yell. "When? ... Uncle

Jack? You're shitting me... Holy fuck! Lucy, turn the TV on."

Something catastrophic is going on, I know, as I rush into the living room, carrying the baby. We sit for over an hour watching the horrors of the Twin Towers going down. Both Pete and I are flabbergasted that such a thing could happen in this country. One of Pete's uncles who's a lawyer working in the North Tower is missing. Pete's cousin in New York City who called us thinks he's dead.

Mia's fussing and I take her off to our bedroom to soothe her to sleep while Pete remains where he is. At about eleven, without a word, he gets up and leaves. I feel down all day, partly because of the tenseness I feel here at home and partly the pictures I keep seeing of people's stunned faces and the destruction in New York.

October

Pete is more attentive to our little girl as she begins to fuss less and sleep more regularly. He's back in our bedroom now even though Mia sleeps there in her crib. She wakes only once per night now, occasionally not at all.

I miss work and I miss our little group. I'm pleased when Pete agrees to invite Bobby and Nancy to dinner. A couple I don't know will be joining us, both Pete's employees.

Jasmine's about 22, a vivacious and pretty brunette who's the receptionist in the repair department of Pete's dealership. She's accompanied by some big wig from Toyota from San Francisco, at least twice the girl's age. At first, I think they're together, but as the evening goes by, it's clear they're not. Jasmine has eyes for only Pete. I notice—how could I not—but, somewhat to my surprise, I'm less jealous than amused.

Bobby is in good form and so is Nancy. Instead of talking about his field, he focuses on Pete's. Until dinner's over and I'm clearing plates, Nancy and I don't get much of a chance to talk. She tells me Swallowtail may have to close. Bookstore sales are down everywhere, she says. One more avenue of escape cut off, I think.

After everyone leaves, Pete says, "That's a hell of a name for a grown man, Bobby, don't you think?"

His remark bothers me. "What's wrong with it, anyway," I say.

"He's a pansy, isn't he."

"I have no idea what his sex life is and I don't care. He's a fantastic person, he really is. You becoming homophobic now?"

Pete looks hostile. "Homophobic," he repeats. "You and your big words. Think you're smarter than me with your college education, don't you. Against homosexuals? That what you're asking me? Damn right I am. They're freaks, that's what they are, gays and dykes. It bugs me when I have to sell cars to them." His look turns nasty when he says, "Tell me something, Luce. Fantastic the guy is, okay. You prefer that kind to me? Is that what you're tellin' me?"

I'm shaking, I'm so mad. I've seen changes in Pete over the years, but I've never seen him quite like this. He's using Bobby to strike out at me. Freaks? I think of little Jannie and I'm burning up, I'm so angry.

With a snarl in his voice, Pete demands, "You gonna answer me?"

"I married you, not Bobby. I've had your children, not his. Doesn't that answer you? As to your attitudes about people's sexual preferences, you can keep them to yourself. I don't want to hear them."

Sneering, Pete says, "Not so sure about you sometimes, girl. You've been acting pretty weird the last few years."

2002

May

"Hey, Claire," Pete comments in our backyard where we're having a barbecue with the Spencers, "you're due in late summer, aren't you?"

"I sure hope so," Claire says. "It's a lot of extra weight to carry around."

"You having twins or what?"

"Well, now that you mention it," Claire says, "we're having a boy and a girl, what you call an instant family."

"Twins!" both Pete and I exclaim at once.

"You're due when, exactly?" I ask.

"Middle of August or thereabouts."

She and Forrest are smiling. I'm glad for them. A lot of work, though, twins are, but I don't say it.

I can't make up my mind about Claire. She's attractive, but she has a little bit of a hard look about her. Sometimes she's soft and warm, other times...

Linda from work phones me to invite me to a goodbye party. Swallowtail Publishing is about to close their doors. Bobby, Linda tells me sadly, has filed for bankruptcy. The living room where I am when I take her call seems to shrink around me as she talks.

We're at the table eating dinner and, without warning, Pete looks over at Alex and says, "Hey there, big man, tell me. Do you still need a babysitter at your age? You look pretty big to me."

Now what's he up to? Alex and Lily are the best of friends and have been since our son was very small. It's clear from the disdainful expression that comes over Alex's face that he's not about to play the little boy before his dad.

"Lily doesn't babysit me anymore. She just plays with me sometimes."

Pete makes an 'I thought so' noise, but lets it go, for the moment anyway. He's a manipulative so-and-so, my husband is.

I'm conflicted when it comes to my duty as a mother. It wasn't that way for me with Alex who thrived since the first day and never cried when I left the house. With little Mia, it's not the same. She's fragile and seems to need more care. Lily says she cries for a long time when I go. Unfortunately, she tells Pete this too.

I feel trapped. I love my children and I want to do what's best for them, but can I do that and be unhappy at the same time? I know other women who have someone at home while they work outside so why can't I?

I know for sure, without bringing the subject up, that if I tell Pete I want to start work again, he'll find some excuse to let Lily go and I'll never get out again. If I'm doing volunteer work of some kind where I'm gone for only hours, work that reflects well on Pete, he won't object so much, at least I hope.

It's been ten months since Mia's birth and she's settled down a lot. Lily's been super helpful with her. I need to meet people, make new friends, have someone to talk to. We see Forrest and Claire once in a while, but that's nowhere near enough. I've got to find something to do outside the house before Pete shuts me down and forces me to get rid of Lily.

July

It's Mia's birthday and I'm making her a chocolate cake when I get the call. They've just formed a new chapter of MADD in Santa Lucia and they're looking for an activity coordinator to work part time as a volunteer. How did they get my name, I wonder. Probably from the public library or hospital where I help out sometimes.

Mothers Against Drunk Driving. That might be something Pete could relate to, especially if there was publicity involved. I agree to meet with the executive director the next day at ten.

Financial support is what our new chapter of MADD is looking for, no surprise. My job is to come up with activities in the city that will drum up funds. The director pats me condescendingly on the shoulder when he sees my face. A fundraiser? Me?

"Don't worry, Lucy," he says, "you'll do wonders. I can tell."

The guy is kind of oily and not so subtle when he looks me up and down. I don't like the looks of him, but it's not his approval I'm looking for but independence.

I smile as I back up a step and tell him I'll do my best. He leers at me. In your dreams, dude, I say to myself as I go into the little cubicle the guy's assigned to me where there's a small desk, a rickety-looking chair and a telephone. There's no window, but the stench of cheap men's cologne sickens me so I close my door. Why aren't women instead of creeps like him running this place, anyway?

No stationery and nothing to write with, I see. Are all MADD offices like this? I dig in my purse for a pad and pen and sit down to think.

Except for something I recently saw on TV, nothing occurs to me, so why not try it.

Who could I get to sponsor a five-mile walk for MADD and how to appeal to Santa Lucia women to participate? I'm so new at this that I don't know where to start, with potential walkers or getting sponsors. And how to publicize the thing? I don't know anyone in this town to appeal to.

I want to work on the project all day long, but I know I have to watch myself. I'm not earning a penny I can point to as the reason for being out. Pete asks me every day what I've been doing and where I've been. When he starts asking me what I have Lily doing apart from babysitting when I'm out, I know I have little time. Either I come up with something he can approve of or he'll demand that I let Lily go.

It might be different if I had money of my own to pay her but I don't. Pete controls all the finances in our home, including bills. Lily is never paid except by him. I have an allowance for food and clothing for the children and myself. Pete's not stingy, really, but there's never enough for me to put aside.

*

I don't dress provocatively when I go out, but I do take care to choose clothing that favors me. Is my choice of mainly men as my initial contacts deliberate? Perhaps. Who cares anyway. Whatever works. Pete's not physically drawn to me as he used to be, but others are. I stroke egos and pretend to be wowed by them and it seems to work. By the end of two weeks of personal interviews, I have pledges from twenty of our best-known merchants in SL.

Then it's time to change the way I look and the way I come across. It's women of well-known charitable clubs that I'll be dealing with. Their backing is surprisingly easy to obtain, especially with the pledges I show them. Now for the coup I'm counting on.

I contact the program director of our local television station and lay the project out to her. She's enthusiastic and promises me a full half hour of prime time. Now for coverage in *The Daily*, Santa Lucia's main newspaper.

One last but by no means least important thing for me to do. Before Pete can question me about my day, I tell him what I've organized and come right out and ask him for a pledge. He frowns at me as though I'm some lowly nobody looking for a handout.

"Let me see those lists." After staring at them for a while, he says, "You contacted these people personally yourself and got these pledges? What did you have to do to get them, anyway?"

I want to slap him, I'm so mad. Why do I have to put up with this from him? Instead of giving him a piece of my mind as he deserves, not a wise move for me right now, I think about a better way to come at him.

"Fine, Pete," I say. "As you can see, there are no other auto dealerships on my list. We should have someone, but I wanted to give you first chance at it, that's all. They're going to feature my project on TV and"—here I knew I had him—"they're going to show a map of the route we're going to take with a picture of all the sponsors in the background. I didn't arrange this, but the editor wants to highlight the sponsors who are contributing the most."

Pete looks coldly at me, but I can see he's calculating. I deliberately gave him not just the sponsors' names but how much each had committed to pay. Pete's scowling at me as he computes.

"And what are you getting out of this?" he wants to know. "You going to be in the paper too?"

"No," I tell him. "I'll be talking about the project on TV."

Pete's head comes up at this and he stares hard at me. I read his thoughts like an open book. How can this nondescript hausfrau of his have managed to do all this? How can he best turn what she did to his advantage? I've put him between the proverbial rock and a hard place, something he doesn't appreciate. He can't tolerate that I'm in control. I wonder what kind of penalty he'll exact from me when all of this is done.

"Give me the name of the person I'm to contact if I want to make a pledge."

I have to work hard to suppress a smile. I may have managed this, but my glee must have been apparent in my voice. "The only person you can contact about this, my love, is me."

Pete's domineering—this I've come to learn—but he's no fool. Again, I read him. Little to be gained by behaving vindictively, at least now. 'Let her be content with her little victory. Her pleasure will be short-lived.'

Pete carries a little notebook with him, no matter where he goes. He reaches in his left shirt pocket and pulls it out. He's not glowering at me anymore. He writes down some figures in his book, looks over at my lists, then writes some more.

With a flourish, he tears out the little page and hands it to me. I look, and I'm not at all surprised that his pledge is the highest I've received.

"So when does this shindig of yours take place?"

"The TV feature's after the news at six this coming Friday, and the article in *The Daily* comes out this Saturday. The photographer will be contacting you this week."

"Fine," Pete says as he gets up. "When does the walk take place?"

"Two weeks from now on Saturday," I say.

"You'll be walking, I assume? Can you get Lily that day?"

"Yes. I've already arranged that with her."

I get another of his dirty looks that as much as says that I should have gotten his permission first. Without another word, he turns around and leaves me in the living room.

September

Big surprise. For the first time in years, Pete brings home flowers on my birthday. Two dozen blood red roses in a gorgeous vase. Their heavenly bouquet fills the house.

Lily helps Alex make a card that looks more like a valentine than anything. I cherish it. She's also baked my favorite kind of cake, lemon chiffon.

Entirely out of character, Pete gives me a big smile and hug. I learn the reason. "I've gotta hand it to you, Luce. That walkathon of yours brought in big bucks. At least ten of our recent sales are due to it. I have to say, you came across real well on TV, none of that dumb blonde bimbo talk I can't stand. You did us proud, babe. You like the roses?"

"I love them," I tell him, and it's true. Pete's been a real bastard toward me the last couple of years, but I still love him. In love? Don't think I can go that far, but I do love him.

Lily's put two candles in the center with eight others in a circle surrounding them. I let Alex blow them out. He's disappointed that it takes him two tries.

Due to my success, Unctuous Duncan, my private name for him, gave me a new office with a window and better furniture. He's looking forward to my next 'escapade,' he says. I grin as I think back to what I said to Jo Ann, the program director at the TV station.

She whispered to me, “Don’t worry, Lucy. I’ll find a way to keep him off the show.” I don’t know what she did, but Duncan wasn’t happy when she called at the last minute to say that I’d be the only one they were going to interview. He doesn’t seem to suspect that it was because of me.

The project’s had some other benefits I hadn’t foreseen. I’ve been invited to join two women’s clubs, both a little pretentious and too upper-crust for me, but hey. The members are the who’s who in town.

Pete doesn’t like it all that much, but he knows these connections are good for him. I think he’s about to make a huge financial move. He’s been making noises about the price he thinks he’ll get for his Toyota dealership that will allow him, with our savings, to go into much more expensive cars, Porsches and Lamborghinis. He’s telling me to expect some tightening of our belts at home. He’s referring to a reduction in my allowance. I don’t see him making any cuts for himself or for the things he does with Alex.

My work with MADD has opened up a new world for me. A year ago, I knew virtually no one in this wealthy city. During these last two months, I’ve gotten to know lots of people in Santa Lucia. Some, I hope, will become good friends.

I’m back to spending nearly the full day out. I feel guilty sometimes about little Mia who seems so forlorn when I leave. She wants cuddling much more than Alex did and still tends to cry rather than express displeasure when she’s upset. She’s not very interactive, which keeps Pete’s focus almost entirely on our son.

I’m what some might call a readaholic. It started when I began going to the library as a place to study. I can’t seem to read enough, as Pete’s constantly telling me.

"Lucy, you're out all day and when you're home, you've got your nose in some damn book. The kids need you. Can't you see that? It's about time you took more responsibility around here. You don't do the laundry, you don't clean, you don't even do the cooking half the time. I'm out twelve hours a day working my butt off while you play around in town, then come home and read. I'm telling you, I've about had enough."

Pete exaggerates as he always does. In the first place, he doesn't like books. He never reads. He's anti-intellectual in most ways. As to our children, I'm the only one, aside from Lily, who spends time with Mia. And, except on weekends when Pete's out with Alex, I'm the one who has most contact with our son.

Pete is right about one thing. Lily is so efficient and so willing to do everything that I've become overdependent on her. I wouldn't have time to be out at all if I didn't have her. I don't know how much longer I'll be able to convince Pete that my activity outside the home is good for him. I don't think he cares a whit about how good it is for me.

2005

February

We rarely have dinner parties anymore. Pete's friends and mine are very different. I'll let it go at that. For some reason, he suggests that we have one, a real party this time.

"Luce, you invite two couples and I'll do the same."

Unusual. I'm pleased. He normally decides who comes. I'll invite Jacqueline Parks, a girl I really like who works at the library where I go, and her husband, Bob, who I don't know. Also Susan Carpenter, who teaches physics at our junior college. She lives with her husband, who could also come. I met him once and really liked him. Both Jackie and Sue have kids. I have no idea who Pete will invite. Probably people associated with his work.

*

Cooking for ten is a bit much for me so Lily agrees to stay until late evening to help me. I'm wrong about Pete's choice. One guy who's very nice but loud works for the postal service. His wife is very quiet. I never do find out what the other guy does. He and his wife don't say much, but they seem pleasant.

Josh—he's the noisy one—keeps everybody in stitches with his stories, a good man to have over, I decide, when others aren't saying much. Since all of us have young kids, the conversation naturally gets around to children, the things they do and how best to raise them.

We've all had a fair amount to drink and the party's going pretty well when Judy, Josh's wife, says, "What I can't understand is women who bring children into the world then leave them at home after a few months so they can go back to work."

"I agree," says Peggy, the wife of Pete's other friend. "Have babies and let somebody else raise them."

Suddenly, everybody's quiet. Pete's staring hard at me, and Sue and Jackie look uncomfortable. Both work outside the home.

"Right on," Josh says. "See what the feminists have done to families." If that loudmouth hadn't sounded off, Sue would have just stayed quiet.

Shooting daggers at Josh with her eyes, she glares at him and says, "There's little difference between guys like you and men in the Middle East. Wifey, keep your mouth shut and behave. Have my babies and take care of them at home. If you've got nothing to keep you busy when they're grown and gone, then keep my bed warm and knit or sew. All this while our men are out most of the time, living it up and having fun." Sue's in battle mode and I'm so proud.

In a quiet but tense voice, Jackie says, "I have to agree with her all the way. We're finally getting rid, partially, at least, of the double standard men try to hold us to."

Peg and Judy are chiming in, but I don't think I hear a word they say. I'm staring at Pete who looks like the cat that got the cream. I watch dumfounded as he raises a hand and everyone goes quiet.

"So, my darling wife," he says, "tell me. You're not unhappy that our maid sees more of our kids than you?"

"And more than you!" I answer back, furious at what he's done.

"More than me, well, yes," he says. "I'm paying the mortgage, aren't I, and earning the money that feeds the family while you gallivant around town making friends."

At this, Jackie and Sue stand up, both turning from the table to leave. Almost to the door, Sue turns around and says, "Lucy, I'm proud to have you as a friend." Though no one's saying anything, it's hard to hear what she says next. "I feel very sorry for you, I do. Thank you for inviting me. I'll be seeing you."

"Well, I never," Judy says. "I'm glad I don't have friends like that."

I want to shake her, I'm so mad. The man who didn't say much during the evening and whose name I never got stands up.

"Pete," he says, "thanks for having us. It's time Peg and I hit the road. We need to get our babysitter home."

Josh and Judy follow suit. I see Lily sneaking out the back door as the last couple leaves. Now there's only Pete and me.

"Well, that was quite a show, wasn't it," he says. Contrary to what I expect, he's calm, as though nothing unpleasant has occurred. I can't believe him. It's almost as though he choreographed the thing. He couldn't have, of course, or so I think, but it seems so.

"Is that what it was for you, a show?"

Pete looks pleased. "Hit a nerve, did we?" he says. "I think Josh just about said it all." What I wouldn't give to wipe that smirk off his gloating face.

Abruptly, his expression changes. That flinty steel look that I see more and more now is back. "I've given you a lot of room over the years, and for what. With that fancy university education of hers, does she have a job that helps support the family while she's out? No, no job. Does her volunteer work she's so big on bring us anything? Not that I know of. Is she at home in the afternoon to greet the kids when they get home from school? Why no, not her. She lets other people do her mothering while she's out hobnobbing with her friends. Tell you something, Lucy. Either you get yourself a lawyer and we get divorced or you shape up around here and be the wife and mother you're supposed to be. Any more of this dillydallying and you're out of here. Got that?"

He stares hard at me for a minute, then he goes on. Derisively, he says, "You're not as strong as your friends who were here tonight, are you. You don't have the guts to fight, do you. You know good and well you'd lose. I'd end up with the house and kids and out you'd go, right on your ass where you belong. Poor Lucy'd have to get a job and work hard for once. How do those apples sound? Understand something. You decide to stay here with us as I'm sure you will 'cause you haven't the guts to do otherwise, be prepared for changes 'cause they're gonna come."

He looks down his nose at me as if I were some creature on the ground, then, as he likes to do sometimes, he spins on one heel and leaves the living room.

I feel humiliated still, but what energy I had is gone. Though Pete was nastier to me tonight than he's ever been, I feel some of what he said about my behavior in and outside the home is true.

And he's completely right about my inability to fight. He might not get everything he thinks he would in a divorce, but I can't take the chance. The thought of being away from my children and my home scares me. Besides, and Pete knows this, there's no way I'd put the children through a separation just so I could get my way.

And, unfortunately, he's right about something else.

What skills do I have to find decent work? The best I could hope for is a minimum wage paying job. So it seems to me, anyway.

Pete can be devious and manipulative as I have learned. He'll use my weaknesses against me to make changes in our relationship and our home that he's wanted for years. I have no choice but to go along with them.

May

What I so deeply feared years ago but am now almost indifferent to is Pete's pronouncement at the dinner table. Mia's dabbling with her food and Alex reaches for the plate of extra pork chops when Pete says, "Alex, what are you doing with that knife?" He asks this with a hint of a smile on his face.

"You know, Dad. I'm cutting off the fat like I always do."

"Cutting off the fat, you say. You don't like fat, do you."

Exasperated, Alex answers, "Dad, you know I don't. I can't stand the stuff. I don't see how anybody does."

Still looking at our boy, Pete says, "Not everybody's smart like that, getting rid of stuff we don't need. I'm afraid we're going to have to be doing a little more of that here at home."

"Like what, Dad? You going to throw out stuff I have?"

"No, no, son, not at all. Far as I can see, you need everything you have. Not true for everybody in the household, though."

Alex, disinterested, goes back to cutting his meat, unaware that Pete's reference to the rest of the household pertains to me. Now what edict am I about to hear?

"The market's down and people aren't buying expensive cars these days. I had to lay off a good man today. We're going to have to make some cutbacks here at home, for the next little while anyway." Pete looks at

Mia when he says, "You still need Lily around here, girl?" Mia looks a little scared and doesn't answer. "Alex, how 'bout you? Do you absolutely need Lily here?"

Alex stops eating and thinks before he answers. "Not really, no. She can't help me with my homework anymore, so, no, not really, no."

"Guess that leaves your mother, doesn't it," Pete says. "I guess I should ask her about Lily, shouldn't I."

I'm not about to object and upset the children. With some apprehension, Alex watches me and waits. Though Mia is far too young to understand what's going on, she's aware of tension in the room, something she's been exposed to frequently since her birth.

"So, mother of Alex and Mia, our little girl, both of them all day in school, what do you have to say. Is Lily truly necessary anymore?"

Pete was lying about profits at his dealership as he knows I know. How often during the past year have I heard him boasting about how good business is. He needn't have bothered with the excuse. Hopefully, Lily who's been with us for a long time won't have a problem finding work. I don't look forward to telling her, though I doubt it will come as a surprise. I don't want to quarrel, and to what end. I have no leverage, none at all.

"We can let her go, Pete, if that's what you prefer."

He's not about to let it drop. Raising his voice a little, he says, "Well, do you need her, do you? If you do, then let's talk about it."

And say precisely what, that I need her so I can keep my job, so I can carry on with the volunteer work I do?

"There's no reason to carry on with this," I say. "I'll give her a month's notice, then let her go."

"A month! Why wait so long? Two weeks will be enough. That's a lot of my money you're willing to throw away."

Pete, always with an angle, with an ax to grind as my father used to say. He wants Alex to see him put me in my place. His son is old enough to learn what the woman's place in the home should be. Pete's callous disregard for someone who's worked tirelessly for us and who is so loyal offends me, but, as he knows perfectly well, I'm not going to force the children to sit through more of this.

"Do what you like, Pete. That's what you'll do anyway."

Before he can reply, I stand up, telling Mia to go wash up and reminding Alex that it's his night to help with dishes. But my husband hasn't finished.

"Mia, do go wash your hands, and Lucy and Alex, I'd appreciate it if you'd sit back down. We have another issue to deal with before we're done."

Wearily, I sit while Alex, who hasn't left his chair, looking troubled, regards both of us.

"Alex," Pete asks, "have you done your homework yet?" Alex shakes his head. "You have quite a lot this year, don't you." This time he nods. "Did you do any before dinner?" Alex says he did, almost an hour. "So you've had no time to play or anything." Our son looks at his father, then at me. "Well, have you?" I can see by his face that Alex is uncomfortable and perplexed.

Finally, he answers, "No, not exactly."

Placing both hands flat on the table, the judge, about to pronounce his verdict, says, "Homework's a darn sight more important than doing dishes. Maybe when school's out in summer, you can pitch in again and give your mother a little help. Otherwise, do some school work when you get home in the afternoon and get out to play for a bit with your friends. After dinner, if you still have homework to do, you can do it then. No more dishes during the school year, okay? In my mom and dad's home, that was woman's work anyway."

I try to keep the dismay I'm feeling from showing on my face, but Alex sees that I'm distressed by this. He can't understand my reasons, but he's unhappy that I'm upset.

"That's okay, Dad," he says. "I don't mind the dishes. They don't take me long anyway, not when

Mom's helping me."

"Absolutely not," Pete says. "It's time I took a hand in this. I don't want to think, when I get home late and you're in bed, that you've had no time for yourself. No more dishes now, do you hear?"

Aware, I'm sure, that his father is attacking me in some way, Alex is unhappy but doesn't know what to do so he just nods.

August

We see quite a lot of Forrest these days since he's one of the coaches for Alex's soccer team. Our son plays center most of the time and scores a lot of goals. We make it to every one of his games this year.

The playoffs end today. Claire and her three-year-olds are here along with Pete, Mia and me. Our daughter doesn't like to sit this long anywhere, but Pete makes her come. Alex assists and his team gets the winning goal. They're tied for first place in their league. Pete's smiling and thumps Alex on the back. The Spencers come to our house for dinner to celebrate.

Mia's at her happiest when she's with other children, especially if they're younger. She adores babies. Trina's one of Mia's favorite little friends. She doesn't pay much attention to little Andy. I'd love to see Forrest and his little family more often, but I'm not so sure Claire would be up for it. There's something standoffish about her.

September

It's late Wednesday evening, my thirty-second birthday, and I just left Pete in our bedroom after the worst fight we've ever had. For the first time in our marriage, he struck me on the face and on my right hand. He demanded sex of a kind I refuse to give.

I'm huddled here on my rug where I come every day, or nearly so, to write. I can't count how many times during the last year or so I've felt down like this and still I've been able to move my pen.

I'm sitting here shivering on our cold basement floor. Forty-five minutes I've been here and, for the first time I can remember, nothing comes. I don't even have the energy to cry.

I'm glad I'm not inclined to read over what I've expressed in the three volumes in my trunk and the fourth here on my lap. I would discover what I already know, that each new volume is sadder than the one before. There's so little joy in what I write these days that my diary doesn't help me anymore. In fact, I believe it hurts to record the things that go on in this house. The more I relate events or conversations that we have, the more depressed I am since I see only isolation and loneliness ahead.

Maybe I'm wrong. Perhaps things will improve. If so, it will bring me pleasure as it once did and I'll come down here again and begin volume five. For now, for the first time since my late teens, I'll put my writing things away.

Chapter 8

2007

October

Two years have passed since I last sat on this rug. Much has happened, most of which I prefer not to think about. I stare at my old trunk, so long untouched, there so much dust that I could write in it. I'm almost afraid to lift the lid for fear that some genie will spring out or, worse, to find that my four volumes have disappeared.

My intentions when last down here were to return if matters here at home had improved or stabilized in any way. They have not. The reverse is true, my life continuing steadily to spiral downward. I've come back down, not because things have gotten better but because I feel I'll have a breakdown of some kind if I don't let some of what's inside me out. I know of no other way than to go back to my diary again for help.

Mia's six and Alex, twelve. My baby's still shy and quiet and rather clingy. Alex, on the other hand, is a strapping boy, very big for his age and strong. He and his father are inseparable.

With Lily gone, I've had to give up my volunteer work at the library and at the hospital. About the only people we ever have over anymore are Claire and Forrest, and not that often. Once a year, maybe. That's a funny thing about Pete I can't figure out. He ridicules my friends and doesn't want them to call or come here, but it's as it's always been with Forrest. He and my old friend are still good together and Pete's okay with Claire too, even though she's definitely the independent kind of female he doesn't like. I wish we could see them more.

Pete's even busier than he was before. He finally bought the Porsche and Lamborghini dealership he was so keen on, which takes a lot of his time. Alex sees him much more than I. The two are heavy into sports, especially in the summertime. Forrest is still one of Alex's soccer coaches and Pete is very active with the baseball team.

With both our kids in school, aside from housework I have to do, I have lots of time to read and think. What, I ask myself nearly every day, led to the miserable situation that we're in? My life has changed so much over the last fifteen years. Pete would say that I'm to blame for this. Am I, or is it that we were just never meant to be together? Pete seemed so different way back then, so happy-go-lucky, easygoing and very loving. How could I have known how old-fashioned in some ways and traditional he was? He must have known that I was the social outgoing type, not a good candidate for the husband's helper stay-at-home kind of wife.

Pete's muttering at the dining room table after dinner while he goes over bills. I hear "too damned expensive" and "not going to keep paying this" and the like. I'm in the kitchen when he calls me. I see at least three receipts or whatever they are with those stupid little pictures of his on them.

"Lucy, look. Paying insurance on your Corolla is money down the drain. What do you use it for now, anyway?"

I've been wondering how long it would be before he decides to take my car away, one more step in his campaign to bind me to the house.

"I use it to get the groceries and to take Mia to her dance lessons." I want to add that the car is my only means of getting to the library for my books, but I know saying this won't help.

"What," Pete says. "To the supermarket two blocks from here? A damn sight cheaper to get a cab for Mia's lessons than pay the upkeep on that car. We need to sell it while it still has resale value. I'm going to put it up on Craigslist, I think. You'll have to take the calls. Can you get your things out of the car so it'll be available on the weekend?"

I say I can.

I feel like a prisoner here. Bit by bit, piece by piece, Pete has robbed me of my independence. He's so intent on isolating me that he's threatening to get rid of the home phone if my friends call me. Alex has his cell and Pete has his, and that's all the family needs, he says.

The groceries, I'm delighted to discover, are not a problem. In fact, I enjoy the walk and I seem to meet more people that way. The taxi works fine for Mia's lessons, too. A little more time consuming, maybe, but that's all. What I really miss are my books. When I'm desperate, I take the bus, which takes the entire morning or afternoon. Pete gets annoyed if he calls the house and I'm not here. I'll have to be careful how I time things or he'll prohibit me from being out of the house that long.

2008
October

I feel like I'm on an emotional roller coaster here. Some days, Pete calls me to tell me he'll be late, other times he just arrives and expects his meal. Today he comes home all lovey-dovey as if we were newlyweds. It's so nice when he's like this and I respond to him. Tomorrow when he arrives, I may get the silent treatment. He'll go on like this for days without telling me what I've done wrong. I try to be nice to him, but he fends me off.

I feel like a total weakling, being vulnerable to him like this. I never know what's going to happen one day to the next. I get conflicting messages from him all the time—you back off from me in any way and I will punish you, but if you try to make up to me, I'll reject you.

2009

March

Pete's in a good mood when he arrives and we sit down to eat. He asks Mia about her day and her face glows while she talks to him. I feel so badly for the child who adores a father who rarely says more than hello to her.

"So, Mia," Pete says. "You're not eating your broccoli. Why not?"

"It's yucky," she says.

Pete looks down at what remains of his on his plate. Conspiratorially, he half whispers, "You know what? I'm not going to eat the rest of mine either. It's overcooked like it usually is. I keep telling your mother to cook it less, but she doesn't listen." Turning to Alex who hasn't touched his broccoli yet, Pete says, "Hey, big guy. You like that stuff?" Pete, using the children to get at me again.

Alex picks up on this. Rather than answering his father, he starts to eat what both Pete and I know he doesn't like. I didn't put that much on his plate to start with. The broccoli I'm eating is al dente.

"No, no, Alex," Pete says. "No need to eat that stuff. Maybe your mother will pay attention to us next time."

Pete frowns as Alex continues eating. Poor Mia, too young to understand and not knowing quite what to do, puts down her fork and sits there. Unhappy with the way Alex responds to him, Pete turns to me.

"Am I going to have to cook and do the shopping too? You're spending too much for groceries, by the way. I'd like you to cut down forty bucks or so per week on what you spend."

If the children weren't with us, I'd tell him to go right ahead and shop himself. As it is, I hunt for sales and buy as little as I can.

Pete's little jibes and tirades wouldn't bother me all that much if he didn't involve the children. After the hundred and seventy-five dollar per month cut in my food allowance, he'll be criticizing me for not preparing enough decent food.

July

Pete comes home late quite a lot these days, past midnight sometimes. Fortunately, he calls me in advance when this happens so the children and I can go ahead and eat. Truthfully, I'm relieved more than worried. It's good to have the children to myself, and there's peace.

It's just after six when the phone rings. 'Not tonight, Pete,' I think, 'not on Mia's birthday.' The last child at her party just left and Mia, eight years old today, can't wait to tell her father about her gifts. I'm thinking about what I can say to him to coax him home when I pick up. There's a man on the other end, but it's not my husband. He sounds angry.

"You Pete Jackson's wife?" he asks.

I hear the quaver in my voice when I say, "Yes I am."

I'm shocked when the next words come.

"Listen up, lady, and listen good." The man has a rough-sounding voice with a Cockney accent. "You tell Jackson to keep his wankin' hands offa Jasmine or I'm gonna sort him out. He won't have such a pretty face when I get done. Got that, lady? Understand?"

Stunned, I hear a click on the other end.

Who's Jasmine and who's that guy and why was he going on about Pete? I'm trembling as I hang up the phone. Mia's standing there, crestfallen, looking up at me.

"What's the matter, Mommy? Daddy not coming

home tonight?"

I ruffle my daughter's hair and tell her that, as far as I know, he is. Mia says, "Yay!" and scampers off to her bedroom. Meanwhile, I stand there shaking while Alex comes into the living room.

"What's going on, Mom? Dad not coming home?"

I repeat that I think he is while my thoughts are racing in my head.

Alex comes toward me. "Mom," he asks me, "what's the matter? You look funny."

What I think is, 'nothing I can talk to you about.' What I say is, "Nothing, love. A crank call, I think. The guy upset me, that's all."

Alex doesn't look convinced. He stands there for a moment, then leaves. I go over to the couch and sit.

Jasmine, Jasmine, Jasmine, then it clicks. Pete's receptionist, the girl who came to our dinner party here. A pretty girl who couldn't take her eyes off of Pete. She has to be the one. Maybe I'm naive, but I've never worried about Pete and another girl. I've never had a reason. Besides, I'm not the jealous type anymore. He flirts with women, they flirt with him. I can't blame them. He's a very handsome man. I think about the times he's home very late. Pete and Jasmine, alone at the dealership. It makes good sense when I consider it.

Strange, the idea of them together doesn't bother me all that much. What does is the possible danger Pete might be in. In a sick kind of way, I realize, I still love the man, just not in the way I used to. The thought of him hurt somewhere makes me shiver.

And what, in God's name, should I say to him? He'll be furious when I tell him. Or, maybe not. Maybe if he sees I'm worried more about his safety than the girl, he won't be angry. I so hate it when he is. He scares me.

December

Very bad news from home. The doctors give Mom only two or three months to live. The cancer has metastasized to her liver. Mom's volunteered to go on an experimental drug regime that might arrest tumor growth, but there's not much hope. Dad's really shaken up. He wants me to come and stay with them for a while. I expect grief from Pete, but he's fine.

"Stay as long as you want," he says. "It's almost the Christmas holidays anyway. Alex can stay here with me. He's plenty old enough to stay in the house alone 'til I get home."

I'm concerned about Alex if Pete's out late. If I say this, he's likely to blow up at me.

Pete agrees to drive Mia and me this coming weekend, which will give me plenty of time to pack. I know Mom and Dad need me and I want to go, but I feel anxious about our son. It'll be the first Christmas I'll be away from him.

I know, without being told, that Pete is doing his best to alienate our son from me. He's helped by the fact that Alex worships him. Pete's already made some headway. Alex ignores me when I scold him about his views concerning girls. Even though I can help him more with his homework, he prefers to get assistance from his dad.

But I know, and this eases me, that Alex is kinder and gentler than his father, and I know he loves me. He loves me, yes, but his love is not respect. Another way in which Pete has won.

I'm dumbfounded when I see Mom. Mia starts to cry. I should have warned her. Mom's skin has a gray tinge. She's so skinny, I can see every bone. She's so weak, she speaks only when she has to. There's a morphine pump attached to her to keep down the pain, Dad says, and she's on new drugs. They said two months, but Dad thinks there's no way it'll be that long. She'll be going to the hospice very soon, he says. Jimmy came and spent two days three weeks ago. He'll return when Dad calls him.

I'm worried about Dad. He's trying to keep his spirits up, especially with Mia here, but I can tell he's down. How will he manage when Mom's gone? He never learned how to cook. I remember how Mom used to shoe him out of the kitchen each time he tried. All he knows how to do is barbecue. He has his dental practice to keep him occupied during weekdays, but how will he manage here at home, alone? I wish he could live with us, but he'd never come. It would never work anyway. Pete's dead set against that kind of thing. He's told me several times that he'd never allow his own parents to reside with us.

I borrow Dad's car—it's good to be behind the wheel again—to shop for presents and to get a Christmas tree. We wouldn't buy one if it weren't for Mia. Dad was quite surprised when he saw her.

"You came just past my knee, Punkin, last time I saw you, and look at you now."

Mia laughs, which is what Granddad wants. It's true. She's grown, grown quite a lot. Since I see her every day, I tend not to notice. I wonder how big she'll get. Mom and Dad aren't tall, but Pete is and so are his parents, and I'm no shrimp. Alex is five feet ten and, to judge by his foot size—twelve—he's not stopping there.

Except for a half hour or so while Mia opens presents, it's gloomy in the house. Mom gets more and more tired day by day and the pain gets worse. They move her to the hospice on the morning of New Year's Eve. Dad intends to spend as much time as he can with her until the end. He'll phone Jimmy and me when it's time to come.

I feel a little guilty that I'm not as devastated as I think I should be about Mom's coming death. I shouldn't be all that surprised since Mom and I were never close. We were always on the opposite ends of things. Come to think of it, she and Dad didn't hit it off all that well. It would have been more obvious if Dad wasn't the quiet type and hated arguments. Mom and Jimmy never got along at all. I felt love from Dad and mainly reproach from Mom.

On January 2, Pete arrives and we drive home.

2010

January

Unbelievable! Mom's home from the hospice. The doctors refuse to commit themselves about long-term effects, but the experimental drugs seem to have stopped tumor growth and cavity fluids. Dad seems hopeful.

May

More good news about Mom. Miraculously, her tumors continue to shrink. Her doctors no longer speak about death around the corner. To the contrary, Dad tells me, her main oncologist thinks that there's a chance that she could go on for years. They can make no predictions at this point since the effects of the new drugs she's on are not yet known. Mom's up and active as she ever was, Dad says. I must find time to go to see them this summer.

It's one of those late nights at work for Pete and we've just finished dinner when the doorbell rings. It's the police. Pete's at Socorro, undergoing minor surgery. He's been badly beaten, the two officers tell me, but nothing critical, they say.

Everyone's in a panic in the house. Mia's crying, Alex is upset and I'm scared to death. Scared of what, I have no idea. I attempt to calm Alex down and give him instructions about making sure Mia gets bathed and into bed. I ask him for his cell phone so I can call him.

By the time the cab comes and I get to the hospital, Pete's out of surgery and bandaged up. He talks to me, but he's woozy. I don't ask what happened to him. I think I know. He tells me anyway.

"Two assholes jumped me as I was leavin' work. They didn't say a goddamn thing. Big bastards, the both of 'em. Christ, I didn't have a chance. One of 'em had brass knuckles, I think, and the other guy hit me with somethin'. They kicked the shit outta me, Lucy, that's what the fuckers did." He says this in an accusatory way as if I'm to blame.

"Do the police have any idea why you were attacked?"

"How the hell do I know," Pete says. "Didn't Alex want to come?"

I stammer, "Yeah, yes, yes he did, but I needed someone to watch Mia."

Pete makes an unpleasant noise. "You shoulda let him come. Kid must be shittin' his pants at home. For Christ sake, Lucy, don't you ever think? What can you do here?"

By now I should be immune but I'm not. Pete knows how to hurt me. As I look at him in his hospital bed in the recovery room, only a part of his face showing through the bandages, I wonder what ever happened to the girl who, a few years ago, would have told him to go straight to hell. She's become a frightened weakling, scared of her own shadow and just about everything.

Wanting to say something, I ask, "Why were you in surgery? Are you hurt bad anywhere?"

"Unless you call two broken ribs and a compound fracture of my left arm just itty bitty things, then, yes. I'm banged up as you can see. The surgery was for my arm. Satisfied?"

"Are they going to keep you overnight?" I ask.

"You kidding me? You'd have to be half dead or worse. No, Luce, you'll have to put up with me at home."

"Good. Then you can come home in the cab with me. Alex and Mia are quite upset. They'll be glad to see you."

"Yeah. At least someone will." Pete's rarely pleasant to me these days, but he rarely speaks to me like this. I'm hoping that it's a guilty conscience and the pain.

"I'm going to go outside and call Alex to let him know," I say.

"You've got Alex's cell phone?"

As I see Pete's right hand reach out, I don't respond. I just take it out of my purse and hand it to him. I'm saddened by his change of tone. Normally, when sick or slightly injured, he wants sympathy. This time, he plays down his injuries and says he's anxious to be home.

"Not to worry about a thing, big guy. Everything's just fine."

It's Pete's way to emphasize to me that it wasn't his wife he wanted there but his cherished son. He needn't have bothered. I'm aware of it.

Pete's experience with the hoodlums changes him. He's darker, somehow, more morose, toward me, at least, and even toward little Mia. I feel so bad for her. For reasons I can't fathom since he's never paid her the least attention, Mia idolizes Pete. She doesn't approach him, but her eyes are on him all the time. The yearning for attention is in her eyes, plain to see.

Pete's even closer to Alex than he was before. His son can do no wrong.

Pete's at the dining room table doing bills when I hear him curse.

"Goddamn it, Lucy, what've you done with our property tax bill? The mail's in a mess! I can't find that bill and the gas and electric bill anywhere. What do you do with our letters, anyway?"

Knowing how sensitive Pete is about this, I'm very careful to put everything that isn't addressed directly to me on the desk in his study. He doesn't do bills there, though. He brings his mail out here into the dining room so I get to hear him complain about the money he has to spend.

From my chair in the living room, I say, "I put everything where I usually do, Pete, on your desk. Letters to the both of us I open and—"

Pete bangs his fist down and pushes back his chair. A moment later, glaring, he's shaking a big finger in my face.

"No more, you won't! I've had enough of your sloppiness, woman, do you hear? Enough!" Clenching his teeth, he says, "From here on out, every single piece of mail goes on my desk, *unopened,* Lucy. Do you understand? You're not to open a single thing, not anything. It's the only goddamn way I'm gonna get my mail. You don't get hardly anything these days, anyway. I'll give it to you if you do. Got that? Don't fuck me over on this, woman, or there'll be consequences you won't like."

Two years ago, I would have been outraged by Pete's prohibition. Now I just sit here, wondering what he'll dream up next. I don't do it, but I suspect that if I went to the table and went through the mail, I'd find those bills, both of them lying there.

June

Alex's room is tidy, not because he is. I couldn't walk in here if I didn't clean up every day. I'm stripping the sheets off the bed when I see the corner of a piece of paper sticking out between the box spring and the mattress. The bottom sheet in my hands, I stare at the paper as if it might bite. Then I reach down and tug at it.

Out comes a glossy magazine. From the cover, I know immediately what it is. I shrink at what I see inside. A little voice inside my head chides me about how this girl has changed. I'd have grinned and doubtless have been aroused way back then. Now the pictures make me sick. Where, I wonder, do teenagers in Santa Lucia find porn like this?

The question is, what to do with it. Talk to Alex about it? I can't. I simply can't. He has no respect for me at all. I think he's sorry for me sometimes, he is, but regard for my status as a parent, none, thanks to his father. I feel apprehensive about talking about this to Pete. I never know quite how he'll be when I raise something he doesn't like. Will he get on Alex for having this? Will he lash out at me? It's important that Pete knows. I'll have to show him.

Pete studies the magazine for a while, flipping

pages. Are those grins he's trying to hide? When he puts the magazine down and looks at me, I know I'm in for it. Why didn't I listen to myself? The expression on his face and his tone are scathing.

Speaking quietly, he says, "I knew a girl once years ago when she was young and still had her good looks who couldn't get enough. Sex-crazed that girl was, you know? Any idea who that girl was? Hmmm? You, babe, that's who." Leaning toward me, a kind of leer on his face, he adds, "As I remember, you wanted it every which way, in the mouth, in the cunt, up the ass. And that's not all, oh no. You wanted it so much that threesomes, foursomes, I don't know what all, were a-okay."

Aghast, I demand, "What are you talking about?"

I'm startled when he reaches out and bunches up the front of my blouse in his fist and pulls. He's angrier than I've ever seen him and his face is close.

"Listen, bitch," he hisses. "Continue playing the innocent with me and I'll bring out pictures to prove my point and spread 'em all over town. First off, though, I'll show them to the kids." Pete's nose is almost touching mine as he says, "I guarantee you, Lucy baby, when Mia and Alex see those photographs, they'll spit on you. They'll never talk to you again."

I'm frightened of Pete more than I've ever been and terrified by what he says. I don't know precisely what he's going on about. Photographs? Photographs of what? Then, feeling pressed down against the ground as if a huge boulder were rolling over me, I know. It has to be about that horrible night in Baja years ago. So Pete lied to me after all.

Malice in his voice, Pete backs away and says, "Remember one thing, Lucy girl. I don't make promises I don't keep. If I say I've got, shall we say, very nasty pictures of our saintly mother here, I've got them. You can take that to the bank."

He settles back in his chair, looking satisfied. Then, suddenly, his face goes dark and he's back breathing on me. "What kind of a mother are you, anyway? You think Alex is a bad kid, do you? When's the last time you caught him drinkin' or takin' dope? Answer me! When? And how 'bout those bad grades in school? Mostly A's if I remember right. What would you have our Alex doin', tell me. Reading homo magazines? Maybe that's it. My God, woman, you make me sick. You're not only a lousy wife, you're a lousy mother! So Alex gets his rocks off on a little porn. So what! He's doin' just about what every other teenage boy in the country does. You gonna crucify him for that? Not on your life, you're not. You mention a word of this to him and I bring out the pictures. Believe me, bitch, once he's seen 'em, he won't want to be around you anymore. You walk around here like some goddamn saint. You keep this crap up and we'll see just how much of a saint you are. You clean his room, that's fine, but you're not to touch any of Alex's things. Not a fucking thing, you hear? Do you hear me, Lucy?"

I'm trembling and he frightens me. I nod. What else can I do? He reaches out and grabs my blouse again. I can hardly get the words out, I'm so scared, but, in a little voice I hardly recognize, I say, "Yes, Pete, I hear you."

"You're damn right you do. Tomorrow when he's in school, you put this back exactly where it was, and that's the end of it." He hands the magazine back to me. "For somebody who's got the morals of an alley cat, you're not fit to tell Alex what to do."

Pete sits back, thinking as he taps his knee. Then he says, "From now on, babe, things are going to change. It's a mystery to me sometimes how I ever hooked up with you. Empty-headed blonde, party girl, nothing serious ever on her mind. Can't keep a job, lets other people do her work at home, hasn't got a clue about what being a good wife or mother is. I had to pressure her into having another baby, and look to Christ what she's done. A mousy girl who's scared of her own shadow and doesn't say a thing to anyone. I've raised Alex, not you, and take a look who *he* is. You've raised Mia and look how *she* is. You're not fit as a wife or mother and you can't do a goddamn thing on your own. It's time I took control around here before this place goes to hell. You can expect changes in just about everything, babe, 'cause they're gonna come."

Sneering at me, he says, "And you know what you can do if you don't like it? You can divorce me if you can manage to do it before I divorce you. I leave it to your feeble brain to figure out where you'll be if that happens."

September

We've just gotten into bed when Pete says, "You know, I've noticed something. You don't give a damn about how you look here in the house, but I've seen you on the weekend when you go out to shop. She fixes up her hair and puts pretty dresses on, doesn't she. Now why is that, babe, tell me."

What can I say to him that won't bring down the roof? That no one pays attention to me here in the house so I don't bother, but people do look at me when I go out. That getting dressed up and looking nice is my only way to know that I'm still someone people might want to know. Hardly, so I don't answer.

"Well," Pete says, "since the lady won't answer me, looks like it's one more thing I'll have to fix." He gets out of bed and goes over to my closet.

I hold my breath. What's he going to do?

My closet is full, mostly of older things that I rarely wear. Out come nice pants, skirts and dresses, shirts and blouses, one by one. Two thirds of them at least end up in a pile in the middle of the floor. Sweat pants and dowdy things like that are all that's left. My throat starts to close as I watch him. All my pretty things to be thrown away. Pete gets back in bed.

"Tomorrow, that stuff goes out. That sexy stuff you're throwing out. Don't screw around with me, Lucy. When I say out, I mean out. Don't you dare hide these things anywhere in the house. On second thought, I'll get rid of them myself tomorrow. Leave them there on the floor." He turns toward me with that special look I know so well. I start to shut off my mind as I always do now when we have sex. "Your face isn't what it used to be, but your body's not bad still. Too bad you can't show it off outside, isn't it. You'd like that, wouldn't you, having men eating you up with their eyes like they used to. Oh you'd like that plenty, wouldn't you. Well, like it or not, Lucy babe, you're my wife, for the present, at least, so if you know what's good for you, you'll do exactly what I say. Now turn over on your front and spread those long legs of yours. Your husband wants somethin' he shoulda had a long time ago."

"Pete, no, please," I say, pleading with him. "I don't want to make love that way."

Is he doing this out of lust or is he doing it to punish me and to show me that he has control?

"Turn over, I said," he repeats to me.

Slowly, I comply, taking the edge of my pillow in my mouth and biting down to keep from crying out.

Contrary to what I anticipate, Pete is careful to prepare me. Again, unlike what he usually does, he enters me very slowly. I detest the feel of him inside me, but it's not as painful as I thought. I feel him ejaculate then withdraw.

"You see, Lucy baby? That wasn't so bad, was it. You came close to finishing yourself, didn't you."

How self-delusional the man is. I haven't had a real orgasm with him in years. Finish that way? How egotistical the man is.

"She doesn't want to answer. Well that's okay. I'm glad she liked it 'cause more of that's gonna come her way."

I feel humiliated but also guilty most of the time. I'm starting to believe, despite myself, that much of what Pete says about me as a wife and mother must be true. I was weak as a teenager in college and little's changed. No, that's not true. I'm weaker than I was in just about every way. Pete and Alex are the strong ones, knowing what and who they are, while Mia and I...

I'm sorting laundry when Sue phones. It's been a long time since I've heard from her. It's nice to hear her voice.

"Lucy, I haven't seen you since, I can't remember when. How are things?"

I give some noncommittal answer.

"Yeah," she says. "More or less the same for me. Sorry I haven't called lately. Listen, Luce. I need a favor. Could I drop in to see you this afternoon, about three, say? Will I be interrupting anything? Your husband won't be there, will he?"

"It'll be great to see you, Sue. Come over, sure. Pete? He won't be home 'til six at the earliest so don't worry."

She arrives at the same time Mia does from school. Sue looks great as usual. We're about the same height and weight, but she makes me feel like a real slob. Her hair is up, a new style for her, and I like her top and skirt.

We chat at the kitchen table for a few minutes, then Sue says, "I hope you don't mind me asking, but would you mind if I take a peek in your clothes closet? There's something special I'm looking for." Before I can put her off, she grins and grabs me by the hand and pulls me up. "Come on, come on, let me take a look. I'm sure you've got it."

"Got what?" I say as she pulls me toward my bedroom.

"You remember that gorgeous dress you wore at your party I came to? You do, don't you?"

I don't, but I figure, what's the use. I'll just have to show her it's not there anymore, whatever she's looking for.

She peeks inside the closet for a minute, then she says, "Come on, Lucy, show me your real clothes. Don't worry. I'll bring it back. It's that gorgeous red dress with all the smocking, you know. My husband's been promoted and we're going to have his boss and people from his work over to celebrate. I've just gotta wear that dress." Tapping her breast, she says, "Got the same problem you do, Luce. It's hard to find things that fit. From the shoulders down, you and I could be twins."

What to tell my friend? Years ago, I'd have been embarrassed, but I don't feel like that anymore.

"These are my clothes," I say. "They're the only ones I have."

Sue sees that I'm serious and her expression changes. "Lucy, what do you mean? You used to have so many nice things. I've seen a lotta them, don't forget. What happened to them all?"

I tell her.

She stares at me for a long time, then says, "I can't believe it. I can't believe someone could do such a nasty thing. You let him?"

I don't answer.

With tears in her eyes, she hugs me. She half whispers, "Lucy, I'm so sorry. Please forgive me for doing this to you. I had no idea. I had no idea. He's not hurting you, is he?"

I shake my head.

She doesn't stay long after that. Sue looks stressed. She doesn't know what to say to me after this. She gives me another quick hug and leaves.

November

I don't read the paper much these days, not as much as I used to, anyway. I bring it in and put it on Pete's chair that he won't let Mia or me near when the phone rings. It's Gloria Wilkins, a name I think I recognize.

"Lucy, isn't that a wonderful thing Pete's done? Have you seen the paper?"

I haven't the foggiest notion what she's going on about and why she's calling me. "The paper? No. I just brought it in. What's Pete done?"

"He hasn't told you about his project? I'm surprised. Read about it in the paper. Your hubby and that gorgeous son of yours are in the middle of the front page."

We hang up and, with real curiosity and a little dread, I go to look.

Pete Jackson, well-known to Santa Lucians, pledges one new automobile per year to be raffled off each Christmas for the Children's Fund. On the first Monday of December of every year, Jackson says, a brand new Toyota or similar SUV will be placed in the middle of the Central Mall, raffle tickets sold as of then at ten dollars each until Christmas day, one hundred percent of the benefits to go to the Children's Fund.

I remember when Pete did this years ago. There's a big picture of him and the mayor shaking hands with Alex in the background. The spread and story are impressive. Whatever Pete's motives might be for doing this, the gesture will be well-received. He contributes to more charitable causes than any other merchant in this city, I hear people say.

Pete and I have sex about two or three times a month, or, more accurately, Pete does. At least once a month, it's anal. He's not gentle anymore when he does this, and it's mechanical in a way. There's no lust or real desire that I can tell. I think it's just another way for him to show his power over me. I go away to another place in my mind each time it happens.

Holding several videos in his hand, Pete says, "Luce, I've got some things here you need to see. A buddy of mine gave me these. Says his wife really gets off on them. It's the only way he can get her hot, he says. We're gonna watch one of these when the kids are both asleep so don't poop out on me."

They're pornos Pete has—I know this—and I don't look forward to watching them with him, but I'm not sure what choice I have. More and more, I find myself capitulating because of my fear of what he'll do if I don't obey him. Often, it's just easier to comply.

"We'll see these in my study and not in the living room," Pete says. "I've got a big enough TV and a DVD player in there."

Alex did say good night, but Pete wants to be sure that neither of the children wander in and see what we're looking at. I follow him in and sit down next to him.

I can't say that what we see during the next two hours really shocks me. What troubles me and makes me a little fearful is how aroused my husband gets by low-budget canned porn. It's obvious to me that none of the low-grade actors we see enjoy the routines that have been choreographed for them.

Halfway through the first video, Pete grabs me by the arm and points to the screen. "Luce, look at what that girl's doing. You could learn to do that, couldn't you? With a little practice, hmmm?"

What I think but don't say out loud is, 'Not for you, Pete, not for anyone would I deliberately choke myself like that.' Best not to react at all, I decide.

"You're gonna do that for me, tonight, maybe."

Better to refuse in bed where there are other options rather than fight it out here on the couch.

The second video's much better done. At least it has a plot and better actors. Two couples, neighbors, it seems, eat together and have after-dinner drinks at a backyard pool. There's even some attempt at intelligent conversation. Predictably, wife of couple A begins flirting with husband of couple B. The other pair reciprocate and, not long after, making out moves to bedrooms. The video ends there with no pornography at all. I'm surprised and glad until Pete turns to me, looking eager and rather earnest.

"Lucy, listen. No sense kidding ourselves, our sex life's not the greatest. A lot of people, sophisticated people, do just what those couples did to get things up and going again. You understand? Get what I mean?"

At his most subtle, Pete's not hard to read. I feel anxious and rather sick. He's got something in mind for us. Knowing him, the planner that he is, he's probably got the other couple.

"Pete, look," I say, "I'm—"

He cuts me off. In a quiet, almost pleading tone, he says, "Now hold on, Luce, hold on. I'm not trying to force you to do anything, not at all."

'Of course not, Pete. You never do.'

"I'd like to try something with you, and you can be the judge. By the end of the evening, if you say no, things end there, and I promise not to complain about it if that's what you do. You know me, Lucy. My promises, I don't break. Do you remember meeting Peter Wilkins and his wife, Gloria, a year or so ago? We met them at a community barbecue."

So that's who the caller was. In fact, I do. She was rather loud, I remember thinking, but I did like Peter, an attractive and soft-spoken man, a teacher at Santa Lucia City College if I'm not mistaken.

"Yes, Pete, I remember them. What about them?"

"Here's what. Gloria comes into the dealership fairly often to visit Pauline, you know, my secretary. We got to talkin' one day, Gloria and me. She told me Peter sees you at the grocery store almost every weekend and can't keep his eyes offa you. No shit. That's exactly what she says. She told me he's seen you at the college several times. So Gloria says, why don't we get together for dinner sometime to get to know each other better."

"You mean, like the couples in your video, Pete. That's what you mean?"

"Okay, babe, like this or not, Peter thinks you're pretty hot and, let's say, I wouldn't kick Gloria out of bed. So what I'm sayin' is simply this. The four of us will probably get along okay. We invite them over and see how things go and, as I promised, if you don't want to get it on with Peter by the end, then they go home and that's the end of it. Now what harm can you see in that, tell me?"

The rational side of me wants to say, 'Lots of things. I'm a married woman, not happily, okay, with two kids and I'm no swinger.' The other part of me that I don't know what to call that has been asleep for a long long time is up and dancing. Licensed to flirt with an attractive man who likes me? Finally appreciated as a woman by someone? Able to have fun, then cut it off when it was time to stop? Why not? After all, Pete and I don't have much to lose, do we.

"Sure, Pete, go ahead and set it up. Let me know when you want to have the dinner."

I almost laugh when I turn to see Pete's face. It's difficult to surprise him. This time I do.

"You mean it, Luce? You'll go along with this? You promise? You're not going to try to make a fool out of me on this?"

"Don't worry, Pete. I look forward to the party. I can't promise you how it will end, but it sounds like fun."

For the first night in so very long, Pete is gentle with me and quiet. He makes no demands on me when we go to bed. As I drift off to sleep, I wonder what catastrophe for us lies ahead.

Catastrophes there may be, but not with the Wilkinses, it turns out. A week or so before Christmas, concerned about our schedule, I ask Pete when this dinner of his is going to be. He glowers at me and shakes his head.

"You'll be glad to hear, I'm sure, that there won't be one. Gloria's all for it but her husband's not. So there you are."

I'm so desperate for social interaction and fresh air that I feel a twinge of regret at what he says, not that I'm proud of it. It probably would have made things worse for us in the long run.

Chapter 9

2011

January

Mom's in complete remission, or so Dad says. The future is still a question mark, her doctors say. The tumors are still there and won't go away, but they're inactive due to the effects of the new drugs. Dad's spirits are back up and things seem to be going well. I feel guilty that I don't go to see them more. I raise the possibility of a visit with Pete, but he always puts me off. Still, that's no real excuse. Jimmy's gone twice as much as I have.

The slightest thing seems to set Pete off these days. He's usually good-humored in the morning. We're just out of bed and getting dressed when he breaks that rule.

"Goddamn it, Lucy, why do I have to keep telling you." From his closet, Pete gathers up all his dress shirts I've washed and ironed and throws them on the floor. "A half inch apart, I've told you a hundred times. Stop bunching them up like that. You do anything you can to bug me, don't you."

I want to tell him he's got too many things in his closet to spread out like that. I don't because it would only make him mad and, to tell the truth, I'm not sure it's really true. I've never really tried to space them out. Passive aggression? Probably.

He demands that the blankets and our sheets be a

half inch from the floor on both sides. I've got to be more careful about this since I never know when he's going to measure. Even so, I only check about half the time.

Things have changed a lot as he said they would. Now I don't go to bed or get up until he says. He makes lists of what I'm to do in the house while he's at work. I buy only what he wants at the grocery store and I cook what he tells me to. If Alex requests something special he likes, I'm to buy it. Mia knows better than to ask.

Once upon a time, Pete asked me to make love. I can't remember exactly when this stopped. Except for the throat thing which we don't try anymore because it hurts me too much, sex is how he wants it and when. He bought another TV and DVD player for our bedroom which he uses to watch porn stuff. When he does this, which is often, it's oral sex he mainly wants and he makes me swallow. I kept a glass of milk under the bed when we did this until he caught me. He doesn't make me turn over on my tummy very much, only when he's mad.

August

It's a gorgeous Saturday afternoon in Santa Lucia and we're at one of Alex's soccer matches. Mia is sitting to my left and Kate, another mother of one of our players, is to my right. Pete's down near the coaches and players somewhere.

It's so nice to be able to talk with another woman, something I don't get to do much anymore. Pete doesn't like me seeing friends. Kate and I are chatting and laughing about something when Pete comes up. He's looking at me in that sidewise way of his. I watch and my insides churn as I see him take off his cap and put it back, bill backwards. He's done this before several times. It's a signal to let me know that he's displeased and I'll pay for my misdemeanor later on tonight. It'll be anal sex. Pete leaves and Kate begins to talk.

"Lucy, I used to see you at the library sometimes.

You don't go there anymore?"

I tell her I'm so busy at home that I don't have much time.

"Yeah, I know what you mean. Something bothering your husband? He looked upset." Before I can tell her no, Kate adds, "I wonder why he turned his hat around like that. Something my two boys do all the time. Nice stop!" she yells.

I don't look at Kate but face straight ahead in case Pete is watching. If I leave Kate alone and talk to Mia, maybe he'll forgive me and things will be okay tonight.

Everybody whoops as Kate's son, the goalie for our team, stops a big one. While she's not looking, I move closer to Mia and start to talk to her.

I can tell by Pete's expression later on at the dinner table that my attempts to placate him haven't worked. He's upset with me and unhappy with the results of the soccer match. Alex hasn't said a word since we got home. It was his failure to pass the ball at a critical moment that allowed the opposing team to win. Tonight, I'll pay the price for both mistakes.

Mia's in tears and she looks frightened as she comes into the kitchen where I'm making breakfast. She grasps my hand and tugs me toward her bedroom. She's trembling. Silent, she points to her pajamas on the floor. I don't notice anything unusual at first, then I see blood.

"Mommy, what's the matter with me? There's blood coming out of me—it got on the bed."

I hadn't raised the menstruation issue yet since Mia is so young. I should have. My first period came just after my eleventh birthday. On the other hand, Mia won't turn ten for another week. Is that menstruation or something else? She's very early, that's all, I think. I'll have to keep an eye on her for the next few days and see. I smile and hug her and sit down with her on her bed. We chat for a little while and she's okay, especially when she learns that the same thing happens to me every month.

Looking a little dazed, Mia asks, "Does that mean I can have a baby soon?"

I laugh and tell her no. She seems let down.

"But I want one, Mommy. I love babies. You said if I'm bleeding like this, I can have one."

Something fierce inside me wants me to grip her by the shoulders and say to her, 'No children until you're thirty and until you're with a man you know super well.' Instead, I bite back my words and tell her to wait right there while I go get a pad if I can find one.

September

Alex will be sixteen in a few days and eligible to take his driver's test. Since the twenty-fourth falls on a Saturday, he'll have to wait until Monday. Pete's been practicing with him for nearly half a year. Both are confident he'll pass.

"Mommy," Mia asks Saturday morning on her brother's birthday, "whose car is that in our driveway? Alex is still asleep."

"Mia, shush up," Pete says. "It's none of your business whose car that is."

Poor Mia cowers as she often does when Pete speaks roughly to her in that way. "Sorry, Daddy," she says and moves away from the front window.

I get up from the kitchen table and go to see. There is another car beside Pete's Porsche that I don't recognize. Pete comes up beside me and lets me know that we're not to discuss the matter until Alex is awake. Pete's obviously bought our son a car for his birthday.

I don't drive much and don't know much about automobiles, but it's plain that the one I'm looking at is expensive. Very expensive, in fact—I'd say many, many thousands. When I compare this gift with the crummy piece of costume jewelry Pete bought last July for Mia's birthday that she wears as though it were pure gold, I burn. How unbelievably unfair the man can be.

To say that Alex is ecstatic when he sees his gift

would be to seriously understate things. Like most boys his age, cars are second only to willing girls. Less than five minutes after he spots the vehicle in the driveway, he and Pete are off. I hear Pete tell him as they're going out the door that it's a BMW sports car, a trade-in less than one year old. I have no idea how expensive a car like that is and I don't want to know.

2012
May

Not yet eleven, Mia's shape starts to change, much sooner than I did. Not that much difference in her face or hair or in her voice, but her breasts are budding early. She won't have the same shape as me. Mia's short as I think she'll always be. I doubt she'll ever go past five two. She'll be curvy as little women often are and she'll have big boobs. It's a shame about her plain face and wispy hair. She has kind of a mousy look, my Mia does, that I doubt will ever really change. Guys will want her for what they can get from her. It makes me sad. She'll be vulnerable because of the way she'll look.

Pete's mowing the lawn in the backyard and I'm cutting chicken up for dinner when the phone rings. Seconds after I pick it up, I start to shake. It's Alex on the phone at the police station. He refuses to tell me what's going on. He wants his dad. Badly frightened, I call Pete to the phone.

He won't tell me what's happened when he hangs up. It's something bad, I know, when I hear Pete say, "Alex did what? Are you kidding me?"

When he puts down the phone, he yells to me to get Forrest to meet him at the police station as soon as he can come. I plead with him to tell me what's going on but he won't. He just repeats what he said before.

I've never seen a trace of tears in Pete's eyes, but they're there when he gets home two hours later. By then, I know pretty much everything because of Forrest's call. I'm so shocked when he explains things that I can't talk.

Our boy robs a liquor store and is now in jail. Alex does this with a friend who gets away and who he refuses to name. It's Kenny, his best friend, it has to be. I'm scared half to death as Pete bunches up his fists and stomps back and forth through our house like an angry lion. He's threatening to go to Kenny's house and slam the boy up against the wall until he "fesses up."

"How dare he leave Alex in the lurch this way," Pete says to anyone who'll listen as he paces back and forth.

Mia's in her bedroom, crying. She ran in there when she heard Pete order me to keep that "sniveling brat" out of here. Pete has no idea or doesn't seem to care how much he hurts her.

We can't sleep, knowing where Alex is and worrying about him.

Sunday around noon, Forrest comes to see us. Things will be much better for Alex, he assures us, if we can convince him to identify the friend. The prosecutor's willing to go easy on this one, given Alex's history, if he tells who his accomplice was.

It turns out that Alex doesn't have to. Kenny goes to the station to give himself up Sunday evening. Alex is arraigned Monday afternoon and Pete puts up his bail.

He's so furious with our son that he won't speak with him. Alex makes things worse by showing no remorse. Pete goes to grab him to shake it out of him, but Alex stands up to him.

I'm afraid something awful is going to happen when Alex says, "Dad, I'd appreciate it if you keep your hands off of me."

Pete's so angry that his face goes red, but he doesn't do anything. I let out a long breath when he spins on one heel and stalks out of the room.

I comfort Mia and get her settled, then I sit down to think. What could have made Alex do such a thing? It's so unlike him. I want to go to him and talk, but he has no regard for me. Pete has taught him well.

*

June

Everything turns out okay as Forrest says. Alex and his friend are on probation with two years of community work to do. To my surprise, Alex seems pleased by this. He and his father seem as close now as they ever were. Neither Pete nor I have any idea what brought on this crisis in our son's life. Could it be his perception of what's going on between Pete and me? I doubt it.

Alex is more excited about the prom than about his high school graduation coming up in two days. His date is a lovely girl from India who we met a year or so ago. I'd be eager too if I were him, but Pete's not all that pleased. Why couldn't his handsome son find a pretty American girl instead?

Pete wants our boy to work for him this summer at the dealership before he goes to college, but Alex told him no. He prefers to work at a museum in Santa Barbara that's more related to what he wants to do. He's going to major either in archeology or in marine biology, he says. I don't find any archeology program in the catalog, but I don't say so. Of three offers he receives, Alex chooses UCSB, I'm proud to say. Pete wants business school and not that "airy-fairy stuff" Alex is going for, but he doesn't say anything, not for now, at least. He's not pleased either about his choice of schools.

October

Things are so different now at home with Alex gone at school. Pete's morose often, getting home well past midnight sometimes. Even on the weekends he's out at night. We stopped going places together long ago. Pete uses Mia's age as an excuse, but that's not really it, as he knows I know.

I feel so sorry for our daughter. She gets good marks but seems to have few friends at school, the very opposite of how I was. She adores a father who hardly knows she's there. Her eyes follow him everywhere he goes when he's at home. She needs a male figure in her life and she has none.

She's blossoming very quickly, our Mia is. In profile, with those well-shaped breasts of hers, she looks fifteen. Already, her hips are wider than her waist. She'll have a luscious body, that one.

2013

January

I miss Alex terribly. Christmas came and he was here and then he went. Otherwise, things at home are much the same. My routine never seems to vary. I have lines in my face now that I didn't use to have and I'm pulling out gray hairs every day. My skin is good, though, and I keep my weight down, for who, I can't imagine.

One thing is different in the house, at least. It's doubtless due to Alex being gone. Whatever the reason, I'm very glad. Pete's finally beginning to acknowledge he has a daughter. Her eyes continue to be on him, and I see Pete watching her. If he gets home in time, he says good night to her, something he's never done. For those few words and his attention, the poor girl often waits up for him.

He's starting to talk to her at the dinner table, more than he talks to me. No matter. It does my heart good to see Mia glow. She literally lights up when he's around.

At long last, he's using pet names with her and bending down to kiss her good night on the cheek. One evening, out of the corner of my eye, I see Mia fling her arms around Pete's neck when he bends down.

I hear him say, "Hey, hey, cutie, what's this? Keep that up and I'm gonna make a mistake some night and take you for some hot girl who I don't know. You wouldn't want that to happen now, would you."

I'm startled, not so much by what Pete said as by the throaty sound Mia makes and the rapt expression on her face.

"You behave like that in school, girl, and you'll have guys all over you. Off you go to bed."

Is there something I should be watching out for here? After a few days go by with no further incidents, no, I think.

Pete can be a first-class asshole as I've come to know, but take advantage of a child, his own daughter? No. He'd never stoop that low.

Nonetheless, I'm concerned. Though Pete is unlikely to initiate anything, Mia, love-starved for her father as she is, may unintentionally start something.

I'd worry less if our family had been normal. Pete's never had a real relationship with Mia in the past. Abstractly, she's his daughter. Concretely, she's a nubile girl who's starved for his attention.

March

I must admit that there've been few signs to support my fears, not that I've witnessed anyway. With Alex away at school, Mia now has Pete's full attention. I exist as a servant to both of them. Mia and I are no longer close. I think she sees me as competition. If she only knew.

Should I be concerned or glad? Pete is rarely home late anymore. Every night during the school week, it's the same. I watch from my chair, not knowing quite what to think, as Mia, close beside her father on the couch, does her homework while Pete watches TV. When she's finished, she hops onto his lap and snuggles up.

Are his occasional caresses entirely innocent? God knows, I hope so.

No way to know other than continue to be watchful as I am.

I have no authority with Mia anymore. Any instruction I give her she ignores. If I get impatient with her, she glares at me as though I have no right. If I persist, she tells her father when he gets home and, in front of her, he scolds me. Mia and I don't interact much anymore.

Bad news from home. It comes as a complete surprise. Mom went to her monthly checkup this week and they told her the tumors were growing again and very rapidly. She's frightened and Dad's in a state. They take her off the drugs that she's been on and are trying something else. Her oncologist tells Mom and Dad that this kind of thing happens frequently. It will be more difficult this time, he says, to slow things down. I'll go to see them like before if things get worse.

May

Mom's going downhill fast, Dad says. There's very little hope this time. He's grateful for these extra years they've had, he tells me. Still, I know he's down. Less than before, maybe, at least I hope.

Pete's so extravagant at times. He and Mia have been out clothes shopping most of the day. He must have bought her a half dozen complete new outfits that she loves, mainly cute skirts with tops and several dresses. I ask her to let me see her try them on, but she says no. I'll see them later, she tells me.

She wears her regular things to school but changes into her pretty things when she gets home. She can't wait to show her father.

Pete's been on me for the last month or so to show Mia how to cook. I've tried, but the child is hopeless in the kitchen. She drops utensils and puts too much salt in everything. If it's something she prepared for dinner that's not quite right, Pete eats it and compliments her. He often criticizes me in front of Mia when I cook, even when everything is fine.

It's Saturday evening and Pete is home. The three of

us are in the living room, he and Mia on the couch watching a TV show while I have a new book and am sitting in my chair. We stay there for about an hour, no one saying very much, when I get up to go find something else more interesting to read.

As I return to the living room, Pete's looking at Mia and says, "Hey, sweetie, come sit on Daddy's lap until this is over."

No coaxing necessary. As though she's been doing it for years, Mia, in one of her new skirts, cuddles up to Pete like a contented kitten. Only, there's something not at all cat-like in what she does. As Pete's arm settles comfortably around her shoulders, Mia, too short to reach his face, presses her forehead against his neck and, tugging down his collar, begins to nuzzle him.

I'm like a startled deer with blinding headlights in its eyes. I want to yell out to stop what our daughter's doing, but I can't seem to speak. I see Pete's eyes pinned on me as though to say, 'Lucy, how dare you look at me that way. What am I doing wrong here anyway? The child's cuddled up to me and being loving. So what.'

I feel my face flush as my eyes drop to my book. I see Pete bend to place a kiss on the top of Mia's head, then gently push her away.

"Show's not over yet," she complains. "You promised."

In reply, Pete says innocently enough, it seems to me, "You're not watching the show anyway, punkin. It's bedtime for you so off you go."

"Do I have to?" Mia whines.

"Yes, you do, so go."

Mia gets off Pete's lap and, petulantly, goes to her room. No more good night hugs for me from her. They stopped months ago.

Pete looks at me for a moment, his expression unreadable, then turns back to the TV. He behaves as though nothing untoward has happened. Is it my paranoia or has there been a change in their relationship of the kind I've been preoccupied about?

The only thing I can reproach Pete for at this point is that he does nothing to discourage the bold behavior of our child. And Mia? There's no way physical desire can account for what she does, not at her young age. Her actions come from raw instinct more than anything, I believe, that tells her how to get attention from a man. If only her body were less developed and the two had had a normal father-daughter relationship, then...

What to do? Two things are sure to happen if I intervene. Pete will punish me and, no doubt about it, I'll alienate my daughter more than she already is. There's nothing I can really say until I have more proof, proof that I hope I'll never have to see.

While we're sitting there in the living room, something occurs to me. How could I not have thought about it before? What if—I would welcome this—he's playing with me? It's distinctly possible that he is. He hasn't done anything overtly wrong. He could be using Mia to get at me. How consoling this would be.

Alex is home but only for a few days. He'll be off shortly to visit a friend in San Diego then be back home for a couple of weeks before he goes to summer school in San Francisco. He says he needs two courses not available at UCSB for his double major. He's agreed to get a degree in commerce. He arranged this with Pete months ago without telling me. I'm sad for Alex when I hear this. He feels obligated to his father to study something he doesn't like. Business is a subject as foreign to him as it would be to me. I'm unhappy too since I'll see so little of him before the next school year starts.

I'm distressed by another thing. Alex can't stand guns of any kind or the uses they're put to, and Pete knows this, yet he's agreed to go to the practice range with his father to learn to shoot. Pete's told Alex repeatedly for years that "anyone worth his salt must learn to handle sidearms."

He told me the same thing when he took me out for a couple of lessons when we got married. I couldn't hit anything so Pete gave up. He and Alex will go out on the two weekends our son is home before he goes to San Diego.

It's Saturday morning and Pete's rummaging in a kitchen drawer. I'm in our room making up the bed when he calls me.

"Lucy, do you have any soft cloths I can use? I need to clean my gun."

Minutes later, he comes in from the garage where he keeps the thing and calls out to Alex to join him. Our son watches, not saying anything, as Pete dismantles the ugly little pistol and lays each part out on the coffee table. He explains how revolvers work and how to care for them.

"Why do you keep a gun like that, Dad? Do you expect to use it?"

I'm in the kitchen when I hear this. Pete's irritated when he replies.

"Don't give me that liberal college crap. Christ! The things they teach you guys. You ever hear of armed robbery in people's homes? It happens, son, it happens. Some guy sneaks into my house at night, I'll use it, damn right I will. Now pay attention to what I'm doing here, okay?"

"I am," Alex says.

I doubt Pete hears the irony in our boy's voice.

June

I want to cry as Alex packs his bag for his short trip south. I've hardly had a moment with him since he's been home, he having so many hours of community work to do. He has a dispensation while he's at school, but when he's home he has to make up for some of the lost time.

He's changed somehow, our boy. He's more distant, more aloof. He doesn't seem to be happy here. This troubles Pete as well as me, but he doesn't say anything. Sometimes—I could be wrong—I think he's afraid in a way of his own son. And—I've seen signs of this many times—I think Alex fears his father.

Pete rarely comes home early on Mondays. Too many things to do at work after the weekend. Exceptionally, he calls at five to say he'll be home at six. At least he phones. I have to hurry since I'd planned dinner for just the two of us at eight.

All goes as normal until nine-thirty when Mia goes to bed. As usual at that hour, I'm sitting in the living room with my book. When Pete bends down to kiss her on the cheek, Mia reaches up and turns his head to take his kiss full on her mouth.

From his startled look—it's genuine—Pete's as surprised as I am. I'm astounded by what my daughter's done. Pete doesn't take her to task as I think he should. His hands on Mia's shoulders, he gazes down at her as she looks adoringly up at him.

"Young lady," he says, stammering, "you surprise me. That was, that was some good night kiss."

The tableau frightens me. Mia standing there, eyes big—and her expression! She looks elated. His hands still on her shoulders, Pete turns her and gently pushes her toward her room. "Off you go now, girl. It's time you get to bed."

I watch her as she reaches the hallway, then turns around. As though no one is here to see, in slow motion, she blows Pete a kiss, then leaves. I want to shake her until her teeth rattle, so angry she's made me. If Pete's not willing to stop this, then I will. I'm so upset that I barely comprehend what Pete is saying.

"That girl's got a lot of her mother in her, wouldn't you say? You need to talk to her. That kind of stuff could get her into trouble."

Pete's trying to play down what has happened, but the truth is on his face, plain to see. That glazed look I know. The man's aroused. I want to run at him and scratch out his eyes. I want to get a butcher knife from the kitchen and stick it into him. I want to run to my baby's room to protect her from the predator in our home. Who does Pete think he's fooling, anyway. He may be conflicted, but I know, even if he doesn't yet, how things will go.

I jump as Pete leaps to his feet and stands over me. His face is bright red and he shakes his fist.

"Wipe that fucking look off your face or I'll wipe it off for you. That screwed-up oversexed mind of yours! You're always looking for trouble, aren't you. You think I'm going to go after her, don't you. It'll be you I go after, lady, and it won't be for sex, believe me. Now get your ass to bed. I'm sleeping in the guest room. I can't stand the idea of being near you." He leaves the living room and I'm alone.

What am I to do? My fury has drained away and left me feeling empty. Did Pete look guilty of anything when he came at me? To be honest, I can't say he did. Aroused most certainly he was, but am I so naive to think that fathers never are? And what about mothers? It never happens?

"Come on Lucy," I say to myself, "get a grip. What is Pete guilty of, given all you've seen. He has a right to be upset. Maybe he was more angry at himself than he was at you."

I try hard to minimize what took place tonight, but it doesn't work. If he allows her to continue doing what she's doing, he'll give in. I'm sure of it. He might resist if Mia was less provocative, but I'm certain as I'm sitting here that she's aware of the effect she has on him. She's bound to push for more rather than back off.

Not much can surprise me anymore about my spouse. But wherever did Mia's wanton behavior come from? I know kids learn a lot of things in school these days, but to see how she was tonight, you'd think she was experienced and in her middle teens. I'll wait until tomorrow when Pete's at work and she's cooled down and I'll talk to her.

*

Mia's just gotten home from school when I go to her room. She looks hostile when I go in. She knows perfectly well why I'm here. She gets sullen as I talk, refusing to answer me. I want to shake her to get through to her, but it would do no good. I can see by her attitude that it's too late.

Frustrated and upset, I say, "Mia, you have no idea what you're doing. You don't understand where this is going to go."

Almost sneering at me, she replies, "You know, Mom, it's just like Daddy says. You're jealous 'cause he loves me more than you."

It's hopeless. There's nothing I can say to her, nothing that will take her away from Pete. She has him eating from her hand and the vixen knows it. I get up from the bed where I'm sitting next to her and go.

Two days go by with no further incidents, doubtless because Pete comes home late. Mia waits up until ten each night, then, sulking, goes off to her room. She ignores me when I tell her to go to bed.

Any doubts I have about the objectives of my daughter are obliterated in a phone call I overhear today. She's in her room and on her new cell phone Pete bought her. She's talking to Cindy, one of her classmates who lives just down the street.

"Why? Don't you like babies? They're so cuddly and they're all your own! ... Why not? What's the matter with them? ... No you're not. You're not too young to have 'em. My mom told me when we get our periods—you've had yours already, right?—we can make babies, real ones of our own... I know that, silly. You have to have a boy. Duh... No, that's not what Jillie said. She said it doesn't hurt when they put it in, least the first time, that's what she told me... I don't know. She wouldn't tell... Oh yes I do. I know where I can get one, but it's a secret. I can't tell. Hey, have you seen my new red dress? My daddy bought it for me. It's awesome!"

The girls hang up shortly after that, but I hear enough. Mia adores babies. She always has. She thinks she's found a way to have one.

At two o'clock next afternoon, the phone call comes. It's Dad. He's crying. He awakes early in the morning and finds Mom dead next to him. He's upset and needs our help. Can I call Jim and can we come? The funeral will be this Saturday.

I feel sad for Dad and more relief than anything for Mom. I call Jimmy who agrees to pick me up this Friday afternoon. We'll come back on Sunday or maybe a little after, depending on how Dad is.

Pete says he's sorry about Mom's death. I know he doesn't really care, but it was decent of him to say. He'll be home for the entire weekend so there should be no problem. If my brother and I aren't back by Sunday, maybe Mia can go to stay with Evie and the kids until we get home. I'm uneasy but I agree. What else can I do?

Funerals are dreadful things. This one's no exception. Dad has friends staying with him on Sunday when we leave so things seem okay.

I'm afraid of what I'll find when I get home, but there was no need. Pete's working in the shed out back and Mia's at Jillie's for the afternoon and dinner. One of the parents will bring her home by eight.

I'm alarmed when, once again, Pete phones at five. Mia's face lights up the moment she hears he's coming home.

Everything starts out as it did on Wednesday of last week, Mia and Pete on the sofa watching a TV program, I, sitting with a book in my easy chair. I can't concentrate, worried as I am about my daughter.

Not ten minutes go by before Mia scoots over close up to Pete who, nonchalantly, puts his arm around her shoulders. She snuggles closer, her head tucked under his arm, her eyes on me. I'm shaken by the look of triumph on her face. 'Oh, Mia,' I think with a sinking heart. I'm losing the one person in my life who's been close to me. I look back at her, sending mental pleas to her to sit up straight and move away. Instead, she presses closer.

Pete fends Mia off when she tries for another kiss. When she reaches up as she did before, he holds her head and pecks her quickly on the cheek.

"No fooling around this time, sweetheart," he says. "It's off to bed with you."

She pouts but goes. I'm relieved, to say the least. Pete dashes a 'See what I did' look at me then goes back to his TV show.

I'm uneasy on Saturday when Pete agrees to take Mia to the movies. They'll go after we finish dinner.

Nothing can happen to her there, I reassure myself as they're going out the door. I expect them to return at about eleven.

Something's happened—I know it immediately—when the two come in. Mia has a soft look about her and Pete is behaving strangely. Fighting back fear of I don't know what, I ask Mia how the movie was.

She looks at me and smiles in the way she did the other night, then says, "The lines were way too long so we went to the drive-in."

"You went where? There is no drive-in anymore."

"Oh yes," she replies as she sits down next to Pete. "There's the one near Cabrillo Jail, isn't there, Daddy."

"There sure is, honey."

I'm stupefied by what happens next. Mia, uninvited, hops onto Pete's lap and the little wanton pulls Pete's face to her.

I feel all cold and nauseous as, unlike what he did before, he puts his arms around her and, pulling her to him, he kisses her. Alright, not on the mouth, but close. No hesitation on his part this time, none at all.

He pulls back from her for just sufficient time to

dart a look at me. There's menace in his eyes. Interfere with him, his look tells me, and I'll be sorry.

I'm afraid of him as I've been for a long time and I have no ally. Mia's not about to give him up. Taunting me, he slowly strokes her arm and continues kissing her on her forehead and cheeks. Mia keeps trying to turn her mouth toward his, but he evades her.

I can't stand this anymore and I jump up to leave when, like a whip, Pete's voice comes at me.

"Sit down, Lucy. Stay there! You're not going anywhere. Get up and I'll knock you on the floor." His sharp tone scares our child and she moves away. "Mia, baby," Pete says in a soothing tone, "it's time for bed. Your mother and I need to talk."

She needs no urging. She glances at me briefly and disappears.

His voice still low but with an edge in it, Pete says, "Lucy, it's time we get some things straight, you and me. It looks like you're about ready to go off the deep end. Before you get too high and mighty around here, it's about time you see some things. Stay here, don't move. I'm going to get something."

Pete returns with a smallish manila envelope in his right hand. With his left, he motions that I am to sit next to him on the couch. His relaxed, almost pleased expression worries me.

"So, babe, you don't approve of the way I am with Mia, do you."

I'm preoccupied about that envelope and what it signifies. Pete never does anything unless it's planned. It's a trap he's laying for me, I know it. Still, I can't hold back.

"Approve?" I hear myself lash out. "Approve while you corrupt our daughter? Do you expect me to stand by while you ruin our baby's life?" I never speak to Pete like this but, once started, can't stop. "Understand this, Pete Jackson. I don't care what you do to me. I don't give a shit. You ever do anything more than you've done to Mia, let me tell you, and you'll be in jail." I'm literally out of breath and limp as a dishrag. Physically and emotionally, I'm a wreck.

As though Pete enjoyed my little outburst, he settles back and smiles. I feel the room grow cold as I realize he's at ease. I haven't seen him look pleasantly at me like that in a long long time. But I'm not fooled. He's planning something very bad for me.

"Lucy, Lucy, Lucy, you amaze me, you know? You used to be kinda smart and a real looker. Now you're a little mouse, scared of your shadow, and you're stupid! You're always complaining about things. Alex stays outta your way and, Mia, well, frankly she can't stand you. You see me being affectionate with her and you flip out. I've been holding off on this, 'cause, well, it's not all that pleasant. Problem is, I think you're about ready to go round the bend and make a lot of unnecessary trouble, so, it's about time I showed you something, something you really need to see. Several things, actually. Might make you change your mind about yelling your head off about what you see."

Pete gets a sly expression on his face. "Thing is, what Mia and me are doing doesn't count for much compared to what somebody else we know likes to do."

I feel a shiver when he says this.

"Before you go shooting off your mouth about nothing, I'd like you to think about whatever you intend to tell people and what they'll think of you once they've seen the pictures. Let's start with these. You're quite impressive, if I do say so myself."

Pete pulls the coffee table closer and lays out four photographs. They're a little yellowed but crystal clear. "The girl in these looks an awful lot like you, doesn't she?"

I can't tear my eyes away from the horrors that I see in photographs that, I'm sure, were taken twenty years ago at that orgy in Mexico. I don't remember any of the grotesque acts in those pictures, but the girl I see in them is definitely me. I feel myself go pale as I look at them. Pete and the others who were at what they called a party must have drugged me to obtain them. I feel a hot flush in my cheeks and deep shame. I'm with an animal in one of those despicable photographs.

Pete's I've-got-you-mouse expression makes me sick. I want to claw him in the face.

"First question," he says. "What do you suppose Alex would think of these?" The room spins. "Second question, kind of important, you'll agree. The people you're gonna talk to about me. You're stupid as a stump, you are, but you're smart enough to know who I am in this town, aren't you. I'm well-established, aren't I. And people like me. Quite a lot, actually. Am I right or wrong?"

I don't answer, not even to shake my head.

"Now comes this scrawny bitch who never sees the light of day, makin' all kinds a accusations. What does her daughter say to all of this? 'My mom's crazy. Nothing's goin' on, not anything.' That's what she says. Then I tell them they've got to pardon my wife who feels guilty about her past. I show them the pictures, then, not because I want to, of course, but to help them understand. Meanwhile, Alex is so embarrassed, he won't come home."

Pete puts the four photographs back in his envelope and turns to me. I feel the blood draining from my face and I'm about to vomit. Pete grabs me by the arm. "Hold on there, babe. I'm not finished yet. You can upchuck all you want when I get done. Can't say I blame you for being sick."

I'm so whipped-feeling and mortified that I can't respond. Though Pete's twisted everything around in a horrid way, he's right about everything he says. No one would believe a word I said, and my children would disown me. I want to get up and rush off to our bedroom, but Pete's not done. To judge from his hard, mean look, bad things are yet to come. He turns half around on his end of the sofa to face me.

"You may not like what Mia does, Lucy, but you're in no position to tell us what to do. It's what Mia needs from me that counts. I don't give a tinker's damn what you think. You're so fucked up that every time I touch her, you think I'm going to rape her, that's how screwed up you are. With all the stuff you've done in your life, woman, you're hardly one to talk. What about that thing you had going with that cute little redhead in Goleta? Didn't think I knew about you and her, did you?"

How dare he bring poor Jannie into this, the only person in my life who truly loved me. I open my mouth to object, but he jabs a finger at me.

"You interrupt me and I'm gonna slap you silly, you got that? So shut up and listen." Pete's angry, and he takes several deep breaths to collect himself. "We started with those pictures, but there's more for you to think about. You interfere with us in any way, and I mean in any way at all, and I'm going to file for divorce and either you or me'll be out of this house, depending on who we get as a judge. Wherever I end up, I'll give you two guesses about where our kids will be. With me, Lucy baby, with me, both of them."

He takes some papers out of the envelope that I think holds only photos. "Here. Look at these. They're separation papers, girl, that's what they are. I had them prepared just in case you go off the deep end. Take a look at them."

My hands shake as I take the single sheet Pete hands me. At the top, in his handwriting, I read *Separation Agreement between Pete Jackson and Lucy Jackson.* I don't read more, I just hand the paper back to him.

"You're not stupid enough to disagree what'll happen if we separate, are you? Didn't think so. You're a lousy mother and, sure as hell, a lousy wife, but you've got just enough sense to know that both of the kids will be with me and out of your reach, okay? Mia will deny everything you say and Alex won't believe a word, especially after seeing these."

Pete waves the envelope in my face. "I know what's best for Alex. I've got him in business school, and, whether you agree or not, I know what's best for Mia. You're no role model for her, that's for sure. So, babe, you wiggle even your little finger and try to make trouble where there isn't any, and you'll be out of our lives for good and on your own. Mia's plenty old enough to say who she wants to live with. So either get on with whatever you're going to do or shut your mouth and behave around here and let us get on with things."

I feel like a truck has slammed into me. I want to scream out about how warped he is, how he's about to traumatize our baby, but I can't. Pete's a bastard in many ways, but he doesn't make promises he doesn't keep. If he thinks I'm going to interfere with him, he'll leave me, and then what help to Mia can I be? Like some chess game, he's thought ahead and sees every move.

I hate him like I've never hated anyone or anything in my life.

Pete's expression changes to something almost conciliatory. He taps me lightly on the knee. "Now, come on Lucy," he says, his tone suddenly more friendly, "give it a rest, why don't you. I'm getting tired of all this, aren't you? So Mia's a little over the top on what she does. She's got a crush on me. Is that so strange? I admit, it's really my fault in a way. I was so focused on Alex for all these years that I hardly knew Mia was around. So I'm paying her attention now. That doesn't mean I'm gonna do the things you think. You've got a habit of getting panicked and spinning out of control. You know that. Let's stop all this crap and get back to being a family."

Pete sighs, gets up and walks off toward our bedroom.

What a helpless weakling I've become. I can't even think rationally anymore. Can Pete get away with everything he says? I don't have the courage to find out. I feel my innards shrink as I think about those pictures.

Even if the authorities paid no attention to them, our children would. Considering where Mia and Pete are right now, she wouldn't speak to me. She'd repeat to everyone exactly what Pete tells her to say. As to Alex, who knows what he thinks of me, not much. I know this by the way he looks at me and what he says.

Whatever would I do all alone? If Pete and the children leave me, I have few friends, no one I can really go to. I have Forrest, I suppose, but he has his own family to take care of, and what could he really do for me anyway? He's a criminal attorney and not in family law.

And something else nags at me. Mia's behavior, as Pete says, is definitely over the top. But is it possible that that's all it is, that I'm making too much of this?

What frightens me and makes me think that I'm seeing things as they really are is that Pete, to my knowledge anyway, has no sex life, not with me, not with anyone. Consciously, he may have no intentions of doing more than he's done. My intuitions scream at me that Mia will know what to do to get at him and that she'll not hesitate.

Alex comes home sooner than we think. He admits to Pete that his friend in San Diego is a girl. She's getting back together with an old boyfriend and doesn't want him around anymore. Secretly, I'm glad. I'll get to see him for a while. He'll be home until the second week in July.

Mia's not happy to have her brother home. I'm pretty sure about the reason. Pete's nervous about Alex seeing things and so he's careful. He'll let Mia sit on his lap for a few minutes, but no caresses or little kisses anymore. Mia keeps asking Alex when he's going to go. She's unpleasant to him as much as she is to me.

We eat dinner at seven-thirty then back to the living room. Alex is in the basement working on something and I'm here with my book. Mia moves to her Daddy's lap where she snuggles down. She's wrapped her right arm around Pete's left and her face is turned toward him. Pete's eyes are on the TV as he strokes her hair. Her attempt to attract his attention sickens me, but this is better than what I've seen.

I don't hear Alex when he comes into the living room. We don't realize he's there until he says, disgust in his voice, "Mia, for God sake. Aren't you a little old to be sitting on Dad's lap like that?"

Pete flinches as though someone's slapped him and he roughly pushes Mia off of him. Looking at Mia, who's shooting darts with her eyes at her brother, Pete says, "Hey, squirt, it's your bedtime. Now off you go."

Mia gives Alex one last resentful look as she goes off. Just before she closes her bedroom door, we hear her say, "I hate you."

Alex, an odd expression on his handsome face, says, "How do you guys put up with that brat, anyway? Who does she think she is?"

No one says a word as our son leaves.

July

I feel unwell most of the time and unwanted here. The only time I can get my thoughts out is when I'm writing.

After the night when Alex came into the living room to find his sister cuddled up on their father's lap, Pete's being cautious. He must have spoken to Mia because she's staying on her end of the sofa until she goes to bed. A quick good night kiss on the cheek is all she gets. I can see she doesn't like it, but Pete's not giving her any choice.

She won't talk to Alex anymore. She just filets him with her eyes. He seems not to notice or not to care. What I fear is what will happen when our son leaves. Mia's been told—I'm certain of it—that things will go back to the way they were when Alex goes.

It's Saturday noon and our son has gone. He'll not be all that far away in San Francisco, but he may as well be on another planet. My stomach's been in knots all day. I'm afraid of what the night will bring.

No waiting until nine o'clock this time. Shortly after we sit down, Pete makes a motion with his hand and Mia's on his lap. Pete makes no pretense. The moment she starts to snuggle up, he's hugging and caressing her as though I'm not there.

Mia climbs up on her knees and throws her arms around her father's neck. With more fervor than I want to hear, she cries, "I love you, Daddy, I love you!"

"And I love you back, sweetheart," Pete says. Teasingly, he tells her, "Those are a lot of sweet little kisses you're giving me."

"I'll give you thousands if you want me to," Mia says.

They haven't come together yet, my intuition tells me, but it's going to happen soon. I can't say why, but I just know. Our daughter's all over him like a bitch in heat. I resent her for this sometimes. If she'd just back off and behave herself, things might be alright.

Does Pete understand that it's not sex she wants but attention and affection from her father who's denied her these things nearly all her life? As a woman and a mother who's watched her grow, I know this, but how many men would continue to turn away from Mia's sexual-like advances?

I don't like leaving the living room when Mia's on Pete's lap like this, but, unusual for me, I have indigestion and I have no choice. Besides, what can they do in the few minutes I'll be gone?

It takes me longer than I expect, and, as I'm coming out of the bathroom, I hear Pete say, "I love you too, sweetheart. I always have. Your mom didn't want another baby, you know that? She wanted an abortion when she was pregnant with you, but I put my foot down. No way she was gonna get rid of my child like that."

So quiet I can hardly hear, Mia says, "Mommy

wanted to get rid of me when I was in her tummy?"

"That's right, my love, she did," Pete says.

My heart jumps in my chest when I hear Mia say, "I hate her! Daddy, I hate her."

I feel my hands bunch up. I want to strangle him.

"Shh, Mia," Pete says. "Not so loud. Don't say anything to her about this. I've had enough of her getting upset around here as it is. You've got me, honey, and you always will. You know that."

Mia says something, but I can't tell what it is. Pete's doing everything he can to take Mia away from me. I'll have no one left, no one.

I'm ashamed and feeling sick at how weak I am. Pete's right. I'm incapable of doing anything on my own. A decent mother would do something to stop what's going on, regardless of what would happen to her after. And here I am, too frightened to intervene.

Pete wants fried chicken tonight and mashed potatoes. I'm beginning to get things together for supper when the doorbell rings. Someone selling something, no doubt. We get a lot of that in this neighborhood.

I'm surprised and glad to see Jacqueline Parks, my friend from the library, the one who spoke up for women at our horrid dinner party. Jacqueline stares at me before coming in.

"Lucy, I didn't mean to gawk. Sorry. It's just that, well, you don't look the same, I mean, oh I'm being so stupid! Pardon me, okay? I haven't seen you in so long and, frankly, I was a little worried, so I thought I'd drop in. I hope I haven't come at a bad time."

I assure her it's fine and that I'm glad to see her. We sit down in the living room.

"Luce, are you okay? Are you ill or anything? You look, I don't know, kind of pale and underfed, sort of. Are you okay?"

"I don't get out enough, Jackie, that's the problem. I've got a lot of stuff here at home to do and all." I'm not convincing as I can tell from Jackie's face.

She looks at me for a few seconds, then says, "Hon, I don't want to interfere or anything, but, you don't look very good to me, not sick, exactly, more depressed or something, I don't know. You just don't look like the Lucy I know."

I nod, but that's all I do.

"Family problems, is it?" she asks.

Sympathy I'm not used to makes me start to cry, even though I try hard to hold it back.

Jackie gets up and comes to sit beside me. "Is Pete hurting you? Is that it?" I shake my head. "Where's your car, Lucy?"

"We sold it. I wasn't using it very much."

"You used to come to the library on the bus. Sorry for all the questions, but, you don't do that anymore. Why not?"

I don't bother lying. "Pete doesn't like it when I'm out of the house that long."

"He doesn't like you seeing anybody, does he," Jackie says.

"No he doesn't," I reply.

There's a glitter in my friend's eyes that I remember seeing at our party. She reaches out and grips my hand.

"Lucy, that man's destroying you. I know he is! You don't have to put up with this. You don't! How many children do you have at home now, one?"

I nod.

"File for divorce and get away from him while you still can! You mustn't put up with this. You mustn't put up with that kind of man. Don't worry about support. You've been stuck here at home for a long time, caring for his children. He's well-off, Pete Jackson is. You'll be fine! You don't have to be kept a prisoner in your own home like this. Think about this, Lucy. I know some good people who can help you with this if you decide."

I look at Jackie for a long time. She's trying to help me, I know that, but it won't work, and I can't tell her why.

Finally, I say, "Jackie, your concern means a lot to

me, more than you know, but there's nothing I can do. I'd tell you why, and I think you'd understand, but there's no way I can. Believe me, I would if I could. I'd give anything if we could solve the problems that we have." I wipe my eyes. "I've gotta stop talking about it now or I'm going to completely break down and that will ruin everything, please believe me."

Jackie squeezed my hand. "All I'm asking is that you think about what I said and you remember that you do have friends who will be behind you, okay? Now I'd better scoot before your husband comes home and I tie into him."

I smile at Jackie and give her a big hug. She hugs me back and tells me to hang in there. She's not giving up on me.

I'll be behind with supper, maybe, but as soon as the front door closes, I sob for easily a half hour, wishing with all my soul that I could follow my friend's advice and take Mia away from here and escape.

Nothing more than what I've already seen happens for the next few nights. I can't sleep, expecting Pete to get out of bed and go to her. But he spends only a couple of minutes in her room each night, not long enough to do anything, not yet.

It's not a question of *if* anymore in my mind, but *when.* It'll happen here in the house, it must. No way Pete will run the risk of being seen. So what's he waiting for?

It's late Thursday afternoon, two days before Mia's birthday, and the doorbell rings. It must be that new paperboy who gets things confused. It's not. It's a shaggy-looking guy who looks like a hippie right out of the 1960s who's holding out something for me to sign. It's one of those plastic computer screen thingies I'm s'posed to write on that says Carrier Pigeon Courier Service at the top. One more of Pete's stupid notes to Mia, I bet. He sends them all the time these days like they're love letters or something.

I sign and the guy who needs a bath hands me an envelope with Pete's logo and business address on it. I'm right. It's addressed to Mia. She's there with me at the door. When she sees it's for her, she grabs it out of my hand and disappears.

I'm on my way back to the kitchen when Mia yells from her bedroom that she's supposed to tell me that her daddy won't be home for supper. He'll get back late so don't wait up. Fine, fine with me. I won't have to put up with the crap that's going on here nearly every night.

I'm afraid of what's happening to me inside. I'm not frantic like I used to be as I watch Pete and Mia in the living room. Neither of them pay attention to me anymore.

Have they beaten me down so much that I've finally given up? Is this what happens to mothers I've read about who know what's going on in their home but who feel powerless to act? Cowards. That's what those women are, too concerned about protecting their own selves.

Is that what I've come to? It's too ghastly to contemplate.

What's Pete waiting for, I ask? I think I know. I'm cleaning our bedroom in the morning when I see the bundle.

It's hidden in the back corner of the top shelf of Pete's closet. It's wrapped in tissue paper from a store. He never brings gifts home, certainly not like that. The longer I stare, the more I need to look. Pete's at work and Mia never comes in here.

I carefully take it down, noting exactly where it is, and examine it. No tape or ribbons or anything written that I can see. I know by the light weight and feel that the package contains clothes.

Very slowly, so as not to tear anything, I unwrap the thing. I gulp and feel my stomach tighten as I look down at a pink satin nightie. I pick it up and hold it out. It's quite small.

Then it hits me. For a moment, I stand there like a statue, not knowing what to do. I know what my monstrous husband has been waiting for. Tomorrow, July 13, Saturday, is our daughter's birthday. She'll be twelve. Pete's been preparing her for this all along. He's promised her she'll be the woman in the house instead of me. Those looks of triumph she's been giving me. How utterly manipulative that man can be.

I rewrap the package and put it back.

Pete's snoring so loud tonight that I know he won't wake up for a while so I sneak out of bed and come down here to the basement to write in my diary one last time. I brush the cobwebs away from my face that are above my trunk where I hide my things and, plugging in my small gooseneck desk lamp and spreading out my little rug, I begin.

It's two o'clock in the morning of July 13, my baby's birthday. I feel wistful in a way and, needless to say, very down as I open the sixth and last volume of my diary. Since my late teens, except for two years I missed, this diary has been my faithful companion. I used to wonder why I bothered, but I no longer do. Without having someone to talk to, especially at bad times like this, I don't know how I could have coped, if coped I have.

If my diary hadn't been here recently to help me vent and point out to myself repeatedly how weak I was, I might have ended up as one of those mothers who turns a blind eye to events at home just to keep the peace. Writing has helped me understand how intolerable such an option would be to me.

Taking a deep breath, I place my book inside the trunk, whispering, "You've been a friend to me in so many ways. Goodbye and thank you for always being here for me."

PART THREE

"There may be times when we are powerless to prevent injustice, but there must never be a time when we fail to protest."

—Elie Wiesel, Nobel Lecture, December 11, 1986

Chapter 10

On our way out the door, my son, Andy, soon to be eleven, dove beneath my left arm and made a beeline for the backseat of my little car. Wise to his maneuvers, I reached out to grab just enough of the back of his shirt to stop him.

"Hey, let me look at you," I said, turning him around. Resignation and reproach was etched on his round face as he slouched.

"That shirt looks like you slept in it, and those shorts—I haven't seen them in the laundry for a while. Back you go and get into something decent and put that stuff you're wearing in the wash, please."

"He must think we're stupid," Trina, Andy's twin sister, commented. "He's always trying to get away with that."

"Hmmm," I rejoined, looking into two large brown eyes that could see into my soul. "You look fantastic, sweetheart, but I'm not so sure about that skirt. It's a little on the short side, don't you think, and besides, this is a barbecue we're going to with two active little girls who'll be all over you in the backyard. Lita who's about three and little Evangelina, you remember?"

Trina looked conflicted. She'd reached the age where what she and her friends wore had become a major factor in her life. At the same time, she was enamored with little children and loved to play with them.

"Yeah," she conceded, shaking her head, "I'd better

change. I'll get grass stains all over this. Anyway, it's not too short."

I could see years of such wrangling ahead with my beloved daughter.

Life was good again, with my children back. The thirty days with their mother in July never seemed to end. The two—my heart warmed to know it—seemed happy to be back home. Andy complained of having missed a whole month of baseball and Trina was glad to be reunited with her friends, but, as was obvious from the countless hugs I received during their first week home, it was me she missed as, God knows, I missed her.

The Martinez family was doing well in their new home, having returned to Santa Lucia just under a year ago. Miguel, whom I defended in a murder trial two years earlier, had a martial arts school that was doing well from all reports, and Isabel was well into her nurse training at the junior college. I'd been delighted to receive their invitation.

The house they rented was on Pueblito Street in an area dubbed Little Mexico. Children played everywhere on poorly maintained but clean streets, and the neighborhood seemed alive and friendly, certainly more so than the upscale area we lived in. As we exited the car, the smells from the cuisine I loved so much were redolent everywhere.

A firm handshake from Miguel, who looked as good as I'd ever seen him, and a big hug from Isabel and we were in. It was a low-cost structure seen only in this part of town. Thrift store furnishings dotted the place with a few pictures and plants. Brightly colored walls made the house look cheerful and lived in. As always, Isabel managed to make the most of little and to keep her home spotlessly clean. In moments, we were outside where, as expected, Trina was rolling around on the grass with the little girls.

"Hombre, it's good to see you," Miguel said. "I'm

sorry we took so long to get in touch. It's just that we only got this house a couple a months ago and the school has been taking all my time."

"You said it, chico," Isabel commented as she joined us, a tray of frosty glasses in one hand and a sizable pitcher in the other. "I never see you. I'm married to martial arts."

"To martial arts?" Miguel retorted. "Is that how you got these two little angels here?"

"*Càllate, mi amor*, and serve these margaritas, please. They're not like Forrest's, remember those, but anyway." A shadow crossed Isabel's attractive face when she realized she'd referred to Claire's and my annual backyard party that would be no more, not with me now single and my ex-wife gone.

To ease her, I said, "I drank a few too many of those margaritas myself, and not just me. I'll be very glad to have one of these."

Isabel smiled, but I could see her sorrow for me in her eyes.

The backyard was about thirty feet by twenty, not large but big enough to accommodate a little patio with a barbecue, table and chairs and a patch of grass. Andy had found a bat-like thing and was swinging it around.

"Hey, watch out with that," I said. "You're going to hit someone."

Meanwhile, the little girls had tugged Trina back inside the house. They wanted to show off some dolls and toys, Isabel explained.

"So, Miguel. Tell me about your school. You attracting clients?"

"It's slow," he said, "but picking up. There's a lot more interest in kids doing martial arts than I thought. I'm lucky I don't have high rent to pay where I am."

The same regret I saw on Isabel's face was mirrored in Miguel's eyes. He must be thinking as I was at that moment about how unexpectedly the grounds beneath our feet can shift and our lives be turned upside down by one event—in his case, the wrongful accusation that he had premeditatedly killed someone, in mine, the unanticipated breakaway by my wife.

Andy, still outside with us and having nothing to do, had been eavesdropping. "What's martial arts?" he asked.

"Oh boy," said Isabel, "here we go."

Walking over to Andy and squatting down to be at his level, Miguel said, "What's that? You don't know what martial arts means? Well, I tell you what. Let me get my iPad and I'll be right back."

Andy knew what iPads were and had wanted an i-whatever for some time, but, on this matter, Claire and I were in accord. Those kinds of distractions our children didn't need. In a moment, Miguel was back.

"Okay. I'm gonna show you what kids your age do at my school, then I'll let you take a peek at what the big guys do, okay? Then you'll know what martial arts are."

For the next forty-five minutes, my son was spellbound. I could see his excitement mount as the video clips went on. I would have had to be developmentally challenged not to perceive what the outcome of this little demonstration was going to be. As I thought, Andy was interested most by the rapid moves and the sparring of teenagers and adults. When Miguel turned his iPad off, Andy's eyes, already big for his small round face, were huge.

Excited, bouncing up and down, he said, "One of those guys I saw made another guy drop his knife. Did you see that? And another guy took away some man's gun, and they only did it with their hands."

"Yeah," Miguel said casually. "I know who the guy in those pictures was. Me."

Andy's eyes got even bigger. "You can do that kind of stuff?"

Instead of replying, Miguel got up and retrieved the bat-like thing Andy had left lying on the grass. It looked something like a hockey stick. Isabel looked reproachful as Miguel took Andy's hand and led him to the patch of grass.

"I'm going to stand here," Miguel instructed, "and you stand here with this. Now I'm bein' serious. I want you to try and hit me with that thing, any way you can. You can go anywhere here on the grass you want to, but I won't move. I promise not to touch you in any way or hurt you, no matter what you do to me. You game?"

Andy's eyes lit up. No coaxing needed.

The look of surprise on my boy's face was priceless as the stick flew from his hands as he swung it. I was watching carefully, but I missed what Miguel did. For a half hour until Isabel called us to the table, Miguel demonstrated maneuvers without ever doing more than causing slight discomfort that didn't faze Andy in the least.

Not for one minute did his eyes leave Miguel while we ate. For once, he stayed quiet. I was under no illusions. I knew what was coming next, especially after Miguel's words.

While cutting his steak, he remarked, "Andy's got a good eye and he's very fast, unusually so, in fact. He puts some of my older kids at the school to shame."

I knew Miguel well enough to know that he wasn't trolling. Nor would he take advantage of a friend. I'd made those same observations while watching Andy play baseball. He was a natural-born athlete.

Miguel's comments brought a flush of pride to Andy's face, but nothing more. The plea I expected didn't come, at least not then. The meal went well, notwithstanding the knife-dulling sinews in the meat. The Martinez budget didn't allow for expensive cuts.

It was good to be with them again. One could see the love between Miguel and Isabel in everything they did. I was glad for them and sad at the same time that I no longer had a spouse to relate to, joyfully or otherwise.

With hugs from everyone and sloppy kisses from little girls, we said good night and made promises about getting together again soon that we'd unlikely keep.

On our way home, Trina yawned while chatting about how sweet Lita and Lina were. Andy was wide awake, but very quiet until we were almost home.

"Dad, I want to be like Miguel is. I want to do what he can do. He said he has a school where kids go to learn things like that. Can I go, Dad, please? Can I? I'll do my homework and anything else you want me to, promise."

I told him that we'd talk it over with Miguel, but it sounded pretty good to me—God, one more thing to distract Andy from his school work. I hoped Claire wouldn't be opposed to the idea.

Lucy had sequestered herself in her house, refusing to take phone calls. I'd have to go unannounced with the hope that she'd let me in.

The house inside looked much the same, grandiose with high-ceiling rooms and ninety degree angles everywhere with little input from architects.

Lucy looked better, dressed in dark slacks and an attractive dove gray three-quarter sleeve blouse. Her blond hair was brushed and down and her face had a bit of color. She'd had three weeks to recuperate since her release from jail. Otherwise, she was the same, impersonal and unforthcoming. Her soft blue eyes revealed no hint of the connection we'd had since our late teens. I was a man with business to conduct with the obligatory cup of coffee in front of him while she, acquiescent for the moment, would be more at ease when I was gone.

"Lucy, there's relatively little more to do with the two trust funds. We will have completed things, ready for your signatures, by the beginning of next week. When the estate has gone through probate, all assets, apart from a little money in your savings account that you've stipulated for yourself, will be funneled equally into both trusts. You'll have to give me instructions about what to do about the house in the event you are convicted with a protracted sentence."

Lucy regarded me as though I hadn't spoken.

"Is something unclear?"

"The house will be sold, of course, and the proceeds put into the trusts. There's nothing about that to discuss." Sitting there like a mannequin, her eyes not having moved at all that I could see, she continued, "Forrest, there's no point in going on with this lawyer game of yours. Of course I'll be convicted and I'll pay the price. I knew that before I shot him and when I confessed. I said not guilty at the arraignment as you told me so I could be freed on bail. You know the reasons. I told you at the start, and I meant every word, I'm not going to drag my children through an unnecessary trial that will only hurt them. There's no need, do you hear? As soon as the trust things are signed and sealed, I'm going to reverse my plea and, what is it that you lawyers say, throw myself on the mercy of the court."

I wanted to take Lucy by the shoulders and shake her. Knowing that would do no good, I tried logic that would probably have little more effect. "I understood you then and I understand you now, but consider this. Put yourself in the judge's place for a moment, please. He's looking for a reason that can at least partially explain why you killed your husband. He may not find that reason strong enough to get you off, but it could be sufficient to reduce your sentence or to justify imprisonment instead of execution."

Looking hard at her and hoping I was getting through, I went on. "The judge in this case has nothing to work with. The perpetrator of the crime appears sane, entirely aware of what she's done, and shows no remorse. Still worse, she refuses to explain her motive. It may be hatred or vengeance or who knows what, but there's no way for the judge to know. Killing for killing's sake is about all that's left. That's a good path to death row and execution." A little overstated, maybe, but worth the try. "You talk about dragging your children through a trial. Do you have any idea how horrific, how traumatic it will be for both of them as they watch over a period of at least a half dozen years while the gears grind with you on death row? Is that the kind of horror you're looking for for your kids? It's time you start to think, Lucy, instead of behaving like an automaton."

Absolutely no change in her expression except the narrowing of her eyes. Lucy said, "I've had enough of this. I'm not putting up with any more. I know what you're trying to do and I understand. But it's no good. You know as well as I do that the State won't kill me. They're that close to abolishing capital punishment here in California, anyway. I'll get a long sentence for killing Pete, that's what I'll get. Meanwhile, my children can carry on with their lives. Forrest, you have your life and your children to take care of. Do that, and let me take care of mine. Next time I see you is when you bring the papers. After that, you do what's necessary to change my plea back, or I'll take care of it myself. Makes no difference to me."

It was like hammering at a granite wall with a wooden stick. Her intransigence was unreal. Her motive had to be very strong. Absolutely the only thing I thought I knew was that she was prepared to sacrifice herself to protect something or someone. I'd have to dig more to see if I could get a glimmer of what that was or she was lost.

Garrett's eyes were still on me as I finished recounting what had happened. He, Bree and I, plus our summer law student, Sylvia, were sitting in my office.

"Forrest, I'm not sure I can think of a single murder case where no motive could be found except with sociopaths and the like. She's got to be protecting someone, but who and why, now that her husband's dead? What could possibly induce her to abandon her little girl—Mia, isn't that her name—and give up her life like this? And she shows no inclination to crack?"

I shook my head. "Not the slightest that I can see, unfortunately. She all but threw me out of her house this morning."

Bree said, "Forrest, you've known Lucy for a long

time. Is there anything about her behavior that seemed strange, strange enough to cause her to think irrationally and to commit murder?"

My chin in my hands, I turned without really seeing her, pondering thoughts I'd had along these lines myself. At last, wishing I could say something that might help, I shook my head. "Except for her refusal to acknowledge me as a friend, she seems perfectly aware. I'm no psychologist, but if she's had a breakdown of some kind or if she's just plain gone around the bend, I can't see it. She's analytical, as much as Lucy ever is, and she knows precisely what she wants. She's obviously convinced that divulging why she killed Pete will change something. What that something is, I have no idea. Ironically, she seems stronger and more determined than I've ever known her."

"So you think she's going to plead guilty after all," Garrett said. "Going to be tough to plea bargain this one. First degree murder, the charge is, right?"

I nodded. "I haven't talked to Vicky about this case at all, but according to the information filed by the DA's office, that's what they've got her down for," I replied.

"Didn't you say you had some connection with the boy?" Bree asked.

I explained that I'd been Alex's soccer coach years earlier and that the two of us got on pretty well.

"And what about the girl? She's twelve, isn't she?"

I shook my head. "I hardly know that one at all. We and the Jacksons visited back and forth once or twice a year, but Mia's the shy type, always stayed in the background near her mother. I could try talking with Alex to see if he has any ideas, but I've got my doubts. He and his father were pretty close and he associates me with his mother more than anyone. I doubt I'd get anywhere with the girl."

"Still," Bree, remarked, "it's worth a try. Right now, we're batting zero."

Again, I nodded, not especially looking forward to either interview.

"The police have doubtless had their go at them," Garrett said. "So, assuming you don't get much from either of the kids, where do we stand on this? Once she signs the trust papers—that's next week, isn't it—will she be our client?"

I felt alarmed as I considered this. Once she cut us loose, there'd be little we could do for her.

"Garrett, I wish I knew, I mean, I wish I knew if there was any way we could hang onto her. If we don't dig up anything in the meantime, I'll do what Lucy wants about the plea, maybe a little slower than she'd like, but I'll do it."

Sylvia, who rarely spoke, asked, "Could we get the plea changed around again if we found something?"

Both Garrett and I shook our heads.

"We'd ruffle a lot of feathers if we tried," Garrett remarked, "and it isn't as though we have a lot of time. Forrest, you and Bree going to handle this?"

Smiling at the third attorney on our team, recently come onboard, I answered, "She's agreed to give me a hand with this so, I guess so. I just hope we'll have something to work with."

I called Jim Evans' home where Lucy's children were and got Evie on the phone.

"Mr. Spencer, I'm so glad it's you. Jim and me, we feel a little up in the air about all this. Is Lucy going to jail? Is Mia supposed to be living with us afterward? Can you tell us what's going on? By the way, call me Evie, okay? Mrs. Evans sounds too weird."

"I will," I said, "if you call me Forrest. All I can tell you at this point is that we're doing our best to see that Lucy doesn't go to jail. She's a long-time friend of mine as I'm sure you know. Our problem, at the moment, is that she's not saying very much. She refuses to tell us why Pete was killed. We believe she's protecting someone, but we have no idea who or why. I hoped that you might help me a bit with this. I'd like to get together with you and your husband if I can."

Hesitating, Evie said, "Forrest—is that what you said your name is—I don't know if you know this, but we didn't get along very well with Pete. I can't tell you why—it's sort of complicated—but we never did. We didn't see them very much and we don't know very much about their lives, we really don't. We thought the two of them were getting along okay. Jim and I, we don't have a clue why she'd kill him. So I don't see how we can be of much help to you."

"Is Alex still with you?"

"He left for a while but he came back. He says he's dropped out of the University of San Francisco or wherever it was he was going up there. Mia's still with us."

"You're managing okay with those two?"

"Well, sorta, we are. We've got the extra rooms, but, it's been three weeks now and we'd like some help, if you know what I mean."

"Yes, of course I do." Jim and Evie must be having to stretch their budget just a bit. "I'll see to it right away. I'll tell you what I'd like to do. If I call Alex and ask him to meet with me in my office, he'll probably turn me down. It'd be better if I could meet him in your home without him knowing that I'm coming. We get along pretty well. Could that be arranged? When is Alex usually there?"

"Pretty much every night. You could come over after supper at about eight, I guess. Is that alright?"

I thanked her and said I would. I'd have to ask Lupe, our almost live-in housekeeper and babysitter, to stay late.

I did a double take as I saw Alex come into the Evans' living room. He looked so much like Pete, a little shorter, less broad in the shoulders and a gentler face, but a big Jackson boy all the same.

"Forrest," he said as he held out his hand. "It's nice to see you." The closed-down expression on his face belied his words. "I know you came to talk to me so let's go in my room."

I waved my thanks to the Evans couple and followed him. Evie had done good things with her home, about seventy years old and in need of work but very neat. The furnishings were a bit threadbare, but in good taste. The house had a warm feeling to it.

With a queen-size bed and handsome furniture, we were obviously in the guest room.

"Pretty nice digs you've got here," I said.

"Yeah. Uncle Jim and Aunt Evie have been real nice to me."

"How's Mia?"

For a moment, Alex didn't answer. He looked troubled. "She's okay, I guess, considering. Like me, she's pretty pissed at Mom. She's changed in a lotta ways. Not the shy mousy little girl I'm used to. Walks around here like she owns the place. I don't know how Aunt Evie puts up with her."

"I understand you've dropped out of school in San Francisco."

"Yeah. Don't need those extra business courses anymore. I'm gonna drop that program. I hated it, anyway. Goin' back to marine biology where I belong."

There was one chair in the bedroom, which I took, while Alex sat on his bed. He looked anything but receptive.

"Alex, I guess you know why I'm here. I don't like bothering you at a time like this, but, to be frank with you, I'm kind of desperate."

That made him raise his head a little, but his guard was up. In a brittle voice, he queried, "Desperate for what?"

Alex had taken on a hostile look. What to say to him that might move him to be compassionate about his mother who, for the present, at least, he probably detested?

"Alex, please don't misunderstand what I'm about to say. I don't justify murder under any circumstances and I certainly don't uphold what your mom did. But I know

Lucy well enough to believe that she would never have done what she did without a compelling reason. She wouldn't give up her children and her life unless she thought she had no choice. We think your mom did what she did to protect someone. Who that someone is and why, we have no idea. That's why I'm here, to see if you know what her motive might have been."

Alex jumped up, trying to control himself. "Forrest," he said with a quaver in his voice, "I'm talking to you because I like you and respect you, but there are some things you've got to know. So, listen up. This is the last time I want to say them." He was gulping as he spoke and the tears were running freely down his face. He was standing ramrod straight.

"It's true that my dad and I haven't been getting along very well this year. He's a control freak and he doesn't like being disobeyed. He's very successful and he wanted me to be the same. He wanted someone to turn his business over to. He made me agree to take business courses. I had to because I was afraid he wouldn't support me in school anymore if I didn't."

Alex's hands went to his face and he started sobbing. "We had problems recently, yes, but I loved him. I loved him a lot. He was a great dad to me, the best a kid could have."

Alex's hands came down and his eyes were blazing. "Now he's dead. Dead for what? Because that bitch killed him, that's why. That's why he's dead. She deserves to get everything they can throw at her, including the needle if it comes to that. You ask me why she killed him in cold blood? At point-blank range? Six bullets? Don't have a fucking clue why, that's what. Probably because she hated him because he wasn't very nice to her. There's your answer. My mom's a selfish airhead. I don't ever want to see her again in my entire life!"

Alex collapsed on the bed and buried his face in his pillow. Sounding more like a young teenager, he said, his voice distorted, "Forrest, how could all this happen to us? We were good, our family. Remember when you were my coach? Things were okay then. My dad's never been very nice to my mom, but things were okay. Now this!"

I felt miserable for him. There was little more I could say and nothing I could think of to do.

I got up and put my hand lightly on his shoulder. I thanked him for talking to me and told him to let me know if there was any way I could help. Then I quietly left the room.

"Just don't talk to me anymore about my mom," came his muffled voice as I closed the door.

Approach Mia now or later? Dejected though I was, I might as well try since I was there.

Evie and Jim must have heard some of my exchange with Alex. They were quiet and sympathetic as they directed me to her room. They'd put her in their finished basement.

When she opened the door, I was dumbfounded at what I saw. When had I seen Mia last? When she was ten years old? Standing before me with an unfriendly expression on her face was no preadolescent child. Had it not been for that face that showed her to be the age she was, I would have sworn I was looking at a girl in her mid-teens, a well-developed one at that.

There was little different from the shoulders up. She was the plain Jane girl I'd always known with dishwater blond hair that looked like it would blow away in the wind. But below her neck, everything had changed. Two ample-sized, perfectly formed breasts, high up, topped a slimming waist below which shapely hips had begun to form. Though age might bring its problems with a compact figure like hers, for the present, her thighs and legs were perfectly formed and spaced. I'd never seen a twelve-year-old so advanced, so, how can I express this appropriately, so alluring.

Mia saw my eyes go up and down and she couldn't have missed the astonishment on my face. She smirked.

"Evie says you want to see me. Why?" None of the good manners I remembered, no invitation to sit down, just insolence of a kind I hoped I'd never see in my twins.

"May I come in and chat a bit with you," I said.

In answer, she pointed to a loveseat in the room and sat down on her bed. Alex was difficult for me. This one was going to be impossible.

"Mia, do you have any idea who your mom was protecting when she killed your father?"

Defiantly, she said, "I don't know and I don't care. I don't want to talk about her anymore. I hate her." From the intensity on her face and in her tone when she said this, I believed her. "I don't want to talk about her at all. So are we done?"

I had little experience in interviewing children. In my line of work, I saw very few, at least, ones of Mia's age. I had no idea what else to ask. I stood up, thanked her for seeing me and left, feeling utterly defeated.

"That one's changed a bit, hasn't she," Jim remarked as he accompanied me to the front door.

"Changed in a variety of ways," I said. "You could have knocked me over with a feather."

"Yeah, me too. She's gonna be a handful, that one. Christ! Who would have expected this? Anything you can do for my sister?"

"Everything we can, but she's not making it easy for us. She won't tell us anything."

"Can't believe my sister would hurt anyone, let alone kill someone. She's gotta have a reason."

"We agree," I said. "If we can find it, we may be able to do something for her." To gain time, I'd do what I could to slow down the drawing up of the trust papers, but there was just so much I could do.

I thanked him and asked him to convey my gratitude to his wife and left.

Another note from the Court, addressed to Resnik and to me. Oddly, there was no reference to a judge, just the order to be at the courthouse at nine forty-five the following Wednesday for Lucy's arraignment. We might or might not find out then the name of our trial judge.

Three days after our unpleasant visit at her home, I had Lucy on the phone.

"We have to go to Court again? I thought we were finished with that stuff. When is it supposed to be?"

"We were able to skip the prelim, Lucy, since you waived your rights, but we can't get out of this. Now that the DA's laid their charge, you have to be arraigned again. It's more or less a formality in your case, but we have no choice. We have to be in court at ten next Wednesday."

"Do I have to be there? Can't you go for me?"

I had been concerned about the second arraignment from the outset when Lucy said she was going to reverse her plea. I wasn't at all confident I could prevent her from doing that this time.

"You have to be there in person, yes."

"Why? Why do they have to have me there?"

"It's like the first time you were arraigned, Lucy. You had to enter a plea, remember?"

"What? You mean guilty or not guilty? Is that what I'm going for?"

With a sinking feeling, I answered, "That and more, yes."

Sighing, Lucy replied, "Forrest, I told you when you were here last time what I'm going to do. Sounds like next Wednesday is a good time to get that done."

"Lucy, look. Can't we—"

"No, we can't. I'm tired of this, Forrest, I really am. It's no good going on like this. I'll see you Wednesday morning and we can get this over with. It'll be a relief, frankly. Can you pick me up?"

Resigned, I answered, "I'll be at your house at nine-fifteen."

I was depressed that day and the next. I wanted to look forward to the weekend with the twins since Claire couldn't take them, but the arraignment loomed ahead. I had no cards to play. My friend for so many years was on a self-destructive path that she wouldn't leave, no matter what I did. I tried to console myself with the virtual certainty that, were there to be a trial, she'd be convicted, but it didn't help. A judge, having little alternative, would sentence her by default.

What could explain Lucy's refusal to let anybody know the reason for what she did? It had to relate to Alex or to Mia, but in what way? Since evidence clearly showed that Lucy had fired the gun, I was inclined to think that it was her daughter who was most involved. But involved how? If Pete had been molesting her, it would be in Lucy's interest to reveal it as she must know. With more time, I might be able to break Lucy down, but as things looked, I wasn't going to have the chance.

Late Friday afternoon as I was about to leave the office, the little phone in my pocket rang. I was surprised to see Vicky's name on my display. It had to be personal or she wouldn't have called my cell.

"Hi Forrest. I'm not at the office as you must know. I left early so I could talk to you. I'd like to chat, but someone's waiting for me outside. It's about Lucy Jackson's case."

If Vicky and I weren't close, it would be a breach of protocol for her to bypass her deputy like this.

"Vic, it's good to hear you. What's up?" Ludicrously, I was speaking almost in a whisper.

"Look. There's no way we're not going to get a conviction if we try this thing. You know we can't offer anything better than murder two, not formally anyway. This goes to trial and she could very well end up with something worse. Help us out here and give your client a break. We'll do what we can to ease things up."

In truth—Vicky knew this as well as I—there was little she could do other than recommending a lighter sentence, which she might do anyway.

"If we go your way, Vic, I send Lucy to prison when I may be able to keep her out. Why don't we wait to see what takes place on Wednesday."

For half a minute, there was only Vicky's breathing on the phone. Frustrated and maybe angry, she said, "Forrest, you are the stubbornest man I know. You're going to hurt your client, and I'm sorry about that. I've gotta go. Bye."

On my way to Lucy's house the following Wednesday, I cast about in my mind for something I could say to her that would make her turn around, if only for a little while. I thought about Vicky's call. It would be a ruse, but if I could use that call...

Lucy was well-groomed, but she'd made no special effort to dress up. In a light blue blouse and dark blue slacks, she could be going to the library. We didn't say much as I drove.

Halfway to the courthouse, I said, "Tell me something. It's hard for me to know based on how you talk. If someone offered you a shorter sentence, would you take it?"

She thought about my question, then frowned. "What are you trying to get me to do this time, hmmm? Haven't we gone over this enough?"

"Lucy, you didn't answer me. Tell me you're not so far gone that a shorter sentence doesn't mean anything to you. It sure as hell will when you get to prison, let me tell you."

"You ever been in a women's jail, Forrest? How do you know what goes on there. And stop making fun of me. I'm no masochist, if that's what you're getting at. I'd like to get out sooner if I could. Of course I would." Rather sarcastically, she went on, "You got some magic up your sleeve?"

"Magic, no. A strategy, perhaps. I got an interesting phone call last Friday afternoon from the DA. I've been dealing with her for years." Tell Lucy that Vicky was a close friend and the lady next to me would go deaf. "They're not that confident about their case. I think they're worried about your motive. They're concerned that something they didn't anticipate might come out in the trial and make them look bad. I'm not saying there has to be a trial. If you absolutely don't want one, then there won't be one. If I'm reading the DA correctly, they may very well sweeten the pot if we put pressure on them at the arraignment and hold off a little before you change your plea. Do you follow me?"

Lucy looked suspicious. For a while, she didn't say anything.

"I'm not sure I can trust you, Forrest. You promise me absolutely that I can change my plea any time before the trial if I want to? How long do I have to wait before I do that?"

How to answer her? I wanted every day I could get, but demand too much and I'd lose her.

"I don't know," I said, "two weeks, maybe three?"

After a short pause, Lucy said, "First week of September at the latest. If there's nothing better by then, I'm gonna change my plea. That make you happy? I'm sick to death of this."

I was relieved, trying to not let it show. "That should do," I said. "If we haven't heard anything positive from the DA by then and you want to go ahead, I'll help you, okay?"

She nodded.

I wanted to see Resnik before bringing Lucy in. She was content to remain in the car.

He was seated in the lobby, tapping a file folder on his lap. He looked as dour as I'd ever seen him. It had to be the judge the court clerks had assigned.

"Who'd we draw," I asked as I sat down next to him.

"Bozo, that's who." The nickname was renowned.

"Conclin?"

Repugnance in his tone, Resnik replied, "Who else! I hope to Christ he's not our trial judge. You know Conclin, don't you?"

"Oh yes. We've jousted a time or two."

What Resnik wasn't saying but I knew was that

he'd had several run-ins with the quirky judge. Fairly recently, if I recalled, Conclin had censured him for something.

"We've got ten minutes. You have the defendant with you, I assume?"

"She's in the car outside. I'll get her. You know Conclin's courtroom number?"

"246b. See you."

Superior court judge Robert Conclin had to be at least sixty-five according to what I knew, but he didn't show it. Attractive in a rugged way, he resembled a wind-burned Arizona rancher, right down to his high boots. He had unusually large light blue eyes that seemed to twinkle most of the time.

The formalities over, looking first at Vicky's deputy then at me, the judge drawled, "Well, if it isn't 'up and coming' and 'down and going.' You feeling down, Mr. Spencer? Nah, don't answer that, no need." Shaking his craggy head and grinning, Conclin continued, "Don't worry, gentlemen, won't be me handlin' this case. I'm just here to see if Mr. Resnik really has one, a case, that is. You boys wanta kick things off or should we sit here for a while and shoot the bull? Doesn't make a hell of a lotta difference to me. I'm outta here anyway, come September."

Disgust evident on his face, Resnik cleared his throat.

"Okay, okay, we'll begin with the youngster here. What you got?"

In a bored, flat tone, Resnik said, to a word, what he had at the first arraignment. Lucy was a villain who'd confessed before witnesses to having killed her husband by shooting him six times in the presence of their child.

As anticipated, two witnesses for the Prosecution testified, the arresting officer and a technician from the forensics lab. By ten-thirty, the session ended and Lucy was bound over for jury trial.

Conclin waved jauntily at us as we left the

courtroom. Under his breath, we heard Resnik mumble, "Cowboy clown" as he stalked away.

Now that the twins were turning eleven, I hoped joint parties might be easier than before. Their birthdays fell on Saturday, normally Claire's week to have them, but the children begged their mother to let them stay with me so they could invite their friends. Claire wasn't happy but she understood. She lived at some distance in a suburb of Los Angeles with her new husband.

I'd have help this time, thank God. Riding herd on fifteen preadolescents wasn't something I was looking forward to alone. Ben, my friend and the PI component of our law firm, who had a softspot for kids, and his girlfriend, Cassie, were eager to join the fray.

Because of disagreement between the twins, I bought two piñatas instead of one. Andy chose the baseball shape and Trina chose a star. At the last minute, I remembered the damn things didn't come pre-stuffed. I dashed out to pick up three huge bags of candy, not something we saw very often in our home.

With the twins' advice, I drew up a list of games that I hoped girls and boys would play without too much fuss. Funny how rapidly attitudes in children about the opposite sex change. Get a group of ten-year-old boys and girls together and the genders will separate, spending most of their time casting insults at the other. Something told me to expect differences with eleven-year-olds.

Trina was going to be in seventh heaven when her birthday came. The day before the party, we got the long-awaited call from our friends, the Hendersons, who lived in Georgia. Anna, their adopted daughter, had been begging them for months to invite Trina to come and stay with them a week. I'd just gotten her back after an interminable month of absence, and now she'd be off again.

Fortunately, Andy wouldn't be let down. He'd been

agitating for over a year to go to a special baseball camp near Ventura. I managed to arrange it for the last week of August when his sister would also be away from home. I bought a new dress and a bright pink suitcase for my daughter and a new pitcher's glove for my son.

On Saturday morning, the children knew it was time for gifts when I told them to stay at the table after breakfast. Trina was eager and doing her utmost not to let it show and Andy was doing his bouncing up and down thing that drove his sibling up the wall.

I brought out two boxes, one with the pitcher's glove and the other with the dress. Andy whooped, threw the glove in the air, then zoomed outdoors to play with it. There were two hours to go before the party.

Trina oohed and aahed over her dress, which, I was pleased to see when she came down to show me, was gorgeous and fit her perfectly. I was well-repaid with hugs.

Calling Andy back, I brought in two more packages, both identical in size. Trina looked bewildered but was delighted by the color of her suitcase. Andy's case was similar but decidedly for a boy. Both children looked mystified. Why would I be giving them suitcases when each of them already had one?

My last trip to my study was for the envelopes, one with Trina's e-ticket and itinerary and the other with the description and papers for Andy's camp.

He recognized immediately what the contents were and jumped around and made a lot of noise. Trina looked puzzled for a few seconds, then she came alive. Tears of joy ran down her lovely face. More rounds of hugs, even one from my boy. Trina wanted to know, again and again, the details of her trip. Would it be okay if she called Anna that minute to let her know? Andy, not to be outdone, had oodles of friends to show his glove off to and to tell about the camp. He scampered out the front door, promising to be back within half an hour.

Cassie, whom I hadn't seen in weeks, and Ben arrived for lunch, which gave us plenty of time to get things ready. Fourteen of the fifteen children came, eight girls and six boys. We three adults chuckled over the indecisiveness of the boys, who couldn't make up their minds whether to taunt or flirt. Most chose the latter. The girls, on the other hand, showed the span in maturity that had already begun. They giggled and smiled no matter what the boys did.

Ben and Cassie stayed for dinner, Ben doing the honors with the steaks and barbecue that he liked so much to do. Apart from sharing kitchen tasks, Cassie and I chatted and made margaritas. The party was a great success.

"Bree, you really have to get this couch out of here. You look like a shrink there behind your desk instead of the hotshot lawyer on our team."

"That couch, good sir, does serve a purpose, I'll have you know. You'd be surprised what people tell me about in here. It's very useful to me, that couch. I'm not about to give it up just because the head honcho of this massive law firm tells me to." The ends of an undeniably appealing mouth turned up as she added, "Besides. Whoever said I wanted to be a hotshot anything, anyway?"

"Why do you always get the last word when I come in here?" I countered as I took my habitual corner of the couch.

Smiling, Bree answered, "Because you want me to."

It could get too comfortable in this place, I mused as I looked back at her.

It was Monday morning, two weeks after my abortive visit to the Evans' home. My friend, who was preparing the trust fund documents, had done everything she could within reason to slow things down. I needed to visit Lucy that afternoon to get her final approval of arrangements and to obtain her signatures. After that, I had to either execute her order to reverse her plea or let her crucify herself on her own, which, needless to say, I wasn't disposed to do.

"Bree," I said, my spirits as low as they'd been in quite a while, "I hope you can come up with something in that fertile brain of yours because I've got no more cards to play." Spreading my hands in futility, I said, "I feel about as useless to my client as I've ever been on a case. I should bring you up to speed, I guess."

"That'd be good if you're expecting anything from this lady who hasn't yet had her second coffee. Can I get you another cup?"

"Oh yeah, that would hit the spot. Then let's go over what we've got. That's not gonna take much time."

Bree was up and brushing me lightly with her skirt as she went by, leaving a just-perceptible fragrance of something coconut- and flower-like in her wake.

Both hands around my steaming cup and Bree settled back in her chair, I reviewed what had taken place during my meeting with Lucy two weeks before and what had happened when I saw her kids.

I was coming to know Brianna Dixon. Though a superb listener, naturally there were moments when she was bored, at which times those perhaps imagined golden specks in her eyes disappeared. Conversely, they were also absent when she was deep in thought. When intrigued by something someone said, she leaned slightly back instead of forward as most of us would do. Unless one were looking for these signs, they'd go unnoticed. When I came to my little skirmish with Lucy's daughter where I spared no details, I saw Bree lean back slightly in her chair. As I suspected, those golden specks that no one else seemed to see were gone. I waited to see how she would process this.

"Lucy wasn't much different at the arraignment, was she."

Disheartened, I shook my head.

Changing tack, she asked, "Do we have any photos of the Jackson girl?"

I shook my head.

"From the way you describe her, Forrest, the girl is unusually appealing for her age."

"Bree, I've got to tell you, she's not the same girl I knew. Appealing? Yeah, I guess she is in a certain way, although the idea makes me kind of sick when I think of how young she is. My God, she's only a year older than my daughter. It's difficult to believe."

"Okay, back to Mia, Forrest. What about her is appealing?"

Describing what I saw was not difficult. Bree nodded.

"And what about her face?"

"Her face, it's, it's kind of plain, I guess. When you look at just her face, she looks Trina's age, no more. But the rest of her. To be absolutely honest, Bree, and it makes me feel funny to use a word like this for a girl her age, she's sexy, her shape, the way she moves, that's the only word. I've never seen such a thing in a twelve-year-old, not that I know of, anyway."

Again, Bree nodded. "I wonder why she was so sullen. You'd think she'd be tearful and devastated. Do you know how her relationship was with her father?"

I thought about this before I answered, trying to conjure up a few things Lucy had let slip.

"All I can say is what Lucy told me. According to what I recall, Pete and his daughter weren't close at all. Pete was entirely focused on his son. I could see that, actually. I don't think I ever saw him even talk to Mia when we were together. As to the last two years," I spread my hands, "I can't really say. Whatever it was, Mia's going to be a real problem."

Bree nodded twice. At that moment, her phone buzzed. She listened for a moment, then handed it to me, whispering, "Evelyn Evans."

"Yes, Evie. This is Forrest. Anything going on?"

"If you consider Mia being two months' pregnant something, then yes there is."

Astounded, I asked, "Pregnant? When did you find this out and how?"

Bree's head went up and down again and I heard her sigh. Evie was in a state.

"She's been sick in the morning for the past few days, but I didn't pay attention, the flu or something. But this morning it was the fifth day. I had enough. I took her to the pediatrician to get checked. At least two months along, the doctor said."

"What did Mia say when she found out?"

"That foolish girl's over the moon about it, that's what she is. The ninny keeps patting her tummy and saying she has it. She has her baby. What, for heaven's sake, would make her do that, tell me? Now what in the world are we going to do with her, Forrest? Jim and I need to know."

"Does Lucy know?"

Sounding at her wits' end, Evie exclaimed, "Are you kidding? She's the last person that girl is going to tell."

"And what about Alex? Does he know?"

"He sure does, and he's furious with his sister because she won't tell him who the father is. We had to hold him back from beating it out of her. She says she'll never tell. What in the world are we going to do? We need to know."

"Evie, listen," I said, thoughts racing in my head. "I think we finally have a big part of the answer we've been looking for. There are going to be some developments now, very soon. If we need you, and I think we will, will you be willing to accompany us to Lucy's to tell her what you've told me?"

"As long as you're there with me, I suppose so."

"Brianna Dixon, my colleague, will be with me. If you can manage it, try to convince Mia to keep this quiet. There are lots of things we have to do now that we know this. We'll be in touch later on today, and thanks for calling me about this. Evie—I can't over-emphasize this—it's very important that you prevent Mia from talking about this with anyone. Can you manage this, do you think?"

"Forrest, I've had just about all I can take from Lucy's brat. She steps out of line just once more around here and I'm going to slap her silly. Don't you worry about her getting on the phone. Just call us back and let us know what's going on, okay?"

I assured her that I would. Letting out a long sigh, I handed the phone back to Bree.

"Well," she said, "I think we know who the protected person was to be and who Lucy was protecting her daughter from."

I nodded, worrying about what was to come. "Now," I said, sitting up straighter with a hand under my chin, "we've got a very different problem."

"Lucy?"

"Yes. Two years ago, I'd have hazarded a guess about how she'd react. At this point, I have no idea. It could break her, for all I know, and make her inaccessible to us. She might be angry and break off contact altogether, or, she might not change at all. I don't have a clue how to approach her."

As usual, something I appreciated a lot about her, Bree thought for a while before responding.

"Forrest, earlier when talking to Evie, you mentioned bringing me with you when you see Lucy. I'm not sure that's a good idea, at least done that way. If I have the right take on this, you're the only person she knows well and trusts, even if she hasn't shown it. Bringing a new person into the picture isn't going to help her. I want to be there to back you up, but I don't think it's wise."

I thought about this for a while.

Bree continued, "A better approach, I think, is for you to go, ostensibly to finish up with the trust papers, then talk to her about what we've learned. It's very possible, probable, I think, that she'll think you're lying, just to stay in touch with her. I can be waiting with Evie in the car outside if you need us. I doubt she'll question her brother's wife."

"That'd be a good idea," I said. "And I think you're right. She won't."

"Before I forget," Bree queried, "there was no preliminary hearing in Lucy's case, was there, just the second arraignment?"

"That's right," I said.

"Why not?"

"She wouldn't go for it, and I didn't feel inclined to press her, since what did we stand to learn from the prosecution had we held one—nothing we didn't already know. Her confession, gunshot residue analysis, fingerprints, the perpetrator found near the victim, that's all they have and need."

Bree nodded. "So, no pre-trial procedures or anything until we go to court? Sorry about all these questions, but I'm still finding my way around in crim law."

"Oh, there's bound to be motions and maybe a little haggling with the DA, but for the moment I'm worried about other things. Once we know a little more—if we ever do—you'll be in on everything, believe me."

All of what Bree said about our approach to Lucy made sense, but it meant that I'd be going it all alone, normally not something that would trouble me that much. This case was different. I was emotionally tied to our client, which complicated things.

Sighing again, I said, "Sometimes, I wish you were just a run-of-the-mill attractive colleague I could drop in on, somebody who didn't have so much common sense."

"Then I really would have to get rid of my couch, wouldn't I," Bree said, smiling. "Sorry to be the bearer of bad news."

"You're not, you're not," I replied as I stood up. "You don't have any idea how glad I am to have you with me on this. My intuition tells me you're going to come in pretty handy."

"Hmmm," she responded, "but you know? You're going to have to stop looking at my eyes the way you do or people are going to talk." Those eyes she was referring to were laughing.

"Yeah, maybe. Anyone ever tell you you have little gold specks in them, kind of like freckles, that are moving all the time. Any idea how distracting a weird thing like that is?" I tried hard to keep my poker face in place.

"I've heard a lotta nutty things before. As a psychologist, one does. But I think that just about tops them all, little golden fishes swimming around in my eyes. That's about the corniest line I ever heard. Forrest, if you must flirt with me, and that's okay, sometimes, be more creative. I'm sure you can."

Was Bree serious? Was I that puerile in what I said? Whether she thought it was a line or not, those specks I saw or thought I saw looked real.

She relented and bestowed one of those heartwarming smiles on me that she was known for.

"Since I assume you'll soon be off to Lucy's, keep me posted so I can arrange things with Evie and be on hand."

I nodded and as I was walking out the door, she said, in that quiet contralto voice of hers, "By the way, just so you know, I'm glad you like my eyes."

A lady to be reckoned with.

Chapter 11

Perspiring, my briefcase tucked under my arm, I rang Lucy's doorbell. She looked less formidable than last time when she let me in.

"So, you've got the papers with you, I see."

"Yes, Lucy, I do."

As I headed for the couch, she stopped me. "No, let's go to the dining room table to look them over. It'll be easier that way. God, I'll be glad to get this over. It's been over a month now."

I continued toward the couch and took my seat. Lucy, frowning at me, stood there.

"As I said, Lucy, I brought the papers. You can look them over and then sign them as you please. I've got something to talk about with you first." My lunch was making ominous rumblings in my stomach.

"No. No more talk. I want to deal with these papers right now and finish up. Come to the dining room table with me, please." The almost-friendly demeanor I witnessed at the front door turned frosty.

Where, I wondered as I pondered what to do, had the hostility and iron-like determination in my old friend come from? I remained where I was. She scowled, then slowly returned to the living room and sat down.

"Make it quick, Forrest, okay? I'm not feeling all that great."

My preference was to be as gentle and sensitive as possible in my approach because of Lucy's situation.

Unfortunately, I didn't think she'd respond well to sympathy and compassion in her current frame of mind. Best be direct.

"Lucy, I learned something this morning that is going to shake you to your roots so don't waste your energy trying to get back at me. You'll need all the resources you have to handle this."

I raised a hand when I saw the fright come on her face. "Your children, the both of them, are fine. They're fine, but there's something you need to know. Mia was seen by a pediatrician earlier this morning, who pronounced her to be two months' pregnant."

Blood drained from Lucy's face and she seemed to fall in on herself. Then abruptly, she straightened up, coming to her feet and glaring at me. Almost hissing, she said, "Of all people, Forrest, I never thought you'd stoop this low to get at me."

Had I not been expecting this, she would have flailed away at me longer than she did. Denial wasn't going to get us anywhere.

I also jumped to my feet, which caused her to pause just long enough to allow me to interject. Speaking sharply, I said, "Lucy, stop this. Evie who took Mia to the doctor this morning is in my car outside. She's with my colleague. If you need to hear this from someone else, I'll bring her in."

For a moment, her hostility remained and her body stayed taut, then, like a pricked balloon, the combative energy that had sustained her since Pete's death was gone. She sank to the floor next to her chair and began to wail.

I pulled out my cell and called Bree.

"There's no point in you two hanging around," I said. "She has no need to see her. Take Evie back to her home and thank her, please. Tell her we'll be in touch later on this afternoon. Thanks to you too, Bree, for being there."

"Hey," she quipped. "What else was this lady with weird green eyes going to do. See you later." The line went dead.

I felt helpless, much as I did when holding a sick child. Who, I wondered as I sat there, wishing I could do something, was my friend weeping for? Was it her violated daughter who was pleased to be carrying her father's baby, for the husband she had killed, or could she be mourning the loss of the vital person she'd once been? We'd so lost touch, Lucy and I, that I couldn't even guess.

We stayed like that for nearly a half hour, Lucy less vocal but crying still, I speculating about how much deeper this quagmire would become and how exceptionally difficult it was going to be to protect my friend. What had begun as a virtually impossible case for us had just taken on dimensions that my sluggish mind could scarcely process. It was well that I hadn't wasted time trying to formulate a defense strategy for a trial whose trajectory would now be different. The prospect of that volatile young girl on the stand was staggering.

And what to do with the woman in front of me? As I remembered her, all the way back to college more than twenty years ago, she had her weaknesses, but at her core, I always thought Lucy to be strong. Self-indulgent, irresponsible at times with a devil-may-care attitude, that was her, but what she felt important, she fought for, and she was loyal. If the connection between her and me was still intact, though undermined and tattered, she might be more willing now to trust and follow me in what we had to do.

She'd ceased crying, but she'd begun to shake, first only her hands and arms, then all of her. In shock? A nervous breakdown? Going to her, I kneeled down and grasped her hands. They were ice cold, a bad sign in my lay view. I gently pulled her to her feet and to the couch where I made her sit down next to me. She followed like an automaton.

Her soft blue eyes that were so pretty under normal circumstances were vacant and looking straight ahead. I doubted very much she was seeing anything. Her face bore no expression that I could read. Physically, she was awake, but, if she was cognizant of my presence, there was no sign. If I couldn't get her to respond, I'd call 911.

I squeezed Lucy's hand. Neither her eyes nor her facial muscles moved. I should stop playing doctor and get her to the hospital.

I let her hand go and was reaching for my cell when, in a flat voice, she said, "Forrest, you realize what this means. I thought he was going to rape her on her birthday. That was July thirteenth. That's what I thought he bought that babydoll nightie for. Two months along, isn't that what you said?"

"Yes, Lucy. That's what Evie's doctor told her."

"Two months along. That means they'd been together a lot earlier than I thought. At least a month." She stayed quiet for a moment, then, just above a whisper, said, "Pete, the bastard, he beat me to it. I would have killed him earlier if I'd known."

Still not looking at me, she went on, the tears starting to fall, "He manipulated her just like me. He made her beg him for that baby. What's my little girl going to do now that her father's dead and there's no one to look after her? Jimmy and Evie, they're helping, but they'll never keep her. They won't! What are we going to do with my baby, Forrest, tell me."

Before I could say anything, she continued, "You know, up to this morning, I was sure that I killed Pete for nothing, can you believe? She adored her father and she adores babies and she wanted his. I thought lots of times that he was just—what's the word I'm looking for— just humoring her. Maybe, when it came down to it, he wouldn't do anything. I was starting to think I killed Pete for nothing. But I didn't, did I. The asshole did exactly as he planned."

Lucy's voice had become more animated and she was looking at me as she talked. "But before you told me today that Mia was pregnant, I didn't know. I had to find out some way whether I'd made a huge mistake, you know? Only one way I could think of, and that was my diary. You didn't know I kept a diary, did you." For the briefest moment, a smile flitted across Lucy's face. "Oh yes, and you're in a lot of it, in the first volume, anyway."

My legal antennae twitched. "You have a diary, not current by any chance?"

"My diary? Oh yeah, I do. Had it since high school. Current? Up-to-date, you mean? My last entry was twenty-four hours before I shot Pete."

"You kept a diary that long?" That seemed improbable to me, knowing Lucy as I did. She wasn't disciplined enough. "Did you keep it up? How detailed is it?"

She said, as though she hadn't heard, "Six big volumes, every page I went through, looking for answers, but it didn't help, not in the long run, it didn't. At least, now it may be a good thing for the kids, Alex, at least. It'll be easier for him to understand what I did."

"Lucy, how detailed is this thing? It goes from high school to the present?"

"I skipped two years, just stopped writing. 2005 to 2007, I think it was. But the most important years are there. Detailed? Find out yourself. I'll give you the volumes before you leave." She reached over and grasped my hand. "I don't suppose you could stay with me for a while. I feel... kinda funny, not all that safe, that's the only way I can describe it... No, I know you can't, not with the twins and all. It feels different... disconnected, sort of, you and me. It's not like it was before, is it."

Hoping I could keep Lucy's attention for just a little longer, I said, "I don't need to tell you that Mia's situation changes everything. You can't protect her anymore, not in the way you wanted to, but you still have two children who need your love and help."

Lucy's tears that had stopped came back. "Forrest, Mia hates me for killing Pete. She'll never speak to me again. It's the same for Alex. He'll—"

"Hold on, Luce. I've known Alex for a long time. I really like him and I respect him. He knows about Mia and he's furious. He doesn't yet know who the father of her baby is, but once he does, if I know him, he'll be over here eventually and want to help. Another thing. Mia's not feeling very charitable toward you right now, you're right. But that girl's got a baby on the way and nowhere to go. Jim and Evie aren't going to want to take on the responsibility. Your children need you, Lucy. Hiding yourself away in some state prison's not an option anymore. We need your help for the coming trial and for your children. Do you follow me?"

She didn't answer for a long time. She looked as though she'd gone to sleep. "I'll do whatever you tell me," Lucy said. "Just promise me, promise me you won't abandon me. I need to know you're near me, Forrest, or I'm not sure I'm strong enough to do anything on my own."

I had only to look at her, weakened and demoralized, to know she required more support than I could give. "Lucy, I'll feel a whole lot better if we can get somebody to stay with you here for a while. I don't want to worry about you here by yourself. What's the name of that nice Filipino lady who used to work for you?"

Patting me on the arm, Lucy said, "Forrest, Forrest, he doesn't change. Thank God he doesn't change. He's always worrying about me, isn't he. Know what? It's kinda nice to have someone fussing over me. It hasn't happened in a long time. Lily's the name of the lady you're thinking about, but she's had a job now for a long time. It'd be so nice if she could come, but she won't be available."

"You could try, or I could call her if you like. Do you have her number?"

"I have her cell number somewhere, I think, but it won't work."

"Please find it for me and let me call, okay? If not her, then we'll find someone else. I'd invite you to stay with us, but..."

Lucy laughed and looked rather wistful. "Like the old days, right?" In a whisper, she added, "I picked a good one, once, but I wasn't smart enough to do what I had to do to hang onto him. I'll go get Lily's number."

I heard her shuffling around in several drawers and had about given up when Lucy returned with a piece of paper that she held out.

"I'm amazed I found this. I hope it's the right number. Maybe she'll know someone."

I pulled out my cell and called.

"Lily Santos," came the voice I thought I recognized. "Who's this?"

I told her who I was, a close friend of Lucy Jackson, and I explained the reason for my call.

"Oh my," she said. "That too bad. I have breast cancer, you know. I sick, well, not too sick but tired all the time. I just have double mastectomy three weeks ago and I been on chemo and radiation for two weeks, Mr. Spencer. They tell me, yes, aggressive treatment necessary for me because cancer in my lymph nodes, you see. I'm so tired half the time. I quit my work three months ago. Lucy, she all alone in the house?"

"Yes, yes she is. Do you think it would be possible—"

"I pack my bag and I come over in a half an hour, maybe less if traffic not too bad. It'll be very nice see Lucy again. Don't worry, Mr. Spencer. I remember where she live. You stay until I get there, in a half hour, okay?"

"We'll be here waiting, Lily. Thank you."

"Lily? Coming over here? How can she?"

I told her.

"Poor thing, poor thing. Lily's not had an easy life. She's actually going to stay with me? Is that what she said?"

Lucy brightened a little when I confirmed this. It was obvious that she feared being there alone.

Psychologically, emotionally, physically, my friend was in bad shape. I was much relieved that someone she liked who knew her well was going to be with her.

"While we're waiting, can I have a peek at that diary of yours?"

"Yeah, sure, my diary. If I can carry it, you can. I was going to throw it out, you know. Maybe it will help Alex understand, least I hope it will. Mia won't ever read it. I'll go and get it."

The house was neat and clean, but there was something about it I didn't like. The homemaker was female, yet the place lacked a woman's touch. Certainly, I could see none of Lucy there.

She was back, laden down with books. They weren't large so much as they were thick. I jumped up to help her with them. Lucy looked as though she was going to fall.

I was astounded by the detail I saw, especially by the amount of dialogue. How could she have remembered what everybody said? I'd begun to wonder if she'd embellished just a little until I found her notes on me and our encounters. There were no word sequences that were unfamiliar or events concerning Lucy and me that I couldn't recall. Some of what I saw must have made me blush.

Laughing a little, Lucy said, "So, Santa Lucia's revered criminal attorney remembers, hmmm? To look at your face, I'd say he does. When I saw the pages you're on now, I didn't blush like you are. I was thinking about how wonderful those times were."

I couldn't wait to tell Bree about what we might have. I knew how she'd respond.

Lily looked much older, even with her wig. She and Lucy, both in tears, hugged for a long time. My mind was racing onto things I had yet to do that afternoon when it was my turn. Lucy took hold of me and showed no signs of letting go. Lily stood back, smiling. After a half dozen kisses on both my cheeks, I managed to disengage.

I was impatient to get a further look at Lucy's

books. I decided to peek at the last volume while still in her driveway in my car. I became angrier as I read, and excited, too, by what her diary might do for us. I was so caught up by Lucy's notes that I'd have been there until dinnertime had my cell been off. It was Bree.

"I started to worry about your health," she said. "Any news? I felt like a crumb, sending you out there, alone."

"News, Bree, is not the proper term."

"Wow! Tell me what you have."

"Better yet, I'm going to show you. I've got six books you need to see, six volumes of Lucy's diary that, I promise you, are going to blow your mind. I'll drop them off to you on my way home, provided you promise to read them all tonight and brief me in the morning. I'd stay and go through them with you, but I've gotta get home to be with the twins. Andy doesn't behave all that well with Lupe, our daytime sitter, when it's near his dinnertime."

"That's just as well. It would be unseemly for a man of your standing to be in my house late into the evening, alone with me, wouldn't it." Was she teasing? I couldn't tell by her voice. "Sounds exciting, what you have. I'll read every page and tell you what I find when I see you tomorrow morning, how's that?"

"Perfect, Ms. Dixon. We wouldn't want your neighbors to get ideas, would we. I should be at your house by five."

My next call was to Jim and Evie. I had nothing substantive to tell them, but they needed to be kept informed. Also, I wanted their permission to return to talk to Mia and to Alex if he was there. I hoped that when I'd finished telling the boy what I believed took place, he'd come to see things differently and eventually feel some empathy for his mother.

Then there was the girl. I'd have to take the gloves off with her this time. She must avoid talking about her pregnancy to anyone until we'd had a chance to read that diary.

Evie's voice boomed over the car speaker as she told me Alex would return within the hour and that Mia was at home. There was no way I'd get the girl to cooperate, Evie assured me. Could Evie attempt to keep them in the house until I arrived without letting either know I was on my way? She'd try.

"Forrest, I'm sorry," Alex said as soon as he saw me, "I don't think we have anything to talk about." Turning to Evie, he said, "You could have told me he was coming."

Showing no remorse, she riposted in a pleasant enough voice, "Alex, Jim and I are glad we can help at a time like this. You're welcome in this house as I'm sure you know, but you're in no position to start giving orders around here. In my home, I do as I want. You know perfectly well that Mr. Spencer is here to help, so have the decency to talk to him."

Alex wasn't happy, but he turned around and led me to his room. I nodded my thanks. Evie had been great.

This time I sat at the foot of the bed while Alex was at the head. How to approach this without antagonizing him? Discuss Mia first.

"Alex, I understand you know your sister's—"

"Going to have a baby, the stupid bitch. Yes I do." He looked hurt and he looked hard. "I'd like to get my hands on the asshole who did that to her. I'd teach him a thing or two."

"She's not telling you who the father is."

"Hell no. I'd beat it out of her if my aunt and uncle would let me."

"No need, Alex," I said in a quiet voice. "I think we know."

Sitting up a little straighter, he asked, "Why? Did she tell you?"

I shook my head. "We haven't run the DNA test yet, but we soon will. I'm very sorry to tell you this, but I think I can say with some certainty that Pete is the father of your sister's baby."

At first, Alex looked stupefied, then angry. "You know, Forrest, I don't know what kind of a game you're playing, but I can tell you, I'm about to kick your ass right out the door." Alex's face was red and he was breathing hard. "I don't get it. You and my dad have been friends for years and now, you turn on him." Alex stood and appeared about to carry out his threat. "My dad would never do a thing like..." For a moment, he remained frozen, his mouth half open, then, much as Lucy had when she heard my news, the energy went out of him and he sat down on the bed. He was looking at the wall. He'd obviously recalled something.

In a matter-of-fact tone, speaking quietly, more to himself than to me, he said, "So that's what all of that was about. Holy shit. Oh my God." He was shaking his head back and forth as he said this. Then he nodded decisively and turned to me. "I came into the living room one night a couple a months ago. I was working in the basement. I had my slippers on so nobody heard me come. I can see it like it was yesterday. What I saw pissed me off. I said so. Shit, there Mia was, snuggled up to Dad like a sex kitten. She was smiling up at him and stroking his neck and face. I couldn't believe it, I just couldn't. They looked like, they looked like lovers, him lookin' down at her the way he was. I didn't see anything like that again before I went back to school, so I forgot about it, at least I sort of did. Mia's changed a lot in the last two years, I'm sure you noticed. She's, she's—"

"Yes," I said. "She has. I'm sure you know what DNA testing is."

Teeth clenched, Alex retorted, "Cut the crap, Forrest. Of course I do."

"I don't think there's any issue about what we'll find. Alex, for lots of reasons, you mustn't hassle your sister about this. She's under a lot of strain and more tumult in the house isn't going to make things easier for Jim and Evie and their kids. You understand this."

He nodded. "Why in the world would I want to talk

to her about this anyway! Jesus, Forrest."

"Good. I'm glad we agree on this. There's something else I need to talk to you about, Alex. It's not an easy thing, and I beg you to listen with an open mind and not interrupt me."

"Can't it wait for another time? You don't want to hear what's going on inside of me. You really don't!"

"I'm sorry, Alex, but this can't wait. As you can imagine, you're not the only one suffering right now." The boy's face went hard. "You may not know but, until today when she learned about Mia's pregnancy, your mother refused absolutely to tell anyone, even me, her friend and attorney, why she killed Pete."

Alex was about to speak, but I cut him off. "She confessed to having shot him and was going to plead guilty and go to prison and to possibly something even worse for premeditated murder. People don't kill other people, Alex, without a reason. But she wouldn't tell us why. My colleagues and I were sure she was protecting someone, but we had no idea who or why, especially now that her husband's dead. Now, of course, we know that reason. She was trying to shield her daughter from sexual assault."

"So why didn't she go to the authorities instead of shooting him?" Alex yelled. "Tell me. She had lots of ways of stopping him instead of killing him."

"I think we're going to have the answers to these questions very soon. I don't think you knew this, but your mom has kept a very detailed diary since she was in high school. It's six huge filled books and it's up-to-date. Unless I'm mistaken, Alex, I think the answers to why she took the extreme action she did will be in that diary that I got just this morning. I can't give you facts at this time, just speculation. This much I can say, and I think you'll agree with me, knowing your mom as you do. She's not a violent or volatile person. If she shot Pete, I believe she thought she had no choice. As I said, we expect to know much more once we've read her diary. All I'm asking you to do at this point is to remember that what she did was intended to protect her child. Give us a couple of days to read what your mom wrote, then, if she agrees, and I'm sure she will, I'll make a full copy of the books for you."

Alex looked broken as he sat there, his face in his hands. Through his fingers I could just manage to hear him say, "She may have had her reasons, Forrest. It may be like you say. Thing is, she shot my dad six times at point-blank range and killed him. That's not something that's easy for me to swallow, no matter how desperate she was. I feel like I've been in a huge earthquake and lost my family. I don't feel sympathy for her or for Mia either. Maybe I'll read the diary, maybe I won't. I'll see. Now, if you don't mind too much, I'd like to be alone. Tell Aunt Evie that I won't be eating dinner. I'm going to stay in my room here for a while."

"Okay," I said as I got up. "Thanks for letting me talk to you about this. As to that earthquake of yours, I don't blame you for feeling the way you do, but remember, three of those four family members are still very much alive."

"She won't let you in," Evie said. "I told you that. If you can wait a few minutes, Jim'll be home from work and we can talk. He really needs to know what's going on."

"Mia's in the bedroom in the basement, isn't she?"

"Yeah," Evie said, "but she won't let you in. That girl is stubborn. She's turned from a mouse into a she-cat."

Not a bad analogy, I thought.

I found the room easily enough and pounded on the door. No response.

"Mia," I said in a loud voice to be sure that she could hear, "I'm going to ask you just once more to open up and then I'll leave. My first stop when leaving the house will be the Child Protective Services. They get pretty shaken up when they hear of young girls who have been raped. You don't want those people nosing around here if you want to keep your baby. So, make up your mind or I'm out of here."

Ten seconds later, the door behind me was closed and I was in the bedroom with her. She was in pajamas that did little to hide what was underneath. Again, she looked defiant.

"Mr. Spencer," she snapped, "for your information, I wasn't raped. I wanted the baby that's inside of me, so there. You've got nothing to report to the Child whatever they are."

Taking a severe tack, I replied, "You, young lady, are going to sit down on that bed and close your mouth and listen. I'm not going to put up with any more of this. Either you do what I tell you to, or I'm going to leave and go straight to the CPS. What's it going to be?"

She glowered at me for a minute or so then sat down.

"Now let's get something straight. You, Mia, are going to listen and listen well and I'm going to be the one to talk. You're very wrong about some important things that you need to know. Are we in agreement here?"

She looked obstinate but less insolent than before. There was more apprehension than anything on her face. Finally, she nodded.

"Good. First, we know who the father of your baby is so there's no need to hide that anymore."

"You can't know! How can you know who it is?"

"Have you ever heard of DNA testing, Mia? There've been tests now for over twenty years that will tell us absolutely who the father is. There's nothing you can do to avoid these tests so let's not waste time. They will identify absolutely that it's your own father who impregnated you."

Mia's face went white. To say that I was on shaky grounds concerning much of what I was going to tell her would be to seriously understate things. I was reasonably confident about most of it, but by no means all.

"Whether you wanted the baby or not, Mia, you're not old enough to legally consent to sex. Anyone in their late teens or older"—I couldn't remember what the actual age limits were—"who touches you in a sexual way is committing a serious crime that we call rape." How little I really knew about these things. "Raped children, and make no mistake, Mia, you are still very much a child, are approached very differently by the authorities." Thank goodness, there was no recorder to preserve my claims. "So, we have rape that is definitely a crime and we have incest which also is. Do you understand what incest is?"

Mia now looked scared and began to cry. I sat down next to her and put my arm around her shoulder. She flinched, but she remained where she was.

"Mia, listen. I didn't come to frighten you. In fact, if you do as I ask, and I'm going to ask you for one simple thing, you have nothing to be scared of. No one's about to take your baby away from you. What I need from you for the next few days is that you keep your pregnancy a secret, that's all. After that, we'll do everything we can to take care of you and protect your baby. I'm a long-time friend of your family, Mia, you know that. You can trust me. You know that too. So, do we have a bargain? You tell no one about your pregnancy, no one at all until I say it's okay. Can you promise this?"

"I won't go to jail for anything?"

"Absolutely not, I promise."

"And I can keep my baby?"

"Mia, I can't tell you at this point. I personally don't work in this area of law, but my colleague has. You'll meet her soon and you'll like her. She'll know for sure. I'll be talking to her tomorrow morning about all this and I'll call you about what she says. I think things will work out in the end, so do as I say and try not to over-stress that baby, okay?"

A watery smile appeared briefly on her troubled face. I gave her another hug and got up to leave.

The young girl looked forlorn as well she might,

unable to foresee the future for herself and for her coming baby and because she must feel dreadfully alone. Doggedly determined though she was to keep her baby, whose provenance in itself could be a problem, she was ill-equipped to cope with the social and practical hurdles she'd have to overcome.

At her bedroom door, I retraced my steps and, kneeling down and taking both her hands, I said, "Mia, something tells me that you're going to be a good mom when your baby comes. You're not alone, even though you may think so now. We'll be here and do our best for you. We're going to need your help to make sure that baby will be as healthy as it can be. You want that, don't you?"

She nodded vigorously, tears still streaming down her face.

"Expecting mothers have to eat carefully, never smoke, or take drugs or even drink alcohol. One of the best things you can do for your baby is to relax and be as happy as you can. Your Aunt Evie will help you and so will a friend of mine who has a little girl. She's very wise about these things. You'll meet her soon, and she'll help you, so you're not alone. We'll be in touch with you tomorrow or the next day, okay?"

"You promise?" came a little voice that might have come from an eight-year-old.

I squeezed her hands and told her, "Yes. I promise. Now don't worry about your brother. He knows, but I've asked him not to bother you on this."

She let out a long breath and her face cleared a bit. She'd obviously been worrying about this.

Jim, Evie and I were seated at the kitchen table since dinner preparations for the family were in progress. Curious about why I hadn't seen the Evans children, Evie told me that she'd sent them to the neighbors to play the last time I came and today to keep them from being underfoot.

"So, what's going on with my sister?" Jim wanted to

know. "Is she going to end up in jail? I suppose she is. My God, that'll kill her."

I recounted what had happened earlier that day and told them about the diary. "It's so detailed," I said, "that I have hopes that it may help us for her defense."

Evie asked, "Is there a defense for people who kill someone when it's planned?"

I said that, in some instances, there was. We were going to try very hard to develop one. Both seemed surprised.

"So you think she's got a chance?" Jim asked.

"A chance, yes. How much of one I can't tell you yet without seeing her diary. We'll know a lot more in a few days."

"I hate to ask you this," Jim said, "but I guess there's no way to know how long we'll have to keep Luce's kids, is there."

"We have to talk about this, I realize," I replied, "but there's little I can tell you at the moment. I have a check for two thousand dollars that Lucy gave me this morning to cover things for a little while." Both looked relieved. "I'll keep in touch with you about developments. Lily Santos who used to work for Lucy is going to stay with her for a while. I talked to Alex and to Mia. I don't expect you should be having any problems from either of them. Please let me know right away if you do."

Bree was standing in her front doorway with little Maya on her hip as I drove up. She had adopted the little girl from India a year ago, I thought she told me. An angelic face was almost lost in a torrent of black hair, easily as thick as Trina's. Bree held out her hand.

"Give, give," she said. "I've been on pins and needles since your call."

"That's a pretty cute girl you've got there."

"Enough stalling, sir. Hand them over."

"And I always thought you were the laidback patient kind."

"Sometimes. Sometimes. Right now, I want those books on your car seat." Bree had a balancing act, managing the six volumes and the little girl.

Past Andy's dinnertime, I could imagine poor Lupe trying to cope with my son's antics and demands and Trina's taunts. In thirty minutes, I'd have the take-out food and I'd be home.

Chapter 12

"Mr. Spencer," Cheryl, our legal secretary, announced as I arrived next morning just before nine, "Ms. Dixon would like to see you right away." Cheryl knew I was aware of this since I was headed straight for Bree's office when I came in, but our sergeant at arms wasn't about to break her rules.

I nodded, said good morning to Nancy and Josephine and continued on my way.

No pleasantries this time, just an index finger pointed at the couch and an expression on Bree's face I had never seen. "Sit," came her curt command, so that's what I did.

Her demeanor, to put it mildly, was unusual. If there'd been flecks I'd seen in Bree's green eyes, either they'd been imaginary or they'd gone to hide. I was looking at one troubled lady. I could see none of the volumes of the diary on her desk, just piles of notes.

Bending forward slightly, putting her elbows on her desk and resting her chin in her hands, she contemplated me, her usually full mouth now a thin line.

In a voice fraught with emotion that was new to me, she said, "Forrest, I'm not sure where to start, maybe by telling you that if she hadn't shot the son of a bitch herself, I would have." Strong medicine from our reflective and mild-mannered Bree. "I was up 'til three this morning, reading and taking notes."

I wished I could look that good when burning the candle at both ends.

In a voice hushed but very tense, she continued, "Lucy's diary is absolutely one of the most extraordinary documents I've ever read. One moment, I was in tears and the next, I felt rage so strong that it scared me. Lucy, like all of us, has her weaknesses, but I've decided I like your choice of girlfriends."

Following her startling declarations, if that's the proper word, Bree's typical control returned and she resumed her normal pose. Her eyes, however, were still on me. "You've heard of battered woman syndrome, of course, haven't you."

I remained where I belonged at the moment, in listening mode, and simply nodded.

"We see more and more instances of successfully arguing BWS as a defense in cases of homicide, I'm glad to say. It's about time society began waking up." Then, her face becoming animated, if still a little tense, Bree leaned toward me again and, this time in a brittle voice that jolted me, she added, "But there's another kind of domestic abuse we hear little about that, in some ways, is worse than physical abuse."

Addressing me as though I was a perpetrator to be dressed down, she carried on, "It's a kind of abuse that destroys one's concept of self, destroys one's identity. I'm talking about psychological abuse, Forrest. Lucy's case is the worst I've ever seen, the very worst. It's the best documented case I know. It's phenomenal how she managed over the years to write all that stuff down and in such detail. You'll cry, I'm telling you, when you read her diary. At the start, she's a lively healthy girl with a real zest for life, attractive and independent. You'll know something about that, won't you."

Her last statement I pretended not to hear.

"Basically, Forrest, over a period of, say, fifteen years, her husband, a scheming manipulator if I ever saw one, systematically broke Lucy down and turned her into the family slave. The only reality she could relate to was the one he forced on her." Bree let out a long sigh and settled back, seeing that I was about to come to life.

Not for the first time, I felt shame at having so long neglected someone I'd convinced myself was close.

Observing the expression that must have been on my face, in a manner much more direct with me than usual, Bree said, "Forrest, please! I understand, but you're not to blame for this. Not to dismiss your feelings, but we've got other important things to focus on."

Had I not seen the softness in her eyes, I might have come back with something that would have been unwise and gotten us off track.

"Psychological abuse," I said, "not something we hear much about in Court. I'll get Sara on it right away, but I've got my doubts that she'll come up with anything significant for this case. I'll have to read the diary, but I suspect I'll find little that's evidentiary that we can use to justify homicide."

"Okay, but what about Lucy's need to protect her child? Can't we use that?"

"Perhaps," I replied, "but it won't be easy. In fact, it will be very difficult. You're talking about defense of another instead of self-defense as the motive for killing Pete. To get that through, you've gotta satisfy several conditions. One of them is almost impossible to establish in a case like this where there was no immediate threat of violence or harm."

"What kind of conditions?" Bree inquired.

I took out my pencil and my little notebook. In a minute or so, I finished writing and looked up.

"Okay, number one." Bree was taking notes. "Lucy reasonably believed that her daughter was in imminent danger of being touched unlawfully." I saw the question on Bree's face, but I carried on. "Second, Lucy reasonably believed that the immediate use of force was necessary to defend against that danger, and the third and most difficult one, Lucy used no more force than was reasonably necessary to defend against that danger."

"Being touched unlawfully? What does that mean?"

"It's a catchall term, but it certainly includes sexual assault. Number one doesn't really pose a problem, not compared with two and three, anyway. Satisfying condition two depends on validating condition three, so let's talk about three first." Looking at my notebook, I said, "Lucy used no more force than was reasonably necessary to defend against that danger, in this case, sexual assault. To establish this, we must show that she had no alternative means to prevent violation of her child. The prosecution will argue correctly that she had a variety of them, none of which involved physical violence."

"And what happens, Forrest, if we can demonstrate that Lucy truly believed she had no choice, that none of the normal recourses available to her would help? What happens then?"

Considering this, I said, "That would take some doing. You'd need hard evidence to establish that. No way one's own statements in a diary would suffice."

"Listen," Bree said, glancing down at her piles of notes, "I believe Lucy was convinced she had no choice and, I think you'll agree once you've read the diary, that we have the potential for showing this. I could summarize what I found right now, but there are things you need to see in Lucy's diary before we discuss them. Can you read it soon, please?"

"Yeah, sure," I said. "We'll need several copies, one of which has to go to the DA."

"Being done. I asked for six copies to be made. I think Josephine's doing that right now. She'll bind them this morning and you'll have your copy before noon," Bree said. "Forrest, I'm sorry I'm so uninformed about all this stuff, but are we under time limits here?"

"I doubt it, not critically anyway," I said. "The diary makes the difference. We'll have to file a motion to continue to get the date beyond the speedy trial constraint. The DA will want thirty days at least to examine the document. And we can argue truthfully that the diary came into our hands only a day ago and that we need time to study it for the defense. The judge will grant us our continuance. How much time we'll get is anybody's guess. I doubt this will be necessary, but if Mia testifies, it'll be to our advantage for the jury."

"If she's showing," Bree cut in, reproof on her face.

"Hey, psycholawyer," I retorted, "in a tough case like this, whatever works."

"Forrest, as you'll see, the diary refers to what must be very compromising pictures that Pete was holding over her. Can you see if Lucy has them? Another thing. She refers to several friends who might be able to help us. Could you get their names?"

"I'm going to have to see Lucy soon anyway so I'll ask her about both those things. In the meantime, I need to get my hands on those books and make some notes. Bree, I've got a couple of other questions that you may be able to help me with."

"I'll try."

"How soon can we run DNA tests for paternity?"

"That depends on which technique you use. The most up-to-date and least invasive involves collecting a minute amount of blood. It's called the SNP test and it's virtually one hundred percent effective as early as nine weeks."

"My God," I expostulated. "Glad Garrett and I didn't know how much was packed away inside that psychologist-cum-lawyer head of yours. We would have had to up your pay."

Smiling, Bree replied, "I'm just getting started. When we're done with this case, we'll have to renegotiate, won't we? Now what's your other question?"

"It's not that likely, is it, that a twelve-year-old mother can keep her baby in this state with all the protective measures we have in place?"

Disparagingly, Bree shook her head. "I know you're good at what you do, Forrest, but your education's lacking, in a few areas, anyway."

"You should have been a school teacher, Bree. You've got that air."

"Spare me. Another male who feels threatened by a woman who knows more than he."

"I think it's him, not he," I said.

"Another area you need to learn about, English grammar. Don't worry, it's he, not him. Now be quiet and listen to what I have to tell you. It could turn out to be important in this case. Here in California, unless it can be demonstrated that a mother, regardless of her age, is seriously neglecting or abusing her child, no one, including Child Protective Services, can take her baby, and I mean no one. We're progressive here in California, Mr. Spencer. And we go further. In the interest of keeping mother and child together, even if they're in a foster home, the State will provide two hundred dollars per month, I think it is, for the child's upkeep and a fee for foster care for the two."

"Is that true? I would have thought they'd take the child away from her at that age to be sure it was well-cared for." I looked at Bree and she looked right back. "You're serious, aren't you," I said. "What you're saying is that Mia, in theory, can keep her baby."

"Did I say in theory? I don't think so. Barring unforeseen circumstances, Forrest, she'll keep her baby."

"Even in a foster home, no less?"

"Even in a foster home."

"You don't believe in overloading circuits, do you."

Bree smiled and I thought I saw some of those flecks come back. "Now go find your Sara, then go home and read."

"Bree—"

"I know, I know, you've already told me. She's not your Sara, but she'd like to be, wouldn't she. Now get out of here and let me get to work. I've got to earn the pittance you people pay me."

As I was heading for my office, Cheryl, ever officious, intercepted me. "I was instructed by Ms. Dixon to give you a copy of the documents she gave me only this morning. Six thick volumes to photocopy there were, if you can imagine."

As I discovered last year, Cheryl could be laidback and fun at parties, but she reverted to a mildly disagreeable stiff neck at work. I sympathized with our two paralegals, who she'd co-opted as her slaves. She had it in for Ben, who ignored her, and, for no reason I could fathom, disliked Bree. Her antagonism toward Sara was intense.

"You do realize my assistants will be at this for nearly the entire day. I'm sorry."

"Well, then, Cheryl, since I ordered those copies made and they're important, it's good to know that you'll be able to lend a hand and speed up the work."

"Mr. Spencer, I have—"

I cut Cheryl off and pointed at Nancy and Josephine and the photocopy machines and said, "Get to it, please. I expect those copies early this afternoon."

No fool, aware that further objections could bring her trouble, she harrumphed and, hands on hips, went to galvanize the girls. Halfway through her admonition that the two would have to hurry, I walked over to the machine. I'd about had enough with Cheryl's domineering attitude.

"Ladies, I'm sorry about this, but it's important that we get these copies out as soon as practical." While looking directly at Cheryl, who was frowning, I said, "Nancy, Josephine, no one's going to be in charge of this process. Cheryl will be working equally with you on this. If there are any problems, see me, please."

Not a good way to maintain a happy camp, but I needed our paralegals to know that Cheryl's domineering days were over.

It was Mia who picked up the telephone. Something wasn't right.

"Good morning, Mia. This is Forrest. Is everything alright?"

For a moment, she didn't answer, then she began to cry.

"Do I need to come over, Mia, or can we talk on the phone?"

In a shaky voice, she said, "The phone. Nobody else is home."

"Alright. Tell me what's the matter."

"Alex says they won't let me keep the baby. He says I'm too young. They'll take it away from me soon as it's born." She was sobbing.

"Mia, stop crying, please, and listen."

No change. I repeated my injunction. Her sobs diminished gradually to hiccups.

"Can we talk? Can you understand me?"

She said she could.

"Remember, Mia, when I told you I have a friend who works with me in our office who knows about these things? She says no one can take your baby, absolutely no one. Alex is upset and saying things he shouldn't. The fact is, he's wrong. We don't separate mothers from their babies here in California. That's what my friend and colleague says, and she knows her stuff, Mia, believe me. We have a lot more talking to do about all this, but you will keep your baby if you take good care of yourself and make sure your baby's healthy."

"You promise? You promise that's what she said?"

I promised.

"I talked to Aunt Evie and she's going to help me about all the things you said. I'll take special care, Mr. Spencer."

"Okay," I said. "A couple of things. Don't fight with your brother and don't worry about what he says. My friend and colleague's named Brianna. We call her Bree. You'll really like her. Everybody does. I'll bring her over to meet you, probably early next week. One last thing. Get a pencil and something to write on that you won't lose. I want to give you my phone numbers so you can call me anytime you need to, okay? And don't forget what I said about not worrying. It's not good for tiny babies who are trying to grow."

"I won't forget, I promise. I feel better now."

What could account for the unusually powerful maternal instinct and drive in a child Mia's age? It had to go far beyond a preadolescent's love of babies. Something seemed unnatural about it. I was sure I'd known pregnant adult women who'd have been far less tenacious about their need to preserve their unborn children. Assuming Mia carried the child to term, what would become of Mia and her little charge, especially if we were unsuccessful, as was all too possible, in getting her mother freed? And even if Lucy were acquitted, what then? Could she help raise a child whose father she had killed?

Apart from these important questions, what role could or should Mia play in Lucy's defense? Issues I couldn't possibly address until I'd read her diary and consulted Lucy's friends.

Finishing the last pages of the first volume—it was nearly four-thirty Tuesday afternoon, time for me to be heading home—I was dumbfounded by the amount of information there. The book read more like an autobiography than a diary.

How, I continued to ask myself as I turned pages, did she manage to get down whole conversations in the way she had? I would never have credited it had I not encountered so many statements of my own that I knew to be accurate beyond any doubt. Lucy had an uncanny memory for dialogue, a fact that added so much richness to what she wrote.

Jannie Stuart. I had vague recollections of having interacted with her several times, but I couldn't pull up the face of someone so important in Lucy's life. Astonishing how we delude ourselves into thinking we really know our friends.

Lucy's words brought me back to what we shared and to who my close friend was as though it was yesterday. Though not eloquent as such, her writing was overwhelmingly evocative, sufficiently so that I felt myself grow red at times.

I was conjuring up pleasant scenes Lucy talked about when there was a light tap at my door. It was Sara, who I'd asked earlier to drop in. I hastily closed my book, but there was little I could do to wipe away the telltale expression that she saw. In mid-stride my research assistant stopped, quietly closed the door behind her and regarded me, a knowing smile on her flawless face.

"To look at you, it's not legal things you've been reading there. Mind if I take a peek?"

Unthinking, I placed a protective hand over Lucy's book.

"Hmmm," came the 'I thought so' noise and her nod. "What goes on behind closed doors!" Sara's games.

More impatiently than I intended, I said, "Sara, it's late and I haven't got time for this. I should have been out of here a quarter of an hour ago."

Again, her nod. "And you would have been if you hadn't been so engrossed." Aware that she'd rankled me, she took her normal seat, took out her notepad and put on her serious look. The ends of her distracting mouth were still perceptibly turned up.

Sara could play, but she was efficiency itself when it came to work. She could write shorthand as fast as I could talk and I had the inestimable pleasure of not having to repeat myself.

Her eyebrows knitting together, she commented, "Psychological abuse. I'm not sure I've ever seen a reference to it in the jurisprudence."

"Probably not," I concurred. "Lots about battered woman syndrome but psychological abuse used as a defense in court?"

Sara slowly shook her head. "I'll dig around and let you know what I find. I'm not optimistic, though." Looking up, she continued, "I hate it when you do this to me, send me looking for things that don't exist."

"Sara," I said, "I do it because I'm confident that, if it's out there, you'll be the one to find it."

I wasn't flattering her and she knew it. She was the best legal researcher I'd ever had.

She got up and was about to go out my door when, again, she stopped. She sniffed, then sniffed again as though she'd noticed something unusual in the air.

Turning back to me, she remarked, "You know, Forrest, if you don't stop spending so much time in her office, you're going to smell like Bree, not something you really want to do."

Before I could respond, she was out the door and gone. I crammed the next three volumes of Lucy's diary in my briefcase and followed shortly after.

The sole topic of conversation at my dinner table was the coming week. Trina was so excited she could hardly eat.

"Daddy, remember when we saw Anna and the Hendersons when they came out here?"

"For the adoption to be finalized, you mean."

"I guess. Anyway, did you see Anna's gorgeous clothes? She's so pretty. I wish I could be like her."

"No, no, you don't," I protested. "Anna's a very pretty girl, yes, but if you changed and you looked just like her, I'd lose the most beautiful girl in the world, so no."

"*Daaaddy*, you know what I mean. I don't have any clothes like her, not anything."

"What, you already threw away your birthday dress? Is that what you did?"

Trina was growing more exasperated by the minute.

"That's all girls think about is clothes," Andy piped. "What good are those stupid things, anyway." He started shadowboxing at the table.

"Settle down, you two. In the first place, Trina, think about your friend and not about all the dresses that she has. If you're going to Georgia just to compare clothes, then we'll cancel the trip until you're a little more mature."

My beloved daughter rarely got upset with me, but she was then. She jumped up and stormed off toward the stairs. I caught her before she got there.

"Young lady, more of this and, I'm telling you, the trip is off. You sit back down and finish up your plate."

My threat was empty as both children knew, but Trina, face set, did return to her chair.

Fifteen minutes later, Trina and I having heard for the tenth time about every activity available at the baseball camp, the twins went off to their rooms while I cleaned up.

Baths over and teeth brushed, stories told or read, by eight-thirty I was ensconced in my favorite chair in the living room and neck-deep in Lucy's books.

I'd decided to leave off taking notes until the second read when I knew better what to underline.

Bree was right. Shortly after opening the third volume, I was struck dumb by Jannie's death and all that it implied. I couldn't go on for a full half hour, choked up and dabbing at a few tears. Poor Lucy. How horrible that must have been, she about to deliver her first baby, and then the news. I had no idea she'd had a female friend like that, and one so good for her.

I could have done nothing to avert the catastrophe in Lucy's life. By then, I'd gone off to law school in Berkeley while Lucy was settling down here with Pete. Did he ever know how close Jannie and his wife were? If so, was his knowledge connected in any way to his behavior with Lucy in Mexico?

Why did I have to be one of those unfortunates who missed people before they left? My children had just returned to me after a very long month away, and there they were, about to be gone again—happily for me, for only a week this time. Still, if I could be lonely as I was then with them in their beds upstairs, how much worse would it be when the house was empty? I had to think back just three weeks to know.

*

Next morning, I gave Cheryl strict instructions that, except for colleagues, I was not to be disturbed—no visitors, no phone calls, unless she considered them important. As a gatekeeper, she was unmatched. They'd have to push aside her not-insubstantial frame to pass.

Except for an hour out to lunch with Ben, a welcome break, I spent all day Wednesday with my nose buried in Lucy's books. The more I read, the deeper my chagrin. The young woman I'd met years ago and had to struggle with myself not to love had been dismantled, bit by bit, by someone who utterly confounded me. I'd been friends with Pete for years, a solid individual in just about every way, a good parent, a seemingly devoted spouse and a first-class citizen of our town. So why degrade and control Lucy in the way he had? Was it to punish her for transgressions we didn't know about? Because she fought persistently against being a hausfrau, as she put it?

With no religious affiliations that I knew of that would have prevented him, why, if he was so unsatisfied, didn't he do what so many others opt for and find himself another wife? He would have had his pick.

I read slowly to ensure that I didn't miss anything that could be important. I finished the last page of Lucy's tragic story at ten-thirty Thursday morning.

Stunned, I sat alone in my office though Bree had attempted to reach me several times. I wanted to talk to her, but not until I'd finished going over the diary at least once. I understood now why she wanted those pictures and anything else Pete might have been holding over her to prevent Lucy from going to the authorities. I started a list of things we had to do that, in just minutes, was discouragingly long.

My phone buzzed. Someone must have had clout at the other end.

"Forrest, this is Allan, Allan Resnik from the DA's

office. You got a minute?"

I was glad that Vicky was staying away from this. She and I would have been in communication by now had she not known that I was fighting for the future of a dear friend. She wasn't giving anything away. Her deputy DA, Resnik, was first-class.

"Sure thing, Allan. What's on your mind?" As if I didn't know.

"That's quite a document you threw at us. I finished reading it last night. We're going to need time to go over this. You know that."

"Yes," I said. "So are we. The first time I knew of it was Tuesday. I filed a motion to continue. You have no objections, I presume?"

"Objections? I insist on it. We'll need another month."

"We'd like more if we can get it," I said. "There's a lot more than the diary to look into. Don't suppose you know who our judge is?"

"As a matter of fact," Resnik replied, "I do. It's Hannah Loewenstein."

"Hannah who?"

"Exactly. She was elected not that long ago. Comes to us from New York. She's as unknown to us as she is to you. I wish it were otherwise. Thanks, by the way, for the note about the girl. Two months pregnant? Is that what you said?"

"That's right, according to the pediatrician who examined her."

"What kind of a continuance are you looking for?"

"Two months or three," I said.

I could hear the wheels turning in Resnik's head. Two months along plus two or three months more. The girl's showing and the defense gets sympathy from the jury.

"Seems a little long. Another month, six weeks, maybe. That ought to do."

"Well, I guess we'll learn something about our new judge, won't we."

"That we will," Resnik said, "that we will. By the way, the defendant mentions pictures her husband had. You wouldn't be keeping those from us now, would you?"

"I have no more knowledge than you about those pictures. But be assured, Allan. If we happen to come upon them, you'll be the first to get a copy. We believe in discovery around here. I must admit, it's nice not to have to be on the begging side for once. Speaking of discovery, I don't think we've heard a thing from you."

After a short dry laugh, Resnik said, "I wouldn't get excited if I were you. As I'm sure you know, there's not a whole lot to divulge."

Laughing too, I said, "Allan, you sound to me like a stand-up kind of guy. But you know something? That's what the people at the DA's office always say. 'You've seen just about everything we've got.'"

"I suppose," Resnik replied. "We'll be in touch." A euphemistic admonition to defense attorneys to stand by for offers we'd be foolish to refuse. Lucy's diary must have stirred up things a little in Vicky's office.

I was going to have to skip lunch and hope I'd find my client home. For all I knew, there was a warrant out for those pictures and anything in the Jackson home that could be used as evidence in the People's case. There was little time to lose.

I called Bree to put off lunch. She countered with an offer to come with me and get a bite to eat afterward. Just as well. It was time she met our client anyway. Next, I called Lucy.

"No, Forrest, no one's asked me about those pictures. To tell you the truth, I have no idea where they are and I'd be just as happy if it stayed that way."

Was Lily still with her? She was. Would it be okay if my colleague, Bree, and I came over for a little while? Sure. She'd like the company.

"What else," Bree asked as I drove, "aside from the photos she talks about, can we get our hands on to demonstrate that Lucy didn't think she had a choice?"

Sighing, I replied, "I'm hoping those pictures exist, that they're as compromising as Lucy said and, more important at this point, that they're locatable."

"Assuming they're what you want and we can find them, they won't be enough, will they?"

I shook my head. "Not on their own, no. We're going to need those separation papers that Pete threatened her with and, much as I hate to do it—"

"You're going to put Mia on the stand. Can we afford to do that? They'll tear her to pieces there."

"Not necessarily, no," I replied. "Judges, at least most I've known, go out of their way to protect young minors in the witness box. Our problem is Mia's reliability. With those three things and assuming we can get at least part of Lucy's diary into evidence, we stand a chance."

"What about her friends?" Bree inquired. "Can't they help us?"

"I don't know, I really don't. It depends who they are, how close to Lucy they were and if she confided in them. From what I saw in the diary, we shouldn't expect much in that department. If Lucy's account is accurate, she had little contact with anyone during the last two years."

Bree nodded. "Yes. That's what I recall as well." Nervously twisting her fingers together in her lap, in a shuddering voice, she added, "God! What must those photos show? I'm not surprised she doesn't want anyone to see them."

"No. Nor am I. Whether she likes it or not, we've got to get our hands on them before the DA does. They get them first, it's anybody's guess when a copy of them will show up on our desks. We need those photographs."

Nothing like her old self, but Lucy did look remarkably improved, groomed as I remembered her and nicely dressed. She'd also taken some trouble with her hair. The strands of gray I noticed when I saw her last were gone. She was still gaunt, but in immensely better shape. Lily, who I'd never seen without a smile, greeted us.

I introduced Bree and watched with amusement as she and Lucy sized each other up. Something subliminal passed between them, I was sure, but I didn't have the foggiest idea what.

Within minutes, Lily had coffee and biscuits on the table.

After obligatory small talk, I said, "Lucy, your diary has been a gold mine for us. It'll be the foundation for our defense."

Nodding and smiling at me, she said, "I'm glad it'll be of use to someone. I never thought anyone would ever read it."

At that point, Bree, pencil in hand, broke in. "You mention several people in your diary who might be able to help us. Their names are Jacqueline Parks, Susan Carpenter and Kate Barns."

Lucy nodded.

"We'd like to get in touch with them if it's okay."

"It's okay with me, I guess, but I doubt they can tell you much."

"Do you have their phone numbers by any chance?"

"For Jackie and Sue, I do, but not for Kate. I haven't seen her for a long time. If she's still married to the guy, you should be able to find her number in the phonebook under Francis Barns. Otherwise, I don't have a clue where Kate is. I'll get Sue and Jackie's numbers for you though."

In a couple of minutes she was back, handing a note to Bree. I continued.

"We're going to shoot for an acquittal. It's no sure thing, but feasible, we think, provided we can pull together sufficient evidence to back you up."

Lucy sat unmoving, her smile fixed in place, apprehension in her light blue eyes. She knew why we were there.

"What we have to establish for the jury, Lucy, is

that you truly believed you had no choice but to kill your husband to protect your child. This will be very difficult for us to do since, in the jurors' minds, you did have choices that didn't involve violence. We have to show that Pete had manipulated you in such a way as to convince you that none of the normal choices we would have would work. If we can't show this, you will very probably be convicted of unjustifiable homicide. Do you understand so far?"

She nodded, her smile gone.

"We need to locate two things with your help before the authorities obtain a warrant to search this house. I doubt very much they'll do this, but they may try. The first thing we need are those photographs you refer to in your diary. Do you have any idea where they are?"

Lucy shook her head, but otherwise made no response.

"Lucy, please. I understand from what you said why you don't want anyone to see those. I can't blame you. No one would. The thing is, they're vital in our case. I want you acquitted, Lucy, not just because you're my friend, but because Bree and I here genuinely believe you didn't have a choice. We also want you freed so that you can help a young girl and an older boy who desperately need you. We have a shot at acquittal, but only just. There's no chance we can succeed in keeping you from prison unless we have hard evidence that confirms what you claim in your diary. Please don't resist us, Lucy. We need your help."

For at least five minutes, there was total silence in the room. Lucy had a far-off look. Otherwise, she didn't move. Lily was upset for her friend, wanting to intercede but, mercifully, she didn't talk. Bree, as usual, appeared calm, though I could tell from the slight movements of her hands that she was as tense as I. Finally, Lucy's choked voice broke the silence. We had to listen carefully to hear.

"Forrest, Bree, you have no idea what you're asking for. You already know since you've read my diary that, when I was in college, I was a bit wild you might say. Sexually, I did a lot of things that some people might not approve of. That's probably why Pete thought I was a good person to drug to get to do things I'd never ever do otherwise, not ever. I still don't understand why he did those things to me. We were so much in love and about to be married and have a baby. Why would anyone do such a thing, tell me?"

We waited until she went on.

"To celebrate me getting my BA, he took me to Baja for a weekend party he said I'd love. I don't need to say more about that. It's in the diary. There were professional porn people there, I'm sure of it. They had to be. They drugged me, that much I know. I was barely conscious, but that's all. They did things to me and... and they made me do awful things, things I can't bear to think about. When I saw those old photographs, I nearly died."

Now, her voice just above a whisper, Lucy added, "you're asking me to show the world what I did. Drugged, yes, but I still did them. Would a girl who wasn't so free with her body as I was have done those things? Not unless she was completely out, she wouldn't. And if she was completely out, the pictures would have been no good and wouldn't have meant a thing."

Now louder, she concluded, "So, those pictures are not really of me and yet they are, and you want me to find them for you. I couldn't show my face anywhere if I did that, not here, not anywhere. I tell you... It would be better if I was dead." Lucy buried her face in her hands and wept.

I looked at Bree and she back at me. We needed those photographs from someone who declared she'd prefer to die were she forced to show them. Unexpectedly, utterly devastated, Lucy stood and faced us.

"I couldn't bring myself to write it down in the diary, I was so ashamed. In one of the photographs you want me to find for you, I'm on all fours and, and, a dog, a dog... Is that what you want to see, my children to see, the whole world to see? Is that what you're asking me?"

Lily looked horror-stricken and Bree was white. Shocking though the pictures Pete had kept must be, what troubled me at that moment was the anguish on Lucy's face. As I cast about in my mind for a way to proceed without the photographs, Lucy turned, as ravaged by despair as I'd ever seen her, and pointed to the hall.

Sounding half strangled, she said, "If the pictures are anywhere in this house, they'll be in Pete's locked desk drawers in his study. He forbade me to ever touch them. You'll need tools from the garage to break them open. It's strong wood. The door's on the right. Now, if you don't mind, I'm going into my bedroom to lie down. Let me know when you're done."

In seconds, she and Lily had left the room. Bree still looked stressed and shaken.

"Stay here," I said. "I can find my way around. I know where the tools are and where Pete's desk is. If the stuff is here, it shouldn't take me very long."

Bree nodded.

I collected a hammer, two chisels and a combination screwdriver, went back in the house and got to work.

Only one of the drawers was locked. Lucy was right. The desk was made of sturdy stuff. I made a real mess of things, but within twenty minutes or so, I had the front panel off the drawer and several embedded splinters and a nasty gash on the side of my right hand.

I found a dozen large, full file folders and two manila envelopes. The first turned out to be an obviously amateur attempt at separation papers. I had to smile at the phraseology and choice of words. Had Lucy been given the chance to scrutinize those papers, she would have recognized them for what they were.

The contents of the second envelope made me feel nauseous. If anything, the images were worse than anything I'd conceived. There were six photos in all with some deterioration due to age, but Lucy, just as I remembered her back then, was unquestionably in all of them. The last in the group was the picture that she feared, so grotesque and vile that I couldn't bear to look at it again.

Curiously, on the back of each was a penciled drawing of Lucy's face, quite good, actually. Since her hairstyle was the same in all of the sketches, it appeared they'd been drawn at the same time.

Any two of those photographs would have sufficed for Pete. The first five went back into the manila envelope and the sixth into my back pocket. Henceforth, as far as I or anyone else was concerned, I'd never seen it. I had no matches and doubted that I'd find any in the house since no one there smoked. I'd burn it at the office or as soon as I got home and flush the ashes down the toilet. Knowingly destroying evidence? Unquestionably, but I wasn't going to lose a second's sleep.

We had everything we'd come for. Pete had unknowingly given us a gift by placing his scrawled signature at the end of each section of the phony separation papers. Bree saw the two envelopes in my hand. I simply nodded. Lucy with faithful Lily at her side came into the living room as I walked in. She glanced down at the envelopes in my left hand then up at me.

Lily exclaimed, rushing forward, "Mr. Spencer, your hand bleeding."

And so it was, more freely than I thought. Lily was back in seconds to dress my wound and to attempt to remove the blood stains from the rug.

"So," Lucy said in a flat voice, "you found them, I see. Congratulations. Now the world will know who Lucy Jackson is."

"Lucy," I said, deliberately hesitating, "I hate to ask you this, but we need corroboration from you that these photographs that I found in Pete's desk are the ones you refer to in the diary. I'm sorry to ask you this, but could you please take a look at them so we know for sure."

Resignation and despair etched on her face, holding

out her right hand, Lucy said, "Give them here."

I handed her the envelope. She took out the photos and examined them, one by one. Looking more and more puzzled, she flipped through them at least three times. Then she looked up at me.

"I'm not sure all the photographs are here. It seems to me, one or two are missing."

'No, Lucy, love,' I thought, 'I'm not about to take away that trace of hope I see forming on your face.'

"If Pete had more, I couldn't find them, and believe me, I looked. What you've got in your hands is all there is in that envelope."

The relief on Lucy's face was plain to see. "These pictures are bad enough, but is this everything people will have to see? You're sure there's nothing else?"

"Tell you what, Lucy," I said. "If you find more pictures you don't like—you didn't hear this from me, okay—just burn 'em up. How's that?"

There was spontaneity left in my friend. For a moment, I was sure she was going to grab me. Instead she handed me the envelope. Then her apprehensive look was back. Pointing to the other envelope in my hand, she demanded, "What's in that? Forrest, let me see what you've got in there."

Smiling, I handed it to her.

"The separation papers. That's what these are, aren't they?"

"That's what Pete intended you to think, anyway," I said. "They're amateurish, but the document that Pete signed a half dozen times corroborates your claim in your diary, which is what we're looking for. All in all, it's been a good day for us. I'm sorry these aren't beauty pictures I've got here, but they're going to help us, believe me. By the way, do you have any idea about how those sketches of you got on the back of the photos?"

Lucy tossed her head in disgust. "What," she said, "you haven't seen those before? They were Pete's calling cards, he used to say, his signature or whatever. Dumb like just about everything else he did."

"Okay, thanks. No, I've never seen them. Didn't know he was some kind of artist. Hang in there, Lucy girl. We're making progress."

Tears came into Lucy's eyes. "Lucy girl, that's what you used to call me, remember?" she said as she came toward me. A second later, her arms were tight around my neck and she was hugging me. I had a feeling I'd have been there for a while longer if it hadn't been for Bree.

The lady in question didn't say very much as we started back. Her eyes, however, were on me. Out of the blue, she queried, "So what did you do with the other photograph?"

"Other photograph?"

She didn't pursue the point. I would have told her were it not for my desire not to involve her with tampered evidence. She understood. I had a feeling that if I took my eyes off the road and looked at her, I'd see those golden specks again.

"That woman's three quarters in love with you. You're aware of that, aren't you?"

"Come on, Bree. She's going through a crisis, and she hasn't had anybody on her team for far too long. Not surprising she'd latch on for a little while."

"Hmmm." Bree's polite way of saying, 'Nonsense.' "Latch on for a little while? You're not very wise when it comes to women, are you. I saw the way she looked at you. Latch on is exactly what she'll do if you let her."

Keeping my eyes on traffic that was heavier than it should have been at that hour, I responded, "What is it, I wonder, that women have that we men don't that enables them to read people's minds. That's an ability I'd like to have."

Bree made another noise. "That's interesting, actually. Some men I know would have immediately spotted Lucy's desire for you. Then there are others who seem oblivious to women's interest in them. Now why do you suppose that is?"

"Your department, Dr. Dixon, not mine. Besides, I think women see a lot of things that aren't really there."

Another Brianna noise, a little more pronounced this time.

It was Friday morning, the end of a long week. Normally, I'd be looking forward to a couple of days with the twins. Not this time. My daughter would be on a plane for the first time in her life and my son would be at his camp. In fact, with both gone and I alone in the house, I'd be impatient to see Monday morning come.

Punctual as usual, taps I'd come to know so well at my office door came right at 9 a.m. Sara started doodling as soon as she sat down across from me. She looked frustrated as she always did when she had little to report.

"Forrest, it's as you said. I couldn't find one instance where psychological abuse was part of the defense strategy in a murder trial, not here in California, not anywhere."

"That's quite alright, Sara. I needed to check it out, just the same. At least you didn't spend your weekend on it this time as you did with another project I gave you not that long ago."

"No, no, not this time. Four hours and I gave up. I had some work to do for Garrett, anyway, so it was okay."

Curious, I asked, "Do you ever do any work for Bree?"

Sara's face took on an odd expression as she shook her head. "No, actually I don't. She never asks me."

I thought it best that I leave that one alone.

As Sara was getting up to go, she said, "I imagine you're happy to have your children back. They were gone all last month, weren't they."

"A damn long month, I have to say. And, yes, I'm delighted to have them back, only to give them up again this weekend. Trina's off to Georgia to visit Anna Henderson. Remember her? And Andy's off to a summer baseball camp. At least it's only a week this time."

Tossing her head in that way of hers, Sara wished me a good weekend as she went out the door.

"Daddy," Andy asked as we were finishing up our spaghetti and meatball dinner I'd had just time enough to prepare, "what airplane do I get to go to my baseball camp tomorrow? It'll be a big jet, right?"

Trina's mouth was opening for a knockdown shot when I grabbed her shoulder.

"Hey, champ, there are no planes from here. Thousand Oaks is way too close, only about an hour or so away. I'll drive you. We drop Trina at the airport and watch her plane take off, then we're on to your baseball camp, okay?"

Andy looked a bit crestfallen, but not for long. He was too excited. "When will I get to fly, Daddy, when? I've never been in a plane before. Not fair that Trina gets to go."

Winking at my daughter, I turned back to Andy and suggested, "Well, tell you what. She doesn't have to take the plane. We'll drive her to Georgia, the three of us. It'll take us almost the whole week to get there and back, but you might like the trip. We can do that, but you'd miss nearly all of your camp. You'd only get about a day or two in, I think. We can do that if you want us to."

Trina was doing her best not to laugh. She snatched up her napkin, covered her face and coughed. Meanwhile, Andy's mental computations were playing across his face.

"Nah, that's okay. She can take her old plane. Who cares. Can't miss any of my camp."

"Okay, that's fine. I'll drive you there and back. It's four o'clock in the morning we're getting up. Shouldn't be much traffic at that hour. Trina's plane to Atlanta leaves at seven forty-five a.m. and we've gotta be there an hour before. If you guys are done, I want to go through your suitcases once more."

Predictably, Trina had twice as much as she needed

and Andy didn't have half enough. The twins were so excited about their coming week that I was afraid they wouldn't sleep. I had to restrain myself from reaching out to hug them as I went through their bags. They couldn't wait to go while I, already, couldn't wait until they got back.

I needn't have worried about my son. Halfway through telling him another made-up story, he was fast asleep. I went into Trina's room to see that she hadn't yet gone to bed.

"Hey, love, four o'clock comes early. It's time to get to sleep. I want to go over the arrangements with you one more time, okay?"

Indulging me, she nodded.

"I know I've told you these things already, but let's go over them one more time. It's your first big trip alone, you know, okay?"

Smiling, Trina said, "And my daddy worries about me, doesn't he."

"He does, and do you know why?"

"Because he loves me almost as much as I love him, that's why."

Now it was my turn to cough, but it sounded like a croak because of the big lump in my throat. What kind of a wuss had I become, anyway.

My daughter, who'd been tuned into me since she was two, wasn't fooled for a second. She slid closer to me, put her head against my shoulder and said, "Okay, Daddy. What do I have to know?"

Pulling her even closer, I said, "Sweetheart, you do know how to make me laugh. Now, the first thing to remember is to call me. It doesn't have to be absolutely every night but—"

"I'll phone every day," Trina said. "What else?"

"LAX is a huge airport with people running around everywhere. You've gotta hang onto me until we put you on your plane, okay? The Delta Air Lines people will put a bracelet on you so everybody knows to keep an eye on you. We'll give your suitcase to the airlines people. You can pick it up again when you're with the Hendersons. They'll know what to do. We'll stay with you until we watch you get on your plane and we see it take off. Okay so far?"

Trina wiggled in confirmation.

"You'll be able to buy lunch and you'll have lots of things to drink. When you get to Atlanta—that'll take about five hours—the airlines people will escort you off the plane and take you to a special lounge called the Sky Zone where you wait for your next flight. Don't forget to change your watch. It's three hours later there."

"I know, Daddy. Anna told me."

"There'll probably be other children there, at the lounge, I mean. You've got about an hour or so to wait for your next plane to Savannah where Norm and Lena and Anna will be waiting for you. The Delta attendants will help you off the plane again and take you to where the Hendersons will be. Now, honey, I know I've told you this before, but—"

"I'm supposed to call you as soon as I'm with Norm and Lena, right?" came Trina's muffled voice.

I was opposed to brain-numbing electronic gadgets that most of my children's peers took for granted. Even so, I would have bought a cell phone for Trina had it not been for Andy's constantly hounding me for one. He'd spend half his life on the damn thing and get nothing important done. Trina had wanted one, but I'd had to tell her no.

"Last thing. When you see the Hendersons, give them the envelope that I'll give you tomorrow at the airport. This is important. It has the letter from your mommy that says it's okay by her that you leave the state. You mustn't lose it, understand?"

Again, the wiggle.

"I'm going to miss my girl. You know that, don't you."

"Of course I do, Daddy, course I do. You won't miss me nearly as much as I missed you though when I was with Mommy in L.A. That was way too long, Daddy. I don't want to do that anymore."

"That's a long time away, so let's not worry about that now."

I felt Trina snuggling closer, about ready to go to sleep.

There it was again in my mind's eye, that soft line between a loving father's care and his emotional dependency upon his children. I knew I stepped over that line sometimes.

Transgression was made the easier by my daughter's unerring sensitivity to me. Since Claire left, I'd not always managed to hide my loneliness from her. Unexpectedly, she'd be at my side and giving me a quick hug before moving on, those hugs coming inexplicably when I needed them the most.

I wanted to remain there and soak her up before she left, but my baby needed to get to sleep. A quick peck on her cheek and I was up. Like her sibling, she was beneath her covers and asleep before I was out the door.

We must have checked every document three times before we bundled into my little car. I'd never seen either of my children this awake at four forty-five a.m. While Andy went on endlessly about his camp and what he'd be doing there, Trina talked about how eager she was to be with Anna and about how awesome her friend was. I doubted that either cared if anyone was listening.

We were at LAX an hour and a quarter early. Andy would have darted off and gotten thoroughly lost among the throngs had I not kept firm hold of him. My daughter, on the cusp of young womanhood, walked sedately beside me as though she flew in airplanes every day. The sparkle in her eyes gave her away.

Her suitcase checked, her bracelet on and her boarding passes in her pocket, we headed for security. Since we'd been given passes, there shouldn't be any problem letting Andy and me through. There weren't. We then went up to another level and began making our way toward Delta's Atlanta gate.

"Why can't we get on one of those walky things?" Andy asked. "They're awesome."

"Because there aren't any up here, dummy," Trina said.

"Come on guys, it's not far from here." Actually, it was, a good half hour's walk. Andy complained every step of the way.

We were at Trina's gate and they were boarding. She beamed when she heard, "Ah, Miss Spencer, here you are. It's Trina, right? Ready to come on board? Jen's waiting to accompany you."

Trina nodded and turned toward me. She took a long look, then reached up to me as I bent down. She kissed me swiftly on the cheek and hugged me. Though she was as excited as I'd ever seen her, she had enough time to whisper, "It's only a week, that's all, and I'll be back. I love you, Daddy. Bye."

Jen had retrieved Trina's bag from the floor and they went down the ramp.

Was I so transparent to that little girl who wasn't so little anymore? Forcing down the lump in my throat that shouldn't have been there, I turned to Andy, who, of course, was nowhere in sight. Before I could hunt him down, a Latina passenger who was boarding stepped momentarily to the side.

In a slightly accented voice, she said, "When I saw the way your child looked at you, it made me want to cry. How wonderful it would be if all parents and children were like that. I have three daughters, and my husband hardly speaks to them." Smiling warmly, she added as she rejoined her queue, "Thank you for letting me see that. Your little boy by the way's over there, trying to get candy out of a machine."

I turned and saw him. When I turned back to thank the lady for her warm words, she was twenty yards away. So maybe that lump that I could still feel wasn't so inappropriate after all. Before Andy could entirely disappear, I moved quickly to apprehend him.

"Alright, MVP, it's your turn."

This time, it was Andy's turn to smile. For the second year in a row, he'd been elected most valuable player on his baseball team. Andy was a first-class pitcher, when he wasn't wild, that is. Everyone had high hopes that the experts at the special camp would help him gain some control.

"You ready to hit the road?"

"Yup yup yup," Andy replied. "Let's get out of here. I like it better outside than bein' in this place."

I agreed.

An hour and a half later, we were all signed in and I'd laid down my second installment of five hundred dollars. According to everyone we talked to, we were lucky to get in. It was Josephine from the office who had told me about this place. Her son, not on Andy's team, had applied but been refused.

Andy kept just far enough away from me to stay clear of hugs. Demonstrations of affection were taboo, especially when in the vicinity of his friends. The best I got was an over-the-shoulder wave as he sped toward his cabin and some guys he knew.

I'd miss my boy, so very different though we two were. Along with baseball, he liked more and more to work with wood, something I genuinely enjoyed. Finding quality time with him was less difficult than it had been.

Chapter 13

My car felt empty as I navigated the Ventura Freeway on my way home from Andy's camp. The last thing I wanted at that moment was to go back to a quiet house. How much more agreeable it would have been to take the road to Ben and Cassie's as I so often did when the twins were gone. The camaraderie, top-notch food and Texas-style drinks were the best remedy I knew for loneliness, an affliction I'd come to know since Claire left.

I'd have to tough it out on my own this time. Ben hadn't been in the office the day before and he wasn't reachable by phone. He and Cassie had to have gone off somewhere, probably to Mexico. They'd be incommunicado until Monday.

It was 3:20 when the phone rang. I should have been buoyed up by Trina's call, but as often happened when the children were away, her voice, the little that I heard, did little to cheer me up. During our brief conversation, she chatting with her friend while she talked to me, I got one word and Anna, three. They were about to get into the Hendersons' car and head for Bimington. She'd call again just before she went to bed. Before I could tell her to phone a little earlier because of the time change, the line was dead.

I found a good-sized T-bone I didn't know I had and

a half dozen Heinekens in the fridge. The one bakeable potato I unearthed had more appendages than I liked, but it would do. I fired up the barbecue in the backyard and set to work. My spirits began to lift a little as beer after beer went down. By my fourth bottle, I had music on outside and was attempting to sing along, not something I was prone to do unless I was in the shower.

At loose ends, I spent the better part of Sunday afternoon replacing the electric starter of my barbecue. The one that came with the machine functioned for about a week. The replacement components didn't work at all. I'd read somewhere that electric igniters in barbecues fail most of the time, so I gave it up and went looking for a beer I might have missed. There were none.

I was contemplating frozen chorizo sausages for my dinner when the house phone rang. Ben and Cassie back? Inviting me to eat?

It wasn't them. It was Sara Pringle. "Forrest, how are things? Did your kids get off okay?"

Reasonable questions, uttered in a matter-of-fact tone, but I doubted there was very much anything matter-of-fact about that girl.

"Yup. Got them both off yesterday. And how are things with you?"

"Okay, I guess," she said, "but they could be better. I'm standing here at the Thai take-out place to pick up dinner for me and a friend and I get this call. She's come down sick with something, food poisoning, she thinks, and she has to bail. So, here I am, our dinners paid for and I've got no place to go. You like Thai food?"

Sara? Here? Alone with me in this house? A tease to get me fired up then pull away or was she serious? In the second it took me to respond, I concluded she'd contrived the visit once she learned from me last Friday that the twins were to be away. Though there was nothing specific that precluded seeing Sara outside work, the generation gap and the differences in our worlds made me hesitate.

My reservations were undermined by the fact that the outstandingly attractive female continued unremittingly to hit on me, to use her language. What, after all, did I have to lose by cavorting with this lovely girl—only my reputation in the office as a respectable, homeloving father who had no time for wanton flirts, and, very possibly, my ability to pursue a relationship with Bree. But the rational part of me was under siege. To start with, I was lonelier than I'd been in a long time. And, it had been far too long since I'd had a woman in my bed.

"I like Thai food very much," I replied, "and I'll be glad to have your company. Do you know where I live?"

"Of course I do. I was at one of your backyard parties a couple of years ago. Remember?"

Remember? How could I forget?

"Good. That works out then. See you in a few," Sara said.

'Alright, Sara girl,' I mused as I went to set the table on the patio. 'You've been coming onto me non-stop, so if you want to play, you've chosen the right day. I may not be up to the studs you're used to, but, I've got fifteen months of abstinence queued up.'

No law office dress tonight. Sara grinned as she saw me take her in. A full head of glossy brown hair, an attractive soft-featured face with sparkling dark brown eyes and pert breasts with no bra that called out to be caressed.

My gaze dropped to a flat stomach and long narrow waist below which were jeans that looked sewed on. My thoughts had leaped far ahead by the time my eyes reached two small sandaled feet. Given her casual dress, I wondered why the fancy purse that seemed oversized.

As I relieved her of two big bags of food, Sara grinned and reached out to give me a little shove. "Tadah!" she said. "I've finally managed to get him to look at me the way I want. You should see your face! We stand around much more like this and the agenda for the evening might have to change a little. I'm glad you like what you see, but I hate to tell you, I'm absolutely starved." Outrageous tease.

I tore my eyes away and, handing back the bags and pointing to the sliding doors to the patio, I said, "The table's set out there. Why don't you spread this scrumptious-smelling food around and I'll get drinks. Wine do for a start?"

"Whatever the intrepid Mr. Spencer's having, I'll have, too."

"Good. I've got a Montrachet that should go well with this."

Outside, Sara said, "I probably brought too much, but, let's see. Here's Pad Kee Mao, noodles stir-fried with chili, herbs and pork. Hope that's okay with you. What else do we have here? Gaeng Keow Wan, that's green curry with chicken, vegetables and tofu. Oh wow, I'm sorry. This is way too much. I got carried away, didn't I. There's Som Tam, green papaya salad if you like that stuff. I love Thai food. Oh no! There's another carton here. Hope you're hungry. This is Lad Na. I think this is stir-fried soft noodles with mixed vegetables and beef."

Sara looked inquiringly up at me. She'd bought far more than we two could eat. I wondered how she knew so precisely what was in each carton until I saw labels on the lids.

"I'm glad you like cuisine like this," I commented. "I know somebody who's going to be eating a lot of it this week."

Sara smiled. "Better more than not enough, I say."

My cautious nature already giving way, I said, "What's that, you don't believe in moderation?"

Grinning, she said, "Not me. You don't either, right? You wouldn't disappoint a girl?"

Shaking my head and smiling, I said, "If what I'm feeling at the moment's any indication, I wouldn't worry too much about moderation on my part if I were you."

Our badinage went on like this for a little while.

Sara was a bit of a gourmand. If she was as voracious in other things as she was with food, I had an exhilarating evening to look forward to. For the present, though, I needed to focus less on my appetizing guest. We had culinary matters to attend to, good wine to drink and conversation to generate that, hopefully, would distract me for a while.

I cleared my throat, looking down at my crowded plate of food, and said, "You know, I assume, how pleased I was to hear that you'd be with us for another year."

With a mouthful of noodles, all she could do was nod.

"You have several offers for law school, don't you?"

"Just two," she responded as she continued to take in food.

"So, which school will you be going to?"

"Stanford. They're good in corporate, and that's what I'll be doing."

"So you're getting out of criminal law, then."

She stopped eating and looked up. "I've never been in criminal law, actually. Frankly, I don't know how you and Garrett put up with it," a comment I'd heard so many times from Claire. "I'll never be a litigator, Forrest. I'm a researcher. You know that. Corporate has a lot more to offer me than criminal law does."

"Yes," I conceded, "I can see your point. I guess you know how much I'm going to miss you when you leave. You're the best legal researcher I've ever had."

Giggling, she said, "How would you know?"

"How would I know what?"

Her dark brown eyes alight, she said, "Well, you've never really had me, have you." A second later, she burst out laughing. "Poor Forrest. You should see his face. He doesn't know what to say. Lighten up! You're with me, Sara, not with Cheryl Bloomfield."

The ludicrous image of our office Nazi there in place of the tantalizing young woman across from me made me laugh so hard, I nearly choked.

Still giggling, Sara said, "She is a piece of work, isn't she. Wherever did you find her?"

Sputtering, I replied, "Don't ask. Let's talk about more pleasant things."

"About pleasant things, let's see." As her glance dropped to her empty glass, I reached again for our second bottle that had more ice water dripping from it than wine inside.

"Just enough for you. I've had all I want."

She didn't quibble. "I love this Cabernet," she said.

I couldn't help it. "Montrachet."

"Cabernet, Montrachet, who cares. It's good. Now where were we? Something pleasant, isn't that what you said?"

I wanted to say pleasantness was Sara Pringle in my house, but I desisted. It seemed trite. "Something pleasant, yes. I'll listen to anything you have to say."

Another grin. "Ah ha. You're pretty sure of yourself, aren't you. Well, let me see." Trying to look serious but not managing very well, Sara asked, "Why do you think I'm here?"

Before I could respond, her hand came swiftly across our little table to cover my mouth.

"No, don't answer, please," she said, laughing. "There's that lawyer look again. It's simple, really. I came to have fun, to do what I've wanted to do for a long time. I came to have sex with you." She paused, holding my gaze, then laughed again. "God, where's my camera! The look on your face! It's priceless. You don't know how to take me, do you. Are you put off by how direct I am?"

Putting her elbows on the table and regarding me, a rather serious expression on her face, Sara said, "I'm no nympho, Forrest, so why do I flirt with you all the time and why am I here right now? Would you like to know?"

"Now that you mention it," I said.

"Well, I'll tell you. You don't have one of those big male egos I can't stand and I prefer men who are more mature. The biggest reason, though, is that I like you. I feel drawn to you, so there. Will that explanation work?"

"Very nicely, thank you." I felt pompous having answered as I had, but I felt good, too. I wanted rather urgently for our meal to end so that I could get close to her. It was the presence of this extraordinary girl and the wine I'd taken in that made me blurt out what I did.

"It's not your directness that puts me off, Sara Pringle. It's that I can't carry you upstairs this minute and get those clothes off of you."

She smiled, looking animated, and clapped two times. "Whoa, not so fast. Something we've gotta do first, okay? You don't have a pen or pencil on you, do you?"

Now what was the minx up to? I happened to have one of the twin's ballpoints in my shirt pocket. She took her paper napkin, unfolded it and turned it over and began to write in letters big enough that I could see, upside down but readable:

Sara's rules
1. If there's no serious make-out time, no sex.
2. If Sara's not excited after making out, no sex.
3. Sara says where, when and how.
4. Sara's the one to finish first.
5. Sara's partner can swallow if he wants to but Sara won't.
6. No artificial barriers during sex.
7. If Sara's flying, her partner can do anything he wants if it feels good to her as long as it doesn't involve drugs, it doesn't hurt and it doesn't involve BDSM.

I had a smile that wouldn't come off my face when she finished writing. It was as well Sara couldn't see what was going on below my waist.

"You have a problem with any of these?" she asked.

"I'll happily be your slave," I said.

She lowered her voice to a whisper and added, "If you're a nibbler—and I like that very much, just so you know—don't bite too hard. I'm kinda fragile."

Shaking her head, she continued, “No, in case you’re wondering, I don’t talk about my little rules with the guys I go out with. Most of them don’t want me to have control.” Her serious expression back again and shaking her head once more, she said, “Actually, Forrest, that’s not the real problem. Can you be patient a little longer while I say something?” She didn’t wait for confirmation. “You probably think I go out with guys a lot, don’t you.”

I said I did.

“You’re wrong, you know. I’d like to, but I don’t. It’s not that I can’t find guys to go out with. Not that. It’s that very few satisfy a special need I have.”

The worry on my face made Sara laugh. “No, no, not that. Don’t get anxious before we start. It’s not that at all. I’ll show you rather than trying to explain. To tell you the truth, most of the time when I go out, I go out with girls.”

Again, my expression must have given away my thoughts. “Me, bi? No way. I’m not into girls. It’s just easier to relate, that’s all. You’ll understand, I promise you. One more thing before we go in, okay? I didn’t tell you the whole truth when I was talking about why I’m here. I’ve been pretty sure for quite a while that you’re one of the few men I’ve met who will know what to do with me. Maybe I’m wrong, but I don’t think so. Whatever you do, don’t worry about what I’m telling you. I’m right. I’m sure I am. It’ll be good, you’ll see.”

Aroused though I was, I felt a tad of apprehension. Know what to do with her? What was she trying to tell me?

Fortunately, cleaning up took only minutes. I was just cognizant enough to put the leftovers in a bag Sara could take home.

Finished with food things, we headed for the living room, I in a state I hadn’t been in for way too long. I asked her if she wanted an after-dinner drink. Instead of answering, she asked for directions to the upstairs bathroom.

While she was gone, I pulled out a bottle of my favorite port rather than going for the scotch. I was looking for a glass in the liquor cabinet when I heard her come back down.

She was an apparition. From the contents of her large black bag, Sara had transformed herself from a casually dressed attractive young woman into a love goddess, quintessentially feminine and breathtaking. In place of her red sleeveless top and sewn-on jeans was a short pale blue negligee. She'd brushed her glossy hair that touched her shoulders. Her feet were bare. Incongruously, she held a bottle in her left hand.

The girl's smile and the loose-fitting garment she had on, diaphanous enough to show there was nothing underneath, made me feel giddy. She made her way noiselessly to the loveseat where I was. She was dream-like, overwhelmingly arousing.

"That's port in your hand, isn't it? Do you like Bailey's Irish Cream?"

I didn't, but I wasn't about to say. I was ready to drink whatever this angel gave me. "Do we need glasses?"

"Actually, we don't," she said. "What we need is for Forrest to get into something loose and comfortable. Can he arrange that while I wait?"

The only thing that qualified was a pair of boxers that Claire had bought for me years ago when I was a bit overweight. I went upstairs to change.

Meanwhile, my enterprising guest had opened up the stereo and found a station with Brazilian jazz. She was seated and waiting demurely for me when I returned. She grinned, then broke out laughing when she saw what I'd put on.

"I like it, I like it," she chirped as I sat back down. "Aren't those Christmas designs I see?"

I wanted to tell her that it wasn't I who chose them when they were on sale, but I was too distracted by her to bother. I hadn't put on a shirt.

"You don't like Irish Cream, why, cuz it's too sweet? Let me try to change your mind."

She removed the top, drank a bit from her bottle and turned to me. Using her finger, she spread some of the liquid over her lower lip, and then on mine, too. Her smile told me what she wanted.

A minute later, I said, "I'd drink a pint of that stuff delivered to me like that."

"Good. Now, give some back to me."

We continued exchanging liquor and luscious kisses for a minute or two more, then put the bottle down.

Sara's nipples, hitherto just perceptible, were reaching out. I was eager to oblige. With a heated girl in my arms and we exploring each other's mouths, my erection was increasingly difficult to ignore. Tumescence is not best hidden by boxer shorts, but Sara seemed not to notice. When I attempted to slide my hand beneath the gauzy material she had on, she gently pulled my hand away.

"We haven't finished making out," she whispered. "Remember rule number two?"

Was that the one about whether or not she'd become aroused? I could tell by the recent change in Sara's fragrance that that wasn't going to be a problem, but I let her take the lead.

Predictably, our kisses became more demanding as did our hands. Still, no touching below the waist.

Sara was now more languorous than before, her eyes slightly glazed and her breaths more shallow. She disengaged and went back upstairs. I was more than ready to swoop her up when, a moment later, she reappeared with a leather pouch in her hand.

Her face slightly flushed, she said, "I've got some pot, some real good stuff. I'm going to have a hit or two if you don't mind."

I didn't since I assumed this would shorten what she kept referring to as our make-out time. When she passed her clip to me, I declined, telling her that the smoke irritated my throat and made me cough. When she smiled and brought her paraphernalia to the loveseat and sat down close to me, it was clear what she had in mind. I didn't want to break the mood.

Couldn't I take in her breaths while kissing her, then exhale quickly without her knowing? I hoped so. I remembered clearly the last time I'd done this. It was with Lucy Evans, decades ago. I didn't know, then, the strong effect the pot would have on me, taken in through Lucy's mouth. Forewarned, forearmed.

With Sara, the experience was sensual and pleasant.

Had I inadvertently taken in the stuff? It seemed so.

Sara put her accoutrements away and, rather than sitting down beside me, she made my temperature and blood pressure go shooting up by pulling up her negligee, spreading her bare legs a little and coming to sit on my lap, facing me. I needn't describe the condition I was in. Her nipples were hard and she was restive. Was this what Sara called making out? Blessedly, that unendurable situation for me was brief. She put her arms around my neck and pulled herself to me, pressing her wet mouth to mine and rubbing herself against me.

After several kisses, hungrier and more frantic than before, Sara whispered rather shakily, "Do you remember rule number two? Don't you think it's time to check?"

What the hell was rule two about? My upper brain was out of order.

"Is Sara ready, do you think?"

That hint didn't require prompting. She was very wet.

Breathless, she said, "Forrest, *now*."

Urging I didn't need. With her arms clinging to my neck and her legs wrapped around my waist, I pressed her close and carried her, with some difficulty, up the stairs. In seconds, her negligee was on the floor as were my boxers.

My God, how best to describe that wild night? I was standing and then I wasn't, having been not so gently pushed backwards onto the bed. With no maneuvering for position by her, no finesse, Sara flew up and was astride me. In a heartbeat, I was as deep inside her as my anatomy would allow.

After an explosive breath, her teeth clenched, she commanded in halting words, "Wait... for.... me... remember?"

Had I not consumed a bottle of Montrachet, and who knew how much of that Irish Cream, I'd never have been able to obey her rule, whatever its number was.

Details here about the next few hours would be self-indulgent. More appropriate are things I could say about my exotic lover.

She was as demanding and controlling as any female I've known and, at the same time, uninhibitedly generous to me. I was gratified to see that she was not averse to breaking her own rules.

If there was a non-erogenous square inch on that girl's body, I couldn't find it. A light caress, a love bite, the feel of my mouth on her anywhere, especially at her center, would send her up, often culminating in orgasms that were as loud as they were strong. Her ability to achieve them so easily was a good thing for me, considering that my thoroughly sated and flagging member, on its own, couldn't have kept her flying for all that time. It was disconcerting that she never stopped to rest.

Sara was exhausted by the end of our lovemaking, two-thirty in the morning if I recall. She could get her skinny jeans and red top back on, but I had to help her navigate our winding stairs. I stopped briefly at the fridge to grab her bag of food, then we headed for the outdoors and her car.

We embraced for a long time without saying anything. Finally, Sara whispered, "It's a good thing, I guess, that I didn't know what I do now. Who knows how much of a pest I would have been. I was right about you, you know. You thought more about me than about yourself when we were loving. I don't get much of that." After more silence, somewhat hesitantly, she said, "You think you could put up with me again?"

I hugged her and kissed her on both cheeks. "You let me know when you've got more Thai food you want to share."

Laughing, she asked, "Only Thai?" Going on, she said, "Listen. I'm going to look pretty bleary-eyed in the morning, but I'll be there at nine."

I took her by the shoulders and gently shook her. "Orders from on high. To my knowledge, there's nothing pressing. Come in when you feel ready. Just don't forget to let Cheryl know."

In a teasing tone, Sara said, "Preferential treatment, Mr. Spencer? Better watch that. People notice."

Hugging her again—I didn't want to let her go—I said, "Thanks for the most spectacular night with a woman I've ever spent. You couldn't have chosen a better time to come."

Laughing again, Sara said, "Didn't I do that lots of times?"

After one more embrace, my research assistant who'd become my lover got into her car and drove away. As I made my way back into the house, I realized that my daughter had failed to phone to say good night. For once, that didn't bother me. The call wouldn't have come at a propitious time.

Why does *après-sex* along with lack of sleep show up sometimes on my face the morning after? I haven't noticed this with other people, but I appeared to be so afflicted, if what I saw staring back at me in the mirror and Claire's irksome pronouncements over the years meant anything. Come to think of it, Ben had made similar innuendoes a time or two.

Repellent though the thought was, if I had any and knew how to apply it, I might almost have resorted to that makeup goop women use to camouflage what they don't want us to see. I had nothing more than a scalding shower and strong black coffee to rely on.

If Sara had the sense to stay at home, I might just pass. In the office, after all, I was known as a quiet man with kids who stayed at home.

Cheryl gazed at me before handing me the envelope. "Are you feeling alright, Mr. Spencer? You look a little... tired."

I assured her and the two office paralegals pretending to be busy behind their desks that all was fine.

"I opened the envelope from the Court since there was no one's name on it. I hope that was alright."

I thought about this for a moment, then I nodded.

In my office, wishing I had Bree's couch where I could take a little nap, I looked at the note Cheryl gave me. I, as lead counsel—my full name was clearly there—was to be in Judge Loewenstein's chambers along with Deputy District Attorney Allan Resnik at ten o'clock Tuesday. That was the next day. Since we'd filed only one motion, there shouldn't be much to do unless the DA's office was going to object or submit something of their own without informing us. Nothing abnormal about that. I preferred to have Bree in on this with me as experience for her, but the order was specific.

God, how I yearned for another coffee. The two I had drunk at home were already burning holes. I kept wiping my face with my hands and yawning to clear my head. Four hours of sleep when I was twenty would have been okay for a night or two, but that was then. What I needed to wake me up was a half hour outside in our fresh sea air, but I had a lot to do, not so much that I couldn't say hello to Ben and drop in for a minute to see Bree.

No mistaking it, that scent, then her open door. The twit had come in to work after all. God help us if she looked half as bad as me. By now, three women would be hard at work in the front office, brewing up the story of the month. Ignore her? Pretend I hadn't noticed and just walk by? Hardly.

I tapped lightly twice as I usually did, walked in and took the one empty chair in the room. I'd have closed the door behind me if it had been my office, but there was no way I could get away with that where I was.

'Sara,' I almost said, 'why couldn't you have remained at home for a few hours, or, better yet, for the entire day.'

To my relief and a measure of exasperation when I saw her face, she looked gorgeous and refreshed, no sign of the wanton who, hours ago, lay tangled in my sheets.

Her eyes dancing as they sometimes did, she grinned and ventured in a concerned tone, "You don't look so good. Bad night? Couldn't sleep or something?"

My expression that mustn't have been that friendly elicited a grin. I wanted to wipe the smirk off of her pretty face. Lurking just behind that thought was the image of Sara, overflowing with desire while facing me on my lap, then attacking me in my bed.

More quietly, she said, "Me, I slept like a baby when I got to bed, into my own, I mean. Not nice of me to keep you up like that." Tossing her head in that way of hers, engulfing me in her scent as she knew it would, offhandedly, she added, "I'll just have to leave a little earlier next time."

Right. Just one more late-night party for Sara Pringle and another romp. Talk about the generation gap and the resiliency of youth. I wasn't in the girl's league. As I got up to leave, feeling frustrated, her flippancy evaporated and that soft sweet look I saw the day before was back.

She leaned forward and said just above a whisper, "I'm still dreaming about last night, you know? It was wonderful for me. I wish everybody I was with was as considerate and gentle as you and made love like that."

Settling back in her chair and putting on a look not

even the formidable Cheryl Bloomfield could reproach, Sara pointed to a file folder on her desk, then pointed to the door. Grinning, she said, "Know where this file comes from? From Brianna Dixon. She was in here just before you came. She'd like it back this morning, so get out of here, Mr. Spencer, so I can get my mind back on my work."

Two warm dark brown eyes were on me as I got up to go. There was tenderness in them that hadn't been there before. But there was also something else. Possessiveness, maybe? The coquetry was gone. Absent, too, were flirtatious gestures I'd come so well to know. She'd crossed that special bridge with me last night where she didn't need those things anymore.

On the one hand, this insatiable girl made me wary. On the other, her sweet words made me feel good and, spent though I was, they made me want her as soon as it could be arranged.

'Hazardous territory, Spencer, not a safe place for you. Get that whatever-it-is look off your face. Somebody's gonna see it, that's for sure. Keep your head on straight and keep your pants zipped up.'

"Jesus, Forrest," Ben exclaimed, "where the hell you been? You don't look so hot. You up drinkin' all night or what?"

Tired of hearing comments about my face, I shook my head and plopped down in a chair. As usual, except for his desk, the office was a mess.

"If you must know," I retorted, "I spent the weekend looking for a couple of friends of mine to have drinks and dinner with. Could I find them? No. Where'd you guys go, anyway?"

"Rosarito Beach in Baja, boyo. Fantastic place to be. Cassie and I go down there every couple months or so. She loves it. Wonders how she ever put up with all that ice and snow. Sorry we missed you. We're havin' a little do next Saturday night though if you wanta come. Steaks, drinks, the normal thing. How 'bout it?"

"Sure thing. Sounds good."

Ben had his stub of a pencil out and had it in his mouth. After another one of those protracted looks, he asked, "Anyone you'd like to bring? There'll be just the five of us unless you've got somebody to make a sixth."

No way I could invite Sara for more reasons than I could count, though the afterward would be nice, and it was a little bit too soon to invite Bree. I didn't know her well enough. She might be a vegetarian for all I knew and she might not drink. I shook my head.

"One of these days, not too long from now, I hope, I'll bring someone. For the time being, it'll just be me. What time should I be there?"

"Bout seven-thirty or eight'll be okay. Yeah. Problem with bein' single is you can't drink. No good in that. You got the kids that night?"

"No. They'll be with their mother."

"Okay then, that settles it. You drink to your heart's content and get up to one of my famous breakfasts. How's that?"

Fine, I reflected, except for that lumpy couch of his. "Good stuff, Ben. Thanks. Hello to Cassie."

Back in my office, I remembered that Trina would be with her mother on Saturday, but not Andy. He'd be coming back home from camp. I'd have to contact Lupe and get her to stay over to babysit.

My one-thirty appointment had arrived, a hand-off from my partner, Garrett, who claimed to have no openings for a month. I suspected he might have other motives if what I'd heard was true, but I owed him. I'd done the same thing to him countless times.

"There's got to be something I can do about this girl, there has to be. She's going to ruin me and my career." From Garrett's sketchy notes, the agitated man in my office did appear to have a problem. "Mr. Austin assured me you could help me."

Fine-boned and slim, dark-haired and graying at the temples, Leon Goodman looked beseechingly at me through gray eyes that wouldn't rest. His hands were in constant motion.

"I'll need a few details from you before I tell you whether or not we can help."

"Yes, of course. I'll tell you anything you want to know, anything." How often had I heard that line before.

"From what I understand, you're an instructor of mathematics at Santa Lucia City College. Is that right?"

"That's right, I am. I've taught there for eight years."

"Apart from teaching evaluations and such, have there ever been incidents of any kind that could be held against you? Any kind, Mr. Goodman?"

Vigorously shaking his head, he said, "None. Not a single one. My evaluations are excellent as well. I can show you."

"From what you told Mr. Austin, one of your female students has accused you of sexual harassment. Tell me specifically what this harassment's all about. Before you do, Mr. Goodman, understand something. Hiding details of any sort—"

"No, no, I'll tell you everything. It's simple, really. Charlene's very concerned about her grades. She wants to go on in science at a university, but her marks are still too low. She's taking extra courses in the summer to make up. She got a C on a test I gave last month and came into see me. It was an objective exam and there was nothing I could do. She was quite upset. A point or two higher and she would have had a B. Next thing I know, I'm called into the Dean's office to talk about the girl's complaint."

"What did she say you did?"

Waving his hands around and looking everywhere but at me, Goodman said, "That's just it, I'm telling you, that's just it. She said I offered to up her grade if she'd make out with me."

"If she made out with you. Where? In your office?"

Hesitating and profusely sweating, Goodman replied, "I don't know, I guess so. I don't know what she meant, I really don't. The whole thing's a lie from start to end. She wanted a better grade and she didn't get it."

"A couple more things," I said. "When students come to see teachers in their offices, are the doors left open or are they closed?"

Almost before my question was out, Goodman declared, "Oh, they're open. Absolutely. I don't know if there's a rule about it, but nobody closes them for reasons just like this."

Too late, Goodman realized what he'd said. He blinked and his face lost some of its color. I didn't need an answer, but I asked anyway.

"Was your door open when she came to see you?"

The man gulped, then said, "You know, now that you mention it, I think she closed it when she came in. She says I went to close it, but I did no such thing. I stayed in my seat."

"One last thing. Does the girl in question have a history of complaints?"

There was no immediate response, then Goodman said in a subdued voice, "The Dean says no. He says there's nothing like that in her file, not in high school either because they checked, and not at the college."

"Since there appear to be no accusations of assault, it's unlikely you'll be formally charged with anything. I'm afraid there's nothing we can do. You're going to have to battle this one out on your own with the school administration. You don't have a union or anything there at the college that might help you?"

Goodman dolefully shook his head.

"I don't know much about these things, but there are mediating services that you might look into."

The man knew as well as I that, without extenuating circumstances, a female's accusation, with or without evidence to back it up, might well carry sufficient weight to destroy a man's career. Guilty or not, I wished him luck. He needed it.

I was exhausted and tempted to leave early, but I

wanted to see Bree about the next day's hearing. My thoughts, as had been happening throughout the day, drifted back to Sara. How had I managed to keep pace with her, voracious as she was? A second go and then a third would find me lacking. Much better to leave her with the positive memory of me she had.

I'd have to struggle against my desire for her, though. The lure of vitality and youth! Who was this forty-year-old fooling? I'd never be able to keep up with that girl, who'd be a challenge for someone half my age. Our worlds were galaxies apart, the music she vibed to, to use her words, the orientation of her friends, she poised to spread her wings and fly while I, postcoitally depressed and lonesome, felt like I was out of gas.

Disgusted with the self-pitying state that I was in, I mentally shook myself as I got up from my chair. Why was I complaining? I had two children I adored, a lovely home, close friends and, hey, enough stuff left to please the most come-on female I'd ever had in my bed. Things could be worse.

Those green eyes and the brain they fed saw too much. My overactive imagination and bad mood, maybe, but wasn't that a hint of mockery on Bree's face? Waving to my corner of her couch, she said, "Somebody told me you'd gone home, sick or something."

Why couldn't women be more direct and just say what was on their mind? But then there were the Sara types.

Sighing and slouching luxuriously on Bree's couch, I inquired, "Is that one of the things in psychology they teach you guys to do?"

"To do? Do what?"

"To be oblique and make things up as you go."

She shook her head. "I did learn to do those things, you're right, but not in psychology. In law school, just like you. Glad you managed to drop in."

With more impatience in my tone than I intended, I said, "Bree, I suspect I was here a good half hour before you were, and between shuffling papers and seeing clients, I've hardly had a minute free."

Making an *O* with those sensual lips of hers and raising both hands, she replied, "Well! I guess we can't kid each other anymore." Lowering her hands and putting on a solemn face, she continued, "For whatever I did, I'm sorry." Unbelievable how chameleon-like women were. Her expression next went to ingratiation. "Is there something I can do for you?"

"Bree, would you knock it off! Okay, alright, I didn't get a lot of sleep last night. Can't understand why that's so important to everybody around here."

Her new expression now contrite, she declared in a conciliatory tone, "I'm sorry, Forrest, I really am. It happens to all of us. It's just that you looked... I don't know... different somehow, that's all."

Fine. She sees it too. Thank my stars that Sara looked alright.

"Apology accepted? Can we be friends again?"

I waved her off. "About tomorrow," I said, "we're to be in chambers at ten o'clock. You were to be in on this, but for some reason, our judge, who no one knows anything about, specified lead counsel only. That's not all that unusual, but I'd have preferred to have you there. Actually, there's not a whole lot to talk about anyway. She'll grant our motion for continuance or she won't, and I can only guess what the DA's up to. They may try to keep the diary out. That wouldn't surprise me. It's not in their interest to have it in." Bree looked disappointed. "I'm really sorry about this. I'd prefer to have you there to back me up, believe me, particularly if there's going to be a challenge about the diary."

"You'll go directly to the court house?"

"No," I said. "I tend to come in a little early these days when the children aren't around—fortunately, not a frequent thing—so I'll drop in at the office for an hour or so, then I'll go."

With a warm smile this time, Bree said, "Well, if you've got a moment before you go, drop in and we can chat."

A letter from Claire, a couple of bills I already paid and a handful of pamphlets awaited me when I got home. My ex-wife rarely wrote, preferring to text me when she had things to say. Open the note and more than likely spoil my evening that wasn't off to much of a start anyway, or have my dinner and maybe a scotch or two, then see what she had to say. Best get it over so I could get on with things.

Forrest,

No greeting anymore, just my name.

I'd appreciate it if the children could be ready on time this week. There's no need to keep me waiting in the car as you usually do. I'll be by at 9:30 this Saturday.

C

Trina would be home, but Claire had obviously forgotten that Andy's baseball camp didn't end until late Saturday afternoon. Certificates would be handed out at that time. He'd be heartbroken if I had to bring him home on Friday. There wasn't much I could do unless I called her to explain since it was her time with the twins. She might capitulate if I phoned, but our conversation would be acrimonious, no matter the outcome. I'd call—I had to—for Andy's sake. It was a lose-lose situation.

We sparred for a while until, as I expected, she gave in. She knew that if she prevailed, she'd see no smile on our son's face that weekend.

Despondent, I wondered why Claire had changed so much these last few months. If not affable, our exchanges had usually been civil when and if we had to talk. She'd become short with me, often to the point of rudeness for no reason I could surmise. I wasn't about to ask. As I was heading toward the kitchen and the fridge, the phone rang.

"Hi Daddy." Trina sounded out of breath. "Bet you

can't guess where we've just been."

I hadn't noticed the gradual change in my daughter's voice, being with her every day as I was. But on the phone, it struck me forcibly. My little girl, the child I'd adored since she was born, was emerging from her cocoon. We'd stay close, we always would, but in a different way. For her sake, I wanted to see her grow. Had I my way, I would have turned the clock's hands back three years or so when I was still her hero.

I had my suspicions about where they'd been, but I replied, "No, my love, tell me."

For the next ten minutes, I was regaled with a blow-by-blow report of the clothing stores Lena and the two girls had been to.

"It's awesome, Daddy, totally awesome. Lena bought me this gorgeous party dress that's almost identical to one she made for one of Anna's dolls. It's so cool and... I just love being here so much, Daddy, playing with Anna and all. She's got such awesome friends. Can Anna come out to visit me some time, can she?"

At last my turn to speak. "Now I guess that depends. Maybe they'd miss her like I miss you. Then what?"

"Oh, Daddy, you know what I mean."

"Of course she can come out anytime she wants. We'll just have to arrange it with Lena and Norm."

A moment or so after, one very excited eleven-year-old girl said her goodbyes and was off the phone.

Instead of taking out a T-bone to thaw, I got the blender down, got my tequila out, several dried-up-looking limes and some cubes of ice and my sea salt. Two large glasses down and the doldrums were on their way.

I met Resnik, dressed to the nines as usual, in the courthouse lobby. Not a speck of dust on him that I could see.

"This should be interesting," he said, the clack of his wingtips echoing in the almost empty hall. "According to things I hear, this lady's got ice water in her veins. Know what they call Loewenstein in New York? The fish. Don't ask me why."

"The fish," I repeated, not overly pleased by what I heard. Sobriquets like that rarely meant good things.

The judge did look somewhat stern behind her desk. Slim and fine-boned, about fifty-five, she had dyed coal black hair tied back in a bun. Beneath a high forehead, her eyes, rather closely spaced, were black as well. A slightly hooked nose sat above generous full lips. A wide jaw with a pronounced cleft chin finished off a rectangular pale face that could have been cut from marble.

There was little warmth in what I saw. Yet there was intelligence and a brightness in her eyes that suggested that her mouth, out of place with the rest, could smile. Loewenstein was corporate in appearance, dressed in a black suit with a snow white blouse. She had beautifully shaped concert pianist's hands. Lucy's six volumes lay in front of her along with two stacks of other papers. I'm not sure what I expected, but it was certainly not the soft feminine voice I heard.

"So, gentlemen, we're here to discuss several things. We might as well begin with Mr. Spencer's motion for a continuance since that seems to be the least contentious issue." Turning her face toward me, she said, "Are we absolutely certain about the date you first saw the defendant's diary?"

"Absolutely certain, Your Honor."

"Very well. Having read through these," the judge said, gesturing toward Lucy's books, "I can understand why you want more time. Mr. Resnik appears to agree on this. The problem is that you, Mr. Spencer, want three months and Mr. Resnik, only one. Tell me, please, why you need three months."

I'd get nowhere by admitting we wanted sufficient time for Mia's pregnancy to be visible when she appeared in court.

"Your Honor," I said, "since you've seen the diary, you'll appreciate how complex this case is. We intend to demonstrate that Lucy Jackson truly believed she had no recourse but to kill her husband in order to protect her daughter. We need to formulate questions for witnesses that will bring this out."

Resnik cut in. "The defense doesn't require that amount of time, Your Honor. Their list of witnesses can't be that long."

"I'm inclined to agree," Loewenstein said. Looking at me, then at Resnik, she suggested, "Two months, gentlemen. Can we agree on that?" Two months would give us just sufficient time to prepare our case, but Mia might not yet be showing. I was prepared to accept the compromise to preserve whatever points I had with our judge for the next issue that was critical for us.

"That will be acceptable to the defense."

Resnik concurred.

"There are a couple of minor matters I have to see to before I have an exact date," Loewenstein said. "My clerk will let you know. Our next problem is more difficult." She tapped each of the six bound volumes on her desk. "Mr. Resnik is strongly opposed to the diary coming in. He claims it's non-evidentiary."

"Exactly, Your Honor. It's hearsay, every page. It can't be used to prove anything, so it must be kept out."

"Your Honor," I countered, "we have no intention of citing the diary to establish facts or to prove that events actually took place. We wish to use it to generate state of mind evidence which is an exception to the hearsay rule, that's all."

"Your Honor," Resnik declared, "as precedent, we have the ruling from the O. J. Simpson trial. Simpson's ex-wife's diary was ruled inadmissible in that trial."

"On the grounds," I stated, "that Nicole Brown was no longer available to be cross-examined on her claims. That problem, obviously, is not present here."

Persisting, pointing to Lucy's volumes, Resnik proclaimed, "Your Honor, anyone could come up with documents like these and say anything they liked. There's no way to verify the reliability of any of it."

Turning her immobile face toward me, Loewenstein said, "Mr. Spencer?"

"Quite to the contrary, Your Honor, the veracity of much of what is written in the diary can be established by testimony and simple research. If it will please the Court, the defense will provide as many witnesses as necessary to establish reliability."

"Mr. Spencer, please do not take up the Court's time with more testimony than absolutely necessary. I have read the defendant's diary from start to end. The extent of detail along with the fact that entries appear for nearly every day make the document appear credible to me. If we exclude it, we'll not do so on the grounds of reliability."

A light sheen of sweat was on Resnik's face. Vicky and her deputy must have dueled over this. Used astutely, the diary could be useful to the prosecution during cross. Obvious to both Resnik and the judge, the presence of the diary in court could significantly strengthen the defense's case. Because of Resnik's lack of fervour, I had the distinct impression that he was in favor of using it and his strong-minded superior was against.

"So," Loewenstein said to me, "it's defense of another that you'll argue and not self-defense, correct?"

"That's correct, Your Honor."

"Very well. On that condition, I will allow volumes four, five and six of the defendant's diary to be used. These volumes will not be permitted into the jury room. I admonish both of you to take care to confine all questions that pertain to the diary in any way to state of mind."

Resnik had a constipated expression on his face.

"There's one more thing I'd like to know before we finish up." Her eyes on Resnik, she said, "I see that there's been no attempt by the DA's office to keep this case from trial. I'd like an explanation, please."

Resnik, uncomfortable, started to speak, then stopped, then found his words. "Your Honor, very frankly, we were waiting for your ruling on the diary."

Loewenstein's brows came together in a scowl. "I'm appalled by what I'm hearing. Does the District Attorney for this county have so little regard for the over-filled agendas of our courts? I expect communication with the defense in this regard within the week. Within the week, Mr. Resnik, within the week. Now, are there any other issues to be resolved this morning?"

We both said no.

"This whole case makes me sick," Resnik said. "We'll be in touch with you shortly with some proposals, at least, I think."

"Right," I said.

From the defense's point of view, we'd gotten off to a good start. But I'd have been very green behind the ears if I thought that meant very much. Loewenstein seemed sympathetic, but there was something about her that, intuitively, I didn't like. And, whether or not he enjoyed his task, Resnik, young and relatively inexperienced though he was, would make things difficult for us, that we could count on. Fortunately, we had lots of time, a good thing since there was a lot of work to do ahead.

Chapter 14

I could see a lot of Bree's curly brown hair and the upper part of her face as she frowned down at pages she was flipping through.

"This looks like something I shouldn't interrupt," I said, standing at her door. She hastily closed the book and raised her head.

"Hey," I chided, "if you're gonna read that stuff, you ought to keep your door closed. People will get ideas."

I was sure I was about to see the bird as her hand came up but, at the last instant, the lady flicked her wrist and gestured toward the couch.

"Alright, so you caught me." Our newest addition to the firm, reputed to always be laidback, was decidedly in a bad mood. "Besides, it's not even nine o'clock. Not everybody begins at ungodly hours like you do."

She slammed her hand down on her desk. "Everyone's been going on about this new book that came out a couple of years ago, women are anyway, raving about how fabulous it is. It's exciting, stimulating, well-written, the reviews say. It's on the bestseller list of the New York Times, not that that means anything these days. So I went out and bought the thing on my way home." This time, the hand fell on the book. "You know, I'm starting to believe people who say our society's in decay. Women everywhere in this country—they've got to be sexually frustrated, I can tell you—are reading and getting off on BDSM. I like to keep an open mind about most things, but this has got to be the worst bestselling crap I've seen."

With a flourish, Bree picked up the offensive volume and sent it sailing past my head into the corner of her office. I bent over to see that it lay neatly in the center of the waste basket.

"Nice shot." Teasing her, I added, "Felt the wind of that going past my head. Remind me not to pick out things for you to read."

No response.

Her face beginning to clear, Bree said, "I need another coffee. You want one?"

"Ms. Dixon, you might as well bring the pot. It's gonna be a long day for us, I'm afraid. You free for a dozen hours?"

She looked quizzically at me. "Been a long time since I've had a request like that. Don't worry, Forrest, I didn't take you seriously. Might have been fun to watch your face, though, if I had. It's your lucky day. I even brought my lunch. Be right back."

It couldn't be perfume that she was wearing, at least, I didn't think so. More like skin cream, shampoo, maybe, or even soap. Whatever it was, the light pineapple-coconut fragrance it cast, I liked. In a moment, she was back, carrying two cups.

Handing one to me, Bree announced, "Now that I've got America's heartthrob out of my system, I'm all yours." She continued on and sat down behind her desk.

Unable to resist, I said, "All mine, you say? And how safe would I be, given what just happened to your last fling?"

Pretending to ponder this, she responded, "Best to think before one leaps, isn't that what they say? Catherine the Great was pretty merciless with her lovers, wasn't she. Now, how do you propose to keep my attention for... how long did you say?"

In answer, I reached for my briefcase. "I wish you could have been with us yesterday at the hearing. I'd like to have gotten your impressions about our judge. I did leave you a voicemail yesterday about it, didn't I? Don't know what's going on with my memory lately."

Bree nodded. "Good, okay. We've got a month and a half until the trial which gives us just enough time and—"

"Mia may be showing by then, won't she," Bree said. "The girl could miscarry at any time, you know, in which case we lose our evidence as to who impregnated her. You remember the SNP DNA test I talked to you about. We should be close to the minimum nine week postconception period by now, even past. Are we doing anything about that?"

"Not yet, no. We're going to have to deal with this right away. You're right. Let's talk more about Mia a little later."

Bree nodded.

"Back to the hearing. As we thought, the DA tried to keep the diary out. Judge Loewenstein read it and agreed that the last three volumes could be brought in on condition that it be used exclusively in conjunction with Lucy's state of mind at the time Pete was killed. I've got the weirdest feeling about this judge though, Bree. Don't ask me why. She's treated us quite well, all in all. I really wish you'd seen her. You might have gotten a different take on her. I'm gonna get Sara to dig up everything we can find on her. We've got enough to handle as it is without ambushes from the bench. I've got this nagging feeling that it's going to be a rough ride, especially for Lucy. The prosecution's going to try to discredit her wherever they can." I pulled out another piece of paper and handed it to Bree. "This arrived just hours after the hearing from the DA."

"Second degree murder?" Bree exclaimed. "They're not willing to go more than that?"

"Seems not. Vicky knows we're not going to accept whatever they offer us so why let the jury know the prosecution's not confident about their case."

Another nod and a brief 'I understand you' noise. "Forrest, I remember what you said before about our defense strategy, but things are still a bit unclear to me.

I must have missed something in my notes."

"Maybe, but the fact that you're having problems shows how hard it's going to be to convey to jurors what we're trying to prove. Actually, it's a good thing you raise this. I'm used to working with evidence, concrete or circumstancial, whatever I can get. This'll be my first experience where we're talking about state of mind instead of facts. I'll be learning right along with you, so you'll have to excuse me if I get a little repetitious or mixed up at times, okay?"

"Agreed."

"Basically, our goal in Court is to convince the jury that Lucy truly believed she had no way to prevent her husband from sexually assaulting their daughter that night unless she killed him. As I see it, our only way to accomplish this is to seek whatever corroborative evidence for this we can by way of testimony from Lucy's friends and family and, of course, by questioning Lucy herself, based on what we know she stated in the diary."

I waited while Bree processed this.

Nodding reflectively, she said, "Okay. So, if I understand you, we don't quote the diary in direct."

"That's right. We formulate our questions based on it, that's all."

"Are we going to put Alex and Mia on the stand?"

"As to Alex, maybe, but I doubt it. He won't cooperate if we try to force him to say anything against his father. As to Mia, God knows I wish we could keep her out. She's volatile and unpredictable, the worst kind of witness for us in court. Trouble is, there are questions only she can answer that the jury has to hear. We have no choice. Based on my brief interactions with the girl, I've got a feeling she's going to be difficult for us."

"How so?"

"For starters, she seems to have made enemies of her family. Mia was very shy when she was younger, but she isn't anymore. She's tenacious about that baby. She thinks people are going to try to take it away from her because of her age. She doesn't trust me and, frankly, I don't trust her. I think she's in a self-protective mode and she'll say or do anything she thinks is in her interest. If I'm right about most of this, it poses problems for us in terms of questions we need answers to."

"Such as?"

"In Lucy's diary, she says several times how afraid she was that Pete would leave her. She was convinced, reasonably, I think, that if Pete left, the children would go with him which would prevent her from protecting Mia. First, would the girl have gone with Pete? Second, and this we have to find out somehow, what were Pete's promises and instructions to her before he died? Did he ever tell her, for example, to deny there was anything sexual between them if she was ever asked? This is vital. If he did so as I suspect, would she ever say so in Court? What can we do to induce her to testify truthfully about these things, especially since she claims to hate her mother? How long did Pete intend to hide his physical relationship with his daughter from Lucy? As you can see, Mia's testimony can have a significant impact on this case."

Bree had a faraway look in her eyes. Disconcertingly, every few seconds as I was speaking, she shook her head. Finally, I just sat back and waited, thankful, once again, that I wasn't the only one to be struggling with the case.

"Why," she asked as though talking to herself, "do I have the impression I'm going to inherit this? Tell me I'm wrong, okay? You wouldn't think of dropping all of this in my lap, now, would you?"

"Thing is, Bree—"

"Yes, yes, I know, she doesn't like you very much, I'm a woman so I might have a better chance of getting closer to her, and what else? Forrest, I hate to say it, but the whole thing doesn't sound very feasible because of her relationship with her mother."

"As things stand now," I conceded, "no, it doesn't. The problem, Bree, is that, without her daughter's corroborative testimony, I doubt very much the diary's going to be anywhere near enough. We'll have to devise a way to get through to her, somehow."

"We, or me? The problem with being a junior member of this firm is that I can't say no." Smiling, she said, "I'm kidding. You know that." A sigh. "Didn't I read somewhere in Lucy's diary that Mia loves babies?"

I nodded.

"Wonder how she'd like Maya. She's about one and a half. Think she'd do?"

I waited.

"Okay. Say I visit the Evans', ostensibly to chat with Jim and Evie, but with Mia too if she'll let me. I just happen to bring along Maya, who loves attention. If Mia takes to her like everybody does, maybe we arrange a little visit to my house so Mia can play with her. We talk about her own baby and how much fun that's gonna be. How's that for a start?"

"You're a wonder, you are," I said. "I'd give you a big hug for doing all of this, but..."

Still smiling, Bree queried, "What, like you give Sara every time she does good work?"

Sunday night's escapade jumped immediately into my head as must have been evident on my face.

Waving a dismissive hand and laughing, Bree remarked, "She needs them more than I do, anyway, so no hugs. I do think the idea's worth pursuing, though, don't you?"

"What, the thing with Mia or the hugs?"

No response. "So, while I'm playing manipulator, what will you be doing?"

My pleasant feeling ebbed away as I thought about Lucy and what we had to do. "Nothing all that demanding. Just my interview with our client who's chomping at the bit to have her sweet daughter back who'll be giving birth to her dead husband's child."

Bree's expression sobered. "Hmmm. Think I'd prefer to watch Mia and Maya play. Before we go on," she said, "what about those awful photos? Can the Prosecution use them as evidence to discredit her?"

"It's not something I'm looking forward to and there is risk, but I suspect we'll be the ones to bring them up. Don't forget. Pete used them to make Lucy think she'd be disbelieved by the authorities if she went to them."

"I understand," Bree said, "but those photos could do more harm than good in the eyes of the jury, couldn't they?"

"Depends somewhat on who the jurors are."

"How so?"

Hesitating, I replied, "Well, if we get mainly older women, for instance, they'll react more negatively to them."

Bree frowned, but she'd understood.

"The risk of using them as evidence is bound to be greater in a place like Santa Lucia. We'll have to brainstorm more about this, I think. The pictures, themselves, aren't evidentiary as such for the prosecution. For them, they don't pertain to their charge of murder. They're relevant only if we bring them out as one of the bases for Lucy's fears. I'm sure the prosecution would like to use them, but I don't think they can."

Bree nodded, looking doubtful.

"So, as I said before, to have a shot at this, we're going to have to make each juror see that, from Lucy's perspective, she believed she had no way out. Naturally, the prosecution will do their best to lay out the options Lucy had. They'll do their utmost to show that no sane informed person could truly believe that help wasn't out there somewhere."

Bree's forehead furrowed. "I'm still puzzled about something, Forrest. Everything you've said so far makes sense. What I don't understand is why we seem to be leaving psychological abuse out of this. Lucy is unquestionably a victim which accounts for what she did, as I see it, anyway. There's got to be some way we can address this rather than just focusing on her beliefs. Can't we do both? I realize the problem of psychological abuse hasn't been raised as a major issue in the courts, but isn't it time someone brought it up?"

"Bree, you know psychological abuse is the problem here. From what you've described to me, I believe so too. The problem is, no one else is likely to. Battering produces evidence that we can use—bruising and follow-up care, police reports and witnesses who can testify to what they've seen. We have no such evidence in Lucy's case apart from what we can infer from her diary."

Far from satisfied, Bree said, "In other words, we can't prove that psychological abuse existed in this case at all. I read you, but that's disgraceful. It's outrageous."

I agreed. "Okay," I said. "Let's go on. Do you recall the three conditions that underlie the defense of another strategy? We talked about that a week or so ago."

"Yes. I checked my notes and they seem pretty clear."

"Okay," I said. "We've got some other things to deal with. We need to find somebody with impeccable credentials who could explain to the jury in simple terms why someone like Lucy might believe she had no options."

Bree was about to say something when I stopped her. "I don't mean someone who can explain what psychological abuse is and what it can lead to. Unless expert witnesses are hard-hitting, clear and brief, juries ignore them. Whoever we manage to find, the prosecution will have one or two of their own experts to counter ours."

Bree nodded, looking pensive.

I continued, "What I'm saying here, I guess, is that such an expert might be talking about aspects of psychological abuse without using the term itself and not using a lot of jargon. We may not be able to find anyone like that. You'll know more than I."

Another nod. "What we're? talking about here," Bree said, "is what's referred to by some scholars as coercive control. I think Lucy is an archetype victim of this form of abuse. Before we get any further into this, let me see what I can find and who might be in a position to help us."

"Sounds good. Find an article that discusses the concept and give it to Sara this afternoon. She'll have everything that's been written on the topic on my desk tomorrow, I promise." Bree looked skeptical.

"You've got a lot of confidence in that girl, don't you."

"You see the kind of work she does and how fast she does it, you would too. You're the better one to run this down, of course, given your knowledge of the field, but not right now. That's why I suggested Sara."

"Hmmm," was all Bree said.

"Moving on, we've got to talk to Lucy. We have to communicate the DA's offer and explain what we've come up with as her defense. I don't look forward to it, but we're also going to have to sound her out about the future of her daughter."

"Yes... well, I think you're going to get further with that one than if I'm along. I've got the feeling she sees me as competition. Forrest, I really think you should go alone."

"Bree," I groused, "you're developing a bad habit, you know that? You're always trying to hook me up with other women."

Smiling, she replied, "You make me laugh, you really do. It never ceases to amaze me how clueless men can be. Now what else is on your list? Can we have lunch first? I'm famished."

"Sure thing. I'll get Nancy or Josephine to get me something."

"No, no, don't bother. I've got enough chicken and other stuff to feed three. I'm one of these lucky people who doesn't have to watch her weight—knock on wood. Think hard before you invite me out to eat. It's going to cost you."

I smiled, thinking that was an invitation long overdue.

For the next twenty minutes while we ate, we

chatted about family things, something we rarely had the opportunity to do at work—how Bree had come to adopt her little girl, what it was like raising twins and how life as a single parent differed from what we'd known. I'd forgotten that Bree's husband had died some years ago from leukemia, having battled with the disease since the age of twenty-eight.

Impulsive I'm not, though sometimes I wish I was. I tend to look behind every tree before I make my move. What caused me to break with tradition that afternoon, I can't say. It might just have been the camaraderie Bree and I enjoyed. More probable, it was my disinclination to be a single at a party. I often left feeling more alone than when I went.

Days before when Ben invited me to join him and Cassie for their barbecue on Saturday, I'd thought about but rejected the idea of asking Bree to accompany me. Ben's parties, as the drinks flowed, tended to get a little bawdy, not something I was confident Brianna Dixon would approve of. I had no idea whether she imbibed and not a clue how she'd respond to just plain talk as my old friend Ben liked to put it.

Perversely, as I began to speak, I realized how little I wanted to offend the lady near me. 'Go figure,' as Ben would say.

"Bree, of course you know Ben. Have you met Cassie Bollinger who lives with him?"

Nodding, munching on an apple, Bree said, "Yeah, sure. I've met her twice, I think, once here at the office and the first time at the firm get-together at a restaurant when I came. Why?"

Clearing my throat, I said, "I know it's not giving you much time, but Ben and Cassie are having a barbecue this coming Saturday night. They've invited me and I wondered if you might like to come."

For the briefest moment, Bree looked startled, then she smiled. "You know, Forrest, for someone who I'd say is on the cautious side, you should take more care about who you casually invite like this. I could be a vegan who doesn't drink. What would you do then?" Her smile was still there and so were those golden specks.

I pointed at the chicken bones on her paper plate.

"Oh yeah, that's right. Forgot about the chicken. But I don't touch a drop. You knew that, didn't you?" Bree's smile remained, but she was thinking. "That sounds like fun. I won't embarrass myself by telling you how long it's been since I've been out. I don't have sitters, not that I can rely on anyway." She was still pondering while she talked, so I waited. Then her face lit up. "Hold on. Let me call someone. She's a single mother with a six-month-old. She knows Maya well."

Without another word, she picked up her phone and dialed. Two minutes later, it was a fait accompli. "We're on. Rita and her baby will stay overnight, so we're good to go. How's that?"

"Do you always work that fast?"

Looking pert and lively, she answered, "When I want to."

"It's been delightful," I said as I stood up to go. "We've both got a lot of work to do. Get that article or whatever to Sara as soon as you can, okay? We need to get going on this right away."

"Don't you worry, Forrest. Your girl will have it in an hour."

"Sara's not my—"

"Go on, get out of here. I have work to do. Thanks for the invitation, by the way. I'll look forward to the party."

'Bree,' I reflected as I left her office, 'I hope I haven't done a crazy thing.'

Since Lucy continued to ignore her cell phone, I drove to her house, reasonably sure I'd find her there. Both she and Lily were at the door when I rang the bell.

I was pleased to see how much better Lucy looked. She was filling out, and the liveliness I associated with her was coming back. There was the hug that was a ritual in our greeting during our late teens. I wasn't expecting the warm kiss. She seemingly wanted our connection back and a little more. Lily announced that she'd be finishing up some baking in the kitchen while we talked.

"Hey, we're going to have to find a better way to communicate," I said. "There may be times when I need to reach you right away. Why don't you let me add a ringtone on your cell that you'll hear only when I call. I really do need to be in touch with you."

Smiling, she replied, "Sounds good. I didn't know you could do that. Hang on a minute and I'll get the phone."

It took me longer than it should have to figure out the thing, but I managed to assign some exotic bird call to my name. We had a good laugh when I called her number with my own phone.

"So, there you are. No more excuses. When you hear that silly bird, you answer, okay?"

She said she would. Lucy frowned as she saw me reach into my blazer jacket for my notebook.

"Do we have to get down to business right away? You have any idea how starved I am for company?"

I did. "Lucy, I can't tell you how glad I am that we're back on a friendly footing. I don't need to tell you how troubled I was when we weren't."

"I'm glad." Back came the smile that conveyed things better left unapproached.

"We've got some urgent things to talk about, and we have to do it right away." I cleared my throat. "Some of this you may not like all that much. I'm going to need your full attention and cooperation here. I promise I'll come back soon for just a social call."

I hoped I was wrong, but I had the distinct feeling that Lucy might be under the misapprehension that she was out of trouble because of the discovery of her daughter's pregnancy. If so, I was going to have to get her turned around. Soft talk and reassurances wouldn't be the way.

"Lucy, you may think that the discovery of Mia's

pregnancy changes things. I'm here to tell you that it doesn't, at least, not yet."

Lucy shrugged.

"The DA has your diary and they've examined it very closely. Mia's pregnancy, assuming we can establish that Pete is the father—"

"Of course he's the father. Who else would it be?"

"Lucy, stop interrupting me and listen! There are some things you don't know and some decisions you have to make. I need your cooperation here. Otherwise, we're not going to get anywhere with this and you'll go to jail for a long, long time. As I was saying, Mia's pregnancy has resulted in only one thing. They are willing to reduce the charge from premeditated murder to second degree, provided you are willing to change your plea to guilty. With second degree, you cannot be executed, but you'll be held in a state prison for a long time. In other words, Lucy, very little in your situation has really changed. Unless we work extremely hard, the prosecutor will very likely get their conviction and you'll go to prison. As your attorney, I'm bound to convey the DA's offer to you. Naturally, my personal preference is that you reject the offer, but the decision belongs to you. Do you understand what I'm saying here?"

I could read nothing in Lucy's face. Her eyes were partly closed as though she were half asleep. Seconds after, she opened them and shifted in her chair.

"You're right, I guess. I thought that Mia being pregnant proved I was right."

"It does, but being right doesn't entitle you to use violence to prevent what happened, not in the eyes of the public, anyway. From their point of view, you had a number of options available to you, none involving murder."

She was about to object when I raised my hand. "I know, I know," I said. "You didn't believe you had those options, and I agree with you. Our objective in court is to convince the jury of this. That brings me to my second point. Your diary is important in many ways to us, but it doesn't prove that events you talk about took place. In other words, it doesn't constitute probative evidence which we normally rely upon in court. What it does establish, in our opinion, is what you believed at the time Pete was killed. We're not declaring self-defense in your case, but defense of another, Mia, of course. For this strategy to work, we have to show beyond a shadow of a doubt that you genuinely believed you had no other way to protect your daughter than to do what you did. What I mean is, we won't be trying to establish facts in court. Our goal is to show what you truly believed to be the case last July thirteenth. If we are successful, if we can get every juror to understand why you believed what you did, there's a reasonable chance that we can get an acquittal, a reasonable chance, that's all. Judges and juries like to deal with facts, hard evidence, not beliefs. So we've got a difficult task ahead of us."

"How can you do that, make them understand, I mean?"

"By asking the right questions to witnesses during the trial."

"I'll be one of those, I suppose."

"Yes, Lucy, the most important one. I'd also like to include close friends of yours if I can."

Lucy frowned at this. "There's no one I can think of except Lily, and she might be too scared. I don't know what she'd be able to say, anyway."

"I said you were the most important witness. That's true, Lucy, but we need someone else to corroborate what you say. We need to put Mia on the stand."

Lucy flinched and looked distressed. "Mia? Do you have any idea what you're talking about? That child hates me. She'd say anything—and I mean anything—to hurt me. She's the last person you want in court. You can't trust her, Forrest."

"Yes, I think you're right, for the moment, anyway. Let me lay it out as we see it, Lucy, and you'll see my point. Pete threatened to leave you immediately and divorce you if you contacted anyone about him and Mia, correct?"

She nodded.

"You'd no longer be in a position to protect your daughter if that happened, right?"

Again, a nod.

"To protect himself, we're quite sure he'll have convinced Mia to deny any physical relationship with him if asked."

Another nod.

"However we manage to get Mia to tell the truth, the Court needs to hear this from her lips. They need to know that Pete programmed his daughter to deny everything. Her testimony to this effect will go a long ways in the jury's minds to understand the no-win situation you were in. Our biggest hurdle right now is to find a way to encourage Mia to tell the truth on the witness stand. Do you understand?"

"Yes, yes, of course I do. It's just not possible, that's all. She'll do anything to destroy me."

"Lucy, think about this. What does Mia want most at this time?"

"That's no mystery. She wants to keep that baby."

"You're aware, I assume, that your brother and his wife aren't willing to keep Alex and Mia on a long-time basis."

"Yes, Forrest, I'm aware of that. Jimmy wouldn't keep them if he had a mansion."

"So, assuming that you're convicted and you go to prison, where do you think Mia would end up?"

Lucy jumped up and began to pace. The ends of her mouth turned down as, silently, she began to cry. "That's one of the things I was scared of most before I shot him, you know that? Where would Mia live? I wasn't thinking about a baby, not then. She'd have to live with poor Dad, I guess. Who else? At least the two of them get along. But with a baby? Good God, Forrest, I don't know. That's a lot of responsibility to put on him." Lucy wrung her hands.

"Alright. From a different point of view. Suppose we

get you off as we hope to. What then?"

Lucy stopped dead and slowly turned toward me, looking almost frightened. I could still see tears on her cheeks. She raised her hands as though to fend me off, then dropped them, returning to her chair. Sighing and forlorn, she said, "Forrest, it just wouldn't work, no matter how much I wish it could. Mia and I, we were close once, not super close as some kids and parents are—I was never all that attentive to her, I know—but even so. Then she changed in so many ways. Pete had a lot to do with it—I know that—but not in everything. She'll never be my little Mia again, never! The girl hates me. We'd never get along. She'd guard that baby with her life, you realize? She'll need help, especially when her baby comes, but she won't let me near her. I wish it wasn't true, but, in a way, she'd be better off with somebody she doesn't know."

I nodded. "Lucy, you could be right in all you say. But you could be wrong. It's possible that the person she'll need most in the world is her mother. She may end up in a foster home anyway, but if we win, would you be willing to try having her live with you for a while, just to see?"

"Yes, yes of course. But she'd have to understand from the start that my slaving days are over. If she doesn't want to live as my daughter and under my authority, then she'll have to consider living some place else. If things work out, when would she come?"

"Not until the trial is over. Otherwise, the jury might think there's collusion between you and your daughter."

Lucy looked relieved. "Thank God. I'm in no shape to deal with that girl right now. You can't believe how much she's changed. I know adolescence does things, but Alex didn't change all that much. Mia's different."

"Okay," I said, "just so we understand each other, if the situation arises, we can tell Mia that you'll accept her and her baby back once the trial is over. Is that correct?"

Lucy hesitated, then nodded.

"Our priority now is you. Don't forget that. Your daughter will be okay, no matter what. It's you we have to be concerned about."

In a softer voice with a little more of her smile back, Lucy said, "It's nice to have someone around who is, concerned about me, I mean."

"Hey," I said as I stood up to go. "I let you down these last two years. If I hadn't, who knows. None of this might have happened."

Lucy shook her head as she approached me. "The way Pete was for the last while, you couldn't have done much, Forrest, really. Next time you come back, let's talk about fun things." Another hug, no kiss this time, and I was out the door, breathing in fresh ocean air.

As I headed for the office, my thoughts jumped back to the nightie Lucy had given me some time ago. Child-size? I couldn't tell. More important at the moment was the stain on what appeared to me to be the back, if the location of the tag meant anything. Did that stain contain DNA and, if so, whose?

Our trial date was set for Tuesday, October 15, according to the note on my desk from Judge Loewenstein's clerk.

Taps at my office door brought a welcome halt to my ruminations. Garrett walked in and, minus his usual greeting, headed for a chair. Trouble of some kind at home. He came to vent and, glad for the interruption, I sat back to listen.

Looking down at his shoes, he let out a long sigh, then said, "Four adults and six noisy kids in our house this weekend. My daughter-in-law popped out twin girls last May, if you can believe, and she can't wait to show them off."

Grinning, I said, "Didn't you tell me just last year how much you adore those kids and how anxious you were to have them come?"

Garrett retorted, "Easy for you to say. You don't even know what a grandchild is. Barb's forcin' me to put up the older children in my study, can you imagine, the only room in the house that's mine... Seriously, why can't our kids come individually with their family instead of invading us all at once? The little ones are cute, don't get me wrong, but the noise. It never stops. I tell you, it never stops. Now, with two little four-month-olds, we're likely to be up all night. You don't have an extra bed a friend could sleep on by any chance?"

Before I could respond which I wasn't going to do, he concluded, "Nah, I take off for your place at night and Barb would have my head." As he stood up to go, Garrett commented to himself, "Gonna have to get those kids of ours into family planning."

Not a minute after came Ben's unmistakable rap at my door. "What's up with him? Looks like he did a couple a weeks ago when his car was towed away."

"No," I said. "He's got a house full of kids this weekend."

"What? That bullshit again? You ever see him playin' with his grandkids? They adore the guy. Damned if I know why somebody'd make such a fuss about somethin' they like so much."

"Got me," I said. "I've never seen him with his grandkids. So how are things?"

"Not bad, 'cept I miss Cassie when she's on a case. She's gone for weeks sometimes. She's due back this Friday. Can't wait, let me tell you. I just hope she makes it by Saturday. Haven't forgotten about the barbecue, have you?"

"Not a chance, Ben. Lookin' forward to it. As it turns out, I am bringing someone if it's still okay."

"Oh yeah? Who?"

"Bree."

That got Ben's attention. "I've been wonderin' about you two."

"Ben, we're just friends, that's all, and don't you forget it when we've had a few."

"Don't worry about me, boyo. Cassie keeps me on a tight leash."

"Anything I can bring?"

"Just an appetite, a big thirst—and your lady." Ben rubbed his hands together in anticipation. "There'll be six of us. There's a younger couple lives just down the road from us. He used to farm, don't know what he does now. His girl's a looker and when the booze hits her, just about any guy's lap will do. They're a lotta fun, but I'll be damned if I can understand why he puts up with her, behavin' like that. Tell Bree to keep an eye out. Gotta go. It's 'bout time I get outta here anyway. See you tomorrow if you're comin' in."

Normally at four o'clock, I'd be packing up my things and headed home to get dinner on. Of late, our large empty house had started to get to me. I looked for any excuse to stay away. Thank God, our place would come alive again when Trina and Andy returned and settled in. My girl would be back late Friday afternoon, only to disappear again the next morning when Claire came for her. At least I'd have Andy for the weekend. Speaking of whom, I'd have to arrange with Lupe that she stay over at our house on Saturday since I'd be out at Ben's. She seemed to prefer that arrangement to sleeping in her little house alone.

Bree was at her computer when I walked in. Her eyes remained glued on her screen as she gestured toward the couch. Frustrated, she said while tapping at her keys, "Damn database keeps timing out on me. I'm almost through."

Ten minutes later, exasperated, she slammed down her laptop lid. "You're lucky to have a minion who does this stuff for you. One day, if I'm ever a partner in this august firm, I'll get me one, you know, some gorgeous hunk who's smart and likes to flirt. Then maybe I can get some serious work done."

"Sounds good if you'll ever make it off his lap."

Bree looked quizzically at me for a moment, then her face fell and she slumped back in her chair. She explained before I had a chance to ask.

"Forrest, we've got a real problem with that girl. While you were at Lucy's, I went over to the Evans' house as I said I would. Evie told me on the phone that Mia was there before I went. I picked up Maya from the daycare and brought her with me. Mia knew we were there, but she refused to even say hello. I didn't even get a glimpse of her... I don't like suggesting this, but is there no way we can put pressure on her to get her to talk to us?"

"We've got to watch out what we say to her, Bree. Resnik may subpoena her. It's unlikely since I can't imagine what he'd gain, but it's possible. Either that or he may just talk to her. If he discovers we've coerced her in any way..."

"Yes, of course."

"We may have an ally, though, who can get to her. Evie hasn't much good to say about the girl. She thinks she's arrogant and uncooperative. Suppose Evie tells Mia she's had enough. Unless she smartens up, she'll put her and her baby out on the street to be picked up by the authorities. In principle, Jim and Evie could do that, couldn't they?"

"As far as I know, yes," Bree said.

Nodding, I continued, "So Evie tells Mia she can either be civil and talk to Bree and Forrest who are trying to help her or she can leave the house. A little coercive, I admit, but... Evie's dependable and certainly bright enough to take the hint, but we'd have to be careful not to coach her. It could come out in court if she's ever called to testify. Now, assume Evie's willing to help us here—if you were Mia, how would you respond?"

Bree frowned. "It might work out, I agree, but then it could backfire, couldn't it. I don't know how quick-witted Mia is. What happens if she decides that it's just a threat that her aunt and uncle would never carry out? What then? I'd expect her to harden up and be less reachable than before."

I thought about this and slowly shook my head. "It could play out that way, I know," I said, "but I doubt it. I think there's a lot of bluster in the girl and she's scared, and I think she feels alone."

"Okay," Bree said. "As to what I'd do if I were Mia, assuming you're right about her, I'd capitulate right away. If fear determines what she does, she's going to conclude that once she's in the hands of the authorities, she'll completely lose control. So best keep below their radar and remain where she is. I can see why Evie would go along with this, but what about Lucy's brother? Will he threaten his niece like that?"

"I think so, once we explain what we're trying to do. If you agree, I'll give them a call to set up a meeting with them."

"On another subject, Forrest, what are we doing about that nightie?"

I'd completely forgotten about the bag in the bottom drawer of my desk.

Looking at me intently, leaning forward, Bree said, "Don't tell me you still have the thing."

"As a matter of fact, I do. It totally slipped my mind. That's happening a little too much these days. Bree, there's that stain on the backside of the nightie."

She nodded just perceptibly but didn't say a word. By the slightly upturned corners of her mouth, I was fairly sure she knew what my dilemma was and had decided not to help. I changed position on the couch and looked down at my hands.

With more than the usual lilt in her low-pitched voice, Bree said, "There something more you want to say?" The vixen.

"If that stain contains DNA—" I stopped when I saw her grin.

"You should see your face." Hadn't there been another female who'd said that to me recently? "The answer to your question is yes. If there's DNA, it could definitely belong to Mia alone or to just the man who was assaulting her or, very possibly, to both. That's something we're going to have to know, isn't it."

Now sitting up quite straight, I rejoined, "You might say so, yes. It's only significant if it's both of them. Can they show who made the stain if it's the two of them, I wonder?"

"I'm sure they can, but I don't know a lot more than you about this stuff. We need answers right away, don't we. We also need to know where the nightie came from. If it's unusual in any way, we may be able to find the store where Pete bought it. They may even be able to tell us when it was sold. In fact, that's likely. Inventories are so computerized these days."

"I'd be like a lost child in the woods," I said, and meant it, "if I was handling this case alone."

"Then Garrett would send me out to find you, wouldn't he?" Tilting her head as she did sometimes and grinning, she added, "Or, just maybe, they'd send someone else, a certain researcher who knows you a lot better than I do."

Before my riposte that wasn't going to be all that nice, Bree's hands came up in mock defense and she smiled. "I'm just kidding you, Forrest. It's just infatuation, I know that."

On whose part, I wanted to ask, but let it drop. Instead, I said, "I'm beginning to think it'll be a good thing when Sara leaves so people around here won't bring her up."

Turning serious, shaking her head, Bree replied, "Who gets teased the most? People who can't help rising to the bait, that's who. You're going to be sad when Sara goes and, from what I've heard, for good reason. You're not the only one around here who sings her praises as a researcher. Sorry if I stirred you up."

"That's okay. If I give you the nightie, can you look into the things we talked about?"

Bree nodded.

"Good. I'll get it from my desk when we're finished here. Jim should be home at dinnertime so I'll call them then to see if they can squeeze me in. I'm going to drop off a copy of the diary for Alex when I go. Hopefully, he'll be willing to look at it. If Evie and Jim go along with our scheme and Mia has responded the way we want her to, I'll aim for tomorrow morning at ten for the both of us at the Evans' place."

"Sounds good. If you can get the nightie, I'll start working on it right away."

Back in Bree's office next morning, I said, "You should have heard Evie. She was happy to go along. Her only problem is that she wishes it was for real. She really doesn't like the girl. From what she told me, she made Mia think about her proposition for an hour before giving her an answer. Evie set us up for eleven. Is that okay with you?"

"That's fine. Now pay attention, lead counsel. I have some news." Bree's eyes looked very green and they seemed to sparkle. "One pink babydoll-style nightie, size four, sold at Parsons Lingerie in Santa Barbara for $236.99—expensive—on July sixth. How's that!"

"Do you know that for sure? How can you tell that it's our nightie and not another one?"

"The tag. And it's exactly as I said. They only carry one each of their high-end items. When one is sold, their computer immediately marks it for reorder with date sold, amount plus tax, etc. No magic here. The name of the store is on the nightie's tag."

"Fantastic. God, do you work fast or what."

"Yeah, well, I'm not finished. I just got a call back from Perkins Diagnostics, the lab where we're going to run the DNA test." Bree looked troubled. "I talked to one of the technicians late yesterday afternoon. She got back to me just now. There can be issues, apparently, but, in principle, two individuals whose DNA is in a stain can be identified. Time doesn't seem to be a factor, especially if the stain is fairly recent. Precise dating is difficult, the lady told me. That shouldn't be an issue, though, I think. According to my notes, Lucy found the unused nightie on July twelfth, so there are only one or two nights possible, aren't there."

"I don't know whether it'll be a problem—I suspect not—but there could be more nights than that involved. It's hearsay as to when the bag in the closet was found. We'll have to think about how we can work all this in. Good work, Bree."

She shook her head and looked down at her notes. "No, not that good, I'm afraid. I'm embarrassed to tell you this and I'm really sorry. I hope I haven't thrown a monkey wrench into things."

"Why? What's wrong?"

"What's wrong is when people go shooting off their mouths about things they don't know anything about. Remember when I talked about the SNP test for paternity?"

Starting to worry, I said, "Yeah, of course. What's wrong?"

Sighing, Bree said, "I was mistaken about how that test works. It can be run as early as nine weeks postconception as I thought and the fetus' DNA can be extracted."

"So what's the problem?"

"I thought they could also get genetic information about the father from the mother's DNA with that test, but I was wrong. They can't. Or maybe they can, but that's not how the SNP test works."

I waited.

Raising her face and regarding me, Bree said, "They need a live blood sample from the alleged father as well."

With a sinking feeling in my stomach, I said, "Oh. That does complicate things a little, yes. So, old blood from a bandage or something like that won't work."

Bree shook her head. "Not for the SNP test, no. The lady I talked to said the blood sample has to be current, just like Mia's. Forrest, does this screw us up?"

"I'm not sure. I know less than I should about testing for paternity. Are there any other tests we can run this early without a fresh sample of Pete's blood?"

"Not that she knew of, no. The best she could offer, if we need something prenatal, is to collect the fetus' DNA between sixteen and twenty weeks postconception by amniocentesis. They get the mother's DNA at that time, of course, and then we need viable DNA from Pete."

More gloomy by the minute, I shook my head. "That'll never work. If I know Mia, she'll never go for an invasive procedure like that. Someone's bound to tell her that it's not entirely safe. And, anyway, the judge is unlikely to let in evidence like that without Mia's authorization."

"She's not old enough to authorize anything, is she? Can't Lucy give permission?"

"Bree, that's another iffy situation. With Lucy as the defendant in a murder trial, it's hard to say what the judge might do. Too many unknowns there."

Twisting her pencil in her fingers and looking down, Bree asked, "So where do we go from here? What about the nightie?"

"Ah yes, the nightie. It's not going to do us all that much good, I'm afraid."

Bree looked distressed. "Why not? I thought you said that looked promising."

"I had my head on backwards when I said that. We may be able to work it in somehow, but it's got its problems. Remember, Pete's not on trial. No one, outside of Lucy's diary, has accused him of having done anything, not sexual assault, not abuse of any kind. The prosecution, maybe the judge, herself, will be opposed to anything evidentiary that we bring against him on the grounds that it's not relevant in the trial. Resnik will never let it through. And, there's the problem I had no business to forget about, chain of evidence. Our lab may corroborate our claim, but could the stain have been manufactured."

At Bree's look of incredulity, I said, "Improbable, I know, but unless you collect evidence in the correct manner and follow protocol, it'll be thrown out. It's not the latter point that's most important, though. We're there to defend Lucy and not to attack the man she killed."

"God, what a mess," Bree said. "Will we ever need to prove Pete's the real father, postnatally, I mean?"

"Good question. For Lucy, someday, maybe. I'll talk to Ben. He'll know about how to get Pete's DNA from clothes and stuff. He's done that sort of thing before."

"Can we switch topics for a while?" Bree suggested. "My head is swimming."

"Fire away."

"You did tell me, didn't you, that Lucy's willing to take Mia in after the trial, right?"

"Yeah, so she said. She's not enthusiastic about having her daughter back, especially in the condition that she's in, but she'll come around, I think. The wild card for us and for Lucy is how Mia will behave."

"Yes," Bree said. "Puberty seems to have hit her pretty hard. I'd feel easier if I knew the girl."

"I'm not sure how much good that would do. I've known her all her life, and she's like a total stranger. I've never been so worried about a witness. She's everything we don't want to see—unreliable, selfish, paranoid, volatile, you name it. Even if we manage to get her confidence, her unpredictability makes her dangerous on the stand. If Resnik rattles her or if we ask a question in the wrong way, she could turn against us, just like that. She's highly emotional and a little schemer, Bree. She's potentially more beneficial to us in court than Lucy is and possibly our worst nightmare at the same time. She could suddenly turn hostile."

Bree nodded. Looking sober, she said, "I can see you like the girl... I don't know how much choice we have. If she's as hazardous as you think, then the soft friendly approach may not work. I don't like to hear myself saying this—it really goes against the grain—but, to keep control, we may have to manipulate her and capitalize on those fears. The idea of treating a young girl like that makes me nauseous."

"I know what you mean," I replied, thinking about how I'd react if someone attempted to maneuver my children in that way. "Machiavelli would be pleased with us, wouldn't he."

"Yes, well, I can do without him in my life, thank you," Bree said. "If we have to exploit the child for our ends, there's nothing keeping us from befriending her. I know I raised the manipulation thing, but if we think about it, as we've said before, it's to Mia's benefit entirely that Lucy remains free. She's a loose cannon, okay, but that doesn't mean she's bad. If she and her mother can reconcile, then things may turn out alright."

"Now who's guilty of rationalizing," I said, laughing. As Bree took on a defensive look, I added, "Hey, I'm kidding. I'm glad we can talk about these things. It's definitely in Mia's interest that we win. However we play this, it's going to take several sessions with her, at least."

Nodding, Bree said, "I wrote up a few questions. Here, take a look. They're intended to make her worry about how she's going to manage to keep her baby safe."

Glancing at the sheet Bree handed to me, I said, "Looks good. You mind starting out?"

Bree smiled. "Did you think I was going to leave this in your hands?"

Mia looked unfriendly as Bree and I sat down at the Evans' kitchen table. Evie's children were at school and she'd gone off to another room.

Contemplating the preadolescent across from me whom I'd known since her early childhood, I said, "Mia, I told you about a lady who works with me, remember? This is Bree. She just happens to know a lot about babies. She's got a little girl a year and a half old."

From the lack of expression in Mia's eyes and her vacant look, we might as well have been speaking to the wall.

"We're not going to keep you very long. We have a

few things to bring up with you, that's all. If you're as smart as I think you are, you must realize that you're not exactly in a good position to bring a new baby into the world. Now, very frankly, Mia, I've got to say, especially given your rude attitude toward everyone, it doesn't really make much difference to me whether you manage to give birth to the baby and keep it or whether they take it away from you."

The girl's eyes flashed at this and she scowled. "Nobody's gonna take my baby away from me. You told me that. You said this lady said so. So what are you talking about?"

"Mia, close your mouth and listen."

I felt Bree's restraining hand lightly touch my arm. This wasn't the tack we planned to take, but I was annoyed at this ignorant scheming child who was not altogether blameless for the situation Lucy was in.

"You keep up this attitude and you're going to have to manage on your own. Jim and Evie have about had it with you. You want to keep that baby, you're going to have to make some decisions, and make them soon."

Mia's face was flushed and she was angry, but not so far gone, I thought, to ignore the precariousness of her situation.

"You may not understand yet that you must make some important choices, but I think you will when you've had time to think about some of the questions we're going to ask. We're not looking for answers from you now. These questions are things for you to think about. That's about all I have to say, for now at least. I'd like you to listen to my friend. As I told you, she has a baby and can appreciate some of the things you're going through."

"Mia," Bree began, "do you have any idea how very lucky you are? You're able to have a baby. Not all of us are."

"So? Lots of people are." Truculent though the girl's words were, her expression appeared less tense.

"I had to adopt my little Maya because I couldn't

have children of my own."

"Why not?" Mia asked.

"Some complicated problem with my ovaries that I never really understood. A lot of women are unable to produce babies. Did you know that?"

Mia shook her head.

Lowering her voice to just above a whisper, Bree continued, "I'd like to show you two pictures of my little girl. Is that alright with you?"

This time, Mia nodded, her plain face definitely more relaxed. Bree took out an envelope from her purse and pulled out two pictures, one of which she held hidden in her hand. In the middle of the table, she placed a photo of a little dark-skinned girl with an attractive young child's face and abundant black hair.

"She's so delicate and pretty," Mia murmured. "I love her skin, but it's not like yours. How come?"

Bree now had Mia's full attention. Still speaking quietly, she answered, "My little Maya comes from India. That's a country that's very far away where most of the people have skin like hers. This is how Maya looks now at sixteen months. I took this picture just last week. Now I'm going to show you what she looked like when she was just four months old, a year ago when I got her." Next to the photo on the table, Bree placed the second that she'd kept concealed.

Mia's eyes grew large and her hands flew to her mouth. My reactions on the outside were less evident, but I was shaken. Only because of facial features could I see that the two photographs were of the same child. Even then, there was ample room for doubt. The baby was jaundiced and emaciated beyond belief. That she'd remained alive was a miracle. No flesh, just sallow skin and bones. She was tiny. Mia took her hands from her face just long enough to say, "What's the matter with her? She looks sick! She looks really sick."

"She was, honey," Bree answered with emotion in her voice. "Maya was undernourished like millions of other babies in the world are. Her mother and father who are still alive look almost as bad as her. They beg on the street for food. Maya was almost dead when I went to India to bring her home."

Pointing to the first photograph, Mia stammered, "But, but how did you make Maya look like that?"

"Nurses and doctors helped me to know what to feed her to make up for what she'd missed. It took a long time, but, as you can see, it worked." There was a quaver in Bree's voice when she added, "My baby may have problems later on in life because of the poor nutrition she got while she was still in her mother's tummy. For now, she's doing fine."

The three of us sat there in silence—Bree, slightly pale—while I recovered from what I'd seen, thoroughly impressed by the perspicacity of my friend. Mia looked stunned, gaping at the photos. Bree cleared her throat as she blinked back tears.

"You might not know this, Mia, but even here in Santa Lucia and in lots of places near here, there are babies born like my Maya was. Most of the mothers of these babies are young, not as young as you, but young, a lot of them on drugs and alcohol and, in nearly every case, they don't eat proper food. So, the poor babies inside these girls and women suffer."

Still staring at the second picture, Mia asked, a tremor in her voice, "Will my baby look like that?"

"No," Bree replied, "no. Not like that. Your baby could suffer, though, if you don't get the proper food or if you smoke or drink or do things like that."

"I don't do those things," the girl assured us.

"I'm glad," Bree said. "Do you know why I showed you these photos, Mia?"

For a moment, the girl across from us didn't say anything, then she shook her head. I could see by Bree's expression that she had the same thoughts as I—high marks for Mia for tenacity, but doubts as to how astute she was.

"The most important thing for you right now is to protect your baby. You need to make sure he or she's healthy when that baby's born. You have to do everything you can to make sure that happens."

Mia's expression became almost fierce, so intense it was. "Yes. Yes. I need to protect my baby. What do I have to do?"

"Do you smoke, Mia?"

After a pause, the girl nodded, and said, "Once in a while, I do."

"Do you do drugs of any kind or drink alcohol?"

"No, no, I don't do those things, not ever."

"First, you must stop smoking as of now. There's strong evidence to show that smoking can have bad effects on your baby."

"Yes, I promise. I won't touch them anymore. I won't."

"You said you don't do drugs or drink."

Mia vigorously shook her head.

"To answer your question, you must eat good food." Bree smiled as she added, "Don't forget. You're not eating for one but two."

Mia smiled.

"I don't mean you have to eat twice as much. What I mean is, there are foods that are particularly good for babies still inside their mothers and foods that are bad for them. You need to be with people who know about such things and who will give you good foods you need to eat. Don't forget what I said. I have a feeling that when your baby's born, you'll be a good mom, but you'll need help. Every new mother does, believe me. I did. My own mom came to stay with me for three weeks. I'd like to be around to see your baby born and to know it's super healthy." If Bree was behaving in a strategic way, she was also genuine.

Mia asked, "But what am I supposed to do? I want to do everything for my little baby that I can."

"Mia," Bree replied, "we're not here to tell you what to do. There are some things you need to think about. Tell you what," she said as though the idea had just occurred to her, "when you're ready, we'll have dinner at my house, the four of us, where you can meet my Maya. Before that, though, you've gotta think about what we're going to say to you. This is important. Evie and Jim have been very good to you and Alex, but they don't have the space to keep you here for a long time. Don't worry, they're not going to throw you out, especially if you're good, but, one day, you'll have to go somewhere else. The question is, where are you going to go?"

All softness had gone from Mia's face. She looked alarmed.

"Let me tell you what usually happens with girls your age who are pregnant and have no place to go. They're placed in foster homes. Do you know what foster homes are?"

Mia reacted as though we'd shaken her. "Foster homes, no," she exclaimed in a loud voice. "I know about those. Daddy and I watched shows about those on TV. They're terrible places for kids to be. I can't go there!"

"Mia, some foster homes are not the best, I agree, but many of them are okay, some even very good. They're not like your own home, okay, but the people who run them do the best they can in situations that are very difficult sometimes. That's very likely where you'll go way before your baby's born."

Mia, distressed and panicked, jumped up, looking first at me and then at Bree. "I can't go to one of those. It wouldn't be good for my baby, would it."

Hesitating, Bree responded, "That's very hard to say. It depends on the people you'd be with. It could work out just fine."

"No it wouldn't. You're just trying to make me feel okay, that's all."

If what Bree was doing was manipulation, it was smooth. It reminded me of what Miguel had told me about good martial artists. They use their opponents' own energy to defeat them.

"Mia, please sit back down," Bree said. "We're talking about this to help you think about what place would be the best for you and your little baby. We don't want answers now. Just think about it for a while and, in a few days, maybe, you can come to dinner at my house as I said, and we can talk about it more."

"You promise? You promise you'll come back to get me and I can go?"

"I promise, absolutely," Bree said. "Now there's one more thing I need to talk to you about before we go. If you end up in a foster home, the authorities will be involved. You understand what I mean by authorities."

Mia said she did.

"They're going to want to know who the father of your child is. Now Mia, listen carefully. Don't get upset with us. It won't do you or your baby any good. We know, of course, who the father is, and that's not a problem for us. If you refuse to tell the authorities who he is, that could make things difficult for you. What I want you to think about is this. It'll make things simpler for everyone, no matter how things turn out, if you're cooperative about this. You'll need to be upfront with everyone about who the father is. If you end up in a foster home, the authorities will run tests to find out who the father is anyway when the baby's born. Do you understand what I'm saying to you?"

Hopefully, I reflected as Bree talked, the girl wouldn't realize we were bluffing. Mia looked belligerent and was unresponsive.

"By the way, Mia," Bree added as we got up to go. "Just so you know, Evie knows a lot about nutrition. She knows what's good for unborn babies, too. So try to follow her instructions while you're still here and remember what I said. The most important thing now for you to do as of this minute is to do everything you can to protect your baby."

Back in the car, I said, "That was some performance. There's no way I could have pulled that off."

Bree smiled. "Well, there are a couple of major attributes you lack—womanhood and being the mother of a young child."

"Guilty on both counts."

Looking reflective, Bree remarked, "You know, I've never seen or even heard of a girl that young with powerful maternal instincts like that. Appeal to those instincts and she's with you. But I have to say, I agree with you absolutely now that I've met the girl. I wouldn't trust her to carry through without that lever. Right now, it's her baby she's preoccupied about, but not far behind is her own self. She makes me anxious. I don't think I know anyone like her. By the way, you've got to give Evie that package for Alex, don't you?"

"How did I manage before you came to us."

I reached for the bundle on the backseat and went back to the house. I explained to Evie what the books were and asked her to give them along with my note to Alex when he came in. She promised me she would.

Chapter 15

I'd gotten through almost half of my inbox by late Thursday afternoon when Sara was at my door. Except for Monday morning, we hadn't met that week.

But for the colorful dangling earrings and her French braid, she looked the same, bright-eyed and full of life.

"Now that's a look I haven't seen before," I said as she sat down.

"That's Tara's doing. She's my cousin. Can't keep her hands out of people's hair. She's been staying with me for a couple of days, down here from Menlo Park. You think I'm energetic, Forrest, I'm nothing compared to her. Anyway, I've dug up some stuff on this coercive control thing. I have nearly a dozen articles on the subject and four people you might want to talk to. They're all on the East Coast. Do you want me to carry on with this or—"

I shook my head. "No, not before Bree sees this stuff. I'll pass it on and she'll probably let you know if there's more to do."

Sara smiled in that coy way of hers. "I'm sure she will. She seems to know what she's looking for. Anyway," Sara said as she rose to go, "have a good weekend if I don't see you before."

I'd long since given up guessing about which of my research assistant's statements had double meanings. I was sure this last one did, but I wasn't inclined to speculate. Though the thought of another tryst with her was exciting, tomorrow night my daughter would be home and Saturday was spoken for.

I picked up the pile of documents Sara left for me to get them off to Bree before she left when I saw the edge of a little piece of paper peeking out underneath the stack, impossible to miss. It was pale green. More of Sara's doodling. I could barely work with her because of this when she first came. She claimed she couldn't think without moving a pencil in her hand. Normally, she took her scribbled notes away. Why not this time?

The only really intelligible thing on the little sheet was a phone number I recognized, her cell. Otherwise, there were a couple of what could be letters and what appeared to be plus signs. The three letters were so stylized as to be barely legible. An *S*, followed by a plus sign, then what could be an *F*. Another plus sign and what surely was a *T*.

The little piece of paper was on its way to my trash can before the objective of my assistant's doodling struck me. *S* for Sara, *F* for Forrest and *T* for the hyperactive cousin. It had to be. The dream of most males on this earth, the chance to have wild sex with two hungry gorgeous girls at once. That dream would become reality if I dialed Sara's number.

I could feel the heat of that billet-doux three feet away. The idea daunted me. 'Be honest, Forrest, it scares you half to death,' remonstrated the voice of reason inside my head. Two insatiable girls of Sara's ilk would have made short work of me at half my age.

Titillating though the proposal was, I would smile and reminisce about last Sunday night and have the good sense to stop while I was ahead. I'd frequent people a little closer to my age who liked juicy steaks, distilled juice of the cactus plant and sex that didn't debilitate me for several days.

With my not-so-little girl due in from Atlanta at 5:10 p.m., I wasn't going to gamble with freeway traffic on Friday afternoon. How often had I been caught in one-hour slowdowns when I'd have been better off on foot. Instead of heading out at two-thirty, which should have given me ample time, I left at one.

LAX was teeming when I arrived at three, thronged with people from all parts of the globe. I would have thought myself to be in a foreign country based on the little English I heard. The air inside was heavy with the smells of unwashed bodies and spicy foods.

With more than two hours to wait, I searched in vain for a little nook away from the din and fetid atmosphere. Eventually, I went back outside and had to settle for a wilted salad and bad coffee in a nearby greasy spoon. I jotted down some ideas about how to approach Mia and her brother the following week, but the ambiance didn't suit. My mind drifted briefly to Sara's note, then, more comfortably, to Vicky and her hideaway. Would I bring my emergency cell phone next time? I'd never get away with it. The thought of her frisking me thoroughly before letting me through her door made me smile.

My attempt to be first in line to meet passengers coming off the plane was thwarted by a packed throng for whom pushing was a way of life. Had Trina missed her flight? Everyone seemed to have deplaned and no sight of her. An anxious-looking woman in her mid-forties and I were the only two persons waiting at the arrival gate.

Just as I was about to say something to her, a tall lady in a Delta uniform caught my eye walking next to a much shorter female who I immediately recognized. Trina, carrying two large bundles, attempted to break away and run to me, but the lady held fast to her. I could see the frustrated expression on my daughter's face as she explained who I was. At about fifty feet away, Trina began calling out to me while I waved at her. When she reached me, she tried to pull her arm free.

The matronly attendant with a no-nonsense demeanor said, "I must see this man's ID first. Those are the regulations." More likely, the woman's private rules.

My creds back in my pocket, I pulled Trina and her bags into my arms while the officious lady mumbled as she endeavored to snip off my daughter's Delta bracelet. Disgruntled, she stepped back while we hugged.

Trina started talking the moment I let her loose and didn't stop until we had her suitcase and were at the car.

"Daddy, it's awesome where Anna lives. I want to go back there soon. Anna's totally my best friend and Lena and Norm, they're both so nice. They bought me lots of really cool stuff cuz Anna told them to. Anna's so gorgeous, Daddy, you know that? She's the prettiest girl ever."

"Oh no she's not," I managed to get in before Trina dismissed my comment with a wave and carried on.

I felt a twinge as I paid for parking and headed for the freeway. Perhaps it was a change in my daughter's hairstyle or the new clothes she wore or, just maybe, the hint of perfume that she'd never had on before that emphasized what, selfishly, I didn't want to see. My baby, who'd been at the center of my life, had stepped across the intangible line between adoring child and young womanhood. We'd always be close, I knew, but with each passing year, less and less the same as it had been.

As I drove onto the freeway, Trina reached up to pull the sun visor down. I blinked and looked again at her left arm.

Alarmed, I exclaimed, "What the hell is that?" It looked like a tattoo of a butterfly.

"Oh that," she said. "I have four of 'em on me. Don't worry, Daddy. They come off in a week."

Then I saw Trina's fingernails. They were hot pink. "Anything else you did at Anna's that I should know about?"

For a moment, she didn't answer. Then, in a wheedling tone I didn't like, she said, "Daddy, could I have my ears pierced?"

I swallowed. She'd ask for a cell phone next. Though I shouldn't have passed the blame to Claire, I answered, "I'm sorry, no. Your mother wouldn't put up with that."

Trina pouted but didn't say anything. She knew what I'd said was true.

To get the smile back on my daughter's face, I said, "So I thought I'd take my favorite girl out to dinner instead of eating at home. That alright with you?"

"Yay! Where do we get to go?"

"That's entirely up to you, sweetheart. What are you hungry for?"

Trina's brow wrinkled, then she said, "I know. Let's go to Chan's on Barrera Street, okay?" I should have guessed.

"At least you choose the best Chinese restaurant in Santa Lucia. It'll be a couple of hours you'll have to wait, okay?"

By the time we broke open our fortune cookies, Trina was half asleep.

"Your body's still on Georgia time," I said. "It's midnight on the East Coast. Better get you home to bed."

"I want to show you all my new stuff, Daddy, but I'm too tired. Can we do it tomorrow morning after breakfast?"

I'd just come back into her room after she'd put on her pajamas and gotten into bed. "I'm afraid not, love. Mommy's coming tomorrow to pick you up. Remember?"

Trina grew somber and she was quiet for a while, then she said, her eyes half closed, "Do I have to, Daddy? I just got home. I want to stay with you, not with them."

"Honey," I responded, "your mommy needs to see you. She misses you just like I do when you're away." Not sure whether I should query her, I asked, "Is there some reason you don't want to go?"

Trina's eyes that had nearly closed slowly opened. She thought about my question. "John—that's Mommy's husband—he's okay, but he doesn't talk to us very much. Andy doesn't like him. He's not nice like you and Norm. That's why I like Norm, Daddy, cuz he's warm and friendly like you. Can't you tell Mommy I'm too tired to go?"

My daughter's disclosure troubled me. Claire seemed more abrupt and less affable of late. Apart from added stress for the twins that we didn't need, I didn't want our children to become alienated from their mother in any way.

"My love," I said, reaching for Trina's hand, "you know something? I wouldn't want to get up in the morning and face the world if I thought you or Andy didn't want to see me. I couldn't stand that. I wouldn't want your mother to have to go through such a thing. No, sweetheart, no. I can't tell her you're too tired. I don't know anything about her new husband, but I know your mommy loves you and she needs to be with you and you need to be with her. You understand, don't you?"

Trina sighed and nodded. "Yeah, I guess so. Maybe it's cuz I'm so tired, I don't know."

I looked down at my daughter, who smiled at me.

"I know what you were gonna say. You were gonna tell me you love me, weren't you."

"You some kind of mind reader, are you?"

"Not really. I just know you, that's all. Besides, you've been telling me that every day all my life, haven't you."

"Guilty as charged," I said as I bent to kiss her just above her nose. "Off to sleep, my angel. I'm glad you're home."

At nine-thirty sharp, Claire pulled in. She was edgy in her voice and in her manner. Trina hugged me and got into the passenger seat of her mother's car. She hadn't taken any of her new things, just her duffel bag.

"Andy will be here at six tomorrow when I bring

Trina back, won't he?" Claire said.

"I'll make sure he is."

A curt nod and my erstwhile spouse and our daughter drove away.

Minutes before I was to leave Santa Lucia to pick up Andy at his camp, the phone rang. It was Miguel Martinez.

"Hey Forrest. I'm here at the camp to see the managers about adding a martial arts class to the activities the camp offers. I can bring Andy back with me if you want me to."

"That'd be great," I said. "Any idea when you'll be here?"

"'Bout sixish, I'd say, unless traffic's bad. That sound alright?"

"Better than alright. It'll give me a chance to fix a decent dinner. Care to join us?"

"Would do, but Isabel's been cooking all day for us so I've gotta be there. See you later on this afternoon."

The only thing my son liked better than Chinese food were barbecued smoked sausage sandwiches with honey mustard. He was working on his second while he recounted the afternoon's events. Next to his plate on our backyard table was his trophy for second best pitcher in his group, a nice prize with twenty-three competing at his age. He looked proud and smiled each time I glanced at it.

"So who got first place?"

"A boy from Russia, Dad. He's awesome! Our coaches say he shouldn't do it cuz he's too young, but he throws wicked curve balls no one can hit. My fastball's better than his, though, my coach says."

"Good stuff. How was your control?"

Andy pretended he hadn't heard. I had my answer. Grinning, I asked, "Didn't bean anybody this time, did you?"

"Nope nope nope," came his machine gun reply.

"Well, that's okay, then. Every good pitcher's a little wild sometimes."

By the time his chocolate sundae had disappeared, that part of it that wasn't on his face and shirt, I'd heard about the entire week, including Andy's overzealous reports of three injuries on the field. He dug inside his shorts pocket and pulled out some sort of badge. I reached for it. Large letters at the top read *VBC* for Ventura Baseball Camp. Beneath were the words *Best Pitcher in Group F.* The last line said *Second Prize.*

"Can you sew that on my jersey, Dad, real soon?"

"Sure can. Is it clean?"

Andy thought for a moment, then shook his head.

"Okay. I'll stick it in the laundry tomorrow and sew it on when it's dry."

It was great to have him back. We rarely had time together at home, just the two of us. Unusual for him, Andy was drooping by seven o'clock, a good thing since I had to be at Bree's at seven-thirty and Ben's at eight. I'd be a little late.

A half hour after, teeth brushed and bathed, he was in his bed, asleep. No tucking in my boy anymore. That little ritual had gone by the boards a year ago.

Lupe, more a member of our family than a sitter, came in as I was about to leave. She did overnights quite often at our house with her own room and personal things that she left there.

"You be back tonight, *señor*, or you be back tomorrow?"

"I'll come back tonight, quite late. No need to worry about Andy. He's asleep."

Lupe grinned. She loved the twins, but had no control over them, especially Andy. She'd have little work to do that night.

"This is quite a fancy car," Bree commented as we headed toward the edge of town. I had the top down.

Grinning sheepishly, I said, "I can't help it. I love Mustangs. It's a bit self-indulgent, but—"

"I think it's great! I haven't been in a fun car like this in, I don't know when. Funny how people are. I'd never have imagined you in this." Coaxing the smile off her face and putting on her serious look, she said, "Something more sophisticated, like a Lexus, or a Cadillac, maybe."

"So that's how the woman sees me, puffed up and pompous."

Her happy expression back, she replied, "No, not at all. I say those things to get a rise out of you and make you smile. I like it when you do."

The breeze played with Bree's curls as we drove along, sending me hints of that tantalizing scent I couldn't identify. In a sleeveless bright green sundress, her feet in sandals, she looked relaxed and out for a good time. I couldn't see any golden specks, but her eyes were sparkling. Had she used lipstick to make her mouth stand out like that?

We'd passed the outskirts of Santa Lucia and were in the countryside. Though rather sparse, there were junipers and pine and some small hardwood trees on both sides of the road. There was little traffic where we were. The air was invigorating, redolent of greenery and the sea.

"Ben lives quite a ways out, doesn't he," Bree remarked.

"About twenty minutes out of town. We're almost there." Catching sight of a run-down house at least a century old, I said, "Even here, real estate is quite expensive."

"More than this girl could afford, I'd say. I'll have to find me a high-paying job somewhere."

"Not til this case is over," I retorted.

"It'll be okay then?"

Feigning impatience and displeasure, I shot back, "No, Brianna Dixon, it won't." I could feel my lips reshape into a grin as I added, "You like to get me going, don't you."

"I told you. I like to see you smile."

*

Ben's party was under way. On about a quarter of an acre, his quaint little house was set well back among the trees. We smelled the steaks and heard laughter before we saw Ben and two people standing near him. They must be neighbors. There was only one car in the driveway. No sign of Cassie's anywhere.

"Bree, darlin'," Ben exclaimed as he approached and gave her a big hug. She looked surprised but not displeased. "Cassie's not back yet, worst luck, but nice to have the flower of the office visitin' us out here."

"Why Ben," Bree replied. "What a nice thing for you to say. You're forgetting Sara, aren't you?"

Ben said, "Bree, honey, you're the real thing. Sara's not a woman yet, just a kid." Turning to me and tapping me on the chest, he said, "Forrest, you old dog, you. Nice to see you've got some sense. Let me introduce you folks around."

As he turned toward the two people we'd seen from the street, an attractive blonde in her late thirties, a little overweight, maybe, came to stand close in front of me. From her flushed face and over-bright blue eyes as well as the fumes that came from her, it was evident she'd started early. For an embarrassed moment, she looked about to kiss me. I moved back a step. Bree was watching and she was smiling.

"I'm Loise. I live just across the road in the next house down. So you're the man Ben talks about all the time. Hmmm. It's nice to have you here."

Moving sideways and reaching for her hand, I said, "This is my friend, Bree. It's her first time out here."

Ben, a tall glass of something frosty in his left hand, stood back and watched. Loise unabashedly eyed my companion up and down, a speculative expression on her pretty face, while Bree looked back at her. I turned to greet the male half of the pair, who'd come up without a sound. He was easily six and a half feet tall and rapier thin with a chiseled narrow face. He had coal black hair and dark blue eyes that had a lazy look.

In a voice like an adolescent boy's, he said, "I'm Julian Sparks. I live with this blonde vampire here. Watch her, you two. She gets a little frisky when the sun goes down."

Nodding, still near me, Loise said, "That's when the party starts, darling, especially with these two here."

"Come on, Lo," her partner urged, "give 'em some space to breathe. They haven't even had their first drink yet."

As they moved away, I heard Loise say, "I like the looks of him, and she looks yummy too, don't you think?"

What had I brought Bree to? Would she be talking to me on Monday morning? Ben came back to life.

"Bree, sweetheart, what's your poison? Tell you the truth, we're only servin' one kinda drink. I call 'em Segalowitz margaritas. You'll like 'em, I guarantee. Just ask this high-flyin' lawyer here. You gotta watch them though, they're kinda strong. Let me get you one."

Clearly charmed by Ben's bon ami, Bree said, "I'll be happy to have one of those, and I don't have to drive."

Loise, a few feet away, made a throaty noise. I was going to have to keep alert. With no more sunlight and another drink, that hungry lady would be all over me or at Bree to pull her onto her lap.

I wasn't sure where Ben bought his meat, but he knew his cuts. His steaks, with just sufficient fat, were always flavorful. He only ever cooked them over charcoal. His baked potatoes, seeded with fresh bacon bits, onion and cheese, were to die for. For these little parties that he held three or four times a year, he baked his own garlic bread. Needless to say, the libations were to my taste.

Bree, it was obvious very soon, was no newcomer to alcohol. By the time she had her plate, she was near the bottom of her second glass. Though half stoked, Ben glanced at her with concern.

"Watch that stuff, sweetheart," he told her. "That's a lotta juice for a itty-bitty girl."

Bree gave him a dazzling smile and said that she'd

be fine. I fervently hoped so.

Julian, who rarely spoke, was an electrician for the gas and electric company. Loise was a manager for Santa Lucia's public library system. As it always does, conversation livened up as drinks went down.

It was remarkable how two people, so very different, could stay together. If Julian said something was, Loise was sure to insist that it couldn't be. If Loise championed someone or a cause, Julian lost little time in proclaiming how ludicrous her position was. If there was physical rapport between the two, they didn't show it.

The good host that he was, during moments of awkward silence, Ben would say something about the weather, about California politics or something about Santa Lucia's lousy cops. Most of the time, though, we were laughing. Bree, halfway through her third tall glass, was quiet and smiled a lot. I chimed in here and there while I nursed my second drink.

It happened during one of those mellow moments when, replete, everyone relaxes and gazes at the stars—everyone, that is, but Loise. The five of us sat more or less evenly spaced apart in a big circle about twenty feet across. The one and a half glasses I'd taken in made me more curious than apprehensive as I watched her stand up and, a little wobbly, make her way toward me.

I wasn't surprised when she nudged my legs slightly to the side and plopped down in my lap. Her inebriated state notwithstanding, that lady knew exactly where on me to sit and how.

Putting her left arm around my shoulders, her drink in her other hand, she bent close and whispered, "Do you like the party?"

Not sure what else to do, I replied in a normal voice, "Do I like the party? Yes I do. The food was great."

Now at a level everyone could hear, her face closer, Loise asked, "Do you like me?"

Before I could say anything, she kissed me on each cheek, then settled on my lips. About ten feet away, Bree was laughing. It was as well that I didn't smoke. A spark in the air around Loise's face and the two of us would have blown up. With nowhere to set my glass and my free hand on the woman's back, I couldn't extricate myself. The librarian was intent on surveying every square millimeter inside my mouth. No help from Julian or from Ben and not a word from Bree, who was apparently entertained.

At last, tiring of my unresponsiveness, Loise withdrew and struggled to her feet. Now it was my turn to be amused. I watched as Loise headed for Bree's chair. Should I rescue her or was it possible that, in her euphoric state, she didn't care?

No sitting on laps this time. A different tack. Putting her glass on the ground, Loise knelt beside Bree's chair, wrapped both arms around her neck and buried her face in her hair. Loise made a satisfied and happy noise. I waited, along with the other men, to see how things played out. Had Bree tried to break away, I would have gone to her aid, but, she appeared content. As I watched Loise's hand come up to stroke Bree's cheek and curls, not without a little disappointment, I began to wonder.

Then, in a soft and friendly tone, we heard Bree say, "Loise, you're lovely and that feels nice, but what I'd really like is for Ben to get me another drink so could you get up?"

Though in his cups, Ben heard. "Comin' up, my love, comin' up. Let her go there, Loise. The woman wants to drink." A moment later, there was a topped-up glass in Bree's left hand.

On her feet and swaying, Loise said, "Come on guys. This is a party and there's not enough lovin' going on." She swiveled her head as though looking for candidates.

This time, I was nervous. Her eyes came back to me while she bent down to take Bree's right hand and pulled her gently up. Now what?

"Come along, love. I know what you want. You've been looking at him all night."

I gulped, but Bree's negative reply that I expected

didn't come. Instead, a little unsteady on her feet, she allowed Loise to lead her straight to me.

"Now do what you should have done an hour ago." Slurring a little, she continued, "Snuggle up on his lap."

I let out my breath as, with a little help from Loise, Bree sat and immediately turned toward me. She was shivering in her sleeveless dress. As to me, I felt a warm contented glow as my arms went around her to pull her close.

Satisfied, Loise commented as she moved away, "Now that's the way two people who want each other ought to be."

Occasionally, someone spoke, often to ward off the blonde, but I wasn't paying much attention. Something very special was going on inside of me as I felt Bree's fragrant hair touch my face. She wasn't trembling anymore. She was possibly asleep, given what she'd had to drink.

Very quietly so she wouldn't hear, I said under my breath, "I've wanted you close to me like this for a long time." The alcohol had put her out. I was glad she had someone staying with her overnight. I felt chagrin and wished fervently I hadn't expressed my thoughts as Bree slowly raised her head.

"I'm glad," she said in that soft low voice of hers. "Here's what I've been wishing for." Up came her hands to pull my face down to hers.

Seconds later, I felt desire, certainly, but stronger was the sense, new to me, of peace and wholeness. It was not unlike what I experienced when returning home after too much time away. Bree's full lips I had gazed at many times seemed to draw me in, warm and soft, so reminiscent of the person I'd come to know. Her quickened breathing and little forays with her tongue said sweet things about the woman who I held.

I have no idea how long we sat like that. It could have been twenty minutes or an hour. By the time Ben tapped me lightly on the shoulder, Bree was sound asleep.

Scarcely able to articulate, Ben whispered, "Loise and Julian left a while ago. You okay to drive?"

"Absolutely," I assured him. "I'm fine." I'd never finished my second drink. "Thanks, old friend. It was... an important time."

Muddled though his thinking processes must have been, he wasn't so far gone to miss the petite figure in my arms. He smiled. "She looks very nice there where she is. Glad you two could come. Take it easy on the road, okay?"

She weighing no more than a hundred pounds, it was easy to pick Bree up and carry her to my car. She awoke when I went to strap her in her seat. Seconds after, her head with all those curls that I'd finally touched was on my shoulder and she was out.

I left the top down because I wanted to let her sleep. There was no wind and it was warm. I drove slowly, not wanting our little trip to end. How nurturing that evening had been for me, and extraordinary too. Had it not been for the amorous Loise, Bree and I surely wouldn't have come together as we had. A wonderful and unexpected thing.

In thirty minutes we were at Bree's home. In no hurry to say good night, I stopped my car adjacent to a field just down the block, something I'd done often as a teenager. It made me grin. I turned my engine off. As I feared, the silence and lack of motion woke Bree up. Would she be unhappy about what happened or would she come to me? The moment I reached for her, she was in my arms.

"I have to go, Forrest," she whispered. "My friend may be looking out the window."

"Maybe," I said, "but she won't see us. I'm down the block."

Bree laughed. I could still hear the alcohol in her voice when she said, "This reminds me of when I was in high school." Then she was kissing me.

Unlike before when she'd been quiet and a little timid, her small tongue was everywhere in my mouth and she was breathing fast. Abruptly, she broke away.

"Lucky, lucky for us," she murmured, "this car is small. I'll get out here and walk down to my house." With more strength than I would have thought she had, she grabbed me around the neck and gave me one more long kiss. She opened the car door and was out.

I sat there and watched her move unsteadily toward her home, where she turned in. 'Good night, sweetheart,' I called out mentally as I drove away. 'Thanks for coming into my life.'

I chatted with Andy at the breakfast table, played ball with him afterward in our backyard and puttered around the house, but the smell of Bree's hair, the feel of her in my arms and the taste of her eager mouth were constantly on my mind.

I was afraid she'd pull away. What had occurred the night before had come too soon. She might want me as I'd discovered I wanted her, but she'd not be ready for someone new this soon, or so I feared. How would she feel in the light of day about a man who, not that long divorced, might still be pining for his wife? Was it my loneliness that made me so susceptible to her or had my intuition when holding her been right about how well we fit?

Our relationship, pushed forward by last night's events, would now be fragile. Press Bree and, reasonably, she'd retreat. Be too cautious as I'd be inclined and she might give up on me. Though she'd been in Santa Lucia for only half a year, vital and attractive as she was, there might be others after her.

I heard Claire's car at twenty minutes after five. She was early and our son hadn't returned from his friend's house yet. 'Please no trouble, Claire,' I whispered to myself as I headed to the front door.

Points for Andy, who was nearly always late. I heard his bike brakes squeak as she was pulling in. Trina, bag in hand and a frown on her heart-shaped face, walked past me into the house without a word. Her brother, doing his best to avoid a hug, was talking without a pause about his camp. Claire looked irritated. Clearly, there'd been some problem with our daughter. After several attempts to interrupt Andy's rapid-fire speech, she managed to break in.

"Honey, that sounds fantastic. You can show me your badge next time I come after your father sews it on." Reaching for Andy who ducked away, Claire said, "Friday night two weeks from now, remember? No games or camps or anything this time, okay? I'm very sorry, love, but I've got to go. I have to be at the hospital by eight, and with Sunday traffic... Come give Mommy a hug goodbye." Unwillingly, Andy went.

Claire hadn't looked at me or said a word. That, in itself, didn't trouble me. What did was the reason for her mood. Something had upset her. I never interrogated the twins. Nor did I squelch the comments they made about their weekends with their mom. I'd hear more than I wanted to when Trina went to bed.

Cheeseburgers on the grill this time, a family favorite. I had my big blender out and was making strawberry shakes when Trina came into the kitchen and sat down. Andy was in his room. My daughter, still with her unhappy look, waited until I'd turned the noisy machine off.

"Daddy, why doesn't Mommy like nice stuff? She used to wear pretty dresses when you guys went out sometimes." I waited. "She got mad at me every time I talked about Anna and what we did. Why does she do that? Anna's family was so nice to me. She wouldn't let me talk about my new clothes or anything. She says I have to get over all that girly stuff. That's what she calls it. Do I, Daddy? Do I?"

I had to be careful how I answered. Contradicting Claire about the validity of her beliefs wasn't the way to maintain the relatively stable arrangements we'd worked out. At the same time...

Standing at the kitchen counter facing her, I said, "Sweetheart, tell me. Why don't you eat what we call junk food?"

Trina didn't answer right away. She knew what I was doing and was searching for a way to short-circuit me. Looking perplexed, she asked, "What do you mean?"

I repeated my question.

Trina looked annoyed. "You're not answering me. You just don't want to go against what Mommy says." As usual with me, she was on the mark.

Abandoning my Socratic strategy, I said, "Look. People have different opinions about things. You know that. We don't eat junk food for good reasons, right? The fact is, most people in this country do eat junk food and they disagree with us or just don't care. Some people smoke and are fine with it. Fortunately, most of us disagree with that and don't. Some people think taking a lot of trouble to fix good food's a waste of time. Just eat what your body needs, they say. We think good food's worth it, don't we."

"Okay, Daddy, I get your point. Mommy doesn't care about cool clothes. But does that mean I'm not 'sposed to?"

I was in a corner. "Alright. Your mother and I have different views about how you dress. I happen to love the way you look in those new things."

The unhappy look went away, replaced by a smile that would melt a block of ice.

"You shouldn't complain, you know. Since you spend most of your time with me, what you and I agree about, you can do. When you're with your mother, try to respect her point of view. Don't force yours on her. You can wear decent things without getting all dressed up, and you can talk about other things than clothes."

She considered this. Nodding slowly, she conceded, "Yeah, I guess... I wish Mommy still lived with us, but me and her would have problems about my clothes and stuff, wouldn't we."

'Yes, my girl, you would, particularly with the stuff,'

I didn't say, 'and you wouldn't be the only one to feel the heat.'

"Let me pour these shakes and we can go outside."

Trina got up and came over to me for a good long hug. She raised the face that I'd cherished since she was small and said, "I'll never live with anybody else, Daddy, you know that, don't you."

"Not until some guy sweeps you off your feet and marries you, you won't, or 'til you go off to college."

Notwithstanding her expression of disgust, the idea was more appalling to me than it was to her. It was wonderful to have my children back home with me.

"Nice to have Bree there at the party, boyo," Ben commented. "Man, can that girl drink. Hope Loise didn't make too much of a nuisance of herself. She upset Bree?"

I shook my head. It was Monday morning, and Ben's office was my first stop.

"Cassie doesn't get along with Loise all that much."

"I'm not surprised," I said. "Where did you find those two?"

"We didn't. They found us. Cassie and me, we were havin' a barbecue outside when up they come. They kept commentin' so much about the smell of the food that I had to get two more steaks and grill 'em up. Whenever we're eatin' outside, those two show up. It's gettin' to be a little wearin' on the nerves."

"That, I can understand." Secretly, I was grateful to Loise. "Thanks for inviting us. I'm really glad we went."

After a little pause and a searching look, Ben said, "So am I from what I seen. We'll have you back pretty soon. Don't know if I told you, but Cassie's in Corpus Christi, Texas. Called out on a case a couple a weeks ago. Christ knows when she'll be back. It's a complicated one, she says. Anyway, we'll do it again before too long. Maybe we'll a gotten rid a Loise and her friend by then."

With trepidation, I went down the corridor to drop

in on Bree. We had things to plan that week. I felt a stab of disappointment as she looked up. As I'd feared, she had a neutral expression on her face, nothing there to suggest where that curly head of hers had been. As was her custom, she gestured toward the couch.

With a smile that failed to reach her eyes, she said, "So how is everything? Both children back?" There was to be no talk of Ben's party, not then, at least.

"Yes, and I'm glad to have them home, believe me. The house is like a tomb when they're not there."

Bree nodded. "I can imagine. I've never had to be away from Maya, I'm glad to say. It'd be very strange not to have her there."

We needed to get off the ice. "I have appointments this afternoon with the three women you asked Lucy about. Two of them seem eager to do what they can. Kate Barns sounds a little doubtful. Have you had a chance to look at Sara's stuff?"

"Yes, yes I did. You're right about that girl. She's resourceful. There were some things she gave us I didn't know about. I'd like to check out a few more things, then we can talk."

"Good. I'm also going to have a talk with Alex. We're meeting Wednesday afternoon. I'd prefer you to be there, but, given our history—"

"No," Bree said, shaking her head. "He's more likely to be responsive with just you there."

Continuing, I added, "Then there's our second meeting with Mia we talked about. Can we discuss that tomorrow morning?"

"Sure. That's fine. In the meantime, I'll get back to what more I can dig up on coercive control."

Whether her final words were an invitation for me to leave or not, I stood up to go.

Barely audible, Bree said, "Bye Forrest. See you tomorrow morning."

Was that a wistful note in her voice or simply preoccupation with her work? No way to know.

*

From what Lucy said, Jacqueline Parks was about our age, but she could have passed for thirty. Though she'd chosen to keep her light brown hair short like a man, the rest, including voice and gestures, was all female. Pretty but for a nose that dominated her oval face, she had a straightforward, friendly look. I warmed to her immediately.

"Mr. Spencer—"

"Forrest, please."

Smiling, she said, "If you call me Jackie. Lucy used to talk about you a lot. You've been friends for a long time, right?"

"Not the kind of friend I should have been," I replied. "Except for the last two years or so, we were pretty close. We've been that way since college days."

"That's what she told me. I wouldn't be too hard on yourself if I were you. From what I saw, I'm not sure anyone could have done that much."

"Why do you think that?" I asked.

Settling back in her chair, her expression gloomy, Jackie replied, "I've known Lucy for... how many years now, five, six? I've watched her steadily go downhill. It was that domineering manipulative husband of hers that was the cause, let me tell you. I don't know what the last straw was that drove Lucy to do what she did, but, whatever it was, the man deserved it for what he did to her."

"Did to her? Like what?"

"Year by year, he tore her down. The Lucy I used to know wasn't there toward the end, last time I saw her, I mean. The bastard took everything away from her. She had no independence left. He took her car, can you imagine? He turned her into a servant for the family in her own home. I tried to convince her to leave the guy. She would have been okay. We could have helped, a bunch of us, but she just wasn't up to it. In too much of a weakened state, I guess."

I didn't doubt anything Jackie said. To the contrary, Lucy's situation was probably much worse than her friend knew. With the possible exception of the incident about Lucy's car, little of what I'd just heard could be used in court.

"Jackie, about Lucy's car. Do you have any idea when Pete took it? Did she tell you?"

Jackie's brows went together in concentration. "Yeah, she did. Let's see. I went to see her on a Monday on my way home from the library. He'd taken it away from her the week before, I think."

"Can you remember when that was?"

"Yes, actually, that's easy. I volunteer once a month to help children with reading problems. I go on Mondays, so... that'd be August fifth last month and, the month before that when I saw Lucy, let's see, July eighth, I think. That's when I saw her. Her husband took the car just the week before."

"Okay," I said. "One more thing. You said that Lucy declined to follow your advice to leave her husband. Did she tell you why?"

"That's a funny thing, you know?" Jackie said. "I've wondered about that. She was crying. She said there were reasons why she couldn't, and she wouldn't tell me what they were. It wouldn't do any good, she said. Do you have any idea what she meant?"

Going around her question, I said, "If we decide that what you've told me can be used in court, can we count on you to testify?"

"Are you kidding? Of course I will. Just call me and I'll be there. It's so unfair what that asshole did! Lucy's a love, she really is, but you know that. Count on me to do what I can."

The next person I saw was Susan Carpenter. She was elegance itself. Everything about her looked regal, from her Patrician nose and high cheekbones to her hairstyle and unostentatious well-tailored suit. Her blue eyes and mouth looked warm, as was her voice. Her figure was a replica of Lucy's, with a bit more weight. I explained again why I'd phoned her.

"I'm glad to help if I can," she said, "but I'm not sure what I can do. I haven't seen all that much of poor Lucy these last few years. I was sorry to hear about what happened in July. By the way, please call me Sue."

"And I'm Forrest. Lucy and I've been friends for a long time. She kept a very detailed diary over the years. I don't suppose you knew."

Sue shook her head.

"Lucy mentions an incident in it that I wanted to discuss with you. You apparently visited her at her home some time ago to borrow an evening dress. Does that ring a bell?"

"I'm afraid it does. I remember that all too well. It was scandalous what that man did."

"Can you explain?"

"If you know Lucy well, you'll know she loved nice clothes. She had a lot of style and the kind of body clothes love. You know what I mean."

I nodded.

"My husband was promoted, yes it was back then, and his office organized a fancy party for him. I went shopping for a new dress, but couldn't find exactly what I wanted. Then I remembered one I saw on Lucy that I wanted to borrow from her for the night since we're the same size... Yeah, well, she didn't have it anymore. The fact is, she didn't have any of her pretty things anymore. Her husband took everything except frumpy stuff away. Actually took her clothes away from her. I couldn't believe it when she told me... Well, in a way, I could. I remembered the guy at a party at their home a friend of mine and I went to. He was the macho type with old-fashioned ways. I didn't like him. Anyway, he took all her nice things away... It made me furious."

"Can you remember when he took the clothes away?"

Sue's forehead wrinkled as she thought back. She shook her head. "I don't know. That was a long time ago."

"It was sometime in 2010, Lucy says in her diary.

Does that help?"

"Yes, yes it does. That's when my husband got his big promotion, that's right."

"Could you figure out the date, by chance?"

She took out her cell phone. A couple of minutes later, she disconnected. "It had to be September seventeenth, that would have been a Friday, cuz the party—my husband looked it up—was on Saturday night of the eighteenth. I would have gone to see her on September seventeenth, a Friday."

"Great," I said. "Would you be willing to testify to all this in court?"

"Absolutely. It's the least I can do for her. Just let me know."

Surprisingly, neither Jackie nor Sue seemed put off by what Lucy did. Perhaps it was not all that strange, given what had happened at the party Sue referred to and what had occurred when they had gone individually to Lucy's home. Would Kate Barns be similarly predisposed?

Settling with some difficulty on the chair, joint problems, maybe, the lady said, "You know, Mr. Spencer, I remember what you said on the phone, but I don't really understand why I'm here. It's for Lucy Jackson, isn't it?"

Just over five feet and close to two hundred pounds, dressed in beige khaki slacks and faded shirt, the woman was the antithesis of the lady who'd just left. Whether due to extra weight or to her temperament, her face had a fretful cast.

"Yes, Ms. Barns. As I told you, we're the defense attorneys for Lucy's case. We're trying to form a picture of her life during the few years that preceded her husband's death."

"His murder, don't you mean?"

"No, actually, I don't mean that. Since you've been good enough to come, I'd explain why we don't believe murder was involved if we had the time. I do appreciate it very much that you're here. As I said, we're trying to get as complete a picture as we can of Lucy's home life for the past few years. We're helped a lot in this by a detailed diary that she kept. It's very useful, but it can't tell us everything. You come up in this diary, and that's why I called."

Barns' head came up at this. "So, what did she say about me?"

"She mentions a soccer game several years ago. According to Lucy, you two were sitting together at this game. She has some nice things to say about your son. Apparently, he was the goalie for the team, a very good one. Alex, as you may remember, was on your son's team. I used to be Alex's soccer coach. That was a long time ago. Anyway, Pete, Alex's father, came up to where you two were, Lucy says—"

"Yes, yes, I remember now. Odd thing that was."

"In what sense, Ms. Barns?"

She looked suspicious for a moment, then she replied, "Men get upset, you know? Least my husband does. Made no sense about Lucy's man, though. Our team was doin' good and Alex was okay, least I think he was. Pete comes up, scowlin' at Lucy to beat the band. Don't ask me why. That's not all that strange, I guess, except for what he does afterwards."

I waited.

"He takes off his hat—one of those with a bill on the front—and, just like my kids used to do, he turns it around the other way. Looked stupid, it really did. I remember askin' Lucy about it at the time. I can't tell you why, but she got real quiet after that. Fact is, she wouldn't talk to me anymore. She just turned around and started chattin' with her little daughter. Kinda pissed me off, if you know what I mean."

"Ms. Barns—"

"Oh, call me Kate. No more a that Ms. Barns stuff. Oughta be Mrs., anyway. You have any idea why Lucy did that to me?"

"I do," I said, "but it'd be better if you see what Lucy

said. Hold on. Let me find the page. I've marked it here."

I opened the sixth volume of the diary and found my spot. I could almost see the steam rising from Kate's head as she read.

"What the fuck? Anal sex? That's what that son of a bitch was doin' to her? I'd a cut him up with my butcher knife, that's what I'd a done. This true, what she's sayin' here?"

"I think, if you read all six volumes here, you'd believe everything she said is true. There was serious abuse in that home, Kate."

"What are you talkin' about, anyway? Whata you mean by abuse?"

I looked at her.

"You're not sayin'—you're not sayin' what I think."

"All I can tell you at this point is that there was serious abuse in that home and Lucy wasn't the one committing it."

"You can't be serious! That little next-to-nothin' girl a theirs?"

"I can't specify the kind of abuse now, Kate. And please don't mention what we've talked about here to anyone, not yet, anyway. I promise you that you're not being misled in any way. I've told you what I did—perhaps I said too much—but I'm hoping you'll agree to appear in court for us and say what you've told me here."

Without a pause, Kate said, "On one condition. I need to talk to Lucy first."

"I have no problem with that at all," I said, "but, please. It's extremely important that you not discuss with anyone what you talk about with her. It could hurt her case."

"I have just one question to ask her. She says one thing, then I'll come. Damn right I'll come. She says the other, I'm not goin' to court anywhere. Can I use your phone?"

"That's fine with me. I'd like to clear it with Lucy, first, if that's okay with you."

"That's fine. Let's get on with it."

A couple of minutes later, Kate took the phone. The conversation didn't last long.

"Lucy, Kate Barns here. Things aren't goin' so good, I guess... Yeah, I know. That's what your lawyer told me. I'm here in his office as he said. Might pop over later on this week, but I've got somethin' to ask you. Was Pete foolin' around with your girl?"

I could hear Lucy's raised voice, but I couldn't make out anything. "Thanks. That's all I need to know. Looks like I'll be seein' you in court. Be my first time. Hang in there, girl. If it'd been me, I'd a done it slow."

From the hard expression on her face and the look in her small eyes, I believed her.

Hoping he'd read his mother's diary, I called the Evans' home to talk to Alex. I waited two minutes on the phone before I heard his voice, no good sign. He sounded tense.

"Did you get a chance to look at the books I left?" I asked.

He said he had.

"Can we get together tomorrow afternoon to chat?"

After a long pause, he replied, "It's too soon. I'm not ready yet. I'm having a real hard time with this. There's... there's a lot in Mom's diary I didn't know. I had no idea." Then, in a rush of words, emotion in his tone, Alex said, "Oh, what the fuck. Go ahead and come. I need to talk with someone about this stuff, anyway. Might as well be you."

Relieved, I said, "Tomorrow afternoon at three be okay with you?"

"Yeah, I guess, but don't say anything about this to Mom, okay? I'm not ready to deal with her right now."

I assured him I wouldn't mention it to her. I doubted Alex could help us concretely in our case. But if there was anything I could do to help bring Lucy and him together, it would be good for both of them.

Next morning, I arrived at the office early. The twins had still been asleep when I let Lupe in and left the house. I had two new clients to interview as well as a third to see, hopefully for the final time. He was a real paranoid who had more cash than sense.

Cheryl, I was glad to see, had grouped my appointments for the morning, leaving me the afternoon to consult with Bree and to visit Alex.

I said no to Ben for lunch. I did have to go out since I hadn't brought anything, but I needed to be alone and think. I was soon to see Bree and I was anxious.

It was as well that I wasn't very hungry. The quality of food at Pilu's Garden had gone down steadily as the popularity of the place increased, a universal in the restaurant industry, it seemed. About all I got for my twenty dollars, aside from a tepid cup of early morning coffee, was a noisy place to sit. I sipped and thought.

I'd been surprised and delighted, too, by Bree's warmth at Ben's. I'd never known quite what to make of her part in the banter we enjoyed, almost from the start. Did she behave in the same way with most men she liked? Was she connected with someone she never talked about? I suspected not, but her cool behavior toward me since the party worried me. Was it a self-protective barrier she'd raised that might come down if I was patient or was her standoffish attitude her means to discourage me? If she was afraid, then afraid of what?

Had she intuited something about the romp I'd had with my assistant just over a week ago? I very much hoped not. Fortunately, I had few skeletons in my closet and, as far as I knew, I had no reputation as a lady's man. Having been out of the courting game for over fifteen years, I had little intuition to guide me. If she wanted nothing romantic in our relationship, I'd know soon enough.

No change in Bree's demeanor. A polite hello, then

straight to business. "I think we may have our man," she said. "He's testified before on battered woman syndrome only, it's true, but he's written a number of interesting things on what some scholars refer to as coercive control. It's a concept that pertains to both physical and psychological abuse. It might be worthwhile giving the man a call."

No, her manner was not the same. Her cool demeanor was more pronounced. No smile this time, no warmth at all. I felt locked out.

Attempting to show indifference to her behavior but not doing very well, I said, "Can you give me a CliffsNotes version of what coercive control is before we go on with this?"

"Sure, I think so. Let's see." Mustering her thoughts, she continued, "Coercive control, as you might guess from the meaning of the two words, involves oppression, particularly of women by their male partners. Basically, it's the strategies men use to isolate and dominate their victims." For the next ten minutes, Bree talked about the concept and how it related to our case. She'd managed to steer me away from her and into legal mode.

"Okay. That seems clear enough. The question is, can we use it?"

Bree looked perturbed. "How can you say that after hearing what I just said?" Her tone was neutral, but she was piqued. "The concept is tailor-made for Lucy's case, absolutely." Bree's face was flushed. She looked indignant.

I raised both hands. "Hey, hey," I said, a bit irritated myself. "Take it easy. You keep forgetting something—two things, actually. There's no question that Lucy's the victim of psychological abuse. That's not at issue. Educating the jury about the nature of this kind of abuse is not what we want to try to do. We'd fail miserably, I assure you. It's Lucy's belief system we must focus on." Bree opened her mouth to interject, but I shook my head and went on. "Yes, I know, coercive control, as you've described it, may have led to those beliefs. That's not at issue either."

Bree appeared to be calming down, but she wasn't happy.

"We use expert witnesses to lend strength to claims we make, I agree, especially when those claims are concrete. Unfortunately, that's not the situation here. That's what makes this case so difficult. We can't talk to the jury very easily about these things. They have to come to it on their own, assuming we can promote this. Are you following me here, Bree?"

Grudgingly, it seemed to me, she nodded.

"There's another thing that I've talked to you about before. Juries tend not to like expert witnesses unless their testimony is very graphic and on something they can relate to. In most cases, after the first five minutes, they tune them out."

"Fine," Bree said, "you have the background in criminal trials, I don't, but how can we show why she had such beliefs without talking about what caused them?"

"Good question. We can't, not directly, anyway. You and I have to work out a careful plan about the issues and questions we're going to raise. Once we do this, we look for holes and decide how to plug them up. We may find in the end that expert testimony may help us."

"So," Bree replied, her normal color back, "first the plan and then our decision about what props to use."

Not thinking about my choice of words, I replied, "That's my girl. That's precisely it."

Though she was quick to get rid of it, a warm smile briefly lit her face.

The temperature in the room came back to normal. I continued, "Regardless what we decide to do, I think it would be a good idea to make your contact. Who are you thinking of?"

"Professor Gordon Chadwick in the Department of Psychology at Pickton College in Charlotte, North Carolina. He's the man I'd call."

Needlessly, I said, "You'll do that?"

Bree couldn't help herself. Tilting her head slightly in that way she had, normally the precursor to a friendly thrust, she said, "You think I should do that instead of you?"

Doing my utmost to keep a poker face and trying to look reflective, I said, "Actually, now that you mention it, the guy may have questions about procedure here that you can't answer. So..."

I seemed to have pulled it off. Bree looked perplexed. Either I was serious or I was playing. It must have been her puzzled look that caused the corner of my mouth to twitch. Instantly, her face relaxed.

In a pretended capitulating tone, she said, "Alright, I'll leave it up to you. I have things to do here, anyway."

At that moment, out of the corner of my eye, I saw Sara standing in the doorway. She looked from me to Bree, then disappeared.

Her lips twitching, trying to hold back a smile, Bree said, "What's with that girl, anyway. She didn't seem very happy about what she saw, did she."

"I only caught a glimpse of her," I said. "She was acting strange, that's true."

Looking pensive, Bree said, "Forrest, forgive me for prying, but I've been curious about this for a while. I've seen how that girl looks at you. Quite a few times, actually. It's her expression that makes me wonder. It's not coquettish, nothing like that. Sorry if I disappoint you. I know how fond of her you are. She looks... how can I say this. She looks speculative, that's the word, like she's trying to make up her mind about which dress to wear. Her expression when she's watching you doesn't exactly go with the reputation you guys have."

Why this interest in the way Sara looks? Feigning ignorance, I said, "Reputation? What reputation?"

At last, the suggestion of a smile on Bree's face. "Tell me, Forrest. Are all men liars like most women are? I think so. You know what I'm talking about. The women around here—don't know about the men—think she's your lover. It's none of my business if she is, but why does she look at you like that? That's what I'd like to know."

I suspected—the thought made me feel good—that Bree wasn't being entirely on the up-and-up with me. It was less Sara's expression than the nature of my relationship with my assistant that was on her mind. Right or wrong, I was going to answer.

"Not because you ask," I lied, "but because I'd like to squash this rumor if it exists. Sara and I aren't lovers and we're not going to be. We live in totally different worlds and she's way too young for me. So, do me the favor of spreading that around here, please. As to Sara's expression, that's no mystery, really, I don't think. My guess is, and I've thought this for a long time, Sara's used to having her way with men, and she gets frustrated if she runs into someone who doesn't give her what she wants."

Now it was Bree who had the speculative look. With dread, I could hear her question about to come. Bree was going to ask me if I'd ever slept with her. But the question never came.

It was amazing how mercurial women were. I needed no instrument to tell me the atmosphere had changed. The smile that I wanted so much to see was back. There might even have been gold specks.

Finally able to relax, I asked, "Any thoughts about seeing Mia?"

"Mia... yes. I was going to bring that up, in fact. Can you arrange to bring her to my house at four this coming Thursday? We could talk to her for an hour, say, then I'll go get Maya so Mia can play with her. How's that?"

"That's fine with me. I have to be home by six-thirty at the latest for dinner with the twins."

"What will you do for food? Is that hour bad for you?"

"I'll make up something later on tonight and freeze it. Six-thirty won't be too late."

Neither of us said anything for several minutes.

Bree seemed at a loss about where to look. She glanced at me, then the items on her desk, at books on shelves around the room, then back at me.

It was she who broke the silence. In her quiet voice, she said, "I learned some things about you last weekend that I like, that I like very much. I needed to tell you that."

"I hope I'm not being too unimaginative if I say the same."

She shook her head. "I'm glad that we have lots of time." No rush-in, rush-out love affair for Bree. Smiling, lowering her voice still more, she added, "But there's no need to wait on things we already know, is there... You look confused. What I mean is, I know how good it felt to be held by you."

I could feel myself smile as I glanced at her open door. Giving me a look that warmed my blood, she gently shook her head. "You'd better let me get back to work before I do something rash. And do get rid of that predatory look before you leave, or we'll have killed one rumor, only to start another."

"At least we'll give this rumor substance," I replied.

"Don't make promises you won't keep."

"I don't do such things," I said, getting up off Bree's couch.

"I'm glad. That's good to know," she said as I headed for her door.

How long had it been since I'd felt so connected to a woman? I'd loved Claire, still did in ways, but I never felt as one with her. Though it was far too soon to know if I ever really would with Bree, the potential with her seemed greater than with anyone I'd known.

Evie met me at her front door. She looked stressed.

"Forrest, before you see Alex, I've got to talk to you about his sister. Come into the sunroom. We'll have privacy out there."

"Is she alright? Has she done something crazy?"

"No, no, nothing like that and she's fine, mostwise,

anyway. Can I get you coffee, or tea or something?"

I said thanks, but no.

"The girl's frantic. She doesn't eat, she doesn't sleep well, she's a mess."

"What seems to be the problem?"

"She's scared shitless that the authorities are going to make her give up her baby. She won't listen to a thing we say. She's worried about where she's gonna live, how she's gonna find good food, she's upset over almost everything. I keep telling her what she's doing's no good for the baby, but she won't listen. You've gotta talk to her. She's right, you know, about where she's gonna live. No way we can keep her here, 'specially if she keeps up like this."

"Is she here this afternoon?"

"Forrest, Mia never leaves her room except when she has to. I told her you were coming. She wants to talk to you, real bad."

"I'm going to see Alex first. He's expecting me in five minutes. Please tell Mia that I'll come to talk with her afterward."

Alex looked listless and drawn. I'd never seen him in wrinkled and dirty clothes. He nodded to me as I sat down on his bed. The room smelled musty and unclean. One of the copies we made of Lucy's diary was on a beat-up chest of drawers.

"Alex, tell me. Did you read the entire thing?"

After a few seconds, he nodded.

"Did you find any incidents that involved you that you think she misrepresented?"

I had two reasons for asking this. Accurate as I'd found her accounts to be about our college years, I had little to confirm that she'd remained truthful about events later on. If Alex were to contradict things his mother said, Lucy's situation would become more complicated, to say the least. If, on the other hand as I hoped, he'd found nothing to discredit her, my question might help him appreciate the significance of the diary for their family. At first, Alex didn't say anything. I wasn't sure he heard.

He shook his head, then said, "No. Nothing."

"I know this isn't easy for you, but it's important, so help me here. Based on what you observed over the years—"

Nearly yelling, Alex said, "I didn't know most of that shit happened. I didn't know my dad did those things to her. I'm sure the fucker did it all. Look at Mia! Jesus, Forrest, what do you want me to say? That my dad was a fucked-up son of a bitch? He was an asshole." Alex began to sob. "Now you happy? You get what you came for?"

I let Alex's outburst run its course. Then I said, "I didn't come here for that, Alex, nothing like that at all. I'm not here to crucify Pete. I'm here to try to make you see that your mother deserves our help. She believed she had no way out, so she took the only path she thought possible to save her daughter. She's suffered a lot. She hasn't stopped. The biggest reason right now is that the two people in the world she loves most won't talk to her. She's convinced you hate her. She needs your support, Alex, and you need hers. I'm her friend, and I'm going to do my best to keep her out of prison. The trial's going to be difficult for all of us. Please think about what I'm asking. Try not to judge your mother too harshly for what she did. Please think about going back to live at your house with her to support her through all this. Can you do that, please?"

"I don't have to think about it, Forrest. I already know what I'm going to do. I called Mom just before you got here to tell her I'm coming back. I still don't like her very much right now, I've gotta tell you that, but it's better than before. I just didn't know about any of this shit, that's all."

The lump in my throat was big as I got up and went around the bed to grasp Alex's hands. I pulled him up and hugged him as he cried.

"Hey champ," a nickname I used with my son and

with Alex when I was his soccer coach, "I'm proud of you for recognizing the truth of what your mother says and for your courage in going home. You be sure to call me if there's anything you need."

Alex pulled free and said, "There's something you could do right now, actually."

"What's that?"

"My bag's packed. I didn't bring over all that much. Can you take me home?"

Smiling—I couldn't help thinking about how Lucy would be feeling then—I said, "You're on. Give me five minutes with your sister and we're out of here."

Mia was in worse shape than Alex, much worse. Her eyes were red from crying and she looked a mess. She was twisting her hands together in her lap as we sat together on her bed.

"Hey there, Mia, I thought we had an understanding. You were going to do everything to protect that baby. You keep this up and you'll miscarry."

Though my threat was undoubtedly nonsense, it was gospel to that preadolescent girl.

"What will make me miscarry? What will?"

I told her.

"I can't sleep and I'm not hungry. They're gonna take my baby away from me when it's born. They will! I know they will."

"Mia, calm down and listen. You remember the lady I was with when we came here? She knows a lot about these things. She used to work in family and child protection law. She's a psychologist and she's a lawyer. She's pretty smart, believe me. She says as long as you can take care of your baby, no one will be allowed to take it away from you. We're here to protect you and your baby, anyway, so don't worry."

"But Alex said—"

"Alex is wrong. I told you that. He's just upset like you. Bree—she's the lady who came here with me last time—she wants me to pick you up this coming

Thursday to bring you to her house so we can talk. Then she's going to bring her baby home so you can play with her. That's two days from now, that's all. That okay with you?"

As rapidly as they'd come, Mia's tears dried up. Eyes big, she said, "Yes. That's good. I get to play with her? You promise?"

"I promise if you keep your promise to me to eat as Evie says and to try to sleep."

"I will. I will. I promise," Mia said.

"Okay now. I've got to go. Alex is going to move back home. I'm taking him there now when I leave."

Surprised, Mia exclaimed, "He is? You are? He really is?"

"Yes. Now be good to that baby of yours and I'll see you in two days."

An altogether positive afternoon from just about everybody's point of view, everybody who counted in our little circle, anyway. We needed every day of good weather we could collect before the storm.

PART FOUR

"In strategy it is important to see distant things as if they were close and to take a distanced view of close things."

— Miyamoto Musashi, *A Book of Five Rings: The Classic Guide to Strategy*, circa 1645

Chapter 16

Lucy must have been carrying her cell phone with the exotic bird call ringtone I had assigned since she immediately picked up. After repeated declarations of how precious to her I was, I was able to say hello.

"He's back home, Forrest, back home with me. He's not saying much to me right now, but that's okay. The important thing is, he's here. How did you manage to get him to come home so quick?"

"It wasn't me, Lucy. It was your diary. Alex just didn't know. Like the rest of us, he had no idea. He'll come around soon enough, you'll see. Just give him a little time. He has a lot to adjust to."

Tearfully, she said, "You have no idea how wonderful it is to have him here. I feel I have something to live for now. Alex is talking about going back to UCSB and taking up where he left off. Isn't that wonderful? I'll miss him when he goes like I did before, but it's so different now. I have a lot of thanking you to do. When will I see you? Soon, okay?"

After mumbling some excuses why I couldn't come right away, I said, "Some advice, Lucy, if you don't mind. Try not to ask Alex too many questions now. It took a lot of courage for him to come back. He did it for you, but he's not ready to talk about things yet. As I said, just give him time. Everything else okay? Is Lily still with you?"

"She's going to be here indefinitely, at least I think

so. Her breast cancer seems to be in remission, thank God, so, here's hoping."

"Good. Bree and I will be in touch with you by the beginning of next week. We have a lot of work on the trial to do. It could be a little later, depending on how much progress we make. Be sure to call me if there are any problems, okay?"

"My only problem right now," she declared, "is getting you over here."

'Not for what you've got in mind, Lucy girl, not now,' I thought. "Say hello to Alex for me. We'll be in touch."

After having spent most of the previous day with Bree, I couldn't very well turn Ben down for lunch. Had I been thinking less about her and more about my old friend's eating habits, I'd have had the sense to ask him what he had in mind. One benefit of the location of our new office was that we were no longer in proximity to Ben's favorite place, one of the few dives left in downtown Santa Lucia. Paying no attention to where we were, just enjoying the fresh air, I ambled alongside Ben.

"No, goddamn it," I expostulated as we stopped and were going through a door. "We're not eating here again. I thought the authorities shut this place down!"

Shrugging, looking innocent, Ben replied, "Find me another place where we can get a table at this hour and we'll go."

He had me. It was almost impossible to find seats at noon without reservations. I resigned myself to a lousy cup of coffee and last week's salad as we pushed our way in. As usual, the odor of blackened deep-fried cooking oil and God knew what else assailed my nose as we sat down.

Harried servers, unaccustomed to tips in Gordy's Diner, were in no hurry to take our orders. My fare, when it finally came, was a lukewarm bowl of dishwater chicken noodle soup and a tepid cup of coffee. Ben, thoroughly at home in greasy spoons, picked up a three-inch-high burger of some kind, surrounded by a massive heap of oily fries. I used to chide him about how long he wished to live, but I'd given up. He wasn't about to go out munching rabbit food, he told me. I knew better than to engage him in conversation until he was done.

His mouth still half full, wiping the grease from his chin, Ben said, "God, the crazy things Garrett gets into."

Intrigued, I waited.

"There's this old couple, gotta be in their early eighties. Live outside a town, not that far from me. 'Cordin' to Garrett, these guys like to hit the sack early and get up with the chickens, if you know what I mean. Trouble starts when some dude moves in next to 'em with a couple a yappin' dogs. 'Parently, they start up barkin' when the sun goes down and keep it up all night. The old geezer, Garrett's client, hoofs it on over there and complains. Says he and his wife can't sleep. Don't do no good. Guy goes over again, not so nice this time, tells 'em they'd better take care of it or he will. The new neighbor just ignores him and the dogs keep up their barkin'.

"So, 'stead a callin' the county or whatever he's 'sposed to do, guy gets out an old Navy Colt that hasn't been fired or cleaned in a hundred years and him and the missus go out in the middle of the night and start blastin' away. He wounds one of the dogs, probably by accident, and on the third shot, damn gun blows up. Hammer comes flyin' out past his ear and nails the old lady in the cheek. Gun registered? Hell no. Guy's had it since he was a kid. Poor bugger's up for illegal possession and I don't know what, all cuz him and his wife couldn't sleep. Can you beat that. Garrett's tryin' to do his best for the old coot but Vicky's hangin' tough. Turns out the guy's wife's so pissed, she's got him sleepin' in the barn."

"Tell you what," I said. "Garrett's got a knack for pickin' up this kinda stuff. He's had more on his plate these last six months than I have so he's been guilt-tripping me into taking things he doesn't like. You tell him, not this time. I've got more than I can handle as it is."

"Tell him yourself. His office is just down the hall from yours. We still meetin' with Bree at two?"

"Far as I know, we are. You get a chance to look into the DNA thing?"

"What do you think they pay me for round here anyway, spendin' time with gorgeous women like certain partners of mine do? Speakin' a which..."

"Cassie back?"

"Cassie, yeah, last night. I'll tell you all about it in a few minutes when we're with Bree." Downing his last sip of milk and dabbing at his face, he said, "We're gonna be late for our meetin' with that sweetheart a yours if we don't get goin'. Hang on to her, boyo. She's the real thing."

Ben cast a jaundiced eye at Bree's couch as we walked in and headed for the hard chair near her desk. I took my normal seat.

"It's been a while since the two of you've been in here," Bree commented, a half eaten apple in her hand. Still hungry with only a cup of coffee in me from lunch, my eyes inadvertently drifted to a large unpeeled banana on the corner of Bree's desk. Simultaneously, my stomach growled.

Looking inquiringly at me, she asked, "Didn't you two just eat?" There no response, she turned to Ben. She was removing the peel from the banana when she asked, "And where was it exactly that you guys went?"

Eyeing the fruit and how she handled it, Ben smirked and said we'd gone to Gordy's.

Looking at Ben's expression then down at her hands, Bree turned crimson, the first time I'd seen her blush. I was barely quick enough to snag the partially-peeled banana that she tossed at me.

Not missing a beat, she continued, "You're going to get food poisoning one day, Ben, you know that, assuming they don't shut that dump down first. No wonder Forrest's hungry. He's got too much sense to touch anything in there."

I had to avert my face to hide my grin. She had to have seen Bo Derek provocatively peeling her banana as she gazed up at Tarzan in that movie. Otherwise, why the sudden color in her face?

"Now, Bree," Ben soothed, "don't get your tail in a knot." He might have used a less explicit metaphor. "It's nice to see someone lookin' out for poor Forrest, here. Guy hasn't a clue how to eat. We'd best get to it, folks. I've gotta be outta here in an hour. Now correct me if I'm wrong," Ben said. "I don't know all that much about this case, but seems like, from what I hear, you need to show who the baby's father is before the trial. Am I right on that?"

Bree had regained her normal color and she looked calm. We were back to business. She looked to me to respond, but I nodded for her to go ahead.

"Ideally, yes, but it's not going to happen from DNA." Before Ben could inquire why, she went on, "There's no way that Mia will agree to getting her baby's DNA before it's born."

"But I thought—"

"I know, Ben," she interrupted. "We were wrong. The SNP test doesn't work the way we thought."

"So what are we doin' here anyway. You can't get the baby's DNA before it's born, no way you're gonna know who the real father is, is there."

Shaking my head along with Bree, I said, "Two things, Ben. It's not clear we have to factually demonstrate who the father is. Hopefully, depending on a number of things, the situation will speak for itself. What we're shooting for is the girl's admission on the stand."

Ben looked incredulous. "You're shitting me, right?" He cast an apologetic look at Bree. "You can't be serious."

I sighed. "Ben, this whole case is a mess. It's unlike anything you've ever heard of in court. Mia could turn hostile and blow our case apart. We've got one month to get her into shape."

"To brainwash her, you mean."

"Essentially, that's right." Bree looked deflated.

"Jesus, guys," Ben remarked half to himself, "I don't like the sound of this. So what do I do with the DNA samples I'm bustin' my butt to get? You're not gonna use 'em, that right?"

"Actually, with a little luck, we will. It all depends on whether or not we can coax our little mother-to-be to go with us to the lab so they can get her DNA. I think the chances of that happening before the trial look pretty good, but you never know with that one. She could dig in and turn us down. Without her okay—"

"Yeah, yeah, I know," Ben said. "Not the first time I've done this stuff."

I nodded. "What I'm afraid of most of all is Resnik. He gets to her at all, even for five minutes, and he'll tell her there's nothing at all that's forcing her to take the test. It'll be a question of whether or not we can convince her otherwise."

"Bugger's probably already gotten to her, don't you think?" Ben said.

"He'd have done that long ago if he or Vicky knew what Mia's like, that's for sure. We're getting together with her tomorrow afternoon at Bree's. We'll know more then. The Perkins Lab have all your stuff?"

"They'd like more, but they've got enough from what they say. Turns out there were a lot of good sources where Pete worked that nobody had touched, so I think we're good."

"Fantastic," I said. "If we can get Mia's DNA in time, then the nightie's goin' in."

"You need to send the thing to Resnik?"

"As part of discovery, yes," I responded. "We'll send it off to him as soon as Perkins Lab's done with it."

As Ben was leaving, he halted in mid-stride and turned around. He looked grim. "Almost forgot to tell you. Three guesses about who dropped in on me last night."

"Cassie's home?" I asked.

"More or less. Aside from a couple a nasty bruises on her chest and a chunk outta her right hand, she's okay."

"What happened?" Bree and I queried at the same time.

Still standing, opening and closing his right hand, Ben said, "Cassie's team was on the heels of some lowlifes who snatched two kids, brother and sister I think they were. Well, they caught up with 'em holed up in a house in Baton Rouge, Louisiana. Cassie and somebody else on the team wanted to split up and approach the house on the QT, maybe try to talk 'em down, but some fucking suit with no field experience who was in charge didn't go for it, stupid jerk."

"No negotiation," I inquired, "nothing like that at all?"

Ben scoffed. "The sons a bitches opened up soon as they saw the Crown Vic. Fucking feds, they never change their cars. May as well of had the siren on. Ended up in a blood bath with kids involved, if you can believe. The team got three of the perps and wounded the fourth who had hold of the little boy. Shithead killed him before somebody on Cassie's team put a couple a rounds through his head."

Both of Ben's hands were clenched. In a growl, he said, "Good thing it was Cassie and not me out there. I'd a put a quiet round between that SAC fucker's eyes. Hadn't a been for him, the kid might be alive."

Bree looked bewildered. "SAC?" she repeated, looking a little pale.

"SAC," Ben echoed, a hard edge in his voice. "FBI lingo for Special Agent in Charge. He'll write it up and change the look a things so he comes off clean. They'll eventually find out what happened though. No way you can keep that stuff quiet for very long. But, by that time, he'll a been promoted to the next level of incompetence. Cassie's so riled up she's spittin' nails and makin' noise about turnin' in her badge. I'll be helpin' her mail the fucker in, let me tell you."

Turning his eyes on Bree, Ben said, "Sorry about the language. I don't get pissed off all that often, but... If there's nothin' else for me to do here, I'll be goin' back home to nurse my girl who's not feelin' so good right now. Don't believe everything you see on TV. Kevlar vests are good, make no mistake. Cassie wouldn't be here otherwise. But two nine-millimeter rounds leave some pretty nasty dents."

Before we could tell him to wish Cassie well, Ben was out the door and gone.

Bree was white and I was shaken. Her face still pasty and with a quaver in her voice, she said, "They killed the little boy? How horrible." In words I could scarcely make out, she added, "And what about the little girl?"

The prospects were too horrific to contemplate.

Bree continued in a tight voice, her visage tense, "Brutality upsets me very much. When I hear about things like this, I have nightmares. I don't know why I react so strongly since nothing bad has ever happened to me. It's like PTSD without the trauma. Does that make sense?"

I nodded, though I wasn't at all sure I'd understood.

We sat there reflecting about what Ben had said for several minutes without saying anything. Daily news reports in papers and on TV of events much more catastrophic reach us with little impact, desensitized as we've become by the frequency and graphic depiction of bloodshed. When violence is less abstract, when someone close to us suffers injury or death, we're jerked from our complacency.

The idea that Cassie could easily have been killed staggered me. And what of the poor family who'd suddenly lost a child, to say nothing of the trauma that might torment the surviving daughter for the remainder of her life. I felt my insides shrink as I had so often two years earlier when Divinity Parker, now Anna

Henderson, had been abducted from our town. The twins would be on their way home from school and I needed to be home.

By the time I was on my feet, Bree was up and headed toward me. I've never ceased to marvel how a quick hug at the right moment can chase away the demons. The darkness and gloom dissipated as I held her.

In her mellifluous contralto voice, she said, "You won't forget our date with Mia at my house tomorrow afternoon, will you?"

"No more than I'm likely to overlook this need I have to consult with you first thing in the morning about how to handle her."

In answer, she made a little contented noise as I left.

Two short years before, Andy would have nearly bowled me over as I came through the front door near dinnertime. Trina would have been clinging to my arm and pressing close. As I walked in, my son, sitting on the couch and engrossed in some sports magazine, briefly raised his head, mumbled something I couldn't hear, then continued flipping pages.

"Hi Daddy," came Trina's greeting from the kitchen. From the odors emanating from where she was, my daughter must have just removed trays of chocolate cookies from the oven. I recalled with nostalgia the years when my presence had been required. No longer. She preferred to do everything on her own.

Cheeseburgers and onion rings was our bill of fare that night, a command performance. Though Trina had few good things to say about fried foods, she consumed stacks of the batter-covered rings as rapidly as her brother, who ate anything whose taste he liked. As usual, the twins competed for my attention about their school day.

Andy's interest in model airplanes was declining, eclipsed by his obsession with martial arts. Apart from baseball, which had ended as of the fall, he spoke of little else. Though Andy would have had it otherwise, Miguel assured me my son had several years to go before he'd be allowed to get into the knockdown stuff. I wasn't especially looking forward to the change in his program that would find me flipped on my back in our yard or lying in a heap, the unenthusiastic recipient of a flying kick or elbow strike.

Whatever happened to good old wrestling, even boxing? For the moment, I felt secure as, after dinner, I watched him perform maneuvers that looked less injurious than difficult to execute.

Trina, finished with her homework and her shower, waited for me in her room. With other changes I'd begun to see in her, I feared that adolescence would soon end a cherished tradition that had started before she'd learned to talk. But no. She still wanted me to read to her and I was to expect this to continue until she left home for college. Attuned to me as my daughter was, she had to know that her declaration would make me happy. *Little House on the Prairie* was her current book of choice.

Prior to Claire's departure well over a year ago, our television set was rarely on except for the evening news. If for no other reason than to have background noise, I found myself turning the set on once the twins were asleep. The house was just too quiet. I'd sit and read as I was doing then with my glass of scotch or port at hand while unseen commercials and movies came and went.

At just before ten, the house phone rang. The ringer was turned low so as not to wake the twins. The voice I heard when I picked up was unfamiliar.

In an agreeable if impersonal-sounding tone, I heard, "Mr. Spencer, my name is John Breconridge, Claire's husband. There's been an accident, but there's no need for alarm. As you must know, I'm a neurosurgeon." My heart jumped in my chest and I felt cold. "Claire's car and another were hit by a public transit bus that went out of control. Claire was injured, but she'll be alright. Unfortunately, the lady and her little boy in the other vehicle were killed."

I couldn't exactly blame Breconridge for the seeming lack of empathy in his tone. How often, in person or on the telephone, had he been the bearer of bad news. Still, the man sounded like he was reading disinterestedly from a script.

"I apologize if I seem to be in a hurry."

In a hurry? The guy sounded half asleep. I wanted to speed him up to hear more about how Claire was.

"The fact is," Breconridge said, "I am somewhat rushed. Claire's concerned about how you tell the children."

'Tell them what, you idiot,' I wanted to spit out. 'Get on with it.' Just as I was about to interrupt him, he continued.

"Claire suffered some severe injuries, none life-threatening, fortunately. She has four broken ribs. One punctured her left lung. That's fully under control now. She has a fractured collar bone, painful but no risk to her. Her most critical injury is a compound fracture of the right femur. No vascular damage there, I'm glad to say. Other than bruises and some contusions, she has no other injuries that we're aware of at this point. She's presently undergoing surgery at the Medical Center here at UCLA for her bone injuries. She was sedated when I last saw her, which was about two hours ago, but lucid enough to give me a message that she's anxious to get to you about your children."

I would like to have gone to see Claire myself, to be sure she was okay. She wouldn't welcome me, preferring that I be with the twins and, no doubt, concerned about the feelings of her husband. Were her condition critical, that's exactly what I would have done, whether or not she had any desire to see me.

"The twins are to be told that their mother had an automobile accident, but she's fine. She'll call them in a day or so to say hello. She wants you to know that it won't be possible for her to care for them for the next six weeks or so. They should be told. I believe I've covered everything Claire wanted."

I was sure he had—an admonition that I should stay away, what I was to tell the twins, and her pronouncement that she'd be off the every second weekend arrangement that we had, the latter, good news for Breconridge, I was sure, and certainly good news for me.

"Yes, Dr. Breconridge, I think you have. Thank you for the call." No need to request that he convey my regards to Claire since he wouldn't bother, and I had serious doubts at that point that she'd care to hear them.

If I was distressed by Ben's account of Cassie's close call, my hands were trembling when I hung up the phone. Claire and I were far less than ideal mates and had been so for a long time. Still, I was attached to her—admittedly, much less painfully than a year before, but attached nonetheless. Was my visceral dislike for Claire's new spouse just plain jealousy or was my reaction toward someone I'd never met based on the cold fish vibes he exuded on the phone? I wanted my snap judgment to be wrong for our children's sake.

What a day. First, the shoot-out that could have taken a friend's life, then an accident that had come close to killing my ex-wife. I'd pour a second drink, a stiffer one this time, watch the news for a few minutes, then head off to bed.

I couldn't have been asleep for more than minutes according to the bedside clock when I heard footfalls. I'd have been alarmed had I not heard the sound before. Slipping on my pants, I went out into the hall to see Andy standing there, appearing wide awake but for the glazed look in his eyes. The first time he'd sleepwalked weeks before, he spoke to me as though I was someone else. I was a little freaked out, as he might have expressed it, when he told me that I was busy in the backyard.

I gently took him by the arm and guided him back to his bed. He'd have no recollection of the event in the morning. One more sign of his mother's absence in his life.

I was surprised the next day at breakfast by the twins' blasé reaction to the news about their mother. True, I played down the severity of Claire's injuries as best I could without making them sound trivial. I was sure that Trina and Andy would have been genuinely distressed had they seen their mother in her hospital room. As things were, Andy was pleased that he wouldn't have to miss any lessons with Miguel for weeks. Trina was more concerned about memorizing lines for a school play she was in than she was in details about the accident.

I felt badly for Claire, who doubtless had foreseen how the twins would react to the news, especially if it had been conveyed to them as she wished. I told them she'd be calling them in a day or so.

"This is like being in my kitchen, only better," I teased as I walked through Bree's office door. "A warm smile, a steaming cup of black coffee and a hot cross bun. I could get used to this."

"You thought I was going to enjoy my first cup and my croissant with you sitting there with nothing?" Feigning a reproach, the slightly upturned ends of her mouth giving her away, Bree added, "Offer a man a cup of coffee and he wants the pot. Make the mistake of giving him a little hug and he wants much more. Are all of you like that?"

Reaching for my cup and settling back on the couch, I replied, "Not always, no. When my Aunt Judy heads for me, all two hundred pounds of her, I do my best to get away. On the other hand, you come toward me with the look you had the other night and I'm liable to pick you up and carry you off somewhere."

"Guess I'll have to be more careful when I'm around

you then."

"Oh well," I said, "the fantasy was nice while it lasted."

"A fantasy? Oh, good. Then you won't mind telling me where that somewhere you were going to carry me off to is."

"I don't mind at all, especially since it's just a dream. It's a place that's very restful where I'd have you completely to myself for, say, eight hours or so, or more?"

"Mr. Spencer, something a psychologist needs to know. Do you fantasize a lot?"

"To tell you the truth, in this case, yes, nearly all the time."

With a sober expression that didn't hide the glint in her eyes, Bree said, "Living in a fictitious world is not such a good thing. We'll have to work on that, I think. Right now, though, we'd better talk about what we're going to do with Mia this afternoon. Have you made arrangements to pick her up?"

"Yeah, well, give me a minute, will you? Right now my thoughts are somewhere else."

"I'm listening."

"Bree Dixon, anyone ever tell you you're a tease? The transition from you to Mia is not an easy one, especially in this case. Hang on a minute while I think. There'll be traffic, so I'm picking Mia up at three-thirty. We should be at your house at four. You're going to get Maya at five? Is that what you said?"

Bree nodded.

"Okay. That should give us plenty of time to chat with the girl, don't you think? How should we go about it?"

"As I see it," Bree replied, "we've got three objectives. The first is getting her to tell us she wants to live at home once the trial's over. That shouldn't be all that difficult, I think. The second may cause some problems. Whether we do it this afternoon or later, we have to entice her to go to the Perkins Lab. Is she old enough, I wonder, to sign her name to such a thing? Won't Lucy have to be involved?"

"Hey, you know more about this than I. If twelve-year-olds in this state as I've heard it said are old enough to get tested for HIV without authorization from their guardians, then I suppose they're old enough for this. Even so, just to cover ourselves, I'll get Lucy to co-sign, all this assuming Mia will go in on her own. I can imagine what your third thing is."

A doleful expression on her face, Bree said, "Honestly, I don't know how best to approach all this. We need her to consent to appear in court in a manner that's not going to hurt us. We need her to openly admit who the father of her child is. We definitely need to learn about any admonitions or instructions Pete gave her to evade inquiries by the authorities if they came. Why do I think it's going to take some kind of miracle to get all this from her?"

"Guessing about what Mia's going to do," I said, "is about as chancy as betting on horses you've never heard of. She'll be no good to us at all if we have to subpoena her. Frankly, the girl scares me half to death. I've never had such a potentially hazardous witness in my career. If she becomes upset by something on the stand, she can literally destroy our case in minutes and, so far, at least, I can't think of a damn thing to do to stop her, assuming we can get her to testify at all. She reminds me of a bomb, just waiting to go off."

Bree nodded, looking lost in thought.

"There's another factor we mustn't overlook," I said. "If Resnik tries to interview Mia before the trial and she allows it, he'll see immediately how susceptible to influence she is. We won't let him wander too far in cross, but he can get his points in and upset her, even if they're stricken from the record. He'll be good at this."

There was silence for a moment while I thought. She must have caught my brain wave before I could get the question out. She vigorously shook her head, then did it again.

"No, Forrest, absolutely not. No chance. I have no criminal trial experience at all; you know that. I did family law which is a different thing. You think Mia's dangerous, get the two of us up there and you'll blow our case for sure."

"Just listen a minute, Bree. Your lack of experience is an important factor, I know, but I think you'll agree that Mia will respond better to you than she will to me which is crucial for our defense. Assuming she'll agree to appear for us, we'll have to be extremely careful about the questions we ask and, more important here, how we ask them. We don't have anyone like Mia to practice on, unfortunately, but we could find someone, I'm sure, who could help us."

"Sara, right?"

In fact, I was thinking of her, yes, which I didn't say. "But we're getting ahead of ourselves here. Much of what we decide to do depends on how Mia reacts to our prompting this afternoon. I think we're going to have to play everything pretty much by ear."

"I agree," Bree replied. "The real problem, and you know this, is that she's utterly unreliable, a loose cannon if there ever was one. Caprice is that girl's middle name."

I nodded. "I'd give just about anything to keep her off the stand. Whatever we do, we're certainly not going to accomplish everything in one day. Our first task, it seems to me, is to gain her confidence, as much as one can with her."

"Yes," Bree commented, "that's going to be a long-range task. One of the first things we have to do is talk about her future living arrangements. We're assuming she'll opt for staying with her mother, aren't we?"

"Damned if I know where else she'd go," I said. "It'll be easier for us if she's determined to return home, something she won't be able to do if her mother's in prison."

"It's somewhat like what we're hoping to do with the jury, isn't it, Forrest—make Mia come to conclusions by herself."

"If we can do it, yes... Do you mind if I change subjects for a while? Talking about Mia gives me a headache."

Smiling, Bree said, "We're not back on this fantasy thing again."

"Nah," I replied, "that's boring stuff. I wanted to invite you and Maya to a barbecue at our house this Saturday. I have the children this weekend and, it looks like it'll be that way for a while. Their mother's been in a car accident that's going to keep her indoors for a few weeks."

"Nothing serious, I hope."

"Serious enough. She's got some major broken bones and a lot of bruising, but she'll be okay, least that's what her husband told me anyway."

Bree contemplated me intently. Her thoughts were evident on her face. Was I still attached to Claire and, if so, how much? It hadn't been that long ago after all that she'd left.

Her smile back, she said, "We'd love to come if I can bring something. What time would you like us?"

"The only thing you have to bring is an appetite and that little girl of yours. Trina will be thrilled. She's always loved little children, especially girls. Five o'clock too early for you?"

"Actually, that sounds good. Maya's not used to going to sleep in other people's homes. We'll have to leave pretty close to nine if that's okay with you."

"That's okay, provided we can make arrangements soon so you can stay later."

"You mean like we did the other night at Ben's."

"That'll be a good start," I said.

"Woah! See what I meant about the dangers in giving hugs?"

"You didn't seem to mind them all that much the other night."

"No, and I'll probably like them even more next time... You know something? I'm beginning to wonder if

I'm a bad influence on you. It used to be when you came in here, we talked almost exclusively about legal things and I learned a lot."

"So, you complaining, Bree?"

"No, not exactly. I just think we should expand our horizons a little, I guess."

"And how do you suggest we do that?"

Tossing her head a little, she replied, "I don't know, do things on the weekends, get together after hours, things like that. You know what I mean."

"It's the after-hours stuff that sounds good to me."

"Oh, get out of here and let me get some work done. You're too distracting with all of your ideas. See you at my place at four, okay?"

I stood there in the middle of her office floor, gazing at her as she gazed back at me. Waving her hands in frustration but not without a little fun, she ordered me to get out of there before she did something rash.

Mia was at Evie's door waiting for me when I pulled into the drive. She looked better than when I'd seen her last, dressed in what appeared to be a new purple tank top, short shorts and sandals. She could still get away with such an outfit since she wasn't showing yet. She'd also managed to do something with her hair that normally looked mousy. It was pulled back from her face in a braid. Her face, to my surprise, was unreadable.

She nodded, mumbled "Hi," and got in next to me.

Resnik had talked to her today or yesterday, the only plausible explanation for her aloof behavior. As we drove along in silence, I was mentally shifting gears, trying to find the best way to penetrate her veneer. If I was right, she'd have been coached to say little of the encounter. Evie would doubtless know of it, but Resnik would have made certain to see the girl alone. He'd have to have used official credentials to get at her. He would have been less interested in obtaining information than in imparting it, I was certain.

The issue, then, given the limited time he'd have

with her, was what he would focus on. It would be the garment and the identification of the stains. If Resnik could prevent anyone from obtaining Mia's DNA, the nightie couldn't come in as evidence of anything. Unless fifteen years in the criminal field were leading me astray, that was what we faced. How best to counter it?

Approaching Bree's house, Mia still inscrutable and silent, I concluded that the not-so-brilliant adolescent beside me would be unresponsive to persuasion. In place of the congenial afternoon Bree and I had hoped for, we would be dealing in cold hard facts, seemingly the only language the girl could understand. This time, it was I who'd have to take the lead.

Bree was quick to perceive the chilly atmosphere. Her smile as she opened her front door faded rapidly to speculation. What, she would be wondering as I had, could have brought about the change. My words in her office that morning would be echoing in her ears.

Quietly greeting Mia, who nodded in return, she suggested we move to comfortable chairs in the backyard. She'd follow us with a pitcher of lemonade. She accompanied us as far as the side of the house with flower planters along the wall and pointed to a cedar gate. Mia and I, wordlessly, continued and settled in to wait.

Patio stones covered every inch of Bree's backyard, there just sufficient space among flower pots for a small barbecue that had seen better days, a round metal table and four padded chairs. In the back corners were what looked to be large fig trees. Bree obviously had a green thumb with plants. I was amused to watch Mia's pasted on indifferent look falter as she got up and wandered among the pots, occasionally bending to touch a bloom.

"They're quite lovely, aren't they," I said.

Her face turned away from me, she answered, "I've never seen such pretty flowers up close like this."

I looked up to see Bree, carrying a large tray. I jumped up to give her a hand as she came down the steps.

"I'm glad you like my flowers," she said in that quiet voice of hers as she poured lemonade and set three tall glasses on the table. Still in slow motion, she sat down.

Exchanging glances, her signal to me was clear. Our roles had changed. I was sure she'd guessed what explained Mia's change in attitude. Had I felt more empathy for the girl, I would have been more conciliatory, which was my nature, rather than how I was that afternoon. I smiled reassuringly at Bree, then turned a sterner face to the girl next to me.

In a tone that matched my look, I said, "Mia, you're aware, I'm sure, that no one's forcing you to be here. In fact, if you prefer, I'll drive you back to Jim's and Evie's right now. You have only to say the word."

Mia's expression didn't change, but nor did she seem inclined to leave.

"I'll tell you what. Bree and I have lots of things to do. You keep up this sullen attitude another minute and we're out of here. You don't want to go back with me, we'll call a taxi, and that'll be the end of it."

Bree just managed to suppress her look of apprehension. This unpredictable child might do precisely what I'd said and we'd lose her. Very possibly, but I was tired of playing games with her.

Mia glowered at me and asked, "What is it that I'm supposed to say?"

I heard Bree let out a breath.

"As I remember, Mia, we asked you to think about where you wanted to live with your new baby." Looking at her in a no-nonsense way, I went on, "Have you done that? Do you have anything to say to us?"

Conflicted feelings played across Mia's face. What, I wondered, had Resnik promised her? Was the girl smart enough to see through his words? If Resnik had indeed talked to her as I was sure he had, what assurances could he have possibly given her without sticking out his neck that would make Mia hesitate like this? I wished I knew.

"I've thought about it, yeah... but I don't want to talk about it right now."

I rarely lost my temper, but I'd had enough. I stood up. Bree looked worried, but made no move to stop me.

"Well," I said, my eyes on Bree, "looks like that settles it. As far as I'm concerned, she can end up in a foster home and do the best she can. Jim and Evie aren't going to hang onto her much longer anyway. Come on, Mia. Let's go. This show is over."

A gamble? Not so much. Resnik was in no position to do much more than inform her that she wasn't legally obliged to do anything she didn't want to. His motivation for doing this would be to disorient her and give her the impression that she was in control. No matter how he couched his words, that's all he could have said.

Mia stayed rooted where she was. In place of defiance was confusion and coming tears. I made no move to console her. I could see compassion in Bree's green eyes where I felt none. Tough love was something I'd never practiced or really approved of, at least not until then. Fortunately, Mia seemed oblivious to Bree.

"Mia, I'm tired of repeating myself. I'll ask you once again. What are your thoughts about where you and your new baby are going to live?"

Now sobbing, looking at her lap, Mia replied, "She probably doesn't want me, but I want to live with my mom if she's not in jail. There's no place else me and my baby can live."

Highly intelligent the girl wasn't, but could she act? Mia's sentimental outburst seemed a little canned.

I changed my mind about bringing Resnik up. It could do no harm.

"Interesting you should say that, Mia. I'm curious about something, and don't lie to me. You do and we're finished here. In case you haven't noticed, I've about had it up to here with you." I'd remained standing. "What did Mr. Resnik suggest to you about where you should live?"

Mia evinced no surprise at my question. Through

her tears, she said, "I can't live with her, even if I want to, cuz she'll be in prison. I'll have to live in a foster home with my baby. He says they'll make sure they find a good home for me."

I sat down. Had my gambit paid off? No way to know with this devious girl. I saw nothing to be gained in directly contradicting what Resnik had said, especially since his prognosis might very well be correct.

Turning to Bree, I said, "Could I have a blank sheet of paper and a pencil, please?"

In a minute she was back, handing both to me. She sat back down and leaned forward to see what I was up to.

"Mia," I said as I was drawing, "I'm no artist so don't poke fun at me. I'm drawing something here that may help you understand something that I don't think is very clear to you."

She remained where she was, but her eyes followed my hands.

Bree lightly cleared her throat. She was looking down at her watch. I'd forgotten entirely about her need to get her little girl. We had momentum now, and there was no way we could interrupt our session. Bree nodded before I could ask my question.

In a low voice, she said, "I'll call my friend at the daycare and ask her to keep Maya for a while. We'll have to cancel our dinner plans, I'm afraid."

I nodded as she got up and I returned to my drawing. At the top, I penciled twelve little circles with mouths and noses to represent a jury. Below and to the left, I wrote *Resnik fights for guilty verdict for L. Jackson.* Then came a straight line beneath which I wrote *Forrest Spencer fights for innocent verdict for L. Jackson.* Below my name, I wrote *Bree Dixon.* At the bottom of the sheet, I penciled *Court of Law.* Bree had returned, nodding briefly, and gone back to looking at what I'd done.

"Mia, scoot closer please so I can explain this to you." She complied. "Now I need you to listen carefully and think about your answers. They won't be difficult. First, do you know what a court of law is?"

"Duh," she said.

"Now don't be smart, just pay attention. Do you know what a criminal court of law is?"

"I think so," Mia said.

"When people are arrested for crimes like what happened with your mother, they must go to court so that people can decide if they are guilty or not. Do you understand this?" A nod. "Alright. See these twelve circles here at the top? In courts of criminal law in California, a jury of twelve people decides if the arrested person is guilty of a crime or if they're innocent. If the jury says they're guilty, then the person who's been accused may go to prison. But, and this happens lots, if the jury doesn't think the person who's accused has really done something wrong, they say not guilty. That means the accused person goes free. Are you understanding me?"

"I think so."

"Good. Let's go on then. How do these people who are in the jury make up their mind about whether or not a person's guilty? I bet you don't know that."

Mia shook her head.

"That's what attorneys like Mr. Resnik and me and Bree are for," I said. "One attorney will do everything he or she can to convince the jury that the accused person is guilty. That's Mr. Resnik's job. He's going to do his very best to show that your mother committed a crime and should go to prison for a very long time. You didn't know this, did you."

Again, Mia shook her head.

"See what I've written here? *Resnik fights for guilty, Forrest and Bree fight for innocent.* Mr. Resnik thinks your mother should go to jail for what she did, Bree and I think she shouldn't. We think she had good reason for what she did. The jury, these twelve people here, will listen to both sides, to Mr. Resnik and then to us, and then they must decide. We're going to do our best to make sure they decide for us. Does that make sense to you?"

Mia looked confused. Finally, she said, "But how can you and that lady say my mom's innocent when she's not? She killed my daddy. I saw her do it."

My God—Mia as a witness for both the prosecution and the defense. Not for the first time, but it would make for hell, especially with a child. I can't say how relieved I was to hear Bree cut in.

"Mia, I'm going to ask you a very important question and I'd appreciate it very much if you could think hard about your answer. Can you do this for me?"

The impact of Bree's gentle and cajoling tone was immediate. Mia's expression softened and she nodded twice.

"Thank you, Mia. I appreciate it. I know this is very hard for you. Now here's my question, two, actually. First question. Do you think there's ever a good reason for killing someone? Now think about this before you answer."

Mia did, then shook her head. "I don't think people should ever kill anybody," she said, "not ever."

"A very good response that most people I like would make. They'd agree with you, okay?"

A nod.

"Now, here's my second question. You think hard about this one, too, okay?"

Another nod.

"This one involves you, Mia, and it involves your new baby, say, two months old. You ready?"

Mia was now leaning forward, her eyes fixed on Bree.

"Alright. Here we go. You're outside in your front yard and your baby's lying on the grass, kicking its hands and feet and enjoying herself. You're very happy while you watch her, right? While your baby's been lying there for a few minutes in the sun, you've been weeding your garden so you've got a big shovel in your hand."

Bree had Mia's full attention though the girl had no

inkling of what was to come. God, was there no end to this woman's resourcefulness?

"Okay. You've got the picture? Your baby's on the grass near you and both of you are in your front yard near the street and you've been weeding. Still with me?"

"Yeah, sure. Then what?"

"Here's what, Mia. Out of nowhere, a man runs up and grabs your baby and starts to run away. There's no one around to help. What's Mia going to do?"

Mia's reaction was close to violent. She leapt up, tipping back her chair and yelled, "I'd hit him with my shovel. I'd hit him with my shovel until he let my baby go. You think I'd let him steal my baby away from me?" Mia's emotions had gone from rage to grief. "My poor baby. He could hurt her, that man could."

Soothingly, Bree continued talking. "Mia, please sit down. Your baby's safe. No one's going to hurt it. Do you understand?"

"Then why did you say those bad things to me?" Another child more perspicacious would have known.

"To protect your baby as you should have done, you used the only weapon available to you, your shovel. You might have easily have killed the man to save your child. Do you think saving your baby from a nasty man is a crime? Do you think you should go to prison because you did what any mother would do? Do you?"

Mute, Mia sat, tears drying on her face.

"Mia, if the situation I described to you where a mother was protecting her baby happened here and the man was killed, the mother would have to go to court. One side, called the prosecution—the one Mr. Resnik's on—would fight for a guilty verdict because a man had been killed, even if it was to protect a baby. The defense—that's what Forrest and I do, defend people—would argue that the mother had no choice to save her baby other than doing what she did. In most cases, the jury would sympathize with the mother and set her free. The situation with your mother is different, but there are many aspects that are the same. We believe we can get an innocent verdict from the jury if things go well. Has what I've told you made any sense to you?"

Mia didn't move or say anything.

"The thing you must remember is this. Mr. Resnik and his people are attacking your mother. We are defending her." Laying a hand on Mia's, Bree said, "You know, we've covered a lot today. I know we were supposed to have Maya here, but it's too late. We'll get together next week, the four of us for dinner so you can meet her and play with her. We'll talk some more then if you're up to it, okay?"

"We have to wait 'til next week?" Mia whined.

"I'm afraid so. Maybe it can be as soon as Tuesday though. How's that?"

"Okay, I guess," Mia conceded. "Maya will be here then?"

"Yes. Maya will be here then, and so will Mr. Spencer, here," Bree said, grinning at me.

"I guess I will. I've gotta take you back now right away so I can get home to my kids. It'll be stop and go with all the traffic."

Once I'd dropped Mia off and was on my way home, I phoned Bree.

"It's a long way from over," I said, "but I think we might just make a team, you and I. That was some scenario you came up with."

"My God, Forrest, you do take risks. Something I'm learning about you. I was sure we'd lost her."

"I'm not much of a risk taker, Bree, not me. Sometimes I wish I was. There was only so much Resnik could have said to her. His goals are to do whatever he can to keep that nightie out and to convince Mia that her mother doesn't have a chance. Accomplish the latter and he'll have her emotionally on his side. Your little scenario was brilliant. The question is, will Mia make the connection between her protecting her baby against a kidnapper and what her mother did. I'd like to think so, but I have my doubts."

"Yes," Bree said, "I'm afraid of the same thing. The child can't see past her nose. Changing the subject, you did hear what I said about Tuesday evening's supper, right?"

"Sure did. I'll get Lupe to stay over."

After a pause, Bree said, "You don't have to do that, Forrest. Nine or ten will do."

"I was just teasing you. Lupe lives at our house more than hers. She usually stays over if I'm going to be out late, like for a nice dinner or a movie or something like that. Please don't worry. I'm not rushing you."

"So if I don't see you tomorrow at the office, it'll be Saturday late afternoon at your house, right?"

"I can always leave a map in your box when I come in tomorrow if you're not receiving visitors."

"No, I get too much paper mail as it is. In exchange for your map, I promise another cup of decent coffee and a bun. Only thing is, if we don't stop doing this, we're going to cause a stir in the office, you know that.

"Like I care. See you tomorrow, Bree, and thanks for bailing us out today like you did."

It was Friday morning. Minutes before I was to meet with Bree, I heard Sara's familiar tap. Had I given her something to do that week? Oh yes, I recalled, I had.

Two things struck me almost simultaneously as she came in and sat down across from me. Her smile was neutral and there was no trace of the scent she always wore. For reasons I had no wish to know about, my research assistant had apparently decided to leave me alone.

"So," I asked, "what did you come up with? I'm curious."

"Forrest, Hannah Loewenstein's been a superior court judge here for some time, hasn't she?"

"Not for all that long, I think. Nobody around here seems to know her. She has to have been elected here, but I have no idea when that was."

"There's not a lot about her I could find in the

jurisprudence. The first reference I could find for her goes back about ten years, so she's no newcomer to superior court. The weird thing is that I could only find about twelve of her decisions for that amount of time. Doesn't seem to be a very active lady."

"Anything you can say about her in particular based on what you've seen?"

"Not really," Sara said. "Four of the twelve were jury trials and the rest were bench trials of hers. About the only thing I can really say about her is that she's unpredictable, going one way in one case and almost in the opposite direction in another. The bad news for you is, there's nothing in the jurisprudence for her in California. Looks like you're going to be her maiden voyage, so to speak."

Bad news, indeed, for both Resnik and us.

"Anything involving battered women or anything like that in her background?"

"Nothing like that that I could see."

Speaking half to myself, I said, "I'll have to get Ben to do a little digging. He's got sources that neither of us really want to know about."

Standing up, looking a little wistful, Sara said, "I'm sorry I couldn't help you more."

"Sara," I said as I always did after sessions like these, "if there was something more out there, you would have found it. At least, we know more than we did."

Before going into Bree, I rang Ben. I was surprised when he answered.

"Cassie kicking you out the door earlier these days or what?"

"I'm a witness in Judge Brown's court today if you must know. I'll probably wait the whole damn day, coolin' my heels, and won't be called 'til tomorrow. What can I do you for?"

I explained.

"Hannah Loewenstein. Never heard a her."

"We neither. That's our problem. What's bothering me for the moment is why, with no experience in this state, they've given her a high-profile capital trial, and we're to be her first case. Sara's got a little history on Loewenstein from New York if you need it. She seems to have tried only one case per year on the East Coast. Wish I knew why."

"Yeah, well, when they get through screwin' around with me in court, I'll get on it. Be back to you when I've got somethin'."

"How's Cassie holding up?"

"She's still pissed at the Bureau but otherwise she's okay. Listen, Forrest, I gotta go. You know the drill."

"Your coffee's getting cold and so is the cinnamon bun I brought," Bree said. "What's the matter? You don't look happy."

I thanked her for the welcome breakfast, took my accustomed seat and recounted what I'd just learned.

"She's never tried a case here in California?"

"Not in superior court, anyway."

Turning serious, she asked, "So we're going to be her first case, is that right?"

"Seems so, yes, unless we exercise our peremptory option to have the judge replaced."

"You can do that kind of thing?"

"Yes, but there are drawbacks. We can also file for disqualification on grounds, but that'd be difficult in this situation since we have nothing to show that Loewenstein would be biased against us. Both sides have one peremptory challenge to the judge assigned. If Ben digs up stuff that we don't like, we may have to go that way. I'd prefer not to if we can avoid it. Unless we've got some pretty substantial reasons against her, she's going to be a little upset, shall we say, if she's replaced. How will those sentiments play out in our next case with her?"

Bree nodded. "I see what you mean. Still, the thought that we're her first case here—"

"Is unsettling, to say the least. Until we hear from Ben, we should leave things as they are." I'd finished my coffee and taken my last bite. "In keeping with that work ethic of yours which you so eloquently expounded yesterday, I think a change of venue is in order, don't you? I mean, when I'm in here, snuggled down on this couch, I can't keep my eyes off of you and stop thinking about all the wonderful things I'd like to do so..."

Throughout my little speech, I'd managed to keep a straight face. Eventually, as Claire had done, Bree would come to recognize the little signs that would give me away, but she hadn't got there yet. There was suspicion in her eyes but bewilderment on her face.

"A change of venue? We can work in here. My door is open, after all."

I can maintain a poker face for a few seconds, but that's all. Smiling at her, I said, "It's true what I said happens to me when I'm in here, but we've gotta go over a few things that are best done in my office, mainly because that's where all the papers are. Plus, green-eyed lady, the more I'm around you, the harder it is to concentrate. I'm thinking my office will help me out."

Smiling in return, Bree said, "I guess we'll see, won't we."

"You know, this is only the second or third time I've been in your office," Bree remarked, eyeing my two client chairs.

Pointing to the one in the corner near the window, I said, "That's where Ben and Garrett sit when they're in here, if that means anything."

With an impish look, she asked, "And where does Ms. Pringle sit?"

"Since you ask, it's the other one. She pulls it closer so she can put her papers on my desk. Satisfied?"

"Hmmm. And if I bring papers with me?"

"Since we don't want you and Sara sharing anything, you can come here and cuddle up on my lap. That way, we're sure to get a lot of work done. You won't have to worry about people in the office since, as I'm sure you've noticed, I keep my door closed. Always have."

Bree took the larger chair in the corner. It dwarfed her.

I laughed. "You look like a schoolgirl sitting there with your curly hair and sundress."

Tilting her head as she did sometimes before a quip, she said, "But I'm no schoolgirl as you should know so let's get to work since that's why we're here." In a voice I had to listen hard to hear, she said, "I have a question before we get to work. Did you think to talk to Lupe about next Tuesday?"

Her query, more a declaration than a question, turned the sexual tension in the room up a notch.

"She'll be very glad to come. She'd live in our home permanently if we let her. I think she gets lonely in that little house of hers even though she has a lot of friends."

Seemingly satisfied, Bree took out her notebook.

Pulling a thin folder from beneath a stack of documents and envelopes, I said, "We might as well start with discovery since that's not going to take us very long. This has got to be about the slimmest pickings from the prosecution in a murder case I've ever seen. Here's the gunshot residue report from the crime lab along with the fingerprint analysis, nothing startling there, and here's the medical examiner's report. I see my old friend Copperstone hasn't retired yet."

I handed the sheets to Bree, who very probably had never seen anything quite like them before.

"What other informative stuff do we have here? The arresting officer's report, and, of course, Lucy's signed confession that we've already seen."

"Not those awful pictures? They're not there?"

"No, no. From the prosecution's point of view, they're not evidentiary as to the crime itself."

"Forrest, how much can this confession hurt us? Lucy admits unequivocally to having killed her husband."

"It happens to be the strongest kind of evidence the prosecution can have. In principle, she could be convicted on it alone. We won't be in court to challenge the confession, especially since Lucy gave no motive for what she did. She had to have stood up under some pretty heavy fire. They'll have pushed hard to get her to tell them why she shot Pete. Without the motive, the weight of the confession is reduced, at least in theory, it is. Our job is to convince the jury that what Lucy did doesn't constitute a crime."

"Yes, yes I understand what our objective is. It's just that looking at this confession, you... you—"

"Don't see how we can possibly get her off. The fact is, Bree, we may fail. Our unorthodox approach may have little impact, depending on who we get for a jury and, I hate to say it, on our unknown judge. She doesn't pronounce the verdict, true, but she'll influence the outcome. Depending on what she does during the trial and her attitude afterward when she instructs the jury, she alone could make or break us if jurors haven't already made up their minds. Let's face it. You and I will be attempting something that's new to the criminal court room when we claim that Lucy's actions were justified, based on premises that her husband had gone to considerable lengths to inculcate in her."

"Premises?"

"Yes," I replied, "such as her lack of credibility in the eyes of authorities in light of Pete's and Mia's denials, the certainty of Pete leaving her if Lucy attempted to interfere in any way and the inevitability that both Mia and Alex would leave with him when he went. And, of course, there's Pete's threat to discredit her with the pictures."

Bree nodded, but I could see that she was troubled. "I understand these things," she said. "We've gone over them a lot. I know you've said how we have to make the jury recognize these things so they can form a picture of what Lucy's state of mind was when she killed her husband. I'm sorry if I'm still confused, but I have only a vague idea how we're going to accomplish this without real evidence aside from those pictures and those ridiculous separation papers Pete gave her. I'm not being very helpful, am I."

Be entirely open with her and tell her of my own doubts? Had our relationship been primarily professional, I might have kept them to myself for fear that she'd lose confidence altogether and be weakened in her ability to contribute. That, need I say it, was not the path I took.

"Bree, look," I said. "It's really the reverse. If you weren't questioning our defense strategy as you are but just following my lead, then, yes, you might not be helping very much. I wish I could reassure you and give you concrete answers. I'd like to lay things out as I normally can and show you, step by step, what we're going to do. Obviously, I can't. If you're confused, it's for the best of reasons. Until things began to fall apart with Mia, I hadn't realized just how much I was relying on her support when on the stand. I'd hoped that we'd find some way to get her to admit things that would strengthen Lucy's case. I was counting on the jury's emotional reaction when they learned that Mia's father had impregnated her. The domino effect, in other words. Establish that fact and sympathy for what Lucy did would rise."

Bree was watching me intently and she nodded.

"But as you know, the wind's not favoring us. It's very possible that Resnik has gained sufficient status in Mia's eyes that he'll maintain control over what she does during the trial. If he does, very simply, we won't have enough, not nearly enough to do much for our client. So, your doubts, I'm sad to say, are well-founded."

Though my own words did little to lift my spirits, I was heartened by the expression on Bree's face. Her distressed look had given way to one of cogitation. I'd been ready to try to buoy her up but, instead, I let her think.

"So," she finally said, "it's what you've implied

before. Mia, in a way, must become our main focus in the trial rather than her mother."

Nodding as I reflected, I said, "I think so. If she were less volatile, more stable, I wouldn't give much for our chances. You and I are going to have to contrive some way to use those bad attributes of hers to our advantage. Any ideas you come up with along the way about how to do that will be very welcome, believe me."

With the ghost of a smile, Bree replied, "I'll do my best. I'll be eager to hear what that fertile imagination of yours conjures up."

"I told you we'd make a team, didn't I."

What had started out as a downward spiral changed form, thanks to Bree's resilience, and, remarkably, had reenergized us. We were back on track.

Tossing her head as though to give herself a shake, she said, "So there's little from discovery that can help us. What have we sent them?"

Clearing my throat and riffling through more papers, I pulled out two copies of a single sheet. "More than they've given us."

She took notes as I spoke aloud.

"They've got the diary, the part of it they're allowed to use, that is—volumes four, five, and six, the important ones. They've got Pete's phony separation papers and, let's see, what else. Of course they've got the pictures. We didn't have much choice in sending them over since we're likely to bring them in."

Bree frowned, still doubtful, but I went on.

"And they have the nightie. Again, no choice. At this point, it's moot since we don't have Mia's DNA. They have the Perkins Lab report on Pete Jackson's DNA and they have the pediatrician's report on Mia's pregnancy. I think that's it."

"Can they hurt us with anything we've sent?"

"Not really. They'll hammer away at Lucy's open and shut confession that she killed her husband premeditatedly. They'll do their best to demonstrate that Lucy could have had help from a variety of sources without having had to resort to violence. And, they know what we're going to argue so they may trot out some expert testimony to discredit what we say about Lucy's state of mind when Pete was killed. They'll see this case as a slam dunk. They're unlikely to get themselves bogged down in expert witnesses and abstract concepts juries don't like. All this brings us to the next issue. Have you seen the prosecution's witness list?"

Bree shook her head.

"Well, don't fall over from surprise. There's nothing very unusual here." Again, I rooted around on my paper-littered desk and drew out two sheets.

"Forrest, how do you ever find anything in here? Don't you lose things? The only desk I've seen around here that's worse is Ben's."

I ignored her. "I'm a very ordered individual, I'll have you know."

A derisive noise from Bree.

"Okay. The prosecution witness list. Usually, there are a lot of people's names there just for show. Some of them they won't call. They're there to make us waste time trying to get info on them. In this case though, I suspect we'll see most of the people on this list. They haven't put names in the order of appearance from what I can see. The arresting officer, for example, is at the bottom. Let's see what we have here. I'm going to move the last name to the top so this list makes some sense.

"One—Sergeant Paul Yublonsky, chief arresting officer. Two—John Murdock, crime lab. I doubt we'll see him. Too bad. I like him. Three—Dr. Alexander Copperstone, medical examiner. I know him well. He's tough but fair. Resnik will try to cajole Copperstone into saying how gruesome Pete's death was, but he won't get far. Four—Lieutenant Kate Schulz, interrogating officer. I know her a lot better than I'd like. She's sneaky and tough as nails. Ben's name for her is Foxy Kate. It'll be interesting to see how she weighs in on this one. Some inexperienced defense attorneys have learned the hard way she's not the sweet old grandmother type she likes to portray. Fortunately for us, she hasn't got a lot to do us damage, at least I hope."

"I know," Bree commented, nodding. "You hate surprises."

"In the courtroom, damn right I do. So will you when you've been in this game for a while. Five—Sharon Lopez, Child Protective Services."

Bree's head came up. "I know her. Yeah, I do. Gray, older lady in her late fifties, rather hard as I recall."

"She'll be there to tell us about all the options Lucy had to protect Mia. Six—Tina Palson, child adoption agency."

In anticipation of my query about whether Bree knew her, she shook her head.

"Seven—Dr. Peter Salmonson, MD, psychiatrist. We'll see him or we won't, depending on who Resnik sees on our list. Eight—Mia Jackson, defendant's daughter."

"Will they call her, do you think?" Bree asked.

"I think so. Ostensibly, they'll put her on the stand as the best witness they could have for what Lucy did. Their real reason will be to elicit sympathy from the jury about the trauma her mother put her through. If I were Resnik, since the People go first, I'd call her, absolutely. We may have to treat her as a hostile witness which is the reverse of what we want. I think a visit to our judge might be a good thing on this. We could move to restrict Resnik's questions strictly to what Mia saw when Lucy shot Pete in the interest of reducing trauma for her in the courtroom. It's certainly worth a try."

By the energy in her nod, it was obvious Bree agreed. "Can I be present at that hearing?"

"Present for sure and potentially very valuable. Hopefully, Loewenstein can fit us in soon. I have some pro forma pretrial motions to file, anyway. This list may change when Resnik sees our list. Not all that much though, I think. Speaking of our list, it's time we drew it up."

Amused, Bree watched me turn over every sheet and document on my desk.

"I have some notes in my office if that'll help," she offered demurely, trying to hide her grin.

As she was getting up, I remembered stuffing a pile of papers in my briefcase the night before. I pulled them out. "You see? I don't lose things, I just misplace them. There's not much here, just a few names I jotted down the other day. Wanna make a photocopy of this?"

She took my sheet and, in what seemed like seconds, she glided back into my office and was settled in her seat.

"Very impressive. You appear quite good at that sort of thing."

She took the bait. In an instant, her pleasant expression gave way to something suggestive of revolt. Then the affable look was back as she shook a reproving finger at me. In a jaunty tone, she said, "Enjoy those moments while you can. I don't want to burst your bubble, but you're really not very good at hiding what you think. Promise you won't be upset with me when I spot one of your phony expressions and just ignore you. That okay with you?"

My turn not to have heard, I said, "Now, as to our non-existent list. Have you had a chance to contact Professor Chadwick? That's his name, isn't it?"

"Yes it is, and we've been in touch. I FedExed him a copy of the diary as you suggested. He says it's the best-documented longitudinal account of psychological abuse he's seen. He says he'll be delighted to help in any way he can. Even though classes have started, he's prepared to fly out here on short notice if we need him."

"That's great. If you don't mind, since we don't know yet quite how we're going to use him, I'll just pencil in his name at the bottom here but, for the moment anyway, we'll leave him off the list."

Since we'd been over this ground before, Bree just nodded.

"Lucy should be our final witness. Not sure what to do with that daughter of hers. A lot will depend upon Judge Loewenstein's ruling on our motion. So, let's concentrate on who we're sure about. One—Jacqueline Parks. She saw Lucy most recently, shortly after Pete took away her car, and tried to convince Lucy to leave him. She's strong."

Bree nodded. "Yes, I remember what Lucy said about her in her diary."

"Two—next most recent, several years ago, actually, Kate Barns, who was at a soccer game and witnessed Pete's strange behavior when he saw Lucy talking to her. She's on the rough and tough side but strong. How much good she'll do us is hard to say. Three—Susan Carpenter. You remember her in the diary?"

Bree nodded.

"When she went back to Lucy's house to borrow a party dress, she discovered that Pete had destroyed them all or given all her nice things away. She'll be good for us. Four—Lily Santos. Lucy says Lily's scared to death of going on the stand. She thinks she'd get confused and say all the wrong things. Unless we get hard-pressed, I'd say we leave her out."

Bree concurred.

"Now things get more problematic. We know what our first three will say and they'll be unshakable, at least I hope so. Mia can appear at the beginning or near the end. It depends a lot on what happens between her and us in the next few days. For the present, let's put her in as number four. I admit I'm a bit at a loss to know what to do with Chadwick. I think you'd better try to get him out here as early as you can next week. I'm counting on him to help us with what best to ask Lucy when she's on the stand."

Bree, looking sober, nodded. "If I could get him here for Tuesday or maybe Wednesday, would that do?" Her expression hadn't changed, but her eyes were locked on me. The little vixen! Would I remember a rather special invitation for Tuesday?

"We've got a lot of stuff on our plates until Wednesday, don't we?" Making no attempt this time to hide anything. I seemed to have passed her little test.

Would Bree be as alluring on Tuesday evening as she was then?

"Now that you mention it, I guess we do. It's a little bit short notice to ask him to come before. Say I try for Wednesday or the latter part of the week. Will that be too late?"

"I don't think so," I said. "Aside from Mia who's unquantifiable at this point and our not knowing how best to use Chadwick, the most critical part of the trial will come when Lucy's on the stand. She should be okay and I think she'll hold up under cross. What's pivotal for us is the kind and sequencing of questions we ask her. To a degree, the same thing applies to Mia. It's especially true in Lucy's case, though. Our questions have to draw Lucy out in such a way that the jury comes to form a picture of her past. I've always thought that jurors are among the most fickle and unpredictable people I know, at least when they're in the box."

Bree was nodding.

"What they're like outside of court, who knows. My defense strategies normally reflect the little I know about jury psychology. I like to think, like any attorney does when I'm addressing jurors, that it's I who have control. For the first time in my career that I can remember, I feel like there'll be a serious mismatch between them and me where I'm the little guy who's begging for their mercy, not a sensation I like very much, believe me. Okay, enough self-pity. Anyone else who should be on this list?"

Bree thought a moment, then asked, "Actually, what about Lucy's son? Could he be of help to us?"

I shook my head. "I don't think so. He hasn't seen all that much during the last two years except that one episode with Pete and Mia. I wouldn't want to try to make him say anything against his father unless it was critical."

"Right. I see," Bree said.

"I can't think of anyone else, at least not now. As soon as we're finished here, I'll draw up a motion to confine the prosecution's questions to Mia to strictly what she saw when Pete was killed. Meantime, if you can get on the phone to Chadwick and arrange an interview with him late next week, we can get on with strengthening this strategy of ours. We've got only a few weeks before the trial starts."

Bree shuddered, doubtless from the daunting prospect of her first day in criminal court.

Chapter 17

It was Saturday, about four in the afternoon, our yard, front and back, redolent with the aroma of barbecuing marinated chicken. Ears of corn in husks along with foil-wrapped potatoes stuffed with butter, cheese, and bacon bits were also on the grill. In the kitchen, Trina was icing her first Black Forest cake. Andy had just come outside to practice new martial arts moves he'd learned, attired in his judogi.

I was feeling good but a little nervous. Bree and her child were meeting the twins for the first time. I wanted the chemistry to be right. How, as the young lady of the house, would my daughter react to an attractive woman near my age who might be competition? Sensible and concerned for my welfare though she was, might Trina feel proprietary about the special relationship we had, grown stronger over the past sixteen months? No matter the care Bree and I took to appear casual, my daughter would sense immediately that we were more than friends.

Were we more than friends? The course of my relationship with Bree would depend in no small measure on how my children responded to her. She would know this. Whatever awkwardness there might be would hopefully be defused by the appearance of little Maya, who would be Trina's sole focus for a while.

Standing on our front porch, watching as our guest extracted her little girl from her car seat, I was confident that Trina would see only that adorable dark-skinned child.

She saw her and smiled, but her eyes were on the mother as Bree's were on her. In an instant, Trina knew more than I could have told her in twenty minutes. Often in my life I had witnessed lightning quick non-verbal communication between women who'd never met. Exchanges like the one that had just occurred were commonplace, it seemed, among females. I was consoled by the warm smiles on Trina's and Bree's faces and soft expression in their eyes. Though my daughter was still a child, she had just taken part in what was obviously an integral social attribute of womanhood.

Maya, not the slightest shy, jumped into Trina's outstretched arms. While I showed Bree the house, my daughter, enchanted by her little charge, went out to the backyard to play.

"Compared to my little house, this is a mansion." Bree looked appreciatively at the hangings and artwork on the walls, but didn't comment. Glancing at me then back at them, she must have intuited, correctly so, that my tastes were less abstract. Claire had selected a few of the paintings, but many of them had belonged to her mother. I liked Bree's quiet intelligence. "This kitchen is amazing! You do all of the cooking, don't you."

"Most," I replied, "but Trina's doing more and more. She used to only bake. It's something we've always enjoyed doing together. These days, I observe much more than advise."

'Well done, Spencer, make Bree feel shy about disrupting your household.'

Just before we went outside, Bree asked if she could see my study. Fortunately, my desk was more or less in order.

Looking around everywhere, she said, "This looks a lot nicer than your office. A couple of cobwebs up there though, see?"

Would Bree be like Claire, who'd tried repeatedly to get Lupe into my study, or like Garrett's Barb with her broom whom he'd had to bar from his precious sanctuary?

'Getting a little ahead of ourselves here, aren't we.'

I'd only completed half my turn toward her and Bree was in my arms, her curly head and face pressed against my chest. Eye contact that I'd seen between her and my daughter wasn't Bree's only way to convey things.

"You keep doing that," I whispered, "and you're going to look pretty disheveled by the time we get out of here."

She made a little noise, made another movement with her hips, then pulled away. "We really do have to get out of here, right now," she said.

I would have been content to hold Bree's hand all the way to the patio, but she, fortunately, had more sense.

Smiling, she said, "I've got a feeling we're going to be under scrutiny today, especially by one alert young lady, and I want her to like me, understand? So behave yourself. Pretend like you don't know me."

"It's clear you don't know much about my little girl."

"Not so little, Forrest, not so little. God, when I think of it, how different those two are—Trina and Mia, I mean."

I couldn't say much in response since we'd come out onto the patio.

My chicken was calling out to be flipped. Had we stayed in the house much longer, we'd have been eating charcoal. From out of the corner of my eye, I saw Trina had resurrected toys from her early childhood, a couple of which I recognized, and had Maya in peals of laughter as the two played under one of our oak trees.

"She's good with children," Bree commented, "isn't she. Maya loves to play, but she tends to be bashful with people she doesn't know. Clearly not a problem here."

Her gaze shifted to Andy, who, a half dozen steps away, was practicing positions and moves he was learning at Miguel's martial arts school. While I shifted things around on my grill, Bree watched him, a rather intent expression on her sunlit face. Standing there at my barbecue, my glance moving from child to child then back to Bree, I felt happy and at peace, more so than I'd experienced in a long time.

My reverie was interrupted when Bree remarked, surprising me, "Andy's unusually agile. He's very precise in his movements and he's very fast. He'll be very hard to take down one day."

My mouth must have been agape. Agile? Precise in his movements? Difficult to take down? What next was I to learn about this gentle lady?

Continuing as though speaking to herself, she added, "I recognize a little of what he's doing but not most of it. I wonder why that is."

"You obviously know a lot more about martial arts than I do," I said. "I doubt you're watching the kind of techniques most people see. From what Miguel, my friend, tells me, he uses a variety of approaches plus a lot of things of his own. It's based on mixed martial arts, he says, then he goes on from there. Miguel's a highly skilled combat instructor. Most of his students are in their later teens and up. He modifies his methods for younger kids he thinks are promising. Andy's not allowed to spar or learn combat stuff at his age, my friend assures me. Personally, I'm not so sure. Andy just started and I'm already in trouble with his mother. I can't blame her, really. Martial arts is the only thing the kid talks about, dreams about, I suspect. Good God, Bree," I went on. "You're about to destroy my image of this sweet woman with tales of black belts and who knows what else."

Laughing, she said, "There's not much of the who-knows-what-else, I'm afraid. I do have a black belt in karate, that's true, but I don't keep it up. Too bad, too. It's good exercise and good for the soul."

Andy saw he had an audience. A born ham, he rapidly shifted from what he'd learned in Miguel's class to maneuvers that were not part of his curriculum. He understood there was to be no sparring and no combat for kids his age, but he wasn't about to wait until his middle teens. He supplemented what he was learning with self-fabricated jumps and kicks and jabs, so quickly executed that I could hardly follow. Some, I had no doubt, might be a little painful if he were to connect with anyone. Miguel, outwardly at least, discouraged these personal forays, but didn't press Andy about them as long as he promised to practice by himself.

"Do you think Andy would mind it very much if I joined him?" Bree asked.

"Andy mind? Are you kidding? That's all the boy thinks about. So, tell me, Bree. Should I be worried about my health if I offend you in some way?"

Smiling, she responded, "Oh, I don't know. I guess that depends on what you do." Her eyes were still on my son, dressed in his judogi that needed washing, while she had on only a pale pink summer dress that didn't reach her knees.

"Can you go out there dressed like that?" I asked.

Enigmatically, she responded as she often did, "We'll just have to see, won't we. Andy," she asked quietly, "mind if I join you?"

Andy abruptly stopped, a bemused expression on his round face. I could read his thoughts. What to make of this lady he didn't know who wasn't dressed to fight and probably didn't know anything about martial arts?

He answered, "Want me to show you some kicks and strikes?"

"You know what," Bree suggested, "I've got another idea. Do you think you could try to trip me or knock me down if I just stand here in place?"

The condescension plain on Andy's face made me laugh. Bree was more discrete.

"Well," she prompted, smiling at him, "could you?"

"Course I can, but Sensei says I'm not s'posed to spar." Looking at me pleadingly, he asked, "Think it would be okay, Dad, just this once?"

Grinning in anticipation, I replied, "Oh, I don't

think Miguel would mind too much. In fact, I think he'd probably like to watch. So go ahead and do your best."

My last comment galvanized Andy. He went into what he probably thought was a threatening pose and faced Bree, there about eight feet between the two.

Excited and eager to show his stuff, he proclaimed, "I'll try not to hurt you when I knock you down."

"Thank you, Andy. I appreciate that. We should start by shaking hands like we're supposed to, don't you think?"

Andy was momentarily nonplussed. Why would the lady know this? They shook solemnly and spread apart.

To my knowledge, this was Andy's first time to have squared off against someone except his instructor. For a moment or two, he was undecided about what best to do. He fidgeted, then charged.

As though she were a top, Bree spun a full three hundred and sixty degrees in a fluid motion so quick it was hard to see. Had one of her feet moved slightly out or was that an illusion? As to Andy, there was no question about where he was—flat on his belly on the ground, about six or seven feet beyond where Bree stood. She'd obviously moved out of his way and allowed his momentum to carry him too far.

"Ha ha," my daughter taunted. "The great martial artist down on his first try."

"Trina," I called out rather sternly, "that's enough. You stay out of this."

My reproach gave back some of Andy's dignity, but not a lot. Slowly he got up and brushed himself off, looking defiantly at Bree's back.

"No fair," he yelled. "You tripped me."

Remaining where she was, her back still to him, she replied amiably, "Isn't that what you were going to do to me?"

Thoroughly humiliated, Andy launched himself again from where he was. That time, I saw all. As he came at her, his right hand shooting out, Bree made a half turn and moved slightly toward me in what had to have taken less than half a second. Grasping Andy's outstretched arm with her right hand, she quickly pulled. My son, helped along prettily by Bree's tug, sailed past her and, for the second time, lay prone on the grass.

I was relieved to see that the only part of Andy that was damaged was his pride. I looked at Bree, who was standing there, hands at her sides, no sign of gloating that I could see. My chicken required attention, but I couldn't take my eyes away. Would my boy resent the woman I was eager for him to like?

Once more, Andy got up, no truculence on his face this time. A secret smile formed on Bree's lips as she approached him.

"You know something?" she said, almost in a whisper. "I have a black belt in karate and I've been doing martial arts since my early teens. I've seen lots and lots of kids in advanced classes, know that? You're the fastest and most natural I've ever seen."

There was no end to this woman's sorcery. Andy, who was trying hard to hold back tears, blinked as his face broke into a wide smile.

"Can we shake again?"

Andy's hand shot out and the two gripped.

"You're going to be very good one day, Andy. It's written all over you, but can I remind you of something?"

Andy regarded her with big eyes and nodded.

Still very quietly, Bree said, within a foot of him, "Know what the most important rule in all martial arts is? Can you tell me?" Before letting the silence get too long, she said, "Never underestimate your opponent. Never."

Andy's head bobbed up and down. "Yeah," he replied, "I hear Sensei say that to the older guys all the time that he lets me watch."

"Thank you for showing me what you can do," Bree said. "I'd like to watch you work out at the dojo some time."

Andy's face lit up. "You would? Can you come soon? I want you and Dad to see how good Sensei is."

"I'm sure I can. We'll talk to your dad about this, but I promise. I'll come soon."

My marinated chicken might have been a little drier than I liked, but it was good. Lots of *oohs* and *aahs* over my Ben-style grilled baked potatoes.

Even more enthusiasm when, proudly transported by my daughter on a large platter, the dessert came out. What I hadn't seen on the top surface of the Black Forest cake was Trina's beautifully designed message to our guests—*WELCOME BREE AND MAYA*—written in white icing. An odd expression came over Bree's face.

Trina looked upset. In a small voice, she said, "Did I do something wrong with the cake or with my design or something? Did I spell Maya wrong?"

Making no attempt to hide her tears, Bree stood up and slowly made her way around the table to my daughter and hugged her. It was obvious that, for a moment, she couldn't talk.

When she could, she said, "Trina, sweetheart, no one's ever given me and my little girl a gift like that. It's too beautiful, too wonderful to eat... Thank you for doing that for us. You have no idea how much it means." Another hug, then, her eyes still dewy, Bree returned to her seat.

I wondered at the strength of her reaction and what would have prompted her to say what she did. Something in her past, no doubt, about which I might or might not ever know.

The only word to describe my daughter at that moment was that she glowed. Until mother and little girl left several hours later, my son's gaze rarely strayed from Bree.

It was almost overwhelming, events I couldn't have contrived if I'd tried. 'Please,' I thought as I carried dishes in, 'don't let so many good vibes, so much good feeling be for nothing.'

After Bree left, Andy spent a few minutes in the backyard, looking like a whirling dervish as he attempted, rather maladroitly, to emulate Bree's spins. Very clearly, she'd made a convert. What could I say to him to prevent him from eulogizing Bree when with his mother? I had to find some way.

When Trina was tucked in and I went in to say good night, she tugged me down to sit next to her on her bed. Though she appeared to have responded well to Bree, she looked quite serious when she gazed up at me. She'd talk when she was ready, so I waited.

In a matter-of-fact voice, Trina said, "You like Bree very much, Daddy, don't you. Do you love her?"

Her last question made me smile and gave me the opening I was hoping for. "Do I like Bree very much? Absolutely, I do, but you knew that. As to your second question, honey, there are only two people in this world I know I truly love. I'm looking at the gorgeous face of one of them, and the other's asleep just down the hall, and that's the truth. I don't lie to you ever, do I?"

Trina, still watching me closely, shook her head.

"Now, will I ever love Bree strongly in the way you mean? Sweetheart, I don't know. I'd sort of need to know that she'd love me back before I'd let myself go there, wouldn't I."

I watched as a smile slowly formed on Trina's lips. "You're very funny, Daddy, you know that?"

"Funny? Why?" I queried though I thought I knew what she was going to say. I'd been discovering of late that women seemed to know my mind better than I.

"You're funny, that's all."

"One thing I can tell you, honey. I'll try very hard not to fall in love with someone you wouldn't approve of."

The response I got was a simple nod as though to say my reassurances on those grounds were unnecessary. If that's what she was thinking, I was glad.

*

How to word my motion to Judge Loewenstein that Resnik be restricted in scope to questions he would pose to Mia on the witness stand? Each time I thought about the girl, how unpredictable and volatile she was, I felt I was holding a sharp two-edged knife, one side of which was too close to me.

With so little personal knowledge about her, Resnik might discover, too late, how hazardous his witness was. On the other hand, if he carefully orchestrated things with no adverse events, Mia's testimony could destroy us. My pencil poised above my blank sheet—I think better when I write things down than with a keyboard—I pondered the wisdom of doing nothing, of allowing the prosecution, unchecked, to go ahead.

If Resnik was less astute and on his own, I might have done just that, not intervene at all and hope that his strategy might backfire. With Vicky at the helm along with her deputy's growing reputation as a litigator, inaction on our part was too risky.

Primary objections to allowing prosecution full scope when questioning their witness, Mia Jackson.

1. Unnecessary interrogation of the witness, due to her young age and to the circumstances of her mother's trial, will traumatize the child.

2. Given the objective of the prosecution to prove that Lucy Jackson willfully and premeditatedly killed her husband, only questions that bear directly on such proof should be allowed.

Based on these two points, I proceeded to draft our motion that, in my view, had a strong chance of being granted, especially given the measures the Court takes to protect witnesses of Mia's age.

I waved the Superman lunch box that I'd purloined from Andy as I headed for Bree's couch. She was tapping away at her computer keyboard when I came in.

"No mooching this time," I said. "I can even share if you don't have enough."

She clicked on the *Send* icon and turned toward me. "No chance of that yummy barbecued chicken left, I suppose," she said, her smile warm enough to chase thoughts of food away. "What on earth are you doing with a Superman lunch box?"

"As a matter of fact, there's darn near two pounds of it in here. Fact is, I didn't bring much else. I would have brought us some of Trina's cake but—"

Bree shook her head. "It would have been in crumbles. It was divine what Trina did. I think I've got some things in my tote bag down here that will go with your scrumptious chicken. You make me feel a little inferior, you know? You're a gourmet cook and I'm just a meat and potatoes girl."

"Hmmm," I said. "Those potatoes and meat sound pretty good to me right now."

With a sham look of reproach, Bree responded, "Is that all men ever think about is sex? You're hopeless like most of the men I've known. What do you say. Let's eat! Thanks, by the way, for a wonderful Saturday afternoon. No way I can match it, but you haven't forgotten about our dinner date tomorrow, have you? You're still picking Mia up as before?"

"I guess so," I said. "We promised her, didn't we, though I think it's a waste of time. We need to talk about that a little more after lunch."

Bree nodded. "Good news about Professor Chadwick," she said. "He'll be in our office this coming Friday morning for the interview. He's very interested in our case and he sounds really nice. He doesn't seem to think it's going to take a lot of time. That surprised me a little, I must say. He's got a flight out of Santa Lucia for L.A. at three o'clock. He'll be staying with friends over the weekend, then flying home. He's got a graduate seminar on Monday afternoon, he told me. Not much time to prep him, is there."

"Seems not," I said, frowning. What could the man hope to do in just two hours? Hoping I was wrong, I asked, "You have any idea what his fee is?"

Bree grinned. "I thought you'd never ask. He refuses to charge a single cent, even for his flights. He said he needed to come out here anyway and this was a good excuse. He seems eager to contribute to our case in any way he can."

Sighing but relieved, I said, "No fee, no control. We'll just have to see what he says, I guess. Doesn't look like we're going to be seeing him on the stand."

Looking mildly disappointed and shaking her head, Bree said, "Guess not. I hope I didn't choose the wrong man for us."

"Don't second-guess yourself on this, Bree. Everything might work out fine. If not, we may still have time to find someone else. We'll just have to wait and see."

Bree looked troubled.

"Now," I said, shifting my position on the couch, "on to something else. I filed our motion with Loewenstein this morning. I put a copy of it in your box. You know the one I'm talking about."

"Yes, yes, of course. You think she'll grant it?"

"Yeah, I think so. Our grounds are pretty good, and she seems to be reasonable." Repositioning myself again, my elbows on my knees and my chin steepled in my hands, I said, "This whole Mia thing is bothering me more and more. Maybe I'm just insecure, but I'm not comfortable with witnesses of ours who surprise us. No attorney is. Frankly, I think we could court Mia for months without knowing how she'll be on the stand. The same goes for the prosecution, of course. They just don't know it yet. You remember Mia's being called as a witness for both sides, right?"

Bree cast me an indignant look.

"Hey, I'm sorry. I just don't do well with loose ends. I can't remember what I've explained to you and what I haven't. It's my fault."

She smiled and waved me off.

"We've been talking about preparing questions for Mia when she's testifying for us, and that we have to do.

Do you know what it means to have a witness of ours deemed hostile?"

Bree looked bewildered. "I should remember that from law school, but it's been so long. God," she exclaimed in frustration, "there's so much about this field that I don't know. Assume I don't, okay?"

"Alright. Except when we're cross-examining a witness for the other side, we're not allowed to ask questions in direct examination that can be interpreted as hints about how they should answer."

"Leading questions," Bree said.

"That's right. We can't lead or badger our witnesses into saying what we want. The other side will object and be upheld by the judge. In cross, opposing counsel can lead and badger to the extent that we allow it, but questions they ask must pertain to issues we raise with our witness during direct, right?"

Bree nodded.

"Okay, now here's the thing. Sometimes we call witnesses who we know don't like us and won't be inclined to help if they can avoid it. Still, as we remind them, they're under oath and may be held in contempt if they lie. If we think this may happen, we can request our judge to have our witness deemed hostile. Okay?"

Another nod.

"Even if someone is our own witness, if they've been deemed hostile, we're allowed, for all intents and purposes, to proceed as though we were cross-examining them with one immensely important difference. We're not restricted to scope as normal since it is we who are examining under direct. To be honest, I think I'd be a lot happier having Mia as a hostile witness. Here's why. First, I think we can now assume that she'll oppose us in any way she can, not something a normal witness of ours would do. Suppose I ask her if Pete is the father of her child. She answers no. Unless she's deemed hostile rather than a normal witness, I'm not allowed to pursue her on this."

"Right," Bree said. "What happens if Mia refuses to

testify for us? What then?"

"Very simple. We subpoena her."

"Do we still have to get her deemed hostile then?"

"It's a good idea, yes. The judge will have our witness list and she'll know who's been subpoenaed, but she may not have checked when Mia takes the stand. So, subpoenaed or not, we don't take chances. We'll get her deemed hostile from the start."

I sat there on the couch for a couple of minutes while this soaked in. Finally, I got my nod. I also got a look of insurrection I'd come to know.

"Okay. I think I understand," Bree said. "We'll have more power and flexibility if Mia's deemed hostile. That makes sense. Here's something else that does. If you think I'm going to get up and question Mia under those conditions, think again. I'll sell groceries in a supermarket before I do that, at least until I learn the ropes. The first unexpected turn and I'd be lost! You must see that."

In fact, I did. She'd objected once before, but she'd not insisted. She was right. She'd be helpless out there if Mia turned on her, which was very likely. I, myself, despite the years of experience I had, didn't like the prospect. I said as much.

"You're lucky you're reasonable, you know that?" Bree said. "Otherwise, we'd have real problems. So," she inquired, "what significance will the judge's ruling have if she grants our motion?"

"A damn good question," I said. "On the one hand, I'd prefer that she grant it since it ties Resnik's hands to some extent. The wild card here is, would it be better to let him go and possibly hang himself? Mia can do as much harm to him as she can to us if he pisses her off and she turns on him. Put it this way. If Loewenstein turns us down, it's going to worry me a little since the elephant in the room gets bigger. We'll just have to keep out of that ubiquitous creature's way. That brings us to tomorrow. Originally, we'd hoped to get closer to Mia and get her confidence. For reasons I've already said, I think that's going to be a waste of time. If she wants to stay in touch with us, that's fine. That can't do any harm, but as to prepping her—"

"No, no, I see your point," Bree said. "It's incredible, the uncertainty in all this that girl breeds. So, basically, we feed Mia and let her play with Maya, then take her home. That right?"

"Think so," I said. I wanted to say something to Bree to tell her how much I was looking forward to what I thought would follow. No need. As I've said before, things that pertained to our relationship seemed to communicate themselves on their own.

It was Tuesday morning, time for me to get in touch with Lucy to see how Alex had settled in. As usual, she responded to her bird call after one ring.

"You coming over? Great! I want to see you. Alex isn't here. He's back in school at UCSB, didn't you know? Guess I didn't tell you."

I wanted to invite her to a surprise birthday party at our house, something I thought would do her a lot of good. Hopefully, I could count on Bree being there. I wanted no mixed signals for the twins.

Lily brought in coffee and freshly baked pastries, then left us. Lucy sat next to me on the loveseat. I'd known her in the past to be superficial at times but not to such a point that she'd ignore important things. Each time I raised the subject, trying to communicate to her how vitally important it was that we rehearse things, that we talk, she waved me off.

"Forrest, can't we discuss all this later and just talk about old times? Don't you remember?"

My frustration must have been apparent.

"Alright, okay. Can you do me a favor, though? I know how important the trial is, even if you don't think I do, but I get so little company and I miss you. Can we talk about social things, anything you want, then go back to the trial at another time? Can we please do this?" She was almost pleading.

Sighing, I said, "Yeah, sure we can, on condition that we get together again soon and focus on getting you ready for the trial. There's a lot more to do about that than you might think."

Smiling, Lucy said, "Thanks. I appreciate it. Now what should we talk about?"

"Well," I replied, "why don't we start with this. We'd like to have you and Lily over to the house next Sunday for dinner, a barbecue if it's nice outside, just like we used to with our two families." I instantly regretted having brought Pete into the picture, but Lucy seemed not to notice. "What do you say?"

"A dinner at your house next Sunday? Sounds good. Why..." Her eyes brimmed over as she turned more toward me and pressed her head against my chest. A moment or two after, she lifted her face to look at me. Still crying, she said, "You remembered, didn't you. Do you have any idea how long it's been since anyone celebrated my birthday?" I felt a twinge of guilt when she said this. "Thank you, love. I don't need to tell you how much that means to me."

I hoped I wouldn't spoil it for her by what I'd say next. "There'll be a bunch of people there, everyone you know, I promise. You'll get to meet Bree's little girl, Maya. She's a little doll."

A brief pause then a big smile. Half laughing, half crying, she said, "You poor thing, worried about how I'd be. That's something I've always treasured in you, Forrest. If you're not already in love with her, you soon will be if she has her way. I envy her, I have to say. She's going to end up with someone I could have had all my life if I'd had a grain of sense. Anyway, the party sounds absolutely wonderful. Lily and I can get a taxi. That won't be a problem."

"We'll see about that later," I said. "I'll be in touch with you by Friday to make final plans. I'm very glad you can come. It's been far too long since you've been at our house. Will Alex be home then by any chance?"

Lucy shook her head. "No, I'm afraid not. He has no

idea it's my birthday."

"He's got a cell phone, doesn't he? You two getting along okay?"

"Thanks to you and everything you did, yes we are. A cell number? Yeah, he does. I'll give it to you if you want."

I nodded and she went to get it.

Though there were still tear stains on her face, my old friend looked happier than I'd seen her in a long time. I got a hug that didn't flatten those outrageous breasts of hers and kisses on both cheeks. The morning had ended well.

So far, the only attendees at Lucy's party would be she, Lily, and we three at home. I had some phoning to do.

Not surprisingly, neither Sue Carpenter nor Jackie Parks were at home. I talked to their voicemails about the project, said their husbands were welcome to join us and asked that they call back. Kate Barns picked up and said she'd be glad to come. She and her "hubby" weren't on speaking terms for the moment so she'd just leave him in the doghouse at home where he belonged. I thanked her, gave her directions and the hour, and said goodbye.

Could I convince the one I wanted most to come to be there? Should I call and probably not hear back or should I text him? I phoned.

"Mom's birthday? This coming Sunday? Shit. I didn't know. Sorry for askin' this, Forrest, but could you tell me who's gonna be there? I mean, not knowing people or anything..."

I gave him names.

Hesitating, he said, "You said the party starts at four. I'm gonna be in Carpenteria with some friends then. If I showed up at six, would that be too late?"

"Absolutely not," I said, delighted that he'd come. "We'll be serving drinks, but I'll hold dinner until you're there. How's that?"

"Thanks a lot," he said. "I'm glad you let me know. I've been wanting to get together with you anyway. I'm back in school now. Mom tell you that? I'm finishing my degree in marine biology. No more of that business school crap."

"Good show," I said. "I'm proud of you. It's good to know you're back in the field you like."

"It's the best, and they've got an awesome program here. It's linked up with San Diego. Tell you more about it later. See you Sunday."

I could already see the surprise and pleasure on Lucy's face when she saw him. Now, I had to get Bree and Maya there. Hopefully, that wouldn't be a problem.

Evie met me at the door just before four. She might have been attractive had she cared for her complexion and her hair and her choice of clothes. She wore faded baggy shorts and one of her husband's work shirts and was barefoot. She was no feast for the eyes, but she was friendly and direct. I liked her.

"Forrest, it's been a while. Come in and sit. You looking for Snootypants who thinks she's too good to talk to us peons?"

What had brought all this on?

Evie clarified. "I don't know if you know this," she said, but Mia's been having visitors, one, in fact. A guy from the DA's office, or so he says."

"Resnik? Tall, slim, well-dressed?"

"That's the one. So you know about him, okay. He's been here, twice, maybe. Ever since, that girl's been impossible. I don't know what the hell he's told her, but she thinks her shi—well, you get my drift. I'm telling you, Forrest, Jim and I are about ready to throw her out. We told her, both of us. She just gives us dirty looks and goes back to her room. We have rights, don't we? I mean, there's nothin' forcin' us to keep her, is there?"

"Nothing I know of. Has Jim talked to Lucy? I take it back. Maybe that wouldn't be such a good idea. The trial's coming up in a few weeks. I don't expect it to last all that long. Any possibility you and Jim can wait until the trial's over and we know what's going to happen to Mia's mother before you put her out? You've got sufficient money—"

"Money's not the problem, Forrest. It's that bitch of a child. It's like she's possessed."

"Okay, listen," I said. "I'm taking her, assuming she's ready, to have dinner at my friend's house where we were last week. I'll tell her that if she doesn't shape up here, you're going to kick her out and she'll end up in a foster home."

Evie's face looked hard. "You can tell her this too. Jim and I have talked about it. Today's Tuesday, right? She hasn't turned over a new leaf around here, say, by Thursday, come Friday, we're phoning the Child Protective Services and telling them to come and get her. We've had it with Pete and Lucy's brat. That's it!"

"Understood, Evie," I said. "Frankly, I don't know how you've put up with her this long. Thanks for the heads-up about Resnik. We suspected that he'd been here."

"Thanks Forrest. It's good to know that this'll all be over soon and that bitch child will be out of here. I'll tell her you're here. She's waiting."

I did a double take when Mia came out. She'd never paid much attention to how she looked. She'd cut her normally long stringy hair to just above her shoulders, which suited her, and she had an attractive blouse and skirt on instead of the ever-present T-shirt and jeans most kids her age wore. She had new high-heeled sandals, nice ones. Where had the funds come from? I'd have to talk to Evie. Resnik surely had nothing to do with it. Vicky would have filleted him then put him out if he'd tried such a thing. The money must have originated with Lucy.

Mia was cool but not unfriendly. As we drove toward Bree's house, she said how much she was looking forward to meeting Maya.

"She should be there not long after we arrive," I

replied.

This made Mia smile.

"Before we get to Bree's though, Mia, I need to talk to you about something."

"No, you don't. I don't have to talk to you at all, not about anything, so let's just go to where Maya is."

Fuming, I slowed, turned down a side street and found a place to park.

"What are we doing this for?" Mia demanded. "I thought we were going to Maya's house."

I had to breathe in and out several times before I spoke. How long had it been since I'd been so angry at someone? Turning to face her—I couldn't have had a pleasant expression on my face—I said, "Has someone given you the impression that Bree and I are your slaves who you can order around as you want? Are you stupid enough to think that Bree has to see you at all, let alone feed you? Can you really be that stupid, Mia, really? Do you think I'm under orders to take you anywhere? Personally, I'll tell you what I'd love to do, that's haul you off to Child Protective Services and tell them to do what they want with you since nobody can put up with you. Now, before I start this car up and take you to CPS, tell me who the hell you think you are."

The girl may not have been that bright, but she couldn't have mistaken the seriousness of what I said. Her face, quite red, went from defiant to angry to confused. Clearly, things weren't going the way she was expecting. Temporizing, she demanded, "What am I s'posed to say?"

"I'll tell you what," I said, "and I'm going to say this only once, so smarten up and listen or you're going to find yourself in a hell of a pickle that'll be your own damn fault. Understand this, Mia. I'm taking you to Bree's because we promised you, that's all. As soon as dinner's over, I'll be taking you back home, and that's likely to be the last time you'll be invited. You're not exactly the nicest guest to have. That's one thing. The second is, I don't know what Mr. Resnik told you or promised you and, frankly, I don't give a damn. I think you're about to learn that he's not all you may think he is.

"The truth, Mia, is that Jim and Evie are about to throw you out. I have a message from them, and I'll say it only once. Either you change your ways very quickly and behave yourself properly as a guest should by this coming Thursday or they're going to call Child Protective Services and have them come and pick you up. What happens to you and your baby after that is none of our affair. If your Mr. Resnik can help you, so much the better. I hope he can. So, like it or not, girl, you're on the street and soon in a foster home if you don't shape up. I'm sick to death of you along with everybody else, so don't expect sympathy from us. All you've done is to cause trouble everywhere you've been.

"Now what you do at Jim and Evie's is your business. I'm washing my hands of you. You had a chance once to go live with your mother once the trial's over. It seems somebody has convinced you that your mother will be convicted and you won't be able to do that. As I said before, we don't really care very much what happens to you anymore, and I'm not sure your mother does. She certainly doesn't appreciate your attitude. So, if Mr. Resnik who's a good guy can help you, go for it. You're going to need all the luck you can get."

For a moment, I thought Mia might become more responsive, but I was wrong. As sullen as I'd ever seen her, she glared back at me. I took out my cell phone and called Bree. I briefly explained what had occurred and expressed my view that nothing good would come from continuing on to her home. Unless she disagreed, I would return Mia to Jim and Evie's.

"I'm sorry, Forrest, but I think we've done all we can do. Take her home, then come back here."

I didn't require urging. As I reversed our direction and headed back toward Jim and Evie's house, the first signs of confusion appeared on Mia's face. I couldn't recall having ever addressed a young person in the reprehensible way I had. Though I'd been angry—an emotion Mia seemed to evoke in nearly everyone—most of what I'd said was for show, my last-ditch attempt to shake sense into her. We'd soon learn from Jim and Evie whether I'd gotten through. It would be revealing, if that's the word, to see how the exchange between Mia and her newfound champion at the DA's office played out. Perhaps we wouldn't know until we were in court.

Bree was an eyeful with her white embroidered blouse and short matching dark blue skirt. She'd put a red ribbon-like thing in her hair which, with her outfit, gave her a peasant girl look.

"You coming in or are you just going to stand there and ogle me?" She didn't seem displeased by my reaction.

"Sorry to be so rude, ma'am. It's just those clothes and... the way you fill them. I'll do my best to behave like a gentleman."

Laughing, walking ahead of me, she said, "Well, no need to carry things too far."

I heard Maya calling out to her in another room. Then she came running in. Though modified considerably to suit a young child, Maya was dressed much like her mother, even to the ribbon in her lustrous hair. Appealing though Bree was, her daughter looked almost more natural in her garb, perhaps due to the darker hue of her skin. Maya stood in front of me, arms out. Charmed, I swooped her up. She flung her arms around my neck and put a sloppy kiss on my chin.

"That's some bashful child you've got here," I said. "What's she like when she's being friendly?"

"Mmm," came Bree's voice from her kitchen, "a little like her mother, maybe."

"Then you're gonna have some problems on your hands in a few years."

"Put Maya down whenever you want to," Bree said. "She'll be pestering you to play with her all afternoon if you don't."

"Don't worry. It's about time we got acquainted. I love children, little ones, big ones."

The womanly creature who was preparing drinks in the next room enchanted me. I thought about Trina's questions and about what Lucy had said earlier that day. Things seemed to be proceeding so rapidly with us, yet was that strictly true? I'd felt myself drawn to Bree and she to me, it seemed, shortly after she came to us. More and more I found myself looking for reasons to be with her. Was our relationship moving all that quickly in light of this?

Maya was sitting demurely on the couch beside me, playing with the ribbon she'd pulled from her hair. Bree came into the little living room with a red wine balloon glass in each hand. The color of what must have been eight ounces in each was off-white. My God, two-thirds of a bottle down.

Seeing the place next to me was occupied, smiling, she turned slightly to her right and sat in a small overstuffed chair across from me. The glass ten inches from my nose, I knew immediately that I was to consume another California Chardonnay I didn't like. A third of a bottle of it, no less. Bree got up and came over to clink glasses.

"To your first dinner at my house," she said. "You do like white wine, don't you?"

'Spencer, for the love of God, lie convincingly for once. This lady's gone to a lot of trouble and she's no fool.'

Metaphorically gulping, I pasted on a smile and said, "It's unbelievable how far California's come with their Chardonnays." The problem, alas, was that they'd not come far enough. "I see you know how—"

Bree burst into laughter and her entire body shook. Sputtering, she said, "I'd better put this down before I spill it. My God, Forrest, you should see yourself." Bree was laughing so hard she could scarcely speak. "It's true I don't know sometimes when you're being serious or just kidding me. Just give me a little time. One thing I do know about you though, and it's very reassuring. You're one of the worst liars I've ever met. Oh, this is too much!"

Grinning from ear to ear, she went on, "I've a confession to make, I'm afraid. I'm no wine connoisseur as you can tell. I'm not much of a connoisseur about anything when it comes to alcohol." Bree began laughing again as though she couldn't stop. "Your face, it was absolutely priceless. God, if I'd only been thinking, I'd have had my camera."

Trying to suppress her mirth, she shook her head. "No, Forrest, please don't look like that. You didn't hurt my feelings in the slightest, really! I'm not laughing at you or, maybe I am but I don't mean to. My confession, right. To show you how much of a clod I am, I didn't even have a real wine glass in the house before yesterday."

Starting to laugh again, then stopping, she continued, "Now what was I to do about wine to drink? I didn't dare buy hard liquor since I'd be completely lost. So I go into the corner liquor store, once I've got my glasses, and I ask this teenager behind the counter—well, at least he looked like one—for a couple of bottles of wine. He looked at me like I was nuts. So I tell him to pick out a couple for me because I don't know anything. But then I start worrying about whether you'll like what the kid gets. I drive to a bigger liquor store downtown and this nice lady takes pity on me. I tell her a little about you and she goes away and brings back four bottles. Two are white that she tells me to chill and two are red. Okay, I'm done. Am I too eager to please, do you think?"

Getting up again, she gently tugged the balloon glass from my hand, went back to pick up hers and told me to follow her into the kitchen. "Maya will be fine there on her own," Bree said.

Embarrassed but relieved, I watched Bree pour both glasses down the sink—a waste, okay, but precisely where they belonged. She opened a cupboard door beneath the counter and pointed to two bottles of red wine that I was to examine. I bent down, not a little apprehensive about what I'd find. Poor white wines are bad. Undrinkable red wines are worse. I needn't have been concerned. Two Margaux, recent but more than acceptable. Acceptable, certainly, but unlikely within Bree's budget.

"We've got something else to look at first before we sit down, okay?" She motioned me to her fridge.

I was stupefied by what I saw. How long had it been since I'd had a good white Graves? Two bottles of it looked back at me. My expression must have said it all. Four bottles of what promised to be good Bordeaux.

Looking jubilant, Bree clapped her hands. "Now, tell me what to do," she ordered.

"Before I say anything else, I want you to promise me to let me pay for at least half of this. Otherwise, I won't drink." That lie was no better than the first, but she had the grace and the good sense to accept. "Tell me something. If I'd been the gentleman you seem to think I am and I'd drunk the Chardonnay without giving myself away, what would you have done with all this wine?"

A little sheepishly, Bree said, "The lady at the big liquor store who helped me? She said if I kept my receipt and the bottles looked untouched, I could bring them back. I shouldn't have told you that but you asked. Now how do we do this right?"

"Please don't be offended by my question," I said, "but do you have any smaller glasses? They don't have to be for wine, not at all."

Bree pointed to cupboards above the sink. I picked out two aesthetically pleasing six-ounce water glasses that would be perfect for the white and placed them on the counter. Next, with reverence, I took out a Graves, opened it and poured each glass two-thirds full. Recorking the wine and returning it to the fridge, I lifted my glass as Bree lifted hers. This time, I was the one to toast.

"To a lady I'm very happy to have in my life."

Bree looked startled for a moment, then smiled, flushing just a little, and touched my glass.

"Now," I said, "when it comes to the meat and potato things, perhaps we'll move to that spectacular red you chose, depending a little on what you cooked."

"Prime rib," she said.

"Then, I'm going to have the pleasure of tasting a good Margaux. You know how to treat a guest, don't you."

Back on the couch, Bree beside me, she said, "So things didn't work out very well with Mia."

I felt ashamed of how I'd behaved, but I told her everything.

Bree slowly shook her head. "No, I agree, it's not like you to talk like that, not at all. Still, how else were you going to get through to her? That pituitary gland of hers is really going wild. Our Mr. Resnik doesn't know it yet, but he's got a real tigress by the tail. It'll be interesting to see how he handles her in court. Not too damaging to us, I hope. Evie's going to phone you on Thursday, you said?"

I nodded. "I'm sorry for the child but, right now, I want to focus on the woman I have my arm around. That okay with you?"

"If I have to answer that," she said, "you should be doing something much less intellectually demanding than what you do. Tell you what. I'm going to refill your glass, then feed Maya. There won't be much conversation going on around here before I do. Then we can eat. She'll play for an hour or so after dinner, then I'll put her down to bed. You'll have my complete and full attention after that, okay? That sound alright?"

Better than alright.

While Bree was feeding Maya, I went to the little vestibule where I'd hung my jacket and got out my cell. Trina answered the phone.

"Hi love," I said. "I'll be home well past your bedtime

so don't wait up. I'm calling in to have Chinese delivered. Should be there in a half an hour or so. Everything okay at home?"

Apart from her brother acting up, things were fine, she told me.

"I'll say good night now, honey, since I don't know exactly when we're going to eat."

"At Bree's?"

"Yes. Let me talk to Andy, please, okay?" I made a good night kiss noise with my mouth. "Hey champ, had a good day at school?"

"Yup," came back his monosyllabic answer.

"It's Chinese takeout for the three of you tonight cuz I won't be home to cook, okay?"

I pulled the phone away to protect my ears. "No, Andy, you aren't allowed to leave the house when Lupe's there. You know that. Now, listen up. I know how you are with Lupe when I'm not there. You also know I'll hear about everything when I get home, right?"

I didn't bring Trina's name into our conversation, but Andy knew I'd get a blow-by-blow description from her of his sins if he misbehaved. I hated making threats, but, under the circumstances, I had little choice.

"I hear of anything I don't like and there'll be no martial arts lesson this Saturday." A low blow, I knew, but the only thing where I had clout. Fortunately, I hadn't had to resort to it before and, with any luck, I'd not have to again.

"Not fair," Andy groused. "Not fair."

"It's not fair for you to terrorize Lupe all night either, so you behave, okay?"

Lupe adored the twins and, however heinous Andy's peccadilloes were, she'd not tell, a fact he was gleefully aware of.

"You make sure you get your homework done. I'll look at it at breakfast tomorrow morning. Got that?"

"Yeah, okay, fine, Dad. See ya."

Bree's meal was simple but very good. The prime rib had a little red, just as I liked it, and the potatoes had just the right amount of butter and garlic. Bree and I got a word in from time to time, but most of our attention was on the child. Though I was not what one would call a permissive parent, I was pleased by Maya's freedom to explore and interrupt when the notion took her, which was most of the time. On my lap or on Bree's or crawling under the table on the floor, she carried on a monologue that rarely stopped.

Not knowing quite how or when the evening was to end, I'd been careful about how much I drank, tempting though it was to do otherwise. The Bordeaux were very good.

Bath over and good night stories read, Bree finally emerged, looking a little flushed. She'd been less abstemious with the wine than I. Standing in the center of the living room, looking this way then that, she appeared to be searching for things to do.

Lamp lights turned down, putting a CD of classical guitar music on the stereo, and straightening an unused chair that wasn't out of place, she made a noise as though out of breath and said, "There. That should take care of everything." Her glance fell on my glass that had at least three ounces left. "Can I top you up?"

I shook my head. "I've got plenty here." Patting the place next to me, I said, "What I'd like is for you to join me."

Her eyes swiveled to take in the room, then she walked over to the couch. Rather than sitting down next to me where she'd been before, she chose the far end. She crossed her legs under her, half turned toward me and smiled, a little tentatively, it seemed to me. I'd not seen typically confident Bree like this, nervous as a schoolgirl, if that simile was appropriate anymore.

Noticing her empty hands folded in her lap, I asked, "Aren't you going to have more of this Margaux? It's a good one."

"My goodness," she said, jumping up. "What's wrong with me. I forgot my glass in the kitchen. I'll be right back."

I heard the cork come out and some heavy duty glugs as she poured. I felt my eyes grow big as I watched the hugely overfilled balloon glass wobble in her hand as she came back. She was carrying at least ten ounces of red wine.

If she downed half that in the next half hour, we'd be saying good night to each other soon and I'd be leaving. I didn't want our evening to end like that. Nor did she, I suspected, though, unless I misinterpreted the apprehension on her face, it was that or commit to something she wasn't ready for. Of more immediate concern was all that wine that was about to overflow.

"Bree," I said in a low voice, "would you mind if I took your glass and poured some of that wine back? We won't be chatting very long if you drink all that up. Do you have a small funnel I could use?"

Bree blushed crimson. "Yes. Yes of course. I'm so sorry, Forrest. I don't know what's come over me. I'll show you where the funnel is, okay?"

A couple of minutes after, there three ounces in her glass instead of ten, we were back in our respective places on the couch. Bree still looked anxious.

Turning toward her at my end as she was turned toward me, doing my best to appear relaxed, I said, "Hey, let's get something understood. I came over tonight to be with a woman I'm growing inordinately fond of who's attractive, and, sexy, I'll admit, but I'm not here to ravish her. I'd like to get to know her better, that's all, so let's stop worrying."

For what seemed a long time, Bree regarded me, sitting very still. At last, she nodded just perceptibly and I could see the muscles in her face relax. Good. She believed me.

I continued, "You know something, Bree, over the last eight months, you've learned quite a lot about me while I've learned virtually nothing about you apart from what you do for us at the office. I'm hoping, the way our relationship is going, that you don't intend to keep this up."

No response.

"Do you?"

Slowly, she shook her head. "You're right, I know," she said. "I can't tell you how much I've appreciated you not pressing me for information. Most men I've known would have by now. I'm ready to tell you anything you want to know about me, even intimate things that I hope you won't ask too much about." Now she was smiling. "You'll probably have to prompt me a little though. I'm not very used to talking about my personal life to anyone, not even my close friends, so there you are. I'll tell you a few things you must be wondering about, then, if you have questions, ask away."

I returned her smile and settled back to listen.

"What you'll want to know about most, I suppose, is my marriage, and, maybe, something about, well, about how I've related to men in the past. There'll be lots of time, at least I hope, to fill in details if you want them, but, basically, I've been married once to someone I thought I was in love with. He died just over three years ago from leukemia. I think I may have told you that. He was diagnosed with the disease two years before his death."

Bree frowned slightly and waved her empty hand as though to dismiss the relevance of what she'd said. "Sorry about these details. This must be confusing. We got married nearly eight years ago when I was thirty. Anyway, he was a very decent and a courageous man."

A rueful expression came onto her face when she added, "Unfortunately, a little like Lucy's Pete, he was much more traditional-minded about women than I thought. Once that became clear to me, we began to grow apart, very rapidly, in fact. He wanted things I just couldn't give, not so much sexually as in lots of other ways. If it hadn't been for his disease, we would have parted sooner."

After a brief pause, Bree continued. "In college, I was in two long relationships. I'm not the short haul type, I guess. Anyway, for reasons not even my therapists could figure out, I lost both of them. The first time it happened, I was eighteen and quite shy. I got very attached to a med student and was with him for two years."

Bree's face had taken on a haunted look. I thought she was going to cry.

"I loved him, quite a lot, actually, and I was sure he loved me. He was always sweet and kind to me. One spring, he went to a conference somewhere in France. He was supposed to be back in two weeks. I didn't hear from him again for almost three years. I was really broken up and dropped out of school for a while. I got tired of waitressing and other jobs I had and went back. I studied really hard and avoided relationships with guys. Finally, though, I got involved with someone else. He was an artist, a painter, the misunderstood genius starving type. I didn't love him all that much, at least at first, but he was in love with me, or so I thought anyway. We lived together, on and off, for almost three years. Then... then," tears were coming to her eyes, "just like the first guy, he dumped me."

A quaver in her voice, Bree said, "To this day, Forrest, I have no idea why he left. We were together and then we weren't. He got together with a good friend of mine."

"Loneliness, hormones, I don't know why, but several years after the second guy left me, I got married, which turned out to be a catastrophe in about every sense."

Bree's body had loosened up and she looked more at ease but she was still distressed. "It seemed like men and I just weren't meant to be. I saw two different therapists, but neither of them helped me. I actually wondered for a while if it was something physical in me that put men off. Tell you the truth, I had a relationship with a girlfriend for a little while before I got married, but I just couldn't get into it. I do seem to attract women. A fair number have come onto me, but it's not my thing." Smiling, looking a little shy, she said, "I think you know that too, don't you."

In answer, remaining where I was, I said, "Yes, I do."

A sober expression on her face, she confirmed, "No, I'm definitely not into girls. What I'm into is what we did the other night at Ben's."

Bree's words and her shy demeanor made me want to reach out for her. She would have come, but at the cost of fragile intimacy that we were building.

Without prompting, she moved close to me with her head resting on my shoulder. I stroked her hair that smelled like fruit and sipped my wine. Her untouched glass was on the end table. Both of us, without putting it into words, were aware of the strengthening of our connection. I wanted to caress her arms and perfectly formed breasts that had never known a baby's pull, but I stroked her hand instead, so warm and so small. As I did, Bree snuggled closer.

'Spencer, for once, your intuition about a woman seems on the mark.'

I might have gotten away with a few more ounces of that wonderful Bordeaux, but best not take chances on the road. I hadn't expected to leave at ten, but Bree was yawning and it was probably a good time to depart.

"Hey, beautiful," I said, "I should be going. I can't tell you how much I'd love to finish the second bottle of that red, but if I did, you'd have to put up with me for the night and that just wouldn't do. What would the neighbors think?"

"Think? Do you think I care? What will you do if I go in the kitchen and bring out that bottle for you? Then what?"

Her provocative questions posed with the certainty that she was safe.

"You keep the wine"—it would have turned bad by then—"for the next time I come, hopefully not too long from now."

At the front door, her small body pressed up against me and our arms around each other, we stood for a quarter of an hour, words entirely unnecessary.

She whispered so I could barely hear, “What part of heaven did you come from?”

Smiling, whispering back, I replied, “Where Brianna Dixons grow.”

After a long minute, she asked, her question again scarcely audible, “Why do I have the feeling that this time it’s right?”

“That’s easy,” I said. “You’re a mind reader. I already told you that.”

My answer must have pleased her for she hugged me tight. Our good night kiss didn’t have the fervor and the heat of others I remembered, but the depth of feeling that it communicated shook us both.

The last thing I heard her say as I opened her front door was, “You realize that the moment you leave, I’m going to be kicking myself all over for letting you go. Thanks for being so understanding.”

“Hey, Bree girl, I want this relationship as much as you so don’t thank me. It’ll happen when it happens and it’ll be wonderful when it does, you’ll see.”

She reached out and grabbed me once again and held on tight, then gave me a little shove.

“I’m about to beg you to stay, so if you don’t want an emotional female clinging to you all night, you’d better go.”

The idea had its appeal, but I chuckled, bent to give Bree one more brief kiss and left.

Chapter 18

On my way to Bree's office the next day, Ben called out to me.

"Got somethin' that may not amount to a hill a beans, but I thought I'd run it by you anyway."

"Fire away," I said.

"The name Jasmine Rees mean anything to you?"

I shook my head.

"Not surprisin'. Cute thing, real hot as the young people like to say. Ran into her at Jackson Motors while scroungin' up samples of Pete's DNA. Don't have a clue who's runnin' the place, but it's still goin' strong. Jasmine, she's the receptionist there. Been workin' there for years, she says. She was real helpful. Seemed kinda funny to me at the time. Woulda thought his people woulda been more loyal to him and all. Turns out, our Jasmine's a pissed-off girl. Don't know why she chooses me to talk to, but she did. She came right out with it. Said she and Pete were havin' an affair. Been goin' on and off for years. Then suddenly she gets this Dear Jane letter just after the fourth a July. Pete didn't tell her why, but he wanted to slow things down for a while. He told her it was nothin' permanent. Course she thinks it's another girl, right? She calls him on it and he dumps her. Don't know if any of that means anything, but—"

"I don't suppose she told you if she still has Pete's note?"

"Sorry, nope," Ben said. "Didn't ask. Girl's really got

it in for Pete. She'll prob'ly talk to you if you ask her nice."

"That could be useful, especially if she kept anything," I said. "I'll try to see her and let you know if we dig up something. She's at Jackson Motors every day?"

"Seems so, boyo. How's Bree?"

What I wanted to say was, 'Wish I knew.' Instead, I answered, "Doing fine, last time I saw her. Thanks for the heads-up. See you."

I felt butterflies as I approached Bree's door. Things had gone well the night before, but could she have decided in the interim to back away? She wanted the relationship, but would her self-protective instincts prevail in the end? Bree was strong in many ways, but also fragile. I was glad there was no need to hurry anything. Unaccustomed as I was to the courting game, I'd have to take care not to become too involved before the path was clear, assuming I was capable of such a thing.

I felt like an infatuated teenager as I hesitated in the doorway to her office.

Her smile widening, revealing the tips of small white teeth, Bree said, "Forrest, you look weird, standing there like that. There a problem about last night?"

"Last night? No. Last night was good," I answered as I went in. "You drink the rest of that red wine when I left?"

She blushed. "If you must know, I did. I loved every drop. Besides, didn't I read somewhere that red wine spoils overnight once it's opened?"

"Whoever wrote that was absolutely right."

"I have an idea," Bree said. "We should compartmentalize."

I blinked. Compartmentalize about what?

Grinning at me, she queried, "Hmmm. Getting second thoughts? Don't worry. I'm thinking about what's best for the firm. It seems to me we're spending too much time gazing at each other and saying silly things while we're here at work, don't you agree?"

I didn't, but I wasn't going to say.

"Now don't get me wrong. I happen to like the way you look at me and I like the things you say, so don't misinterpret me. All I'm suggesting is, we find more time outside the office to do these things. Can we do that?"

"Absolutely, as long as you don't mind me finding every excuse I can to see you."

"Try me. Now what are we supposed to be doing here?"

"Tell you what, Bree," I said as I stretched. "My coffee didn't do a thing for me this morning. I've gotta get some fresh air or I won't be of any good to anyone. I'll be back in fifteen minutes.

"I bike to work. It helps."

"Yeah, well, you live a lot closer to the office than I do and you've got a lot less weight to schlep around."

"Excuses," Bree quipped. "You're overweight by what, three pounds?"

'How fast females take over your life,' I almost said but didn't.

"You have my notes on my interviews with Sue Carpenter and Jackie Parks, don't you?"

"Yeah, I do," Bree said. "You gave them to me last week."

"Can you prep them while I see Kate Barns?"

"She's the shoot and ask questions later type, isn't she."

"She's outspoken and she won't be taking any guff from the prosecution if that's what you mean. We should talk a little more about Chadwick. You haven't heard anything further from him, have you?"

"No. Not a word. I share your misgivings about him, but I don't know what to suggest at this point."

"Well, as we said before, we'll just have to wait until

he's here. I know how relevant the concept of coercive control is to you, but I'm having problems seeing how we're going to fit it in. Scheduling things that aren't absolutely necessary may hamper us, and that makes me nervous."

"I agree with you, actually," Bree replied. "The difficulty of what we're trying to do is beginning to sink in. Wish I could have cut my criminal trial teeth on something else."

I nodded. "On my way to see you," I said, "Ben stopped me. He had some info that could turn out to be important." I briefed her on what he'd told me.

"Not so surprising that Pete was cheating on her, but what does that have to do with us?"

"Very likely nothing. I doubt Jasmine kept the note. But if she did and she's willing to share it with us—"

Bree's head bobbed. "I said you were devious, didn't I. You'd use the note to stir Mia up in court. You were right about Machiavelli. He'd be very proud of us."

"Yes, maybe," I responded while I thought, my eagerness to check things out increasing as possible scenarios took shape. "I've got to run this down and do it right away. We don't want to get our hopes up, but if she still has that note and she's willing to give it to us or let us make a copy, it could be hugely significant to us. If you don't mind, Bree, I'm going to Jackson Motors right away to try to see her. With any luck, I'll be back by lunch, maybe a little later."

Looking resigned, Bree said, "I'd like to go with you, but it'll probably be better if you go alone. You'll get more from her if I'm not along."

Though not much consolation, I replied, "If everything goes well, then you and I are going to start your compartmentalizing this evening at the best restaurant we can find."

"Sounds good. I'll set up appointments with Sue and Jackie while you're gone. I'll call my friend, Rita, to see if she can stay with Maya for a few hours."

Jasmine Rees was a honey blonde with hair just past her ears, a knockout in just about every sense. She had an unblemished peaches-and-cream complexion. Sultry and languorous of movement, she was a woman very much at home with men. It was not hard to picture Pete, attractive in his own right, there close beside her. How old could she have been, twenty-eight, twenty-nine?

When she spoke, I was jarred by her brittle and grating voice. "I'll get Nina in to watch the desk for a few minutes if you want," she said. "Can't spare a lotta time cuz we're real busy this afternoon. You can always come back another time, though."

"Ms. Rees—"

She shook her head and smiled. "I'm Jasmine."

"Right. Thanks. I'm Forrest." Seeing her puzzled look, I continued, "Yeah, like the trees."

She laughed. It was difficult to reconcile the braying sound with Jasmine's beauty.

"My partner, Ben Segalowitz, was here recently. Do you remember him?"

The girl's eyebrows came together, then she nodded. "I think so. The old bald guy with the funny accent? That him? The one who took away a couple a Pete's hats and some shirts of his?"

"He's the one," I said. "He told me about you. Said you were very helpful."

She let out a derisive snort. "Listen, Forrest, that's your name, right? Your partner didn't have a clue. I was glad to get rid of all that crap. Reminded me of the jerk every time I saw one of his things."

I nodded. "I can imagine," I said. "Ben told me Pete wasn't that nice to you. That true?"

Her eyes narrowed as she regarded me. Did her expression reflect suspicion or dislike for her old boss? It was the latter.

"That asshole didn't know the meaning of the word nice. I don't know what your partner told you, but I prefer not to talk about Pete if you don't mind. I should be gettin' back to work now, you know? No tellin' how much longer I'm gonna have this job. This one pays good. It'll be hard to find somethin' like it." She was about to show me out.

"Jasmine, you really like this job?"

She frowned again, giving her lovely face an unpleasant look. "What's it to you?" she growled, her voice like rough sandpaper. Pete's note, if it still existed, was growing indistinct.

As a last-ditch ploy, a poor one, I said, "I happen to be a close friend of the owner of this company. She'll be pleased to know if you were helpful, especially if you have anything against her husband, Pete."

We sat there for what must have been a minute, she searching my face with unfriendly eyes.

At last, Jasmine said, "What can a woman who's goin' to prison do for me. Tell me that."

"I can't speak for Lucy Jackson about who she'll keep on here, but I can say this. At our law firm, we believe Mrs. Jackson will go free. I can't say right now why we're convinced of this, but if you follow the trial, you'll understand soon enough. Second, if you do your work well here and you've helped us, I'm quite confident she'll keep you on."

After some hesitation she waved a hand and said, "Fuck it. What the hell. What is it you want. I'm not doin' that bastard any favors."

"Ben said you told him about a note Pete sent to you."

"Oh, that. I tore it up. Is that all you came here for?"

Deflated, wondering what blow we'd suffer next, I asked, "Jasmine, are you sure you threw it out? It's really quite important."

Impatience in her expression and her tone, she retorted, "Yeah, why not? You think I'm gonna hang on to shit like that? I mighta stuck it in my black purse to throw it out later, but I'm sure I didn't."

"Look," I said, "I really appreciate your help. Is that purse around here and do you think you could take a look?"

Jasmine got up and turned around and left without a word. She'd dismissed me and gone back to work. I realized more acutely as the minutes passed how useful that little piece of paper might have been during direct examination with Mia on the stand. If it had contained what Jasmine told Ben, in seconds, we might have undone Resnik's careful programming and Mia's own resolve. Yet one more step back with no clearance to go ahead.

Lethargically, I got up and headed toward the outside door. As I reached it, I heard my name.

"Mr. Forrest? Mr. Forrest?"

I turned to see a short plump young woman in her late teens, as plain as Jasmine was breathtaking. She was holding out something in her right hand. Timidly, she said, "Jasmine, she told me I was s'posed to give you this."

I felt my heart beating in my ears as I reached for the crumpled scrap of paper. The moment I took it, the girl turned and was gone. I made my way outside and headed for my car. How precarious our situation was, dependent as we were on such slim hopes.

The note was handwritten on Pete's letterhead. My eyes dropped to the bottom of the wrinkled sheet, where there was a dime-sized sketch of a woman's face. I'd seen drawings like it before, but I couldn't remember where. No doubt about it. It was a miniature of Jasmine's face, the sketch not perfect by any means but unquestionably her. Then I remembered. On the back of each of the six grotesque pictures I'd unearthed in Pete's desk was a drawing of Lucy's face. The size and style were identical to the sketch I was gazing at.

Jasmine baby... can't tell you how good the lovin' was last night... sorry I can't be with you tonight like you asked me but it's Mia's birthday tomorrow and I promised her I'd spend some time with her this Friday... father's duty... I'm coming back into the office though this coming Sunday... Try to be here about seven-thirty after dinner and I'll make it up to you... Sweetheart I'm sorry to tell you this but we're gonna have to cool it a little for a while... I got some overnight trips to make and got more problems at home again... they never stop.... trust me baby... by the end of the summer, things'll be like they were before... I'll miss our lovin'... you're the sexiest girl ever... don't go flashin' them eyes at anybody else while we're not together... Sorry I had to write all this in a note but I had to leave the office early this afternoon and I couldn't find you anywhere... Nina said you were out somewhere.

Love ya... PJ

It looked like what I remembered of Pete's handwriting. We'd have to get some other samples. I felt a little thrill as I conjured up Mia's face, suffused with rage as she took in the note. Presented to her in court along with actual pictures of her father's paramour, she'd feel abandoned and betrayed. Uncharitable of me to put the child through that? Unquestionably, but, compared with what her mother would suffer if we lost, I could justify it. I folded the potentially explosive document and put it in my briefcase.

By the time I reached the office, the plan Ben's tip had kindled had begun to form. I made photocopies of the note, then told Cheryl to put the original in the vault. Bree, who was munching on another apple, looked up as I walked in. I handed her the sheet of paper and watched her read.

A moment later, sounding reflective, she remarked, "The existentialists were right about how irrational and chaotic our world is. We keep looking for something to help us in this case, then, out of the blue, comes this. It makes me feel kinda small, you know?"

I had to play over what I'd heard to comprehend what she'd said.

"A philosopher too, no less. What next?"

Bree eyed me. "No, seriously. The best laid plans and all that. Doesn't it bother you sometimes how much we rely on luck? What's the probability that Jasmine would still have this note, then talk about it to Ben? Who'd predict that you'd end up with it, tell me."

"Whoa, slow down," I said. "Metaphysics. Don't get me started. We got a break, I admit, but I don't agree about how much chance accounts for it. Ben knows we're working on Lucy's case. He has a nose for things like this. At Jackson Motors, he picks up on something that may or may not be relevant and he passes it on to me. This happens a lot with him. I rely on it."

A wry expression on her face, Bree said, "Okay, okay. I didn't mean to go off track. So what can we do with this?"

I laid out my embryo of a plan. She made an 'I see' noise and tapped the note. "I'm assuming this doesn't have to go to Resnik. Please tell me that it doesn't."

"No, no. It's not evidentiary in any way except for Pete's infidelity, but the jury will never see it. We'll distribute copies to the prosecution table and to the judge just before we show the note to Mia. Resnik will pick up on what we're up to and do his best to keep the note out. He'll know that Mia's reaction to it could derail his strategy. He'll call for a sidebar, a conference with the judge. Loewenstein will know we'll push for a mistrial if she blocks us."

Bree looked skeptical. "Seriously, would we get away with that?"

"Maybe, if we have to," I said, "but it wouldn't be in our interest. We would have lost the element of surprise."

Still dubious, Bree replied, "If I were Resnik, I'd argue that the note is defamatory concerning Pete, who's not on trial, and that it's intended to inflame the witness. If I were the judge, I'd block it."

"It could play out like that, absolutely. Let it not be said that judges have no power in situations like these. Loewenstein makes me nervous, I have to say. It's hard to know which way things will go."

Looking solemn, Bree asked, "I know you want to sabotage Mia in direct, but will the note be enough, especially with Resnik constantly interrupting to calm her down?"

"You're developing good instincts. We'll make a criminal defense attorney of you yet."

Bree's voice had an edge. "Forrest, please. Don't be condescending. It doesn't suit you. The things I've just mentioned would certainly apply in family court. Frankly, I don't see why it should be different in a criminal trial."

"I'm sorry. I don't know, Bree. My experience doesn't help me much with this. As I've said before, basing our strategy on state of mind evidence is new for me and I've never had someone like Mia for a witness. We're walking a tightrope here. No question about that. I wish it were otherwise. To answer your question, the note, on its own, might not be enough, I agree. We've got something else though. See that sketch at the bottom of the sheet? That's Jasmine, a damn good likeness, too. Pete drew it. I'm sure of it. The guy had talent. It's identical in style to the little sketches of Lucy on the backs of the pictures we found at her house. Remember those?"

Bree nodded.

"We need to get a couple of good photos of Jasmine at her workplace that we can show to Mia before the note. She'll make the association right away between those photos and the sketch. She'll have seen drawings like that before. What we don't want to do," I continued, "is to get her riled up before we're ready. To start with, we're gentle with her in cross during Resnik's case in chief. We avoid asking or saying anything that might upset her."

"Won't Resnik wonder about the soft approach?"

"I'm sure he will. He'll know we've got something that's coming later. Anyway, we go on in the same way when she's on the stand for us in direct, treat her gently and not alert her to anything. A little later during our questioning, we ask Mia if she knows who Jasmine Rees is and we show her the photographs. It's quite possible she'll recognize her right away if Pete ever took her to work with him. We can then follow up with a sample of her father's handwriting to make sure she knows it's his. It's possible she won't recognize it, but I doubt it. How many notes from him will she have received. A bunch from someone she adored. After that comes the note."

"Forrest, I understand what you're trying to do, but it's wild! She'll go ballistic. She may very well become hysterical, in which case the Court may hear nothing but a lot of rage and noise. The judge will shut us down. She'll have to. She won't allow Mia to just yell and scream, will she?"

Sighing, unable to contradict her, I replied, "Make that a thin wire we're on, not a rope. All I can say is, when you've got nothing else to work with, you go with what you have. Pretty paltry, I know. I think it's time we bring Garrett and Ben in on this. Ben doesn't have much experience with kids, but he has a knack for going to the heart of things. Don't be surprised if he comes up with a better way to come at this. As I've said, we need all the help we can get. You okay with this?"

"Totally. It'll be interesting to brainstorm with them. It'll be my first time."

Trina greeted me from the kitchen as I walked in. "Monica's invited me for a sleepover this Saturday, Daddy. Is that okay? Mommy's still not coming to get us yet, is she?"

Andy came racing down the stairs, dressed in his freshly laundered gi.

"Why are you wearing that?" I asked. "You're going to get it dirty."

He ignored me. "No fair, Dad, Trina sleeping over." Fidgeting, he complained, "She does it all the time and I have to stay at home. Can I go too if I find somebody to stay over with?"

I sighed. One more Saturday alone. Even with their mother still recuperating, it seemed as though I hardly saw the twins. Hanging up my blazer and putting my briefcase away, I went into the kitchen and sat down. Andy, still jouncing, hovered near.

Exasperated, I said, "Would you please stop jumping around like that and go sit down or do what you need to do to find someone. Where does Monica live, Trina? Do I know her?"

"Daddy," she grumbled, "why do you always ask me that? I'm not a baby anymore."

"You always act like one when Dad's home," Andy taunted.

Trina gave her brother a dirty look.

"You're not a baby, no," I said, "and you're not nearly old enough to be telling me you're staying over with someone I don't know. I either know the girl or I get in touch with the parents. You already know that, don't you. So who is this Monica, anyway?"

My preadolescent daughter bore an expression I didn't like. She looked put out. As she'd done occasionally since childhood, she stomped her foot.

"Way to go, Dad. Poor Treeny"—one of his nicknames for his sister she couldn't stand—"doesn't get her way. Yay!" He stuck out his tongue.

"Andy, that's enough," I ordered, seeing that my daughter was about to run at him. My son was wiry and getting stronger, but he knew better than to take on his twin if she was upset with him. "Alright now. If that's all you can tell me about Monica, then no sleepover."

Resigned, Trina said, "She's our new vice-principal's youngest daughter. You met her when school started last year, remember?"

"What, the girl with... with—"

"White hair, yes. She's the one. She's one of my best friends. I really like her."

My baby doing what she'd always done. I felt chagrined. Since the first or second grade, she'd been befriending classmates who remained on the social fringe because they differed in some important ways from their peers. Monica, as I recalled, was an albino child. I'd seen her during opening week hovering near her mother, who'd just been taken on as an administrator in the twins' school. How to express approval without being condescending?

I said, "Alright then. I do remember her. That's fine. Do you know where she lives?"

"Sure I do. I've been there lots of times before. You just forgot, that's all. Can you drop me off on your way to Andy's class?"

I nodded. "What time will you be home?"

"Monica's parents invited me to a picnic the next day on Sunday at Buena Vista Park. I prob'ly won't be home til about three or so. Is that okay?"

At that moment, I wished she had a cell phone. "That should be okay. Remember to get in touch with me if there's a problem. Can you give me a call before you head off there?"

The indignant look was back, justifiably this time, maybe. It wasn't easy for me to loosen ties. I needed to recognize my daughter's growing maturity and sense of responsibility. I shouldn't worry too much in that regard. She'd help me.

"Okay, okay, honey, I'm sorry. Don't worry about that call."

For a moment, Trina regarded me, then, of a sudden, she was hugging me. I was still an open book.

Going to the refrigerator to get out scallops and shrimp for our evening meal, I looked for my boy, who'd disappeared. I could hear bits and pieces of an excited conversation he was having on the upstairs phone. A moment later, he hurdled down the steps. Grinning broadly, he came rushing up to me.

"Guess what," he exclaimed, hopping from foot to foot. No guess was necessary. He'd talked some kid and his parents into inviting him.

"LC says I can come. I can go, right? Trina's going."

Fifteen minutes home and I felt besieged. "LC. Who the heck is that? Sounds like the name of someone's dog."

"Nah. I slept over there before lotsa times. You just don't remember. LC's real name is Lyle." Seeing me hesitate, Andy added, "You know, Dad. He lives in the Andersons' old house just down the block. LC's dad teaches the sixth grade at our school. Why do you remember all a Trina's friends and you don't remember mine?"

Wearily, I said, "Sorry. Must be age. So when are you leaving and what time will you be back?"

Connivances and calculations raced across Andy's face. He said, "'Bout two or three like Trina, okay?"

I was in a bind. I thought I knew who LC was, but I wasn't certain. My son was not averse to a bit of conning if he could get away with it. Having given Trina the green light, could I reverse direction and demand LC's phone number? Andy's eyes were fixed on me.

"Hey champ, listen," I said, trying for conciliation in my tone. "I'm not sure I know this LC guy. I've never seen him here at the house, that I know. The name Lyle doesn't ring any bells. I'm afraid I'll have to call his parents before I can say okay."

Andy looked accusing.

"I know who Monica is. I remember her, but I've never seen LC, or at least I don't think so."

A sour expression on his face, Andy groused, "It's embarrassing if you call them."

"Sorry about that, but unless I talk with them, you're not going and that's final."

Andy spun on his heel and ran up to his room. Seconds after, he was back down, his eyes alight and his grin back. He wasn't one to hold a grudge. He handed me a torn piece of paper.

The moment Barbara Goldman said hello, I placed her. In fact, I'd seen Lyle several times at picnics and at Andy's baseball games. All was well.

"Am I still supposed to watch you this Saturday at

martial arts?"

"Yup, but Sensei lets us go at four. I can go to LC's after that."

"Sounds good."

I'd have to find something to do on the weekend. I wasn't going to spend Saturday night alone. Was it too soon to invite myself back to Ben's?

I was grinning next morning as Kate Barns walked out my office door. Resnik would do well to not trouble her. She was tough as nails and she was pissed. Pissed at men in general, it seemed to me, but no matter. At the trial, she'd be after Pete Jackson's balls and anyone else's who was foolhardy enough to get in her way. I was still chuckling as I went off to talk to Bree.

"And what's that smirk about?"

"Kate Barns, that's what," I said. "If Mia's the worst witness I can think of, Kate's the best, in the entertainment category, anyway. I could do without the trial, but that's one cross-examination I'm looking forward to. Resnik's tough, but Kate will eat him up for lunch."

"Mmhmm. I expect my interviews with Sue and Jackie will be less amusing. Seems like you get all the fun."

"So which of our witnesses would you like to take—Mia, Lucy, Kate, Chadwick if we use him?"

The expressions that played over Bree's face made me laugh. She slowly shook her head. "Okay, alright. I'm not ready for that stuff yet, I guess."

"Then why don't you defend our motion in Loewenstein's chambers this coming Monday. That shouldn't put you off too much."

"I didn't know you were so vindictive. I take back what I said about not having fun."

"Seriously, I do think you should be the one to speak for us on Monday. You may have more impact with our judge. Not just that. I think you should take Kate and Jackie in direct. You may have to rein Kate in a bit, but you'll be fine. It's about time you got your feet wet."

Though reticent, Bree agreed.

"To change the subject," I said as I munched on a seafood-filled soft taco from the night before, "I've arranged for a birthday party for Lucy at my house this coming Sunday. You'll know everybody except Alex, Lucy's son. Not that many coming, actually. I'd really be happy if you and Maya could be with us."

A smile in her eyes and on her lips, Bree said, "You looking for a little backup, maybe?"

"You've got it. Can you come?"

The smile bigger, she replied, "I wouldn't miss it. I'll be right beside you every minute."

"There's a couple of other things, in keeping with your concern about the firm, you understand."

Her head tilted slightly, Bree inquired, "Now what would those things be?"

Shifting on the couch so I could look directly at her, I said, "I know it's last minute, but could you get a sitter for tonight? I promised you a dinner out if we got Pete's note, remember?"

Smiling, she said, "It's done. Rita's coming over after work. She's good until about ten o'clock. Will that do?"

"Perfect! As to the second thing, Andy has a public demonstration class in martial arts this coming Saturday that'll be outside. I'm supposed to go."

Before I could add something, Bree replied, "We'd love to come. I can bring Maya, right?"

"Of course you can. That's great. It'll be nice for Andy to have his little fan club."

Bree nodded and watched me. The vixen. She was waiting.

"Why don't the two of you come over for dinner after that. The twins will both be out on sleepovers, so..."

The smile was still there when Bree said, "You don't do things halfway, do you. This is shaping up to be one fun weekend. I must warn you about Maya, though. She's not the best at settling down in other people's houses." Putting a hand on her cheek and tilting her head again, musing, she added, "What are people going to think when they arrive at your house on Sunday for the party and they see me and Maya there? Don't fool yourself. There won't be a woman there who won't know."

"That bother you?" I asked.

"Not if it doesn't bother you. I may seem conventional to you, Forrest, but I'm really not."

"That's good because I'd like people to get used to seeing you with me."

We were silent for a while, neither of us wanting to break the spell. But there was work to do and less time than I liked to get it done.

"Before I forget," I said as I got up to leave, "we won't be able to meet with Ben and Garrett until next Wednesday. One or the other's tied up til then."

Bree nodded. "That's fine. We should probably brainstorm a little more before getting together with them anyway. Out you go. It's not as though we're going to be missing each other very much. Sue Carpenter's due here in a few minutes and I need to review her file."

Trina's face looked back at me from my office wall. Two years had elapsed since Claire and I took the twins to a photography studio to get their portraits. Two years, months before Divinity Parker's disappearance. Then the bombshell about Claire. More recent, Lucy's catastrophe. Unpredictability, a sure path to paranoia, I reflected as I gazed at my young daughter's face. Bree's offhand remarks about chance occurrence made me shiver, not something I could afford to think about too much. I turned away from the large photograph and reached for the telephone.

"Lucy," I said, letting out a breath, "you remember about Sunday, don't you? Is three okay for you and Lily?"

"You think I'd forget the first birthday party I've had in I don't know how many years? I've been thinking about it since I saw you. You didn't invite Bree, did you?" She was laughing. "Poor Forrest. He doesn't know what to do with all these women after him. Three o'clock's just fine. Lily's got her car. She'll drive us."

Good. I was about to tell her I'd send a taxi for them. "We're looking forward to it. Supposed to be a nice day. See you on Sunday."

As I was hanging up the phone, Bree walked in. "Professor Chadwick just called. He'll be here in a half hour."

"I was beginning to wonder if he was going to show. Is this the first time he's called?"

"No, actually," Bree replied. "He phoned late yesterday afternoon. I forgot to tell you. Should we meet here? Your office isn't that inviting." Cheeky woman.

"I agree. The conference room would be more comfortable and it's easier to serve coffee in there. I'll talk to Cheryl and open up the room. You'll bring him in when he arrives?"

"You think my suit's business-like enough?"

I grinned. She had on a form-fitting earth-toned blazer and skirt that fell just past her knees and a blouse that, while not décolleté, did little to hide her appealing shape.

"I don't know," I said, standing up. "These women who fish for compliments. You look perfect and you know it. Now go take care of Chadwick."

Except for two large windows and some paintings by local artists whose work I didn't like, the walls of our plush little conference room were lined with shelves of dog-eared journals and law books. Someone with good taste had selected the rectangular oak table, six cushioned chairs and the Turkish rug beneath. It couldn't have been Cheryl. The lighting, too, was nice, soft and indirect. There was a whiteboard at the far end of the room.

Nancy brought in a tray with a fancy French cafetière and three porcelain coffee cups with what looked like a solid silver sugar bowl, cream pitcher plus tiny spoons. I had no idea we had such ostentatious stuff. There came Josephine behind Bree and Chadwick with a platter loaded with big croissants. There was little resemblance between what lay on the table and our ultra-practical reception area and offices. The tableau did little to minimize the incongruity. Passive aggression on Cheryl's part—my comeuppance for not having made arrangements with her the day before.

I placed our pretend witness in the head chair and I sat across from Bree. Chadwick was rotund with a friendly round face and brown eyes that reflected good humor and intelligence. I had to suppress a smile at his efforts to hide gray hair and his bald spot with pitch-black dye and a comb-over, unusual for someone who cared little about his dress. The man must have endured unrelenting taunts from his schoolmates because of the most cauliflower ears I'd ever seen. To add to this mélange was a deep basso profundo voice that was warm and pleasant.

"Let's be done with this Professor stuff," he boomed. "I'm Gordon and you're Bree, aren't you?"

"I am, and this is my friend and colleague, Forrest. I didn't know we were going to be fed like this. Feel free to serve yourself."

Like me, Bree must have noted the gleam in Chadwick's eyes. Without ceremony, he covered a napkin with two croissants and poured coffee that smelled strong. I wasn't sure I could cope with another brew like that, but I didn't hesitate. Bree did the same. We left the pastries to our guest.

Pleasure evident on Chadwick's face, mouth half full, he exclaimed, "Whoever set this up has my gratitude. It's my second breakfast, but hey. If you two will give me a minute to indulge myself, we can get on to other things."

Normally, I'd take the lead with prepared questions, not easy in this case since we weren't sure what to ask. It seemed evident from exchanges between him and

Bree that he knew we were not focusing on coercive control during the trial. Nor, as he must have been aware, did we intend to raise the problem of battered woman syndrome, the second area in which he specialized. By his own conditions, his contribution was to be pro bono, limited to brainstorming with us. Best to start out with what the professor had to say.

Leaning forward, looking at Bree then at me, elbows on the table, Chadwick said, “I don’t need to tell you I’ve given this case a lot of thought. It’s too bad we can’t use it as an entrée for psychological abuse in the courts, along the lines of what we’re slowly managing to do with battered woman syndrome. Based on your client’s extraordinary diary, there’s no issue at all in my mind that her decision to kill her husband to protect her daughter was the result of prolonged systematic undermining of her sense of identity. Especially during the last two years, she’d become increasingly isolated and made to believe she was powerless to do anything without her husband.” Chadwick’s sentences were long and complex, as though he were delivering a lecture. “I’m no expert in criminal law,” he said, “far from it, but the more I thought about this case, the more difficult, it seemed to me, that you’d make much headway with the jury by trying to demonstrate what happened to Lucy in psychological parlance. Jurors, in my experience, prefer concrete events and facts rather than abstract concepts.”

First my nod, then came Bree’s.

“With battered women, the situation’s different. We frequently have police reports, physical evidence, corroboration by friends and family, hard data in other words. I’m preaching to the choir here, I know. These things you don’t have.” He spread his hands. “I feel like I’m letting you down on this and I’m sorry. Suggestions are about all I have.”

“Gordon,” I said, “we’ll take whatever we can get.”

“You are putting your client on the stand, I assume?”

“We don’t have much choice.”

"How reliable will she be as a witness, do you think?"

"She's stronger than she was two months ago. She'll be okay with us in direct. How well she'll hold up under cross is a question, as always. The prosecution will do their best to discredit her and demonstrate she had non-violent options."

Chadwick nodded. "I'll bet," he commented. "What I have to say isn't going to surprise you all that much. It bothers me to admit this given what we're trying to do." Chadwick frowned, scratched his nose, then continued. "It's not clear to me that bringing up psychological abuse and coercive control during the trial is going to bear much fruit."

I concurred with him. It was reassuring to know he was able to separate his interests and biases from the particulars of our case. I asked Chadwick to explain.

"Well, to start with, it took me longer than it should have to understand what you meant by a defense strategy based on your client's state of mind. I was putting theoretical considerations before what I know about juries. That's not unusual for researchers like me, I'm afraid." Chadwick paused to pour himself another coffee. "Your job, as I finally came to see it, is to get jurors to understand what her beliefs were at the time of the shooting and what accounted for those beliefs. What I'm saying, I guess, is that the only way you're going to get through to jurors is to expose them to real-life situations they can understand and relate to. The question is, how does one do that. By asking your client questions that'll bring things into the open, at least, so it seems to me."

Bree and I nodded in agreement. Nothing new so far. Chadwick pulled over the notepad and pencil I'd put at his place and began to write, speaking his sentences aloud as they appeared.

"Question: What kind of a reputation did your husband have in Santa Lucia? Can you give examples? Was he the type to inspire confidence? Do you think people in the community would have considered him to be strong?"

Resnik would object on the grounds that Lucy's husband's profile wasn't relevant. I'd contend that the questions pertained to our client's state of mind, not an argument difficult to make if our judge was even moderately sympathetic.

Going on, Chadwick pronounced, "Do you have a reputation in the community? Why not? In your diary, you often speak of yourself as being weak. Explain why you said this. Did you open mail? If not, why? Did you have a cell phone? Why not? Did you have a car? When did your husband take it from you? Did you maintain contact with your friends during the last two years? Why not? I've got a few more examples," Chadwick said. "Who handled the finances at home? Did you have money of your own? An allowance?

"Question: What kind of social activities did you engage in outside the home? Explain. In your diary you talk about the disappearance of your clothes. Can you elaborate? You also talk about the disappearance of your car. Can you explain? Do you have friends who call you or visit you at home? Why not? Was your husband socially active? Examples?

"Can you describe your relationship with your son? And what about your relationship with your daughter? Why do you say 'up to the last year'? What about your daughter's relationship with her father? Did anyone but you ever witness their affectionate behavior toward one another? Did you complain about the situation to your husband? Did you ever threaten to go to the authorities? What do you believe would have happened if you'd complained to people outside your home that he was about to sexually assault your daughter? If your husband had left you, would your children have stayed with you or would they have gone with him? Why did you kill your husband?"

Putting down his pencil and looking up at us, Chadwick asked, "Bree, you told me, didn't you, that you'll be allowed to refer to the diary during questioning?"

"When Lucy's on the stand, yes, and only questions based on volumes four, five and six."

"Right. These questions aren't comprehensive by any means, but they suggest one way of approaching things. Your client's responses to prompts like these will be a lot more telling than anything I might say. I'm sorry I'm not able to be of more help to you."

I was about to speak when Bree broke in. "Personally, I find your ideas very helpful. I had a general idea about what we were going to cover. Your examples give me something to focus on."

"Same thing for me," I said. "Your questions will be a good guide for us. We had to get around to this, but I've been avoiding it."

"Don't blame you," Chadwick said. "As long as your judge allows your questions, you may be in better shape than you think."

"That's the issue," I replied. "She's an unknown quantity. She's a little scary, actually. About the only thing we've learned about her is she's inconsistent."

Chadwick looked commiserative.

Grinning, I added, "Now that Bree has a good model to work from, I can't wait to see what she comes up with."

Rolling her eyes at me then smiling at our guest, she complained with no trace of lament in her tone, "That's the problem with being the junior member of this firm. I get everything no one else wants to do." She was at ease with Chadwick, her demeanor fostered by his sidelong glances at her chest. Was she flirting? I thought so. I hadn't seen this side of her, apart from how she was with me.

In good humor, though I thought I could see a hint of desire in his eyes, Chadwick replied, "What makes me think you're not put upon that much. Not getting that vibe at all." Adopting a more serious look, he prompted, "So where do we go from here?"

I'd been tempted to get the Mia problem on the table, but I'd held back. Chadwick had no close-up knowledge of the girl. For other than Bree's input, best wait for our upcoming discussion with our colleagues. We needed Garrett's legal background and Ben's no-nonsense take on what to do with volatile Mia on the witness stand.

Chadwick closed his notebook with a snap. Instead of the chat on theories that we'd expected, he'd given substance to only vague thoughts we'd had before on what to do with Lucy in direct. Though there was nothing novel in what he'd laid out, his thoughts were helpful on two counts. Chadwick's questions, based on his grasp of key points of the diary, provided us with something to critique and augment rather than having to start fresh. Even more important was his strong support for our defense strategy. I was pleased and so was Bree.

"I hope you're not tied up for the next couple of hours or so," I said. "You can't come out to California without sampling Santa Lucia's seafood. Can we take you out to lunch with us?

Chadwick beamed. "Wonderful. Thank you. What we get back where I live all tastes processed. I don't get to the West Coast near enough."

"Well, you should like this place," Bree said, standing up. "It's a tiny café on the waterfront called Mira's." All smiles for I wasn't sure whose benefit, she chirped, "Forrest's taken me there only once, but that's about to change."

Chadwick looked at her and then at me and grinned. "I was right when I said you didn't look that abused, wasn't I."

The meal was superb as it always was at Mira's, but the little restaurant was noisy. Not to be foiled as I'd been before, I'd reserved our places a week early. I savored my British Columbia oysters on the half shell and delighted in my fresh-caught halibut while Bree and our guest had their first abalone steak. If we'd heard nothing about coercive control during the morning, my companions showed no such reserve at lunch. I listened with half an ear. Bree saw me looking at my watch when it neared two.

I stared blankly at the note on my desk from Judge Loewenstein. Though I was happy for the quiet, the two glasses of Sauvignon Blanc I'd drunk for lunch did little to help me think. We'd know more about the mystery woman after our meeting with her and Resnik the coming Monday. Bree had agreed to defend our motion to restrict the scope of the prosecution's direct examination of Lucy's child. How vigorously should she argue?

Initially, it seemed a good idea to tie Resnik's hands since the wily prosecutor would guide Mia down paths where she'd be induced to prevaricate. In light of our new plan to ambush Mia with her father's note, I was less sure about the wisdom of our motion. Resnik didn't really know the girl and how volatile she could be. One wrong turn by him and she could erupt and veer off course. Unpredictable as the girl was, to whose advantage would her outburst be?

And, what if Loewenstein denied our motion? Too many questions for my head that felt stuffed with cotton wool. With Bree's overnight visit on Saturday and the party for Lucy the day after, there wouldn't be much time on the weekend to consider them. I'd have to manage.

Little Maya was walking in circles around our blanket on the grass as Bree and I watched outdoor demonstrations of different age and skill groups at Miguel's martial arts school. Except for a few children, the sixty or so observers around us were very quiet.

Unlike baseball games and soccer matches where noise was the rule, eyes were glued on participants and their instructors. Five paired older teenagers were sparring, if that was the proper word. Miguel moved from pair to pair, occasionally stepping in to replace someone to demonstrate something or to correct.

"Forrest, I'm surprised your friend allows his younger students to watch this. It's, it's not sparring they're doing out there. They're fighting. Look," she exclaimed. "That young man over there flipped that teenager on his back! That's risky! You're going to allow Andy to do this stuff?"

What I'd seen troubled me as well. If Claire got wind of what was going on there, she'd demand that I pull Andy out. At that moment, I wasn't so far from doing that myself.

"No. I don't think so. Miguel's letting younger students in because he needs the revenue, I think. The problem is, it's jujitsu and the rougher stuff that interest him. He opened his new school just recently and is kind of feeling his way, it seems to me."

"Maybe so," Bree said, "but that's hard combat stuff and someone's going to get hurt. Your friend's so fast, I can't see a lot of what he does. Remind me not to spar with him. I've never seen anyone like that. He may be a nice guy and all, but out there, he looks dangerous. He moves like people who are trained to kill in special forces. You know about them, don't you?"

I shook my head. "I don't know much about any of this stuff," I said.

"No," Bree replied. "I don't think you do. Andy's class is coming up next, isn't it?" she asked.

"I think so. I'm glad I saw this, actually. I don't want Andy getting too attached to this kind of thing. Fighting for fighting's sake's not what I want him into."

Shaking her head reflectively, Bree said, "No, Forrest, you really don't. For people who are naturals, and there is such a thing, it can become addictive. I've seen it."

There were fourteen children in Andy's group, all about his age. We watched attentively for about a half hour.

Then Bree said, "There's no rough stuff here, okay, but your Miguel's teaching these kids basic skills they'll need to move up to what we just saw. There's no elegance in what they do. It's pure technique and reaction time... Do we have to stay when Andy's finished?" She looked upset.

"No. We can leave right away. Listen, I'm really glad you pointed these things out to me. By the time I got around to really worrying about it, it might be a little late."

"Yes, well, I'm glad you react the way you do. I can't stand violence, not of any kind. Fighting upsets me. It always has."

On our way to his friend's house, Andy chattered incessantly about how "great" his sensei was and about how "awesome" the older guys had been. He seemed not to notice how preoccupied Bree and I were. Maya had fallen fast asleep in her car seat.

After we'd dropped Andy off, Bree asked, "Do your children have a lot of sleepovers?"

"Not all that many," I responded. "It's when Trina does, Andy doesn't and the reverse. It can be a problem. When Trina's staying over at a girlfriend's and it's just Andy and me at home, he acts like he's lost his best friend. It's my job to entertain him, he thinks. They used to play together a lot when they were little. Not now. They just argue."

"With just one," Bree rejoined, "I won't have that problem, will I."

A statement or a question? Steering clear, I shrugged as we pulled into my driveway.

Josephine looked up from her keyboard and smiled as I walked in Monday morning. I smiled back and sniffed fresh-brewed coffee.

"I didn't expect to see anyone at this hour," I said. "Do you come in often at eight o'clock?"

"Only when I have a lot of work. Mr. Austin is in court this week and he also has a hearing. I'm quite behind."

My eyes moved to the space that Nancy's desk used to occupy. Puzzled, I asked, "You'll be moving into the office we set up for you two, right?"

Josephine shook her head and blushed. "Actually, if you and Mr. Austin don't mind too much, I'd prefer to be out here. The new office doesn't have any windows. I worked in there for a day or so. I felt closed in. Do you mind if I stay out here?"

"Not at all," I replied. "If you prefer, stay out here if the coming and going doesn't bother you too much."

"Thanks. I like it here. Can I get you a cup of coffee? It's dark Colombian."

"Smells wonderful. That's not what Cheryl usually makes, is it."

Another smile. "No, it's not. Tell you the truth, that's one of the reasons I come in early. You take it black, don't you." Before I could answer, she was up and pouring.

In just under two hours, we were to be in Loewenstein's chambers. As I reached for my notes on the motion I'd written, I thought back to the weekend.

First, the unsettling demonstration at Miguel's school. Had Bree not been there to point out the obvious, I wondered how strong my reaction would have been. Though Claire was certainly no fan of martial arts, she would eventually capitulate and go to watch Andy in his class. If, perchance, she were to witness another demonstration like the one we'd seen, I'd be in for real trouble for a long time. I was going to have to find some way to extricate us from a potentially contentious situation.

I still couldn't decide whether to be put off or pleased by how our Saturday night had ended. From the time we arrived home until just before we went to bed, Bree had been flirtatious and affectionate. Several large margaritas for each of us, Ben's recipe, had smoothed the way. I'd been careful not to say anything in anticipation of lovemaking.

Just as well. When we'd gone upstairs, as though she'd thrown a switch, a curtain, almost palpable, dropped between us. Bree had stammered as she tried to apologize, standing stiffly outside Andy's room where Maya slept. I reached to comfort her.

"Hey there," I told her. "Let's not end our visit like this. We'll do this when you're ready and not until, okay?"

Her smile was fleeting. Gently, I'd led her to Trina's room.

On Sunday, before and during Lucy's party, which was a big success, she'd been very warm, always staying close to me. Bree and Maya left without a word about the night before.

As I gazed at Trina's picture on my office wall, only half seeing her, I knew the denouement of that evening was going to trouble us. My already more than friend and almost lover was no spinster who hadn't experienced sex. Could she have problems in that regard? Not according to our time at Ben's. She'd been willing and very eager. Had it not been for then, I'd be worried.

Bree had to be confused as well, at least so it seemed to me. It had looked as though she'd been expecting throughout the evening to go to bed with me. She'd be convinced that I'd become frustrated and impatient, even though I'd tried hard to avoid conveying such. She'd be in self-protection mode when I next saw her, which would be in minutes. There was little I could see to do other than support her.

Josephine's dark Colombian was creating havoc in my stomach as I approached Bree's office. It was nine. I stopped in her doorway as I saw the odd expression on her face. No smile, no frown. She looked strained. I could hear the tension in her voice. She was about to tell me that we had to break it off.

"Forrest, do you mind very much if we move to your office? I need to talk to you and we can't do that here."

She was going to tell me she was leaving us.

"Ah, sure," I croaked, my mouth bone dry. "Let's go."

As was my habit at the office, I closed my door. Bree drew the smaller chair that Sara used close up to my desk and she sat right across from me. Her expression hadn't changed, her full lips pressed together in a straight line as she regarded me.

"I know we have to go over the motion now, but I need to say something first."

I waited, wishing I had a glass of water.

Frowning, Bree said, "This won't take long... I've been thinking a lot about Saturday night and the way I was. I thought about how I feel and what I want every day, especially when I'm near you, and I'm pretty sure it's just a case of the jitters. We haven't got time to discuss this anymore right now, and besides, I don't really want to. I'm going to tell you what I want to do and you're not going to try to stop me, understand?" She tempered her statement with a little smile. "I want to make love as much as you do, maybe more. Can you come over to my house tomorrow night for dinner?"

Like a balloon that quickly loses air, I felt the tension in me drain away. Feeling the smile form on my face, shaking my head, I said, "No, no need to do that Bree. I'm glad to hear you say what you did, but there's no hurry. We don't—"

"Answer me, please. Can you come over tomorrow night?"

I was relieved, yet I was hesitant to agree. Rather than put Bree off, determined as she was, I decided to go along. If slowing things down turned out to be necessary, primed as I was, I was sure I'd realize in time. The prospect was exhilarating.

As we left our building and walked toward the courthouse, Bree touched my arm. She looked troubled.

"Forrest, I don't see how we can continue to argue this, our motion, I mean."

"You want me to handle it?"

"No, no, not at all. That's not what I mean. Don't

you see the inconsistency between what we plan to do with Mia on the stand and what I'm supposed to say to Loewenstein?"

I'd been wrong. She wasn't dwelling upon our weekend. I'd worked long enough with Bree to understand that she verbalized only after a lot of thought.

Temporizing while I pondered what she'd said, I replied, "What kind of inconsistency?"

"Okay. I stress Mia's vulnerability as grounds for restricting the scope of Resnik's questions to her in direct. Then what happens when we're in court and Mia's our witness? We expect our judge to give us permission to upset her. Don't you see? That's not going to work!"

I stopped walking and looked at her. The hazards of allowing turmoil in our private lives to blunt our thought processes. I felt as though I was in an elevator shooting up and down. If we proceeded with our motion, we'd defeat ourselves. How much damage to ourselves would we do if, at the eleventh hour, we withdrew it? We continued walking. I swallowed.

"Christ, Bree," I exclaimed, thoroughly humiliated, not by her but by my lack of insight. "Thank God one of us is on the ball."

I could see relief on Bree's face. "Good," she said. "I was afraid... I was afraid you'd want to push ahead because it was too late to do anything."

"We'll have to cut our losses. We'll have to withdraw the motion, don't you agree?"

"I do," She said. "I don't see that we have a lot of choice."

I nodded. "I don't think it'll look very good if I pawn this off on you with the judge and Resnik. I'll be the one to withdraw it."

"I can do that, Forrest, really, I can."

"Thanks, but no thanks. You've done a lot for us already."

Resnik was waiting outside our judge's chambers

when we arrived. He almost bowed. "So this is the lady I've been hearing about," he said. "I wish my colleagues had your attributes."

'Not the lady to say that to, Resnik,' I would have said had he and I been alone.

Nonchalant, it appeared to me, Bree contemplated him. "You don't want to let your boss hear you talk like that. She wouldn't like it."

Feigning chagrin, Resnik replied, "You've got that right. She wouldn't. I won't tell her if you don't."

The door opened and Judge Loewenstein's clerk stood there. "Good morning Mr. Resnik, Mr. Spencer. Judge Loewenstein's ready for you." Looking at Bree, she asked, "Are you with them? I don't think the judge is expecting you."

Unruffled, Bree said, "I'm Mr. Spencer's colleague. I'm Bree Dixon, co-counsel."

The sober-looking young woman in her middle twenties nodded once and disappeared. A minute later she returned to tell us to go in.

Loewenstein was much as I'd seen her the first time, garbed in the same black suit and white blouse. The only part of her that appeared to move as we three took our seats were her dark eyes.

"Ms. Dixon, you're working with Mr. Spencer, my clerk tells me. Thank you for coming." Loewenstein's eyes cut to me then to Resnik. "I'm sorry to rush you this morning, but I have a dentist appointment in an hour."

We watched as the judge picked up a sheet from her desk. I was struck once again by the incongruity between the judge's gentle voice, almost lyrical, and the alabaster frozen quality of her face. Her body language was very stiff.

"I presume you have a copy of this, Mr. Resnik?"

Vicky's young deputy said he did.

"Mr. Spencer, do you want to say anything further on this motion?"

Clearing my throat, I said, "Yes, your honor, we do. We wish to withdraw our motion at this time."

Resnik turned his surprised face toward me. Loewenstein's expression didn't change.

"I apologize to the Court and to the prosecutor's office for the tardiness of our request. Our decision was last-minute."

As though what we'd done was routine, the judge said, "Very well. Do we have anything else to discuss?" Hearing nothing, she continued, "Good. Unless something does come up, the next time I'll see you is on the fifteenth at the trial."

Chapter 19

Later that Monday afternoon, waiting at home for the twins to return from school, I felt lethargic and down. I was still reeling from Bree's epiphany on the street. She'd maintained focus despite turbulence in our relationship while I'd allowed my mind to drift. I'd made mistakes before in my career, but they'd rarely come one after another. I was overdue for a vacation.

As usual on school days, Lupe had juice and snacks ready for the children. She'd left quietly minutes after I arrived. For the many hundredth time, I thought about how fortunate we were to have her. We'd never had to look for babysitters since the twins' births. Lupe preferred staying overnight at our house rather than going home.

My spirits rose as I thought about the next evening. Though I was uneasy about Bree's determination to forge ahead, I reasoned she, more than I, should be the one to gauge her needs and trepidations. It was as well that I'd have to drive back home. I'd limit myself to two glasses of wine, which should allow me to keep myself in check.

"This time, I'll buy the wine," I said as we left the office. "I never paid you for what you spent, did I."

Bree waved me off. If she was nervous about our upcoming evening, she didn't show it. "I'm late to pick up Maya. Can you stop to get a baguette?"

I smiled and nodded.

Unlike the first time, I helped make dinner. Bree, a recipe book at her elbow, deveined shrimp, chopped large scallops and made Italian pasta sauce while I minced garlic, chopped red and yellow onions and made green salad. We were a half bottle down in a good Chianti Classico with a second standing by. Maya was weaving in and out between our legs.

Bree and I sat on the couch after dinner, her daughter snuggled up between us. We took turns reading to her from a stack of children's picture books. Apart from little excited noises she made when she saw animals she recognized, Maya was quiet. Bree's strategy had worked. In less than a half hour, the child was asleep.

I'd known, moments after I arrived, that something in Bree's manner was different. Several times during our preparation of the meal, she'd reached out to lightly touch my hand, my shoulder, then my cheek. There'd also been something in her voice when she greeted me.

Any fears I'd had about the remainder of the evening evaporated as I saw how she looked at me with Maya's drooping head against my arm. Amused, I perceived less desire in her startlingly green eyes than something proprietary.

It was 3 a.m. when I left, tired but exhilarated. Only hints of apprehension and shyness during our lovemaking. She'd been warm and searching in my arms, as eager as I to cement our physical connection. I was euphoric as I drove home. More than any other time in my life, I felt spiritually at peace. We'd crossed the Rubicon, the first major step for both of us that would hopefully heal wounds and bring some happiness.

"Boyo, up shit creek again in a boat plum full a holes," came Ben's sardonic comment, his eyes going back and forth between glossy photos of Jasmine and

Pete's note. "Ain't gotta clue what to do with this."

During the past half hour in our conference room, Bree and I had taken turns laying out our problem.

Garrett, a pinched expression on his hound dog face, contemplated us. I could read his thoughts. Wouldn't it be better to bet on the red or black instead of putting everything we had on one sole number? In principle, I agreed with him. Bree, who was sitting close beside me, touched my hand beneath the table.

"Too damn chancy," Ben added. "I know why you guys are doin' what you're doin', but things could go tits up." Recalling himself, he added, "Sorry, Bree. It's just these perdicaments Forrest gets himself into. And to think, I'm the one who started all this with that Jasmine woman. Oughta learn to keep my nose clean. Christ! That Jackson girl's a loose cannon waitin' to go off."

Glancing down once again at the photos and the note, his forehead puckering into a thoughtful frown, he said, "There's something else about this case that bothers me. You knew this Pete character pretty well, Forrest, so maybe you can answer this for me. I hope so cuz it makes no damn sense." Ben picked up his pencil, which prompted the rest of us to do the same.

"Number one. We got this Pete Jackson guy with more money than Croesus who's got just about everything, 'cept maybe a happy home life. He's well-known, well-liked in Santa Lucia and has a good reputation."

We were writing down nearly everything Ben was saying.

"Guy's a handsome devil, must have women after 'em all the time, drives a Porsche that's gotta cost over a hundred grand and has a lovely home."

Ben waved a hand at us as though we were about to object. To the contrary, we'd long since learned that when Ben resorted to pencils, we didn't interject. We listened.

"I know, I know, you don't have to tell me. Just cuz a guy's got it all, doesn't mean he's happy. But here's what's stumpin' me. From everything I've heard, the guy seemed fine. He's got himself a gorgeous mistress and who knows how many others. In other words, lose that reputation of his, bad rumors about him start goin' around and he stands to lose a lot, 'specially with that high-flyin' business of his.

"Number two. The guy gets sexually involved with his adolescent daughter and knocks her up, unfortunately not all that an uncommon thing to do. Does the guy go to bed with her cuz he's not gettin' any sex?" Ben picks up the glossy photos and waves them at us. "I'd say that's not the case, wouldn't you? Is he havin' sex with his daughter cuz he's in love with her?" He points to Pete's note to Jasmine, copies of which we all have. "Doesn't seem to be the situation, does it, not accordin' to what he says to his girlfriend, anyway.

"And number three, the one that's causin' me all the trouble. Pete's no kid. He knows what condoms are, prob'ly used 'em all the time with his girlfriends. He also knows his daughter wants a baby more than anything. So he gives her one, just like that, no precautions, no nothin'. Say his wife never complains about it. Some mothers don't. That baby's gonna grow up in Pete's home for all to see, least we think so. Say the kid's a boy and he looks like Pete. What are people gonna say. Now I ask you, for a guy who has everything to lose, who could easily end up in prison because of sexual assault and incest, why... why do such a stupid thing? The guy wasn't goin' off the rails, least nobody thought so, so why put himself in a situation like that? He couldn't get away with claimin' that it was somebody else's kid, least not for long. Pete couldn't have been dumb enough not to know about DNA.

"So, I'm thinkin', there's somethin' very serious about this case that we're not gettin'. The whole thing makes no sense, no sense at all. Question is, whatever Pete's plans for the girl and the baby were, will they influence the outcome of this case? Is there any chance Lucy knows somethin' she's not tellin'? If she doesn't, we may never have the answer to what Pete's ideas were, but I sure as hell wish we did." Ben laid his pencil down and glanced at each of us.

Though I was sure that his questions had occurred to all of us at one time or another—they certainly had to me—the odd thing was they had never arisen in previous discussions, perhaps because they seemed insoluble. Nagging, of course, was the distinct possibility that the prosecution had knowledge about these issues that we did not.

I felt as though someone had laid a sandbag across my shoulders. Most troublesome in this case for me was the absence of facts that could help us and the number of variables over which we had no control. All we could hope at this late point was that Pete Jackson's inexplicable behavior would remain a mystery until the trial was over.

Garrett inclined his head. "Returning to questions of strategy, your approach does make me a little nervous," he said. "You're counting a lot on Loewenstein's support. I wouldn't allow those photos or the note in if I were her. It's not the way to go, I think. Too risky."

We'd reached much the same conclusions, Bree and I, only to return to the same point.

"We recognize the dangers," she said, "don't think we don't, but here's the problem. If Resnik keeps control of Mia throughout the trial, the jury will hear the girl deny everything we and Lucy say about what was going on. You guys can see that, right?"

"You two are forgettin' somethin," Ben declared. "That little wild cat's pregnant. That oughta be enough for the jury, right?"

Garrett gloomily shook his head. "Not really, no," he rejoined. "Unless you can show whose baby it is, and it seems we can't, it won't be enough. Resnik will say the defense is taking advantage of Mia's unfortunate situation by dragging the murdered victim into it. If the girl holds to her story and denies her father was involved, he'll probably get away with it. It's a conundrum, that's for sure. I don't know what to tell you."

Disconsolate, the four of us sat there.

Minutes after, removing the pencil stub from his mouth, Ben said, "Okay. We can't let Rodriguez's play toy get away with that, for damn sure." Ben and Vicky had never been good friends. "Who you gonna call first, Lucy or the girl?"

"We'd thought of putting Lucy last," I answered.

"She'll hear her daughter testify, but the girl won't be allowed to hear any witnesses, including her mother, that right?"

"Correct," I replied.

"Got it. So, how's this? Say you put the daughter last. That way, your client won't be all riled up by what her daughter says when she testifies, okay?"

Not okay, I reflected, thinking about Lucy's pessimistic attitude. If anything, she needed to be stirred up.

Ben continued. "Say you don't show the girl these photos or the note. You question her about her pregnancy—how far along is she, why she's keepin' the father's name a secret. You're treatin' her like a hostile witness, so you can say all that, right? You ever get the pediatrician's affidavit?"

"She refused to divulge anything," I answered, "on the grounds of confidentiality. So—"

Garrett broke in. "The woman Mia's staying with—forgot her name—she'll testify about what happened at the pediatrician's office, won't she?"

I said I thought so.

"It might be a good idea to fit her in between Lucy and her daughter to get that on record."

Ben agreed. "Good way to find out if the girl's lyin' or tryin' to hide somethin'."

Bree nodded.

"Okay, say you do all that. That'll support your client's story. If things go south, use these," Ben concluded, tapping the photos and the note. "That way, you can save yourself a lotta grief."

Bree was nodding enthusiastically. "I like that," she said. I was glad to see her participating. "We use our original strategy as a backup. Much better."

Later, in her office, Bree remarked, "That was helpful, wasn't it. I feel easier, don't you?"

"I do," I said, "but I'm beginning to wonder if I'm losing it. You had to bail us out with Loewenstein. Then Ben points out the obvious that I should have seen. Disconcerting, I've gotta say. How about going on vacation with me after the trial?"

Bree regarded me solemnly, but the gold specks were back. "You'll have to talk to the head honchos of the firm. I don't think I've got enough time yet. Does sound like fun though. What will you do about Trina and Andy?"

"I've got an answer back already from the main office. You've got two weeks, three if you need them. As for the twins, Trina will be okay. According to her, she's got friends whose parents would love to have her. Andy's a bit more of a problem. If you're okay with this, I'll look into it."

"Two weeks will do just fine. There are perks being with you, I'm finding out. The only thing is, I'll have to bring Maya. Is that okay with you? I don't have any choice, really." Uncomfortable, Bree shifted in her chair. "It's not that I couldn't find someone to be with her. I wouldn't want to, I guess, not when she's so young."

I thought about what she'd said. There was no way Claire or I would have left our children at that age. I smiled. "Maya's part of you so she has to come, doesn't she," I said.

Bree got up and came to sit beside me on the couch. "So where are we going, hmmm?"

She and I spent the rest of the afternoon working on Chadwick's list. His points were useful, but coming up with questions of our own was difficult. We disagreed at nearly every turn on sequencing and phrasing. In a remarkably short time, Bree had become bolder.

Two days after, I was on Lucy's porch with only generalities to discuss. It was pouring rain. She greeted me with a big smile and waved me in.

"The party last Sunday was wonderful, Forrest, it truly was. It was great that you got Alex to come. How's Bree?"

"She's good," I said. "I haven't seen her in a while." Her absence during the past two days had seemed long to me. "She's at a psychology conference at UCLA."

Lucy eyed me. "She's good for you, you know? Don't lose her."

Wanting to change the subject, I said, "I don't plan to. How are things?"

She shrugged. "Nothing much has changed. I've gotta get out of this house. Problem is, I don't know anyone to talk to. I've been out of touch too long. I phoned up Jackie and Susan and Veronica, but they're all busy, least that's what they said. You think they don't want to see me anymore?"

My reassurances had no visible impact. Something troubled me as we looked for things to say. I realized what it was. Lucy exhibited none of the concern I was accustomed to in my clients before their trial. Insouciance wasn't going to help her in the eyes of jurors, to say nothing of our lady judge. I had to find some way to shake her up.

Pleasantries over, we sat there, staring at one another. Physically, she was responsive, but passive otherwise. Her blasé demeanor would be interpreted by everyone in court as unconcern and overconfidence. Little sign of a woman psychologically abused. How to get through to her.

"You hear anything from Jim or Evie?" I asked her.

"Not a thing," she replied caustically, "not a goddamn thing. You'd think my brother would keep in touch, wouldn't you." Hesitating, she queried, "You hear anything?" A covert bid for knowledge about her daughter.

"I talked to Evie just yesterday," I said. "Mia's calmed down a lot, she told me. I haven't seen her in a while, Mia, I mean. I can't say we ever got on that well."

"You and everybody else. I can't believe what she's turned into. She used to be little Miss Mouse, remember?"

I did. That was exactly how she'd been. I nodded. "I don't think I've talked to you about this yet. The prosecutor's going to call her as a key witness. A guy from their office has kept in touch with her."

"I'll bet," Lucy quipped. "I wonder what they're cooking up."

"Not that hard to predict," I replied. "We're also going to call her as a witness, Lucy. You need to know that. I want to ask you something."

Looking wary, an expression I'd seen often since Pete's death, Lucy said, "Ask me what? I don't like your questions lately."

"I get the impression you don't care very much about what happens to you at your trial. Think about what I'm saying. I need to know. Does it bother you that you could go to prison?"

Lucy's eyes narrowed and the ends of her mouth went down. It made her look ten years older. With a sharp edge in her voice, she exclaimed, "So if I tell you I don't give a fuck, you'll drop me, is that it?"

"Come on, Lucy. You know better. I don't deserve that. Please answer me."

As had happened several times before during our encounters that summer, her face drooped and her hostility drained away. She appeared hollowed out. "Yeah, you do deserve better. I'm sorry. I don't know what to say to you. And no. Of course I don't look forward to going to jail. Who would. But that's what's gonna happen. You know that as well as I do."

"No, Lucy, I don't. We should have talked more about this earlier. I'm sorry. I seem to be doing a lot of stumbling around these days."

Lucy heaved a sigh. "Forrest, Forrest, you're too hard on yourself. Your head's been in the clouds, that's your problem. I wish I was there with you, feeling good, I mean. It's hard to mix love and work, isn't it."

I had to have had a rueful expression on my face as I smiled at her. "I guess," I said. "You know, Lucy, it's time we cleared up some things. I've told you this before, but I'll say it again. It's important, so please listen. I admit that I'm biased in your case. That's not just because you're my friend. It's because I don't think you're guilty. If I thought you were, I'd be negotiating with the prosecutor's office for a reduced prison sentence. Ethically, that's all I could do. Do you follow me?"

She regarded me but didn't answer.

I went on. "We're not plea bargaining. Our defense strategy is to convince the jury that you had no choice when trying to protect your daughter. Pete threatened to disgrace you if you attempted to stop him by going to someone outside your home. That's right, isn't it? He also threatened to leave you and take the kids. He convinced you about these things, didn't he. He shamed you into thinking that no one would believe a word you said against him. These are some of the things we need to demonstrate. Am I off track here?"

Lucy's face was inscrutable, but her eyes hadn't left me.

"Don't be confused. How Pete died is not at issue here. We're not trying to make people think you didn't kill him. What we want to do is establish that, in your mind at the time, you believed you had no choice. You believed this because of the way Pete manipulated you over the years. Does what I'm saying make sense to you?"

I was disheartened by the blank look on Lucy's face. I'd waited too long to go over the case with her; one more error on my part. She'd convinced herself she'd be condemned to prison for killing her husband.

Her head slightly bowed, in a flat tone, she said, "No one will believe that, Forrest. I'm glad you do, but nobody else will."

"Maybe," I said, "but I think you're wrong. If we present what happened to you in the proper light, we think jurors will relate to your need to shield your daughter from incest. The case is no slam dunk, I'll grant you that. We have Mia's unpredictability to contend with and we're dealing with a kind of evidence juries aren't very accustomed to." Gross understatements on my part. "Still, with some luck, we think there's a good chance you'll go free."

"You know something," Lucy responded, looking at her feet, "it'll be easier if I think the worst. That way—"

"No. You're wrong. That attitude in court isn't going to help you. It'll give jurors the wrong idea about you. That will hurt us, Lucy. I'm not saying you have to be enthusiastic or lively. The prosecutor's going to be making all kinds of accusations as you might expect. People in the jury box will have their eyes on you while he does this. If you look too hangdog, they're likely to think you're guilty or you're scared. You'll have to pretend much of the time, but that's always how it is in cases like these."

Lucy slowly nodded. "I'll have to be an actress, right?"

"Not always," I said, "but most of the time, yes."

"You'll have to help me then. It shouldn't be all that difficult, you know? I've been pretending most of my life."

"We have a few weeks before the trial. Bree and I will be over lots of times before then to prepare you."

Lucy responded with a wan smile.

"Is Lily still with you?" I inquired. I hadn't seen her.

Lucy made an *O* with her lips and blew out her breath. "Thank God, she is. She's out shopping. I couldn't get through this without her."

"Do you hear from Alex?"

"Once in a while. He calls me sometimes. It's not

easy for him, Forrest."

I nodded. I got out my pocket calendar. "Okay if Bree and I come at ten o'clock this coming Monday?"

"Of course you can. I'll look forward to it, even if I don't like your questions. I'm pathetic, aren't I." With another sigh, she added, "I'll be happy when all this is over."

I fervently hoped so.

Cheryl, who'd been complaining to someone, turned toward me as I came through our main door. She looked harassed. The reason sat slouched in one of our spartan chairs in the reception area.

It was Leon Goodman. I'd hoped not to have to deal with him again. He was at my heels.

"You said they wouldn't prosecute me, now look at this." Goodman's face was contorted.

Sighing, I reached for the sheet of paper he was waving. Charlene Robinowitz, Goodman's student, had accused him of sexual assault. If nervous movements and restless eyes counted for anything, the man, pressed up against my desk and too close to me, was guilty.

"I said nothing of the sort," I replied. "If I remember correctly, I said you probably wouldn't be charged since no one had accused you of anything when I last saw you. They obviously didn't hold you."

"Obviously," Goodman retorted. "I'm out on my own recognizance. Thank God someone believes me. So what do I do now?"

I thought a moment. "You'll have to wait for your trial, I suspect. Plea bargaining isn't likely to get you anywhere in this instance."

"What do you mean, trial? Do you realize what that'll do to my reputation? I'll never get a teaching job again, you understand?"

'You should have thought of that before when your student was in your office and you closed your door,' is what I wanted to say to him.

"I'm not the judge or jury, Mr. Goodman. I'm your

attorney, that's all, unless you'd like to consult someone else." I could smell Goodman's sweat and feel his breath on my neck.

Fidgeting and wiping his face with his hand, he said, "I'm here, aren't I? So what am I supposed to do?"

"I'll talk to the prosecutor's office and see if we have any wiggle room, but don't count on this. I don't suppose you've tried to settle this privately?"

Sputtering, Goodman railed, "What, pay her? Is that what you mean?"

"Just asking. Call me in a week and I'll let you know what I find out."

"It'll take you that long?"

Standing up, I said, "A week at least. It could take longer. I'm going outside for a breath of air."

Looking frustrated and hostile, Goodman preceded me out my office door. I could hear the man trying to enlist our office manager's support. He'd get short shrift.

In fifteen minutes, I was back. During my absence, Cheryl had placed a message on my desk.

I groaned. I'd been so distracted by the Jackson case and my personal life that I'd completely forgotten about Manny Valenzuela's upcoming B and E bench trial on Monday. I'd have to call Lucy to cancel the appointment I'd just set up with her.

My consolation, if I was entitled to think of it that way, was that Manny already had two strikes against him. Having coached him would have done little good. I'd have no trouble finding him. He'd been locked up at the county jail for the last ten months. If I continued on my present path, I mused as I left for home, someone was going to suffer.

I mentally shook myself. I had just under three weeks before Lucy's trial, which loomed like a huge mountain.

PART FIVE

"Are we masters or victims? [...] Do we shape the world, or are we just shaped by it?"

— Salman Rushdie, *The Satanic Verses*, 1988

Chapter 20

Garrett, Bree, Ben and I were again in our conference room. It was a week before Lucy's trial. There was little to report.

"So," Ben said, reaching for his coffee cup that had BS stamped on the side, "Vicky toss in the towel yet?"

"Not hardly," I rejoined. "She's far from doing that."

Garrett shuffled papers, among which were copies of our witness lists. "Forrest, you're not big on testimony, are you," he said. "You had about the same number in the Martinez case if I recall." As the public prosecutor at the time, he'd remember.

"That's not normal, I gather," Bree surmised.

Garrett slowly shook his head. "In a murder trial of this magnitude, no. Try two or three times that number."

"Yup," Ben added with a grin. "Guy likes to get things done fast, just like I do."

"I'll mention that to Cassie next time I see her," Bree retorted.

"Dr. Leon Silvergold," Garrett drawled. "Where have I seen that name before?"

"He's from Santa Barbara, isn't he?" Ben inquired. "I think I know that dude. Long-winded like most shrinks. He testified for us once in Ventura way back when, didn't he? Do we really need him?"

"We don't have much choice," Bree said. "We're using him to counter Resnik's guy."

Ben scowled. Psychiatry was an anathema to him.

Garrett ran his index finger down a sheet of paper. "Friends we know and love. Good to see Alex Copperstone's still on the job. He's a good man, actually."

Ben's eyebrows came together. "Can't say the same 'bout Katy. No offense, Bree, but you're not doin' cross with her, are you?"

Bree laughed. "I'm no masochist, don't worry. I'm a lamb, remember?"

There was a glint in Ben's eyes and his mouth twitched.

"What have you guys decided to do about your opening comments?" Garrett asked. I was glad to hear his inclusive language.

"We'll open after Resnik," I said. "With Mia on the stand in the case in chief, it'd be too risky to wait."

Nods from the two men across from us.

"You staying in touch with the girl?" Garrett asked.

Bree answered, "I wish we could. She's in a difficult situation. Mia doesn't want to see us and... there's not a lot we can say to her."

"She still okay with Lucy's brother?" Garrett inquired.

"Seems so," I said, "last time I checked, anyway. It's tough for all of them, especially Evie."

"That kid was mine," Ben exclaimed, "I'd teach her a thing or two, let me tell you."

Frowning, Bree gently remonstrated, "It's not that easy. I'm sure she feels everyone's abandoned her."

"Yeah, may be, but she's not exactly helpin' her situation. Be a damn sight better for everybody if she says who the father of her kid is, not that we don't know already."

"I'm in court next week," Garrett told us, "but look for me after that. I should be there before Resnik finishes up. Forrest," he went on, "there's something missing in this witness list of yours. Say everything goes as planned with Mia and you get all you need from her.

You'll have solved one major problem. But what about demonstrating that Lucy had no other recourse at all to protect her daughter than to commit homicide? Resnik's calling people to show Lucy had people to complain to if she really wanted to. Who are you depending on to demonstrate she didn't? No one I can see on this list of yours. I've never been involved in a case like this so I don't know much, but what happens if a mother complains to the police that her daughter's being sexually assaulted by her father and both the girl and the husband say that's wrong? I don't think anyone in this state in a situation like that can force a preadolescent girl to be physically examined, but shouldn't you pin this down? Seems critical to me."

I rapidly perused my list. Another mid-life moment? I felt more than a little sheepish.

"Your mind's on too many other things, boyo," Ben commented, his eyes coming to rest on Bree. Grinning, he said, "Hey, I know the one you want. Put old Katy on the hot seat as a hostile witness and make her squawk."

Garrett and I simultaneously shook our heads. "We've got to plug in someone here but not her," I said. "Captain Lonigan would be good if we could get him."

Garrett smiled at that. "Damn good idea. See what you can do. Wonder how long he's managed to stay off the witness stand. Better get out that subpoena pretty quick though or Resnik's going to complain." Turning to Ben, he asked, "You'll be at the trial, won't you?"

"For moral support if for nothin' else."

"How's Lucy been since Friday?" Bree asked me on our way to see her. "You haven't mentioned her."

"Not all that well, I think. I talked to her on the phone last Monday and she seemed down. She's discouraged more than anything."

Bree looked down at her lap. "I don't know how I'd react if I were her. Her case is very iffy, isn't it."

In response, I said, "We've got to breathe life into her some way. I'll be damned if I know how though."

*

Lily met us at the door. She told us Lucy was asleep. She said she'd wake her up.

"Forrest, Bree, I'm sorry. I didn't hear my alarm." Lucy looked droopy-eyed, as though she'd slept the clock around. She had on a bathrobe. "Lily will get coffee and muffins she made this morning, if you like. I'm not hungry."

We'd planned to go over questions once again, but in light of Lucy's depressed state, I hesitated. We'd been through them already a half dozen times.

"Alex called me yesterday," she informed us. "He wanted to know if he should come next Tuesday. I told him no. He has his studies, and he doesn't really want to come. What about Mia?" Lucy asked. "She's coming? I suppose she has to."

"Not at first, no," I replied. "She'll only be there when she has to testify. That'll probably be at the end of the People's case, a couple of weeks from now, I expect. She won't hear anybody's testimony. You're the only witness who'll hear everyone."

Lucy nodded. "I wish I could stay home like she can," she said, "til they need me." We made no comment.

"We'd like to go over the questions at least one more time before next Tuesday if we can. What day is best for you?"

There was no humor in Lucy's smile. "You tell me when you want to come and I'll be up this time. No more than once though if you don't mind. I hear those damn questions in my sleep."

"Friday morning at ten?" I prompted.

"That'll be okay, I guess. You've gotta bring Bree too, like today. I can put up with all this easier when she's here."

No one in the room missed the ruefulness in Lucy's expression that belied what she'd said.

"I'm concerned about her, Forrest. She's declined a lot, just in the past month."

Bree and I had stopped for a coffee on our way back to the office.

"Yes she has. She's acting as though the trial's over and she's been convicted. She keeps going downhill like this..."

Bree nodded. "She needs support... company. She's lonely. Good thing she has Lily. I know it would be difficult for him with his classes, but could Alex help, maybe?"

I mulled over what she said. I contemplated my half empty coffee cup.

"I don't know," I replied, musing. "What could he do, come home? I don't think Lucy would allow him to. The trial could conceivably drag on for weeks. He'd lose a term, maybe more." I shook my head. "Lucy'd never go for it, even if Alex agreed to come, and that's no sure thing."

Bree considered. "We'd need him here for what, two weeks? It's the impact of the case in chief on Lucy you're concerned about, isn't it?"

"That's right."

"Okay," she continued. "That shouldn't interrupt him too much if he makes arrangements and brings his books home. I think it's important that he be here, for a little while at least."

I agreed. "I've got his cell number. I'll call him. Happy?"

Bree smiled, then put her serious look back on and placed her hands flat on the table. "Forrest, I'm getting nervous about taking Sue and Jackie. I need to get my feet wet, I know, but not at Lucy's expense. I feel every minute of the trial will be critical, don't you agree?"

I said, "You think I'll be calm when I go into the courtroom? I'll have butterflies just like you. Of course you're anxious. I'd be disappointed if you weren't. Jackie and Susan shouldn't be that difficult in direct."

"It's not direct I'm worried about. It's when Resnik cross-examines them that I'm bothered about. He'll know I'm a novice and take advantage of it. You know that. You can't rescue me every time he asks something he shouldn't and the judge allows it."

I pondered. "No, I can't, but there shouldn't be all that much he can squeeze out of them. You'll know soon enough if Resnik strays off course. You can force him back. Don't worry. If you want off the hook after your first witness, I'll take over. That okay with you?"

Bree thought about it, then nodded as her smile returned. "Okay. One last thing. Where are we going when all this is over?"

"You know about Cabo San Lucas?" I asked her. "It's a beautiful place on the ocean, not that far from here. We wouldn't lose a lot of time in transit. I'll give you a couple of websites and you can let me know what you think."

"Daddy, I don't like this pasta sauce. It tastes funny. How come?"

It was Friday at dinnertime. Trina had made veggie pasta and garlic bread while I cleaned up our yard. Andy was at LC's for another sleepover. My daughter was ill-disposed toward housework, but she loved to cook, a predilection she'd had as of school age. How to tell her?

Pretending surprise, I said, "I don't know, honey. What spices did you use?" 'A little heavy on the thyme,' I'd almost said.

"What I usually put," she replied as she rolled spaghetti on her fork. "Oregano and basil and... thyyyyme," she pronounced, drawing the last word out.

"Mmm?"

Trina regarded me, almost accusingly. "That's what it is, isn't it, too much thyme."

"Maybe," I responded, trying hard not to laugh. I'd always had to be circumspect with her as her sous-chef. She had a discriminating palate but a sensitive ego in the kitchen. "I wouldn't worry about it too much. It's very good otherwise."

Disgruntled, she said, "I don't want the rest of this."

"Come on now. You've hardly touched your food. You have to eat." As happened nearly always when she wasn't happy with what she'd done, Trina pushed things around her plate while I cajoled, then she scraped what she had left in the garbage.

"When is Maya coming over again, Daddy? She's so cute."

My back was to her as I loaded the dishwasher. "What about her mother?"

"Bree too. You know what I mean. I like her too. You're in love with her, aren't you?"

I turned around. Temporize or tell her? "I think so, baby. I think so. You see pretty much everything, don't you."

Trina nodded. "It's kinda obvious."

"I suppose it is. Does that bother you?"

"No, not really."

Was that nonchalance? I sat down across from her. "I want to ask you something," I said. "Bree and I are thinking about going on vacation when the trial's over. We'll be gone for two weeks if we go. What do you think about that?"

Trina looked solemn for a few seconds. "Just you and Bree? All that time?"

Hastily, I added, "Maya too, of course."

"Daddy, you know what I mean."

I did. Trina's half smile was too knowing. Was our little tête-à-tête to turn to birds and bees? I hoped not. I wasn't ready. I felt faint as I thought about it. Claire should be the one to speak to her about such things. Trouble was, Trina wasn't at ease about intimate things with her mother.

I cleared my throat. "I can't take you or Andy out of school. You know that, right? So we'll have to find some place for you to stay while we're gone."

My diversion worked. Trina's expression changed as wheels began to turn. "Monica's mother said I can stay with them anytime I want to. Jessica wants me over too. Can I call them?"

Relieved, I said, "No, love, not yet. We don't know when we're going to go. It depends when the trial finishes up. It'll probably be in a month or so. You can talk about it with your friends when you're at school. If you get invitations, I'll need to speak to the girls' parents. You understand that, right?"

"Yeah, I know."

"As to the weekend, I'll call Bree tonight and see if she wants to come."

I stared at the cordless phone on my lap as I thought about Alex. The only sound in our large house was the tic-toc of the grandfather clock in the corner of the living room. Trina had gone to bed.

How to approach Lucy's son? Though he empathized with his mother, he'd taken pains to maintain some distance between the two of them. School had been his refuge. I doubted I could break through his veneer.

He answered on the third ring.

"Hey Alex. I'm going to be in the Santa Barbara area this weekend. Any chance we could get together while I'm there?"

After a few seconds, Alex said, "Yeah, I guess so. Do you mind telling me what it's about? I'm sorta busy on Saturday."

"How about Sunday, then?"

More silence and a sigh. "I live in Isla Vista next to the university near Goleta. You know where that is?"

"I do," I said. "It's nice out there. I've got your address. Noon or so okay with you?"

"I guess so," came his lackluster reply. "See you then, okay?"

Sipping the remainder of my port, my thoughts moved from my probably wasted trip to Goleta to Andy and Miguel. My son's enchantment with my friend's brand of martial arts was growing. Bree's reaction to the demo class we'd observed had continued to trouble me. I'd thought fleetingly about shifting the burden to Claire, an easy cop-out for me since she'd be strongly opposed if she were aware of what was going on. Not a conscionable thing for me to do. She was not to blame for my predicament.

With each successive class, it would be harder to extricate Andy without serious resentment on his part, perhaps long-lasting. I had to do something. Talk to Miguel? He'd be impervious to my concern. He might ask me if I found him violent. That I didn't should be my reference point for danger, he'd argue. I'd give it a bit more time, then intervene after the trial.

I called Bree.

"Hi love," she said. "Didn't expect to hear from you this soon. How long has it been since I saw you, five hours?"

"I talked to Alex. I'm going to Isla Vista to meet him this coming Sunday."

"You taking the twins?" Before I could answer, she chirped, "Oh, I get it. This is a ruse to get me to come to your place tomorrow isn't it. What time should we be there?"

"No ruse, sweetheart, not mainly, anyway. If you can stay over and watch Trina and Andy while I'm in Santa Barbara, that'd be great."

In a teasing tone, Bree asked, "And where am I to sleep? And how 'bout Maya?"

"Both of you in the guest room, of course, where else."

"I was afraid of that. I'll bring salad and dessert. Five o'clock tomorrow be okay?"

"We'll look forward to it. Trina put me up to this, you know."

It'd been some years since I'd been in Isla Vista. A residential community, it had grown. Low-rise apartment complexes everywhere with attractive landscaping, all within walking distance of the beach.

As I searched for Alex's apartment, I flashed back to my undergraduate years at UCSB when I'd met Lucy. How buxom and full of life she'd been then. We met Pete during our final year. He was her Adonis. So much had happened since. Had I been able to peek into the future and change it, I would have pursued Lucy more vigorously and, very possibly, married her.

Alex didn't invite me in. Instead, he led me to deck chairs on a kind of veranda at the back of his building. He'd met me at his door with two cans of beer in hand. The sea air was wonderful. We sat and sipped our drinks.

"I come out here a lot," Alex said, seemingly relaxed. "It's quiet."

I nodded. "The place brings back memories. I used to go to school here a long time ago. That's where I met your mother."

"I know. She told me about it. Several times. You're here about her, aren't you."

"Yup," I said. "I'm glad to see you again, but it's her I came to talk about."

"So what's going on, Forrest? Do I want to know?" He appeared less resistant than resigned.

"You know Lucy's trial begins next week." I waited.

At last, he shook his head. Either he hadn't been in close touch with his mother or she hadn't told him. I decided to come right out with it.

"Alex, we need your help. Your mother's not doing very well. She's convinced herself that she'll be found guilty, no matter what we do. Our problem right now is that her feelings show on her face and in her body language. She's not guilty and she knows this, but the jury's going to believe she is by the way she looks."

"Yeah, I imagine so," Alex remarked in a flat voice. "So, what am I supposed to do about this. I don't get it."

"She needs someone to be with her for a little while, someone she loves."

Alex's face was wooden.

"I'm not talking about a long time, just to get her through this patch. A couple of weeks, maybe. That should do."

Still no response. I watched seagulls diving at bits of

garbage here and there. They were raucous.

"I'm studying here, you know? I've got midterms coming up." Abruptly, Alex stiffened and he grew tense. "Goddamn it, Forrest, I don't want to get involved. Can't you understand that? My dad was a total asshole, my sister's screwed up and my mom's a murderer. In a couple a weeks after the trial starts, everybody around here's gonna be lookin' at me like I'm some kinda freak, and you want me to get mixed up with that. What the fuck!" he yelled at me.

Mute, I watched as the air went out of him and his body sagged. Tears were running down his face. Helpless, I sat there. Alex wiped ferociously at his face as though to rub off skin.

Looking at his feet, he said, "Sorry to say that about Mom. It's not true what I said. I know what it's like to feel alone, believe me. It's been that way for me for a long time, least it seems. How long do I need to go?"

Out of empathy, I would have hugged him if he'd been my boy. He was hurting.

"A couple of weeks or so if you can manage," I replied. "It would mean the world to your mother, I think."

Alex inclined his head. "I can probably get my exams delayed, for a little while, at least. If I have to stay longer than two weeks, I'll lose the term, even the year because of courses I'll be missing."

"Your mother wouldn't want that, believe me... You can make it back to Santa Lucia on your own?"

Alex contemplated me quizzically. "What, you gonna send a limo to get me? Jesus, Forrest, give me a break. I'm not a kid anymore."

We sat, not speaking for a while, I lost in my thoughts. I hadn't expected Alex to capitulate. That he had was reassuring, provided we could get Lucy to agree. She might be unwilling to be the reason for her son's leaving school, even temporarily.

"No classes tomorrow, Forrest. It's a holiday. I can't see my profs until the day after. Wednesday noon's the earliest I can be there."

Better than I'd hoped. "That's great. You'll go to your mother's house?"

Alex nodded.

"Lucy, don't be stubborn. Alex will be here on Wednesday as I told you."

I'd come alone since Bree had no one to be with Maya because of the holiday. As I'd feared, Lucy was being obstinate.

"You made him come, didn't you. I know you did."

"I didn't make Alex do anything. He made up his own mind. He's not a child anymore, Lucy. He made up his own mind about this. He said he can come for two weeks or so without much trouble. You need him here. You know that."

Lily, normally in the background, approved in compressed English. "Your son good for you, I think so. Mr. Spencer right."

Lucy turned back to me. "You sure it'll only be two weeks? I won't let him ruin his school year just because of me."

"That's what we talked about, yes," I said. "He has no intention of abandoning his studies, not from what he told me."

Lucy's recalcitrance had lost momentum. Her face gradually assumed a soft expression. In a quiet voice, she said, "Thank you, Forrest, thank you. I can't wait to see him... Two weeks. I don't think I've ever had him to myself that long. It'll be wonderful."

Lily bobbed her head and smiled. Everyone would be sorry to see Alex head back to school, but his time with his mother would have helped her immeasurably. It would also improve their relationship, I believed. Lily brought out scones and rich dark coffee.

"All rise. The superior court of Santa Lucia County is now in session, the Honorable Hannah Loewenstein presiding." The bailiff, who had to have been a tough female prison guard in her last life, glowered as she scanned the crowded courtroom.

Our judge sat motionless at the bench, her hands hidden by the top of the raised desk. Her garb was identical to what I'd seen twice before.

Resnik, looking almost foppish, was at the prosecution table with two people I didn't know, both of whom were dressed to the nines.

At the defense table Lucy was seated to my right. Her blond hair was conservatively styled, pulled back in a bun, and her navy blue blazer and skirt attractive but simple. There was little she could have done to play down her ample top. Next to her was Ben, his eyes pinned to the comely court reporter. Bree sat to my left.

Behind us in the first row of the gallery was the press, most of whom I knew, including reporters from the *L.A. Times* and the *San Francisco Chronicle*. Santa Barbara and Ventura counties were well-represented. I'd also recognized many members of the public as we came in, a significant number of them trial groupies.

There were too many warm bodies in the room, the air conditioning designed for half our number. I could just hear Loewenstein's oversized ballpoint pen strike the table. She had to rap several times.

"Before we get underway, I want to say several things. As you will have noticed, I don't have a loud voice. Don't expect me to compete with yours. I will not hesitate to clear the room if you oblige me too. Anyone who is disruptive in my court will be ejected and barred from returning here. Please do not test me on this."

As it had been before for Bree and me in her chambers, only the judge's lips moved as she spoke.

"I have imposed a gag order on everyone participating in this trial, including all witnesses as well as the police."

I swiveled my head to see consternation in the front row. Reporters had doubtless hoped that the judge, whom they'd not seen before, would fear displeasure of the press.

"I will hold anyone who violates this order in severe contempt. Now for the final matter. I wish to remind everyone that attempting to influence jurors is a serious offense, punishable by fines and imprisonment. No one is exempt from prosecution."

The unusual tongue-lashing evoked more disgust than apprehension in the audience. Loewenstein's puppet-like manner perplexed me as well as Resnik from what I could see.

As though on cue, twelve jurors filed in, followed by three alternates who took their seats in the back row of the jury box. We had dueled for two exhausting days with Resnik. He'd hoped to impanel chiefly men, who might be less sensitive to spousal abuse, while we wanted the reverse. We eventually left Loewenstein and the jury selection room with nine women and three men as primary jurors, ranging in age from twenty-three to sixty-four. The alternates were all male. Though Bree was a neophyte in the criminal courtroom, she was masterful in her advice about whom to choose. Never again would I be without a psychologist during the selection process. I had to lean forward to hear our judge.

"Mr. Resnik, are the People prepared to open?"

"The People are, Your Honor," he replied. Resnik, like a cat, glided to his feet. He cut an impressive figure, lithe and graceful. He had a handsome narrow chiseled face and alert hawkish eyes that conveyed the impression of a bird of prey. If there was a speck of dust on his dark gray tailored suit, I couldn't see it. The clack of his wingtips sounded loud as he positioned himself midway between the jury box and the prosecution table.

His speech crisp and business-like, swiveling his head to take in everyone in the courtroom, he said, "Your Honor, ladies and gentlemen of the jury, members of the press, and observers in the gallery, my name is Allan Resnik." Gesturing casually with his right hand, he continued, "Allow me to introduce my colleague, Elisa Alvarez, who will be assisting me in this trial. Beside her is Hugh Malory, who's a detective on the Santa Lucia police force."

Resnik turned and walked slowly to what naval captains would dub the quarterdeck, the area immediately in front of the jury box that I had trod up and down so many times. The sheaf of paper in his left hand was at his side. Facing the fifteen jurors, he began, "Good morning."

Everyone in the box nodded, several echoing his greeting.

"At approximately nine-thirty in the evening of July thirteenth of this year, Pete Jackson was murdered in his home before the eyes of his adolescent daughter. Murdered in cold blood, I say to you, not killed by accident. To plot to kill someone is bad enough, but before one's child?"

Extracting a sheet from the papers in his hand, Resnik held it up. "This, members of the jury, is a copy of the confession by the defendant. In it, she states, and I quote, 'I planned to kill my husband. I shot him six times with his revolver.'" Drawn out, he repeated Lucy's statement. "Remember this because it is the most important thing you're going to hear in this trial. Pete Jackson, well-known and much-liked in Santa Lucia, married and the father of two loving children. For those in this courtroom who may not know who the defendant is, permit me to point her out."

Disdain etched on his face, Resnik, in an unusual move, came to stand about four feet from us at the defense table, directly in front of Lucy. He glared down at her for fully ten seconds, then contemptuously turned around and went back to where he'd been.

I was surprised that Resnik, no novice, had ignored protocol in high-profile trials where physical movement by attorneys required approval by the judge. He couldn't have missed the slight pucker above Loewenstein's eyebrows as he'd approached us. Theatrics or an alpha's bid for dominance?

Again facing jurors, he said, "Before I summarize

the People's case and outline what we intend to prove here, I need to say several crucial things you need to know. Of all forms of evidence a prosecutor can put before you, an untainted written confession is the strongest kind. It is so powerful, in fact, that we literally need nothing else, not the motive of the killer, not precisely when the assault took place, not even witnesses who saw the crime. But, because of things the defense would have you believe in trials like this, we must often call upon additional expert testimony of our own to demonstrate the emptiness of their claims."

Were Resnik less cautious, less generic, we'd have cause to interrupt.

"Second," he went on, "you're going to hear a lot about the defendant's state of mind when she committed homicide. Remember one critical thing as you hear what the defense has to say. At no time has it been advanced by them or by anyone that the defendant was not of sound mind when she killed her husband."

Fifteen pencils were busy in the jury box.

"No insanity, no memory blackouts, no post-traumatic stress disorder to excuse what she did. Now, for what the People will demonstrate to you in this trial. Earlier, I used the word tainted. A confession may be said to be tainted if an alleged perpetrator has been physically or psychologically abused in any way to coerce that person to claim events that are either untrue or confess events that person prefers not to reveal.

"We will show beyond a reasonable doubt that the defendant was not pressured in any way by anyone, including the police, to say anything she didn't wish to prior to her confession. You will see portions of the video of the interrogation of the defendant at the police station that will clearly establish for you the conditions under which the confession was obtained. We will present testimony from the arresting officer as to what he observed and did when arriving at the defendant's home. An expert from the police crime lab will review evidence that corroborates the defendant's claim that she shot her husband. Santa Lucia's Medical Examiner will discuss cause of death. You will hear a recognized authority from Child Protective Services who will spell out options other than homicide that were available to the defendant.

"As I mentioned before, you will hear much during this trial about the defendant's state of mind. To avoid confusion about this, we will call upon the expertise of a renowned psychiatrist. Finally, ladies and gentlemen, you will meet the defendant's young daughter, who saw her father butchered before her eyes."

Lucy beside me made a choking noise. Her face momentarily scrunched up, but she quickly recovered.

"The evidence we will present is so massive, so overwhelming that we'll have no choice but to call for the maximum penalty law will allow for premeditated murder. You, the jury, must be our conscience, society's conscience in this case. I beg you not to allow yourselves to be led astray from your central task, that is, to be certain that we do not license murder, not in the second degree, not in the first degree, not murder of any kind. Thank you."

Nothing scintillating in Resnik's remarks, but concise and hard-hitting. Jurors had been impressed, to judge from the copious notes they took. Assuming their opening was well-planned and -executed, the prosecution would retain the benefits of first blood drawn. It was going to be an uphill fight. Loewenstein's pen sounded through the hubbub.

"Very well, Mr. Resnik. Mr. Spencer, will the defense open at this time?"

"The defense will, Your Honor, thank you."

Not a flicker in the judge's face. As though she were acknowledging someone who'd handed her a tissue, she said, "Good. Thank you."

As I'd reflected often during my career, the relationship between jurors and attorney was very different from what existed between a college teacher and her small class. Optimally, mature students came to learn, endowing much of what the instructor said with truth. Juries, on the other hand, were there to decide between good and bad, their decisions far too frequently more sociopolitical than logical.

I'd heard colleagues say jurors liken us to smooth-tongued salespeople. However one may wish to characterize the relationship, it was less an exchange of knowledge than a contest in which acting ability and charisma often won. We relied heavily on feedback from jurors to know whether we were getting our point across, how credible our witnesses appeared—very simply, how much they liked us. It was disconcerting in the extreme to lack this feedback. From the puzzled expression I'd seen on Resnik's face after his opening, I was confident he felt the same as I.

Fifteen faces looked back at me as I approached the jury box. Moderate interest and a few smiles was the most I saw. It was as though I was to address speakers of another language. The only common denominator I could see between them and me was the casualness of our dress. None of the six men in front of me wore ties and the women—exceptionally so, I thought—hadn't gone out of their way to catch our eye.

The first thing I did was remove my blazer. It was stuffy in the courtroom. An omen? Four of the men and three women did the same. The neighbor next door was the figure I wished to emulate.

Seeing their pencils poised, I began, "Ladies and gentlemen, I doubt very much you'll need to take notes in what I have to tell you. As you can see," I said, raising my empty hands, "I have none. What I have to say is simple, something all of you will understand without the need for legal jargon and expert witnesses. You'll see and hear them anyway since they're an integral part of our justice system, but you won't need them, I promise you, not when you learn why we're here. After you've heard everybody talk, we'll ask you to retire as a compassionate group of human beings who will look inside your hearts to see what you would have done in the situation you'll hear about. We believe what you will discover there will bring us justice."

I hoped the friendlier vibe I perceived came from my informal style rather than from relief from the overheated room. If so, I'd exploit it as best I could.

"I need to introduce you to some important people. More than her share of the brains in this defense team lies under that curly brown hair at the far left of our table over there. Bree Dixon has been with me in this from the start. To her right past my empty chair is Lucy Jackson, the defendant in this case, and, I'm proud to say, a longtime friend."

Conflict of interest? I didn't give a damn.

"Ben Segalowitz is to Lucy's right, another friend who's the gumshoe in our outfit and the best PI I've had the pleasure of working with."

Turning back to the jury, I made brief eye contact with each person in the box, rotated my head to regard Lucy, then looked back at them.

"What my colleague told you earlier is true. Ms. Jackson did shoot her husband as she confessed to the police. We're not here to try to convince you otherwise. The question is why she did this, why a woman of sound mind who was a mother and a wife in a lovely home would knowingly kill anyone, let alone her spouse. You will eventually be asked to decide whether or not Ms. Jackson's reason was justifiable.

"Several of you shake your head. No homicide is justifiable, you may think. If that were the case, if our laws called for punishment for homicide of any kind, you'd have nothing to decide. The perpetrator would automatically receive whatever penalty those laws prescribed. We don't hold our soldiers responsible when they execute other men, planned or otherwise. We don't penalize Special Operations personnel who are licensed by agencies of our government to kill terrorists. We don't hold our police officers responsible when they defend us, even though we carefully scrutinize what they do. If a father awakes to the noise of a burglar in his home who is harming one of his children and that father attacks the intruder and kills him, are we likely to imprison that man for protecting his family?

"Ladies and gentlemen, look at me. Do I look like a violent man to you? I abhor violence. I don't like it on TV, in movies or even in the news. I'm not saying to you that we should try to justify killing a human being except in extreme circumstances. The defense's aim in this trial will be to demonstrate to you how extreme the conditions were that led to the death of Ms. Jackson's husband.

"Lucy Jackson is a mother of two, a college boy in his latter teens and a girl of twelve. Shortly before her husband's death, she believed her daughter to have been or about to be sexually assaulted by her father. She wanted desperately to contact authorities to investigate, but, for reasons you will come to know, she felt blocked at every turn. She believed at the time the only recourse she had to shield her child from incest was to kill her child's father.

"In short, we will demonstrate how, year after year, Pete Jackson so restricted the social life and freedom of movement of his wife to cause her to feel completely powerless. You will see, yourselves, the forces she had arrayed against her. Thank you."

Several jurors had nodded or shaken their heads as I spoke, indicating little of what they thought. When I'd finished, their faces were as blank as they'd been before. I fervently hoped the emotional component of those people was softer than their outside, or we were lost. Aside from a sympathetic glance from Bree, the only comment I received when returning to our table came from Ben.

"Where'd you guys dredge up those zombies, anyway?"

The judge was speaking. "Mr. Resnik, will the People call witnesses at this time?"

Rising, Resnik answered, "The People will, Your Honor, thank you."

Loewenstein motioned him to go ahead. The bailiff echoed Resnik's call.

Sergeant Paul Yublonsky, the arresting officer if my notes were accurate, came through the door of the witness room and made his way to the stand. He was tall and lanky in his wrinkled police uniform. In his middle forties, his face was correspondingly long and pallid with a receding hairline. Clearly bored and appearing half asleep, he sat down and was promptly sworn. Resnik approached him.

Once he established who Yublonsky was, he said, "Sergeant, thank you for being here. Would you please tell the Court what your role in this case has been."

The officer fished in his breast pocket for his notes. His tone as indifferent as his face, Yublonsky said, "At about twenty-two hundred hours in the evening of July thirteenth, my partner and I were ordered to proceed to 1415 Sycamore to investigate an alleged homicide."

Resnik tried to interrupt, but the man ignored him.

"A Mrs. Lucy Jackson came to the door when we rang the bell and let us in."

This time, Resnik stopped him. "Sergeant Yublonsky, do you see that woman in this courtroom? If so, can you please point her out."

The officer turned to his left, said, "Right there," then waved casually toward Lucy.

"Thank you. Please tell us what you remember about how she looked." Not how she actually looked, but how his witness thought she looked. Resnik was being careful about his choice of words.

Yublonsky's visage didn't change as he scratched his nose. "Ordinary, I guess," he said. "Nothing unusual, I'd say."

"No surprise, no anxiety, nothing like that?" Leading, but not worth standing up about.

"No, don't think so. She looked normal to me."

"Thank you. Tell us what happened once you were in the house."

A solemn expression on her face, Lucy looked on.

"We followed the woman to an upstairs hall at the back of the house. She told us it was her husband lying there on the floor. She said she'd shot him."

"Was he dead?"

Yublonsky sniffed. "With a bullet in his forehead and bloody holes in his chest? I'd say so."

"Did you touch the body?"

The sergeant heaved a long sigh and shook his head. "No, Mr. Resnik, we didn't touch the body. We're not rookies."

"Resnik's an asshole," Ben murmured above his breath. "Thinks cops are skum."

"What did you do then?"

"We arrested Mrs. Jackson and Mirandized her. I did a gunshot residue test on her, then we took her to the station."

Resnik frowned in frustration at his witness's unresponsiveness. As a prosecutor, he was good but lacked experience in the courtroom with homicide. Santa Lucia didn't spawn many of them. Resnik would have to learn to be more specific in his questions to laconic police officers.

After several seconds, he said, "Can you tell us anything about the weapon the defendant used?"

"Yeah. We bagged it and took it in."

Ben laughed out loud. I saw Alvarez glare at him. A muscle in Resnik's otherwise impassive face twitched.

As though he'd just thought of it, Resnik retrieved a folder from his table and requested permission to approach the witness. Loewenstein told him to go ahead. He handed the folder to Yublonsky.

"Sergeant, do you recognize this document?"

The witness looked at it briefly then nodded. "Yes I do. It's my arrest report."

"Thank you," Resnik said, taking back the papers. "Let this report be marked as People's Exhibit Number One."

"So marked," the judge replied.

So intent we were on the little tableau, more

amusing than important, several of us at the defense table started at the sound of Loewenstein's lilting voice.

"Do the People have any more questions for this witness?"

"No further questions, Your Honor," he replied. "Your witness, Mr. Spencer."

I picked up my notes and made my way toward the witness box. "My name is Forrest Spencer, Sergeant. I won't keep you long."

Detached, Yublonsky regarded me.

"I'd like to return to a question Mr. Resnik asked you. You said that Mrs. Jackson looked normal to you. Is that right?"

Resnik was on his feet. "Objection. Asked and answered."

"Your Honor," I retorted, "goes to the defendant's psychological state at the time."

Loewenstein considered my reply, then rejected it. "Sustained. The last question will be stricken from the record and the jury will disregard it. Continue, Mr. Spencer."

The judge might have been listening to music through invisible headphones, so in another world she seemed. I went on.

"Did you or your partner ask Mrs. Jackson who shot the man on the floor or did she volunteer the information?"

"We didn't ask that," Yublonsky said. "She told us herself."

"She admitted this herself with no prompting. Thank you."

Resnik made to object, then relaxed.

"On another topic, you said you bagged the weapon the defendant said she used. Was it on the floor, somewhere else? How did you come by it?"

Seemingly indifferent to the implications for the People's case, the sergeant replied, "It was on the dining room table. The woman showed us."

"So, to summarize," I said, "you've testified that the

defendant seemed normal, she admitted on her own that she shot her husband and that it was she who pointed out the weapon."

Remaining seated, feigning exasperation, Resnik interjected, "Counsel's testifying, Your Honor. The witness has already responded to these issues."

Resnik was right. He had. It mattered little to me whether or not Loewenstein acceded to his objection. The jury had heard me.

"Sustained," she said. "If you have nothing more to ask this witness, Mr. Spencer, please sit back down."

"A few more questions, Your Honor, if the Court please. Sergeant Yublonsky, tell us. Did Mrs. Jackson say at any time while you were with her why she shot her husband?"

"No, she didn't."

"Other than Mrs. Jackson and her husband, was there anyone else in the house when you arrived?"

Resnik's head came up.

Finally a change in Yublonsky's face. "Yes, the daughter, I think it was."

"Did you address her?"

"We had no reason to. She was cryin', anyway."

"Can you tell us where she was when you saw her?"

Yublonsky looked annoyed. Impatient, he said, "Standin' in a doorway, mighta been a bedroom, I don't know."

"Think carefully, Sergeant," I said. "What kind of clothes did the girl have on when you saw her?"

From nonchalance to truculence, Yublonsky riposted, "How would I know. We had other things on our mind."

Doing my best to appear skeptical, I put my notes down on the podium and eyed him. He shifted in his seat. Ben was grinning while Bree and Lucy watched me. Yublonsky moved around again in his seat.

"She had something pink on, I guess. A nightie or somethin', maybe."

"A pink nightie, you said, thank you. One more

question, please."

Though the sergeant had neither performed badly on the stand nor revealed anything significant to weaken Resnik's case, he clearly thought he had. There was a light sheen of sweat on his face.

"During the time you and your partner were with her, did Mrs. Jackson resist you in any way, before or after her arrest?"

"No," came the man's terse reply.

"Thank you, Sergeant." Glancing up at the judge, I said, "No more questions for this witness, Your Honor."

"Very well," Loewenstein said. "Redirect, Mr. Resnik?"

He answered, "No, Your Honor, thank you."

"Call your next witness, please."

"That woman's in a straight jacket," Ben whispered. He was referring to the judge.

Resnik rose. "John Murdock," he called out, to be repeated a second later by our sandpaper-voiced bailiff.

Ben and I had seen the man many times before. The Assistant Director of Santa Lucia's Crime Lab looked nerdy, a blue-gray stubble on his round baby face with inexpressive washed-out blue eyes. He was in army green cargo pants with a faded blue golf shirt. He was no stranger to the courtroom. He pulled out his notes as he gave his oath.

Formalities over, Resnik went straight to business. "Mr. Murdock, are you familiar with the case involving the defendant in this trial? If so, in what capacity?"

In a monotone, much like his predecessor, the witness replied, "Routine stuff, GSR, prints, things like that."

Bright and able though he was, Resnik's eye on the upper echelon in the prosecutor's office had distracted him from fundamental work details concerning interrogation. Neither Yublonsky nor Murdock, languishing in witness rooms, appeared likely to render up more than asked for. Improbable that we'd see such errors in cross.

Glancing at a note card for a moment, Resnik said, "Thank you. Let's begin with GSR. Even though the jury probably knows what that is, please explain the procedure and tell us what you did."

Murdock sighed. It was as well for Resnik that his first witnesses were relatively unimportant. "If things are done right after a shooting and the perp's in custody, the officer wipes the palms of their hands with cotton swabs with diluted nitric acid. We're lookin' for barium and antimony."

Stony faced, Resnik pursued, "What are barium and antimony for?"

Murdock looked up, frowning. He was manifesting his disgust. If the hotshot prosecutor didn't know the ropes, let him stew.

"They show up particles in the hands that tell us if a sidearm's been fired in them recently."

"Is that what a gunshot residue test consists of, Mr. Murdock?" There was a touch of sarcasm in Resnik's tone.

Loewenstein had surreptitiously picked up her pen.

"That's right."

Deciding to paste a semblance of a smile on his face lest his frustration show, Resnik continued, "Very well. Did the arresting officer in this case provide your lab with GSR evidence and was the test performed?"

"Absolutely, he did. The results were positive."

"May I assume that positive results indicate that the defendant fired the murder weapon?"

More for form's sake than for substance, I stood to object. "No foundation, Your Honor. No evidence that murder has been committed. Matter for the jury."

Loewenstein eyed me for a few seconds, then, in what sounded in her barely audible voice like disgust, she said, "Sustained, Mr. Spencer. Rephrase your question, Mr. Resnik."

Murdock didn't wait. "As far as we're concerned, yes it did. That and the fingerprints on the gun ties it up, doesn't it."

"Two last questions, please. What kind of a weapon was used?"

"Six-shot revolver, thirty-eight caliber, Smith and Wesson."

"How many shots had been fired that night?"

"Six shots, Mr. Resnik, all six."

"Six shots, you say. Is that a common thing for someone to discharge all bullets in a gun?"

Standing up again, I said, "Calls for speculation, Your Honor. Beyond the expertise of this witness."

In a flat voice that contrasted markedly with the lyrical quality I'd heard when Loewenstein and I'd first met, the judge said, "Sustained. The previous statement will be stricken from the record and the jury will disregard it."

Resnik retreated to his table and took an envelope Alvarez handed to him. "Your Honor, may I approach the witness?"

Again, Loewenstein signaled him to proceed.

"Mr. Murdock, I have here an amalgamation of the tests that was sent to me by the crime lab performed on the defendant. Would you kindly review it and attest to its accuracy?"

Murdock's examination of the two sheets inside was cursory to say the least. "Looks fine to me," he said.

"Thank you," Resnik replied. "Let this summary be marked as People's Exhibit Number Two."

The judge waved her hand in acknowledgement. "Any more questions for this witness, Mr. Resnik?"

Poker-faced, doubtless perturbed with his poor start, he replied, "Nothing more, Your Honor." Turning to me, in a mocking voice, he added, "Your witness."

I could see little gain in treating the jury to greater details about Pete's death. "No questions for this witness, Your Honor, Thank you."

No more hurriedly than when he'd come, Murdock got up and left.

Loewenstein's pen came down. "We will reconvene at two o'clock. Court adjourned."

Voices came up quickly and people scrambled for the door.

"Well, girl," Ben inquired, chewing on a fresh-made two-inch-thick sandwich, "how was your first day in court, criminal court, I mean?"

Bree had invited us back to her house for lunch. Lucy had gone back home with Lily to rest.

Still at her kitchen counter slicing roast beef, over her shoulder, she said, "It's a lot to comment on. What did I think of what?"

Ben had too much in his mouth to answer.

"Lucy seemed okay, didn't she," Bree added.

"Thought Resnik had more on the ball," Ben mumbled. "Guy looked like a greenhorn up there."

Smiling at Bree in thanks for the overcrowded plate she'd given me, I shook my head. "He's gotta learn that the police aren't always the best witnesses, but don't sell him short. He has the instincts of a predator. I've seen him take strong people apart in cross. Vicky told me once he's got ice water in him."

Sitting down to join us, her eyes on me, Bree asked, "So what's your take on things?"

"Too little's happened. The testimony of Resnik's first two witnesses doesn't really amount to much."

"What about the judge? She's an odd one, isn't she."

"I don't know what to make of her," I answered. "I didn't when I met her and I still don't. You get anything from her, Ben?"

"Nope. She looks like a mannequin up there with a face somebody painted on. Not someone I'd trust, I can tell you."

I nodded, trying to get my mouth around Bree's immense sandwich. "Funny thing," I commented. "First time Resnik and I were going to her chambers, he told me a little about her. She apparently had an odd nickname back east."

"What's that?" Ben asked. "Robot?"

"The fish."

My companions looked bemused.

"Exactly. I can't put the two together either. What bothers me a little more is some stuff Sara dug up a few weeks ago. In the decisions she found, there wasn't much consistency. She couldn't get a reading on her."

"Maybe she's just a free thinker," Bree suggested.

Ben and I shook our heads.

"I don't think that's quite the way Sara meant it," I said. "I've got a feeling both sides are in for some surprises."

"Could be, boyo, could be. Tell you one thing. Resnik pussyfoots around with Copperstone like he did the others, he'll be in for it. Old Alex is comin' up next, isn't he?"

I said he was.

"Will he be of any use to us?" Bree queried.

"I doubt it. No more than the first two. We wouldn't hear from him at all if they didn't have to formally specify cause of death in court.

"He's a crusty bugger, but I like him," Ben remarked. "Nobody's toy, that one."

I grinned.

Dr. Alexander Copperstone, Santa Lucia's Medical Examiner, was in the witness chair that might have been built for him, so often had he sat there over the years. In a dark blue blazer and blue-and-white-striped tie, in his sixties, he looked distinguished and very fit. Straight-backed with sharp blue eyes and white hair he'd had since I'd met him ten years before, he bespoke authority. My last encounter with him had been at the Martinez trial.

To forestall Resnik's lengthy introduction, we stipulated to his credentials.

Wasting no time, Resnik said, "Dr. Copperstone, according to the report I have here, it was you who performed the autopsy on Pete Jackson. Is that correct?"

"It is."

"Please tell the Court how Mr. Jackson died."

"The decedent was shot multiple times at short range," the ME said. "Six rounds in all were fired, one or two of which killed him."

"Your Honor," Resnik requested, "may I approach the witness?"

Loewenstein motioned to him to go ahead. Meanwhile, Alvarez distributed a glossy photo to the judge, one to the jury where it made the rounds and another to us at the defense table. We'd seen it months ago as part of discovery. Resnik asked that it be marked as People's Exhibit Number Three.

Copperstone looked up as Resnik's hand came out. "I don't need a copy of that, young man," he said. "I have several right here."

Stymied momentarily, Resnik looked down at his photograph, then let it fall to his side. "Very well. Please explain from your perspective what the picture shows."

Copperstone nodded, seemingly appreciating Resnik's forthright approach. He said, "To begin with, one of the rounds penetrated the forehead above the bridge of the nose and the left eye, causing massive damage to the left hemisphere of the brain. That bullet would have killed Jackson instantly if he was not already dead. The second round of interest went through the left side of the sternum and perforated the left ventricle of the heart sufficiently to cause death. The four remaining bullet holes appear at various places in the chest and abdomen. For someone who has never shot, it is way too unlikely that all six rounds even hit him."

"Yes, thank you. You stated, 'shot at short range.' How did you determine this?"

"There were traces of powder burns around each of the six entries, either on Jackson's clothing or, in the case of the head shot, on his skin."

"One final question, Doctor. Apart from the six gunshot wounds you spoke of, did the autopsy reveal anything else the Court should be aware of?"

I raised a mental eyebrow to the potentially loaded

question for which I doubted very much Resnik had answers. There was a trace of a sardonic smile on Copperstone's lips.

"Well now," he drawled, "let me see. Little alcohol if I remember, no drugs, I think, what else could I have missed?"

Resnik looked flushed. "No more questions, Your Honor. Your witness."

Ben made a derisive noise through his nose that pulled a reproachful look from the judge. I jotted an admonitory note and passed it in front of Lucy to my right. My partner smirked.

"No questions for this witness, Your Honor, thank you," I said, remaining in my chair.

The ME was dismissed, an exceptionally short stint for him. He looked pleased as he exited the courtroom.

It was three-thirty at the end of the first day of trial. We'd been waiting in the conference room for Garrett, who'd phoned to say he'd been held up in court. There wasn't a lot more to talk about since we'd been at Bree's.

"Resnik keeps on droppin' the ball," Ben remarked, "this one's gonna be in the bag. You see Copperstone's face?"

"What I mainly saw was Loewenstein's, Ben. Cool it, will you please? We don't know where that lady's at. There's no sense in antagonizing her."

"Yeah, yeah, okay. I didn't like the way Resnik treated Yublonsky, that's all."

"The sergeant wasn't all that helpful, Ben, was he," Bree commented.

"Maybe not. Resnik's green behind the ears and he thinks cops are just there to screw around with. I know the type."

"Anyway," I said, leaning back in my chair, "fun starts tomorrow. Kate Schulz is up."

"Look out fancy boy," Ben said, chortling. "Old Katy's gonna chew you up and spit you out before you know what hits ya."

Chapter 21

Though I could recall individuals we interviewed during the selection process, jurors seemed amorphous to me when seated as a group in the jury box. Not a one stood out for me. Perhaps it was because nothing noteworthy had yet occurred in the trial.

The atmosphere in the courtroom on the second day was almost cheerful, incongruous though that was for a murder trial. Bree, wearing a musk-like perfume I liked but didn't recognize, looked expectant as did Lucy, I was glad to see. Ben's face was sober as he contemplated the empty witness stand. Their garments still eye-catching but more subdued, Resnik and his little entourage must have concluded their designer clothes might be inappropriate in light of jurors' preference for more casual dress. All members of the press were busy writing.

Bree nudged me and whispered, "Did Alex ever show?"

I turned to Lucy. "So how's Alex settling in?"

Her eyes sparkled with unshed tears and, for the first time in weeks, her smile was unrestrained. "Forrest,"—she reached under the table to tightly grip my hand—"I can't tell you what him being at home means to me." Her smile faltering, she added, "I wish it weren't so late for us."

I punched her in the arm. "Hey, hey, none of that. We've got a good chance here, I've told you that."

Bree's eyes had shifted to the prosecution table. "So I finally get to see the harridan at work. I know I shouldn't say this, but I'm kind of looking forward to it, based on everything I've heard about her."

Scowling, Ben faced her. "Be glad you've never had her grilling you. This is no sideshow, Bree."

"No," she responded in a contrite voice. "I'm sure it's not. I'm sorry."

Lucy reached over and lightly poked her. "Ben's a sourpuss," she said, smiling. "Don't listen to him."

"We'll see who listens to who when Katy's on the stand," came his curt response.

I kept a blank face though I felt much the same. The woman was intimidating.

In words only I could hear with voices all around us, Bree murmured, "Ben doesn't like the Lieutenant very much, does he." She clearly hadn't heard the standing rumor.

Not unexpectedly, both Bree and Lucy looked surprised as Lieutenant Kate Schulz, turning her head right and left and smiling, ambled toward the witness box. Outmoded blue-gray hair was pulled back to reveal a lined wrinkled face that gave no hint of inner steel. Crowding sixty-five, she'd continued to gain weight over the years. She appeared to look forward to the proceedings. Compared to the major role she played in the Martinez trial where I'd seen her last in court, she'd have little to do here, at least so it seemed to me. She must know this, so why her anticipation? She made me nervous.

Resnik smirked as we offered to stipulate to her credentials. He intended to leave no doubt in jurors' minds about the Lieutenant's extensive background in homicide and her expertise as an interrogator.

"Lieutenant Schulz, if you recognize the defendant in this courtroom, would you point her out to us, please."

Turning briefly and pointing toward Lucy, she said, "She's right there."

"When did you first meet her?"

No longer smiling but still pleasant, Schulz answered, "At twenty-two forty-five hundred hours on July thirteenth of this year in an interrogation room at the police station where I interviewed her."

"Would you please tell the Court what transpired there."

The Lieutenant actually grinned. "About the easiest thing I've been asked to do, Mr. Resnik. I don't even need my notes."

Old Katy hadn't come to court just to say yea and nay. Since there might be little to challenge her, she would put on a little show.

Feigning surprise, Schulz announced, "Never saw a defendant so much in a hurry. I'd barely told her who I was and she wanted to get down to it. She wanted to confess, right there. Now you know, when that happens, I get suspicious. I'm thinkin' the person's confessin' for someone else, you know? So I tell her to slow down and remind her of her rights."

As choreographed, Resnik raised a hand. Addressing Loewenstein, he said, "With the Court's permission, we'd like to play two short segments of the video of the defendant's interrogation."

Loewenstein glanced at her watch as though it were near noon. It was fifteen minutes after ten. "How long are those segments, Mr. Resnik?"

"About three minutes each, Your Honor," he said.

"Go ahead."

Malory, having cued up his machine, raised his remote control. A screen came down and lights in the front row dimmed. A moment later, the Lieutenant's left profile appeared along with a clear frontal image of Lucy. Schulz was speaking, a yellow pad and pencil before her on the table.

"Hold on, Mrs. Jackson. No one's in a hurry here."

Out of the corner of my eye, I could see Ben grimace at Schulz's pretended nonchalance.

"You've been arrested for homicide. You're aware of that, correct?"

Lucy was frowning and waving the Lieutenant off.

A little more severe, Schulz said, "Mrs. Jackson, be quiet for a minute and listen to me. Before you confess to anything around here, I want to be sure you're aware of your right to have counsel present."

"The cop who arrested me already told me that," Lucy said, still frowning.

"Yes, I know he did. That was then. This is now. You don't have to say a single word more without an attorney present if you don't wish to. We'll terminate this interview right now if you wish to make that call."

Lucy impatiently shook her head.

"I want it verbally on record. Do you wish to have counsel present?"

"I do not."

"Very well," Schulz said, all signs of affability gone. She picked up her pencil.

Malory stopped the video.

"The second segment takes place near the end of the interview," Resnik explained.

The screen lit up. The scene had changed very little except for the pen in Lucy's right hand and a sheet of paper in front of her.

"Before you write down and sign what you've just told me," Schulz said, "I'll ask you this once again. You insist that you shot and killed your husband. Why did you do this?"

Lucy made no response.

"Very well, go ahead."

The video camera's resolution was insufficient to display what Lucy wrote, but it was obvious that she was writing. It was also evident when she signed her name at the bottom of the almost-empty page. The wide angle of the camera showed the Lieutenant exiting the room, reentering shortly after with a man in uniform with a sergeant's insignia who witnessed Lucy's signature.

Malory pressed a button and the video stopped. The fluorescent lights just above us came back on and

Resnik returned to the podium.

"Let these video segments be marked as People's Exhibits Four and Five, Your Honor."

"So marked."

"Lieutenant, does the term 'crime of passion' mean anything to you?"

"Yes it does."

"Can you explain, please."

Schulz shifted in her seat and settled back, her eyes moving to the jury box then to Resnik's face. "I assume we're talking about homicide," she said.

"Homicide, that's right."

"The majority of murders in this country, Mr. Resnik, occur because of anger or jealousy. Alcohol's usually involved. Men kill other men in bars, they kill women at home, you get the picture. Most often, these crimes are not premeditated. Does that help?"

"Yes, thank you," Resnik replied. "Have you interrogated persons guilty of such crimes?"

"Many times," Schulz said, "more than I can count."

"In your experience, would you say the defendant in this trial committed a crime of passion?"

This called for a conclusion beyond the expertise of the witness, but it was not in our interest to object. Resnik's eyes flicked expectantly to me then back to Schulz.

"A crime of passion," the Lieutenant voiced for the benefit of the jury, "I'd say not. She showed no signs of being sorry for what she did. That's one of the first things you see. She didn't give excuses, not a one, something else you look for. Most of all though, she gave the impression she'd do it all again if she had to. Besides, she told me she planned to kill him."

Schulz seemed pleased with her little speech, Resnik less so. He would have preferred concise short answers rather than a diatribe that we might pick apart. As a hardened veteran of the courtroom, Schulz's loquacity surprised me.

Stepping back from the podium, Resnik said, "No

more questions for this witness at present, Your Honor, but I request the right to recall her if necessary."

Schulz's face darkened.

"Very well," Loewenstein replied. "Please remain available for recall, Lieutenant Schulz. Your witness, Mr. Spencer."

I had but two questions, both of which would raise Resnik's hackles. Ben was fiddling with our machine as I took my place at the podium.

Before I could address her, Schulz put on her grandmother look and said, "Forrest Spencer. Nice to see you. It's been a while, hasn't it?"

'Not nearly long enough,' I would have said aloud if we'd been alone.

"Good morning, Lieutenant Schulz." Turning to our judge, I continued, "Your Honor, with the Court's permission, we'd like to show a two-minute segment of the video we just saw. May we do so?"

Loewenstein motioned to us to proceed.

My eyes on the jury, I explained, "In this short segment, Lieutenant Schulz is asking Ms. Jackson why she killed her husband. Please listen carefully to this exchange."

The screen still in place, lights dimmed and the video segment started. Lucy looked harassed and the Lieutenant was bearing down as could be seen from the intent expression on her face.

"Mrs. Jackson, you've already told me several times you shot your husband. What I want to know is why." Schulz's tone was hard.

"I can't tell you," Lucy said.

"You can't or won't!"

"I won't. I have my reasons, believe me, but I can't say."

Resnik was on his feet and calling out. "Objection, Your Honor, objection. This segment contains material beyond scope of direct. Counsel is free to call this witness for his own case." Resnik was vehement.

I signaled to Ben to halt the video. The judge's pen

rapped twice though it was hardly necessary. No one was talking.

In her low-modulated voice, Loewenstein said, "Beyond scope, Mr. Resnik? I don't think so. You are responsible for your questions as well as your witnesses' responses, are you not? Overruled. Carry on, Mr. Spencer."

Nodding in approval, Ben pressed the button.

"When you shoot someone," Schulz insisted, "there's a reason. I want to know what it is. You're being ridiculous."

By way of answer, Lucy glared back at her interrogator and said, "I'll confess to killing my husband as I said, but I don't have to say why. That's all."

Our video segment ended there. I gathered up the few notes I'd made. "One last question, Lieutenant Schulz."

Her face inscrutable, she'd gone from amused witness to combatant.

"In your explanation to the Court about crimes of passion, you gave examples, one of which was, and I quote, 'they kill women at home.'"

Dismissively, Schulz waved her hand and retorted as Resnik jumped to his feet, "Mr. Spencer, please. I was giving an example, that's all."

Meanwhile, Loewenstein heard the objection I'd foreseen.

"Counsel continues to go beyond scope of direct." Resnik was red-faced. "I move that the video segment we just saw be disallowed and stricken from the record. Mr. Spencer must—"

For the first time, there was genuine displeasure on the judge's face. Not a sound in the courtroom. "Mr. Resnik. I'm growing tired of your impudence. Am I incorrect, or did I already address this issue a moment ago. If you need instruction in court procedure, then I suggest you relinquish control to Ms. Alvarez or to another in the prosecutor's office. Now sit down or you're going to find yourself in contempt. Mr. Spencer, you may carry on."

Resnik promptly sat, looking pale.

"Serves the puppy right," came Ben's low-voiced comment that I could hear from the podium.

"My colleague," I said, "has pointed out your extensive experience as a police officer in homicide. As a recognized expert, I ask you to estimate the number of men who kill women at home versus the number of women who kill men at home."

Resnik made as if to rise, saw the judge's countenance and sat back in his seat.

Schulz frowned as her eyes narrowed. "I've handled a lot of cases, yes, but I don't keep track of such things. You'll have to go to records to get that."

I let a few seconds go by before I prompted, "You mean that the numbers are sufficiently close that you can't give an educated guess? Is that what you're telling this Court, Lieutenant Schulz, really?"

Again, Resnik would have broken in had he not just been squelched. Schulz's face at that moment was pugnacious, as I'd seen her two years earlier at the Martinez trial where she'd been caught off stride. What I wanted from her wasn't critical in the People's present case as she knew well, but it was galling. Nonetheless, she let it go.

"Fine. If it'll satisfy your feminist persuasions, more men kill women than women kill men. Is that what you want to hear?"

"Since we're on this topic, if the Court will indulge me, I have two more questions. May I go ahead, Your Honor?"

"You may, Mr. Spencer, but keep it brief."

"Have you interrogated women who've confessed to killing their husbands at home, Lieutenant Schulz?"

"A few."

"Would I be correct to say that nearly all of these cases involved repeated physical abuse by husbands?"

"In most cases, yes. They did. I don't have a lot of experience in that area, you know."

"One final question, Lieutenant Schulz. Are you aware of any women who confessed to killing their husbands in their home who refused to give the reasons for what they did?"

I was flagrantly beyond scope on this one as was evident on Resnik's and Alvarez's angry faces. I was shamelessly exploiting errors the two had made and hoping Loewenstein was sufficiently interested in the subject to let it through. I wasn't likely to get free passes like that again.

Canny as well as smart, Schulz sensed she was on soft sand. Finally, she shrugged. "I'm not aware of any cases like that, no."

I could see no reasons to want the Lieutenant back. "No more questions, Your Honor," I said with a silent thanks to lady luck.

Her unruffled demeanor back, Loewenstein said, "Redirect, Mr. Resnik?"

His agitation conspicuous in his omission of the honorific, he replied, "No thank you."

Not a good day for him. From long experience, I knew our turn would come.

"The witness is excused. Court is adjourned until ten o'clock next Monday morning."

Bree's mouth was compressed as we dodged photographers and wended our way outside. "Can we go have lunch some place it's quiet? I feel tense."

"It's not all that close, but we might get to Teresa's before the rush. How's that?"

"Teresa's sounds good. There wasn't anybody there last time we went. Let's go."

We got a big smile as we walked in. Teresa might have been Lupe's sister, nearly as round as she was tall with dark-skinned indigenous Mexican features. She cooked, served and managed her six-table little restaurant single-handed. I'd known her for at least five years. We were the sole patrons but for a Mexican worker in threadbare clothes.

"You two sit down right here at your special table, no? I don't write so good so I tell you what we have today."

"Surprise us, Teresa," Bree said. "Everything you serve is good. Bring us some water though, okay?" To me, she said, "God, what I really need is a stiff gin and tonic."

"No alcohol served here, love, as you know. Water'll have to do. What's the problem?" The morning in court had gone relatively well for us.

"You and Schulz. It was scary."

"Scary? In what sense? Kate can be pretty daunting, I grant you, but—"

"No, not that," Bree broke in. "I was paying close attention, believe me, but the questions you asked her never occurred to me! I would have had no idea what to say to her up there."

"Want to know something? I wasn't sure myself until Resnik played those clips."

"Forrest, I'm sure of it. I'll never be a litigator in this field. I found it super stressful and I wasn't even up there. I watched you taking notes. You've gotta be quick on your feet or you'll miss things. It's a lot different in family law. We plan everything out before. We know what we want, we know what the other party's gonna ask for. We even talk to the opposing lawyer sometimes to work things out. It's... it's more civilized, know what I mean?"

I thought I understood. I had great respect for Bree's intellect and logic, but I had speculated on occasion about whether or not she possessed the instinct good prosecuting and defense attorneys had to probe for weaknesses and go for the jugular under fire. Some lawyers were better suited to work behind the scenes. I put my hand on hers and lightly squeezed.

"Hey, it's a bit early to toss in the towel. Tell you what. If you're still having qualms about taking Sue and Jackie when we start our case, I'll pick them up, okay?"

Bree let out a breath. "I kept thinking while you

were questioning Schulz about what Resnik was going to do to me in cross. He's intimidating."

"Okay. It's a deal," I said. "We had a little excitement in court today, but not all that much, really. If Resnik hassles Kate Barns when she testifies, we may see a spark or two. The gallery won't sleep through that encounter, I can tell you that. I doubt we'll see much more action until Mia's on the stand, though. That's when things will get interesting... Here's Teresa with our food. I'm starved."

Despite my preoccupation with Lucy's trial, I couldn't shake memories of Miguel's martial arts demo weeks before that Bree and I had seen. As the two of us had feared, Andy was becoming fixated. Exceptional for him, he completed his school work as soon as he arrived home to be sure he had enough time to practice before supper.

I'd finally summoned the courage to call Miguel. We'd arranged to meet for lunch. He'd tried to lure me to his house with Isabel and the girls, but I'd demurred.

"So, amigo," he said as I sat down across from him. "So serious all of this. You finally going to invest in my little company?" His grin was friendly, but his eyes were troubled.

What could I say to my erstwhile client who'd been through so much, to my friend who was doing his best to support his wonderful little family? What words could I use to convey my concern for my son?

"What's up?" he asked.

I'd have to come right out with it. "Miguel, my son's in love with what you do, too much so. It's all he thinks about. Being able to put someone down is what he talks about all day. Very frankly, it's got me worried."

No surprise on my friend's face, just a nod and a long sigh. "You're not the first to come to me about this, you know? It was the demo, wasn't it. Four kids dropped out after that. I think I'm about to lose several more."

My friend's face was sad as he contemplated the red

and white checkered tablecloth. I didn't know what to say.

"Thing is, Forrest, the young students pay the bills. The older ones—you saw some of them—they only come once a week and they don't pay much except the beginners... You know what's funny? I'm not a violent person. I don't like to hurt people. I really don't. You believe that, don't you?"

I nodded.

"It's true, I don't, but I love what it takes to do that, the moves, I mean. Does that make any sense to you?"

"In a way it does," I answered. "Kinda like a person who loves how guns are made and how they work without wanting to shoot someone."

"Yeah, sorta like that, I guess. The difference is, in what I'm good at and like to do, I end up knocking people around. I have to. They get hurt sometimes. It's in my blood, Forrest. I can't explain it."

"You don't have to, friend," I said. "It's nothing to be ashamed of. It represents a primal instinct in us. Properly controlled as you practice it, it shouldn't cause any harm—it shouldn't, that is, if students come to it as adults."

"You want to pull Andy out, don't you." Miguel raised a hand to forestall me. "You're afraid that he'll want to learn to fight as I do and it could lead to things, bad things. You could be right. I know that. I'm just not sure what to do. Like I told you, parents are startin' to leave the school, 'specially after what they saw at the demo. I'm not gonna have a choice. I'll have to shut down the place and get another job somewhere, teachin' kids, prob'ly. How 'bout that?" As he spoke, the animation I'd come to associate with him was gone. The martial arts school he'd taken over had been his dream.

Playing for time while I thought, I asked, "What kind of an arrangement with the original owner of the school do you have? Didn't you say he was your partner?"

Miguel regarded me briefly before answering.

"Kinda like that, yes," he said. "He was never askin' very much cuz he knew I was so into it, and I think it made him feel good to help. He's too old to do stuff like that anyway, least he says so."

So far, Miguel hadn't told me anything I didn't know.

"I hope you don't mind me asking," I said, "but, you have a contract with him, some kind of understanding?"

Miguel's eyes narrowed slightly as he looked at me. "Yeah, we do, but why you asking? Not sure I like the sound of this."

Retreating to safer ground, I said, "I consider you a close friend and I'm a lawyer. Do you need more of an explanation than that?"

My rejoinder made him laugh. "Okay, okay, sorry. I'm just a little sensitive about this these days. I appreciate your concern. Isabel's supportive as always, but she doesn't understand the financial end of things. And, to make matters worse, she's, a, she's—"

I smiled and slapped my hand down on the table as the server came. No need for confirmation of the pregnancy. I could see it on his face. I congratulated him and Isabel before turning to the girl. We both ordered chicken salads.

Shrugging, Miguel said, "Isa told me last week we were gonna have another one. Women! I didn't think they were s'posed to get pregnant when they were still nursin'. Angie just started walking and she's still in diapers. Can you beat that?"

I was fervently glad I didn't have to. Three kids under four years old, my God!

"So back to my question if you don't mind," I said. "What kind of an arrangement do you have with the guy?"

"Pretty simple, really. I either buy him out, building, supplies and all, for thirty grand or I pay him thirty percent of my net for as long as it takes."

I thought about Miguel's school, the interior and the grounds. "That's pretty generous, far below market value, I'd think."

"Guy has all the money he can use. He absolutely loves martial arts, a lot like I do, and he wants to help as I said."

I nodded. "You say young students—kids, really—will make or break your school. Don't get me wrong here, but couldn't you develop special classes that take the best from all the martial arts that would be defense rather than combat oriented? Is such a thing possible?"

Before he could respond, I went on. "Say you could. Then, on the side, out of the kids' way and where parents wouldn't see, you continue to do what you do with older guys who want the rougher stuff. You wouldn't have to advertise that part. Given your reputation, you'd have lots of candidates."

Miguel looked rueful. "Some good ideas, Forrest. There's just one thing you've left out of it. Money. First place, I'd have to hire somebody to teach the kids since that's not what I like to do. I like kids and all, but I'm not into the kind of things they and their parents usually go for. I'd have to renovate the building, maybe, so we could do both things. No way my partner's gonna go for a scheme like that."

Nodding, I said, "I understand. Answer me this, though. Would the scheme have a good chance if you had the backing?"

Miguel contemplated me for a long time. Looking almost stern for him, in a quiet voice, he said, "I understand why you want to pull Andy out. As I said, you're not alone. Yes, of course we're friends. I hope we'll always be, but do me a favor, please. Let's leave it at that. You find different classes for Andy and I'll carry on the best I can." He looked down morosely at his uneaten salad. "I'm not really hungry anymore so, if you don't mind, I'll get back to the dojo. I've got some cleaning up to do."

I'd lost my appetite as well. An idea had germinated in my mind, but to attempt at this moment to make it grow in his would be fruitless. I had Miguel's pride to contend with. There had to be other ways.

"I'm not going to pull him out right away," I said as I got up. "I'd never hear the end of it at home if I did. Give my love to Isabel and the girls. Remember to congratulate her for me about the new one."

It was Monday morning, four days after the second day of the trial. I'd just sat down next to Bree at the defense table when Lucy slipped in beside me. My apprehension had been misplaced about how she'd appear in court. Whether it was Alex who'd buoyed her up or something else, she looked good in a pretty high-necked dark green dress that would raise no eyebrows. Her profuse blond hair hung down just past her shoulders, appealing but not styled to attract attention. Best of all, her large blue eyes were clear and she looked pleasant.

"Lucy," I said, "come to court like that every day and we're halfway there. Be sure to keep your attention on the jury, especially when you think Resnik's coming after you. Know what I mean?"

With a wry smile, she replied, "That's kind of obvious, isn't it. Is Ben always late? It's almost ten."

Just then, looking haggard and his clothes smelling of wood smoke, Ben joined us. Glancing briefly at me as he snapped open his briefcase, he growled, "Don't ask. Rough weekend."

In my old friend's idiom, those words meant an overabundance of strong margaritas and at least two overnight parties. I wondered where Cassie'd been. The bailiff was calling court to order.

Surprise. Elisa Alvarez, Resnik's co-counsel, was heading toward the podium. Vicky must have wanted her recent acquisition in the prosecutor's office to cut her teeth in direct examination of a witness who'd be no threat to the People's case.

Like her male colleague, she was tastefully dressed in a dark well-tailored suit and immaculately groomed. There the resemblance stopped. Where Resnik moved with feline grace, Alvarez's short legs caused her to appear choppy when she walked. Contrasting with her stocky man-like body was an exceptionally lovely face with what had to be naturally curly dark hair. She had a sensuous mouth, pixy nose and almond-shaped brown eyes. The mismatch in her features was emphasized in her voice.

"Sharon Lopez," came the attorney's loud and low-pitched call.

Iron Woman, Ben's name for the bailiff, boomed out the name and the witness filed in to take her seat and be sworn.

I looked down at my list. Child Protective Services, a woman in her middle fifties with mannishly short gray hair with a round face and thin-lipped mouth. She wore thick glasses. Like hundreds I saw every day in the street, she was short and considerably overweight. She had that unmistakable officious look.

Alvarez dutifully took her witness through her paces—how long she'd been established in Santa Lucia, her experience and training for working with children, how long she'd been attached to Child Protective Services. "Thank you for coming, Ms. Lopez. We're grateful to have someone with your background here."

This obviously not the first time she'd testified, relaxed, she nodded and smiled.

"Child Protective Services," Alvarez said, "works extensively with abused children, do they not?"

"That's correct, we do," Lopez responded. "In fact, that's primarily what we do."

"Can you explain to the Court how abused children come to your attention."

"Well, in many ways. Teachers, neighbors' complaints, the police. Our information comes from many sources."

"Yes, thank you," Alvarez said. "What does your office do when you hear of an abused child?"

Lopez pursed her lips. "My goodness, that depends on so many things, age of the child, type of abuse, it's difficult to say without particulars."

Resnik must have given his colleague free rein. "But you do investigate complaints, correct?"

"Why yes, of course we do. That's our job!"

Previously bent over the podium, Alvarez straightened up. "Allow me, Ms. Lopez, to pose a hypothetical situation which should help us understand the kind of work you do. Please make your answers hypothetical as well, alright?"

"I'll try," Lopez said. All of this, of course, had been rehearsed.

"A mother calls your office and complains that her daughter is being sexually abused. What would your people do in such a situation?"

Lopez seemed to puff up with self-importance. "This happens frequently, Ms. Alvarez, believe me. Someone from CPS would arrange to visit the home to investigate."

"How long would it take for you to respond?" Alvarez prompted.

"That depends on a number of factors, but it doesn't take more than a day, usually."

"You say you'd investigate. Can you tell us what investigation on your part means?"

"Certainly," Lopez said. "We'd interview the mother first to see what's going on, then we'd talk to the child, assuming she's old enough. Unfortunately, Ms. Alvarez, that's not always the situation. It's atrocious the things men will do to young girls."

"Assuming the child is old enough to be interviewed, what then?"

"If the situation warrants, we call in our specialists to gather forensic data and we demand that whoever assaulted the child be charged. It's as simple as that, Ms. Alvarez."

"Let me get this straight. Earlier, you said that you receive complaints and information from various sources that you follow up on. Is this correct?"

"Absolutely. It's as I said."

"So, is it reasonable for the Court to assume that a complaint from almost anyone would eventually reach you so that you could act upon it?"

Lopez hesitated. "That may be overstating things, Ms. Alvarez. Almost anyone, you say. I'd correct your statement to say that any complaint, submitted in person or in writing or even on the phone to the authorities, would likely reach us."

"Yes, I see. Thank you. So, if I've understood you correctly, any mother who's concerned about sexual assault of her daughter has a good number of options open to her to complain. Is that correct?"

"Certainly, she does," Lopez replied.

Alvarez glanced back briefly to Resnik who gave a slight nod.

"Thank you, Your Honor," she said. "Your witness, Mr. Spencer."

"Ms. Lopez, I'd like to take up where my colleague left off with our hypothetical situation if that's alright with you."

The lady from the CPS stared back at me as though I were a vulture. I had to smile, so ludicrous she looked.

"Relax," I told her. "I'm just an attorney like the rest. I have a few questions for you, that's all."

Her frozen expression didn't change.

"I assume you get complaints from mothers sometimes about sexual assault that turn out to be incorrect. Is that right?"

Lopez's lips barely moving, she conceded, "It happens."

"How does your office determine if the mother's right?"

Lopez considered this. "We talk to the child, what else. That's not always easy. You understand this. Depending on the circumstances, children, boys as well as girls, shy away from talking about sexual things, especially if they've been threatened."

"Yes, that makes good sense," I said. "But tell me. Do people like you with your experience and special training develop a sense about whether a child is holding back?"

"Calls for a psychological conclusion," Resnik declared as he stood up, "that's beyond the ability of this witness."

"To the contrary, Your Honor," I said. "We would hope professionals from Child Protective Services to have just this kind of capability. How else could they function."

"Overruled, Mr. Resnik," Loewenstein said. "Do carry on, Mr. Spencer. I'm interested in what this lady has to say."

I could almost see Lopez puff up with self-importance. Another error. Resnik had all but impeached his witness, inadvertently thrusting her into our camp. Vicky would have little sympathy for him.

"Would you like me to repeat my question?" I asked.

"No, no, not at all," Lopez crowed. "I remember exactly what you said. I can't tell you we're always right, but if we didn't have a sense that something wasn't right when we're talking to an abused child, we couldn't function. We simply couldn't."

Again, I thanked her, which yielded a smile. I wasn't beyond a little blarney when the occasion called for it.

"I must thank you for the clarity of your testimony, Ms. Lopez. It's been immensely helpful."

Everyone could see Resnik wanted in the worst way to interject, but he'd tied his hands. As long as I didn't stray from issues he'd raised in direct, I was free to say more or less what I liked in cross, provided I wasn't over-argumentative or grandstanding. As luck would have it, his witness was prepared to eat out of my hand.

"From what you say," I carried on, "you must also develop a sense that tells you a complaint is unwarranted, due to an overprotective or overanxious mother, maybe."

Lopez's head bobbed up and down. "That happens all the time. You have no idea how often we're called out on false alarms."

A muscle twitched in Resnik's face, a tic I'd seen before, and his hands opened and closed, opened and closed. He needed no help to understand where we were going.

"You may think this is obvious, but could you please tell the Court how you determine when a mother's complaint is unfounded."

"As I said before, we talk to the daughter, assuming it's a girl involved. It takes a pretty good actress to hide something like that from us."

"So," I said, "if I understand you right, if a preadolescent girl is convincing when she tells you she hasn't been sexually assaulted and there are no signs to the contrary, you're likely to believe her."

Lopez hesitated before she replied. "Understand something, Mr. Spencer. Just because a preteen girl says nothing is wrong, that doesn't necessarily mean she's telling the truth. The problem is, we can't force the child to undergo physical examination in this state unless she gives permission. Even with a physical examination, we can't always tell. If the girl and the father say there's nothing wrong, regardless what the mother tells us, unless we've got solid proof of some kind to the contrary, we have to let it go. What choice do we have?"

"Ms. Lopez, thank you. You've been very helpful. No more questions for this witness, Your Honor."

"Redirect, Ms. Alvarez?"

Resnik answered for her. "No more questions. May I approach the bench, Your Honor."

Since we were not included in the powwow, it must concern Resnik's witness roster. It did. A minute later, court was adjourned until the following morning. We learned later from the judge's clerk that Tina Palson, the People's sixth witness, had been abruptly dropped. Dr. Peter Salmonson, a psychiatrist, the seventh scheduled to testify, would be available only the next day.

Lucy disappeared in the crowd with Lily before I could say goodbye. Ben agreed to join Bree and me for lunch.

As we exited the courthouse and breathed fresh air, Bree reached out to grab Ben's arm. "No way we're going to Gordy's, that dump, if that's where you're heading."

Turning back to her, looking down at his watch, he inquired, "Where is it you highfliers want to go at this hour of the morning? Half the joints aren't open yet. Besides, the places you guys go, they want twenty bucks for a cheeseburger."

Airily, she rejoined, "See you later on at the office then or tomorrow."

Continuing the charade, Bree and I turned left at the corner. "I don't think they serve burgers at Nellie's, do you?"

"I doubt it," she said, laughing.

Ben snorted as he followed behind us.

At eleven-thirty, we were in luck. We found a nice table in the shade on the patio.

I chose a seafood salad that I'd enjoyed before and Bree went for a fruit plate. Ben's frown deepened as he scanned the menu.

"Christ, what kinda place is this? What's a slider anyway, and what the hell is a Portobello panini? Sounds like something the Italians go for. I don't see a decent piece a meat anywhere here. I'm not eatin' rabbit food, I'll tell you that."

Bree laughed. "I think there's an open-faced roast beef sandwich here somewhere. Yeah, here it is." Grinning, she added, "Comes with green salad, your choice of dressing. No fries, I'm afraid. Least it's healthy."

"How come every health nut I know looks sick?"

Our orders came in under fifteen minutes.

Dubiously eyeing his gravy-covered sandwich, Ben said, "Thought you said Resnik was some kind of hotshot. Vicky oughta be more careful. And who's that

Alvarez chick he's got? She looked scared shitless up there."

Bree'd put her fork down to listen.

"Don't sell Resnik short, Ben. I know him. He's had a few false starts, but that doesn't mean much as you know. As to Alvarez, people have to start somewhere. Who'd have guessed Lopez would turn out to be good for us?"

Disgruntled that he couldn't pick up his food, Ben had grabbed knife and fork and was digging in.

More appetizing than my food, smiling with her hair moving gently with the breeze, Bree said, "We're ahead so far, don't you think?"

Removing a tail from a large shrimp and popping it into my mouth, I reflected. "In one sense, yes," I said, "if you're counting trial points. It's not that little victories like today's don't have impact. But the big elephant in the room doesn't notice them all that much. He makes his mind up based on other things, some visceral, some emotional. We never count our chickens until the verdict's in."

Bree lost her happy look. "Your invisible elephant is the jury, I assume."

I nodded. "In truth," I said, "I don't think this trial's really started yet. Something else. For the first time in my career, I haven't a clue what's going on in jurors' minds."

"I've been watching them a lot," Bree remarked. "They look attentive. Some even look amused."

"Yes, I've seen that too, but how are they going to relate to abstract concepts like state of mind? That's the issue. I'm used to making adjustments in the way I talk and ask questions according to how the jury looks." I sighed. "Maybe it'll get better as we get into it. I hope so."

"The psychiatrist comes on tomorrow?" Bree asked.

"So it seems. Resnik's funny. Renowned is the word he used about the Doctor in his opener. He's renowned, alright, as a professional witness, he is. He'll testify to just about anything. Resnik knows this. He's put him in to muddy up the water. God knows what Salmonson will say up there."

"Can he hurt us, do you think?"

Ben made a derisive noise. "Don't they always? Never once heard a shrink do anything but confuse things. You actually gonna put Silvergold on the stand, Forrest? He's better than most, but still."

"I can't tell you at this point," I said. "So much depends on Mia when she's up there. If she holds up and all goes as Resnik plans, then Dr. Silvergold has to come in."

We finished up our meal, not talking very much, and returned to the office and our work.

If Resnik had run the gauntlet with his fiery boss the previous day, it didn't show. He looked alert and ready for his seventh witness.

There wasn't a vacant seat in the gallery I could see. Loewenstein's gag order notwithstanding, the press was rampant with speculations, centering most on the twelve-year-old who was shortly expected to appear.

Noise subsided as court was called to order and Dr. Peter Salmonson came in. I'd last seen him two years earlier in a Ventura court. He'd made efforts to remain in shape despite his years, but time had played havoc with his face. His jowls were pronounced below a bulbous nose that was crisscrossed with little veins. His impressive stature and good taste in clothes couldn't camouflage a visage that had seen too much hard life. I remembered those penetrating dark blue eyes.

Five minutes of credentials weren't enough. By the time Resnik had enumerated the tenth of his psychiatrist's publications, jurors were chatting quietly among themselves.

"Dr. Salmonson, since the jury will be hearing much from the defense about what they're calling state of mind, could you please explain to the Court in simple terms what state of mind is."

The witness smiled. "It would be nice, Mr. Resnik, if every question posed to me were that easy. Strictly speaking, state of mind exists as long as there is evidence of mental functioning."

"So," Resnik paraphrased, "state of mind always exists as long as we're alive."

"It's more complex than that, Mr. Resnik, but basically, that's right."

"Is it correct to say that state of mind varies from time to time with every individual?"

"Most certainly it is. To keep things manageable, I'm going to confine my remarks to people who suffer from no psychopathology, that is, to people we call normal. Our state of mind will often vary according to our mood. It may change if something wonderful has happened to us or something bad. Repeated negative experiences with someone, for example, may cause one to become overcautious, which will affect their state of mind." This was a path down which Resnik didn't want to go, always a risk with professionals who tended not to follow scripts.

"Yes, thank you, we understand. In most instances, Doctor, is one's state of mind likely to be long-lasting, for months, for years, say?"

Though Salmonson would lecture on as long as allowed, he knew why he was there. He'd been paid to be aware. Without a hesitation, he stated, "In most cases, no. They're temporary. People with mild depression couldn't function very well otherwise."

Resnik was content. His vague concept of state of mind had been rendered vaguer. "Your witness, Mr. Spencer."

"Dr. Salmonson, permit me if you will to return to your statement a moment ago about the short-term effects of state of mind."

The witness could see I held a scholarly journal in my hands. He waited.

Opening it to a marked page I said, "Your Honor, may I approach the witness."

She motioned for me to go ahead. I handed the open journal to Salmonson.

"Doctor, would you please read aloud the title of this article and the author's name."

Hesitating briefly, he said, "Anomia as a Corollary of Recidivism. Peter Salmonson, MD."

"Objection, Your Honor. Irrelevant. Counsel's fishing."

"Mr. Spencer?" queried Loewenstein.

"Goes to the witness's credibility, Your Honor. Moments ago in direct, he claimed state of mind is something we associate with short duration. I contend he makes precisely the opposite claim in the published article he wrote in the journal he holds."

"Very interesting, Mr. Spencer, a fairly serious charge. Overruled, Mr. Resnik. Let's hope Mr. Spencer doesn't hang himself. Please proceed."

"Gladly, Your Honor. Thank you. Though jurors may perfectly well understand the meanings of anomia and recidivism, would you kindly define each of these words for us. Begin with anomia, please."

Salmonson's jowls seemed to droop further and he was sweating. "Anomia is a term used in sociopsychology to denote feelings of alienation towards one's culture or subculture."

"Thank you," I said. "By feelings of alienation, I assume you mean feelings of rejection or dislike."

"That would be correct."

"In the article you published in the journal in your hands, you report the results of an extensive study in which you found long-term prisoners to suffer from anomia, that is, dislike or hatred, for people on the outside. Is that correct?"

Tersely, Salmonson said it was.

"You go on to say that these feelings increase, often lasting a lifetime. Is that correct?"

Again, he said it was.

"You argue, convincingly, I must say, that prisoners' anomia accounts in part for their need to return to prison, for recidivism, that is. Doctor, let me ask you as a professional. Would you say that anomia is a long-term state of mind brought on by conditions of prison life?"

Sighing as he put the journal in his lap, Salmonson said, "Yes, Mr. Spencer, I would say it is."

"To summarize, Dr. Salmonson, you agree that negative conditions that exist over time can alter a sufferer's long-term state of mind."

"That can happen, yes."

"No more questions for this witness, Your Honor."

Resnik's face, closed down, echoed what I'd said. But for one final witness, the People's case should be done.

Chapter 22

Because of Loewenstein's gag order, the public had limited access to information about trial participants, an altogether salutary thing from my point of view. The press was free to comment. Opinions about the trial ranged from "lackluster" to just "plain dull," there too little drama in the proceedings they associated with high-profile murder cases.

The butterflies that were habitually with me during the first few minutes were active as Bree and I pushed through throngs to get to our seats. We could just hear Garrett's greeting as he found a space in the second row behind the press. To Ben's annoyance, he'd been called away on some emergency in Lompoc where he'd be for at least the day.

The buzz of voices in the crowded courtroom was stronger, everyone anticipating twelve-year-old Mia's presence on the witness stand. The stress Bree and I felt was evident on Resnik's and Alvarez's faces. How much more anxious would they be if they really knew the girl.

Lucy had dark circles beneath her eyes and she looked tense. We'd attempted to prepare her as best we could, but she refused to listen.

"You don't know any more than I do what's gonna go on up there," she'd said. "How can you tell me what to expect? Alex by the way's not gonna come. He says he can't stand to see his sister. We'll just have to get through this, whatever happens."

Lamentably, Lucy had been right. No one, including Resnik, could predict what was to occur that morning.

The judge's clerk stopped for a moment at the prosecution table, then came toward us. Counsel and co-counsel for both sides were to proceed immediately to chambers.

Loewenstein invited the four of us to sit. With no suggestion of tension in her soft voice, she said, "I'm sure you know why we're here. I've spoken with your witness, Mr. Resnik, yesterday and this morning. She seems calm and able to answer questions, even those concerning her parents. If I thought otherwise, I'd never let her appear in open court. Frankly, I'm less concerned about her than I am about how you're going to interact with her. I hardly need tell you that we're dealing with a child who must be treated very carefully. I appreciate the importance of this witness for both the prosecution and the defense, but you must understand this. It is our duty to protect this child in whatever way we can from trauma that results from trials like these. I will not tolerate the slightest abuse of her, not in any form. If she gets seriously upset or if any of you become argumentative with her or attempt to confuse her, I will immediately adjourn until such time as more appropriate arrangements for her testimony can be made."

Loewenstein's hands became restless and her face took on a troubled look. She continued, "I'm not asking you to oversimplify your questions. She's old enough to understand and answer them. Nor do you have to be overcautious about what you ask her as long as you don't raise subjects that you know will alarm her. I'm relying on you for this." The judge looked stressed. "Perhaps I should have insisted upon alternative arrangements. Further accommodations for the child as a witness. Yes, perhaps."

In almost a whisper, she added, "Just use softer gloves than you're used to if you can. Thank you for your attention. Oh, and one more thing. Please try not to intervene on procedural grounds unless absolutely necessary. Exchanges like that will just confuse the girl. That will be all for the present."

Ordinarily, outside the judge's chambers, Resnik and I might have exchanged pleasantries, if for no other purpose than to lighten the atmosphere. He didn't look at Bree or me as we left, and Alvarez looked constipated as she strode ahead.

The bailiff called court to order and the jury filed in. All eyes in the courtroom were on the door to the witness room.

A hush fell as Mia came into view and, as rehearsed, headed directly toward the stand. The prosecutor's office had taken care with her appearance. Her normally stringy dishwater blond hair was neatly combed and pulled back in a ponytail. It did good things for her plain face. She had on low-heeled black sandals with tight-fitting black pants and an attractive pink top that, in the current style, fell halfway to her knees. It did little to hide her appealing shape. She displayed no apprehension as she was sworn. Lucy's eyes were glued on her pregnant daughter, whom she hadn't seen in three months, her expression tense.

"She's showing," Bree whispered. "Not too much, but you can tell. Just look at the women in the jury box."

I was more preoccupied about the fixed stares of the men. However much Resnik might have tried to conceal it, Mia exuded sexuality in the way she looked and the way she moved. I was glad of our majority of women on the jury.

Resnik gathered his notes and made his way to the podium. His confident air was gone. He looked tentative as though this were his first time in court. "Good morning, Mia. My name is Allan Resnik."

In a matter-of-fact tone, Mia replied, "I know who you are. I've only seen you a thousand times."

A few laughs from the jury box and tittering from the gallery, which seemed to distract Resnik.

"I know this place looks pretty new to you, but

there's no reason for you to be scared, okay? No one's going to bother you here."

Mia looked around the courtroom then back at the man she'd come to know. "You're funny, you know that? Why should I be scared, anyway. There's nothing scary in here."

I doubted very much Resnik had any children, especially a child Mia's age.

"Nothing scary, Mia. You're absolutely right. Now I'd like to explain a couple of things to you that you probably already know, but I need to say them anyway, okay?"

No response.

"Alright. First thing."

Resnik's Adam's apple bobbed up and down. Keyed up though I was, I felt sympathy for the man. He was totally out of his depth.

"I'm going to be asking you some questions and you're supposed to answer them, not by nodding or shaking your head but in real words. You understand that, right?"

She nodded. Resnik blinked, but didn't correct her.

"Second thing, you must think carefully before answering each question and you must tell the truth, all the time. You do understand what we mean by the truth, right?"

"You already told me that lotsa times. I understand what telling the truth means."

"Now here's the last thing and it's important. This is a courtroom and we have a judge who you already met. We must be respectful at all times. We don't get mad, we don't yell, nothing like that. You're a witness. Your job is to answer the questions we ask you the best you can. Okay? You do understand these things, don't you?"

"Course I do," Mia said. "Go ahead and ask me."

"Okay. Let's start. What is your full name?"

"Mia Josephine Jackson."

"How old are you?"

"Twelve, going on thirteen."

"Where do you live?"

Mia thought about this, then answered, "With my aunt and uncle here in Santa Lucia, but I don't remember the house number."

"That's okay. We don't need it. You have girlfriends at school, I presume."

"Yeah, course I do. You already know that."

"Can you give us the names of some of them?"

Resnik was doing his best to establish a rapport between himself and his witness. Unfortunately for him, his smiles that appeared contrived and his body language had little effect on a young girl who wasn't in the slightest intimidated. How had they managed to relate before, I wondered.

"Yeah, I guess," Mia said. "There's Cindy, she's my best friend. There's Jessica and, oh yeah, there's Tammi."

"Good. That's fine." Resnik licked his lips. "What about boyfriends? Do you have any?"

Either the question was unexpected or Mia wasn't inclined to answer. After a long pause, she said, "Yeah, a couple. So?"

Calculations raced across Resnik's face. Annoy her, maybe worse, or drop it? He did the latter. "Very good," he said. "Now can you tell us where you go to school."

Again, Mia hesitated. Her expression petulant, she said, "I don't go to school this year. I have tutors."

"You have tutors instead of going to school. Can you tell us why?"

Though Bree and I were writing down verbatim almost everything both said, up to that point, at least, I could discern no direction in Resnik's questions.

"Cuz the kids will make fun of me, that's why."

Bree noticed it the moment I did. "He's upsetting her," she whispered in my ear.

I made a low noise of acknowledgement in my throat but kept my face blank.

Mia was talking. "I'm pregnant. I can't go to school. I thought you knew that."

No news to us or to Resnik, of course, but it was like a bombshell in the room. The hubbub subsided only when Loewenstein rose as though to clear the court. Resnik looked distraught. He dared not turn his star witness over to me without getting more from her, but how to do that without losing her? The sole course he saw open to him was to forge ahead.

"How far along are you, Mia? Can you tell us?"

Tersely, she replied, "Four months."

Once again, he licked his lips and cleared his throat. "Mia, do you know who the father is?"

I could feel the rise in Mia's energy from where I was as could Bree, who nudged me. If Resnik was to obtain anything of importance from her, he'd better do so quickly. He was about to lose control, not something that would be in anyone's interest, certainly not ours.

Perturbed and growing more so by the moment, she snapped, "Course I do."

"Right," Resnik charged on. "Will you tell us who the father is?"

I, along with everyone in the courtroom, held my breath.

"No," came Mia's immediate clipped answer.

Was Resnik expecting this? His next question revealed that he was. "Why won't you tell us, Mia?"

Still upset but maintaining a modicum of control, she said, "Cuz he'll get in trouble."

'Well done, Resnik. You braved the flames and came out the other side unscathed.' Had the man been content to finish there, he might conceivably have prevailed. Emboldened, very deliberately, Resnik turned to gaze at Lucy for several seconds.

This move had apparently not been in the script. Mia, momentarily confused, turned in the witness box to lock eyes with her mother. Choreographed, this was not. In alarm, Bree grabbed my arm.

Hissing in my ear, she demanded, "What's he doing! Look at that child's face!"

Hatred blazed from it like nothing I'd ever seen.

Loewenstein craned her neck but couldn't see everything from where she was. Lucy had collapsed and torrents of tears were running down her face. Resnik was calling out Mia's name. Her face still contorted, she turned back to him.

Doggedly pursuing her, his voice higher in pitch and animated, he demanded, "Do you know who your mother thinks the father of your baby is?"

Too late, Resnik saw his mistake as blood suffused Mia's face and she leapt down from the witness chair and stood as the bailiff bore down on her.

"Course I do," she yelled. "She hates me and she's jealous. My daddy loves me more than her. He loves our baby. He promised me we could keep it and I'd be the mommy and he'd be the daddy." Whirling toward us at our table and jabbing a finger toward Lucy, she screamed, "That's why she killed him. She didn't want me and him to have our baby in the house!" At the top of her lungs, Mia screamed epithets while the bailiff's strong arms pulled her from the courtroom.

There was pandemonium. Lucy's gut-wrenching sobs were lost in the tumult. Loewenstein was standing and waving both arms and mouthing something to no effect. It was utter chaos until the bailiff returned, heading for the crowd with truncheon in hand, her bellows audible above all the noise.

Seconds later, there was quiet in the courtroom. The judge was back behind the bench, her veneer of detachment gone. Astonishingly, Resnik had regained his cool.

In a voice clear of emotion, he stated, "Your Honor, the People rest."

Three rapid taps of Loewenstein's pen and chatter died. Though still soft but now with a quaver, the judge said, "Mr. Spencer and Ms. Dixon, is the defense ready?"

Glad that Loewenstein had included Bree, I nudged her. Startled but looking pleased, she announced, "The defense is, Your Honor."

"Court is adjourned until ten o'clock tomorrow

morning. Defense counsel, to my chambers, please."

At Bree's quizzical expression, I said, "Mia's on our list of witnesses. She's going to want to know what our intentions are, I think."

"My God, Forrest. We're not going to call her, are we?"

"Not unless you'd like a turn with her on the stand," I rejoined.

Bree shuddered.

Loewenstein had our witness list in her hands when we came in. "Sit down, please," she said. "I see you wish to call Mia Jackson as a hostile witness. You may do so, but under very different circumstances. The child will have someone she designates with her at all times, and all interactions will be conducted by closed circuit TV. There will be no repetition of what occurred this morning."

I cleared my throat. "After what was divulged this morning, Your Honor, we have little more to learn from her. We've removed the child from our witness list."

Loewenstein nodded. Though she'd redonned her figurative body mask, she seemed warmer somehow, more human. "I'm relieved to hear it," she said. "It was shameful what happened earlier. You two bear none of the blame, of course." She contemplated us for a moment before going on. "I hardly need tell you that this case is far from over." Her eyes moved to Bree then back to me. "You'll have a lot of work to do of an unusual kind." After another pause, she said, "Thank you both for coming."

Garrett was chatting with the bailiff when we came out. The lady was animated.

"Almost got to knock some heads this time," she groused. "People are chickenshits, you know that, Garrett? Soon as they see my billy, they back off like a lotta sheep. Almost decked one of those reporter creeps though. Got too much in my face. Anyhoo, how you doin' now you're on the wrong side of the fence? Hear you're workin' with this Spencer guy. Mm-mmm. And who's this sweet thing he's got with him?"

All of us were laughing, more from nervousness than anything, I trying hard to remember the lady's name. Paula, that was it.

"See you around. Got work to do." She spun on her heel and left.

"Woof," Bree exclaimed when the bailiff was out of earshot. "I wouldn't want that woman after me!"

"You sure?" I teased. She smacked me.

"I need to chill," she said. "I'm emotionally exhausted. You guys mind if we don't have lunch out? Can we just get some sandwiches and coffee and hang out in one of our offices? Would that be alright?"

Garrett and I agreed.

A half hour later, the three of us with our food and drinks were seated in Bree's office, by far the coziest in our suite. With the three of us in there, I had no opposition when I closed the door.

"We had a little confab with the judge, Garrett," Bree said as she stabbed at her salad with a plastic fork. "I think she was trying to tell us something, Forrest, don't you?"

"You think she's sympathetic toward our case," I said.

"Maybe? Didn't you hear what she said?"

"I did. She's more consistent and logical than I thought she'd be, that's true, but sympathetic? I suspect she's more worried about the impression she makes than about our client. She likes to see herself as unassailable, objective, neutral, you get my point. She's probably concentrating on what she'll be saying to the jury about how to interpret the law on homicide in this state."

"Yes," Garrett commented, looking thoughtful. "You've got one major problem out of the way concerning Lucy's credibility as to incest. You've still got the biggest hurdle to overcome. How do you get the jury to forgive premeditated homicide. You're gonna have to show that Lucy had no support system at all to protect her daughter, a pretty tough thing to do, given the number of agencies we have around here for just about everything. Not exactly the best time to say it, I guess, but I have to tell you, I've got serious doubts that you'll pull it off on state of mind alone. I understand your position on this, but, to be blunt, state of mind, as Resnik's gonna try very hard to show, is just another term for ignorance."

"Isn't this a cheerful bunch," Bree commented. "Nice to have you in for lunch finally, Garrett, even if you come in to shoot us down." Bree's half smile took the edge off her remark.

"Fact is, Bree, I think he's right. What Garrett's saying, I think, is even if a woman's been badly abused, physically or psychologically, she still knows how to call 911. We have to demonstrate beyond a shadow of a doubt that, no matter who Lucy called or went to, there'd have been no help. State of mind and psychological abuse play into it but, in the end, it's our ability to show she had no recourse—not that she thought she didn't, but that she really didn't."

"That's it in a nutshell," Garrett said. "With that seemingly insoluble task, I leave you two to your devices. Don't get disheartened, Bree. I said seemingly insoluble. The guy you're teamed up with has a habit of pulling rabbits out of hats. What's that they say? It's not over til the fat lady sings."

"That's one of the stupidest sayings I've ever heard," Bree riposted. Then she smiled. "Anyway, don't you worry about me. You think Forrest keeps secrets from me anymore? I know exactly what he plans to do. Don't bet against him like Ben does."

Looking very serious, Garrett said as he was leaving, "That, Bree, I'm not about to do. It does look like I'll be free tomorrow morning and afternoon, by the way, so I just may get to see what you two are up to. Barb's gonna peel me like a carrot and cook me up if I don't get out a here. See you tomorrow mornin'."

"By the way, Forrest," Bree asked as soon as

Garrett had gone, "did you see Lucy after they took Mia out? Things got so hectic that I lost sight of her."

"That friend of hers is really something. By the time the furor had died down, Lily had her out of there. Strictly speaking, Lucy wasn't supposed to leave, but no one noticed. Court had been adjourned anyway."

"Will she be okay, do you think? She was utterly devastated by what Mia did."

"I know she was. I think we should go see her this afternoon."

Distressing though her daughter's outburst had been for Lucy, as her defense team, we had reason to be encouraged since we'd been absolved of the burden to prove incest. No one in the courtroom, especially the jury, could any longer question the legitimacy of Lucy's fears.

Fortuitous though the incident had been in one sense, it had been catastrophic in another. The loathing for her mother that had emanated from Mia's eyes offered little hope for a meaningful relationship between the two in the foreseeable future, if ever. Much of the girl's hostility, of course, lay at Pete's door, but by no means all. Mia's overpowering instincts to safeguard her coming baby were also involved, but there was more. With the rapid onset of puberty had emerged characteristics that, to my untutored eye, appeared disturbed.

Were we able to obtain an acquittal, what then? Would Lucy be harnessed for years with a conniving, ungrateful daughter with her child who would be a constant reminder of the past? How free would Lucy be to pursue a life of her own? All valid questions, but none so important as the immediate one facing us.

Of a sudden, Bree was curled up on my lap and crying. "I've never seen raw hatred like that in my life," she murmured, sobbing against my chest. "Please God, don't ever let anyone look at me like that, especially my daughter."

As I stroked Bree's back and held her, I reflected

about how fragile and unpredictable our relationships with loved ones could be when things we don't expect occur.

"With a little luck and lots of TLC," I said, "that's not going to happen to either of us. We adore our kids too much."

Bree quieted and we held each other for a while.

Lifting her head, smiling through her tears, she urged, "Come on. We need to comfort Lucy. She can't be in very good shape right now. Where do you suppose Mia got off to, by the way?"

"I don't have a clue. I'll call Evie and see if they've heard from her or to phone us in a while if they haven't."

Shortly after, we were in the car on our way to Lucy's. In that way women have, Bree had banished all signs of our emotional encounter moments earlier, no redness in her green eyes, not a hair out of place and no wrinkles in what should have been a rumpled blouse. She'd even freshened up her perfume.

"So much for all our plans to derail Mia on the stand," I said.

"I'm sorry about this morning," Bree replied, "but I'm awfully glad it wasn't us. I would have hated to go through with it."

I wholeheartedly agreed. However we might have justified our scheme, it would have constituted abuse of a child not yet in her teens. Resnik's overeagerness to extract as much incriminating information as he could from Mia about her mother had relieved us of the onerous strategy we'd conceived.

"Hey Forrest, come on in. Hi Bree." For the first time in I couldn't remember how many years, it was Alex at the front door. "I'll tell Mom you're here." We were left to find our way inside.

"He doesn't look very good, does he," Bree said.

I sighed. The house smelled like burned food and garbage that wanted taking out. "He sure doesn't. He wasn't at the trial this morning, was he?"

"Forrest, I don't think I've seen him once. Didn't you say he refused to be there with Mia?"

"Oh yeah, I remember."

Lucy, in sweat suit and slippers, came into the living room, Lily nowhere in sight. She looked broken, her face slack and eyes cast down. Alex had not returned. She sidled to her customary chair and sat, showing no inclination to interact. Mia's tirade seemed to have taken the spirit out of her. What to say? Bree, too, was at a loss for words.

After a heavy silence, Lucy said in a flat voice, "Lily's gone to the pharmacy for me. She'll be back in a little while. Alex is in his room. He's packing up to leave, I think."

Christ, one hurdle then another. There was no way Lucy could go into court like this. We'd have to file a motion for a continuance for a few days with Loewenstein, assuming she'd grant it. That shouldn't be a problem since, as she'd demonstrated with us, she wasn't averse to skipping potential court days. But with the momentum we'd inadvertently accumulated that morning, it was a poor time to delay the trial. We needed to proceed immediately to the issue of Lucy's lack of options to shield her child.

My thoughts racing, I turned to Bree and said quietly, "Can you hang on a minute here? I want to talk to Alex for a minute."

She whispered to me to go ahead. Lucy hadn't moved, seemingly impervious to us.

I was sure I knew where Alex's room was. His door was open. Head bent, he was seated on his bed. I went to join him.

"I never did get to thank you for coming back home like this."

"For all the fucking good it's done," he answered. "She was okay for a few days until that screwed-up sister of mine came into it. She's an airhead, a total bitch." Alex was trying hard to blink back tears. "She's always been like that, but my dad? That's what I can't understand! He had everything, fucking everything going for him, and he had to go and mess around with her. And now the bitch's gonna have his baby! Jesus, Forrest, can you beat that? And where do you think that cunt is gonna live? Right here with Mom, that's where, cuz Mom still loves her and she needs to take care of her. I swear, Forrest, if I see Mia just once, I'm gonna strangle her, all the trouble she's brought us. If you get Mom off, and I really hope you do, and Mia and her brat come to live here, I'm gone. I'll see Mom other places, but I'll never come back here until that bitch and her kid are out of here."

I wanted to respond, to some measure in defense of Mia, but what could I say that wouldn't vilify his father more than I already had?

"Alex, there's no way we can resolve all of this right now. Our immediate concern is your mom's future. Given what went on this morning in court, I think we've got a shot at getting her acquitted or something reasonably close to that. It could still easily go the other way, though. One thing's certain. If we don't give it everything we've got in the next few days, she's likely to go to prison for a long time. I don't need to tell you that your mom's a good person and she doesn't deserve that. Right now, she's in real bad shape. There's no way she can go to court like she is. If we have any chance at all, we need to finish this thing up right away. However we do it, we've gotta get Lucy's morale back. She's afraid you're about to leave."

I could see nothing in the bedroom that suggested this.

"Alex, please. I think the trial could be over in a week. We need you to be here for her and to do everything you can think of to cheer her up." Half kidding, I said, "Drug her, get her half soused, do what you have to do, but make sure she's in court with us before ten tomorrow morning, please! Can you do that?"

Alex regarded me without saying anything for a

while. Finally, he asked, "What happened in court this morning that got her all shook up?"

Collecting my thoughts as rapidly as I could, I said, "Mia was on the witness stand today. Perhaps you knew that. The prosecuting attorney didn't know her very well. He asked her a few too many personal questions, and she flipped out. She said some... not so pleasant things about your mom that really upset her."

"So that's what happened," Alex said. "Thought it was something like that. She came home a total wreck, I can tell you." His chin cupped in his hands, he studied the carpet under his feet. Scarcely audible, he said, "I'm glad she's got a friend like you. She wouldn't have a chance if she didn't, would she." Nodding twice, he continued, "Yeah, sure. I'll do what I can. I'm not taking off. That should help. I'm not going with her to the trial though, you know that. Lily'll take her and bring her back, but I'm staying here."

Much relieved, I replied, "That should be fine. Bree and I will leave you with her now if you don't mind. We've got a bunch of things to do before court tomorrow. I'll phone back later on this afternoon to see how things are, okay?"

"That's fine," Alex answered, getting up from his bed. "I'll come out with you."

Returning to the office, Bree announced, "Forrest, I'm sorry about this, but I've decided. Don't try to change my mind." I knew and expected what was coming. "I don't want to question Sue or Jackie. There's far too much at risk as Garrett said. We've gotta show that jury somehow that premeditated homicide's not always a crime. We need experience and intuition of a kind I just don't have. You aren't too disappointed in me, are you?"

"Of course not. Resnik's lost the first battle in this war, but he'll do everything in his power not to lose the second, the most important one, in fact. Frankly, Bree, I'm glad to see you recognizing your limitations in this instance rather than going out there overconfident, especially in a sensitive case like this. I'm glad to have you with me in no matter what capacity."

She seemed pleased. Tilting her head briefly against my shoulder and reaching out to touch my hand as I drove, she murmured, "I'll always be next to you, you know that."

I'll make no attempt here to communicate how much her gestures and words meant.

Adjectives in the press about the trial had changed. "Exciting" and "unique" were among words I saw.

The atmosphere in the courtroom was also different. Anticipation showed on most faces in the gallery and the level of conversational noise was high. Resnik and Alvarez appeared alert, continuously exchanging notes. Inexplicably, Malory was gone.

At our table, as was the case each day, the two women were in different clothes. Bree was decked out in earth tones that she liked while Lucy wore an attractive pale pink top and long black skirt I'd not seen before. Happy the lady to my right was not. But nor was she downcast, I was pleased to see. Alex had been good to his word.

"You actually got Cap Lonigan to agree to come?" Ben exclaimed. "Either somebody up there loves you a lot or someone's out to get you. I'm bettin' that it's the last. That guy never shows up in court."

"Well, we haven't seen him yet," I said, "but we snuck the subpoena through."

"Who'd you send to do the dirty deed?" Ben demanded.

A little shamefacedly, I admitted I'd sent Sara.

"You dog, you," he exclaimed, grinning. "A little below the belt, but, hey."

"Wasn't that the idea," Bree commented, laughing.

"We'll see if the guy shows up," Ben responded. "Ten bucks says he won't."

No one took him on.

From the bench Loewenstein inquired, "Mr. Spencer and Ms. Dixon, is the defense ready to begin its case?"

This time I was the one to reply. "The defense is, Your Honor. We wish to call Ms. Jo Ann Phillips."

She was by no means a star witness for us. Her function was to help us build a portrait of Lucy that was to change significantly over time as we hoped to show.

"Nice scenery," came Ben's low-voiced remark. "Who's she?" He glanced at his witness list and nodded.

"Ms. Phillips," I said, "my name is Forrest Spencer. I'm on the defense team for Lucy Jackson as you doubtless know."

The lady smiled and nodded. I looked into warm gray eyes in an attractive oval face surrounded by an abundance of dark brown hair that must have been a challenge to blow-dry. She was tastefully dressed in a knee-length black skirt and leaf-green blazer with matching blouse. What I liked most was the natural message she conveyed that "I'm a 'what you see is what you get' kind of person." Altogether charming.

"So everyone here knows you two are acquainted, could you please point out who you believe Ms. Jackson is."

Still smiling, the lady turned to Lucy, waved and said hello. Lucy smiled back at her.

"Ms. Phillips, can you tell the Court when you first met Ms. Jackson and under what conditions."

She pursed her lips and looked reflective. "Gosh," she said, "it's been so long, twelve years or so, I think, 1999, 2000, something like that. I was a program director for one of our TV stations at the time. That's right. Lucy came to see me about a fundraising project of some kind, don't remember what. We really hit it off, like some people do, you know? She was all fired up on this project thing, real lively. I saw her quite a lot for a while after that. It was a long time ago, but I still remember."

"Did she ever share any problems with you that she was having?"

Quick to respond, Phillips answered, "She wasn't the complaining type, not like some people. The one thing I remember was that she felt frustrated sometimes that her husband didn't want her to work outside the home. Lucy was the independent type, I can tell you. She just wasn't your model of the stay-at-home wife at all."

"Do you remember if she had children?"

The lady's brow furrowed briefly, then she said, "Yeah, a boy, I think. She liked to show me pictures of him."

"One last question, Ms. Phillips. Other than the work problem you referred to, did your friend seem well-adjusted or unhappy?"

Resnik wasn't going to let this pass. "Objection, Your Honor. Calls for a psychological conclusion beyond the expertise of this witness."

"Sustained," came Loewenstein's laconic response. "The question will be stricken from the record and the jury will ignore it. Carry on, Mr. Spencer, if you please."

Jo Ann Phillips had played her minor role. "Your witness, Mr. Resnik," I said.

He wasted no time. "As you said earlier, Ms. Phillips, it's been almost fifteen years since you've seen the defendant, hasn't it."

"Yes, yes it has," came her subdued response.

"So it's fair to say, isn't it, that you know virtually nothing about her personal or family life since then."

Phillips hesitated, then said, "I guess that's right, I don't. I wish we'd kept in touch."

"Nothing about her personal or family life," Resnik repeated. "What about her work history during the last fifteen years? Can you tell us anything about that?"

Phillips slowly shook her head.

"For the court record, please answer yes or no."

"I know nothing about that, no."

"In fact, Ms. Phillips, all you really have are memories from a long time ago. You really know very little about the defendant's life at all, do you."

Abject, the witness sat there unresponsive for several seconds. Resnik was content to wait, aware that her hesitation was to his advantage.

"No," Phillips finally conceded, "I don't."

A note of ridicule in his tone, Resnik said, "No more questions for this witness, Your Honor."

"Redirect, Mr. Spencer?"

"None, Your Honor," I replied.

Jo Ann Phillips cast a long sympathetic look at Lucy as she walked slowly toward the exit.

Bree touched my elbow. "Resnik won't have such an easy time with our next one, will he."

I couldn't suppress my grin. "Who knows? Maybe she'll have taken a happy pill."

Bree snickered.

When I heard Ben's, "Who the hell is that," I couldn't help but laugh. Kate Barns was wearing the same beat-up work clothes she had on when I'd seen her last in my office.

"Fuck me," Ben whispered to Lucy's right.

Maybe you, not me, I wrote in a note and passed it down. Lucy chuckled as she handed it to him. Ben made an obscene noise with his mouth.

The moment of levity wasn't limited to our table. There was tittering throughout the courtroom as Kate, in wrinkled beige khaki slacks and faded plaid men's shirt, shambled toward the witness box. Any good mood tablets she might have taken had to have worn off. Her round puffy face looked decidedly out-of-sorts. Beware, Allan Resnik. Not a lady to trifle with.

Other than what might have been a nod, Kate made no response to my greeting. Then, abruptly, she said, "Can we get this over, Mr. Spencer? I'm expecting the TV man this afternoon."

"It shouldn't take all that long," I assured her. "Do you see Lucy Jackson in this courtroom? If so, would you kindly point her out."

An 'Are you some kind of idiot' expression crossed

her face, then she turned in her seat and rudely pointed an index finger at our table.

"Of course I know her," she quipped. "Why do you think I'm here?"

"Yes, thank you. How long have you known Lucy Jackson?"

More civilly, she replied, "'Bout six years or so, I guess."

"In what situation did you see her most?"

"The only time I ever saw her was at soccer games where my son played. I thought you knew that."

"I did, but we need this information for the Court, so answer the questions as best as you can, please. Was Ms. Jackson alone when you saw her at these games?"

"Of course not. Her son was on my boy's team. She usually brought her daughter with her. Oh yeah, I forgot. Her husband came to the games sometimes. He was a coach when they needed him."

"Can you please describe how you came to know her."

"We sat together a bunch a times. We went together to a lotta games, you know?"

"Was there anything unusual about your time together with Lucy Jackson that you can remember?"

Kate made a face. "Too bad we can't talk normal in here or I'd tell ya exactly what happened sometimes. Like you told me to, I'll try to keep it clean."

More chuckling in the gallery.

"Like I said, Lucy and I, we sat together and talked sometimes, 'bout lotsa things. For some reason I could never figger out, her husband didn't like us carryin' on. We weren't doin' nothin', just yackin', that's all. He'd get real pissed sometimes, come up on the bleachers where we were and stand there next to Lucy, starin' at her. Not talkin' to her or anything, just glarin', if you get my drift. Then, like some schoolkid, he takes off his baseball cap and flips it around toward the back. Know what I mean? He was always frownin' when he did that. Lucy'd go all quiet and move away a little and wouldn't talk to me no more. Made no sense."

"Did that sort of thing happen more than once?"

"'Bout half the time, I'd say. Wasn't just with me it happened either."

That, Kate hadn't told me. Nor was it in Lucy's diary.

"Made no difference who she was talkin' to, he'd see her doin' it and up he'd come if he was at the game. 'Nother thing. Okay. Most of us at those games were women, I admit it. Some guys came too though. Never saw Lucy sittin' next to one of 'em, not ever. Her husband with that cap of his turned around backwards, he looked like an idiot, I can tell you. I asked her once why he did that, but she wouldn't say anything. She just turned away. I'd tell you what I think of him, but not in here, I guess."

"One last question, if you don't mind. About how many years ago did all this start?"

Kate reached up to scratch her head and frowned. "I don't know, let's see. My boy's nineteen now and he was a junior in high school when he started playin' soccer, so musta been three or four years ago. All that crap with her husband didn't start right away though. That was only in the last couple a years, I think."

I thanked her and turned her over to Resnik.

"Ms. Barns, is it all that strange that a husband should come up on the stands to chat with his wife and daughter? You make Pete Jackson sound like a villain for doing that."

Kate gave him a scathing look. "Resnik, is that what your name is? Well, listen up. Course there's nuthin' odd about someone's husband comin' up to say hello durin' a game. Happens all the time. But when some dude comes marchin' up, looks all pissed off and doesn't say a word, stands there glarin' at his wife, then, for no reason, slowly takes off his cap and turns it 'round the other way and stays there for another minute, glarin', then takes off, I'd call that weird, wouldn't you, or are you one of those kinds a guys who'd do somethin like that. Are you?"

Resnik blinked. "Ms. Barns, I'll remind you we're in court and not on a soccer field."

"It's called a pitch," Kate snapped.

Momentarily, Resnik looked confused. "You're not here to make comments of your own," he said, "but to answer questions. Please keep your personal observations to yourself. You said Mr. Jackson came up to see his wife not just with you but with other people. Would you be prepared to give us their names?"

A mistake by Resnik, or was there something he knew that we did not?

Kate's grin was wolfish. "You want names, Resnik? I'll give you names, and you know something else? I'll bet they'll all say the same damn things as I did. You want names? I can remember them. Got a good memory for names. I'll write 'em down, you give me a paper and pencil."

Mentally, I smiled. Resnik had put his foot into a fresh one.

"Not at present, thank you. We'll contact you if we need them."

"In a pig's eye, he will," Ben muttered.

"I'll let you in on somethin' else that really bothered me, you know?"

Resnik tried to stop her, but by the time he'd turned his face to the judge for help, Kate had finished what she had to say.

"Back then at those soccer games, Lucy's daughter was just a slip of a thing, like a little mouse she was. Never once did I see her father say a thing to her or even smile at her when he came up on the stands. A real asshole, that one."

Disgusted, Resnik said he had no further questions.

"Redirect, Mr. Spencer?" Loewenstein inquired.

I said no and Kate was released. The judge adjourned court until two that afternoon.

"That guy better start chalkin' up some points or your..."—he was about to say girlfriend as he always had but prudently changed his mind—"Vicky's gonna hang him out to dry."

All the points in the world weren't going to help us, I reflected. We somehow had to convince an aloof jury to disregard California's penalties for premeditated homicide. In light of Mia's disclosures that morning concerning her physical relationship with her father, I had fewer fears about long-term imprisonment for my client. Incarceration, however, remained a probability unless we could clearly demonstrate to jurors that Lucy genuinely believed there was no one who could help her protect her daughter.

Jacqueline Parks had smiles for everyone in the courtroom as she walked through the door of the witness room and made her way to the stand. Though I knew her to be forty, she seemed closer to her early thirties in trendy clothes and attractive pageboy hairstyle. I couldn't decide whether her eyes that were always moving were brown or hazel. She had a friendly look.

Thanking Jackie for having come, I said, "You know the defendant in this trial, don't you. Could you point her out to us, please."

As Jo Ann Phillips had done, Jackie turned, smiled at Lucy and said hello.

"Could you please tell the Court how long you've known each other?"

"It has to be ten years, at least," Jackie said.

"How did you two meet?"

"I was a volunteer in the central library where I used to see her every week. She used to ask me for advice on what to read. We'd go out for lunch sometimes and talk about books and things."

"Assuming you've known each other for ten years, that would have been back in 2004. Does that sound correct?"

"About then, yes, I think so."

"Thinking back to that time, how would you describe Lucy Jackson as a person, from a behavioral standpoint, I mean."

Resnik made to object, but doubtless decided he had insufficient grounds. My question did not require expertise on the part of the witness. Jackie thought for a moment before she spoke.

"She was friendly, easygoing, fun to be around. Nothing jumps out at me, at least not then. Actually, there was something I should mention. I've always been into clothes, you know? Been that way since I was small. Lucy was the same. She looked good in everything."

"Did the two of you talk on the phone at that time?"

"Occasionally, but not all that much. Just to arrange lunch dates and things."

"Was your relationship with Lucy Jackson pretty much the same in 2007?"

Without hesitation, Jackie said, "No. It wasn't the same at all."

"In what ways were things different?" I asked.

"First off, I hardly ever saw her at the library anymore. She came sometimes, but I didn't see her much. I volunteered in the mornings and she had to come in the afternoons."

"Any other differences?"

"You'd have to really know Lucy to know what I mean. She used to be bouncy, really lively, a lotta personality. 2007, 2008, she seemed to have lost her umph. Oh yeah. She used to wear really pretty skirts and dresses and nice blouses. A few years later, she was almost always wearing pants. She just didn't seem to care all that much anymore."

"Okay, fine. If you don't mind, let's jump ahead three years more or so to, let's say, 2011. Did you see Lucy Jackson much at that time?"

Jackie's face grew somber. "Fact is, Mr. Spencer, I hardly ever saw her then. She wouldn't answer when I phoned and she didn't come to the library anymore. I wasn't volunteering then but I still went pretty regular."

"Were you curious about why you'd lost contact?"

"Yeah, sort of, I was. I guess I thought she just

didn't want to see me anymore so why bother. We didn't get back together until recently."

"Until recently," I echoed. "How did that come about?"

Jackie seemed distressed. "It was just last summer. I don't really know why I went, I just did. I decided to drive to her house. I'd been there lots of times."

"What happened?"

"I couldn't believe it. Lucy looked a wreck. I could barely make her talk. Finally, she asked me in, but she didn't want to, I think."

"Did she tell you what was wrong?"

"I kept asking her, but she kept shaking her head and saying no. She said no one could help her with her problem."

"What problem?" I queried.

"That's just it! She wouldn't tell me. Finally, I got it out of her that it was about her marriage, but that's all she'd say. I kept telling her she didn't have to live like that, that people could help her. She'd be okay, but she kept repeating that nobody could help her with her problems. I asked her where her car was. She told me her husband took it away from her just days ago. I felt sick about it all, I can tell you."

"You're absolutely sure she didn't tell you what kinds of problems she was having."

"The only thing I found out from her was that her husband took her car and that the woman who worked for them for years and helped with the children had been let go. Lucy's husband fired her, she told me."

"Again, Ms. Parks, thank you for coming. Your witness, Mr. Resnik."

It looked as though he intended to bypass Jackie altogether, flipping through notes. Finally, Loewenstein had to call out to him.

"Mr. Resnik, would you kindly—"

"I apologize, Your Honor. I do have a question or two if you will permit." Resnik rose and moved to the podium, his eyes pinned on Jackie. "You did say you hadn't been in touch with the defendant hardly at all during the last three years, did you not?"

"That's right."

"I, and I'm sure the jury, would like to know why, after three years being out of touch, you suddenly decided to visit her at her house. Why did you do that, Ms. Parks?"

Though Bree had discussed this issue several times with her, Jackie's face grew puzzled. "It was a whim, I guess. I hadn't heard about Lucy from any of my friends and I hadn't seen her anywhere. I guess I just wanted to see if she was okay."

"So, if I have this picture right," Resnik stated, "you saw the defendant only once during the last three years. Is that true?"

"Yes. I already said so."

Resnik considered his witness for several seconds, his eyes remaining briefly on her hair, then going to her face and momentarily to her front before returning to her eyes. His scrutiny had a clinical aspect.

"Tell me, Ms. Parks, and I beg you not to be offended by my questions. They have no such intent, believe me. Does your hair always look like you just emerged from the stylist? Is your face always so beautifully made-up? And are your clothes always so well-coordinated?"

Though the slight flush on Jackie's face was evidence of pleasure, her wary expression showed she was no ingenue. There was no suggestion of a smile on her attractive face. I was about to object on the grounds of the ambiguity of the compound question when Jackie beat me to the punch.

"If you're asking me, Mr. Resnik, if my husband sees me like this every morning, I can tell you that he does not."

"Ah. So you admit, Ms. Parks, that you're not always at your best, that there may be times when you'd prefer not to be seen by other people."

By then, I'd had enough. "Objection, Your Honor.

Counsel is entirely beyond scope. I fail to see—"

"Enough, Mr. Spencer," the judge retorted. "I agree. If you have nothing more cogent to ask this witness, Mr. Resnik, then kindly sit down and allow us to carry on."

"Your Honor, if you please. One or two more short questions and the motive for my earlier ones will be clear."

Loewenstein regarded him. "Very well. I'll give you a little leeway, but that's all."

"Thank you, Your Honor. To continue where we were, Ms. Parks, will you agree that there may be times when you're alone at home during the morning and you have no plans to go out and you've made no particular attempt to appear attractive. Would you agree to this?"

Aware of Resnik's intent and disgusted, Jackie replied, "As I'm sure you know, Mr. Resnik, such days exist for everyone, me included."

"You saw the defendant only once during a period of three years when, according to your own words, she neither expected you nor wanted you to come into the house. Couldn't that have been one of the defendant's bad days, so to speak? Couldn't that have easily been the case?"

"I'm sure what I saw that day wasn't exceptional," Jackie said.

Rather sternly, Resnik admonished, "It's not your opinions we're looking for, Ms. Parks. You've given great weight in your testimony to the unkempt appearance of the defendant when you saw her, obviously attempting to convince the Court that that was her normal state."

"Objection, Your Honor. Counsel's testifying."

"Sustained. Mr. Resnik's last statement will be stricken. The jury is directed to ignore it. Mr. Resnik, I've about run out of patience with this monologue of yours. Either finish up or let this witness go."

"Ms. Parks, you testified that you attempted to get the defendant to talk about her marriage when you went to see her that one time. Allow me to pose a hypothetical question to you. If you were having marital problems, are you one of these people who would be willing to discuss these problems, even with someone who dropped in on you just like that, someone you hadn't seen in years? Would you do that?"

Jackie's pretty mouth became a thin straight line. She was angry that Resnik had managed to trivialize what she'd said. She sat for nearly fifteen seconds, searching for an apt response. She found none. Finally, bowing her head slightly, she replied, "No, no I guess I wouldn't."

"One other thing," Resnik said. "You spoke of the loss of the defendant's car and the fact that she no longer had her maid. Couldn't both these events simply be a way to economize, Ms. Parks, instead of punishments by the husband as you make out?"

For a moment, Jackie appeared as though she hadn't understood, then her expression changed. "Mr. Resnik, are you serious? Do you know anything at all about Pete Jackson? Economizing measures. Is that what you said? Let's see. Jackson takes Lucy's car away and fires her maid while he drives around a two-hundred-thousand-dollar Lamborghini. Oh, and let's not forget the super expensive sports car he gives his son Lucy told me about when I was there. Is that what you call economizing, Mr. Resnik?"

Since there were no further questions on either side for the witness, Jackie, dejected and sad for Lucy, left the courtroom.

"She socked it to him, didn't she," Bree commented, "but we're not doing all that well, are we. Am I ever glad it's not me up there asking questions."

"Poor Jackie," Lucy said. "She was trying to help me up there and that asshole kept—"

I shook my head. "No, Lucy, not an asshole. He was just doing the best with what he had to work with, which wasn't much. So far, we haven't given him anything to get his teeth into. Our three witnesses up to this point, plus the next one, are sort of setting the stage for us for our big push that comes at the end."

I'd liked there to have been more substance to what I'd just said. It would have been good if Jo Ann, Jackie, Kate and, finally, Susan could have been more than props. We needed more than a few character witnesses who, as Resnik had justly said, had only marginal knowledge of Lucy's recent life. Our case was going to hinge almost entirely on the two last people I'd be calling to the stand, a dismaying prospect since so much could go wrong.

"Still can't believe it," Ben remarked, "you snaggin' the captain like you did. He'll actually be here tomorrow?"

"Nope, don't think so. Loewenstein's clerk told me the judge'll be out of town til next Monday. She's going to call a recess."

"No shit! You watch. Give that bugger a few days to diddle with and he'll worm out of it, you'll see. Guy never shows up in court, not for nobody. When's the last time you saw him there?"

My old friend and partner played many roles in and out of court, comic relief not the least important of them. That day, I'd like to have shut him up about Lonigan, who was to be our secret weapon if things worked out. He absolutely had to be there.

"He'll come if I have to drag him by the ears," I said. "You'll see."

"A hundred a my hard-earned dollars say he won't."

If for no other reason than to buoy up my flagging confidence, I did a rare thing for me. I took him up on his bet. His grin looked a mile wide. Judge Loewenstein's voice broke into my reverie.

"We do have sufficient time for another witness, Mr. Spencer, should you wish to call one."

Before I could respond, Resnik rose. "Sidebar, Your Honor, if you please."

"Will lead counsels be enough or do we need the entire team?" the judge asked.

I mentally grinned. The four of us gathered around

the bench would look portentous and a little silly. Still, it was considerate of her to ask.

Resnik and I got up.

"Keep it down, gentlemen," the judge admonished. "The court reporter doesn't need to be in on this. What is it you need, Mr. Resnik?"

"Your Honor," he said, "I'd like to know if the defense's next witness is going to waste the Court's time as the last three have. Mr. Spencer's case may be weak, but this is ridiculous."

Inscrutable as ever, Loewenstein's eyes swiveled to me. "I must say, I tend to agree," she commented, her lips barely moving so no one but us could hear. "I'll want a very solid reason from you, Mr. Spencer, if you intend to carry on as before. I don't like wasting the Court's time. You know that."

"Your Honor," I responded, "as will be obvious to both you and my colleague here, our three previous witnesses and the one to come have not been called for evidentiary reasons. The defense claims, as you will recall, that the defendant acted to shield her daughter in the only way she believed available to her. It is vital that we establish as best we can why Mrs. Jackson was convinced that she had no other choice. The four witnesses we will have heard today are here for background to help us do this. I assure the Court that our focus will shift dramatically with our last two witnesses when court resumes. Please remember, Your Honor, we are seeking to establish the defendant's state of mind when she killed her husband rather than providing evidence of the more conventional kind."

"Very well," Loewenstein replied, "as long as you confirm you will be looking for more substantive information with your final witnesses."

"That I can promise you."

We thanked the judge and the two of us returned to our respective tables, a smug and rather arrogant expression on Resnik's handsome face.

*

Susan Carpenter, near forty, looked statuesque as she made her way to and settled in the witness chair. Regal might have been a better word with her Patrician nose and high cheekbones, her impeccable hairstyle and tailored suit. From the neck down, she could have been Lucy's twin in just about every sense. She was the CEO for a recently established medical appliance company in Santa Lucia.

In much the same way as her three predecessors, Sue immediately identified Lucy at our table.

"To dispense with unnecessary questions later, let me ask you. Have you been in much contact with Lucy Jackson during the past three years?"

"No I haven't. We seem to have lost touch with one another."

"Did you see much of her before, 2010, 2011?"

"Sometimes. I used to visit her at home a fair bit, for selfish reasons, I must admit, but we enjoyed each other's company."

"Can you explain what you meant by selfish reasons."

Sue looked down briefly at her ample breasts then back at me. "It doesn't take a rocket scientist to see that Lucy and I look a lot alike, from here on down at least," she said, touching her shoulders. "It's, it's not always easy to find good fits in decent shops. Clothes are either too big here or too small there, you get my point." Everyone in the courtroom did. "So, I used to go to Lucy's to borrow dresses and things. We entertained a lot back then because of my husband's job. It's different now."

"May I ask why you went to Ms. Jackson's house in particular?"

Sue smiled. "Easy. She had gorgeous things. Lucy knew how to dress. Clothes loved her. She didn't go out all that much anymore so she was glad to share."

"Ms. Carpenter, I called you here to recount an incident that we believe will tell the Court something important about the defendant's life. Are you aware of the event in question?"

Sue's head came up and her eyes grew hard. "I went to Lucy's house on a Friday afternoon. It was September seventeenth, 2010, I remember."

"Before you go on, Ms. Carpenter, can you tell us why you'd remember a precise date like that back in 2010?"

"No problem. The company was giving a big party for my husband because of his promotion. He's the owner now. Anyway, I couldn't find the party dress I wanted. Couldn't find it anywhere at any price. I thought Lucy might just have something like it so I went over there."

"Was she expecting you?"

Frowning, Sue said, "Yeah, I think so. I called her before I went."

"Did she have the dress?"

"Did she have the dress?" Sue parroted. "Lucy didn't have a damn thing. I made her show me."

"What do you mean, she didn't have a thing? She must have had clothes to wear?"

"Her dresses, all those gorgeous dresses and skirts and blazers and even some party gowns she bought and her husband bought her were all gone, every one."

"Gone where?" I asked.

"The bastard threw 'em out. She told me, one night, he tore all of her pretty things out of her closet and got rid of them."

"Got rid of them where?"

"She didn't know, at least she didn't tell me."

"Do you know why he threw them out?"

"Damn right I do. Lucy's pretty and she's got a nice body. Pete, her husband, complained men looked at her when she wore her pretty things so he got rid of them. All he left her was crummy stuff no self-respecting woman would wear outside the house. Didn't keep him from catting around, oh no, but he wouldn't let her out the door."

Not bothering to rise, Resnik called out, "Objection,

Your Honor. Witness is embroidering."

"Sustained," Loewenstein said. "The last statement by the witness will be stricken. Ms. Carpenter, kindly refrain from expressing your opinions and just answer the questions."

"Ms. Carpenter," I asked, "you were in Lucy Jackson's bedroom, correct, and you saw her closet?"

"Absolutely, I did. I saw every single thing in there."

"Were there any attractive clothes left that you could see?"

In a tired voice, again failing to rise, Resnik declared, "Objection. Question asked and answered."

"Sustained," the judge said. "Do you have anything else for this witness, Mr. Spencer?"

"No further questions, Your Honor."

"Mr. Resnik?"

Pausing, contemplating Sue as though she were some oddity, he answered, "There's nothing we're likely to learn from this witness, Your Honor. No questions."

"Very well," came Loewenstein's stock reply. "The witness is free to go. Court is adjourned until ten o'clock next Monday morning."

Lucy turned to me. "Forrest, for the love of God, when will this be over? It's awful how they're treating old friends of mine who only want to help."

"Not long now, Luce," I answered. "One more day, possibly two of trial, that's all."

"Then the jury comes back with their verdict, right?"

I nodded.

"Yeah, well, we all know what that's gonna be. I know I agreed to have supper out with you and Bree, but I'm too pooped. I just want to go home and lay down for a while."

"Is Alex still there with you?"

"Oh yeah, he is. He's been wonderful, him and Lily. Can we make dinner sometime this weekend?"

I gave a rueful smile. "You've obviously forgotten how kids control your life. I have to find out what Trina and Andy are up to before I can commit to anything, but we'll be in touch. We should be able to work something out."

Bree smiled at her. "We'll get together, don't worry," she said.

Lucy chuckled. "Looks like kids aren't the only ones you have to pay attention to."

Still smiling, a contented look on her face, Bree replied, "He's adjusting pretty fast, I'm glad to say. I think he kinda likes it."

Chapter 23

Weekends at the Spencer home bore little resemblance to what they'd been. I used to count on them for quality time with the twins. No longer. The older Andy and Trina grew, the more difficult it became to rouse them from their beds on Saturdays and Sundays.

Rarely were the three, or even two, of us sharing popcorn on weekend nights as we watched videos in our living room. One twin or the other, too often both, were out on sleepovers. Ball games with Andy in the backyard or culinary ventures with Trina still occurred, but only if their friends were unavailable.

Though I missed our time together, these changes did allow me more one-on-one time with Bree, which I was glad to have.

I'd learned of the twins' plans days before, which allowed me to wangle a Saturday evening dinner invitation at Miguel's and Isabel's. Andy was on a friend's family's last camping weekend for the year. Trina had invited her new friend, Sylvia, to stay with her at home with Lupe as complicit chaperone. I looked forward to seeing the Martinez family and even more to my night with Bree with only sleeping Maya for company.

As was his custom, Miguel handed me a frosty glass

of beer as I walked through his front door. It was followed up by hugs from the three females in the house, two of whom reached just past my knee. The house was redolent with Isabel's kitchen magic. No simple tacos, enchiladas, rice and beans for her. Though a Chicana, her cooking, especially her sauces, were more reminiscent of central Mexico than California. She was a true artist.

"I know you may not want to hear this, Forrest, but Andy's turning out to be one of my star students. He's a natural if I ever saw one. You're lucky we don't go for all those colored belts and tests and crap or you'd be broke, you know?"

"Yeah, I expect so. Tell me something, Miguel. Isn't there usually a philosophical or meditative component to most of the martial arts? I always thought so."

"Absolutely," Miguel said. "It's probably not a good thing, but recently, we're not focusing as much on that stuff. Problem is, kids and older guys wanta learn how to fight. They don't give a damn about the other stuff."

"But that other stuff, as you call it, can be important, can't it?"

"Of course it can, in many ways, in fact... You ever see any of these mixed martial arts fights on TV? They're pretty rough, I can tell you. That's what people are wanting to see, amigo, the hard stuff. It's in all of us men. It just comes out in different ways."

I nodded, thinking about what he'd said. "But surely," I rejoined, "a lot of parents aren't looking for hard stuff for their kids. Don't they see martial arts as a good physical and mental exercise?"

"Most do, yes. I agree with you. It's something I'm having trouble with as you know. That's probably one of the reasons you're here tonight, right? You want to pull Andy out."

I shook my head. "No, you're wrong. I don't want to pull Andy out. But I don't want him to just focus on technique either. Andy needs structure in his life. He needs discipline. I don't want him to be in school all day, dreaming about how he's going to put someone on the mat. His mother would crucify me if she thought I was letting him do that."

Miguel sipped his beer and regarded me sadly. "That's what you want and that's what most people want, I know. I studied those things when I started martial arts years ago and I really liked it. I liked it then. It's not that I'm against the moral and philosophical principles they teach you. They're good things for all of us. My problem is, probably cuz I got so good at it, I got interested in technique, mainly, and that's how I still am. Trouble is, nobody, 'cept people in the military, can earn a living doing that, not around here. People don't have the money to learn it, and there's no real use for fighting skills like that here anyway. Good thing, I guess."

Isabel must have guessed that Miguel and I needed quiet. Despite her work in the kitchen, she was keeping the girls close to her.

"Are there people here in Santa Lucia who are willing to take lessons in combat of the kind you like to teach, enough to keep your interest?"

Thinking about this, he said, "Oh yeah, they exist alright, just not a lot of 'em. And, most of the guys who are aren't all that reliable. They pay up okay, but they don't always show up for training." Miguel's expression turned vexed. "Forrest, why all these questions? What are you getting at? Spill it!"

"I will, if you promise to listen for a few minutes and not interrupt."

He considered, then shrugged. "Fire away."

"Okay," I began, not entirely sure how to proceed. "It seems to me, we've got several things that are clear here. We've got an established martial arts school that has the potential to be successful. We have an owner who's highly trained and skilled and obviously a good teacher. We have two different student groups, one interested in martial arts in general and the smaller one, interested in acquiring combat skill. Am I on target so far?"

Miguel nodded.

"Okay. So much for the positives. For the negatives, because of his own interests, the owner's not able to easily keep the two groups separate in his mind. He tends to think of the younger and larger group as trainees for the smaller combat group. Is that a fair assessment?"

Miguel had begun to scowl. "Fair, maybe," he said, his eyes narrowing, "but what's all that got to do with us? That's what's botherin' me right now."

"I remind you, Miguel, you promised not to interrupt. Let me explain. If you designed the courses and you had another instructor who could take most of the first group, you could focus on the combat group where your interest lies. That way, you could keep the two groups separate if you tried. You could put a minimum age for starting combat instruction, for example, say, eighteen. That way, parents with younger kids wouldn't have to worry."

Miguel's resistant attitude hadn't changed.

"As I see it, to accomplish all this, you'd need to do three things. First, you'd have to pay off your silent partner so you'd own the school outright. Second, you'd have to renovate the school to accommodate the two separate student groups who could be trained, each separate from the other. Third thing, of course, you'd need financial backing."

Miguel waved dismissively. "You think I'm into robbin' banks, Forrest? Why don't we just stop talkin' about all this and drink beer and shoot the bull. Be a shitload more profitable than what we're doin' here."

"I'm almost done. Three more short things and then I'll quit. I promise. First thing, I'd like Andy to keep working with you or, at least, under your direction. I think you're good for him. Second thing, I'd like very much to see that school project of yours work. Assuming it's a success, there'd be enough money for Isabel to keep up her nursing studies which would be a real good thing.

Third, I'd like to invest in the project, not as a partner or anything but just as a financial backer. I'm no money expert, far from it, but I've got a good feeling the scheme will work. If it does, you pay me back over time with modest interest and we both win. If the project doesn't make it, then, you can't say you didn't try. As long as you assure me that you'll run the two schools separately as we talked about, that's all the word I need. There'll be no one looking over your shoulder or telling you what to do. I've got a hundred thousand dollars to invest in a startup which is yours if you want it. Would that be sufficient to pay off your partner and rebuild the school?"

Miguel still looked grim, but there was a speculative gleam in his eye. We sat there for a couple of minutes, not talking.

Finally, Miguel said, "I might not be in a position to pay you back anything for a couple of years, Forrest. I'd have to build up a clientele first. The interest would mount up."

"Not at today's rates, it wouldn't," I responded. "I'm not looking for a sure thing, financially speaking. I'd like to speculate on a venture that appeals to me that I think will work. If it doesn't, then it doesn't, no one's fault. The thing is, Miguel, if you really think this could fly, then go for it."

Shaking his head as though it was a doubtful thing, he said, "I'll have to talk this over with Isabel tonight, you know that."

"Of course you do. If she agrees as I hope she does, then we'll draw up what minimal papers we have to and the money will be available to you after that."

I was about to ask for another beer when Isabel appeared in the kitchen doorway. She had a very determined look as she contemplated her husband.

"I won't say anything to Forrest right now cuz I'll start to cry," she said. "Miguelito, tonight we gonna have a special dinner to celebrate. We don't need to talk tonight. It's your dream, mi querido, you know that. It'll work out, you'll see." Looking at me, she said, "Your glass is empty. I bring you another one." Lita and Evangelina were tugging at Isabel's skirt and whining as she left the living room.

"And who says women don't wear the pants, mi amigo," Miguel rejoined, excitement reflected in his eyes. "I guess you know, you just made one Chicana very happy."

Ben, Bree and I had gathered in my office at just before nine on Monday morning, an hour before court was to begin. Ben was looking at our shortened witness list.

"So you took off Silvergold? Good thing. How come?"

"Due to my ignorance about the rights of minor children in this state, we've had to make some last-minute changes in strategy, beneficial to us, actually. Originally, we were going to argue that Lucy killed Pete because she'd been led to believe she had no recourse."

"This state of mind thing of yours and Bree's."

"That's right. We weren't going to try to prove she didn't have a choice, but that she thought she didn't."

"Pretty shaky stuff," Ben commented.

I nodded.

"You're right, it was," Bree said. "It turns out that, because of California child protection laws, Lucy really didn't have a choice in the matter, strange as that seems. As someone who was in family law before, I should have known this. It would have saved us a lot of grief. It's a technicality in a way, but an important one in our case."

"What," Ben exclaimed, "you're gonna try to convince the jury that Lucy had no choice but to plan to kill the guy to protect her daughter? None of this belief stuff. She had no choice. You guys gone off the rails? You'll never make it. No way." Ben genuinely looked distressed.

"Not off the rails, old friend," I riposted. "Back on them where we should have been. Don't feel cut out.

We've just come to this ourselves. Since we're not focusing on state of mind very much anymore, we don't need our psychiatrist to distract us."

"That's about the only smart thing I'm seein' in all this. So it's down to two, Cap Lonigan, assumin' he'll appear which he won't, and Lucy, that right?"

"That's right," I said. "I've gotta tell you a little story that'll amuse you, Ben. Apparently Lonigan sent a note to the Court that, because he was required elsewhere, he'd have to send a subordinate. That note didn't seem to impress Loewenstein all that much. According to the judge's clerk, who was nice enough to phone me Saturday morning, her boss sent a note back to Lonigan, informing him he'd be heavily fined for contempt if he didn't honor the subpoena. She didn't tell me how much the fine would be, but she seemed pretty sure Lonigan would be there."

"You're joshin' me. That didn't really happen."

Bree was looking at me strangely. "The judge's clerk?" she asked. "She phoned you at home on the weekend? You didn't tell me that. Anyway, guess we'll all find out in about an hour if he comes, won't we."

"Christ, this thing could end today then, less you're countin' on keepin' Lucy up there for a long time."

"Today, no," I countered. "I doubt it. Don't forget, we have closing arguments that Loewenstein'll put over to the next day. Probably just as well."

Ben rubbed his hands together. "I might just lose my hundred bucks, but this is somethin' I'm lookin' forward to, least I think, unless you guys go off the deep end up there."

Struggling to keep a straight face, I said, "It should be exciting. Bree's going to take Lonigan and I'm taking Lucy."

Months earlier, it would have taken minutes for Bree to settle down. Her stunned expression lasted all of two seconds. Ben knew me too well to react.

"Just don't embarrass me up there," Bree ordered. "The judge associates me with you. I kind of like her."

*

Ten o'clock came and went. Everyone was there but Captain Lonigan. The bailiff's echoed call yielded silence, then nervous shuffling in the gallery. My stomach was in knots as I watched Loewenstein read a note handed to her by her clerk.

In the subdued courtroom, she announced, "Court will be in recess for fifteen minutes. Jurors are to wait in the deliberation room."

The judge stood up and returned to her chambers. The buzz of speculative voices increased.

Ben, grinning broadly and looking over at me, chided, "What did I tell you. Easiest hundred bucks I ever earned. I wonder who they'll send." His grin widened. "Maybe you'll have another go at old Katy. Wouldn't that be somethin'!"

I could have hugged Bree. She, smiling sweetly, said, "If I didn't know better, Ben, I think you might like that. Does Cassie know about her?"

An unspoken expletive on his lips, with disgust, he turned away.

"So what happens if he doesn't come?" Lucy asked.

"Whether or not Lonigan shows up, we'll eventually get someone high up enough in the force who can address rules and policy. That's mandatory for our case."

Things settled down as Loewenstein returned, the jurors, like puppies, following in after her. A moment later, the witness door opened and in walked Captain Lonigan.

"Well, I'll be damned," Ben whispered. "The old man actually showed up."

No need for the judge's pen. The sounds of breathing and the air conditioner were all we heard. The police captain, in full uniform with two gold bars on his shoulder, settled in the witness box and was sworn. He'd be prominent in tomorrow's press.

"Your Honor," I said, "I would request that this witness be deemed hostile."

Loewenstein's response was immediate. "So

deemed."

I could now proceed as though I were examining Lonigan in cross, allowing me to lead, contradict, even badger, provided I didn't overplay my hand.

We spent the first five minutes establishing his credentials, which were impressive. It was he who was in command of Santa Lucia's police force. His immediate superior was our police chief. Like upper-echelon officers in the military, every aspect of Lonigan bespoke authority. He was thoroughly at ease, courteous yet brisk. Normally, witnesses of his stature were aware of the reasons for which they'd been called. In the present instance, I suspected this might not be true. I went straight to the point.

"Captain Lonigan, my questions to you presume expert knowledge about rules and policies that govern our police force. The knowledge you have that may best serve the Court may be what instructions you would issue to your officers in certain situations. Does this seem acceptable to you?"

Smiling affably, the captain said, "That depends what you ask, I guess. What is it you'd like to know?"

"Let's begin, if we may, with a situation that would probably be routinely handled by your officers, who'd see no need to trouble you about the matter."

Lonigan waited.

"A woman calls to complain that she believes her adolescent daughter is being sexually assaulted by the girl's father. Would you tell the Court, please, what would typically happen in a case like that?"

Lonigan nodded. "Officers would be dispatched to investigate the complaint." The witness, infrequently though he might appear on the stand, was a pro. He answered no more than the question he was asked.

"Very well. Thank you. What form would that investigation take?"

Though Lonigan's outward demeanor hadn't changed, his eyes left little doubt that his mind had gone into high gear. Policy and general rules that were to be interpreted if necessary were one thing. Discussion of procedure turned up microscopes that often revealed unpleasant things. Temporizing, the Captain replied, “That depends on the situation as I’m sure you know, Mr. Spencer. If only the woman calling in the complaint is home, that would be one thing. If—”

“Excuse me if I interrupt you, Captain. To save time, I’ll be more specific. The mother calls and, as you have explained, officers arrive to investigate. They find three people at home, the mother who telephoned, her daughter and her husband. The mother continues to insist that assault is taking place while the daughter vehemently denies it. The husband, a highly reputable and well-known man in Santa Lucia, confirms his daughter’s position. He attributes his wife’s complaint to her being overwrought. In such a case where the adolescent daughter insists that nothing is going on, with the backup of her well-known father, what would your investigating officers do?”

Lonigan, in no hurry, thought about this for a while. Resnik’s and Alvarez’s eyes were glued to him.

“Mr. Spencer,” Lonigan finally said, “you’re aware, of course, that the daughter’s and father’s denials don’t prove the mother’s wrong, do they. Quite the reverse, in fact. The woman’s fears could be very valid.”

“All very true, Captain, but you didn’t answer my question. Given the denials in the case I cited, what would your officers do?”

“They’d probably take a report with statements from the three and submit the case to Child Protective Services for further investigation. That’s what they’d likely do.” Lonigan concluded his statement with a confident nod.

“So, let me be sure I understand you, Captain. Your statement sounds very reasonable, but I want to be sure I have it straight. Your officers sent to investigate don’t actually investigate at all, according to you. They file a report and a recommendation to the CPS. Did I get it right?”

Again, the barely perceptible flicker in the captain's eyes. He sensed trouble, but of a kind he couldn't see. "Mr. Spencer, you know as well as I do that I don't make the laws. My job is to enforce them. Without a warrant, my officers are not allowed, without probable cause, to search for evidence. The CPS is much better suited to handle such things."

"Understood, Captain Lonigan, understood. Tell me. Would your officers react differently if the daughter agreed with her mother and accused her father of assault? What would happen then?"

"Ah, now that's an entirely different story. In most situations, if the child confirms assault and is willing to provide evidence and the father is present, the officers would very probably arrest the father and take the child in for medical examination."

"Very clear, Captain, thank you. What would happen if the only person submitting a complaint were the daughter herself and not the parents. What then?"

"Again, if the daughter's willing to provide names, evidence and such, she'd be taken in for medical examination in most cases and we'd attempt to apprehend the person accused of assaulting her."

"This has all been very helpful, thank you. Earlier, you said that your officers would very probably send a recommendation of some kind to Child Protective Services to follow up, correct?"

"That's right. They're the people who are trained to handle things like this, much more than we are."

"Very well. Do you know a person who works for the CPS named Sharon Lopez?"

I could see that Resnik wanted to derail this discussion whose objective he clearly understood. I'd been scrupulously careful, however, despite my latitude with hostile witnesses, to word my questions as unambiguously as I could, allowing him little room to intercede. To object and be rebuffed would not help him.

Lonigan's face lit up. "Why, yes, I know her well. She's the perfect person for cases like these. You should be talking to her instead of me. You'd learn more."

"Assume, Captain, that CPS people came to the home, as suggested, to investigate. What would you expect them to do that your officers could not do?"

Lonigan stammered for a moment, then said, "Look, Mr. Spencer, to be frank with you, I don't know all that much about their rules and procedures. I don't know exactly what they'd do. I assume they'd find out if assault had taken place, regardless of what the girl or the father said."

"Captain, it may interest you to know that we did precisely what you suggested. Ms. Lopez testified before you did. She told us that, without the consent of a twelve-year-old girl, nothing whatsoever could be done. We have since reviewed the California statutes that require consent from a girl who's reached that age that we can show you if necessary. Basically, if the twelve-year-old refuses to be examined or denies that assault has taken place, the CPS's hands are tied, seemingly as much as your officers' are."

At last, Resnik rose to his feet. "Objection, Your Honor. Counsel for the defense continues to take every possible occasion to testify. He's preaching rather than asking questions."

"Overruled, Mr. Resnik. I'd like to hear the remainder of this discussion."

Disconsolately, Resnik sat down.

"So, tell me, Captain. Are we to understand that even if incest is occurring in a woman's home that her daughter and husband deny, neither our police force nor our Child Protective Services can prevent this unless the girl agrees to cooperate? Is this conceivable?"

Lonigan's face had reddened and he was agitated. He couldn't have been pleased by the prospect of headlines and his picture on the front page. Leaning forward, in a raised voice, he proclaimed, "That's not at all what I said. You've turned my words around. We do everything we can to protect our citizens in this city, especially our children." He glared at me.

"Captain Lonigan, I believe that. I believe that's exactly what you do. I have not asked these questions to discredit the police or the CPS, both of which deserve our support and admiration. Allow me, please, to ask one more thing. May I do that?" I didn't require his permission, of course, but I hoped to calm him down to get on record what I needed him to say.

Letting out a long breath, he said, "Fire away, counselor, fire away."

"Thank you. If, as in the hypothetical case I have cited here, neither the police nor the CPS could intervene because of the refusal of the girl to cooperate, who else could the mother go to in order to get protection for her child?"

Another long sigh. Lonigan looked in vain to Resnik, who could only shrug. He fell back on platitudes.

"You've raised a situation that rarely happens. We do the best with what we have, but we can't possibly cover every base. I don't need to tell you that. What police force can?"

"With respect, Captain, could you please answer my question. Would you like me to repeat it?"

Waving me off, he said, "No, no, I know what you asked. In a case like that, I can't tell you what a woman in that situation could do. She'd surely have friends who could help her, the church maybe. As I said before, we don't make the laws that bind our hands sometimes. We're paid to uphold them. What else can we do?"

"So, Captain Lonigan, to summarize what you and another expert have said in this courtroom, a woman in the hypothetical situation I raised couldn't expect support from the authorities to prevent violation of her child."

Lonigan sat mute and rigid in the witness chair, unwilling to say more to crucify himself in the press. I waited ten seconds or so to allow the silence to have its impact on the jury, then thanked the witness and turned him over to Resnik for cross.

"Captain Lonigan, I have one question for you,

that's all. When we're desperate for help in non-life-threatening situations, has the environment in which you and I live become such a jungle that we can justify the premeditated killing of someone to solve our problem? Is that what we've come to?" Objectionable language on Resnik's part, but not worth contesting.

Now back in his comfort zone, Lonigan boomed out, "Most certainly not. Premeditated murder is still a crime, Mr. Resnik, no matter how you dress it up. You plan to murder someone, you pay the cost."

"Thank you very much for coming, Captain. No further questions."

Her small voice sounding far away, Loewenstein asked, "Redirect, Mr. Spencer?"

I declined. Lonigan got up, his dignity retrieved, and left. Court was adjourned until two o'clock that afternoon.

We had two hours before court reconvened, not enough time to find some quiet place for lunch to go over things one last time with Lucy.

Minutes after leaving the courthouse, the three of us were comfortably installed at Bree's, our sandwiches, fruit and juices awaiting us in the fridge. All of us would have been happier with chilled white wine. We sat cozily in the living room.

"Lucy," I said, "we're further along in our case than I thought we'd be at this point. Here's why. We've had three major hurdles to overcome. Number one, were you justified in your fear that your husband had or was going to sexually assault your daughter? That issue, as you know, no longer exists. Number two, given the probable agreement between father and daughter to deny everything, did you have any help available to you at all to shield your daughter from probable incest? We've come a long ways with testimony at the trial to indicate that, in your particular case, the authorities could not have intervened, that is, there was no assistance available to you. So far, so good. The third hurdle, as Mr. Resnik's one question to Captain Lonigan revealed, is whether, help available or not, killing someone was justifiable as your solution. Since neither your life nor Mia's was in jeopardy, strictly speaking, legally, it is not. Our job this afternoon and tomorrow morning during closing arguments will be to convince the jury that, legal or not, your action was the only reasonable one you had. This will be a hard sell unless we can demonstrate to jurors how scheming and manipulative Pete was to ensure his interests and his safety. We need jurors to put themselves in your place and ask themselves what they themselves would have done. We need to demonstrate that imprisoning a mother who needs to care for her abused daughter and her coming child is inhumane and unreasonable."

We took a minute out to sip our drinks, each of us with an eye on the wall clock.

"Remember, Lucy. You're on the witness stand to tell your story, the first time the jury will have heard it. Try to maintain your cool and let the jury see your face. They'll listen to us, yes, but, especially, they'll be watching you. 'Is this woman on the up and up or is she putting us on.' You understand me."

Lucy nodded.

"To make sure we stay on track and give your story direction, I'm going to be asking you quite a lot of questions about specific things, most of which you refer to in your diary. Say what you have to say, but don't take too long. Jurors can be like children in terms of attention span. Another thing. Don't lie or tell half truths. Resnik hasn't shone very brightly in this trial so far, it's true. But don't be fooled. He'll be looking for every inconsistency he can find to use in cross. I'll not allow him to wander off into territories of his own, don't worry. But he'll have a lot to ask, most based on what you will have said to me. If you need a glass of water or you need to pee, say so. There's no point in being uncomfortable up there. While I can't guarantee this, I'll stay as close to the questions as I can that you already know. If you say something I wasn't expecting and I need you to clarify, I may have to go off track a little, okay?"

Again, Lucy nodded. "God, Forrest," she said. "One lousy glass isn't gonna do us any harm, is it?" This made Bree smile.

"Best way I know to give Resnik what he wants," I said. "We'll drink tomorrow, how's that?"

Our easiness together and the friendly atmosphere in Bree's house had helped. Lucy appeared more or less relaxed given what lay before her. I was just plain nervous.

While not as wholesome as she might have looked in her twenties, Lucy, with Sue Carpenter's assistance, had achieved a simple attractive look in a loose-fitting deep wine-colored dress with a respectably high neckline. Her blond hair fell just past her shoulders.

Her brother, Jim, and his wife, Evie, were in the gallery, where Garrett had also managed to find a seat.

Picking up three volumes of Lucy's diary, I accompanied her to the witness box where she was sworn, then moved to face her at the podium. The courtroom, every chair occupied, was quiet.

"For the record, state your name, please."

"Lucy Evans Jackson."

"Is Evans your middle name?"

"It's my maiden name. I use it sometimes."

"How old are you, Lucy?"

"I just turned forty."

"And your profession?"

Hesitating briefly, Lucy replied, "Housewife."

"Are you married?"

"Until July thirteenth, I was."

"To whom?"

"Pete Jackson."

"For how long?"

"We were married nineteen years." Some murmuring from the gallery that soon subsided.

"Do you have children from this marriage?"

"I have two, a daughter, twelve, and a boy, nineteen."

"Their names, please?"

"My daughter's name is Mia and my son's Alex."

"Do you reside in Santa Lucia and, if so, where?"

"At 1415 Sycamore Street."

"How long have you lived at that address?"

"I think we moved there in 1999."

"Thank you." Turning to the judge, I said, "Your Honor, may I approach the witness?"

As was her habit, she motioned me ahead. I walked up to Lucy and handed the three volumes to her.

"Do you recognize these?" I asked her.

Looking at them briefly, she answered, "They're three of the six volumes of my diary, the most recent ones."

I took them back and retraced my steps to the podium. "How long have you kept a diary?"

"Since I was about seventeen, I think."

Feigning surprise, I asked, "You've kept the diary up for all this time?"

"All but for two years that happened three or four years ago."

"Can you tell the Court why you kept a diary for that long, which is a rather unusual thing?"

"I liked to write down what I did some of the time but, mostly, it was my way to talk about people in my life. My diary also helped me think when I had problems."

"Would you say it's a diary with a lot of detail or is it sketchy?"

"Well, I didn't write in it every every day, but it's pretty detailed, I'd say."

"Did you write it for someone else to read?"

Lucy shook her head even though I'd told her a hundred times not to. "No. I just wrote it for myself, not to keep secrets or anything like that, just as a way for me to talk to myself about my day."

"Lucy, I've put you on the witness stand to help the jury form a picture of your family life, especially during the last three years when there have been so many changes. To form this picture adequately, jurors need to know more about you and something about your two children and your deceased husband. With the Court's indulgence, I'll begin my questions with him. What kind of work did your husband do?"

"He sold high-end cars like Porsches and Lamborghinis. He was the owner of Jackson Motors."

"Would you say he was well-known in Santa Lucia?"

"Very much so, yes. He was involved in a lot of charity work in this city."

"Would you say he was someone to inspire confidence?"

"People trusted him. He was very popular."

Glancing at the jury, I could see everyone was attentive, some taking notes. "Was your husband socially active, by that I mean, did he often go to city functions, parties and such?"

"Quite often, yes, sometimes on weekends."

"Were you socially active, either in his company or on your own? Remember we're talking about the last three years."

"Socially active?" Lucy echoed. "Hardly at all. I didn't know anyone, didn't go out anywhere except for groceries."

"Do you have friends who call you or visit you at home?"

"During the last three years, hardly at all."

"Lucy, would you consider yourself to be antisocial, or self-sufficient as it's sometimes called, where people don't seek out friends much?"

Lucy bent forward, her expression hard as though she hadn't heard this question before. "Me? Antisocial? That's a good one. Mr. Spencer,"—Bree and I had worked hard to make Lucy use my last name—"fifteen years ago, maybe even ten, people would have laughed at you if you asked me that. By nature, I'm one of the most social people you'll meet."

"In your diary, especially during the last three years, you often speak of yourself as being isolated. Please explain what you meant by this."

Lucy sighed and seemed to sag in her seat. "I'll make this as short and sweet as I can. How do I express this? I have a lot of respect for women who love raising kids and who work at home. I'm just not one of them. I love kids but I need to be independent and work outside the home. I've always been like that. I didn't know this when we got married, but my husband wanted a stay-at-home wife who took care of our children and our home. We went round and round about this, but he finally won. Slowly but surely, he turned me into a hausfrau by making me completely dependent on him and by cutting me off from the world."

I had to call out her name to stop her. "Let's return to your word, isolated. In what way were you isolated?"

"He didn't want me going out with the girls, going out anywhere, actually. Even when he went to parties on weekends, he preferred to go alone. He was rude to my friends on the phone or when they came over, so they stopped calling or visiting."

"Who handled the finances at home?"

"Are you kidding?" Lucy said. "He wouldn't let me touch a cent. I used to pay the bills but, then he insisted on paying all of them."

"Did you have any kind of an allowance or anything?"

"For groceries, yes, and God help me if I went over it."

I'd have to reign in Lucy. She was emerging as the resentful wife.

"What about the mail? Did you open it when it came?"

"I used to, but these last few years, he wouldn't let me touch anything, not even things addressed to me, without him seeing them first."

"Did you or your children have cell phones?"

In derision, Lucy sniffed. I'd not seen this belligerent side of her. "Mia and Alex did. I didn't. Pete said I didn't need one. No one was going to call me anyway, he said."

"Did you have a car, Lucy?"

"I used to until Pete took it away from me. Said I didn't need it, and it cost too much anyway."

"In your diary, you mention an incident about your clothes. Do you know what I'm referring to?"

Lucy seemed to intuit that she was coming on too strong. She lowered her voice and attempted to relax. "I told you I bought our groceries. Somebody must have told him they'd seen me in a store and that I looked good. Pete was the jealous type. He couldn't stand the idea of other men looking at me. One evening, he got out of bed and went to my closet. He pulled out every pretty thing I had and threw them in a pile on the floor. A lot of the stuff I'd bought years ago with my own money. All I had left was sweat pants and stuff that I wouldn't be caught dead in outside the house. He took all my pretty clothes away and I never saw them again. That's what I was talking about in my diary."

The jury that, hitherto, had been non-reactive was no longer so. I could see indignation and outrage on at least half a dozen women's faces in the box.

"Now, Lucy, I'd like to move to another topic. This one concerns your children. How would you describe your relationship with your son, Alex, during the past three years?"

"I love my son," she said. "I love him very much, but there's something you must understand. He idolized his father and his father adored him. They had an excellent relationship for a dad and son, at least til Alex started going to university. Pete wanted him to study business and join him in the company and Alex wanted to work on marine biology. Even so, they still got along well. You ask about my relationship with Alex. He loved me too, but his father criticized me so much around the house and made me look so small that it was easier for Alex just to avoid me. Otherwise, Pete would get jealous and get after him. So, to be honest, Alex loved me, but he preferred his father. They'd been super close since Alex was a baby."

"Thank you. Now what about Mia, your daughter, during the past three years? What can you say about her?"

"That's a different story, completely different," Lucy said. "Mia adored her father. She did since she was a baby, but he wouldn't give the child the time of day, probably cuz she didn't say all that much and, very frankly, she wasn't all that pretty to look at. Alex was his ideal child. Mia and I were close until about the age of ten when she started to change, and I mean change. Overnight, she went from a kinda mousy little girl nobody noticed into, into, what can I say, a sexpot. Her face and hair didn't change much but the rest of her sure did. I developed fast when I was young, but nothing like that. Then, all of a sudden, her father—who she still adored, even if he ignored her—started to pay attention. Poor Mia didn't understand why, but she was in heaven. Finally, her father liked her and wanted to be with her, more and more. The closer they got, the further away from me she went. It got so bad this last year that she wouldn't even speak to me unless she wanted me to do something for her."

"Even though you weren't as close to your daughter as you once were, weren't you pleased that your daughter was finally developing a relationship with her father?"

"At first, yes I was. It was wonderful to see Mia so happy, so glad to see him when he came home from work. But, the situation changed. He was pulling her on his lap and hugging and kissing her in ways he shouldn't. Mia's no fool. She soon learned the kind of power she had over him and she used it. There's something you have to know about my daughter. She's in love with babies. She's been that way since she was a little girl. What she wanted most in the world was to have one of her own, even if she was only a kid herself. She was going to get that baby and it was obvious that, if he could get away with it without being punished, he was going to give it to her."

"Lucy, did anyone else witness this overly affectionate behavior between father and daughter?"

"Alex did once. He was working in the basement and came upstairs while the three of us were in the living room. I was in my normal chair and Mia was curled up on Pete's lap and... and..."

"That's alright. Did you ever complain to your husband about what was going on?"

"Several times, I did. Of course I did. It was driving me crazy."

"Did you ever threaten to go to the authorities if he didn't stop?"

Again, leaning forward and looking at me intently as though we hadn't talked about these things before, she snapped, "Of course I did. Who do you take me for?" No one could have assumed Lucy's response to have been an act. It was too spontaneous.

"Alright, Lucy," I cajoled, "settle down. Please tell the Court what happened when you threatened this."

Less aggressive but still a bit harsh, Lucy said, "He laughed. The bastard laughed at me."

"Then what happened," I prompted.

"He brought out these marriage separation papers he said he'd had made up and showed them to me. He said that if I tried to interfere in any way with him and Mia, he'd file the papers and we'd separate. Two things would happen then, he said. First, no one would do anything about my complaint because he and Mia would deny everything. He was so well-known and -respected in the city that everyone would believe him anyway. Second thing, who did I think the kids would want to live with? He was right about that. I knew that. Both of them would go with him. How would I watch over Mia then, he asked me."

"Lucy, listen carefully and give your answer very

clearly because it's the most important question I'll ask you. Why did you kill your husband?"

Lucy sat stock-still with a haunted expression on her face. With bitterness, leaving a space between each word, she declared, "Pete planned everything to make it impossible for me to get help. I didn't know he'd already made her pregnant. I was sure he intended to so I shot him. I had no idea what else to do." Lucy slumped in the witness chair, emotionally exhausted.

I might convince Loewenstein to put off the cross-examination until the next morning, but I doubted it. Resnik, notes in hand, was prepared to pounce. He would vigorously contest any effort I might make to delay. She saw my concern and waved and nodded to assure me she'd be okay. I smiled at her and returned to the defense table.

In an accusatory tone, even snide, Resnik said, "Ms. Jackson, when I look at you and certainly when I listen to you, I don't get the impression of a weak person. Tell me. Do you consider yourself as weak as you make out in your diary and in your responses to Mr. Spencer's questions?"

We'd spent countless hours with Lucy, going through as many scenarios as we could conjure up as to what Resnik might ask her. This was especially difficult since the range of questions we needed to ask her gave him so much latitude. She tired of this soon as anyone might, this deciding us in the end that the best advice we could give was to think carefully before she answered and to tell the truth as she saw it.

Unlike what she'd experienced with me when on the stand, she could rely on the prosecution's relentless attempts to trip her up in order to make her appear unbelievable. If Resnik set traps of which he was eminently capable, we said nothing to Lucy about the improbability that she would detect them. Her best strategy, we told her, would be to analyze his questions as best she could and to answer them as openly and calmly as possible, never forgetting that, at this eleventh hour, jurors were likely to be alert and watching her.

After several seconds elapsed and Lucy hadn't responded, Resnik continued, "If you don't like that question, then try this. Would a weak person have the guts to take a loaded revolver in both hands and fire it point-blank at someone she'd planned to kill? Would she?"

Lucy trembled. He was forcing her to experience what she lived in nightmares. At last, in a timid voice, looking down at her feet, she said, "I don't know. I don't know what to tell you."

"There's something else that troubles me, Ms. Jackson. At least twice, according to your diary and to testimony in this court, two close friends came to visit you. In both instances, so you say, these friends expressed great concern about your welfare. One, very recently, said you had friends who would be glad to help you with your problems. You had only to call on them, the woman told you. Yet you refused to say a word, first with one and then the other. Now I ask you, Ms. Jackson, how likely does that situation appear to you? We've got a woman who fears greatly for her daughter and is offered help but turns it down. Does that seem a likely story to you, Ms. Jackson?"

Again, Lucy faltered, badly shaken and probably having forgotten what the question was, if it could be called such. Resnik was pleased to wait, knowing the defendant's silence would lend power to his query. I had no choice but to intercede.

"Objection, your Honor. Counsel is grandstanding. He's intentionally upsetting and confusing the witness with questions that aren't really questions. I request that counsel be directed to formulate real questions in clear language and that he be ordered to cease browbeating the witness."

"Counsel, approach the bench," the judge commanded.

Resnik and I went.

"If Mr. Spencer hadn't spoken up," she said, "I would have. If I hear one more statement by you, Mr. Resnik, of the kind you've begun with, you will forfeit your right to cross-examine. I should inform you that I have already filed a complaint about your behavior in this trial with the California Bar. I have likewise communicated with the public prosecutor. If you have genuine questions for the witness, then proceed or we will adjourn and move to closing statements in the morning. I'm aware of your excellent reputation, Mr. Resnik. I sincerely hope you don't allow yourself to damage it. Be so good as to carry on."

The twitch in Resnik's face was back and he was pale as, God knew, he had a right to be. While it was questionable about how far the Bar would go with the judge's complaint, there was no doubt at all about how Vicky would handle it. Her fair-haired boy was in for some rough bumps.

Lucy had regained some control by the time Resnik returned to his post, doubtless heartened by Bree's just visible thumbs-up and little smile. Where, I wondered, would Vicky's deputy go from here.

In a tone more conciliatory, Resnik said, "I'm curious about something, Ms. Jackson, that I hope you can clarify. In her testimony, Lieutenant Schulz said you refused to state why you killed your husband. I'm sure the jury would like to know the reason for this as much as I would."

"Mr. Resnik, I shot my husband before he'd had a chance to violate my daughter, or so I thought mistakenly at the time. If he was dead and she hadn't been sexually assaulted, I thought, no one would know about their relationship. My daughter wouldn't have a reputation to carry around for the rest of her life. Do you understand?"

Resnik considered this, then nodded. "Something else. Handguns are harder to use than it looks on TV. Yet you seemed to manage with no difficulty. The revolver was fully loaded and you fired every round. I'm curious why you didn't have more problems with that gun? Did you practice on a firing range somewhere to make sure you could handle it when the time came to use it?"

"No, not at all. Pete tried to teach me how to shoot around the time we got married, but I didn't like it so he quit. The only other time I ever saw the ugly thing is when he got it out and took it all apart for Alex. Our son didn't like guns either."

His plan of aggressive attack derailed, Resnik seemed at a loss about what to do. I couldn't blame him. I had objected, more to bring a moment of relief to beleaguered Lucy and to lower temperatures than to halt Resnik's offensive. I had no inkling of the immense impact my insubstantial objection was to have. Nor, alas for him, did Resnik. Loewenstein's intense response broke his stride, forcing him to abandon his strategy to break Lucy down by testosterone and rhetoric. On the spot, he had to forge another plan. I was grateful it was not I up there.

"I'm still troubled by this lack of help thing. You have friends who offer to be there for you. Your husband, given who he was, had a lot to lose if unsavory rumors about him got around. You honestly don't think he would have backed off if several of your friends approached him and threatened to reveal him if he didn't leave his daughter alone?"

"Mr. Resnik, I admit your question sounds reasonable but, unfortunately, not under my circumstances. You asked me to tell you what would have happened if my friends did that. I'll tell you exactly what would have happened, so listen, please." She said these things in a reasonable, calm tone. "The first thing he would have done is threaten them with slander for even openly discussing events potentially damaging to him without evidence. He'd demand what evidence they had, which, of course, would be none. They'd be scared to death and run. They'd know he had the means to sue them if he wanted to. Then he'd come home and demand a separation. He'd ask the kids where they wanted to live, which, of course, would be with him, and I'd be alone. That would have been my last chance to watch over my daughter. To tell you the truth, Mr. Resnik, I think Pete hoped I'd do such a stupid thing so he'd be good and rid of me. There's your answer."

'Well done, Luce, well done.'

"Another question if you don't mind." Unusual language between prosecutor and defendant. "You testified that your son saw your daughter on your husband's lap. Did he react to this?"

"He was disgusted, yes."

"Do you think he knew what was going on?"

"No, I don't think he did. I don't think he thought his father capable of such a thing."

Though I was grateful for the unexpected gift, I sympathized with my colleague at that moment. He was truly at a loss about what more to ask. Had there been the issue about whether or not Lucy had pulled the trigger, he would have had much to say. As it was, all he could challenge was whether what she'd done was justifiable. He'd clearly run out of gas.

Resigned, he told Loewenstein he had no more questions. I said I had no need to redirect. Voices in the gallery rose sufficiently at Resnik's announcement to bring the judge's pen down three times. We could just hear her say that she'd hear closing arguments the next day at ten. Court was adjourned until then.

Small though the waterfront seafood restaurant was, Mira's managers had found a secluded room we didn't know existed where the six of us sat for dinner to decompress. Garrett, Ben, Bree and I were there along with Lucy and Lily, whom we'd had literally to pull into the car to accompany us. We'd agreed—uselessly, need I say—to talk of anything but the trial. Our pact held until the first drink arrived.

"Hey boyo," Ben demanded, halfway through his first glass, "what the hell did Loewenstein say to cut

Resnik off at the knees? That guy was shittin' bricks! What'd he do to piss her off?"

I'd thought about this almost continuously since court had been let out that afternoon. "Not a lot of doubt about it, I think, based on what she said. She'd given us strict instructions about how to deal with Mia, whom she'd preferred to have had in closed session, that was clear. We were to avoid issues that could upset the girl on the stand. Resnik ignored the judge's directive when he started asking questions about the father of her baby, especially the last one that caused the blowup. Loewenstein's already sent a complaint about this to the Bar and to Vicky."

Garrett's face grew long. "I doubt he'll have to worry very much about the disciplinary committee of the Bar. Vicky, now? That's another matter. She can be a little unforgiving."

Waving the server over for another drink, Ben exclaimed, "Did you see the poor bugger's face? He looked like death warmed over."

Lucy, also with a new glass, said, "The guy was really after me, wasn't he. Are all prosecutors like that?"

"I don't think that's Resnik's normal style," I responded. "This case has been tough for him—in principle, one easy enough to win, but difficult to argue. For him, it must have been a little like shadowboxing. He's a decent guy and a good litigator from all I've seen."

"Yeah, well," Ben commented, "tell that to his boss. He'll be needin' all the support he can get right now."

"Things aren't over, guys. Don't sell him short. He knows how to talk to juries. Speaking of which, don't let me order more of this excellent white Burgundy. I've gotta go home with a clear head."

Bree smiled and nudged me, which elicited laughter around the table.

"I think a certain very lucky lady's watching out for you," Lucy said as she tipped up her glass. "No such restrictions on me, guys. I've got my Lily here to drive me home. Besides, didn't I hear Ben's paying for drinks?"

"You've got it, babe," he said. "That was one bet I was glad to lose. I 'spect I'll be leavin' a lot more than a hundred bucks for booze, but who cares. I'll get a taxi if I have to."

"Where's Cassie?" Bree asked. "I haven't seen her in a long time. She didn't hear about Kate Schulz, did she?"

'Don't go too far, baby,' I wanted to say. 'He can't stand Lieutenant Schulz and hates to have his name connected with her.'

No admonition needed. Ben's visage, suddenly stern and unfriendly, was enough. Realizing she'd stepped out of line, she reached across the table to squeeze his hand. "Ben, I apologize. I had no business saying that and I won't again."

"That's alright, sweetheart," he said, his expression softening, there already the beginnings of a slur in his voice. "You're an angel. Cassie's off on a case in Arizona, by the way, or she'd be here."

Bree and I left Mira's about eight o'clock, she off to her home and babysitter and I to my study with work to do. The twins would be preparing for bed when I got there.

It was even-Stephen in the press, near half believing Lucy would be exonerated, the remainder convinced that her sentence would be light. The reporters hadn't treated Allan Resnik very well and had been less generous yet with Lonigan. His picture looked lugubrious on the front page.

On cue, Resnik, garbed impeccably as usual, rose and walked to the jury box, there nothing the slightest arrogant in his demeanor. I needed no clearer signal that his approach had changed. Devised by his superior or conceived by him, I couldn't know, but a deviation there would surely be, in objective, in delivery style, possibly in both. He had but one note card in his hand.

"Ladies and gentlemen, this case is the simplest and yet most complex I've had to deal with in my career.

Normally, it is our task to defend evidence we have presented to convict a defendant of a crime, in this instance, premeditated murder. Did he or she do the deed or not. Trials sometimes take months to decide such things. But that's not the issue here. The defendant herself has freely confessed to having killed a man. At no time has the defense attempted to prove otherwise.

"So, knowing that she's guilty of having premeditatedly killed her husband, are we here to sentence her? Clearly not. That is not my job, not yours. That task is the exclusive domain of the judge. So, if not to determine whether or not the defendant pulled the trigger, and, if not to sentence her, then why are we here? That, ladies and gentlemen of the jury, is the question. As I view it, what you must decide is whether or not what the defendant did was justified. Should she be held responsible or not for what she did?"

Resnik began to slowly pace up and down what I have referred to here earlier as the captain's quarterdeck, glancing at his sole note card.

"Put another way, given the horrific circumstances under which the lady was, are you to issue to her a special license to kill in order to protect her daughter? Listen to me. I have no wish to add to the defendant's agony. She has clearly suffered much as I'm sure you'll agree. But, fellow citizens, you have not been convened here to express sympathy or pity for someone. You are here as our society's safety net, as our conscience to ensure that we do not allow ourselves to stray from laws that protect us. Your job is to ensure that we remain resistant to arguments that homicide is a viable solution to problems that we have.

"We must refuse to grant licenses to kill, no matter the provocation, for to do otherwise is to guarantee that, for our children and grandchildren, murder by the government and by private citizens will become commonplace. I appreciate whatever compassion you may have for the defendant, but I beg you to remember what your true purpose for being here is. That purpose is not to send a message to society that, under certain circumstances, premeditated homicide can be justified. Thank you."

Twelve implacable faces watched Resnik's back as he returned slowly to his table. The hushed gallery released a collective breath as he sat down.

There was nothing charismatic or emotion-rousing about Resnik's remarks. As I sat reflecting during the ten-minute recess before I was to speak, it seemed to me that Resnik had acted wisely by appealing to jurors' sense of responsibility and integrity. I had some rapid reconfiguring to do if I was to undermine what he'd done.

Though there were sotto voce comments around the defense table as I got up, it was Bree's whispered words that I heard.

"There's a difference between legality and humanity. Make them ask themselves what they would have done if someone was attacking their own child."

"Ladies and gentlemen, like my esteemed colleague, I'll be brief. Before I move to my final points, which, I promise you, will be short, I need to address two concepts raised by Mr. Resnik. They were important ones.

"The first concerns what he referred to as a license to kill. Since I touched on this before in my opening remarks, I won't dwell upon it here other than to say that it is to offend your intelligence to suggest that such licenses don't exist, all issued by federal, state and municipal governments with the aim of protecting us. It would be equally condescending to suggest that you are unaware of unofficial operations by divisions of our federal government to track down and kill terrorists whose goals are to harm us. In other words, most of us are okay if licenses to kill come from our governments.

"Mr. Resnik also spoke of our need for a public conscience. He did so well. But, I ask you, conscience about what? Are we to be concerned only about the enforcement of our laws, or do humanity and social justice play their parts? Why do you think juries like you exist instead of computers that could be programmed to dole out penalties for crimes? Juries exist to ensure justice, that's what, to be as certain as we can that our rules are as humane as possible, that these rules don't penalize the wrong persons.

"Alright. Enough. I said I would be brief. In just hours, you'll be deciding the fate of Lucy Jackson. You won't have reams of material to go through nor tons of evidence. What you will have is time to think. That's what I am begging you to do. You know by what you've seen and heard that Lucy Jackson had no place to go for help. You've heard this from the police and from the CPS. You've heard what would have occurred had Lucy gone to her friends for help. You've heard Lucy's daughter confess to carrying her father's baby—her father who, she says, desired it. When you're deliberating the fate of this child's mother, ask yourselves this, please. Whether or not help were immediately available, if, as fathers or mothers, you caught someone in your house at night who was carrying away your child, would you stand by with the hope that your child might eventually be found? If you were certain that help were not at hand, would you let matters take their course or would you take action to protect your child?

"There's another issue I implore you to consider. Unfortunate as the matter is, Lucy's daughter is carrying her father's baby, to whom she'll give birth in months. Who will care for this badly abused child, and who will help this child care for her own? The public? Is it just, is it humane to imprison the mother of this pregnant adolescent who's soon to give birth? Is it just to condemn a woman who was prepared to sacrifice her life to protect her child?

"Mr. Resnik's correct when he insists that we must be responsible about the enforcement of our laws. I insist that we must also be responsible to the people whom these laws serve. Thank you."

Juries are notoriously capricious in the verdicts they render. The pundits are so often wrong. The twelve faces I saw as I turned away had lost their self-righteous look. Instead, they appeared contemplative. A good sign? Hard to know. Would they take an hour to reach their verdict or take days? A lot of fingernails would be chewed to stubs in the interim.

The judge first directed the jury to proceed to the deliberation room to receive instructions. She then courteously thanked everyone for coming as though it had been a spectacle of some kind, then adjourned. She reminded us that the gag order would remain in effect until the verdict was in.

I went to shake Resnik's hand. "Tough job," I said. "Don't lose sleep about Loewenstein's complaint. They rarely go anywhere unless they're really serious. It was good to work with you."

"Hey thanks," he replied. "It's your buddy, Vicky, I'm concerned about, not the Bar. I learned a lot in this trial. I have you to thank for a lot of that."

I waved him off. "Vicky doesn't carry grudges and she's smart. She's not going to hurt one of her rising stars. Go home and have a drink. That's what I'm going to do."

I made supper for the twins, but I couldn't eat. Supervising them as they finished homework and prepared for bed distracted me, at least for a little while. I poured myself a double scotch and settled back, only to hear the house phone ring.

"I couldn't eat a thing," Bree said. "How 'bout you?"

"Pretty much the same. I'm hoping what I'm holding in my hand will help me get to sleep. I talked to Lucy and she seems fine, believe it or not. I'll never understand that woman."

Bree laughed. "All the more time for learning to understand me. Call me later if you can't sleep."

We exchanged I love yous.

*

Nothing was accomplished at the office in the morning while we waited, a phenomenon I was all too familiar with. Garrett, Ben, Bree and I were in and out of each other's offices a dozen times before the call came in the middle of the afternoon. We were to be in court in a half hour to hear the verdict.

My butterflies were back and Bree's smile forced. Ben cracked jokes as we walked to the courthouse. Lucy and her entourage waited outside for us. Evie, exceptionally, had a nice dress on. Jim looked frazzled. Mia was at their home with her tutor, so they said. The courtroom was full when we went in.

Following formalities, the jury filed in. I could read nothing whatsoever in their faces, a bad sign for me. When had I last obtained an acquittal without smiles? I turned my attention to Loewenstein, who'd just received a sheet of paper from the jury foreperson.

She'd done spectacularly well to hide her feelings throughout the trial, to a fault, it seemed to me, since she often appeared bored. I felt Bree grab my hand with surprising force. She'd seen it too, a slight parting of the judge's lips that morphed into a real smile. Before the verdict could be read, there was instant uproarious applause from everyone in the courtroom, including Resnik and his colleague and—the first time I had witnessed this—the jurors. Though the non-guilty verdict appeared in the official record, I was not convinced that it was ever formally read out.

People were crying and hugging everywhere, everyone but Lucy.

She did smile once when, turning to Bree, she proclaimed, "Sorry, girl, but this time he's mine."

Bree laughed as the cameras caught a very warm kiss and hug.

"Thank you for being there for me," Lucy whispered. "You're the only one who would have been except for Jannie."

Epilogue

My dear Jannie,

Yet another letter to you since who else do I have who I can bear my soul to? As I do nearly every night when everything is quiet, I sit down to write, almost like I used to do in my diary, hoping, I guess, that putting things down in words will clarify things for me somehow. Maybe talking to you will be more useful to me than the diary was.

You never knew about my diary, did you. Your name is in it nearly everywhere, you'll be glad to know, until... until you went away. I can't think of that terrible day or I'll start to cry and have to put this letter down.

You won't believe where I sit when I write to you like this. I'm in my favorite chair in the living room, right across from where I used to watch Pete cuddle Mia in his lap. Why do I put myself through this, Jannie, why? There are lots of other places where I could go to write, but I come back here every time.

Something else that makes no sense. I dust and clean every day like I used to, but, otherwise, I haven't changed hardly a thing in the house since Pete died over a year ago. I feel like he's watching everything I do, just waiting for something to complain about. I'm sorry to use words in front of you that I know you don't like, sweet Jannie, but I can't help it. I hate him! I hate him like I've never hated anything before. He's dead. He's not in my life any more, so why do I keep behaving like his slave?

Can you see me, love? I'm tearing up a little, I know—I usually do when I talk to you—but I'm also smiling. There is one big difference in this house. I already told you, probably. It's something I should have done a long time ago, but I just couldn't. Remember that beautiful painting your parents sent to me with the little lovebird in the tree? But of course you do. I hid it in my trunk in the basement to keep it away from Pete. I wanted to take it out when he died, but every time I looked at it, I got so sad and lonesome that I had to put it back.

Did you do something to that painting to help me, Jannie? I wonder sometimes. The next time I took it out to look at it, I felt different. Honestly, I thought I could hear your voice and feel you reaching out to comfort me. That's how I feel every day now when I look at the little lovebird in the tree which, of course, is you.

You're everywhere in the house. You didn't know that either, did you. The one I love the best is the original painting that's on my bedside table. That's where I say good night. I made two copies the same size for other rooms. And, oh yeah, I didn't tell you. I have a miniature I carry around with me in my purse. The one I look at most, though, is an enlargement I had made that's on the living room wall here next to me. It helps me feel like I'm in touch with you when I write.

You know about Forrest and his Bree, of course. They read my diary and they know who you are and what you mean to me. They're the only ones who understand the meaning of the painting. I think I see tears in Bree's eyes sometimes when she looks at it.

Everybody tells me I should sell the house. Too many bad memories here. Why don't I do it? I can't stand the place. Mia doesn't like it either. Alex swears he'll never come back here again. He says it's his sister's fault, but I wonder if it isn't the house he doesn't want to see.

Jannie, none of this makes sense. This place used to be my prison until Pete was gone. Forrest unlocked the gates when he got me off in court, but look at me. I'm still here in my cage like a bird who's scared to leave. The doors and windows are all open now, but they may as well not be. Jannie, you'd know, wouldn't you? Is it possible Pete's spirit holds me here? I know that sounds ridiculous, but that's how I feel sometimes, locked in here forever. The idea frightens me. My therapist tells me I shouldn't think about these things since they're not real, but what does she know about such things?

Some things here have improved, I guess you'd say. Mia's better. She finally lets me hold and change the baby. She still doesn't allow anyone else but me and the pediatrician to touch her. She's a sweet thing, Mia's baby is. You won't believe me when I tell you what her name is. Mia's best friend—it's her only friend now, really—is Forrest's twelve-year-old daughter whose name is Trina. Mia named her baby after her. She wants her friend, Trina, to be her child's godmother. I forgot. Mia lets Trina hold her whenever she wants to.

You know what I was afraid of most when the baby was born? Mia wouldn't allow an ultrasound so we didn't know the sex. I was scared it would be a boy who looked like Pete. The weirdest thing ever, Jannie. She looks more like me than anything. She had a ton of dark hair when she was born, but it's turning light. Everyone says she'll be blond and have lots of hair like me. She has big eyes that keep changing color. The doctor's sure they'll be light blue like mine. A true generation skip, he says. How horrible it would have been if the baby looked like Pete, can you imagine?

I've already told you, haven't I, how crazy and wild Mia was a year ago. She's changed. She's a lot more like she used to be when she was little. She's softer and very quiet. She scares me though. She seems locked inside herself. She never cries and she never tells anyone how she feels. She looks closed-down if you understand what I mean. The only good thing is that she's a lot nicer to me now, almost loving sometimes. She refuses to talk to therapists. We keep trying.

Forrest and his family help a lot. Trina has Mia and the baby for overnights sometimes, and Trina comes to see Mia over here. When Mia goes to Trina's there's another girl there sometimes, even two. Mia seems to get along with them. The girls adore her baby which helps a lot.

I feel so bad for Alex and I miss him. He graduated from UCSB last June and will be doing graduate work in marine biology next fall in San Diego. Like I said, he won't come here. I drive up sometimes to see him in Goleta and it's good, but I'm always sad when I have to leave. He has friends, but he seems lonely.

Did I tell you my Lily passed away. I'm sorry if I repeat myself so much, but I can't remember, day to day, what I've told you. She was fine until just over two months ago, in remission, her doctors said. Then, suddenly, her breast cancer or whatever she had flared up and, a few weeks later, she was gone. I was devastated. If it hadn't been for Forrest and Bree who came over a lot to be with me, I don't know what I would have done.

Oh, Jannie, something absolutely wonderful and hilarious. I've already talked to you about who Bree is, Forrest's girlfriend, a real darling. She's a whole lot nicer than his first wife, Claire. She has the cutest little three-year-old girl named Maya. She adopted her from India, I think. Anyway, they organized this big backyard party like Forrest does pretty much every year. This time, it was to celebrate his friend Ben's birthday.

Forrest's summer parties usually start around seven

or so. Not this time. There were lots of kids, including baby Trina, so they had to start things at four. There must have been thirty people there, including children. As usual, Forrest had it catered so he could do the drinks. All that got kinda complicated with twelve-year-olds and such.

Anyway—I can't get the smile off my face right now as I think of this—just before dinner was s'posed to start and Forrest's famous margaritas were coming out, Forrest rang a bell to get everyone's attention. Everybody had to have a paper cup with something in it to toast his friend, so we all filled up and waited. Bree was there beside Forrest with somebody nobody knew. She'd just come in, apparently. Even Forrest's kids were fooled. The rest of us were, I can tell you. That lady nobody knew was a pastor from a nearby church. That party wasn't to celebrate Ben at all. It was to celebrate the marriage between Forrest and Bree which took place on the spot.

We all stood in a circle around the three, singing songs and holdin' our drinks in one hand, punch mainly, and hanging on to some part of our neighbor to the right with our other hand. Forrest and Bree spoke the most beautiful vows I've ever heard and, five minutes later, they were married. The place went nuts, I can tell you. Trina and Andy, Forrest's kids—they're twins, remember—knew the marriage was coming soon but they didn't know exactly when. Things got pretty noisy around midnight but, instead of cops, neighbors kept comin' to join us. I've never seen Forrest so happy in my life. He used to be my love once way back when, Jannie. You remember that, don't you. Anyway, it was just plain fantastic. First time I'd ever seen a wedding in a backyard like that.

I sold Pete's business, did I tell you? Put it this way. Money's not going to be a problem for us for a long time. That's the ridiculous part about all this. Okay, some things could have gone better in my life, but I've got a lot more than most people do and look at the stupid situation I'm in. I just don't seem to have the energy to do anything other than keep up the house. I've gotta find a way to get out of here and back into the world. I'm only forty-one, Jannie. That's not too old to start again, is it? One good thing, at least. If I take the trouble to dress up right, men still look at me. Okay, I know, it's sex they're looking for, but it's something. Now don't look at me like that.

Something I almost forgot to say. I've gotta quit soon anyway cuz my hand's getting tired. A couple of things, actually.

Way back a few years after I married Pete, a sweetheart of a guy gave me a job. He was a small-time book publisher at the time. I haven't seen the guy for years. Last I heard—it made me sad—he had to go bankrupt and leave the publishing business. Anyway, the other day, just by chance, I met him filling up for gas. His name is Bobby Burke. He's the nicest guy. Anyway, over a cup of coffee, he and his brother who's divorced—he's real nice too—told me they're looking for a cheap bookstore to buy. There's no real money in that anymore—they admitted it—but they can't stay away from books. So, what to you think they want to do—invest in a bookstore. First time I've been excited about anything since Forrest's wedding. They want me to come in with them. The problem is, the store they're looking at is in Santa Barbara. If I back them for half of the selling price which I can do, no problem, we can have it, including stock.

Jannie, I want to do it, but I'm scared. Scared of what? I don't know.

I couldn't even consider it if Mia wasn't ready to go back to school. She was out last year with tutors because of the baby. She's willing to go, she says, if we can find somebody to watch Trina who she can have confidence in and she likes. I've got a feeling that's gonna be difficult. We've only got a couple of months before school starts. It's a possibility, don't you think? Talk to me, Jannie. I'll never have the courage to break away from here unless you help me. I know that.

With love to you always,

Lucy

Afterword

When I began this book, Lucy Jackson was to be portrayed as the archetypal victim of psychological abuse by her husband, abuse that led her to believe that her sole means to shield her daughter from incest by her spouse was to kill him. There was to be no doubt about who fired the gun or about whether or not incest was involved. My outline for the novel entailed two objectives, the second of which turned out to have been impractical to pursue.

First, I wanted to demonstrate that psychological abuse in marriage can be as devastating and far-reaching as battered woman syndrome with consequences easily as severe. By including Lucy's diary in the manuscript, I hoped to show how, over time, abuse-induced loss of self-esteem and personal identity made it easier and easier for her partner to brainwash her and to inculcate in her beliefs that, as a mate and mother, she was powerless.

Second, I wished to illustrate why psychological abuse of the kind Lucy suffered should be viewed in a court of law as exculpatory evidence to vindicate her having taken her husband's life. The defense would have argued that Lucy's perception of her options, other than the one she took to shield her daughter, was shaped entirely by coercion and threats by her abusive spouse. In short, the defense's case would have relied upon state of mind evidence rather than more conventional physical evidence of the kind used to defend battered women. Could the jury be persuaded to accept that Lucy believed she had no choice but to resort to homicide to protect her child? Even were they sympathetic and convinced, would jurors be willing to set aside the penalties for premeditated homicide in her case? Daunting questions, both.

Defensible though my second objective for the novel was, it was clear to me from the start that my protagonist, Forrest Spencer, could hope for little more than some reduction in his client's prison term. Psychological abuse, to say nothing of evidence emanating from state of mind, has not yet found solid footing in our courts. To expect juries to cope with unfamiliar abstract concepts is, as yet, wishful thinking.

With each successive chapter, my novelist's license to invent of little use to me at that point, I grew more uneasy. I was less worried about proposing new foci for our criminal courts than I was about the overall impact of a guilty verdict that was sure to ensue from my contrived defense strategy. The aim of the book, after all, was not to highlight deficiencies in our judicial system. Rather, I wanted to emphasize the need to be more inclusive in the courts in what we consider to be abuse if justice for psychologically abused women is to be obtained. Would condemning Lucy to years of prison in my story have accomplished this? Perhaps, but I doubted it. Well beyond the point of no return in the novel, I began casting about for another way.

Happily for me, I discovered, well into the book, how progressive some of California's child protection laws are. Except in extreme circumstances—for example, child abuse by the young mother or severe malnutrition—no one in that state can take a twelve-year-old girl's child from her. In fact, California will pay extra costs to support the baby along with her mother in foster care. Nor, as made explicit in the book, may a twelve-year-old girl be forced to undergo physical examination that pertains to sexual acts or pregnancy except in extreme situations. These felicitous provisions in California's laws became my bolt-hole, giving Lucy at least a shot at absolution by the jury. Hopefully, it will not be long before defense strategies as set forth in this novel will succeed.

Having followed developments in the courts in which some severely battered women have been exonerated from killing their injurious spouses, it seemed eminently reasonable to me that defenses equally robust could be mounted to defend psychologically abused women as in Lucy's case.

I did not come to these conclusions on my own. For the scant knowledge I have in this area, I am indebted to scholars who focus on physical and psychological abuse and to victims who have had the courage to share their stories.

Learn how a marriage partner, over time, can take control of their spouse's life:

Coercive Control: How Men Entrap Women in Personal Life by Evan Stark, Oxford University Press, 2009

"Psychological Abuse of Women: Six Distinct Clusters" by Linda L. Marshall, Journal of Family Violence, December 1996, Volume 11, Issue 4, pp 379-409

"Re-Presenting Woman Battering: From Battered Woman Syndrome to Coercive Control" by Evan Stark, Symposium on Reconceptualizing Violence Against Women by Intimate Partners: Critical Issues, 58 Albany Law Review, 1994-1995

Read what victims themselves say about how abuse began and how powerless they became to resist:

I Just Lost Myself: Psychological Abuse of Women in

Marriage (hardcover) by Valerie Nash Chang, January 19, 1996

Walking on Eggshells: Living with Psychological Abuse and Codependency by Mckenzie Brown, published by Trafford, 2012

Acknowledgements

Apart from my sweet wife who has been present from the conception of this book to the completion of the last page, Cate Preston whom I sorely miss as friend and assistant has contributed to the novel in so many ways. Cate, though I wish you well in your graduate studies at Kingston University, it would be pleasant and reassuring for me to know that you'd be near as I begin my next project.

How does a treasured sibling who knows so much about what good writing is convey her concern about whether I'm getting sufficient sleep after she's read a chapter I've sent to her? Sharron Harris who reads prodigiously and who has taught English literature and writing for many years gets away with this. She'll say this doesn't happen much anymore because I've had the good sense to follow her advice as I struggled with the transition from formal to creative writing.

Though we sometimes disagree about how best to express something, she's taught me so much about the need for immediacy and uncomplicated language. I owe much of whatever progress I've made in that direction to her. Thanks, Sharron, for your unending encouragement and help. It's nice to have one more excuse to go out to the West Coast to visit you.

Long before my editor sees the manuscript, the

more perspicacious member of this Neufeld couple has to vet what I have done. "This word went out twenty years ago," my spouse will say, or "Your character wouldn't express herself like that." And here I thought I was a realist when I write. Verisimilitude is Heather's long middle name. Thank you, my love, for seeing all the things I should but don't.

About the Author

As a student and then university professor of linguistics and psychology, I learned to write as a scientist, a not-unpleasant task if a little tedious at times. If there was creativity in my written work, it came not from my imagination or my desire to play with language but from whatever theoretical insight I might have to offer at the time. Brevity, precision and clarity in research reports will always prevail over idiosyncrasies in style. I learned the scientific writing craft, if that it can be called, thereby acquiring habits I would later find very difficult to break.

Addicted to fiction as I've always been, I could not but be aware of the gulf that lies between the novelist's and the scholar's use of language. Until I attempted to bridge that gap, I had no idea of how wide the chasm was. After decades of research in my fields, I craved the freedom to exploit the power of language to evoke human feelings and emotions that have little place in most scientists' quest for knowledge. How extraordinary for a writer would it be to encapsulate in just pages much of the story of a person's life that could encompass more than what a close friend of many years might impart.

Lofty goals for someone schooled as a writer of research reports. How to achieve immediacy and pull my reader in with my overly formal-sounding language and sentences that are too complex? How to ignore years of experience in the artificial environment of the research laboratory when attempting as a writer to create characters in a novel who seem real? While trying to assemble a toolbox very different from the sort to which I was accustomed, my greatest struggle has been to exchange the professor's formal mindset for one more suited to storytellers.

Though the goal of most fiction is to entertain, an objective that surely needs no defense, as many of our favorite authors have demonstrated, the genre also serves as a vehicle for raising consciousness about important social issues as well as offering valuable insight into sensitive areas of human relationships. And, good writing remains the best means I know to ensure that our language remains rich. If I am able, it is these latter aims that I will continue to pursue in my books.

I live in Ottawa, Canada, with my wife Heather, an immigration lawyer. When not writing, I may be in the kitchen indulging my love of preparing international cuisine, reading or listening to music or journeying to remote regions of the planet at the behest of my travel-loving spouse.

As Heather continues to remind me, my endeavors at home find me too often at my keyboard, too immersed in my imaginary world. I defend myself by occasionally printing out and handing over readers' letters I receive. For an hour or so, she is mollified.

To find out more about what I'm up to and what my current rant's about, do visit my website at **www.geraldneufeld.com**.

More gratifying to me as must surely be true for any author will be a personal note from you, whether or not you liked a book of mine you've read. Unless one's a writer who loves to appear on radio and TV and give talks about themselves everywhere—I'm not one of those—we novelists may get little feedback other than obligatory praise from friends and terse reviews. It is what our readers truly think that really counts, so drop me a line if you're so inclined. It'll keep me at my keyboard a little longer, maybe, but I'll be happy.

My email address is one of those easy ones:
gerald@geraldneufeld.com.

CPSIA information can be obtained at www.ICGtesting.com
Printed in the USA
LVOW05s0414051214

417228LV00005B/9/P

9 780985 44648